# THE
# JOURNEY TO
# THE WEST

# THE
# JOURNEY TO
# THE WEST

VOLUME TWO

*Translated and Edited by* Anthony C. Yu

*The University of Chicago Press* CHICAGO AND LONDON

Chapter 27 of this volume appeared in a slightly
different form in the *University of Chicago Magazine* 70,
no. 1. © 1977 by The University of Chicago.

THE UNIVERSITY OF CHICAGO PRESS, CHICAGO 60637
THE UNIVERSITY OF CHICAGO PRESS, LTD., LONDON
© *1978 by The University of Chicago*
*All rights reserved. Published 1978*
*Phoenix edition 1982*
*Printed in the United States of America*

89 88 87 86 85 84 83 82   2 3 4 5 6

*Library of Congress Cataloging in Publication Data*

Wu, Ch'eng-en, ca. 1500–ca. 1582.
   The journey to the west.

   Translation of Hsi yu chi.
   I. Yu, Anthony C., 1938–   II. Title.
PL2697.H75E596   1976   895.1'3'4   75-27896
ISBN 0-226-97146-5 (cloth)
      0-226-97151-1 (paper)

*For Nathan and Charlotte Scott*

# Contents

# Acknowledgments

I wish to express my gratitude to the John Simon Guggenheim Memorial Foundation for the award of a Fellowship (1976–77), during which period I was able to complete the translation of this volume of *The Journey to the West*. My special thanks are due to Najita Tetsuo, Director of the Center for Far Eastern Studies at the University of Chicago, for his support and provision of needed research funds; to Mrs. Susan Fogelson, for expert assistance in the preparation of the manuscript; and to Mr. Ma Tai-loi of the Far Eastern Library, the University of Chicago, for invaluable help in research.

Amid the Three Islands Sun Wu-k'ung seeks a cure;
With sweet dew Kuan-shih-yin revives a tree.

Hold fast in life the "sword" above the "heart."[1]
Remember the "long" beside the "suffering."
It's common to say the sword's the law of life,
But think thrice to root out both anger and pride.
"The noblest"[2] is peaceful—this came from long ago;
"The sage loves virtue"[3]—this truth's for all times.
The strong man will meet someone stronger still,
Who will, however, come to naught at last!

We were telling you about the Chên-yüan Great Immortal, who grabbed Pilgrim and said, "I know your abilities, and I have heard of your reputation. But you have been most deceitful and unscrupulous this time. You may indulge in all sorts of wizardry, but you can't escape from my hands. I'll argue with you all the way to the Western Heaven to see that Buddhist Patriarch of yours, but you won't get away from having to restore to me the Ginseng Fruit Tree. So stop playing with your magic!" "Dear Sir!" said Pilgrim, laughing. "How petty you are! If you want the tree revived, there's no problem. If you had said so in the first place, we would have been spared this conflict." "No conflict!" said the Great Immortal. "You think I would let you get away with what you have done?" "Untie my master," said Pilgrim, "and I'll give you back a living tree. How's that?" "If you really possess the power," said the Great Immortal, "to make the tree alive again, I'll go through the proper ceremony of 'Eight Bows' with you and become your bond-brother." "Relax!" said Pilgrim. "Let them go, and you can be certain that old Monkey will give you back a living tree."

The Great Immortal reckoned that they could not escape; he therefore gave the order to free Tripitaka, Pa-chieh, and Sha Monk. "Master," said Sha Monk, "I wonder what sort of tricks Elder Brother is up to this time." "What sort of tricks?" said Pa-chieh. "This is called

the trick of 'Pulling Wool Right over Your Eyes.' The tree is dead!
You think it could be cured and revived? He's just putting out some
empty formula for show. On the pretext of going to find medicine to
cure the tree, he will flee and take to the road all by himself. You think
he has any care for us!" "He won't dare leave us behind," said
Tripitaka. "Let's ask him where he is going to find the cure." He called
out, "Wu-kung, how did you manage to deceive the Immortal Master
and have us freed?" "Old Monkey is speaking the truth, only the
truth," said Pilgrim. "What do you mean by deceiving him?" Tripitaka
asked; "Where will you go to find the cure?" Pilgrim said, "According to an old proverb, 'The cure comes from the seas.' I want to go
now to the Great Eastern Ocean and make a complete tour of the
Three Islands and the Ten Islets. I want to visit all the Immortals and
Aged Sages to ask for a method of revivification that will revive the
tree for him." "How long do you need to be away before returning?"
said Tripitaka. "Only three days." "All right," said Tripitaka. "As you
said, I'll give you three days. If you return by that time, everything
will be fine. If you don't come back after three days, I'll begin reciting
that 'Old-Time Sūtra'!" "I hear you! I hear you!" said Pilgrim.

Look how he quickly straightened his tiger-skin skirt. As he walked
out the door, he said to the Great Immortal, "You need not worry, sir.
I leave now, but I'll be back very soon. But you must take good care
of my master; see that he lacks none of the three meals and the six
teas of the day. If my master's clothes become soiled or wrinkled, wash
and starch them. Should he want anything, old Monkey will settle the
account with you when he returns. I'll finish puncturing all the pans
for you! If my master's face pales even a little, I won't take him back;
and if he becomes a trifle thin, I'll not leave this place." "Go, go," said
the Great Immortal. "I'll see to it that he won't starve!"

Dear Monkey King! He mounted his cloud-somersault quickly and
left the Temple of Five Villages, heading straight for the Great Eastern
Ocean. Moving through the air like lightning and meteor, he soon
arrived at the immortal region of P'êng-lai. He lowered his cloud and
took a careful look below: it was a lovely place indeed, for which we
have a testimonial poem. The poem says:

A great land divine, the sages' domain,
This P'êng-lai island-group calms the winds and waves.
Its jasper towers' cool shapes dip into the sky;
Its tall arches' bright reflections float on the sea.

Mists of five colors veil the jade-green sky;
On the gold turtle stars and moon shine from on high.
The Queen of the West comes here frequently
To bring peaches to those Immortals Three.

Before he had finished looking at this divine scenery, Pilgrim was already entering P'êng-lai. As he walked, he saw three old men playing encirclement chess in the shade of some pine trees outside the White-Cloud Cave. The one watching the game was the Star of Longevity, while the two playing were the Star of Blessing and the Star of Wealth. Pilgrim approached them, crying, "Old brothers, receive my bow!" When the Three Stars saw him, they pushed away the chess board and returned his salutation. "Great Sage, why did you come here?" they asked. "I came especially to have some fun with all of you," said Pilgrim. "I heard that the Great Sage, who forsook Taoism to follow Buddhism," said the Star of Longevity, "had won back his freedom to protect the T'ang Monk on his journey to seek scriptures in the Western Heaven. He must be traveling over rugged roads every day. Where would he find time to have fun with us?" Pilgrim said, "To tell all of you the truth, old Monkey has run into a little obstacle halfway on the journey to the West. That's why I came to request some assistance, but I don't know whether you are willing to help me or not." "At what place?" asked the Star of Blessing. "What sort of obstacle? Tell us plainly so that we may decide." "We were stopped while passing the Temple of Five Villages at the Mountain of Longevity." "The Temple of Five Villages is the divine residence of the Chên-yüan Great Immortal," said one of the three old men, who were astonished. "Could it be that you stole and ate his ginseng fruits?" "So I stole and ate them," said Pilgrim with a laugh. "How much could they be worth?"

"You ape!" said one of the three old men. "You are dumb! A man who takes one whiff of that fruit will live to be three hundred and sixty years old; he eats one and he'll last forty-seven thousand years. That's why it bears the name of 'The Long-Life Grass of Reverted Cinnabar.' The level of cultivation in Tao of that Great Immortal far surpasses ours! With such a thing in his possession, he can easily have the same age as Heaven, whereas we still have to nourish our spermal essence, cultivate our breaths, fortify our spirits, harmonize the tiger and the dragon, catch the *k'an* to fill up the *li*—in short, we have to spend a lot of time and effort just to attain immortality. How could you say, 'How much could they be worth?' Throughout the whole world, that's the only kind of spiritual root there is." "Spiritual root! Spiritual root!" said Pilgrim. "I have already uprooted it!"

"What do you mean by 'uprooted it'?" said the three old men, greatly alarmed. Pilgrim said, "When we went to the temple the other day, the Great Immortal was not home, and only two lads received my master. They served him two ginseng fruits, but my master did not realize that they were fruits. Thinking that they were infants not yet three days old, he absolutely refused to eat them. The lads took them away and ate them without bothering even to share them with us. So, old Monkey went and stole three of the fruits for us three brothers to eat, but those two lads, without any sense of propriety, kept on calling us thieves. Old Monkey got mad and gave the tree a blow with his rod. When it fell to the ground, the fruits on it disappeared, the branches snapped, the leaves dropped, and it died with all its roots exposed. The lads tried to imprison us, but old Monkey broke their lock and left. Early next morning, their master came back and gave chase; we had a few rough exchanges with him which led eventually to a fight. In a flash, he flipped open that sleeve of his and bagged all of us. We were bound and shackled, interrogated and whipped for a whole day, but we managed to escape again that night. He caught up with us once more and took us captive. Mind you, there was not an inch of steel on him! He had only that yak's tail to parry our blows, but none of the three weapons of us brothers could even touch him. And so he gave us more of the same treatment, wrapping my master and my two younger brothers in cloth coated with varnish but putting me in a pan of boiling oil. I then showed him my special talent for escape, but not before I had punctured his pan. When he saw that he could not hold me captive, he became somewhat intimidated, and that was when I sweet-talked him into freeing my master and my brothers with the promise that I would revive his tree for him. That's how we came to a temporary truce. When I remembered the saying, 'The cure comes from the seas,' I decided to pay you three, old Brothers, a visit in this lovely place. If you have any formula to cure the tree, please pass it on to me at once so that I can rescue the T'ang monk from his ordeal."

When the Three Stars heard these words, they became distressed also. One of them said, "Monkey, you're completely ignorant of people! That Chên-yüan-tzŭ is the patriarch of earthly immortals, while we belong to the elder branches of divine immortals. You may have some sort of position in Heaven, but you are only an irregular number in the Great Monad clan, and you have yet to become an authentic member. How could you possibly expect to escape from him? If you had killed some beast or bird, some insect or scaly creature, all you would need is one grain of my millet-elixir and it would be revived. The ginseng fruit, however, is the very root of all divine trees. How could it be healed? There's no cure for it!" When Pilgrim heard that there was no cure available, his brow became completely furrowed. "Great Sage," said the Star of Blessing, "though there is no cure here, there may be one in another place. Why are you so dejected?" Pilgrim said, "Of course, I don't mind going to another place to seek a cure. It would have been a small matter indeed, even if I had to journey to the edge of the seas or make a complete tour of the thirty-six Heavens. But that Elder T'ang of mine, who is neither tolerant nor magnanimous, has given me a limit of three days. If I don't return with something after three days, he'll start reciting the Tight-Fillet Spell." "Good! Good! Good!" said the Three Stars, laughing. "Had it not been for this little means of control, you would be crawling all over Heaven again!" Then the Star of Longevity said, "Relax, Great Sage. Don't worry. Though that Great Immortal is our senior, he does know us. As we have not visited him for a long time, and as it is for the sake of the Great Sage, we three shall go and call on him right now. We'll express your concern to the T'ang monk and tell him not to recite the Tight-Fillet Spell. Three days, four days—what's the difference? We won't leave them until you come back with the cure." "Thank you! Thank you!" said Pilgrim. "Please get on with your journey, old Brothers. I'm off." So the Great Sage took leave of them, and we shall say no more of that.

We tell you now about the Stars, who mounted the auspicious luminosity and went straight to the Temple of Five Villages. The crowd at the temple was milling about when suddenly the cries of cranes could be heard in the sky to announce the arrival of the three elders. You could see

A sky lit up by sheens of auspicious light,
As sweet, unending fragrance filled the air.
Colored mist—a thousand strands—veiled the feathered gowns;
Fleecy clouds in petals held up the Immortals' feet
(As green phoenixes flew

And red phoenixes soared).
Their sleeves sent a scented breeze to sweep the earth;
Their staffs, like hanging dragons, brought laughter gay;
Their beards swayed before them like medals of jade.
Their blithe, youthful features showed no grief or care;
Their strong, healthy frames were those of the blessed.
They held tallies of stars
To fill up the sea-mansions;
From their waists hung the gourds and precious scrolls.
Ten thousand decades—so grand was their age.
On the Three Islands and Ten Islets they freely lived.
They came to this world often to grant their boons
And increase man's blessings a hundredfold.
The whole, wide world
Bright with glory and wealth!
To have now endless blessing and endless life!
Three elders riding on halos saw the Immortal Great:
What boundless peace and blessing filled the hall!

When an immortal lad saw this, he ran to make the report, "Master, the Three Stars from the sea have arrived." Chên-yüan-tzŭ was just chatting with the T'ang monk and his disciples. Hearing the announcement, he went down the steps into the courtyard to receive the visitors. When Pa-chieh saw the Star of Longevity, he grabbed him and said with a laugh, "You blubbery old codger! I haven't seen you for a long time, and you still look so dashing! Why, you didn't even bring along a hat!" Taking off his own monk's cap, he plopped it on the head of the Star, clapped his hands, and roared with laughter. "Fine! Fine! Fine!" he cried. "As the saying goes, 'Put on the cap to increase riches!'" Throwing away the cap, the Star of Longevity snapped back, "You stupid coolie! You have absolutely no manners!" "I'm no coolie," said Pa-chieh, "but you are all knaves." "You are a stupid coolie all right," said the Star of Blessing, "and you even dare to call people knaves?" "If you are not the knaves of some household," said Pa-chieh again, laughing, "how is it that you come bearing the names 'Increase Age,' 'Increase Blessing,' and 'Increase Wealth'?"

At that moment, Tripitaka ordered Pa-chieh to step back while he straightened his clothes quickly to greet the Three Stars, who in turn saluted the Great Immortal as a senior colleague before they dared take a seat. After they were seated, the Star of Wealth said, "We apologize for not coming to pay our respects for such a long time. We came now especially to see you since we learned that the Great Sage Sun had caused some disturbance here." "Has Pilgrim Sun been to P'êng-lai already?" asked the Great Immortal. "Yes," said the Star of Longevity. "As he had damaged the cinnabar tree of the Great Immortal, he came to our place to seek a cure. When he found out that we didn't have any, he went elsewhere in search of it. He was afraid, however, that he would exceed the time limit of three days set by the holy monk and provoke him to recite the Tight-Fillet Spell. That is the reason why we came to see you and to ask you for an extension of the limit." When Tripitaka heard this, he said repeatedly, "I won't recite it! I won't recite it!"

As they talked, Pa-chieh came running in again to tug at the Star of Blessing. Demanding that he be given some fruits to eat, he began to give the Star a complete search, poking into his sleeves, frisking his waist, and even lifting up the hem of his robe. "What sort of bad manners is that, Pa-chieh?" asked Tripitaka with a laugh. "I'm not ill-mannered," said Pa-chieh. "This is called 'Every Turn's a Blessing.'" Tripitaka again ordered him to leave. As he slogged towards the door, Idiot turned and stared fiercely at the Star of Blessing. "Stupid coolie!" said the Star. "How have I offended you that you should be so mad at me?" "I'm not mad at you," said Pa-chieh. "I'm just doing what they call 'Turning Your Head to Look for Blessing'!" When Idiot went out of the door, he ran into a little lad holding four tea-spoons while searching in the hall for the cups with which he could present tea. Pa-chieh grabbed the spoons and ran into the main hall; picking up a sonorous stone, he began to strike it wildly with the spoons as he pranced about. "This monk," said the Great Immortal, "is becoming more and more undignified!" "I'm not undignified," said Pa-chieh, laughing. "This is called the 'Joyful Festivities of Four Seasons.'"[4]

We shall now stop telling you about the pranks of Pa-chieh and turn instead to Pilgrim, who mounted the auspicious clouds to leave P'êng-lai and soon arrived at the Fang-chang Mountain. It was a lovely mountain indeed, for which we have the following testimonial poem.

The soaring Fang-chang, a Heaven by itself—
The primal palace where immortals meet.
Light from purple towers brightens three pure paths;

The scent of flowers floats up with five-colored mists.
Gold phoenixes themselves often pause on the pearly arch.
But who forces the jade juice[5] to flood the agaric fields?
Pink peaches and purple plums newly ripened
Announce in truth an aeon's change among the gods.

Pilgrim lowered his cloud, but he was in no mood to enjoy the scenery. As he proceeded, he was met by a gentle scented breeze and by the sounds of black cranes. Then he saw in the distance an immortal, from whom

Ten thousand motley rays shot out to fill the sky.
Colored mists drifted up with endless shafts of light.
His red phoenix's mouth held flowers ever fresh;
His green phoenix soared with canorous cries.
His luck, great as the East Ocean; his age, like a mountain.
He looked like a boy with sound, healthy frame.
His vase kept the cave-heaven's ageless drug;
A seal old as the sun hung from his waist.
He brought blessings to mankind many times,
And saved the world a few times from distresses.
King Wu summoned him to add to his age.
He always attended the Festival of Peaches.
He taught various monks to break their worldly ties,
Revealing to them like lightning a great way.
He did cross the seas to wish a man long life;
He saw Buddha often at Spirit Mountain.
His holy title: Supreme Ruler of the East,
First among the immortals of smoke and mist.

Somewhat shamefacedly, Pilgrim Sun met him and said, "Supreme Ruler, I'm raising my hands!" The Supreme Ruler hastened to return the salutation, saying, "Great Sage, forgive me for not going to meet you. Please come to my place and let me serve you tea." He then took the hands of Pilgrim and led him inside. It was truly a divine palace, where there were countless arches studded with pearl-oyster shells, jasper pools, and jade terraces. As they sat down to wait for their tea, a little lad stepped out from behind the jade screen. "How was he dressed?" you ask.

His body wore a Taoist robe of lustrous hues;
He tied a bright silk sash around his waist;
He wore a silk head wrap to tread the Dipper;[6]

His feet had straw sandals to tour fairy haunts.
He refined his real, primal self
To cast the original shell.
Merit achieved, he could play as he pleased.
He found out the true source of spirit, sperm, and breath;
His master knew him, there was no mistake.
He fled from fame, glad to have now an ageless life—
The months, the seasons had no hold on him.
Passing the winding corridors
To ascend the royal towers,
He found three times divine peaches from the sky.
With fragrant clouds he came from behind jade screens,
This little immortal was called Tung-fang Shuo.[7]

When Pilgrim saw him, he laughed and said, "So, this little crook is here! But there's no peach at the Supreme Ruler's place for you to steal and eat." Tung-fang Shuo bowed to him and replied, "Old burglar! Why did you come? There's no divine elixir at my master's place for you to steal and eat."

"Stop blabbering, Man-ch'ien," cried the Supreme Ruler. "Bring us some tea." Man-ch'ien, you see, was the religious name of Tung-fang Shuo. He hurried inside to fetch two cups of tea. After they had finished drinking, Pilgrim said, "Old Monkey came here to ask of you a favor. Will you grant me that?" "What favor?" said the Supreme Ruler. "Please tell me." "I recently became guardian of the T'ang monk on his westward journey," said Pilgrim. "We were passing by the Temple of Five Villages at the Mountain of Longevity, where we were insulted by two young lads. My anger of the moment made me topple their Ginseng Fruit Tree, which led to T'ang monk being detained for the time being. That's why I came to ask you for a cure. I hope you'll be generous about the matter." "You ape," said the Supreme Ruler. "You really don't care for anything except to cause trouble everywhere. The Chên-yüan-tzŭ of the Temple of Five Villages, with the holy title of 'Lord, Equal to Earth,' happens to be the patriarch of earthly immortals. How did you manage to offend someone like him? That Ginseng Fruit Tree of his, you know, is the grass of the reverted cinnabar. If you had stolen it and eaten it, you would be guilty already. Now you have gone so far as to knock the tree down. You think he'll let you get away with that?" "Exactly," said Pilgrim. "We did escape, but he caught up with us and scooped us up in his sleeve as if we were handkerchiefs. It's a troublesome affair: since I could not prevail, I had to promise him that the tree would be cured. That's why I came to beg you." The Supreme Ruler said, "I have one grain of the great monad reverted cinnabar of nine turns. It can be a cure for all the creatures in the world, but it cannot cure trees. For trees are the spirits of earth and wood, nourished by Heaven and Earth. Moreover, the Ginseng Fruit Tree is no tree of the mortal world; if it were, you might find a cure for it. But the Mountain of Longevity happens to be a Heavenly region, and the Temple of Five Villages is a cave-heaven of the West Aparagodānīya Continent. And the Ginseng Fruit Tree produced there is a spiritual root which came into existence at the time of creation. How can it be healed? I have no cure, none whatever!"

"If you have no cure, old Monkey will take his leave," said Pilgrim. The Supreme Ruler would have liked to offer him a cup of jade nectar, but Pilgrim said, "This is emergency business; I dare not linger." He then mounted the clouds to proceed to the island of Ying-chou. This, too, was a lovely place, for which we have a testimonial poem. The poem says:

The elegant pearl tree[8] aglow in purple mists;
Arches and towers of Ying-chou touching the sky;
Green hills, blue waters, and fair coralline blooms;
Jade nectar, red steel,[9] and the hard iron stone.
The five-colored jade cock calls up the sun from the sea;
The red phoenix, ageless, breathes in scarlet mists.
In vain mortals seek to grasp the scene in the vase,
That eternal spring beyond the world of forms.

Our Great Sage arrived at Ying-chou, where before the red cliffs and beneath the pearl trees sat several figures with luminous white hair and beards, immortals of youthful complexion. They were playing chess and drinking wine, telling jokes and singing songs. Truly there were

Hallowed clouds all filled with light;
Auspicious mists with fragrance afloat;
Colorful phoenixes calling at the cave's entrance;
Dark cranes dancing on top of the mountain.
Jadelike lotus roots and peaches went well with wine;
Magic pears and fire dates prolonged the years.
Each one of them had no need to heed any royal summons,

Though the divine record had each of their names.
Wholly at ease, they could wander and play;
With no work or care, they could do as they pleased.
The months, the years had no hold on their lives;
Throughout the great world they were completely free.
How lovely were the black apes
Who came in pairs, bowing, to present the fruits!
How friendly were the white deer
Who lay down two by two with flowers in their mouths!

Those old men were enjoying themselves when our Pilgrim walked up to them and cried, "How about letting me have some fun too?" When the immortals saw him, they quickly rose to greet him. We have a poem as a testimony, and the poem says:

The spirit roots of the Ginseng Fruit Tree snapped;
The Great Sage called on the gods for the wondrous cure.
As scarlet light poured from the divine grove,
He was met by the Nine Elders of Ying-chou.

Recognizing the Nine Elders, Pilgrim said laughing, "Old Brothers, how content you are!" "If the Great Sage in years past had persevered in the truth," said the Nine Elders, "and had not disrupted Heaven, he would be even more content than we are. But you are all right now. We heard that you had returned to the truth to seek Buddha in the West. Where do you find such leisure to come here?" Pilgrim then gave a thorough account of his efforts to find a cure for the tree. Astounded, the Nine Elders said, "You cause too much trouble! Just too much trouble. Honestly, we don't have any cure." "If you don't," said Pilgrim, "I shall take leave of you."

The Nine Elders asked him to stay and drink some jade nectar and eat some lotus root. Pilgrim would not sit down but, standing, drank a glass of nectar and ate a piece of lotus. He then left Ying-chou swiftly and headed straight for the Great Eastern Ocean. Soon the Potalaka Mountain came in sight. Dropping down from the clouds, he went straight to the top of the mountain, where he saw the Bodhisattva Kuan-yin giving a lecture to the various celestial guardians, dragon-ladies, and Mokṣa in the purple bamboo grove. As a testimony, we have a poem which says:

The sea-mistress city's tall with dense auspicious air.
Here you see countless marvelous things.
Know that the thousand vague and varied forms

All come from a small, soundless part of a book.[10]
The Four Noble Truths[11] conferred will bear right fruit:
The Six Stages,[12] when listened to, will set you free.
This young grove[13] has its pleasures special and true:
Fruits full of fragrance and trees full of flowers.

The Bodhisattva was the first to notice Pilgrim's arrival, and she asked the Great Mountain Guardian to go meet him. As he came out of the grove, the guardian shouted, "Sun Wu-k'ung, where are you going?" Raising his head, Pilgrim cried: "Bear rascal! Is Wu-k'ung the name for you to take in vain? If old Monkey hadn't spared you back then, you would have been a corpse on the Black Wind Mountain. Today you are a follower of the Bodhisattva, for you have received the virtuous fruit and you have been made a resident of this immortal mountain so that you can listen frequently to the dharma teachings. Now, with all these benefits, can't you address me as 'Venerable Father'?" That Black Bear, you see, had indeed attained the right fruit, but the fact that he was made a guardian of the Potalaka and given the title "Great Guardian" was something that he owed to Pilgrim. So he really could not do anything but smile and say, "Great Sage, the ancients said, 'The princely man does not dwell on old faults.' Why mention my past? The Bodhisattva asked me to come meet you." Our Pilgrim at once became solemn and earnest as he followed the Great Guardian to bow down to the Bodhisattva in the purple bamboo grove.

"Wu-k'ung," said the Bodhisattva, "where has the T'ang monk reached in his journey?" "The Mountain of Longevity, in the West Aparagodānīya Continent," said Pilgrim. "In that Mountain of Longevity," said the Bodhisattva, "there is a temple of Five Villages, which is the home of the Chên-yüan Great Immortal. Did you come across him?" Banging his head on the ground, Pilgrim said, "It was all because of your disciple, who did not know the Chên-yüan Great Immortal at that Temple of Five Villages. I offended him by damaging his tree, and he in turn held up my master, preventing him from making any progress in his journey." "You mischievous monkey!" scolded the Bodhisattva, who already had knowledge of the whole affair. "You don't know any better! That Ginseng Fruit Tree of his is the spiritual root planted by Heaven and nourished by Earth. Chên-yüan-tzŭ himself is also the patriarch of earthly immortals, and even I must be somewhat deferential to him. Why did you damage his tree?" Bowing low again, Pilgrim said, "Your disciple was truly ignorant. The day when we arrived at the temple, Chên-yüan-tzŭ was not home, and only two immortal lads were there to receive us. It was Chu Wu-nêng who discovered that they had these fruits, and he wanted to try one. Your disciple stole three such fruits which we three brothers divided up among ourselves. When the lads found out, they kept on chiding us until I became so angry that I pushed down the tree. Their master returned the following day and caught up with us; after he had scooped us up with his sleeve, he had us bound and whipped, interrogating and torturing us for a whole day. We escaped that night, but he caught up with us again and took us captive as before. Two or three times it went on like this, and when I became convinced that it was impossible for us to flee, I promised him that I would heal the tree. I have just made a complete tour of the Three Islands seeking a cure from the sea, but none of the immortals was able to give me one. That's why your disciple has come to bow before you in all sincerity. I beg the Bodhisattva in her compassion to grant me a cure, so that the T'ang monk can soon journey toward the West." "Why didn't you come see me earlier?" said the Bodhisattva. "Why did you go looking instead on the islands?"

When Pilgrim heard these words, he was secretly pleased and said to himself. "What luck! What luck! The Bodhisattva must have a cure!" He went forward again to beg some more, and the Bodhisattva said, "The sweet dew in my immaculate vase can heal divine trees or spiritual roots." "Have you tried this before?" asked Pilgrim. "Indeed," said the Bodhisattva. "When?" asked Pilgrim. The Bodhisattva said, "Some years ago Lao Tzu had a wager with me: he took my willow twig and placed it in his elixir-refining brazier until it was completely dried and charred. Then he gave it back to me, and I stuck it in my vase. After one day and one night, I had my green twig and leaves again, as lovely as before." Laughing, Pilgrim said, "I'm lucky! Truly lucky! If a scorched willow could be revived, what's so difficult about a tree that has been knocked over?" The Bodhisattva then gave this order to the rest of her followers: "Maintain your vigilance in the grove. I'll be back soon." She left, balancing the immaculate vase in her hand; the white parrot flew ahead of her, while the Great Sage Sun followed from behind. We have a testimonial poem, and the poem says:

The world can't describe such sacred, golden form:
She's the merciful One who dispels our woes,

She met the stainless Buddha in kalpas past;
An active body she has now achieved.
She calms the sea of passion in many lives;
Her moral nature is wholly unsoiled.
The sweet dew, long charged with true wondrous power,
Will bring life eternal to the precious tree.

We now tell you about the Great Immortal, who was just having lofty conversations with the Three Elders when all at once they saw the Great Sage Sun drop down from the clouds and shout, "The Bodhisattva has arrived. Come meet her quickly! Come meet her quickly!" The Three Stars, Chên-yüan-tzŭ, Tripitaka, and his disciples all hurried out of the main hall. Stopping her sacred cloud, the Bodhisattva first exchanged greetings with Chên-yüan-tzŭ before bowing to the Three Stars. After the ceremony, she took the seat of honor as Pilgrim led the T'ang monk, Pa-chieh, and Sha Monk to bow to her. After that, the various immortals in the temple also came to greet her. "Great Immortal," said Pilgrim, "there's no need for further delay. You may as well prepare the table of incense at once and ask the Bodhisattva to heal that fruit tree of yours." Bowing low to thank the Bodhisattva, the Great Immortal said, "Why should the trivial affair of this plebeian be such a concern to the Bodhisattva that she would take the trouble of coming here?" "The T'ang monk is my disciple," said the Bodhisattva. "If Sun Wu-k'ung has wronged you, it's only reasonable that he should make recompense and return your precious tree." "In that case," said the Three Stars, "there's no further need for polite talk. May we ask the Bodhisattva to go to the garden and see what can be done."

The Great Immortal gave the order to prepare an incense table and to sweep the grounds in the rear garden. The Bodhisattva was asked to lead the way, followed by the Three Elders, Tripitaka, his disciples, and the various immortals of the temple. When they arrived at the garden, they saw the tree lying on the ground—with the soil around it turned up, its roots exposed, its leaves fallen, and its branches dried up. "Wu-k'ung," cried the Bodhisattva, "stretch out your hand." Pilgrim stretched out his left hand. Dipping the willow twig into the sweet dew of her vase, the Bodhisattva then used it as a brush and drew on the palm of Pilgrim a charm that had revivifying power. She told him to place his hand at the base of the tree and watch for the sign of water spurting out. His hand closed tightly, Pilgrim went to the base of the tree and placed his fist on the roots. In a little while, a clear spring welled up from the ground. The Bodhisattva said, "That water cannot be touched by any instrument containing any one of the Five Phases. It must be scooped up by a jade ladle. Push the tree back up into an upright position; pour the water over it from the top down. The bark and the roots will grow back together again; the leaves will come out, the branches will turn green, and the fruits will appear." "Little Taoists," said Pilgrim, "bring me a jade ladle, quickly." "Your humble Taoist lives in a rural area," said Chên-yüan-tzǔ, "and there is no jade ladle available. We have only jade tea cups and jade wine goblets. Can they be used?" "As long as they are made of jade," said the Bodhisattva, "and capable of bailing water, they will be all right. Bring them here." The Great Immortal asked the little lads to take out some thirty jade tea cups and some fifty wine goblets with which they scooped up the clear water. Pilgrim, Pa-chieh, and Sha Monk raised the tree into an upright position and covered its base with topsoil. They then handed the jade cups one by one to the Bodhisattva, who sprinkled the sweet liquid onto the tree with her willow branch as she recited a spell. Before long, she stopped sprinkling, and the tree turned green all at once with thick leaves and branches. Twenty-three ginseng fruits could be seen on top. Clear Breeze and Bright Moon, the two lads, said, "When we discovered our loss the day before, we came up with only twenty-two fruits even after we had counted them over and over. Why is there an extra one today after it has been revived?" " 'Time will disclose the true intent of man,' " said Pilgrim. "Old Monkey took only three the other day; the fourth one dropped to the ground and disappeared, for as the local spirit told me, this treasure would become assimilated once it touched earth. Pa-chieh kept hollering about my skimming something off the top, and that was how my act was discovered. Only today is this whole mess cleared up."

The Bodhisattva said, "That's why I didn't use any instrument containing the Five Phases just now, for I know that this thing and the Five Phases are mutually resistant." Highly pleased, the Great Immortal asked for the gold mallet at once and had ten of the fruits knocked down. He then invited the Bodhisattva and the Three Elders to go back to the main hall, where a Festival of Ginseng Fruits would be given in their honor. The little immortals duly set the tables and took out the cinnabar trays, while the Bodhisattva was asked to take the seat of honor in the center. The Three Elders were seated at the table to the left, the T'ang monk was placed at the right, and Chên-yüan-tzŭ as the host took up the seat down below. We have a testimonial poem which says:

At the Longevity Mountain's ancient cave,
The ginseng fruits ripen every nine thousand years.
The spirit root upturned, shoots and branches are hurt;
The sweet dew quickens, fruits and leaves are made whole.
All are old friends whom the Three Elders gladly meet:
Friends foreordained the four monks find by luck.
Now they have learned to eat the ginseng fruits;
They'll all be immortals who never age.

Presently the Bodhisattva and the Three Elders each ate a fruit. Finally convinced that this was a treasure of the immortals, the T'ang monk also ate one. Each of the three disciples also ate one, and Chên-yüan-tzŭ himself took one to keep his guests company. The last one of the fruits was divided among the other residents of the temple. Pilgrim thanked the Bodhisattva and the Three Stars, who went back to the Potalaka Mountain and P'êng-lai Island, respectively. Chên-yüan-tzŭ also prepared some vegetarian wine for a banquet, during which he and Pilgrim became bond-brothers. As the proverb says, they would not know each other if they had not fought; but now the two families have become one. Happily, master and disciples spent a restful night there. Thus it was with that Elder, who was

Lucky to have tasted the grass of reverted cinnabar;
His long life would bear the ordeals of ogres.

We do not know how they will part the following day, and you must listen to the explanation in the next chapter.

*Twenty-seven*

The Cadaver Demon three times makes fun of Tripitaka T'ang;
In spite the holy monk banishes the Handsome Monkey King.

We were telling you about Tripitaka and his disciples, who made preparations to leave the next morning. Our Chên-yüan-tzŭ, however, had become such a fast friend of Pilgrim since the two were made bond-brothers that he refused to let them leave. He gave orders instead that they should be feted for five or six days. Ever since he took the grass of the reverted cinnabar, the elder's spirit had been strengthened and his body made more robust; he felt as if his entire physical frame had been renewed. As he was intent on acquiring the scriptures, he refused to stay, and so they departed.

After taking their leave, master and disciples took to the road and soon came upon a tall mountain. "Disciples," said Tripitaka, "the mountain ahead appears to be rugged and steep, and I fear that the horse may not be able to proceed so easily. Every one of you should be careful." "Have no fear, Master," said Pilgrim. "We know how to take care of everything." Dear Monkey King! He led the way; carrying his rod horizontally across both his shoulders, he opened up a mountain path and led them up to a tall cliff. They saw

Peaks and summits in rows;
Streams and canyons meandrous;
Tigers and wolves running in packs;
Deer and fallow deer walking in flocks;
Countless musks and boars massed together;
A mountain swarming with foxes and hares.
The huge python of a thousand feet;
The long snake of ten thousand feet.
The huge python blew out awful mists;
The long snake belched dreadful air.
By the road thorns and thistles sprawled unending;
On the peak pines and cedars grew resplendent.
Wild hemps and creepers filled their eyes;

Fragrant plants reached up to the sky.
Light descended from the northern pole;
Clouds parted at the south pole star.
Ten thousand fathoms of mountain holding old, primal breath;
A thousand peaks stood august in the cold sunlight.

The elder on the horse became fearful, but our Great Sage Sun was
ready to show off his abilities. Wielding the iron rod, he let out such
a fearful cry that wolves and serpents retreated, that tigers and
leopards took flight. Master and disciples thus journeyed into the
mountain. As they reached the summit, Tripitaka said, "Wu-k'ung,
we've been traveling for almost a day, and I'm getting hungry. Go
somewhere and beg some vegetarian food for me." "Master, you
aren't very smart!" said Pilgrim, attempting to placate him with a
smile. "We are in the middle of a mountain, with no village in sight
ahead of us nor any inn behind us. Even if we had money, there's no
place for us to buy anything. Where do you want me to go to find
vegetarian food?" Irritated, Tripitaka began to berate his disciple.
"You ape!" he cried. "Don't you remember what sort of condition
you were in at the Mountain of Two Frontiers? Pinned down by
Tathāgata in that stone box, you could move your mouth but not
your feet, and you owed it to me for saving your life. Now that you
have become my disciple by having your head touched and receiving
the commandments, why are you not willing to exert yourself a bit
more? Why are you always so lazy?" "Your disciple," said Pilgrim,
"has been rather diligent. Since when have I been lazy?" "If you are
that diligent," said Tripitaka, "why don't you go and beg me some
vegetarian food? How can I journey if I am hungry? Moreover, this
mountain is filled with pestilential vapors, and if I become ill, how can
I hope to reach Thunderclap?" "Master," said Pilgrim, "please don't
get upset. No more words. I know that yours is a proud and haughty
nature. A little offense and you will recite that little something spell!
Dismount and rest awhile. Let me find out whether there's any family
for me to beg some vegetarian food."

With a bound, Pilgrim leaped up to the edge of the clouds. Using
his hand to shade his eyes, he peered all around. Alas! The journey to
the West was a lonely journey, one with neither villages nor hamlets.
There were abundant trees and shrubbery, but there was no sign of
human habitation. Having looked around for some time, Pilgrim saw
toward the south a tall mountain, where on the eastern slope there

seemed to be some tiny specks of red. Lowering his cloud, Pilgrim said, "Master, there's something to eat." The elder asked what it was, and Pilgrim said, "There's no household here for me to beg for rice. But there's a stretch of red on a mountain south of here, and I suppose that must be ripe mountain peaches. Let me go and pick a few for you to eat." Delighted, Tripitaka said, "For a person who has left the family to have peaches is already the highest blessing!" Pilgrim took the alms bowl and mounted the auspicious luminosity. Look at that brilliant somersault, with cold vapor trailing! In an instant, he was heading straight for the peaches on the south mountain, and we shall speak no more of him for the moment.

Now, the proverb says:

A tall mountain will always have monsters;

A rugged peak will always produce fiends.

In this mountain there was indeed a monster-spirit, who was disturbed by the Great Sage Sun's departure. Treading dark wind, she came through the clouds and found the elder sitting on the ground. "What luck! What luck!" she said, unable to contain her delight. "For several years my relatives have been talking about a T'ang monk from the Land of the East going to fetch the Great Vehicle. He is actually the incarnation of the Gold Cicada, and he has the original body which has gone through the process of self-cultivation during ten previous existences. If a man eats a piece of his flesh, his age will be immeasurably lengthened. So, this monk has at last arrived today!" The monster was about to go down to seize Tripitaka when she saw two great warriors standing guard on either side of the elder, and that stopped her from drawing near. Now, who could these warriors be, you ask? They were, of course, Pa-chieh and Sha Monk. Pa-chieh and Sha Monk, you see, might not have great abilities, but after all, Pa-chieh was the Marshal of Heavenly Reeds and Sha Monk was the Great Curtain-Raising Captain. Their authority had not been completely eroded, and that was why the monster dared not approach them. Instead, the monster said to herself, "Let me make fun of them a bit, and see what happens."

Dear monster! She lowered her dark wind into the field of the mountain, and, with one shake of her body, she changed into a girl with a face like the moon and features like flowers. One cannot begin to describe the bright eyes and the elegant brows, the white teeth and the red lips. Holding in her left hand a blue sandstone pot and in her

right a green porcelain vase, she walked from west to east, heading
straight for the T'ang monk.

> The sage monk resting his horse on the cliff
> Saw all at once a young girl drawing near:
> Slender hands hugged by gently swaying green sleeves;
> Tiny feet exposed beneath a skirt of Hunan silk.
> Perspiring her face seemed flower bedewed;
> Dust grazed her moth-brows like willows held by mist.
> And as he stared intently with his eyes,
> She seemed to be walking right up to his side.

When Tripitaka saw her, he called out: "Pa-chieh, Sha Monk, just
now Wu-k'ung said that this is an uninhabited region. But isn't that
a human being who is walking over there?" "Master," said Pa-chieh,
"you sit here with Sha Monk. Let old Hog go take a look." Putting
down his muckrake and pulling down his shirt, our Idiot tried to affect
the airs of a gentleman and went to meet her face to face. Well, it was
as the proverb says:

> You can't determine the truth from afar.
> You can see clearly when you go near.

The girl's appearance was something to behold!

> Ice-white skin hides jadelike bones;
> Her collar reveals a milk-white bosom.
> Willow brows gather dark green hues;
> Almond eyes shine like silver stars.
> Her features like the moon are coy;
> Her natural disposition is pure.
> Her body's like the willow-nested swallow;
> Her voice's like the woods' singing oriole.
> A half-opened *hai-t'ang*[1] caressed by the morning sun.
> A newly bloomed peony displaying her charm.

When Idiot saw how pretty she was, his worldly mind was aroused
and he could not refrain from babbling. "Lady Bodhisattva!" he cried.
"Where are you going? What's that you are holding in your hands?"
This was clearly a fiend, but he could not recognize her! The girl immediately answered him, saying, "Elder, what I have in the blue pot
is fragrant rice made from wine cakes, and there's fried wheat gluten
in the green vase. I came here for no other reason than to redeem my
vow of feeding monks." When Pa-chieh heard these words, he was
very pleased. Spinning around, he ran like a hog maddened by plague

to report to Tripitaka, crying, "Master! 'The good man will have Heaven's reward!' Because you are hungry, you ask Elder Brother to go beg for some vegetarian food. But we really don't know where that ape has gone to pick his peaches and have his fun! If you eat too many peaches, you are liable to feel a bit stuffed and gaseous anyway! Take a look instead. Isn't that someone coming to feed the monks?" "Coolie, you're just clowning!" said an unbelieving T'ang monk. "We've been traveling all this time and we haven't even run into a healthy person! Where is this person who's coming to feed the monks?" "Master," said Pa-chieh, "isn't this the one?"

When Tripitaka saw the girl, he jumped up and folded his hands. "Lady Bodhisattva," he said, "where is your home? What sort of family is yours? What kind of vow have you made that you have to come here to feed the monks?" This was clearly a fiend, but our elder could not recognize her either! When that monster heard the T'ang monk asking after her background, she at once resorted to falsehood. With clever, specious words, she tried to deceive her interrogator, saying, "Master, this mountain, which turns back serpents and frightens wild beasts, bears the name of White Tiger. My home is located due west of here. My parents, still living, are frequent readers of sūtras and keen on doing good works. They have fed liberally the monks who come to us from near and far. Because my parents had no son, they prayed to the gods, and I was born. They would have liked to marry me off to a noble family, but, wary of helplessness in their old age, they took in a son-in-law instead, so that they would be cared for in life and death." Hearing this, Tripitaka said, "Lady Bodhisattva, your speech is rather improper! The sage classic says, 'While father and mother are alive, one does not travel abroad; or if one does, goes only to those places one regularly visits.'[2] If your parents are still living, and if they have taken in a husband for you, then your man should have been the one sent to redeem your vow. Why do you walk about the mountain all by yourself? You don't even have an attendant to accompany you. That's not very becoming of a woman!" Smiling broadly, the girl quickly tried to placate him with more clever words. "Master," she said, "my husband is at the northern fold of this mountain, leading a few workers to plow the fields. This happens to be the lunch I prepared for them to eat. Since now is the busy season of farm work, we have no servants; and as my parents are getting old, I have to run the errand myself. Meeting you three distant travelers is quite by accident, but when I think of my parents' inclination to do good deeds, I would like very much to use this rice as food for monks. If you don't regard this as unworthy of you, please accept this modest offering." "My goodness! My goodness!" said Tripitaka. "I have a disciple who has gone to pick some fruits, and he's due back any moment. I dare not eat. For if I, a monk, were to eat your rice, your husband would scold you when he learns of it. Will it then not be the fault of this poor monk?" When that girl saw the T'ang monk refuse to take the food, she smiled even more seductively and said, "O Master! My parents, who love to feed the monks, are not even as zealous as my husband. For his entire life is devoted to the construction of bridges and the repairing of roads, in reverence for the aged and pity for the poor. If he heard that the rice was given to feed Master, his affection for me, his wife, would increase manyfold." Tripitaka, however, simply refused to eat, and Pa-chieh on one side became utterly exasperated. Pouting, our Idiot grumbled to himself: "There are countless priests in the world, but none is more wishy-washy than this old priest of ours! Here's ready-made rice, and three portions to boot! But he will not eat it. He has to wait for that monkey's return and the rice divided into four portions before he'll eat." Without permitting further discussion, he pushed over the pot with one shove of his snout and was about to begin.

Look at our Pilgrim! Having picked several peaches from the mountain peak in the south, he came hurtling back with a single somersault, holding the alms bowl in his hand. When he opened wide his fiery eyes and diamond pupils to take a look, he recognized that the girl was a monster. He put down the bowl, pulled out his iron rod, and was about to bring it down hard on the monster's head. The elder was so aghast that he pulled his disciple back with his hands. "Wu-k'ung," he cried, "whom have you come back to hit?" "Master," said Pilgrim, "don't regard this girl in front of you as a good person. She's a monster, and she has come to deceive you." "Monkey," said Tripitaka, "you used to possess a measure of true discernment. How is it that you are talking nonsense today? This Lady Bodhisattva is so kind that she wants to feed me with her rice. Why do you say that she's a monster?" "Master," said Pilgrim with a laugh, "how could you know about this? When I was a monster back at the Water-Curtain Cave, I would act like this if I wanted to eat human flesh. I would change myself into gold or silver, a lonely building, a harmless drunk, or a beautiful woman. Anyone feebleminded enough to be attracted by me I would lure back to the cave. There I would enjoy him as I pleased, by steaming or boiling. If I couldn't finish him off in one meal, I would dry the leftovers in the sun to keep for rainy days. Master, if I had returned a little later, you would have fallen into her trap and been harmed by her." That T'ang monk, however, simply refused to believe these words; he kept saying instead that the woman was a good person.

"Master," said Pilgrim, "I think I know what's happening. Your worldly mind must have been aroused by the sight of this woman's beauty. If you do have the desire, why not ask Pa-chieh to cut some timber and Sha Monk to find us some grass. I'll be the carpenter and build you a little hut right here where you can consummate the affair with her. We can each go our own way then. Wouldn't that be the thing to do? Why bother to undertake such a long journey to fetch the scriptures?" The elder, you see, was a rather tame and gentle person. He was so embarrassed by these few words that his whole bald head turned red from ear to ear.

As Tripitaka was struck dumb by his shame, Pilgrim's temper flared again. Wielding his iron rod, he aimed it at the monster's face and delivered a terrific blow. The fiend, however, had a few tricks of her own. She knew the magic of Liberation through the Corpse.[3] When she saw Pilgrim's rod coming at her she roused her spirit and left, leaving behind the corpse of her body struck dead on the ground. Shaking with terror, the elder mumbled, "This ape is so unruly, so obdurate! Despite my repeated pleadings, he still takes human life without cause." "Don't be offended, Master," said Pilgrim, "just come see for yourself what kind of things are in the pot." Sha Monk led the elder near to take a look. The fragrant rice made from wine cakes was nowhere to be found; there was instead a potful of large maggots with long tails. There was no fried wheat gluten either, but a few frogs and ugly toads were hopping all over the place. The elder was about to think that there might be thirty percent truthfulness in Pilgrim's words, but Pa-chieh would not let his own resentment subside. He began to cast aspersions on his companion, saying, "Master, this woman, come to think of it, happens to be a farm girl of this area. Because she had to take some lunch to the fields, she met us on the way. How could she be deemed a monster? That rod of Elder Brother is quite heavy you know. He came back and wanted to try his hand on her, not anticipating that one blow would kill her. He's afraid that you might recite that so-called Tight-Fillet Spell, and that's why he's using some sort of magic to hoodwink you. It's he who has caused these things to appear, just to befuddle you so that you won't recite the spell."

This single speech of Pa-chieh, alas, spelled disaster for Tripitaka! Believing the slanderous suasion of our Idiot, he made the magic sign with his hand and recited the spell. At once Pilgrim began to scream: "My head! My head! Stop reciting! Stop reciting! If you've got something to say, say it." "What do I have to say?" asked the T'ang monk. "Those who have left the family must defer to people every time, must cherish kindness in every thought. They must 'Keep ants out of harm's way when they sweep the floor, and put shades on lamps for the love of moths.' And you, you practice violence with every step! Since you have beaten to death this innocent commoner, what good would it do even if you were to go to acquire the scriptures? You might as well go back." "Master," said Pilgrim, "where do you want me to go back to?" The T'ang monk said, "I don't want you as my disciple." "If you don't want me as your disciple," said Pilgrim, "I fear that you may not make it on your way to the Western Heaven." "My life is in the care of Heaven," said the T'ang monk. "If it's ordained that I should be food for the monster, even if I were to be steamed or boiled, it's all right with me. Furthermore, do you think really that you have the power to deliver me from the great limit? Go back quickly!" "Master," said Pilgrim, "it's all right for me to go back, but I have not yet repaid your kindness." "What kindness have I shown you?" said the T'ang monk. When the Great Sage heard this, he knelt down immediately and kowtowed, saying, "Because old Monkey brought great disruption to the Celestial Palace, he incurred for himself the fatal ordeal of being clamped by Buddha beneath the Mountain of Two Frontiers. I was indebted to the Bodhisattva Kuan-yin who gave me the commandments, and to Master who gave me freedom. If I don't go up to the Western Heaven with you, it will mean that I

Knowing kindness without repaying am no princely man.

Mine will be forever an infamous name."

Now the T'ang monk, after all, is a compassionate holy monk. When he saw Pilgrim pleading so piteously with him, he changed his mind and said, "In that case, I'll forgive you this time. Don't you dare be unruly again. If you work violence again as before, I'll recite this spell over and over twenty times." "You may recite it thirty times," said Pilgrim, "but I won't hit anyone again." Helping the T'ang monk to mount the horse, he then presented the peaches which he picked. The T'ang monk indeed ate a few of the peaches on the horse to relieve his hunger momentarily.

We now tell you about the monster who got away by rising up into the sky. That one blow of Pilgrim's rod, you see, did not kill her, for she fled by sending away her spirit. Standing on top of the clouds, she gnashed her teeth at Pilgrim, saying spitefully to herself, "The last few years I have heard nothing but people talking about his abilities, but I've discovered today that his is not a false reputation. Already deceived by me, the T'ang monk was about to eat the rice. If he had just lowered his head and taken one whiff of it, I would have grabbed him and he would have been all mine. Little did I anticipate that this other fellow would return and bust up my business. What's more, I almost received a blow from his rod. If I had let this monk get away, I would have labored in vain. I'm going back down there to make fun of him once more."

Dear monster! Lowering the direction of her dark cloud, she dropped into the fold of the mountain further ahead and changed with one shake of her body into a woman eighty years old, having in her hands a bamboo cane with a curved handle. She headed toward the pilgrims, weeping each step of the way. When Pa-chieh saw her, he was horrified. "Master," he said, "it's terrible! That old dame approaching us is looking for someone." "Looking for whom?" said the T'ang monk. Pa-chieh said, "The girl slain by Elder Brother has to be the daughter. This one must be the mother looking for her." "Stop talking nonsense, Brother," said Pilgrim. "That girl was about eighteen, but this woman is at least eighty. How could she still bear children when she was sixty-some years old? She's a fake! Let old Monkey go have a look." Dear Pilgrim! In big strides he walked forward to look at the monster, who

Changed falsely into an old dame,
With temples white as snow.
She walked ever so slowly
With steps both small and sluggish.
Her frail body was most slender;
Her face, a leaf dried and wilted.
Her cheek bones jutted upward;

Her lips curled downward and out.
Old age is not quite like the time of youth:
The face is wrinkled like lotus leaves.
Recognizing the monster, Pilgrim did not even bother to wait for any discussion; he lifted up the rod and struck at the head at once. When the monster saw the uplifted rod, she again exercised her magic and her spirit rose into the air, leaving behind again the corpse of her body struck dead beside the road. The sight so frightened the T'ang monk that he fell from his horse. Lying on the road, he did not speak another word except to recite the Tight-Fillet Spell back and forth exactly twenty times. Alas, poor Pilgrim's head was reduced to an hourglass-shaped gourd! As the pain was truly unbearable, he had to roll up to the T'ang monk and plead: "Master, please don't recite anymore. Say what you have to say." "What's there to say?" asked the T'ang monk. "Those who have left the family will listen to the words of virtue to avoid falling into Hell. I have tried my best to enlighten you with admonition. Why do you persist in doing violence? You have beaten to death one commoner after another. How do you explain this?" "She's a monster," said Pilgrim. The T'ang monk said, "This monkey is babbling nonsense! You tell me that there are that many monsters! You are a person lacking any will to do good, one who is only bent on evil. You'd better go." "Master," said Pilgrim, "are you sending me away again? All right, I'll go back. But there's something which I find disagreeable." "What do you find disagreeable?" asked the T'ang monk. "Master," said Pa-chieh, "he wants you to divide up the luggage with him! You think he wants to go back empty-handed after following you as a monk all this time? Why don't you see whether you have any old shirt or tattered hat in your wrap there and give him a couple of pieces."

When Pilgrim heard these words, he became so incensed that he jumped up and down, crying, "You loud-mouthed overstuffed coolie! Ever since old Monkey embraced the teachings of complete poverty, he has never displayed the least bit of envy or greed. What are you talking about, dividing up the luggage?" "If you show neither envy nor greed," said the T'ang monk, "why don't you leave?" "To tell you the truth, Master," said Pilgrim, "when old Monkey lived at the Water-Curtain Cave of the Flower-Fruit Mountain five hundred years ago, he was hero enough to receive the submission of the demons of seventy-two caves and to command forty-seven thousand little fiends.

I was quite a man then: wearing on my head a purple gold cap, putting on my body a red and yellow robe, tying around my waist a jade belt, having on my feet a pair of cloud-treading shoes, and holding in my hands the compliant golden-hooped rod. But ever since Nirvāṇa delivered me from my sins, when with my hair shorn I took the vow of complete poverty and followed you as your disciple, I had this gold fillet clamped on my head. If I go back like this, I can't face the folks at home. If Master doesn't want me any more, please recite the Loose-Fillet Spell so that I may get rid of this thing from my head and return it to you. I'll find that most pleasant and agreeable then. After all, I have followed you all this time; surely you would not deny me this bit of human kindness!" Greatly taken aback, the T'ang monk said, "Wu-k'ung, I only received the Tight-Fillet Spell in secret from the Bodhisattva. There was no Loose-Fillet Spell." "If there was no Loose-Fillet Spell," said Pilgrim, "then you'd better still take me along." The elder had no alternative but to say, "You'd better get up. I'll forgive you one more time, but you must not do violence again." "I won't dare do so," said Pilgrim, "I won't dare do so." He helped his master to mount up once more and then led the way forward.

We now tell you about that monster who, you see, had not been killed by Pilgrim's second blow either. In midair, the fiend could not refrain from praising her opponent, saying, "Marvelous Monkey King! What perception! He could recognize me even when I had changed into that form! These monks are moving on rather quickly; another forty miles westward beyond the mountain and they will leave my domain. If some demons or fiends of another region pick them up, people would laugh till their mouths crack up, and I would eat my heart out! I'll go down and make fun of them one more time." Dear Monster! Lowering the dark wind again into the fold of the mountain, she shook her body and changed herself into an old man. Truly he had

Flowing white hair like P'êng Tsu's,[4]
And beard more frosty than the Age Star's.
A jade stone[5] rang in his ears,
And gold stars flashed in his eyes.
Holding a curved dragon-head cane,
He wore a light crane's-down cloak.
Grasping in his hands some beads,
He chanted a Buddhist sūtra.

When the T'ang monk on his horse saw this old man, he was very pleased. "Amitābha!" he cried. "The West is truly a blessed region! This dear old man can hardly walk, but he still wants to recite the sūtras!" "Master," said Pa-chieh, "stop praising him. He's the root of disaster!" "What do you mean the root of disaster?" said the T'ang monk. Pa-chieh said, "Elder Brother killed his daughter as well as his wife, and now you see this old man groping his way here. If we run smack into him, Master, you'll pay with your life since you are guilty of death. Old Hog is your follower, so he'll be banished to serve in the army; Sha Monk carries out your orders, so he'll be sentenced to hard labor. But our Elder Brother, of course, will use some kind of escape magic to get away. Now, won't that leave the three of us here to take the blame for him?"

Hearing this, Pilgrim said, "This root of idiocy! Won't this kind of absurdity alarm our master? Let old Monkey go and have another look." He put away his rod and went forward to meet the fiend. "Aged Sir," he called, "where are you going? Why are you walking and reciting a sūtra as well?" Our monster this time somehow misread, as it were, the balance of the steelyard, and she thought that Great Sage Sun was after all an ordinary fellow. Hence she said, "Elder, this old man has lived here for generations. My whole life is devoted to doing good and feeding the monks, to reading scriptures and chanting sūtras. Fate did not give me a boy, and I had only a girl, for whom I took in a son-in-law. This morning she went off to take rice down to the fields, and we fear that she might have been made food for the tiger instead. My old wife went searching for her, but she, too, did not return. In fact, I have absolutely no idea what has happened to them. That's why this old man came seeking to see if they have been harmed in any way. If so, I have little alternative but to take back their bones and have them buried properly on our ancestral site." "I'm the ancestor in pulling pranks!" said Pilgrim laughing. "How dare you sneak up on me and try to deceive me with something up your sleeve? You can't fool me. I can see that you are a monster." The monster was so startled that she could not utter another word. Wielding his rod, Pilgrim was about to strike, but he said to himself: "If I don't hit her, she's going to pull some trick again, but if I hit her, I fear that Master will recite that spell again." He thought to himself some more: "But if I don't kill her, she can grab Master the moment she has the opportunity, and then I'll have to make all that effort to save him.

I'd better strike! One blow will kill her, but Master will surely recite that spell. Well, the proverb says: 'Even the vicious tiger will not devour its own.' I'll have to use my eloquence, my dexterous tongue, to convince him, that's all." Dear Great Sage! He recited a spell himself and summoned the local spirit and the mountain god, saying to them, "This monster made fun of my master three times. This time I'm going to make sure I'll kill her, but you must stand guard in the air. Don't let her get away." When the deities heard this command, neither dared disobey it, and they both stood guard on the edge of the clouds. Our Great Sage lifted up his rod and struck down the demon, whose spiritual light was extinguished only then.

The T'ang monk on the horse was again so horrified by what he saw that he could not even utter a word, but Pa-chieh on one side snickered and said, "Dear Pilgrim! His delirium is acting up again! He has journeyed for only half a day and he has slaughtered three persons!" The T'ang monk was about to recite the spell when Pilgrim dashed up to the horse, crying, "Master! Don't recite! Don't recite! Just come and take a look at how she looks now." There was in front of them a pile of flour-white skeletal bones. "Wu-k'ung," said the T'ang monk, greatly shaken, "this person has just died. How could she change all at once into a skeleton?" Pilgrim said, "She's a demonic and pernicious cadaver, out to seduce and harm people. When she was killed by me, she revealed her true form. You can see for yourself that there's a row of characters on her spine; she's called 'The White-Bone Lady.'" When the T'ang monk heard what he said, he was about to believe him, but Pa-chieh would not desist from slander. "Master," said he, "his hand's heavy and his rod's vicious. He has beaten someone to death, but, fearing your recital, he deliberately changed her into something like this just to befuddle you."

Indeed a shilly-shally person, the T'ang monk believed Pa-chieh once more and started his recital. Unable to bear the pain, Pilgrim could only kneel beside the road and cry, "Don't recite! Don't recite! If you have something to say, say it quickly." "Monkey head!" said the T'ang monk. "What's there to say? The virtuous deeds of those having left the family should be like grass in a garden of spring: though their growth is invisible, they multiply daily. But he who practices evil is like a whetstone: though its ruin is invisible, it diminishes daily. You manage to get away even after beating to death altogether three persons only because there's no one here to oppose you, to take you to task in these desolate wilds. But suppose we get to a crowded city and you suddenly start hitting people regardless of good or ill with that mourning staff of yours, how would I be able to go free from that kind of great misfortune caused by you? You'd better go back." "Master," said Pilgrim, "you have really wronged me. This is undeniably a monstrous spirit, bent on hurting you. I have helped you to ward off danger by killing her, but you can't see it. You believe instead those sarcastic and slanderous remarks of Idiot to such an extent that you try to get rid of me several times. The proverb says, 'Anything can't repeat itself three times'! If I don't leave you, I'll be a base and shameless fellow. I'll go! I'll go! It's no big deal, in fact, for me to leave, but then you will have no man to serve you." Turning angry, the T'ang monk said, "This brazen ape is becoming even more unruly. So you think that you are the only man around here? Wu-nêng and Wu-ching, they are not men?"

When the Great Sage heard this statement about the other two disciples, he was so deeply hurt that he could not but say to the T'ang monk, "O misery! Think of the time when Liu Po-ch'in was your companion as you left Ch'ang-an. After you delivered me from the Mountain of Two Frontiers and made me your disciple, I penetrated ancient caves and invaded deep forests to capture demons and defeat monsters. I was the one who, having experienced countless difficulties, subdued Pa-chieh and acquired Sha Monk. Today, 'banishing Wisdom just to Court Folly,' you want me to go back. That's how it is: 'When the birds vanish, the bow is stored; when the hares perish, the dogs are cooked.'⁶ All right! All right! There's only one thing left for us to settle, and that's the Tight-Fillet Spell." The T'ang monk said, "I won't recite that again." "That's hard to say," said Pilgrim. "For when the time comes for you to face those treacherous demons and bitter ordeals, and when you, because Pa-chieh and Sha Monk cannot rescue you, think of me and cannot stop yourself from reciting it, I'll have a headache even if I'm one hundred thousand miles away. I'll have to come back to see you, so why don't you let this matter drop now."

When the T'ang monk saw that Pilgrim was so long-winded, he became angrier still. Rolling down from his horse, he told Sha Monk to take out paper and brush from one of the wraps. Fetching some water from a brook nearby and rubbing out some ink with an ink-slab on a rock, he wrote at once a letter of banishment. Handing it over to Pilgrim, he said, "Monkey head! Take this as a certificate. I'll never want you as a disciple. If I ever consent to see you again, let me fall into the Avīci Hell!"[7] Taking the letter of banishment, Pilgrim said quickly, "Master, no need to swear. Old Monkey will leave." He folded up the letter and put it in his sleeve. Attempting once more to placate the T'ang monk, he said, "Master, I have followed you after all for all this time because of the Bodhisattva's instructions. Today I have to quit in midjourney and am not able to attain the meritorious fruit. Please take a seat and let me bow to you, so that I can leave in peace." T'ang monk turned his back and refused to reply, mumbling only, "I'm a good priest, and I won't take the salutation of an evil man like you!" When the Great Sage saw that the T'ang monk refused to answer, he resorted to the magic of the Body beyond the Body. Pulling three pieces of hair from the back of his head, he blew on them a magic breath and cried, "Change!" They changed at once into three Pilgrims, who along with himself surrounded the master on all four sides. The master tried to turn left and right, but he was unable to dodge anymore and had to receive a bow from one of them.

Jumping up, the Great Sage shook his body and retrieved his hair. Then he gave the following instructions to Sha Monk, saying, "Worthy Brother, you are a good man. Do be careful, however, that you don't listen to the foolish nonsense of Pa-chieh. You must also exercise caution on the journey. If there should be a time when a monster catches hold of Master, you just say that old Monkey happens to be his senior disciple. When those clumsy fiends of the West get wind of my abilities, they'll not dare to harm my master." "I'm a good priest," said the T'ang monk, "and I'll never mention the name of an evil man like you. Go back." When the Great Sage saw that the elder simply refused to change his mind, he had no alternative but to leave. Look at him:

In tears he kowtowed to part with the priest;
In grief he took care to instruct Sha Monk.
He used his head to dig up the meadow's grass
And both feet to kick up the ground's rattan.
Like a wheel spinning he entered Heav'n and Earth,
Most able to overleap mountains and seas.
All at once he completely disappeared;
In no time he left on the way he came.

Look at him! He suppressed his outrage and took leave of his master by mounting the cloud-somersault to head straight for the Water-Curtain Cave of the Flower-Fruit Mountain. As he was traveling, alone and dejected, he suddenly heard the roar of water. The Great Sage paused in midair to look and discovered that it was the high tide of the Great Eastern Ocean. The moment he saw this, he thought of the T'ang monk and could not restrain the tears from rolling down his cheeks. He stopped his cloud and stayed there for a long time before proceeding. We do not know what will happen to him as he goes away, and you must listen to the explanation in the next chapter.

## Twenty-eight

At Flower-Fruit Mountain a pack of fiends hold assembly;
At the Black Pine Forest Tripitaka meets demons.

We were telling you about the Great Sage, who, though he was
banished by the T'ang monk, was nevertheless filled with regret and
nostalgia when he saw the Great Eastern Ocean. He said to himself:
"I haven't come this way for five hundred years!" This is what he
saw as he looked at the ocean:
Vast, misty currents;
Huge, far-reaching waves—
Vast, misty currents that join the Milky Way;
Huge, far-reaching waves that touch the pulse of Earth.
The tide rises in salvos;
The water engulfs the bays—
The tide rises in salvos
Like the clap of thunder in Triple Spring;
The water engulfs the bays
As violent gales that blow in late summer.
Those old, blessed dragon-drivers[1]
Would travel no doubt with knitted brows;
Those young, immortal crane-riders
Would surely pass by anxious and tense.
No village appears near the shore;
Few fishing boats hug the water.
Waves roll like a thousand year's snow;
Wind howls as if autumn's in June.
Wild birds can come and go at will;
Water fowls may stay afloat or dive.
There's no fisher before your eyes;
Your ears hear only the sea gulls.
Deep in the sea fishes frolic;
Across the sky wild geese languish.

With a bound, our Pilgrim leaped across the Great Eastern Ocean and soon arrived at the Flower-Fruit Mountain. Lowering the direction of his cloud, he stared all around. Alas, that mountain had neither flowers nor plants, while the mist and smoke seemed completely extinguished: cliffs and plateaus had collapsed and the trees had dried and withered. How had it all become like this, you ask. When Pilgrim disrupted Heaven and was taken captive to the Region Above, this mountain was burned to total ruin by the Illustrious Sage, Erh-lang God, who was leading the Seven Bond-Brothers of Plum Mountain. Our Great Sage became more grief stricken than ever, and he composed the following long poem in ancient style as a testimony. The poem says:

I view this divine mountain and tears fall;
I face it and my sorrows multiply.
The mountain, I thought then, would not be harmed;
Today I know this place has suffered loss.
Hateful was that Erh-lang who vanquished me,
That heinous Little Sage who oppressed me.
In violence he dug up my parental tombs;
With no cause he broke up my ancestral graves.
All Heaven's mists and fog are now dispersed;
The whole land's wind and clouds both dissipate.
The tiger's roar is heard no more on eastern peaks;
The white ape's cry is still on western slopes;
The northern gorge has no trace of fox or hare;
All deer have vanished from the southern glen.
Green rocks are burned to form a thousand bricks;
The bright sand's changed to a pile of dirt.
Tall pines outside the cave have fallen down;
Green cedars before the cliff are thin and scarce.
*Ch'un, shan, huai, kuei, li,* and *t'an*[2] all are scorched;
Peach, pear, prune, plum, almond, and date are gone.
How could silkworms be fed with no mulberry?
Midst few bamboos and willows birds cannot live.
Well-formed rocks on the peak have turned to dust;
The brook's water has dried up—all is grass.
No orchid grows on parched earth below the cliff;
Creepers o'erspread the brown mud by the road.
To what region have birds of past days flown?

To which mountain have the beasts of old retired?
This gutted spot that snakes and leopards loathe!
This blasted place that cranes and serpents shun!
It must be for evil deeds in former times
That I should this day suffer so much pain.

As the Great Sage was thus expressing his grief, seven or eight small monkeys suddenly leaped out with a cry from among the tall grass and bushes on the slope. They rushed forward to surround him and kowtow, shouting, "Father Great Sage! You've come home today?" "Why aren't you all having a little fun?" said the Handsome Monkey King. "Why is everyone in hiding? I've been back for quite a while, and I haven't seen even the shadow of one of you! Why is that?" When the several monkeys heard these words, every one of them began to weep. "Since the Great Sage was taken captive to the Region Above," they said, "we have been suffering from the hands of hunters, truly an unbearable affliction. How could we withstand those sharp arrows and strong bows, those yellow hawks and wicked hounds, those ensnaring nets and sickle-shaped spears! To preserve our lives, none of us dares come out to play; instead, we conceal ourselves deep in the cave dwelling or take refuge in some distant lairs. Only in hunger do we go steal some grass on the meadow for food, and in thirst we drink the clear liquid from down stream. Just now we heard the voice of our Father Great Sage, and that was why we came to receive you. We beg you to take care of us." When the Great Sage heard these words, he became more distressed. He then asked, "How many of you are there still in this mountain?" "Young and old," said the monkeys, "altogether no more than a thousand." The Great Sage said, "In former times, I had forty-seven thousand little monsters here. Where did they go?" The monkeys said, "When Father left, this mountain was burned by the Bodhisattva Erh-lang, and more than half of them were killed by the fire. Some of us managed to save our lives by squatting in the wells, diving into the brook, or hiding beneath the sheet iron bridge. When the fire was extinguished and the smoke cleared, we came out to find that flowers and fruits were no longer available for food. The difficulty in finding sustenance drove another half of the monkeys away, leaving those of us to suffer here in the mountain. These two years saw our number dwindle even further by more than half when hunters came to abduct us." "For what purpose?" said Pilgrim. "Talk about those hunters," said the monkeys, "they are truly abominable! Those of us who were shot by arrows, pierced by spears, or clubbed to death they took away for food to be served with rice. The dead monkeys would be skinned and boned, cooked with sauce and steamed with vinegar, fried with oil, and sauteed with salt. Those of us who were caught by the net or the trap would be led away live; they would be taught to skip ropes, to act, to somersault, and to do cartwheels. They would have to beat the drum and the gong on the streets and perform every kind of trick to entertain humans."

When the Great Sage heard these words, he became terribly angry. "Who is in charge in the cave now?" he asked. "We still have Ma and Liu, the two marshals," said the little fiends, "Pêng and Pa, the two generals: they are in charge." "Report to them at once," said the Great Sage, "and say that I've returned." Those little fiends dashed inside the cave and cried, "Father Great Sage has come home!" When Ma, Liu, Pêng, and Pa heard the report, they rushed out of the door to kowtow and to receive him inside the cave. The Great Sage took a seat in the middle as the various fiends all lined up before him to pay homage. "Father Great Sage," they said, "we heard recently that you had regained your life so that you could protect the T'ang monk on his journey to the Western Heaven to acquire scriptures. Why are you not heading toward the West? Why do you come back to this mountain?" "Little ones," said the Great Sage, "you have no idea that the T'ang monk is wholly ignorant of who is worthy and who is foolish. For his sake, I caught fiends and overcame demons throughout the journey, using all my abilities. Several times I slew a monster, but, accusing me of doing evil and violence, he disowned me as his disciple and banished me back here. He even wrote me a formal letter of banishment as proof that he would never want to use me again."

Clapping their hands and roaring with laughter, the monkeys said, "Lucky! Lucky! What do you want to be a monk for? Come home and you can lead us to have a few years' fun. Quick! Let's bring out the coconut wine for the reception of Father." "Let's not drink wine yet," said the Great Sage. "Let me ask you, how often do those hunters come to our mountain?" "Great Sage," said Ma and Liu, "there's no telling of time. They are here every day to make trouble." The Great Sage said, "why aren't they here today?" Ma and Liu said, "Just wait and you'll see them come." The Great Sage gave this order:

"Little ones, go up to the mountain and bring me the rocks that have been burned to small pieces. Pile them up around here in piles of thirty or sixty pieces. I have use for them." Those little monkeys were like a cloud of bees; they swarmed all over the mountain and brought back the rock pieces and piled them together. When the Great Sage saw that, he said, "Little ones, go hide in the cave. Let old Monkey exercise his magic."

Our Great Sage went straight up to the peak to look around, and he saw over a thousand men and horses approaching from the southern half of the mountain. Beating drums and striking gongs, they were holding spears and swords, leading hawks and hounds. When the Monkey King stared carefully at them, they appeared to be most ferocious indeed. Dear men! Truly fierce! He saw

Fox skins covered their heads and backs;
Silk brocades wrapped around their torsos;
Quivers full of wolf-teeth arrows;[3]
And carved bows hung on their thighs.
The men seemed mountain-prowling tigers;
The horses, like brook-leaping dragons.
The whole group of men led their hounds,
As hawks perched on all their shoulders.
They hauled fire cannons[4] in baskets.
They had also eagles most fierce,
And hundreds of poles with birdlimes,
And thousands of forks to catch rabbits;
Dragnets like those used by bullheads,
And lassos tossed by King Yama.
They yelled and shrieked altogether,
Causing confusion far and near.

When the Great Sage saw those men swarming up his mountain, he grew terribly angry. Making the magic sign with his fingers and reciting a spell, he drew in a breath facing the southwest and blew it out. At once a violent wind arose. Marvelous wind!

It threw up dust and scattered dirt;
It toppled trees and cut down forests.
The ocean waves rose like mountains;
They crashed fold upon fold on the shore.
The cosmos grew dim and darkened;
The sun and the moon lost their light.

The pine trees, once shaken, roared like tigers;
The bamboos, hit abruptly, sang like dragons.
All Heaven's pores let loose their angry breaths
As rocks and sand flew, hurting one and all.

The Great Sage called up this mighty wind which blew up and scattered those rock pieces in every direction. Pity those thousand-odd hunters and horses! This was what happened to everyone of them:

The rocks broke their dark heads to pieces;[5]
Flying sand hurt all the winged horses.
Lords and nobles confounded before the peak,
Blood stained the ground like cinnabar.
Fathers and sons could not go home.
Could fine men to their houses return?
Corpses fell to the dust and lay on the mountain,
While rouged ladies at home waited.

The poem says:

Men killed, horses dead—how could they go home?
Lost, lonely souls floundered like tangled hemp.
Pity those strong and virile fighting men,
Whose blood, both good and bad, did stain the sand!

Lowering the direction of his cloud, the Great Sage clapped his hands and roared with laughter, saying, "Lucky! Lucky! Since I made submission to the T'ang monk and became a priest, he has been giving me this advice: 'Do good a thousand days, but the good is still insufficient; do evil for one day, and that evil is already excessive.' Some truth indeed! When I followed him and killed a few monsters, he would blame me for perpetrating violence. Today I came home and it was the merest trifle to finish off all these hunters." He then shouted, "Little ones, come out!" When those monkeys saw that the violent wind had passed and heard the Great Sage calling, they all jumped out. "Go down to the south side of the mountain," said the Great Sage, "and strip the dead hunters of their clothes. Bring them back home, wash away the blood stains, and you all can wear them to ward off the cold. The corpses you can push into the deep mountain lake over there. Pull back here also the horses that are killed; their hides can be used to make boots, and their meat can be cured for us to enjoy slowly. Gather up the bows and arrows, the swords and spears, and you can use them for military drills again. And finally, bring me those banners of miscellaneous colors; I have use for them."

Every one of the monkeys obeyed these instructions.

Pulling down the banners and washing them clean, the Great Sage then patched them together into a large banner of many colors, on which he wrote the following words in large letters: The Flower-Fruit Mountain Rebuilt, The Water-Curtain Cave Restored—Great Sage, Equal to Heaven. A flagpole was erected outside the cave to hang up the banner. Thereafter, he gathered together more fiends and beasts by the day, and he stored up all kinds of foodstuff. The word "monk" was never mentioned again. As he enjoyed wide friendship and great power, he had no trouble in borrowing some sweet, divine water from the Dragon Kings of the Four Oceans to wash his mountain and make it green again. He next planted elms and willows in front, pines and cedars in the back; peach, pear, date, and plum—he had them all. He then settled down to enjoy life without a care, and we shall speak no more of him for the moment.

We now tell you about the T'ang monk, who listened to Crafty Nature and banished the Monkey of the Mind. He mounted his horse to head for the West as Pa-chieh led the way in front, while Sha Monk poled the luggage in the rear. After they passed the White Tiger Ridge, they came upon a large forest, full of vines and creepers, green pines and cedars. "Disciples," said Tripitaka, "the mountain road is already rough and difficult to negotiate. And now we have a thick and dark pine forest. Do be careful. I fear that we may run into some fiends or monstrous beasts." But look at Idiot! Rousing his energies, he told Sha Monk to take hold of the horse, while he himself used his muckrake to open up a path in front and led the T'ang monk directly into the pine forest. As they journeyed, the elder stopped the horse and said, "Pa-chieh, I'm getting really hungry today. Where can you find me some vegetarian food to eat?" "Please dismount, Master," said Pa-chieh, "and let old Hog go find some for you." The elder descended from his horse; Sha Monk put down his load and took out the alms bowl to hand over to Pa-chieh. Pa-chieh said, "I'm off!" "Where to?" asked the elder. "Never mind," said Pa-chieh. "Once I go, I will

Drill ice for fire[6] to find your maigre,
And press snow for oil to beg your rice."

Look at him! He left the pine forest and walked toward the West for over ten miles, but he did not come upon even a single household. It was truly a place more inhabited by tigers and wolves than by

humans. When Idiot became tired from walking, he thought to himself: "When Pilgrim was here, whatever that old priest wanted he got.
Today, it's my turn to serve, and it's like what the proverb says:

You know the cost of rice and firewood when you run a house;

You realize your parents' kindness when you bring up a child!
Where in the world can I go to beg for food?" He walked some more
and became rather drowsy. He thought to himself, "If I go back now
and tell that old priest that there's no place here for me to beg for
vegetarian food even after traveling all this distance, he won't believe
me. I must find some means to while away another hour or so before
I go back to answer him. Well, well! Let's take a nap here in the
grass." Idiot indeed put his head in the grass and lay down. At the
time, he thought that he would doze for a while and then get up, but
little did he realize how fatigued he was from all that walking. Once
he lay down his head, he fell into a deep, snoring slumber.

For the time being, we shall speak no more of Pa-chieh asleep in
this place. We tell you instead about that elder in the forest, who grew
so restless and anxious that his ears became flushed and his eyes
began to tic. He turned quickly and said to Sha Monk, "Why hasn't
Wu-nêng returned from his trip to beg for food?" "Master," said Sha
Monk, "don't you understand? When he sees how many families
there are in this region of the West who love to feed monks, he's not
going to worry about you, is he, especially when he has so large a
stomach! He's not going to come back until he's completely filled!"
"You are right," said Tripitaka. "But if he is staying at some place
just to satisfy his hankering for food, where are we going to meet
him? It's getting late, and this is no place to live. We better find some
lodging." "Don't worry, Master," said Sha Monk, "you sit here and
let me find him." "Yes, yes," said Tripitaka, "it doesn't matter
whether there's food or not. But it's important for us to find a place to
stay." Grasping his precious staff, Sha Monk left the pine forest to
search for Pa-chieh.

The elder, sitting alone in the forest, became so weary and fatigued
that he had to force himself to summon enough energy to get up.
Putting the luggage together in a pile and tying the horse to a tree,
he took off his wide splint hat, stuck his priestly staff into the ground,
and straightened his clerical robe in order to take a walk in this
secluded forest just to rid himself of his depression. He looked at all the
wild grass and untended flowers, but he did not hear any chattering

of birds heading homeward. The forest, you see, was a place of tall grass and small paths. Because he was rather confused he soon lost his way. He had, to be sure, wanted to dispel his boredom in the first place, and to find Pa-chieh and Sha Monk in the second. Little did he realize that they were proceeding westward, whereas he himself, after going in circles for a while, was heading south. As he emerged from the pine forest, he raised his head and saw all at once flashes of golden light and colorful mists ahead of him. He looked more carefully and found that it was a bejeweled pagoda, whose golden dome was gleaming in the rays of the setting sun. "This disciple truly has no affinity!" he said to himself. "When I left the Land of the East, I made a vow to burn incense in every temple, to worship Buddha when I saw an image of Buddha, and to sweep a pagoda if I came upon a pagoda. Isn't that a golden pagoda which is so brilliant over there? Why didn't I take this road before? Beneath the pagoda there must be a temple, inside of which there must also be a monastery. Let me walk over there. It's all right, I suppose, to leave the white horse and the luggage here since there is no one passing by. If there's any space there, I'll wait till my disciples return and we can all ask for lodging for the night."

Alas, the time of that elder's misfortune has indeed arrived! Look at him! He strode forward and went up to the side of the pagoda. There he saw

Boulders ten thousand feet tall;
A large bluff reaching the green sky:
Its roots joining the thick earth,
Its peaks sticking into Heaven.
Several thousand trees of all kinds on both sides;
A hundred miles of snarled creepers front and back.
Bright flowers on grass tips, the wind had its shadows.
In the clouds' cleft of flowing water the moon had no base.[7]
Fallen logs rested in deep streams;
Dried tendrils entangled bare summits.
Beneath a stone bridge
Flowed a bubbling clear stream;
On top of a terrace
Grew flourlike white blossoms.
When seen from afar it seemed the Paradise of Three Isles;
When you drew near it appeared like the lovely P'êng-lai.

Purple bamboos and scented pines enclosed the mountain brook;
Crows, magpies, and monkeys cut through the rugged ridge.
Outside a cave
There were herds of wild beasts coming and going;
In the woods
There were flocks of birds leaving or returning.
In lovely green the fragrant plants thrived;
Radiantly the wild flowers bloomed.
This region, nonetheless,[8] was an evil place.
It was the elder's bad luck to come barging in!

The elder strode up to the door of the pagoda and found a mottled
bamboo curtain hanging inside. Walking inside the door, he lifted up
the curtain to proceed further when suddenly he saw before him a
monster asleep on a stone couch. "How does he look?" you ask.

Indigo face,
Long white fangs,
And a big gaping mouth!
Tousled hair on the head's two sides
Seemed as if it had been dyed red by rouge.
A few stubs of deep purple beard
Bore the look of lychee sprouting.
A nose curvate like a parrot's beak,
And eyes glowing like the morning stars.
His two huge fists
Had the shape of a monk's alms bowl.
Two blue-veined feet
Forked like branches dangling down a cliff.
Half covered by a light yellow robe,
Better than the silk-brocade cassock,
He still grasped a scimitar
Which gleamed and glittered.
He slept on a slab of stone
Both flawless and smooth.
He had led young fiends to make formations like ants,
And old demons to rule with order like bees.
Look at his awesome bearing,
When all his subjects
Raised the cry, "Father!"
He had made the moon his third friend as he sipped his wine;[9]

He had felt the wind grow beneath his arms as tea was poured.
Look at his vast magic power!
In the twinkling of an eye
He could tour all the Heavens.
In his wild woods screeched birds and fowls;
In his dens slept dragons and snakes.
Immortals tilled his fields to grow white jade;
Taoists calmed his fire to raise cinnabar.
A door of a small cave
Did not, of course, lead to the Hell, Avīci;
But such an ugly monster
Seemed truly a bullheaded yakṣa!

When the elder saw that kind of appearance, he retreated in horror
as his body turned numb and his legs, flabby. He tried to turn and
run, but just as he got out of the door, the monster, who was a rather
alert creature, opened his demonic eyes with golden pupils and
shouted, "Little ones, go see who is outside our door!" A little fiend
stuck his head out the door and saw that it was a bald-headed elder.
He ran quickly inside and reported: "Great King! It's a priest outside.
He has a round head and a large face, with two ears hanging down
to his shoulders. He has a bodyful of tender flesh and very fine skin.
He's a good-looking priest!" When the monster heard these words, he
laughed aloud, saying, "This is like what the proverb says: 'Flies on
a serpent's head—food presented by itself!' You, little ones. Chase him
down and bring him back here. I have great rewards for you." Those
little fiends rushed out of the door like a swarm of bees. When Tripitaka saw them, his mind wanted him to go like the arrow and his feet
wanted to fly; but he quivered and shook, and his feet were numb
and flaccid. Moreover, the mountain road was rugged, the forest was
dark, and it was getting late. How could he possibly move fast
enough? The little fiends ran him down and hauled him back bodily.
Truly, it is like

The dragon in shallow water teased by shrimps,
The tiger on level ground mocked by dogs.
A noble venture may have many snags.
Who's like the T'ang monk when he faces the West?

Look at those little fiends! After having carried the elder back and put
him down outside the bamboo curtain, they ran happily to make this
report: "Great King, we have caught the monk and brought him

back." The old monster stole a glance at Tripitaka and saw that he had an erect head and a handsome face. He was indeed a good-looking priest. The monster thought to himself, "Such a good-looking priest must be someone from a noble nation. I can't treat him lightly. If I didn't show him some power, would he willingly submit to me?" Like a fox affecting the authority of a tiger, he all at once bristled up his red hairs and whiskers while his eyes split wide open. "Bring that monk in!" he bellowed. "Yes, sir!" the various fiends shouted in response, as they shoved Tripitaka inside. As the proverb has it,

Standing beneath low-pitched eaves,

How could one not bow his head?

Tripitaka had no choice but to fold his hands and greet him. "From what region are you, monk?" said the monster. "Where did you come from? Where are you going? Tell us quickly!" "I'm a monk from the T'ang Court," said Tripitaka. "Having received the imperial decree of the Great T'ang Emperor to seek scriptures in the West, I passed by your noble mountain and decided to seek an audience with the sage beneath this pagoda. I have no intention to disturb Your Eminence. Please forgive me. When I return to the Land of the East after acquiring scriptures in the West, your illustrious name will be recorded gratefully for posterity." When the monster heard these words, he roared with laughter, saying, "I said to myself that you were from a noble nation. So you are indeed! You're exactly the person I want to eat! It's marvelous that you presented yourself here. Otherwise, I might have missed you. You are ordained to be the food of my mouth. Since you have barged in here all by yourself, I couldn't let you go even if I wanted to. And you couldn't escape even if you wanted to!" He then ordered the little fiends, "Tie up that monk." The little fiends rushed forward and fastened the elder firmly with ropes to the Spirit-Soothing Pillar.[10]

Grasping his scimitar, the old monster asked again: "Monk, how many persons are there in your entourage? Don't tell me you dare go up to the Western Heaven all by yourself!" When Tripitaka saw him picking up the scimitar, he said candidly, "Great King, I have two disciples named Chu Pa-chieh and Sha Monk. They all left the pine forest to go beg for food. I have, moreover, one load of luggage and a white horse, which I left in the forest." "That's luckier yet!" said the old monster. "Two disciples including you make three, and there are really four of you if we count the horse. That's enough for a meal!"

"Let's go and catch them too," said the little fiends. "Don't go out," said the old monster, "but shut the door instead. After begging the food, those disciples would bring it to their master; when they can't find him, they will surely come seeking right up to our door. The proverb says, 'Business at one's own door is easier to handle.' Let's take our time and catch them then." The little fiends indeed closed the front door.

We speak no more of Tripitaka who met disaster; we tell you instead about Sha Monk, who left the pine forest looking for Pa-chieh. He walked for over ten miles but did not see even a village or hamlet. He went up to a knoll to look all around when suddenly he heard someone speaking in the grass down below. Pushing the tall grass apart hurriedly with his staff, he found Idiot inside talking in his sleep. Sha Monk gave one of the huge ears a hard tug and cried, "Dear Idiot! Master told you to beg for food. Did he give you permission to sleep here?" Idiot woke up with a start, mumbling, "Brother, what time is it?" "Get up, quick!" said Sha Monk. "Master said that it didn't matter whether there was food or not. He told us to try finding a place to stay instead."

Picking up the alms bowl and toting his muckrake, Idiot walked back stupidly with Sha Monk. When they reached the forest, their master was nowhere to be seen. Sha Monk began to berate him, saying, "It's all because of you, Idiot, for taking such a long time to find some food. Master must have been seized by a monster." "Brother," said Pa-chieh laughing, "don't talk nonsense. This forest is a pure, lovely place and it definitely cannot harbor a monster. It must be that that old priest cannot sit still and has gone sightseeing somewhere. Let's go find him." The two of them picked up the hat and the priestly staff before they left the pine forest, leading the horse and poling the luggage as they searched for their master.

It happened that the T'ang monk at this time was not yet destined to die. Having looked for him for some time to no avail, his two disciples saw beams of golden light coming from the south. "Brother," said Pa-chieh, "the blessed will only receive more blessings! Master, you see, must have gone to that bejeweled pagoda over there which is giving off that light. Who will dare to be inhospitable at a place like that? They must insist on preparing vegetarian food and his staying to enjoy it. Why aren't we moving? We should get there and have something, too." "Elder Brother," said Sha Monk, "you can't tell whether it's a good place or not. Let's go and have a look first." The two of them walked boldly up to the door of the edifice and found that it was closed. Across the top of the door was a slab of white jade on which were written in large letters the following words: Casserole Mountain, Current-Moon Cave. "Elder Brother," said Sha Monk, "this is no monastery. It's a cave-dwelling of a monster. Even if Master were here, I doubt if we could see him." "Don't be alarmed, Brother," said Pa-chieh. "Tie up the horse and stand guard over our luggage. Let me question them." Holding high his muckrake, Idiot went forward and shouted, "Open the door! Open the door!" The little fiend who was standing guard inside opened the door. When he saw the two of them, he ran quickly to report: "Great King, business is here." "What sort of business?" said the old monster. "There is a monk with large ears and a long mouth outside our cave," said the little fiend, "and there is also another monk with the gloomiest appearance. They came calling at our door." Greatly pleased, the old monster said, "They have to be Chu Pa-chieh and Sha Monk! Ho-ho! They know where to look all right! How did they manage to find our door so swiftly? Well, if they appear so audacious, let's not treat them casually. Bring me my armor!" The little fiend brought it out and helped him put it on. Grasping the scimitar, the old monster walked out of the door.

Pa-chieh and Sha Monk were waiting outside the door when they saw this savage fiend emerge. "How did he look?" you ask.

Green face, red beard, and floppy scarlet hair.
His yellow gold cuirass both sparkled and gleamed.
A belt inlaid with ribbed shells wrapped his waist;
A silk sash wound tightly round his armored chest.
The wind howled when he stood idly on the mount;
The waves churned when he, depressed, would roam the seas.
A pair of hands with veins both brown and blue
Grasped firmly the soul-snatching scimitar.
If you would learn this creature's given name,
Remember Yellow Robe, two famous words.

That Old Monster Yellow Robe came out of the door and asked at once, "Where are you from, monk, that you dare cause this racket before my door?" "My child," said Pa-chieh, "don't you recognize me? I'm your venerable father! I'm one sent by the Great T'ang to go to the Western Heaven, for my master happens to be the royal brother, Tipitaka. If he's in your house, send him out at once. That'll

spare me having to level it with my rake!" "Yes, yes," said the fiend
with a laugh, "there's a T'ang monk in my house, and I haven't
denied him any hospitality either. I was just preparing some buns
filled with human flesh for him to enjoy. You two can go inside and
have one also. How about it?"

Idiot indeed would have gone inside immediately if Sha Monk had
not pulled him back, saying, "Elder Brother, he's deceiving you. Since
when did you start eating human flesh again?" Only then did Idiot
realize his mistake. Raising his muckrake, he brought it down hard
on the monster's face. The monster stepped aside to dodge the blow
and then turned to meet him with uplifted scimitar. The two of them,
summoning their magic powers, mounted the clouds to fight in midair. Sha Monk abandoned the luggage and the white horse; wielding
his precious staff, he joined the fray also. At this time, two fierce
monks and one brazen monster began a savage battle on the edge of
the clouds. Thus it was that

The staff rose high, met by the scimitar;
The muckrake came, blocked by the scimitar.
One demon warrior used his power;
Two divine monks displayed their might.
The nine-pronged rake, how truly heroic!
The fiend-routing staff, ferocious indeed!
Their blows fell left and right, in front and back,
But squire Yellow Robe showed no fear at all.
See his steel scimitar shining like silver!
And, in truth, his magic power was great.
They fought till all the sky
Was fogbound and beclouded;
And in midmountain
Stones cracked and cliffsides collapsed.
This one, for the sake of his fame,
How could he give up?
That one for the sake of his master
Would surely show no fear.

The three of them closed in again and again in midair for scores of
times but a decision could not be reached. Though each of them cared
for his life, none of them was about to be separated. We do not know
how the disciples manage to rescue the T'ang monk, and you must
listen to the explanation in the next chapter.

*Twenty-nine*

Free of his peril, River Float arrives at the kingdom;
Receiving favor, Pa-chieh invades the forest.

The poem says:
   Vain thoughts cannot be destroyed by force.
   Why must you seek or hope for Suchness?
   Cultivate before Buddha the self-existent mind—
   Are not illusion and enlightenment the same?

   Enlightened, you reach the Right in an instant;
   Deluded, you sink into ten thousand kalpas.
   If you can cultivate one thought joined with Truth,
   Sins vast as Ganges' sand are stamped out.

We were telling you about Pa-chieh and Sha Monk, who fought with
that monster for over thirty rounds but a decision could not be
reached. Why not, you ask. If it were a matter of matching abilities,
you needn't speak of two monks. Even if there were twenty monks,
they would still be unable to withstand that monster. It was only
because of the fact that the T'ang monk was not yet fated to die that
his followers could count on the help of certain deities. Pa-chieh and
Sha Monk, therefore, were assisted in secret in the air by the Six Gods
of Light and Six Gods of Darkness, the Guardians of Five Quarters, the
Four Sentinels, and the Eighteen Guardian-Spirits of monasteries.

   For the moment we shall speak no more of the battle between the
three of them. We tell you instead about the elder, who was weeping
piteously in the cave and thinking about his disciples. As tears fell
from his eyes, he said to himself, "Wu-nêng, I don't know in which
village you have met a friend of truth and are enjoying being fed. O,
Wu-ching! Where have you gone to search for him, and how will you
be able to meet him? Will you two realize that I met a demon, that
I'm suffering here? When will I see you both again? When will I
escape from this great ordeal so that I can reach the Spirit Mountain
soon?" As he was giving voice to his grief in this manner, he suddenly

saw a woman walk out from inside the cave. Holding on to the Spirit-Soothing Pillar, she said, "Elder, where did you come from? Why are you bound here by him?" When the elder heard this, he turned his teary eyes to steal a glance at her and found that she was about thirty years old. "Lady Bodhisattva," he said, "no need for further questions. I must have been fated to die when I entered your door. If you want to devour me, go ahead. Why bother to question me?" The woman said, "I don't eat people! About three hundred miles west of here is my home, a city by the name of the Precious Image Kingdom.[1] I'm the third princess of its king, and my childhood name is Hundred Flowers' Shame. Thirteen years ago, on the eve of the fifteenth of the eighth month, I was enjoying the sight of the moon when this monster-spirit kidnapped me and brought me here in a violent wind. I was forced to become his wife for all these thirteen years and to bear his children. It was impossible, of course, for me to send any news back to the Court, and I couldn't see my parents even though I thought of them frequently. But where did you come from, and how did he catch you?" "This poor monk," said the T'ang monk, "is someone sent to acquire scriptures in the Western Heaven. I was taking a walk when I bumped into this place. Now he wants to catch my two disciples also so that we will all be steamed and eaten together." "Elder, please don't worry," said the princess with a smile. "If you are a scripture pilgrim, I can save you, for the Precious Image Kingdom is right on your main path to the West. All I ask of you is to deliver a letter for me to my parents and I'll ask my husband to let you go." Nodding his head, the T'ang monk said, "Lady Bodhisattva, if you can save the life of this poor monk, I shall be glad to serve as your messenger."

Quickly running inside, the princess wrote a letter and had it properly sealed. She then went back out to the pillar and untied him before handing him the letter. After he was freed, the T'ang monk held the letter in his hands and said, "Lady Bodhisattva, thank you for saving my life. When this poor monk reaches your kingdom, he will certainly deliver the letter to the king. I fear, however, that such a lengthy separation will make it difficult for your parents to recognize anything from you. What shall I do then? They would not accuse me of lying, would they?" "No fear," said the princess. "My parents have no son; all they have are us three sisters. When they see this letter, they will look after you." Tucking the letter deep into his sleeve, Tripitaka thanked the princess again and started to walk out. "You can't go out the front door!" said the princess, tugging at him. "Those monster-spirits, great and small, are all outside waving the banners and beating the drums and gongs to assist the Great King, who is at this very moment fighting with your disciples. You'd better leave by the back door. If the Great King seizes you, he will at least interrogate you. But if the little fiends catch hold of you, they may slaughter you on the spot without further ado. Let me go instead to the front and speak a word on your behalf. If the Great King is willing to let you go, your disciples can take that as a favor and leave with you." When Tripitaka heard these words, he kowtowed to the princess before taking leave of her. After walking out of the back door, he dared not proceed; instead, he hid himself in some bushes and waited.

We tell you now about the princess, who had devised a clever plan. She ran out the front door and pushed her way through the vast throng of monsters. All she could hear was the jangle of weapons, for Pa-chieh and Sha Monk were still doing battle in midair with that fiend. The princess shouted, "Lord Yellow Robe!" When the monster king heard the call of the princess, he abandoned Pa-chieh and Sha Monk and dropped down from the clouds. Holding his scimitar with one hand, he took the hand of the princess with the other and said, "Mistress, what do you want?" "Husband," said the princess, "I was sleeping just now within the silk curtains, and I saw in my dream a golden-armored deity." "That golden-armored deity," said the demon, "what does he want at my door?" The princess said, "During my youth when I was living in the palace, I made a secret vow that if I found a good husband, I would ascend the famous mountains, visit the immortal abodes, and feed the monks. Since I married you, ours had been such great happiness that I never had the opportunity to mention this to you. Just now that golden-armored deity came to demand that I fulfill my vow; he was shouting at me so vehemently that I woke up with a start. Even though it was all a dream, I made haste to come to tell you about it. Then I saw a monk all tied up on that pillar. I beg you, husband, to be compassionate for my sake and spare that monk. Just regard the matter as if it were my feeding the monks to redeem my vow. Are you willing?" "Mistress," said the fiend, "you're so gullible! I thought it was something important! All right! If I wanted to eat humans, I can catch a few anywhere. This one monk, what does he amount to? I'll let him go." "Husband," said the princess, "let him go out the back door." The monster said, "What nuisance! Just let him go. Why bother about the back door or front door?" He gripped his steel scimitar and shouted, "You, Chu Pa-chieh! Come over here! I'm not afraid of you, but I won't fight with you anymore; for the sake of my wife, I'm going to spare your master. Go quickly to our back door and find him so that you can leave for the West. If you ever trespass our territory again, I will not spare you."

When Pa-chieh and Sha Monk heard these words, they felt as if they had been released from the gate of Hell! Leading the horse and poling the luggage, they darted like rodents past the Current-Moon Cave. When they reached the back door, they cried, "Master!" The elder recognized their voices and answered from the thorny bushes. Sha Monk parted the grass and picked up his master, who mounted the horse hurriedly. So,

Almost harmed by the vicious blue-faced spirit,
He met by luck the zeal of Hundred Flowers' Shame.
The scorpaenid has from the golden hook escaped:
He wags his head and tail to swim with the waves.

Pa-chieh led the way in front while Sha Monk brought up the rear. They left the pine forest and proceeded on the main road. Look at the two of them! Still bickering and grumbling, they were trying to put the blame on each other, and Tripitaka had to spend all the time attempting to pacify them. At night they sought a place to rest; when the cock crowed they looked at the sky. Stage by stage, they soon traveled some two hundred and ninety-nine miles. When they raised their heads one day, they saw a beautiful city. It was the Precious Image Kingdom, a marvelous place indeed!

How boundless the clouds!
How vast the journey!
Though the land is beyond a thousand miles,
Its condition is no less prosperous.[2]
Auspicious mist and smoke surround it;
Bright moon and clear wind befriend it.
Green, towering distant mountains
Spread out like a painted scroll;
The flowing stream, surging and bubbling,
Throws up pieces of white jade.
Arable fields, joined by roadways and paths;

Worthy of food, dense sprouting rice crops;
Hooked by the fisherman, three winding brooks of a few house-
    holds;
Gathered by the woodsman, one load of pepper-wood from two
    hills.
Each corridor and each rampart
Are made strong as if by metal and liquid;[3]
Every house and every home
Vies with one another in felicity.
Nine-tiered towers rise like palace halls;
Layered terraces soar like beacons.
There are also the Great Ultimate Hall,[4]
The Bright Cover Hall,
The Burn Incense Hall,
The Text-Viewing Hall,
The Policy-Proclaiming Hall,
And the Talent-Engaging Hall—
Every hall lined with jade threshold and gold steps,
With civil and military officials.
There are also the Great Light Palace,
The Bright Sun Palace,
The Longlasting Pleasure Palace,
The Bright Clear Palace,
The Memorial-Establishing Palace,
And the Never-Ending Palace—
Each palace, with its chimes, drums, pipes, and vertical flutes,
Releases its boudoir sorrows and springtime griefs.
There are in the forbidden courtyard
Young, fresh faces like flowers bedewed;
There are on the palace moat
Slender waists like willows dancing in the wind.
On the broad boulevard
There may be one who is capped and sashed,
Who, elaborately dressed,
Mounts a five-horse chariot.
At a secluded spot
There may be one holding bow and arrows
Who, pushing through fog and clouds,
Would pierce a pair of hawks.[5]

Alleys of flowers and willows;
Towers of pipes and strings:
Spring breeze here's no lighter than at Lo-yang Bridge!
Our scripture-seeking elder
Recalls the T'ang Court and his bowels almost burst;
Our disciples, flanking their master,
Rest in a post-house and become lost in their dreams.

There was no end to the sight of such fine scenery at the Precious Image Kingdom. Master and disciples, the three of them, brought the luggage and the horse to a post-house and rested.

Afterwards, the T'ang monk walked to the gate of the Court and said to the gate official, "A priest from the T'ang Court has arrived to seek an audience with the Throne and to have my travel rescript certified. Please make this report for me." The Custodian of the Yellow Gate hurried inside and went before the white jade steps to say, "Your Majesty, there is an illustrious monk from the T'ang Court, who wishes to have an audience with you in order to have his travel rescript certified." When the king heard that an illustrious monk had arrived from such a great nation as the T'ang, he was very pleased and consented at once. "Summon him to come in," he said. When Tripitaka was summoned before the golden steps, he went through an elaborate court ceremony to pay homage to the ruler. None of the civil and military officials lining up on both sides of the Court could refrain from saying, "Truly a man from a noble nation! What exquisite manners!" The king said, "Elder, why did you come to our Kingdom?" "This humble monk," said Tripitaka, "is a Buddhist from the T'ang Court. I have received the decree of my emperor to go to acquire scriptures in the West. The travel rescript which I received originally should be certified once I arrive at the kingdom of Your Majesty. This is the reason why I dare intrude upon your Dragon Presence." "If you have the rescript from the T'ang Son of Heaven," said the king, "bring it up here for me to look at." Presenting it with both hands, Tripitaka placed the document on the imperial desk and unfolded it. The rescript says:

The travel rescript of the T'ang Son of Heaven, who succeeds
under the guidance of Heaven to the throne of the Great T'ang
Empire in the South Jambūdvīpa Continent. Though we humbly
acknowledge our poor display of virtue, we are the lawful

descendant of a great heritage. In the service to the gods and
the government of men, we try to be vigilant night and day, as
if we were approaching a deep abyss or walking on thin ice.
Some time ago, we failed to save the life of the Old Dragon of
Ching River, for which we were chastised by the Most High
August One. Our soul and spirit, drifting in the Region of
Darkness, had already become a guest of impermanence. But,
because our allotted age was not yet exhausted, we were indebted
to the Ruler of Darkness, who released us and returned us to
life. Thereafter, we convened a grand mass and established the
truth-plot for the dead. It was at this time also that the One
who saves from afflictions, the Bodhisattva Kuan-shih-yin,
revealed to us her golden form, and enlightened us with the
knowledge that the West had both Buddha and scriptures,
able to redeem the dead and deliver the orphaned spirits. For
this reason we now commission Hsüan-tsang, master of the law,
to traverse a thousand mountains in order to acquire such
scriptures. When he reaches the many nations of the West, it
is our hope that they will not extinguish the goodly affinity and
allow him to pass through because of this rescript. This is a
necessary-to-be-sent document.[6] An auspicious day in the
autumn of the thirteenth year, in the Chên-kuan period of the
Great T'ang. An imperial document. [There were also the marks
of nine precious seals on it.]

When the king read it, he took the jade seal of his own nation and
stamped it before handing it back to Tripitaka.

After he thanked the king and put away the travel rescript, Tripitaka said, "This humble priest came first of all to have the document
certified, and secondly to present to Your Majesty a family letter."
Delighted, the king said, "What kind of family letter?" "Your
Majesty," said Tripitaka, "the third princess was kidnapped by the
Yellow Robe Fiend of the Current-Moon Cave at the Casserole
Mountain. This humble priest met her by chance and it was she who
asked me to send you this letter." When the king heard this, his eyes
brimmed with tears. "Thirteen years ago," he said, "we lost our
princess. For that, we banished countless officials, both civil and
military, and we did not know how many ladies-in-waiting and
eunuchs we had caned to death throughout the palace. For we
thought that she had walked out of the palace and lost her way. Since

we did not know where to look, we interrogated countless households in the city, but there was not a trace of her. How would we
know that a monster had kidnapped her? When I receive this word
today, I cannot hold back my grief or tears." Thereupon Tripitaka
took out the letter from his sleeve and presented it. When the king
took it and saw the address on the envelope, his hands turned feeble
and could not open the letter. He therefore gave the order to have the
Grand Secretary of the Hanlin Academy[7] come before the throne
and read the letter. The Grand Secretary ascended the steps as all the
civil and military officials before the Court and all the imperial concubines and palace ladies behind the Court listened attentively. Opening the letter, the Grand Secretary began to read:

The unfilial daughter, Hundred Flowers' Shame, touches her
head to the ground a hundred times before the Dragon-Phoenix
Palace to honor Father King of the highest virtue. Long may
he live! I bow also before the Bright Sun Palace to my Queen
Mother, Queen of the Three Palaces, and to all worthy ministers,
both civil and military, of the entire Court. Ever since it was
my good fortune to have been born into the queen's palace, I
have been indebted to you for the countless acts of grievous
labor you undertook on my behalf. I regret that I have not done
the utmost to please you, nor have I discharged with all my
strength my filial duties. It was on the fifteenth day of the eighth
month thirteen years ago that Father King, on that lovely
evening and auspicious occasion, gave his gracious command
that banquets be prepared in the several palaces so that we
might enjoy the moonlight and celebrate the glorious Festival of
Immaculate Heavens. During the moment of festivity, a sudden
gust of fragrant wind[8] brought forward a demon king with
golden pupils, indigo face, and green hair who took hold of your
daughter. Mounting the auspicious luminosity, he carried me
away directly to an uninhabited region midway in the mountain
and absolutely forbade me to leave. He exploited his fiendish
power and forced me to become his wife; I had no alternative
but to suffer such ignominy for these thirteen years. Two monster
children were born to me, all seeds of this fiend. To speak of
this, in fact, is to corrupt the great human relations and to
pervert our morals. I should not, therefore, send you such an
offensive and insulting letter, but I fear that there would be no

explanation should your daughter pass away. As I was thinking
of my parents with deep sorrow, I learned that a holy monk
from the T'ang Court was also taken captive by the demon king.
It was then that your daughter wrote this letter in tears and
made bold to obtain release for the priest, so that he might
deliver this small document as an expression of my heart. I beg
Father King in his compassion to send his noble generals
quickly to capture the Yellow Robe Fiend at the Current-Moon
Cave of the Casserole Mountain and bring your daughter back
to the Court. Yours will be the deepest favor to me. Please
pardon my disrespect in writing this letter in haste, and
whatever has not been said I hope to tell you face to face. Your
disobedient daughter, Hundred Flowers' Shame, kowtows again
and again.

When the Grand Secretary finished reading the letter, the king burst
into loud wailing; all the three palaces shed tears and the various
officials were also overborne by grief.

After the king had wept for a long time, he asked the two rows of
civil and military officials, "Who dares lead the troops and captains
to capture the monster for us and rescue our Hundred Flowers
princess?" He asked the question several times, but there was not a
single person courageous enough to answer. Like generals carved
out of wood and ministers molded with clay, they all turned dumb!
Sorely distressed, the king wept till tears streamed down his face,
whereupon many officials prostrated themselves and memorialized,
saying, "Your Majesty, we beseech you to desist from your sorrow.
The princess was lost, and for thirteen years there had been no news
from her. Although she met by chance the holy monk from the T'ang
Court so that she was able to send us this letter, we are still not fully
informed about her situation. Moreover, your subjects are merely
mortal creatures. We have studied military manuals and tactics, of
course, but our knowledge is limited to placing troops in formations
and pitching camps in order to protect the frontiers of our nation from
any invasion. The monster-spirit, however, is someone who comes by
the fog and goes with the clouds. Unless we could meet him face to
face, how could we attack him and rescue the princess? The scripture
pilgrim from the Land of the East is, we believe, a holy monk from a
noble nation. As a priest

Whose vast power tames dragons and tigers,
Whose great virtue awes demons and gods,
he must know the art of subduing monsters. As the proverb says, he
who comes and tells of another's affair is himself involved in the affair.
Let us ask this elder to subdue the monster and rescue our princess;
this is our safest policy."

When the king heard these words, he turned quickly to Tripitaka
and said, "Elder, if you have the ability to release your dharma power
and catch the monster so that my child can return to the Court, you
need not go worship Buddha in the West. You can let your hair grow
again, for we will become bond-brothers with you. You may sit on
the dragon couch with us and enjoy our riches together. How about
it?" "This poor monk," said Tripitaka hurriedly, "knows a little of
chanting the name of Buddha, but truly he does not know how to
subdue monsters." "If you don't," said the king, "how dare you go
seek Buddha in the Western Heaven?" No longer able to hide the
truth, the elder had to mention his two disciples. "Your Majesty," he
said, "your poor monk would find it very difficult indeed to come here
if he were all by himself. I have, however, two disciples, most capable
of opening up a pathway in the mountains and building bridges when
we come upon the rivers. They have accompanied me here." "You
are an insensitive monk," said the king, chiding him. "If you have
disciples, why did you not bring them to see us also? When they enter
my court, even if we had no intention to reward them, we could
provide at least some food." Tripitaka said, "The disciples of this poor
monk are rather ugly in their appearances, and they dare not enter
the Court without permission. For I fear that they might cause too
great a shock to your Majesty." "Look at how this monk talks," said
the king with a laugh. "Do you think really that we'll be afraid of
them?" "It's hard to tell," said Tripitaka. "My elder disciple has the
surname of Chu, and his given names are Wu-nêng and Pa-chieh. He
has a long snout and fanglike teeth, tough bristles on the back of his
head, and huge, fanlike ears. He is coarse and husky, and he causes
even the wind to rise when he walks. My second disciple has the surname of Sha, and his religious names are Wu-ching and Monk. He is
twelve feet tall and three span wide across his shoulders. His face is like
indigo, his mouth, a butcher's bowl; his eyes gleam and his teeth seem
a row of nails. With looks like that, how could they dare enter the

Court without permission?" "Since you have now given them a thorough description," said the king, "we wouldn't be afraid of them. Summon them in." He then gave the order that an invitation by a golden plaque should be sent at once to the post-house.

When Idiot saw the invitation, he said to Sha Monk, "Brother, you were saying previously that we should perhaps not deliver that letter. Now you can see what benefits delivering that letter can bring. It must be that after Master had delivered the letter, the king said that a messenger should not be lightly treated and insisted on giving a banquet for him. He has no stomach for that sort of thing, but at least he's considerate toward the two of us by mentioning our names. That's why a golden plaque has been sent to invite us. Let's go and have a good meal then, and we can leave tomorrow." "Elder Brother," said Sha Monk, "we still don't know the true reason for this. Let's go and find out." They therefore turned over the luggage and the horse to the care of the post-house master. Taking their weapons with them, they followed the golden plaque into Court and went before the white jade steps. Standing on the left and on the right, they made one bow and then remained erect without moving again. Every member of those civil and military officials was deeply shaken. "These two monks," they said, "are not only ugly, they are downright uncouth! How could they see our king and not prostrate themselves? After one bow, they just stand there and remain erect. It's preposterous! It's preposterous!" Pa-chieh heard this and he said, "Don't complain, all of you. That's how we are! At first glance, we may appear ugly, but after a while, you'll get used to us."

When the king saw how hideous they were, he was immediately frightened. By the time he heard what Idiot had said, he was shaking so hard that he fell down from his dragon couch. Fortunately, there were attendants nearby who took hold of him and helped him up. The T'ang monk was so terrified that he knelt before the Court and kow-towed without ceasing, saying, "Your Majesty, this monk deserves ten thousand deaths, ten thousand deaths! I said that my disciples were ugly and that they should not be granted an audience because it might injure your dragon body. Now, they have indeed alarmed the Throne." Still trembling, the king went forward to raise up the priest, saying, "Elder, it's a good thing that you told me about them before. If you hadn't, the sudden sight of them would have scared me to death!" After he had calmed down, the king said, "Elder Chu and

Elder Sha, which one of you is good at subduing monsters." Foolishly Idiot answered, "Old Hog knows how." "In what way?" said the king. "I am the Marshal of the Heavenly Reeds," said Pa-chieh. "Because I transgressed Heaven's decree, I fell to the Region Below where luckily I could embrace the truth and become a monk. Since our journey from the Land of the East, I have been the one most capable of subduing monsters." The king said, "If you are a celestial warrior who has descended to Earth, you must know very well the magic of transformation." "I shouldn't boast," said Pa-chieh, "but I do know a few little tricks." "Try to change into something for me to have a look," said the king. Pa-chieh said, "Give me a subject, and I'll change into its form." The king said, "Change into something big then."

That Pa-chieh happened to know thirty-six kinds of transformation. He stood before the steps and showed off his ability; making the magic sign with his fingers and reciting a spell, he shouted, "Grow!" He straightened his torso and at once attained the height of eighty or ninety feet just like a path-finding deity. The two rows of civil and military officials shook in their boots; the ruler and the subjects of the entire kingdom were terror-stricken. One of the palace guardian-generals managed to ask, "Elder, when will you stop growing? Is there a limit to your height?" Idiot could not refrain from spouting idiotic words. "It depends on the wind," he said. "It's all right if the east wind is blowing, and the west wind is okay too. But if the south wind rises, I'll bore a great hole in the blue sky!" Horrified, the king said, "Retrieve your magic. I know your power of transformation." Squatting down, Pa-chieh changed back into his original form at once and stood before the steps. "Elder," asked the king once more, "what sort of weapons do you intend to bring with you to do battle on this expedition?" Pa-chieh took out his muckrake and said, "What old Hog uses is a pronged rake." "That's shameful!" said the king with a chuckle. "We have here whips, maces, gilt bludgeons, mallets, scimitars, spears, halberds with crescent-shaped blades, battle-axes, swords, halberds, lances, and battle sickles. You can pick anything you like and take it with you. How could you regard that rake of yours as a weapon?" "You have no idea about this, Your Majesty," said Pa-chieh. "This rake may seem a rather crude instrument, but it is one which has stayed with me since my youth. When I was commanding some eighty thousand sailors in the naval department at

the Heavenly River, I relied solely on the strength of this rake. Now
that I have descended to this mortal world to accompany my master,
that which

Plows through the mountain dens of tigers and wolves
And overturns the water homes of dragons and serpents
is this rake!"

When the king heard what he said, he was most delighted and re-
assured. Turning to some of his ladies in the Court, he said, "Bring
me my own special wine. Take the whole bottle, in fact, so that we
can send the elder off properly." He then poured a goblet of it and
presented it to Pa-chieh, saying, "Elder, this cup of wine is for the
labor you are about to undertake. Wait till you capture the monster
and bring back our little girl. We shall have a huge banquet and a
thousand pieces of gold to thank you." Idiot took hold of the cup in
his hands; though he was a rude and rowdy person, he could act
courteously when he wanted to. Bowing deeply to Tripitaka, he said,
"Master, you should be the first one to drink this wine. But since it is
the king who bestows it on me, I dare not refuse. Please permit old
Hog to drink this wine first. It should help inspire me to catch the
monster." Idiot drained the goblet with one gulp before filling it again
to hand it to his master. Tripitaka said, "I don't drink. You brothers
may take it." Sha Monk went forward to receive the cup, while the
clouds sprouted beneath Pa-chieh's feet and lifted him straight into
the air. When the king saw this, he said, "So Elder Chu knows even
cloud soaring!"

Idiot left; after draining the goblet also with one gulp, Sha Monk
said, "Master, when that Yellow Robe Fiend caught you, two of us
could only battle him to a draw. If Second Brother goes by himself
now, I fear that he may not be able to withstand him." "You are
right, disciple," said Tripitaka, "you may go to lend him some assistance." Hearing this, Sha Monk leaped up and left soaring on the
clouds. The king became alarmed and caught hold of the T'ang monk,
saying "Elder, please sit with us for a while. Don't you go away too,
soaring on the clouds." The T'ang monk said, "Pity! Pity! I can't even
move half a step like that!" At this time, the two of them chatted in
the palace, and we shall speak of them no further.

We tell you now about Sha Monk, who caught up with Pa-chieh,
saying, "Elder Brother, I'm here." Pa-chieh said, "Brother, why did

you come?" "Master told me to come help you," said Sha Monk. Highly pleased, Pa-chieh said, "Well said and welcome! United in our minds and efforts, the two of us can go catch that monster. It may not be much, but we'll spread our fame a little in this kingdom." Look at them:

Swathed in hallowed light they passed the kingdom's edge;
Borne by auspicious air they left the capital.
They went by the king's decree to the mountain cave
To catch with all diligence the monster-spirit.

In a little while, the two of them arrived at the mouth of the cave and lowered the direction of their clouds. Raising his rake, Pa-chieh delivered a blow on the door of the Current-Moon Cave with all his might: at once a hole about the size of a barrel appeared in the stone door. Greatly startled, the little fiends standing guard at the entrance opened the door immediately and found that it was the two of them. They ran inside to make the report, saying, "Great King, it's terrible! The monk with a long snout and huge ears and the monk with the gloomiest complexion have returned and busted our door." Surprised, the monster said, "These two have to be Chu Pa-chieh and Sha Monk. I spared their master already. How dare they come back and wreck my door!" A little fiend said, "They must have left behind something and returned to get it." "Rubbish!" cried the old fiend. "You leave something behind and then you go and break down someone's door? There has to be another reason." He quickly put on his armor, grasped his scimitar, and walked outside. "Monks," he shouted, "I have already spared your master. For what reason do you dare come back and break down my door?" Pa-chieh said, "You lawless monster, you have really done something all right!" "What?" asked the old demon. "You abducted the third princess of the Precious Image Kingdom to this cave and forced her to be your wife," said Pa-chieh. "It's been thirteen years, about time that you give her up. I have been decreed by the king specially to capture you. Go inside quickly and come out again after tying yourself up. That'll save old Hog from having to raise his hands." When that old monster heard these words, he grew enraged. Look at him! Noisily, he ground his teeth together; round and round, his eyes glowered; furiously, he lifted his scimitar; with deadly aim, he brought it down hard on Pa-chieh's head. Pa-chieh stepped aside to dodge the blow and returned one with his pronged rake. Immediately, Sha Monk wielded his precious staff and rushed forward to join the battle. This conflict waged on the peak was different from the one before. Truly,

Wrong words and irksome speech arouse one's wrath;
Malice and rancor make one's anger grow.
The scimitar of this big demon king
Slashes at the head;
The nine-pronged rake of that Pa-chieh
Confronts him at the face.
Sha Wu-ching unleashes the precious staff;
The demon king parries this weapon divine.
One savage fiend
And two godlike monks
Move back and forth, taking their time to fight!
This one says, "You defraud a nation and are worthy of death!"
That one says, "You're wrongly indignant at someone's affairs!"
This one says, "You raped a princess and brought her country shame!"
That one says, "It's none of your business, so stop meddling!"
It is all because of a letter sent
That both monks and demon are not at peace.

They battled for eight or nine rounds before the mountain, and Pa-chieh began to weaken steadily; he could hardly lift his rake and he was rapidly losing his strength. Why couldn't he prevail against the monster, you ask. When they fought previously, you see, there were the dharma-protecting deities who gave the disciples secret assistance because of the T'ang monk's presence in the cave. That was why they fought to a draw. At this time, however, all the gods had gone to the Precious Image Kingdom to guard the T'ang monk, and the two disciples by themselves could not withstand their adversary. Idiot said, "Sha Monk, you come up and fight with him for a while. Let old Hog go shit first!" Not showing the slightest care for Sha Monk, he dove right into a thicket of bramble bushes; without regard for good or ill, without any concern that the thorns were pricking his face and tearing up his scalp, he rolled right inside and lay down, refusing to come out at all. Only half of his ear was left outside, so that he could hear the rattle[9] and learn how the battle was faring.

When the monster saw that Pa-chieh had run away, he went after Sha Monk. Completely flustered, Sha Monk did not even have time to try to escape, and he was seized by the monster and hauled back to the cave, where he was bound hand and foot behind his back by the little fiends. We do not know what will happen to his life, and you must listen to the explanation in the next chapter.

*Thirty*

The evil demon attacks the true Dharma;
The Horse of the Will recalls the Monkey of the Mind.

We were telling you about the fiend who, having had Sha Monk firmly bound, did not proceed to kill him or beat him. He did not, in fact, utter so much as an abusive word to his prisoner. Holding on to his scimitar, he thought to himself instead: "The T'ang monk is a man from a noble nation, who must know the meaning of propriety and righteousness. How could he possibly send his disciples to try to seize me, when it was I who spared his life in the first place? Aha! It has to be some sort of letter sent by that wife of mine back to her kingdom, and that's how the news is leaked! Let me go ask her." Turning savage all of a sudden, the monster wanted to kill the princess.

The princess, alas, was still in the dark about the whole matter. After putting on her makeup, she was walking along when she saw the fiend approaching with bulging eyes and knitted brows, fiercely grinding his teeth together. Smiling broadly, she said to him, "Husband, what's bothering you so terribly?" "You filthy bitch!" cried the fiend. "You don't have any regard for human relations! When I first brought you here, you didn't utter half a word of protest. You had silk to wear and gold to put on; whatever you needed I went out to procure. You have been enjoying the goods of all four seasons and my deep affection every day. Why do you still think only of your parents, with no care at all for our marriage?" When the princess heard what he said, she was so terror-stricken that she knelt on the ground at once. "Husband," she said, "why are you speaking such words of separation today?" "I don't know whether it's you or I who wants separation!" said the fiend. "I caught the T'ang monk and wanted very much to enjoy him. Why did you promise him release before you even consulted me? The fact of the matter had to be that you wrote a letter in secret and asked him to deliver it for you. If it weren't so, why did those two monks come fighting back to my door and demand your return? Didn't you do all this?" "Husband, you

wrong me," said the princess. "Since when did I send any letter?"
"Still trying to deny it, huh?" said the fiend. "I've caught some one
here who's going to be a witness." "Who's he?" said the princess. The
old fiend said, "Sha Monk, the second disciple[1] of the T'ang monk."

Now, no human person is likely to accept death willingly even if
death is near. Determined to deny everything, the princess said,
"Husband, calm yourself and let us go question him. If there were a
letter, I would gladly let you beat me to death. But if there were no
such letter, wouldn't you have slain me unjustly?" When the fiend
heard these words, he did not wait for further discussion. Stretching
forth his indigo hand which had the size and shape of a winnow, he
grabbed the princess by those ten thousand locks of long, lovely hair
and pulled her all the way to the front. He threw her to the ground
and then went forward, scimitar in hand, to question the prisoner.
"Sha Monk," he bellowed, "since the two of you dared fight up to our
door, I ask you this: was it because this girl had sent a letter back to
her country that the king told you to come?"

When the shackled Sha Monk saw how furious the monster was,
hurling the princess to the ground and threatening to kill her with the
scimitar, he thought to himself: "Of course she sent a letter. But she
also saved my master, and that was an incomparably great favor. If
I admitted it freely, he would kill the princess on the spot and that
would have meant our repaying kindness with enmity. All right! All
right! Old Sand,[2] after all, has followed Master all this time and I
haven't made the merest of merit. Today, I'm already a bound captive
here; I might as well offer my life to repay my master's kindness." He
therefore shouted, "Monster, don't you dare be unruly! What kind of
letter did she send that made you want to accuse her and take her
life? There was another reason for us to come to demand from you
the princess. Because you had imprisoned my master in the cave, he
had the chance to catch a glimpse of the princess, her looks and her
gestures. By the time we reached the Precious Image Kingdom and
had our travel rescript certified, the king was making all kinds of
inquiry about the whereabouts of his daughter with a painted portrait
of hers. He showed my master that portrait and asked us whether we
had seen her on the way. When my master described the lady he saw
at this place, the king knew it was his daughter. He bestowed on us
his own imperial wine and commanded us to come here to take you
captive and bring his princess back to the palace. This is the truth.

Since when was there a letter? If you want to kill someone, you can kill old Sand! But don't harm an innocent bystander and add to your sins!"

When the fiend heard how heroically Sha Monk had spoken, he threw away his scimitar and lifted the princess up with both his hands, saying, "I was quite rough with you just now, and I must have offended you deeply. Please forgive me!" He helped her straighten her hair again and reset the bejeweled ornaments with great tenderness and amiability, hugging her and teasing her as they walked inside. He then asked her to take a seat in the middle of the chamber and apologized again. The princess, after all, was a rather fickle woman; when she saw how penitent he became, she, too, had a change of heart. "Husband," she said, "if you have regard for our love, please loosen those ropes on Sha Monk a little." When the old fiend heard that, he ordered the little ones to untie Sha Monk and lock him up instead. After he was freed and locked up, Sha Monk stood up, secretly pleased and thinking to himself: "The ancients said, 'Kindness to others is really kindness to oneself.' If I were not kind to her, she wouldn't make him untie me, would she?"

The old fiend, meanwhile, asked also for wine and food to be served as a means of making further amends to the princess and calming her fears. After drinking until they were half tipsy, the old fiend suddenly changed into a brightly colored robe and girded a sword on his waist. "Mistress," he said, caressing the princess with his hand, "you stay home and drink some more. Look after our two kids and don't let Sha Monk get away. While the T'ang monk is still in the kingdom, I'm going there to get acquainted with my kin." "To get acquainted with what kin?" said the princess. "Your Father King," said the old fiend. "I'm his imperial son-in-law and he's my father-in-law. Why shouldn't I go and get acquainted?" The princess said, "You can't go." "Why not?" said the old fiend. The princess said, "My Father King did not win his empire by might on horseback; he inherited it from his ancestors. Since he ascended his throne in his youth, he hasn't even left the gate of the city. We have no violent men with looks so savage and gruesome as yours. If you meet him, you might scare him and that wouldn't be a good thing. It's better that you not go to get acquainted." "If you put it like that," said the old fiend, "let me change into a handsome fellow and go there." "Change and let me look at you first," said the princess.

Dear monster! Right before the dining table, he shook his body once and changed into a very comely person. Truly he had

Most elegant features
And a rugged physique.
He spoke like a mandarin
And moved with the grace of youth.
Gifted as Tzŭ-chien,³ he could rhyme with ease;
He looked like P'an An⁴ when they tossed him fruits.
He put on his head a crow-tail cap,
His hair gathered in smoothly;
And wore on his body a lined, white silk robe
With wide, billowy sleeves.
Beneath his feet were patterned black boots;
Around his waist shone the five-colored belt.
He had the true bearing of a striking man:
Handsome, tall, dignified, and full of strength.

The princess was most pleased by what she saw. "Mistress," said that fiend laughing, "is it a good transformation?" "Marvelous! Marvelous!" said the princess. "Just remember this: once you enter the Court, many officials, both civil and military, will no doubt invite you to banquets, since it's my Father King's policy never to reject any relatives. You must be extra careful when you drink not to reveal your original appearance. For once you show yourself in your true form, you don't look that civilized." "No need for all that instruction," said the old fiend, "I know what to do."

Look at him. He mounted the clouds and soon arrived at the Precious Image Kingdom. Lowering their direction, he went before the Court and said to the guardian of the gate, "The third imperial son-in-law came especially to seek an audience with the Throne. Please report this for me." The Custodian of the Yellow Gate went before the white jade steps and made the report, saying, "Your Majesty, the third imperial son-in-law has come to seek an audience with the Throne. He is outside the gate of the Court and awaits your summons." The king was just conversing with the T'ang monk; when he heard of the third imperial son-in-law, he asked his ministers, "We have only two sons-in-law. How is it that there is a third?" "The third imperial son-in-law," said several of the ministers, "must be that monster." "Shall we summon him in?" asked the king. Already apprehensive, the elder said, "Your Majesty, it's a monster-spirit! If he's not a spirit, he will not be intelligent. He must know the future and the past, for he is able to mount the clouds and ride the mists. He'll come when you summon him, but even if you did not, he would come in anyway. You might as well summon him in so that we might be spared any kind of hassle."

The king gave his consent and ordered the fiend be summoned before the golden steps. He, too, went through an elaborate performance of court ritual to pay homage to the king. When all the officials saw how handsome he was, they dared not consider him a monster-spirit; being of fleshly eyes and mortal stock, they regarded him as a good man instead. When the king saw how lofty and dignified he appeared, he also thought that this was a man of distinguished abilities, fit to govern the world. "Son-in-law," he said, "where is your home? What region are you from? When did you marry our princess? Why did you wait until today before coming to be recognized as our kin?" "My lord," said the old fiend, kowtowing, "your subject comes from a household east of this city, in the Current-Moon Cave of the Casserole Mountain." The king said, "How far is your mountain from our place?" "Not far," said the old fiend, "only about three hundred miles." "Three hundred miles!" said the king. "How could our princess possibly get there to marry you?" With clever words and the intent to deceive, the monster-spirit replied, "My lord, your subject has been fond of archery and riding since his youth, for I earn my livelihood by hunting. Thirteen years ago, I led scores of houseboys up to the mountain, and we were just sending out our hawks and hounds when we saw a large, striped tiger. It was going down the slope of the mountain carrying a young girl. It was your subject who shot the tiger with a single arrow and brought the girl back to our village, where she was revived with some warm liquids. When I questioned her about her home after saving her life, she never mentioned the word 'princess.' Had she declared that she was the third princess of your Majesty, would I dare be so insolent as to marry her without your consent? I would have tried to enter the golden palace and seek some kind of appointment, however lowly, in order to be worthy of her. Because she claimed, however, that she was a girl from some peasant household, your subject asked her to remain in my village. We seemed to be ideally suited for each other, and we were both willing; that's why we've been married for these thirteen years.

After our wedding, I was about to slaughter the tiger and use it to fete the relatives. The princess, however, requested me not to do so, and she put her reason aptly in these poetic lines:

Heaven and Earth made us husband and wife;
With no broker or witness we were wed.
Red threads[5] did bind our feet in previous lives:
That's why the tiger is our go-between.

Because of what she said, your subject untied the tiger and spared its life. Claws flailing and tail wagging, it ran away still carrying the arrow wound. Little did I anticipate that after a few years, the tiger thus spared managed to become a spirit in the mountain through self-cultivation, bent on seducing and hurting people. Some years ago, your subject had heard of several scripture pilgrims, all priests sent by the Great T'ang. The tiger, I think, must have taken their lives; he probably got hold of the travel documents and changed into one of their forms to come here to deceive my lord. My lord, the person sitting on that brocaded cushion over there is none other than the tiger which carried away the princess thirteen years ago. He is not a real scripture pilgrim."

Look at that capricious ruler! His foolish, undiscerning eyes of the flesh could not recognize the monster-spirit; instead, he regarded that entire specious speech to be the truth. "Worthy son-in-law," he said, "how could you tell that this monk is a tiger, the one which carried away our princess?" "My lord," said the fiend, "what your subject feeds on in the mountain are tigers; what he wears are also tigers. I sleep with them and rise with them. How could I not recognize them?" "In that case," said the king, "make him appear in his true form." The fiendish creature said, "Please give me half a cup of clean water, and your subject will make him appear in his true form." The king ordered an official to fetch the water for the imperial son-in-law. Taking the cup in his hand, the fiend got up and went forward to exercise the Dim-Eyes, Still-Body Magic. He recited a spell and spat a mouthful of water on the T'ang monk, crying, "Change!" The true body of the elder at once became invisible; what everyone saw in the palace was a ferocious striped tiger instead. In those worldly eyes of the king and his subjects, the tiger truly had

A white brow and a round head,
A striped body and lightning eyes.

Its four huge paws
Were straight and rugged;
Its twenty claws
Were hooklike and sharp.
Sawlike teeth filled its mouth;
Pointed ears joined its eyebrows.
Savage, it bore the form of a big cat;
Raging, it had the shape of a brown steer.
Steel hairs stood rigidly like silver strips;
A red tongue, daggerlike, belched nasty air.
It was indeed a striped, ferocious thing,
Blasting the palace with its awesome breaths.

When the king saw it, his soul melted and his spirit fled, while many of his subjects were frightened into hiding. A few courageous military officials led the captains and guards to rush forward and began hacking away with their weapons. If it had not been for the fact that the T'ang monk this time was not yet fated to die, even twenty monks would have been reduced to minced meat. Fortunately, he had at this time the secret protection of Light and Darkness, the Guardians, the Sentinels, and the Protectors of the Faith in the air. For that reason, the weapons of those people could not harm him. The chaos in the palace lasted until evening, when the officials decided to capture the tiger alive and lock it up with chains before placing it in an iron cage. It was then stored in one of the palace chambers.

The king then gave the decree that the Court of Imperial Entertainments prepare a huge banquet to thank the imperial son-in-law for saving him from the monk. After the officials retired from Court, the demon entered that evening into the Silver Peace Hall, where eighteen young palace ladies attended him; they sang, danced, and poured his wine for him. Sitting all by himself at the head table, he had on both sides of him all those lovely beauties. Look at him drink and enjoy! By about the hour of the second watch, he got drunk and could no longer refrain from mischief. Leaping up all of a sudden, he laughed hysterically for a moment and changed back into his original form. He grew violent then and grabbed one of the girls playing the p'i-p'a[6] with that big winnowlike hand of his. With a crunch, he bit off her head. The other seventeen palace girls were so terrified that they dashed madly for hiding and shelter. Look at them:

The palace ladies panicked;
The maids-of-honor took fright—
The palace ladies panicked
Like rain-struck hibiscus bearing the night rain.
The maids-of-honor took fright
Like wind-blown peonia dancing in the spring wind.
They smashed their *p'i-p'as*, eager to live;
They broke their zithers, fleeing for life.
They dashed out the doors, not knowing north or south!
They quit the main hall, flying both east and west!
They scraped their jadelike features;
They bruised their lovely faces.
Everyone scrambled for her life;
Each person darted for safety.

Those people ran out, but they dared not even scream or holler for fear of disturbing the Throne so late at night. Quaking and shaking, they sought to hide beneath the eaves of the low palace wall and we shall speak no more of them.

We tell you now about that fiendish creature who sat in the hall, pouring wine and drinking all by himself. After draining a glass, he would haul the bloody corpse near him and take a couple of bites. As he was thus enjoying himself inside, the people outside the palace began to spread a wild rumor that the T'ang monk was a monster-spirit. All the hubbub soon reached the Golden Lodge post-house. At that time, there was no one at the post-house except the white horse, which was consuming hay and feed in the stall. He was originally the dragon prince of the Western Ocean, you recall, but because of past offense against Heaven, his horns were sawed off and his scales were shorn. He was changed into the white horse so that he could carry the T'ang monk to acquire scriptures in the West. When he suddenly heard people saying that the T'ang monk was a tiger spirit, he thought to himself, "My master is definitely a true man. It had to be that fiend who changed him into a tiger spirit in order to harm him. What's to be done? What's to be done? Big Brother is long gone, and there is no news from either Sha Monk or Pa-chieh." He waited until it was about the second watch, and then he said to himself, "If I don't try to rescue the T'ang monk now, this merit will be undone. Finished!" No longer able to contain himself, he bit through the reins and shook off the saddle; all at once he changed himself once more into a dragon and mounted the dark clouds to rise into the air. We have a testimonial poem for him, and the poem says:

The priest goes West to seek the World-Honored One,
Though foul and fiendish vapors clog the way.
Tonight he's a tiger, what hopeless ordeal!
The white horse drops reins his master to save.

In midair the young dragon prince saw that the Silver Peace Hall was aglow with lights, for there were eight huge candelabra standing inside with all their candles lit. As he lowered the direction of his clouds, he looked carefully and saw the monster seated alone at the head table and gorging himself with wine and human flesh. "What a worthless fellow!" said the dragon with a laugh. "He has shown his hand! He's revealed himself! It's not very smart, is it, to eat people! Since I don't know the whereabouts of Master and I have only this lawless demon before me, I might as well go down there and have some fun with him. If I succeed, I might be able to catch the monster-spirit first and then rescue my master."

Dear dragon prince! With one shake of his body, he changed himself into a palace maid, truly slender of body and seductive in appearance. She walked swiftly inside and bowed to the demon, saying, "Imperial son-in-law, please don't hurt me. I came to pour wine for you." "Pour then," said the fiend. Taking up the wine pot, the little dragon began pouring until the wine was about half an inch higher than the rim of the goblet, but the wine did not spill. This was, in fact, the Magic of Water Restriction used by the little dragon, though the fiend did not know it even when he saw it. "What uncanny ability you have," he said, highly pleased. The little dragon said, "I can pour and make it go even higher." "Pour some more! Pour some more!" cried the fiend. The little dragon took the pot and kept on pouring, until the wine rose like a pagoda of thirteen layers with a pointed top; not a drop of it was spilled. The fiendish creature stuck out his mouth and finished a whole goblet before he picked up the carcass and took another bite. Then he said, "You know how to sing?" "A little," said the little dragon, who selected a tune and sang it before presenting another goblet of wine to the fiend. "You know how to dance?" said the monster. The little dragon said, "A little also, but I'm empty-handed, and the dance won't be attractive." Lifting up his robe, the fiend unbuckled the sword he wore on his waist and pulled the blade out of the sheath. The little dragon took the sword from him and began to dance in front of the dining table; wielding the sword up and down, left and right, she created intricate patterns of movement.

Waiting until the fiend was completely dazzled by the dance, the little dragon suddenly broke the steps and slashed him with the sword. Dear monster! He lunged sideways and the blow barely missed him; the next thrust of the dragon was met by a candelabrum made of wrought iron and weighing about eighty or ninety pounds which the monster picked up in a hurry. The two of them left the Silver Peace Palace as the little dragon changed back to his original form to do battle with the fiend in midair. This battle in the darkness was something! "How was it?" you ask.

This one was a monster born from the Casserole Mount;
That one was a chastised true dragon of the Western Ocean.
This one gave off bright light
Like white lightning;
That one belched out fearsome air
Like bursting red cloud.
This one seemed a white-tusked elephant let loose among mankind;
That one seemed a golden-clawed wild cat flown down to earth.
This one was a Heaven-upholding jade pillar;
That one was a golden bridge hung across the ocean.
The silver dragon flew and danced;
The yellow demon jumped up and down.
The precious sword, on left and right, did not slow down;
The candelabrum, back and forth, went on and on.

After the two of them had fought at the edge of the clouds for about eight or nine rounds, the little dragon's hand grew weak and his limbs turned numb. The old demon, after all, was strong and powerful; when the little dragon found that he could no longer withstand his adversary, he aimed the sword at the monster and threw it at him. The monster, however, was not unprepared for this desperate move; with one hand, he caught the blade, and with the other, he hurled the candelabrum at the little dragon. Unnerved, the dragon did not duck fast enough and one of his hind legs was struck by it. Hastily he dropped down from the clouds, and it was his luck that the imperial moat was there to save his life. Chased by the demon, the little dragon dove headfirst into the water and all at once became invisible. Whereupon the demon took the sword and picked up the candelabrum to go back to the Silver Peace Palace; there he drank as before till he fell asleep, and we shall speak no more of him for the moment.

We tell you instead about the little dragon, who hid himself at the bottom of the moat. When he did not hear a sound after half an hour, he gritted his teeth to endure the pain in his leg and leaped up. Treading the dark clouds, he returned to the post-house where he changed once more into a horse and lay down in the stall. He looked pitiful indeed—completely soaked and wounded on his leg! At this time,

> The Horse of the Will and the Ape of the Mind are all dispersed;
> The Metal Squire[7] and the Wood Mother are both scattered;
> Yellow Hag is wounded, from everyone divorced;
> With reason and right so divided, what can be achieved?

Let us say no more about how Tripitaka met disaster and the little dragon encountered defeat. We tell you instead about that Chu Pa-chieh, who, since abandoning Sha Monk, stuck his head deep into the bushes and lay there like a hog snoozing in a pool of mud. The nap, in fact, lasted till the middle of the night, and only at that time did he awake. When he became conscious, he did not even know where he was at first; only after he rubbed his eyes and collected his thoughts a little did he manage to cock his ears to listen to whatever might be happening. Well, what happened was that

> This deep mountain had no dog barking;
> These spacious wilds lacked even cock crowing.

Looking up at the stars, he figured that it was about the hour of the third watch and he thought to himself: "I would like to try to rescue Sha Monk, but 'One silk fiber is no thread, and a single hand cannot clap!' Okay! Okay! Let me go back and see Master first. If I could persuade the king to give me some more help, old Hog would return to rescue Sha Monk tomorrow."

Idiot mounted the clouds quickly and went back to the city; in a little while, he reached the post-house. The moon was bright and people had become quiet at this time, but he searched the corridors in vain to find any trace of his master. All he saw was the white horse lying there: his whole body was soaked and on one of his hind legs was the mark of a bruise about the size of a pan. "This is doubly unfortunate!" said Pa-chieh, greatly startled. "This loser hasn't traveled. Why is he sweating like that, and with a bruise on his leg? It must be that some evil men have robbed our master, wounding the horse in the process." The white horse recognized that it was Pa-chieh; assuming human speech suddenly, he called out: "Elder Brother!" Idiot was so shaken that he fell on the ground. Pulling himself up, he was about to dash outside when the white horse caught hold of the monk's robe by his teeth, saying again, "Elder Brother, don't be afraid of me." "Brother," said Pa-chieh, still shaking, "why are you talking today? When you talk like that, it has to mean that some great misfortune is about to descend on us." The little dragon said, "Did you know that Master had landed in a terrible ordeal?" "No, I didn't," said Pa-chieh. The little dragon said, "Of course, you didn't! You and Sha Monk were flaunting your abilities before the king, thinking that you could capture the demon and be rewarded for your merit. You didn't expect that the demon was so powerful and you were the ones no doubt who were beaten. At least one of you could have returned to give us the news, but there was not one word from either of you. That monster-spirit had changed himself into a handsome scholar and broken into the Court to present himself to the king as an imperial relative. Our master was changed by him into a ferocious striped tiger, who was then taken captive by the officials and locked up in an iron cage in one of the palace chambers. When I heard how Master suffered, my heart felt as if it had been stabbed by a sword. But you were gone for nearly two days, and I was afraid that any further delay might mean that Master would be killed. So I had no choice but to change back into my dragon body to go and try to rescue him. When I reached the Court, I couldn't find Master, but I met the monster in the Silver Peace Palace. I changed into the form of a palace maid, trying to deceive him. He asked me to do a sword dance, during which I tried to slash him. He escaped my blow and defeated me instead with a candelabrum. I tried desperately to hit him when I threw the sword at him, but he caught it instead and gave me a blow on my hind leg with that candelabrum. I dived into the imperial moat and saved my life; the bruise on my leg was caused by the candelabrum."

When Pa-chieh heard these words, he said, "Is that all true?" "You think I'm deceiving you?" said the little dragon. Pa-chieh said, "What are we going to do? What are we going to do? Can you move at all?" "If I can," said the little dragon, "what then?" "If you can move at all," said Pa-chieh, "move into the ocean then. Old Hog will pole the luggage back to the Old Kao Village to pick up my wife again." When the little dragon heard this, he clamped his mouth onto Pa-chieh's shirt and refused to let go. As tears fell from his eyes, he said, "Elder Brother, you mustn't become indolent." "Why not?" said Pa-chieh. "Brother Sha has already been caught by him, and I can't beat him. If we don't scatter now, what are we waiting for?" The little dragon thought for some time before he spoke again, tears streaming down his cheeks, "Elder Brother, don't mention the word, scatter. If you want to save Master, you have to go and ask a person to come here." "Who is that?" said Pa-chieh. The little dragon said, "You'd better hurry and mount the clouds to go to the Flower-Fruit Mountain, so that you can invite our Big Brother, Pilgrim Sun, to come back. Most certainly he has dharma power great enough to subdue this fiend and rescue Master, avenging at the same time the shame of our defeat."

"Brother," said Pa-chieh, "let me go ask someone else. That monkey and I are not on the best of terms, you know. When he killed that Lady White Bone back there on the White Tiger Ridge, he was mad at me already for wheedling Master into reciting the Tight-Fillet Spell. I was just being frivolous, and I didn't think that the old priest would really recite it and even banish him. I don't know how he hates me now, and I'm certain also that he won't come back. Suppose we have a little argument then: that funeral staff of his is pretty heavy, you know. If he doesn't know any better at that moment and gives me a few strokes, you think I'll be able to live?" The little dragon said, "He won't hit you, because he is a benevolent and righteous Monkey King. When you see him, don't say that Master is in peril; just tell him that Master is thinking of him and deceive him into coming. When he gets here and sees what's happening, he will not get mad. He will want most certainly to have it out with the monster-spirit instead. Then the demon will surely be caught and Master will be saved." "All right, all right!" said Pa-chieh. "You are so dedicated; if I don't go, it'll mean that I'm not dedicated. I'll go, and if indeed Pilgrim consents to come, I'll return with him. But if he is unwilling, then don't expect me, because I won't be coming back either." "Go! Go!" said the little dragon. "He will certainly come."

Idiot indeed put away his muckrake and straightened his shirt. He leaped up and mounted the clouds, heading straight toward the East. It so happened that T'ang monk was not yet fated to die. The wind was blowing in the right direction; all Idiot had to do was to stick up his huge ears and he sped across the Eastern Ocean as if sails were hoisted on him. The sun was just rising when he dropped from the clouds to find his way in the mountain. As he was walking, he heard someone talking. He took another careful look and found Pilgrim sitting on a huge boulder in a mountain valley. Before him some one thousand and two hundred monkeys lined up in ranks, all shouting "Long live our Father Great Sage!" Pa-chieh said, "What pleasures! What pleasures! No wonder he doesn't want to be a monk and wants only to come home! Look at all these goodies! Such a huge household, and so many little monkeys to serve him! If old Hog has a large farm like this, I'm not going to be a monk either. Since I've arrived, what shall I do? I suppose I'll have to see him." But Idiot was in truth afraid of Pilgrim, and he dared not show himself openly. Sliding down the grassy meadow, he crawled stealthily into the midst of those thousand-odd monkeys and began to kowtow also along with them. He had no idea how high the Great Sage was sitting and how sharp his vision was. Having seen everything all at once, the Monkey King asked, "Who is that barbarian in the ranks who's bowing in such a confused manner? Where does he come from? Bring him up here!" Hardly had he finished speaking when the little monkeys, like a swarm of bees, pushed Pa-chieh to the front and pressed him to the ground. Pilgrim said, "Barbarian, where did you come from?" "I dare not accept the honor of your questioning me," said Pa-chieh, his head lowered. "I'm no barbarian, I'm an acquaintance." Pilgrim said, "All the monkeys under the command of the Great Sage here have similar features, not like that lubberly face of yours. You must be some fiendish demon from another region. If so, and if you want to be a subject of mine, you should have first presented us with your name and the particulars of your age and antecedents on a card so that I can take your roll when you are assigned to our ranks here. But you haven't even done that, and you dare kneel here to bow to me?" With his head and snout lowered, Pa-chieh said, "Oh, for shame! I'll show you my face! I have been a brother of yours now for a few years, and you still claim that you don't recognize me, calling me some kind barbarian!" "Raise your head and let me have a look," said Pilgrim with a chuckle. Sticking his snout upward, Idiot said, "Look! Even if you can't recognize me, you can at least recognize this snout of mine!" Pilgrim could not refrain from laughing and saying, "Chu Pa-chieh." As soon as he heard this, he jumped up, crying, "Yes! Yes! I am Chu Pa-chieh." He thought to himself also: "If he recognizes me, then it's easier to speak."

Pilgrim said, "Why aren't you accompanying the T'ang monk to go fetch scriptures? Why are you here? Could it be that you, too, have offended Master and he banished you also? Do you have any letter of banishment? Let me see it." "I didn't offend him," said Pa-chieh, "and he didn't give me any letter of banishment. Nor did he dismiss me." "If there's no letter and he didn't dismiss you, why are you here?" said Pilgrim. Pa-chieh said, "Master has been thinking of you; he told me to come and invite you to go back." "He didn't think of me, nor did he invite me," said Pilgrim. "He swore to Heaven that day and he wrote the letter of banishment himself. How could he think of me and ask me to go back? I definitely will not go back." Pa-chieh lied conveniently, saying, "He really did think of you! He really did think of you!" "What made him think of me?" said Pilgrim. Pa-chieh said, "As Master was riding on the horse, he called out at one point, 'Disciple.' I didn't hear him, and Sha Monk claimed that he was somewhat deaf! Master at once thought of you, saying that we were worthless and that only you were smart and alert enough to answer once you were called, to give ten replies to one question. That's how he thought of you, and he has sent me specially to ask you to go back. Please do so, at least for the sake of his expectation and for the sake of my having traveled all this distance." When Pilgrim heard these words, he jumped down from the boulder. Taking the hand of Pa-chieh, he said, "Worthy Brother, sorry that you have to travel such a great distance to come. Let's you and I go and have some fun." "Elder Brother," said Pa-chieh, "this place is quite far away, and I fear that Master might be kept waiting. I don't want to play." Pilgrim said, "After all, this is your first time here. Take a look at least at my mountain scenery." Idiot dared not persist in his refusal and had to walk away with him.

The two of them proceeded hand in hand, while the little monsters followed behind to go up to the highest spot on the Flower-Fruit Mountain. Marvelous mountain! Ever since the Great Sage's homecoming, it had been completely made new by his labor these few days. You see the mountain

Green as carved jade,
Tall like a cloud-scraper.
All around there are tigers crouched and dragons coiled;
On four sides are frequent calls of apes and cranes.
At dawn the clouds blockade the summit;

At dusk the sun is poised above the forest.
The flowing stream murmurs like tingling girdle-jade;
The brook sounds drop by drop a psaltery note.
Before the mountain are ridges and tall cliffs;
Behind the mountain are flowers and dense woods.
It touches the jade-girl's hair-washing bowl above;
It joins a branch of Heaven's River down below.
This cosmos-formed beauty surpasses P'êng-lai,
A true cave dwelling born of primal breaths.
Even master artists find it hard to sketch,
Nor can wise immortals depict it all.
Like openworks carved finely fantastic rocks
In fantastic colors soar up at the top.
The sun moves in a thousand purple rays;
Auspicious air forms countless strands of red mist.
A cave-heaven, a blessed place among mankind:
A mountain full of fresh blossoms and fresh trees.

Delighted by the endless splendor of the scenery, Pa-chieh said, "Elder Brother, what a lovely place! Truly the number one mountain in the whole world!" "Worthy Brother," said Pilgrim, "think you can pass the time here?" "Look at the way Elder Brother talks!" chuckled Pa-chieh. "This precious mountain is a cave-heaven, a land of blessing. How could you say, pass the time?" The two of them chatted pleasantly for a long time before descending from the peak. They met on the way several little monkeys, all holding purple grapes, fragrant pears, bright golden loquats, and dark red strawberries. Kneeling by the road, they cried, "Father Great Sage, please have some breakfast." "My Brother Chu," said Pilgrim laughing, "has a huge appetite, and he doesn't take fruits for breakfast. Nonetheless, please don't be offended by such trifles; use them as snacks and take a few." Pa-chieh said, "Though I have a huge appetite, I do as the natives do anywhere. Yes, by all means bring them up here. I'll try a few for taste."

The two of them ate the fruits, and the sun was fast rising high. Afraid that there might not be enough time to save the T'ang monk, Idiot tried to urge his companion, saying, "Elder Brother, Master is waiting for us. Please hurry and go." "Worthy Brother," said Pilgrim, "I'm inviting you to have some fun with me at the Water-Curtain Cave." Pa-chieh at once declined, saying, "I appreciate your kind thoughts, Old Brother, but Master has waited for a long time already.

There's really no need for us to enter the cave." "In that case," said Pilgrim, "I daren't detain you. I'll say good-bye right here." "Elder Brother," said Pa-chieh, "aren't you going with me?" Pilgrim said, "Go where? This place of mine is neither governed by Heaven nor controlled by Earth. I'm completely free here. Why shouldn't I enjoy this? Why should I become a monk again? I will not go. You have to go back by yourself. And please tell the T'ang monk that once he has dismissed me, don't ever think of me again." When Idiot heard these words, he dared not press any further, for he was afraid that Pilgrim's temper might flare and he would then receive a couple of strokes from the rod. He had no alternative but to take leave meekly and find his way back.

When Pilgrim saw him leave, he ordered two agile little monkeys to follow him and to find out what he was going to say. Indeed when that Idiot descended the mountain, he did not cover more than three or four miles before he turned around and pointed his finger at the direction of Pilgrim. "You ape," he cried, "you don't want to be a priest! You choose to be a monster instead. What an ape! I came here with good intention to ask him to go back, but he refused. All right! If you don't want to go, you don't have to!" He took a few steps and began his castigations again. The two little monkeys ran back to report: "Father Great Sage, that Chu Pa-chieh is rather sneaky! He's ranting at you as he walks away." Pilgrim grew angry and shouted, "Seize him!" All the little monkeys rushed after Pa-chieh and pushed him to the ground. Clutching at his mane and tugging at his ears, pulling his tail and grabbing his hair, they hauled him bodily back to the cave. We do not know how he will be treated or what will happen to him, and you must listen to the explanation in the next chapter.

*Thirty-one*

Chu Pa-chieh provokes the Monkey King to chivalry;
Pilgrim Sun with wisdom defeats the monster.

> Righteousness joined to fraternal feelings,
> The dharma returning to its own nature:
> Docile Metal and Gentle Wood will perfect the right fruit.
> Ape of the Mind and Wood Mother form the elixir true,
> Both ascending to the world of ultimate bliss,
> Both arriving at the gate of undivided truth.[1]
> Sūtras are the main path of self-cultivation;
> Buddha should unite with one's own spirit.
> Brothers, elder and younger, form the kinship of the three;
> Friends and demons correspond to the Five Phases.
> Exterminate the Sixfold Path[2]
> And you'll reach the Great Thunderclap.

We were telling you about Idiot, who was caught by those monkeys; pulling and tugging at him, they ripped open his shirt as they hauled him away. Over and over again, he muttered to himself, "Finished! I'm finished! This time, I'm going to be beaten to death!" In no time at all, they reached the entrance of the cave, where the Great Sage was sitting again on top of the boulder. "You overstuffed coolie!" he shouted. "You should have just left. Why did you abuse me?" Kneeling on the ground, Pa-chieh said, "Elder Brother, I did not abuse you. If I did, I would bite off this tongue! I only said that if you didn't want to go, I would go back to tell Master and that would have been the end of it. How would I dare abuse you?" "How could you possibly deceive me?" said Pilgrim. "If I pull up this left ear of mine, I can find out who's speaking up in the Thirty-third Heaven; if I pull down this right ear of mine, I can discover how the Ten Kings of Hell are settling the cases with the judges. You were maligning me as you walked away, and you thought that I couldn't hear you?" Pa-chieh said, "Elder Brother, now I know. You are something of a crook and a shakedown artist! You must have changed into some kind of creature

and followed me. That's how you found out." "Little ones," cried
Pilgrim, "select for me a large cane! Give him twenty strokes on his
shanks as a greeting; then give him another twenty on his back.
Thereafter let me use my iron rod to send him on his way!" Pa-chieh
was so terrified that he kowtowed at once, saying, "Elder Brother, I
beg you to spare me for the sake of Master." "O, Master is so just and
kind!" said Pilgrim. "Elder Brother," said Pa-chieh again, "if not for
the sake of Master, at least for the sake of the Bodhisattva, please
forgive me."

When Pilgrim heard him mention the Bodhisattva, he relented
somewhat, saying, "Brother, if you put it that way, I won't hit you
for the moment. But you must be honest with me and not try to
deceive me. Where is that T'ang monk facing an ordeal that has
caused you to come and call for me?" "Elder Brother," said Pa-chieh,
"there's no ordeal. He is truly thinking of you." "Coolie, you must
love to be beaten!" shouted Pilgrim. "Why are you still trying to dupe
me? Though old Monkey's body has returned to the Water-Curtain
Cave, his heart follows the scripture monk. Our master faces an ordeal
with each step of the way; he is fated to suffer at every place. You
better tell me quickly, or you'll be whipped!" When Pa-chieh heard
such words, he kowtowed and said, "Elder Brother, I did quite clearly
attempt to deceive you into going, but I had no idea how smart you
were. Please spare me from a beating and let me tell you standing up."
"All right," said Pilgrim, "rise and talk." The monkeys took away
their hands and Idiot, jumping up at once, began to look wildly left
and right. Pilgrim said, "What are you doing that for?" "To see which
road is wide and smooth so that I can run," said Pa-chieh. "To
where?" said Pilgrim. "I'll let you have a three days' head start, and
old Monkey still has the ability to chase you back. You'd better speak
up! If you get me mad again, I won't spare you this time."

Pa-chieh said, "To tell you the truth, Elder Brother, since you left
us, Sha Monk and I accompanied Master to go forward and we arrived
at a black pine forest. Master dismounted and told me to go beg for
vegetarian food; because I didn't find even a single household after
walking a great distance, I got a bit tired and napped a little in the
grass. Sha Monk, I didn't realize, also left Master to try to find me.
You know that Master couldn't sit still, and he took a walk by himself
in the forest to enjoy the scenery. When he got out of the forest, he
saw a luminescent jeweled pagoda of yellow gold, which he thought

was some sort of monastery. He didn't know that there was a monster-spirit beneath the pagoda, who had the name of Yellow Robe, and he was caught by the fiend. Later, when Sha Monk and I returned to look for him, we saw only the white horse and the luggage, but we didn't see Master. We searched until we went to the door of the cave, where we fought the fiend. Meanwhile, Master met a saving star inside, who happened to be the third princess of the Precious Image Kingdom, abducted some time ago by that fiend. She wrote a letter to her family and wanted Master to send it for her; that was the reason why she persuaded the monster to let Master go. When we arrived at the kingdom, we presented the letter, whereupon the king asked Master to subdue the monster. Elder Brother, you should know. How could that old priest subdue any monster? It had to be the two of us again who went back to do battle, but the magic power of the fiend was tremendous and he seized Sha Monk instead. I managed to escape by hiding in the grass. Thereafter, the monster changed him-self into a handsome scholar to gain admittance into the court and imperial recognition. Master, on the other hand, was changed by him into a tiger. That evening, it was fortunate that the white dragon-horse revealed himself to go search for Master; he didn't find him, but he saw the fiend drinking in the Silver Peace Palace. Changing into a palace maid, the dragon poured wine for him, did a sword dance, and was about to use that opportunity to try to kill the monster. He was wounded instead by him with a candelabrum, and it was the dragon who told me to come get you. He said that Elder Brother was a just and benevolent gentleman, one who would not dwell on old wrongs and would be willing to go and save Master. I beg you, Elder Brother, remember the thought of 'Once a teacher, always a father,' and do try to save him."

"You Idiot!" said Pilgrim. "At the time of my leaving, I told you again and again that if Master were caught by a monstrous demon, you should tell him that old Monkey was his eldest disciple. Why didn't you say so?" Pa-chieh thought to himself, "To ask a warrior is not as effective as to provoke a warrior. Let me provoke him a bit." He said therefore, "Elder Brother, it would have been better had I not mentioned you. Once I said something about you, the monster became even more impudent." "What do you mean?" said Pilgrim. Pa-chieh said, "I said, 'Monster, don't you dare be insolent, and don't you dare harm my master. I still have an elder brother, who is called Pilgrim

Sun. His magic power is great and he is especially capable of subduing monsters. When he gets here, he'll make you die without picking a place for burial.' When that fiend heard my words, he became
more aroused, crying, 'Who's this Pilgrim Sun that I should be afraid
of him? If he shows up, I'll skin him alive, I'll pull out his tendons, I'll
debone him, and I'll devour his heart. He might be thin, this monkey,
but I'll still chop him to pieces and fry him in oil.'" When Pilgrim
heard these words, he became so enraged that he jumped up and
down, madly scratching his cheeks and pulling at his ears. "Who is
this that dares abuse me thus?" he bellowed. Pa-chieh said, "Elder
Brother, calm yourself. It's the Yellow Robe Fiend who is thus abusing
you. I was just giving you a rehearsal of what he said." "Worthy
Brother," said Pilgrim, "get up. I've got to go. If that monster-spirit
dared abuse me so, it would be impossible for me not to subdue him.
I'll go with you. When old Monkey caused great disturbance in the
Celestial Palace five hundred years ago, all the divine warriors of
Heaven would bend their backs and bow to him when they saw him.
Every one of them addressed me as the Great Sage. This fiend is truly
impudent. He dares abuse me behind my back! I'll go, I'll catch him,
and I'll smash him to pieces to avenge myself for being so insulted.
When I've done that, I'll come back." "Exactly, Elder Brother," said
Pa-chieh. "You go and catch the monster first, and when you have
avenged yourself, you can then decide whether you want to come
back or not."

Leaping down at once from the boulder, the Great Sage dashed into
the cave and took off his monster garment. Tucking in his silk shirt
and tightly fastening his tiger-skin skirt, he walked right out of the
door holding his iron rod. Startled, the various monkeys barred the
way and said, "Father Great Sage, where are you going? Isn't it better
that you look after us and have fun with us for a few more years?"
Pilgrim said, "Little ones, watch what you are saying. My accompaniment of the T'ang monk is no private matter, for Heaven and Earth
know that Sun Wu-k'ung is his disciple. He didn't banish me back
here; he told me to come home and relax a little before joining him
again. That's what this whole thing is about. You all must take good
care of our property and don't fail to plant the willows and the pines
in due seasons. Wait till I finish accompanying the T'ang monk and
taking the scriptures back to the Land of the East. After that merit is
achieved, I'll return to enjoy the joys of nature with you." Each
monkey obeyed the instructions.

The Great Sage then mounted the clouds with Pa-chieh to leave the cave and cross the Great Eastern Ocean. When they reached the western shore, he stopped the cloudy luminosity, saying, "Brother, please stop for a moment and let me go down to the ocean to clean up my body." "We are in a hurry," said Pa-chieh. "Why do you need to clean up your body?" Pilgrim said, "You have no idea that the few days since I went back there have caused me to pick up some monster odor. Master loves cleanliness, and I fear that he might be disgusted with me." Only then did Pa-chieh fully realize that Pilgrim was utterly sincere. In a moment the Great Sage finished bathing and mounted the clouds again to proceed westward. Soon they saw the luminescent gold pagoda, to which Pa-chieh pointed and said, "Isn't that the house of the Yellow Robe Fiend? Sha Monk is still inside." "Stay in the air," said Pilgrim, "and let me go down to his door to see what I can do about fighting with the monster." Pa-chieh said, "Don't go, the monster is not at home." "I know," said Pilgrim. Dear Monkey King! Lowering his auspicious luminosity, he went straight to the entrance of the cave in front of which he found two young boys playing field hockey. One was about eight or nine years of age, and the other was over ten years old. As they were playing, Pilgrim rushed forward and, with no regard at all for whichever family they belonged to, grabbed them by the tufts of their hair and picked them up. Terrified, the boys began to brawl and scream so loudly that the little fiends in the Current-Moon Cave ran to report to the princess, saying, "Lady, some unknown person has carried off the two young princes." The two boys, you see, were the sons of the princess and the monster.

When the princess heard that, she ran out of the cave, where she saw Pilgrim holding the two boys. Standing on top of a cliff, he was about to dash them to the ground below. "Hey, you!" screamed the horrified princess. "I have no quarrel with you. Why did you take them away? Their old man is rather mean, and if anything happens to them, he won't let you get away with it." "You don't recognize me?" said Pilgrim. "I'm Pilgrim Sun Wu-k'ung, the eldest disciple of the T'ang monk. My younger brother, Sha Monk, is in your cave. You go and release him, and I'll return these boys to you; two for one, you're getting a bargain already." When the princess heard what he said, she went quickly inside and told the few little monsters guarding the door to step aside. With her own hands, she untied Sha Monk. "Princess, you'd better not untie me," said Sha Monk. "When your fiend comes home and demands the prisoner from you, I fear that you would take the blame again." The princess said, "Elder, you are my benefactor; not only did you send a letter to my home in my behalf, but you also saved my life. I was trying to think of a way to release you when your eldest brother Sun Wu-k'ung showed up at the door of our cave. He told me to release you." Holla! When Sha Monk heard Sun Wu-k'ung, those three words, he felt as if his head had been anointed with mellow wine, as if his heart had been moistened with sweet dew. Joy flooded his countenance; his whole face lighted up with spring. He did not behave like someone who heard the announcement of a person's arrival, but rather like someone who had just discovered a block of gold or jade. Look at him! Flapping his hands to brush off the dust on his clothes, he ran out the door and bowed to Pilgrim, saying, "Elder Brother, you have truly descended from Heaven! Save me, I beseech you." "O, you Sandy Bonze!" said Pilgrim with a chuckle. "When Master recited the Tight-Fillet Spell, were you willing to say a word for me? You were just as much a braggart! Why aren't you accompanying Master to go to the West? What are you squatting here for?" "Elder Brother," said Sha Monk, "no need to talk like that anymore. A gentleman forgives and forgets. We are commanders of a defeated army, hardly worthy to speak of courage. Please save us." Pilgrim said, "Come up," and Sha Monk leaped up to the cliff.

When Pa-chieh who was standing in midair saw Sha Monk coming out of the cave, he dropped down from the clouds, crying, "Brother Sha! You've had a hard time!" Seeing him, Sha Monk said, "Second Elder Brother, where did you come from?" Pa-chieh said, "After I was defeated yesterday, I went into the city at night where I learned from the white horse that Master was in great difficulty. He was changed into a tiger by the magic of Yellow Robe. The white horse suggested to me that I should go ask Big Brother to come back." "Idiot," said Pilgrim, "let's not chitchat. Each of you take one of these boys and go into the Precious Image City to provoke the fiend to come here, so that I can slay him." "Elder Brother," said Sha Monk, "how do you want us to provoke him?" Pilgrim said, "The two of you should mount the clouds and stand above the Palace of the Golden Chimes. Don't bother about the consequence: just hurl the boys down to the ground before the white jade steps. If anyone asks you whose kids they are, just tell them that they are the sons of the Yellow Robe monster caught by the two of you. When the fiend hears this, he will certainly want to return here. I don't want to fight with him inside the city because our battle will scatter cloud and mist, throw up dirt and dust. The officials of the Court and the city's whole populace will then be disturbed." "Elder Brother," said Pa-chieh with a giggle, "the moment you do anything, you start to bamboozle us." "What do you mean?" said Pilgrim. Pa-chieh said, "These two kids, after having been seized by you like that, are already shocked beyond cure. Just now they cried till they became voiceless; after a while, they will die for sure. If we hurl them to the ground from the air, they'll turn into meat patties. You think the fiend will let us go once he catches up with us? He will surely make us pay with our lives, while you get away scot free. There's not even a witness against you! Aren't you bamboozling us?" "If he tangles with the two of you," said Pilgrim, "just lure him here. We have a smooth and wide battlefield at this place, and I'll be waiting for him." "Exactly, exactly," said Sha Monk. "Big Brother is right. Let's go." Riding on the power and assurance of Pilgrim, the two of them picked up the boys and left.

Pilgrim leaped down from the boulder and went before the door of the pagoda. "Hey, Monk," said the princess, "you are completely unreliable. You said that you would give me back my boys once your younger brother was released. Now that he is, you are still detaining my boys. What are you doing here instead?" Pilgrim smiled to her and said, "Don't be offended, princess. You have been here for a long time, and I thought that we should take your sons to present them to their maternal grandfather." The princess said, "Monk, you'd better behave! My husband, Yellow Robe, is no ordinary person. If you have frightened my boys, you should try to comfort them first."

"Princess," said Pilgrim with a chuckle, "do you know what is considered a crime for a human being living in this world?" "I do," said the princess. Pilgrim said, "You are a woman! What do you know?" "Since the time of my youth in the palace," said the princess, "I had been taught by my parents. I recall an ancient book said, 'Set against the Five Punishments are some three thousand crimes, but none is greater than an unfilial act.'"[3] Pilgrim said, "You are precisely an unfilial person. Remember:

O my father,[4] who begot me!
O my mother, who had nursed me! . . .
Pity my father and mother,
How hard they toiled to bear me!

Therefore, filial piety is the foundation of a hundred virtuous acts, the source of all morality. How could you entrust your body to be the

mate of a monster-spirit and not think of your parents at all? Haven't
you committed the crime of an unfilial act?" When the princess heard
these words of rectitude, she was so embarrassed that she blushed for
a long time before blurting out her reply, saying, "The words of the
elder are most righteous. How could I not think of my parents? But all
my troubles began when the monster kidnapped me here. His orders
are very strict, and I cannot travel at all. The distance, furthermore,
is great and there is no one able to send word for me. I wanted to
commit suicide, but I was afraid that my parents would suspect that
I had eloped with someone, and the whole matter would not be cleared
up. I had, therefore, no alternative but to prolong my fragile existence.
Indeed, I am a great criminal in this whole wide world!" When she
finished speaking, tears streamed down her face. Pilgrim said,
"Princess, there's no need for you to sorrow. Chu Pa-chieh did tell me
that you wrote a letter and you saved my master's life. You did
express your thoughts for your parents in the letter. Now that old
Monkey has arrived, you may be assured that he will catch the
monster for you and bring him back to court to see the Throne. You
can then find a worthy mate and look after your parents in their old
age. How about it?" "Monk," said the princess, "don't look for certain
death. Those two younger brothers of yours were quite tough, but
they could not overcome my husband, Yellow Robe, during the fight
yesterday. Now look at you! You look like a ghost with more tendons
than bones! You look like a crab or a walking skeleton! What kind of
ability do you have that you dare speak of catching the monster?"
Laughing, Pilgrim said, "You really don't have much judgment, and
you can't discriminate between persons. As the common saying has it,

    A urine bladder, though large, has no weight;

    A steelyard weight, though small, licks a thousand pounds.

They may look big, but they are useless: creating wind resistance as
they walk and wasting cloth when they put on clothes. They may be
big as a mountain but they are hollow inside; they may be wide as
door frames but they are slack of torsos; and they may eat a lot but
food won't do them any good. I, old Monkey, am small, all right, but
hardy." "You really have the skills?" said the princess. "Nothing that
you have ever seen," said Pilgrim, "but I specialize in subduing
monsters and taming demons." "You'd better not get me into trouble,"
said the princess. "Certainly not," said Pilgrim. "If you are able to
subdue monsters and tame demons," said the princess, "how will you
go about catching him?" Pilgrim said, "You'd better be out of sight, or

else I can't really move when he gets here. I'm afraid that you still have a lot of feelings for him and can't give him up." "What do you mean by not giving him up?" said the princess. "My remaining here is not of my choice!" "If you have been husband and wife for thirteen years," said Pilgrim, "you can't be wholly without affection. But when I see him, I won't be fooling around: a stroke of the rod will be a stroke, and a punch will be a punch. I have to slay him before I can take you back to court to see the Throne." The princess indeed followed Pilgrim's advice and went off to a secluded spot. Her marriage to the monster, moreover, was fated to end, and that was why the Great Sage made his appearance. After he had the princess hidden, the Monkey King shook his body once and changed into the form of the princess to enter the cave and wait for the monster.

We tell you now about Pa-chieh and Sha Monk, who took the two boys to the Precious Image Kingdom and dashed them to the ground before the white jade steps. Alas! They were reduced to two meat patties; their bones were all crushed and blood splattered all over. "Terrible! Terrible!" cried the officials in court. "Two persons have been thrown down from the sky!" "These boys," shouted Pa-chieh from above, "are the sons of the monster, Yellow Robe. They were caught by old Hog and Brother Sha."

Still under the effect of wine, the fiend was sleeping in the Silver Peace Palace when he heard someone shouting his name. He turned over and looked up: there were Chu Pa-chieh and Sha Monk standing on the edge of the clouds hollering. The monster thought to himself: "If it were just Chu Pa-chieh, I could understand this, but Sha Monk was tied up in my house. How could he get here? Why would my wife let him go? How could my boys land in their hands? Could it be that Chu Pa-chieh, fearful of my unwillingness to do battle with him, is using this to trick me? I can take the bait and go fight with him. Hey! I'm still hung over. If he gives me a whack with his rake, I'll lose all my credibility. Let me go home first and see if they are indeed my sons or not. Then I can speak to these monks."

Dear monster! Without taking leave of the king, he headed straight for his cave in the mountain forest to investigate. At this time, people in the court knew full well that he was indeed a monster. For, you see, he ate one of the palace maids during the night, but the seventeen others who escaped made a thorough report to the king after the hour of the fifth watch. Since he left so abruptly, they knew all the more that he was without doubt a monster. All the king could do was to order the many officials to guard the specious tiger, and we shall speak no more of them for the moment.

We now tell you about the fiend, who went back to the cave. When Pilgrim saw him arriving, he at once devised a plan of deception. He blinked a few times and tears began to fall like rain; stamping his feet, pounding his chest, and calling for the boys all the time, he bawled lustily in the cave. So sudden an encounter made it impossible for the fiend to recognize that this was not his wife. He went forward instead and embraced Pilgrim, saying, "Mistress, why are you so upset?" With artful invention, with imaginative fable, the Great Sage said tearfully, "Dear Husband! As the proverb says,

If a man has no wife, his wealth has no boss;

If a girl has no mate, she's completely lost!

After you went into Court yesterday to present yourself to the kinfolks, why didn't you return? This morning Chu Pa-chieh came back and robbed us of Sha Monk. Furthermore, they took away our two boys by force despite my desperate pleadings. They said that they would bring the boys into court also to present them to their maternal grandfather. Half a day has gone by already and there's no sight of our boys or even news of whether they are alive or dead. And you didn't turn up until just now. How could I part with my babies? That's why I'm so broken up." When the fiend heard those words, he grew very angry, saying, "Did that really happen to my sons?" "Yes," said Pilgrim, "and they were taken away by Chu Pa-chieh."

The demon was so incensed that he jumped about madly, crying, "Undone! Undone! My sons have been dashed to death by him! They can't be revived! The only thing left is to catch that monk and make him pay with his life. Mistress, don't cry. How do you feel now? Let's take care of you first." "I'm all right," said Pilgrim, "but I miss my babies so much, and all that weeping has caused my heart to ache." "No need to worry," said the demon. "Get up first. I have a treasure here; all you need to do is to rub it on the painful spot and it will not hurt anymore. But you must be careful not to fillip your thumb onto the treasure, for if you do, my true form will reveal itself." When Pilgrim heard this, he said, smiling, to himself, "This brazen creature! He's quite honest; even without torture he has made a confession already. Wait till he brings out his treasure. I'm going to strike at it with my thumb and see what kind of monster he is." Leading Pilgrim, the fiend took his companion into the murky depth of the cave before spitting out from his mouth a treasure having the size and shape of a chicken egg. It was an internal elixir, formed crystalline white like a śarīra.[5] Secretly delighted, Pilgrim said to himself, "Marvelous thing! God knows how many sedentary exercises had been performed, how many years of trials and sufferings had elapsed, how many times the union of male and female forces had taken place before this internal śarīra was formed. Today, it's a great affinity that it has encountered old Monkey!" The monkey took it over. Of course, he did not have any pain, but he rubbed it deliberately on his body somewhere before filliping his thumb at it. Alarmed, the fiend immediately stretched forth his hand to try to snatch it away. Think of it! This monkey is just too slick and shifty a character! He popped the treasure in his mouth and with one gulp swallowed it whole. The demon raised his fist and punched at him, only to be parried by the arm of Pilgrim. With his other hand, Pilgrim wiped his own face once and changed back to his original appearance, crying, "Monster, don't be unruly! Take a look! Who am I?"

When the fiend saw what he saw, he was greatly shaken, saying "Gosh, Mistress! How did you manage to bring out a face like that?" "You impudent imp!" chided Pilgrim. "Who's your mistress? You can't even recognize your own ancestor!" Suddenly understanding, the fiend said, "I think I know you." Pilgrim said, "I won't hit you just yet, take another look." The fiend said, "Though you do look familiar, I just can't think of your name at the moment. Who indeed are you? Where do you come from? Where have you moved my wife? How dare you come to my house to cheat me of my treasure? This is most reprehensible!" "So you don't recognize me," said Pilgrim. "I am the eldest disciple of the T'ang monk, and my name is Pilgrim Sun Wu-k'ung. I'm also your old ancestor of five hundred years ago!" The fiend said, "No such thing! No such thing! When I caught the T'ang monk, I found out that he had only two disciples named Chu Pa-chieh and Sha Monk. No one had ever mentioned that there was someone by the name of Sun. You must be a fiend from somewhere who came here to deceive me." "The reason why I didn't accompany the two of them," said Pilgrim, "was because my habitual slaying of monsters had offended my master. A kind and compassionate person, he dismissed me when I slaughtered one too many. That's why I was not traveling with him. Are you still ignorant of your ancestor's name?" "How feckless you are!" said the fiend. "If you were banished by your master, how could you have the gumption to face people here?" Pilgrim said, "You impudent creature! You wouldn't know about the sentiment of 'Once a teacher, always a father,' nor would you know that 'Between father and son, there's no overnight enmity.' If you plan to harm my master, you think I wouldn't come to rescue him? And you didn't stop at that; you even abused me behind my back. What have you got to say to that?" "Since when did I abuse you?" said the fiend. Pilgrim said, "Chu Pa-chieh said you did." "Don't believe him," said the fiend. "That Chu Pa-chieh, with his pointed snout, has a tongue like an old maid's! Why do you listen to him?" "No need for such idle talk," said Pilgrim. "I'll just say that during old Monkey's visit to your house today, you have not shown your distant guest sufficient hospitality. Though you may not have food and wine to entertain your visitor, you have a head. Stick it over here quickly and let old Monkey beat it once with the rod. I'll consider that my taking tea." When the fiend heard this, he roared with laughter, saying, "Pilgrim Sun, you've miscalculated! If you wanted to fight, you shouldn't have followed me here. The various imps under my command, young and old, number in the hundreds. Though you may have arms all over your body, you won't be able to fight your way out." Pilgrim said, "Don't talk rot! And don't mention a few hundreds! Even if you have hundreds of thousands, just call them up one by one and I'll slay them. Every stroke of my rod will find its mark. I guarantee that they will be wiped out! Exterminated!"

When the monster heard these words, he quickly gave the order and called up all the monsters before and behind the mountain, all the fiends in and out of the cave. Each holding weapons, they lined up thickly and completely barricaded the several doors inside the cave. When Pilgrim saw this, he was delighted. Gripping his rod with both hands, he shouted "Change!" and changed at once into a person having three heads and six arms. One wave of the golden-hooped rod and it changed into three golden-hooped rods. Look at him! Six arms wielding the three rods, he plunged into the crowd—like a tiger mauling a herd of sheep, like an eagle alighting on chicken coops. Pity those little fiends! One touch, and heads were smashed to pieces! One brush, and blood flowed like water! He charged back and forth, as if he had invaded an uninhabited region. When he finished, there was only one old monster left, who chased him out the door, crying, "You brazen ape! You are nasty and noxious! You dare oppress people right at their own door!" Spinning around, Pilgrim waved at him, crying, "Come! Come! It's no merit until I've struck you down." Lift-

ing his scimitar, the monster aimed at his opponent's head and hacked
away, as dear Pilgrim brandished the iron rod to face him. This time
they fought on top of the mountain, halfway between mist and cloud.

Great Sage had great magic power;
The demon had vast abilities.
This one struck sideways with the raw iron rod;
That one raised aslant the steel scimitar.
The scimitar rose softly, and bright mist glowed;
The rod parried lightly, and colored clouds flew.
Back and forth it circled to protect the head;
Round and round it turned to guard the body.
One followed the wind to change his looks;
One shook his body standing on the ground.
This one widened his fiery eyes and stretched his simian arms;
That one flared his golden pupils and bent his tigerlike waist.
Coming and going, they fought round and round—
Rod and scimitar giving blow for blow.
The Monkey King's rod conformed to battle art;
The fiend's scimitar followed the rules of war.
One had always worked his skills to be a demon-lord;
One had used his vast power to guard the T'ang monk.
The fierce Monkey King became more fierce;
The violent monster grew more violent.
Heedless of life or death they fought in the air,
All for T'ang monk's quest for Buddha from afar.

The two of them fought for over fifty rounds, but a decision could not
be reached. Secretly pleased, Pilgrim thought to himself: "The
scimitar of this brazen monster is quite a match for the rod of old
Monkey! Let me pretend to blunder and see if he can detect it." Dear
Monkey King! He raised the rod above his head with both his hands,
using the style of "Tall-Testing the Horse." The fiend did not perceive
that it was a trick. When he saw that there was a chance, he wielded
the scimitar and slashed at the lower third of Pilgrim's body. Pilgrim
quickly employed the "Great Middle Level" to fend off the scimitar,
after which he followed up with the style of "Stealing Peaches beneath
the Leaves" and brought the rod down hard on the monster's head.
This one blow made the monster vanish completely. He retrieved his
rod to look around, but the monster-spirit was nowhere to be seen.
Greatly startled, Pilgrim said, "O my child! You can't take much

beating! One stroke, and you're dead! But even if you were beaten to death, there had to be some blood or pus left. Why isn't there a trace of you? You must have escaped, I suppose." Leaping up quickly to the edge of the clouds, he stared in all four directions, but there was not the faintest movement anywhere. "These two eyes of old Monkey," he said, "can see everything anywhere. How could he vanish just like that? Ah, I know! That fiend said that he recognized me somewhat, and that meant that he couldn't possibly be an ordinary monster of this world. Most likely he was a spirit from Heaven."

Unable to suppress his anger, the Great Sage somersaulted all at once and leaped up to the South Heavenly Gate, wielding his iron rod. P'ang, Liu, Kou, Pi, Têng, Hsin, Chang, and T'ao, the celestial captains, were so startled that they bowed on both sides of the gate and dared not stop him. He fought his way in and arrived before the Hall of Perfect Light. Chang, Ko, Hsü, and Ch'iu, the Divine Preceptors, asked him: "Why did the Great Sage come here?" "Because I accompanied the T'ang monk until the Precious Image Kingdom," said Pilgrim, "where there was a demon who had seduced the princess and sought to harm my master. Old Monkey waged a contest with him, but as we were fighting I suddenly lost him. I don't think he's an ordinary fiend of Earth; he has to be a spirit from Heaven. I came especially to investigate whether any monster deity has left the ranks." When the Divine Preceptors heard this, they entered the Hall of Divine Mists to make the report, and an order immediately was issued to take the roll among the Nine Luminaries,[6] the Twelve Branches, the Five Planets of the Five Quarters, the numerous gods of the Milky Way, the Gods of the Five Mountains and the Four Rivers. Every one of the Heavenly deities was present, for none dared to leave his post. The investigation was then extended beyond the Big Dipper Palace, and the count, back and forth among the Twenty-eight Constellations, had turned up only twenty-seven members. Revatī, the Wood-Wolf Star,[7] was missing.

The Preceptors returned to report to the Throne, saying "Revatī, the Wood-Wolf Star, has left for the Region Below." The Jade Emperor said, "For how long has he been away from Heaven?" "He was absent for four muster-roll calls," said the Preceptors. "The roll is taken once every three days, so today is the thirteenth day." "The thirteenth day in Heaven," said the Jade Emperor, "is the thirteenth year on Earth." He thereupon gave the order for the Star's own department to recall him back to Heaven.

After having received the decree, the Twenty-seven Constellations went out of the Heavenly Gate and each of them recited a spell, which aroused Revatī. "Where was he hiding?" you ask. He was actually a celestial warrior into whom the Great Sage had struck terror when he caused great disturbance in Heaven before. Just now, the Star hid himself in a mountain stream, and the water vapor had covered up his monster-cloud. That was why he could not be seen. Only when he heard his own colleagues reciting their spells did he dare emerge and followed the crowd to return to the Region Above. He was met by the Great Sage at the gate, who wanted to hit him, but fortunately the other Stars managed to put a stop to it. He was then taken to see the Jade Emperor. Taking out the golden plaque from his waist, the fiend knelt below the steps of the hall and kowtowed, admitting his guilt. "Revatī, the Wood-Wolf Star," said the Jade Emperor, "there is boundless beauty in the Region Above. Instead of enjoying this, you chose to visit in secret another region. Why?" "Your Majesty," said Revatī the Star, kowtowing, "please pardon the mortal offense of your subject. The princess of the Precious Image Kingdom is no ordinary mortal; she is actually the jade girl in charge of incense in the Spread Incense Hall. She wanted to have an affair with your subject, who was afraid, however, that this act would defile the noble region of the Celestial Palace. Longing for the world, she went first to the Region Below where she assumed human form in the imperial palace. Your subject, not wanting to disappoint her, changed himself into a demon. After I occupied a famous mountain, I abducted her to my cave dwelling where we became husband and wife for thirteen years. Thus 'not even a sup or a bite is not foreordained,' and it is fated that Great Sage Sun should accomplish his merit at this time." When the Jade Emperor heard these words, he ordered that the Star's golden plaque be taken away from him; he was then banished to the Tushita Palace to be a paid fire-tender for Lao Tzu, with the stipulation that he would be restored to his rank if he made merit, and that he would be punished further if he did not. When Pilgrim saw how the Jade Emperor disposed of the matter, he was so pleased that he bowed deeply to the Throne. Then he said to the other deities, "All of you, thanks for taking the trouble." "This ape," said one of the Preceptors, laughing, "is still so uncouth! We have taken captive for him the monster-god, and instead of showing his gratitude to the Heavenly Grace properly, he leaves after only taking a bow." The Jade Emperor said, "We count it our good fortune already if he doesn't start any trouble and leaves Heaven in peace."

Lowering the direction of his auspicious luminosity, the Great Sage went back directly to the Current-Moon Cave of the Casserole Mountain, where he found the princess. As he was just giving her an account of all that went before, they heard Pa-chieh and Sha Monk shouting in midair: "Elder Brother, save a few monster-spirits for us to beat too." "They are all finished," said Pilgrim. "In that case," said Sha Monk, "nothing should detain us here. Let's bring the princess back to court. Brothers, let's do the magic of Shortening the Ground."

All the princess heard was the rushing of wind, and in a moment, they were back in the city. The three of them brought the princess up to the Palace of the Golden Chimes, where she bowed reverently to her parents and met again her sisters. Thereafter, the various officials all came to pay their respects. "We are truly beholden to Elder Sun," said the princess to the Throne, "whose boundless dharma power subdued the Yellow Robe Fiend and brought me back to our kingdom." "What kind of monster is that Yellow Robe?" asked the king. Pilgrim said, "The son-in-law of Your Majesty happens to be the Star Revatī from the Region Above, and your daughter was the jade girl in charge of incense. Because of her longing for the world, they both descended to Earth to assume human forms. It was no small thing that they should consummate a marriage contracted in their previous existence. When old Monkey went to the Celestial Palace to report to the Jade Emperor, it was discovered that the fiend had not answered the muster-roll for four times. This meant that he had left Heaven for thirteen days, and correspondingly thirteen years had passed on Earth, for a day in Heaven is a year down here. The Jade Emperor ordered the Constellations of his department to recall him to the Region Above, where he was then banished to work for further merit in the Tushita Palace. Old Monkey was then able to bring back your daughter." After the king had thanked Pilgrim for his kindness, he said, "Let's go and take a look at your master."

The three disciples followed the king and descended from the treasure hall to go into one of the chambers in the court, where the officials brought out the iron cage and loosened the chains on the specious tiger. Everyone still saw the tiger as a tiger, but Pilgrim alone saw him as a man. The master, you see, was imprisoned by diabolical magic; though he understood everything, he could neither walk nor open his eyes or mouth. "Master," said Pilgrim, laughing, "you are a good monk. How did you manage to end up with a fearsome look like that? You blamed me for working evil and violence and banished me. You claimed that you wanted to practice virtue single-mindedly. How did you acquire such features all at once?" "Elder Brother," said Pa-chieh, "please save him. Don't just ridicule him." "You pick on me in everything," said Pilgrim, "and you are his favorite disciple. Why don't you save him? Why do you ask old Monkey instead? Remember what I said originally, that after I had subdued the monster to avenge myself from his abuse, I would go back." Sha Monk drew near and knelt down, saying, "Elder Brother, the ancients said, 'If you don't regard the priest, do regard the Buddha.' If you are here, I beseech you to save him. If we could do so, we wouldn't have traveled all that distance to plead with you." Raising him with his hands, Pilgrim said, "How could I possibly be content not to save him? Get me some water, quick!" Pa-chieh rushed back to the post-house and took out the purple gold alms bowl from the luggage. He returned and handed to Pilgrim the bowl half-filled with water. As he took the water in his hand, Pilgrim recited a magic spell and spat a mouthful of water on the tiger. At once the diabolical magic was dispelled and the tigerish illusion was broken.

After the elder had appeared in his original body, he recovered sufficiently to open his eyes and recognize Pilgrim, whom he took hold of with his hands immediately. "Wu-k'ung," he cried, "where did you come from?" Standing to one side, Sha Monk gave a thorough account of what had taken place, and Tripitaka was filled with gratitude, saying, "Worthy disciple, I owe you everything! I owe you everything! Let's hope that we'll reach the West soon. When we return to the Land of the East, I'll report to the T'ang emperor that yours is the highest merit." "Don't mention it! Don't mention it!" said Pilgrim with laughter. "Just don't recite that little something, and your living kindness will be most appreciated." When the king heard this, he also gave thanks to all four of them before preparing a huge vegetarian banquet for them in the Eastern Palace. After they had enjoyed these royal favors, master and disciples took leave of the king and headed for the West. The king led all his ministers through great distance to send them off. So it was that

The king returned to the palace, his empire secured;

The monk went to worship Buddha at Thunderclap.

We do not know what took place thereafter or when they reached the Western Heaven. You must listen to the explanation in the next chapter.

*Thirty-two*

On Level-Top Mountain the Sentinel brings a message;
At Lotus-Flower Cave Wood Mother meets disaster.

We were telling you about the T'ang monk, who acquired again the service of Pilgrim Sun; master and disciples thereupon embarked on the road to the West, united again in heart and mind. After they had rescued the princess of the Precious Image Kingdom and been sent off by its king and officials, they journeyed without ceasing, taking food and drink when they hungered and thirsted, resting by night and traveling by day. Soon it was again the time of Triple Spring, a season when

Light breezes blow on the willow green as silk,
A lovely view most fit for verse.
The times hasten the bird songs;
The warmth kindles the flowers,
Spreading blossoms everywhere.
A pair of swallows comes to the *hai-t'ang*[1] court,
A time indeed to enjoy the spring:
The red dust on the Purple Path,[2]
The strings, the pipes, and the silken gowns,
The games and the passing of wine cups.

As master and disciples walked and enjoyed the scenery, they found another mountain barring their way. "Disciples," said the T'ang monk, "please be careful. We have a tall mountain before us, and I fear that tigers and wolves might be here to obstruct us." "Master," said Pilgrim, "a man who has left the family should not speak as those who remain in the family. Don't you remember the words of the *Heart Sūtra*[3] given to you by that Crow's Nest Priest: 'No hindrances, and therefore, no terror or fear; he is far removed from error and delusion'? Only you must

Sweep away the filth of your mind,
And wash off the dust by your ears.
Without tasting the most painful of pain,
You will never be a man among men.

You mustn't worry, for if you have old Monkey, everything will be all right even if the sky collapses. Don't be afraid of any tiger or wolf!" Pulling in the reins of his horse, the elder said, "Since I

Departed Ch'ang-an that year by decree,
My one thought was seeing Buddha in the West—
That bright, golden image in Śārī-land,
Those jade-white brows[4] in the pagoda blessed.
I searched through the nameless waters of this world;
I climbed all the mountains unscaled by man.
Fold upon fold the mists and waves extend,
When can I myself true leisure attain?"

When Pilgrim heard what he said, he roared with laughter saying, "If Master wants true leisure, it's not that difficult! When you achieve your merit, then all the nidānas[5] will cease and all forms will be but emptiness. At that time, leisure will come to you most naturally." Hearing these words, the elder had to be content to put aside his anxiety and urge his horse on. Master and disciples began to ascend the mountain, which was truly rugged and treacherous. Marvelous mountain:

The tall, rugged peak;
The sharp, pointed summit.
Within the deep, winding brook—
Beside the lone, rugged cliff—
Within the deep, winding brook
You hear water loudly splashing as a serpent turns;
Beside the lone, rugged cliff
You see the big mountain tiger wagging its tail.
Look above:
The jutting peaks stab through the green sky.
Turn your eyes:
The canyon's deep and dark as the empyrean.
Start climbing:
It's like a ladder, a stair.
Walk down there:
It's like a moat, a ditch.
It's truly a weird, hillocked range;
It's indeed a steep-banked precipice.
On top of the hillocked range
The herb-picker is wary of walking;
Before the precipice

The woodsman finds it hard to move an inch!
Foreign goats and wild horses madly gallop;
Wily hares and mountain bulls seem to form in ranks.
The mountain's height does hide the sun and stars;
One often meets strange creatures and white wolves.
Through dense grassy path the horse can hardly pass.
How could one see Buddha at Thunderclap?

As the elder pulled back his horse to survey this mountain, which was
so difficult to ascend, he saw a woodcutter standing on the green
slope above. "How was he dressed?" you ask.

His head wore an old rain hat of blue felt;
He had on him a monk-robe of black wool.
The old rain hat of blue felt:
Indeed a rare thing to ward off sunlight and mists;
The monk-robe of black wool:
A sign of utter contentment rarely seen.
His hands held a steel ax polished highly;
He tied his machete-cut firewood firmly.
The spring hues at the ends of his pole
Quietly overflowed in all four seasons;
His carefree life as a recluse
Had always been blessed by the Three Stars.[6]
He resigned himself to grow old in his lot.
What glory or shame could invade his world?

That woodcutter

Was just chopping firewood before the slope,
When the elder came abruptly from the East.
He stopped his ax to go out of the woods
And walked with big strides up the rocky ledge.

In a severe voice, he cried out to the elder: "The elder who is going
toward the West, please stop for a moment. I have something to tell
you. There is a bunch of vicious demons and cruel monsters in this
mountain devoted to eating travelers who come from the East and go
toward the West."

When the elder heard what he said, his spirit left him and his soul
fled. He shook so violently that he could hardly sit on the saddle.
Turning around quickly, he shouted to his disciples, "Did you hear
what the woodcutter said about the vicious demons and cruel
monsters? Which of you dare go and ask him in greater detail?"

"Master, relax!" said Pilgrim. "Old Monkey will go and question him thoroughly."

Dear Pilgrim! He strode up the mountain and addressed the woodcutter as "Big Brother" before bowing to him with folded hands. The woodcutter returned his greeting, saying, "Elder, why did you people come here?" "To tell you the truth, Big Brother," said Pilgrim, "we were sent from the Land of the East to go to acquire scriptures in the Western Heaven. That one on the horse is my master. He is rather timid; when he heard just now what you said about vicious demons and cruel monsters, he asked me to question you. For how many years have there been demons and monsters. Are they real professionals, or are they just amateurs? Let Big Brother take the trouble to tell me, so that I may order the mountain god and the local spirit to send them away in custody." When the woodcutter heard these words, he faced the sky and roared with laughter saying, "So, you are really a mad monk!" "I am not mad," said Pilgrim, "and this is the honest truth." "If you are honest," said the woodcutter, "how dare you talk about sending them away in custody?" Pilgrim said, "The way you are magnifying their power, the way you have stopped us with your foolish announcement and silly report, could it be that you are somehow related to these monsters? If you are not a relative, you must be a neighbor; if not a neighbor, you must be a friend." "You mad, impudent monk!" said the woodcutter, laughing. "You are so unreasonable! My intentions were good and that was why I made a special effort to bring this message to you, so that you could take precaution at all times when you journey. Now you are blaming me instead. Let's not say just yet that I don't know anything about the origin of those monsters. But suppose you have found that out, how would you dispose of them? Where would you send them away in custody?" "If they are demons from Heaven," said Pilgrim, "I'll send them to see the Jade Emperor. If they are demons of Earth, I'll send them to the Palace of Earth. Those of the West will be returned to Buddha; those of the East will be returned to the sages; those of the North will be returned to Chên-wu;⁷ those of the South will be returned to Mars.⁸ If they are dragon spirits, they will be sent to the Lords of Oceans; if they are ghosts and ogres, they will be sent to King Yama. Every class has its proper place and direction, and old Monkey is familiar with all of them. All I need to do is to issue a court order, and they will be sent off in a hurry. Even at night!"

The woodcutter could hardly stop his scornful laughter, saying, "You mad, impudent monk! You must have made a pilgrimage to some place and learned some paltry magic of drawing up charms and casting spells with water. You may be able to drive away demons and suppress ghosts, but you have never run into such vicious and cruel monsters." "In what way are they vicious and cruel?" said Pilgrim. The woodcutter said, "The length of this mountain range is about six hundred miles, and it's called the Level-Top Mountain. In the mountain is a cave by the name of Lotus-Flower Cave. There are two old demons in the cave who had portraits made with the intent to catch the priests, and who had names and surnames written down because they insisted on eating the T'ang monk. If you have come from another region, you might get by, but if you are in any way associated with the word "T'ang" you'll never pass here." "We are exactly those who have come from the T'ang court," said Pilgrim. The woodcutter said, "And they specifically want to devour you." "Lucky! Lucky!" said Pilgrim. "How would they like to eat us?" "Why do you ask?" said the woodcutter. "If they want to eat me headfirst," said Pilgrim, "it's still manageable, but if they want to eat me feetfirst, it'll be more bothersome." The woodcutter said, "What's the difference between eating you headfirst and feetfirst?" "You haven't experienced this," said Pilgrim. "If he eats me headfirst, one bite will kill me, of course. Even if he were to fry, sauté, braise, or boil me thereafter, I wouldn't know the pain. But if he eats me feetfirst, he can start by munching on my shanks and then proceed to gnaw on my thighs. He can devour me up to my pelvic bones, and I still might not die in a hurry. Will I not be left to suffer bit by bit? That's why it is bothersome." "Monk," said the woodcutter, "he is not going to spend all that effort on you. All he wants is to catch you and have you bound in a large steamer. Once you are cooked, he'll eat you whole!" "That's even better! That's even better!" said Pilgrim, chuckling. "There won't be pain; I have to endure a little stuffiness, that's all." "Don't be so sassy, monk," said the woodcutter, "for those monsters have with them five treasures which possess tremendous magic powers. Even if you happen to be the jade pillar that holds up the sky, or the golden bridge that spans the ocean, if you want to protect the priest of the T'ang court and pass this place safely, you will become dizzy." "For how many times?" asked Pilgrim. "At least three or four times," said the woodcutter. Pilgrim said, "That's nothing!

Throughout a year, we must have become dizzy for seven or eight hundred times. These three or four—what's that to us? A little dizziness and we are through."

Dear Great Sage! He was not at all afraid. Eager only to accompany the T'ang monk, he abandoned the woodcutter and returned with big strides to where the horse was standing before the mountain slope. "Master, it's nothing serious," he said. "There are a couple of puny monster-spirits, to be sure, but people around here are rather timid and overly concerned. You have me, so why worry? Let's get going! Let's get going!" When the elder heard what he said, he had no choice but to proceed. As they walked, the woodcutter vanished. The elder said, "Why did that woodcutter who brought us the message disappear all at once?" "Our luck must be rather poor," said Pa-chieh, "we have met a ghost in broad daylight." "He must have crawled back into the forest to find firewood," said Pilgrim. "Let me take a look." Dear Great Sage! He opened wide his fiery eyes and diamond pupils to scan the mountain far and near, but there was no trace of the woodcutter. He raised his head and suddenly saw the Day Sentinel on the edge of the clouds. Mounting the clouds, he gave chase immediately, shouting several times, "Clumsy devil!" When he caught up with the deity, he said, "If you had something to say, why didn't you present yourself and speak plainly? Why did you have to put on all that transformation to make fun of old Monkey?" The Sentinel was so frightened that he bowed before he said, "Great Sage, please do not take offense at my tardiness in bringing you the news. Those fiends do have great magic powers, and they know many ways of transformation. It's up to you to use all your cleverness, to exercise all your divine intelligence to guard your master carefully. If you are the slightest bit negligent, you can't get through this road to reach the Western Heaven."

When Pilgrim heard this, he drove away the Sentinel, though the words he kept firmly in his mind. Lowering the direction of his cloud, he returned to the mountain. As he saw the elder proceeding with Pa-chieh and Sha Monk, he thought to himself: "If I give an honest account of what the Sentinel said to Master, he will weep for sure. He's so weak! If I don't tell him the truth, I can put something over him and lead him forward. But as the proverb says, 'Going all of a sudden into the swamp, you can't tell whether it's deep or shallow.' If Master indeed were to be taken by the monsters, won't old Monkey be asked to expend his energy again? Let me take good care of Pa-chieh instead. I'm going to make him go and wage a battle with those monsters first and see what happens; if he wins, we will consider that to be his merit. If his abilities are no good and he is caught by the monsters, there will still be time for old Monkey to go rescue him. I can display my powers then and further spread my fame." As he was thus deliberating with himself, using the mind to question the mind, he thought again: "I fear that Pa-chieh is so lazy that he will refuse to volunteer his service. Master, moreover, is so protective towards him. I'll have to use my gimmick."

Dear Great Sage! Look at the chicanery he's resorting to! Rubbing his eyes for a while, he managed to squeeze out some tears as he walked back facing his master. When Pa-chieh saw that, he cried out at once, "Sha Monk, put down your pole. Bring the luggage over here and we two will divide it up." "Second Elder Brother," said Sha Monk, "Why divide it up?" "Divide it!" said Pa-chieh. "You can then go back to the River of Flowing Sand and become a monster again. Old Hog will return to the Old Kao Village to see how my wife is doing; we can sell the white horse and buy a coffin for Master in preparation for his old age. All of us can scatter. Why bother about going to the Western Heaven?" When the elder heard this on the horse, he said, "This coolie! We are still journeying. What's all this babble?" "Only your son babbles!" said Pa-chieh. "Don't you see that Pilgrim Sun is weeping over there as he walks toward us? He's a stalwart fighter who's not afraid of the ax, the fire, or the frying pan, who can penetrate Heaven and pierce the Earth. Now he has put on a cap of sorrow and arrived in tears. It has to be that the mountain is rugged, and that the monsters are truly vicious. How then do you expect weaklings like us to go forward?" The elder said, "Stop this nonsense! Let me question him and see what he says." He therefore asked, "Wu-k'ung, if you have something to say, let's discuss the matter face to face. Why are you so distressed all by yourself? Are you trying to frighten me with that tearful face of yours?" "Master," said Pilgrim, "just now the one who brought us the message happened to be the Day Sentinel. He said that the monster-spirits were most vicious, making this place a difficult one to pass through. It is indeed a treacherous road through a tall mountain. I don't think we can go through it now; we may as well wait for another time." When the elder heard these words, he was greatly shaken. Tugging at Pilgrim's tiger-skin skirt, he said,

"Disciple, we have covered almost half the journey. Why are you speaking such discouraging words?" "I'm not undevoted to our cause," said Pilgrim, "but I fear that the demons are many and my strength is limited if I have no help. As the saying goes, 'Even if it's a piece of iron in the furnace, how many nails can you beat out of it?'" "Disciple," said the elder, "you have a point there. It is difficult for a single person to handle this matter, for as the military book says, 'The few cannot withstand the many.' But I have Pa-chieh and Sha Monk here, both my disciples. I permit you to command and use them as you wish, so that they can serve as your helpers, someone to protect your flank. Only you should work together to clear up a path and lead me across this mountain. Will we not then be attaining the right fruit?"

All that legerdemain of Pilgrim, you see, was aimed at eliciting from the elder these few words. He wiped away his tears, saying, "Master, if you want to cross this mountain, Chu Pa-chieh has to agree to do two things for me. Only then will we have about a third of a chance to get by. If he doesn't agree to help me, you might as well forget about the whole matter." "Elder Brother," said Pa-chieh, "if we can't do it, let's scatter. Don't drag me down." "Disciple," said the elder, "let's ask your Elder Brother first and see what he wants you to do." Idiot indeed said to Pilgrim, "Elder Brother, what do you want me to do?" "The first thing is to look after Master," said Pilgrim, "and the second is to go patrol the mountain." Pa-chieh said, "Looking after Master means sitting right here, whereas to patrol the mountain means taking a walk somewhere. Do you want me to sit a while and walk a while? How can I do two things at once?" "I'm not telling you to do two things at once," said Pilgrim, "but to select one only." "That's easier to decide," said Pa-chieh chuckling, "but I don't know what's involved in looking after Master or in patrolling the mountain. Tell me something of my duties and I can then carry them out accordingly." "To look after Master," said Pilgrim, "means that if he wants to move his bowels, you wait on him; if he wants to journey, you assist him; if he wants to eat, you go to beg for vegetarian food. If he suffers from hunger even slightly, you'll be beaten; if he pales a little, you'll be beaten; if he loses some weight, you'll be beaten." Horrified, Pa-chieh said, "This is terribly difficult! Terribly difficult! To wait on him or to help him to walk—that's nothing; and even if I have to carry him bodily, it's still an easy matter. But if he wants to send me to beg for food, I fear that there might be those on this road to the West who can't recognize that I'm a monk seeking scriptures. They might think that I'm a healthy hog just reaching maturity and then have me surrounded by many people with brooms, rakes, pitchforks, and all. I'll be taken to their homes, slaughtered, and cured for the new year. Wouldn't that be like meeting the plague?" "Then go and patrol the mountain," said Pilgrim. "What does that involve?" said Pa-chieh. Pilgrim said, "Go into the mountain and find out how many monsters there are, what kind of mountain this is, and what kind of cave there is. We can then make plans to pass through." "This is a small thing," said Pa-chieh. "Old Hog will go patrol the mountain." Hitching up his garment at once, Idiot held high his muckrake and strode energetically up the road leading into the mountain.

As he watched Pa-chieh leave, Pilgrim could not suppress his giggles. "You impudent ape!" scolded the elder. "As a brother, you haven't shown the least bit of sympathy or kindness. You are constantly envious of one another. With all that base cunning, all that 'clever talk and pretentious appearance,'9 you have managed to trick him into the so-called patrolling the mountain already. Now you are even mocking him with your laugh!" "I'm not mocking him," said Pilgrim, "because there's another meaning in my laughter. You see that Pa-chieh has left, but he will not go to patrol the mountain, nor will he dare to face the monsters. He will go instead somewhere to hide for a while and then come back to deceive us with some story that he has made up." "How do you know that about him?" said the elder. Pilgrim said, "I suspect that's how he will behave. If you don't believe me, let me follow him and find out. I can also lend him some assistance in subduing the monsters, and see at the same time whether he is earnest in seeking the Buddha." "Fine! Fine! Fine!" said the elder, "but you must not play tricks on him." Pilgrim agreed and ran up the slope of the mountain. Shaking his body once, he changed into a tiny mole-cricket, indeed a delicate and lightsome transformation. You see

Thin wings dance in the wind without effort;
A small waist sharp as a pin.
He darts through rushes and the floral shades
Faster than even a comet.

Eyes that are shining bright;
A voice that's soft and faint.
Of insects he's one of the smallest:
Slender, shapely, and sly.
A few times he rests idle in the secluded woods—
His whole body out of sight,
Lost to a thousand eyes.

Spreading his wings, he flew with a buzz up there, caught up with Pa-chieh, and alighted on his neck beneath the bristles behind his ear. Idiot was intent on traveling; how could he know that someone had landed on his body! After walking for seven or eight miles, he dropped his muckrake, turned around, and faced the direction of the T'ang monk. Gesturing vehemently with hands and feet, he began to let loose a string of abuses. "You doddering old priest!" he said. "You unscrupulous pi-ma-wên! You sissy Sha Monk! All of you are enjoying yourselves, but you trick old Hog into stumping the road. All of us seeking the scriptures hope to attain the right fruit, but you have to make me do this so-called patrolling the mountain. Ha-ha-ha! If there are monsters known to be in this place, we should have taken cover and tried to get by undetected. But that's not sufficient for you; you have to make me go find them instead! Well, that's your bad luck! I'm going to find some place and take a nap. When I am through sleeping, I'll go back and give you a vague story about having patrolled the mountain, and that will be that!" It was the good fortune of the moment for Idiot. As he walked further along, carrying his muckrake, he discovered a clump of red grass in the fold of the mountain. He crawled inside at once and used his muckrake to create for himself some sort of floor mat. Lying down and stretching himself, he said, "O joy! Even that pi-ma-wên is not as comfortable as I am now!" But Pilgrim, you see, who had stationed himself behind his ear, heard every word. No longer able to contain himself, Pilgrim flew up and decided to badger him a little. With one shake of his body he changed again into a small woodpecker. You see

A fine bill iron hard and glossy red
And bright, gleaming patterned plumage.
A pair of steel claws sharp as nails,
He likes the quiet woods when he's famished.
He loves best the dried trunks worm-rotted;

He cares, too, for the lonely, old tree.
Round-eyed, fan-tailed, he's very perky—
The noise of his pecking bears hearing!

This creature was neither too big nor too small, weighing perhaps
only several ounces. Armed with a red bronze-hard bill and black iron
claws, he hurtled straight down from the air. Pa-chieh was just sleeping soundly with head upturned when his snout received a terrific
bite. So startled was Idiot that he scampered up at once, madly shouting, "A monster! A monster! He stabbed me with the lance! Oh, my
mouth is sore!" He rubbed it with his hands and blood spurted out.
"That's weird!" he said, "I'm not involved in any happy event. Why
has my mouth been painted red?" He stared at his bloody hands,
muttering to himself confusedly, but he could not detect the least
trace of movement around him. He said, "There's no monster. Then
why was I stabbed by a lance?" He raised his head to look upward
and suddenly discovered a small woodpecker flying in the air. Gritting
his teeth, Idiot shouted: "You wretched outcast! Isn't it enough that
pi-ma-wên should oppress me? Why must you, too, oppress me? Ah,
I know! He must not have recognized that I'm a human, thinking
instead that my snout is a charred, rotted tree trunk with worms
inside. He's looking for worms to eat and that's why he gives me a
bite. Let me hide my snout in my chest." Tumbling on the ground,
Idiot again lay down to sleep. Pilgrim flew down once more and gave
the base of his ear another bite. Alarmed, Idiot jumped up, saying,
"This wretched outcast! He's really harassing me! This must be
where his nest is located, and he's worried that I have taken his eggs
or offspring. That's why he's harassing me. All right! All right! All
right! I'm not going to sleep anymore." Poling his rake, he left the red
grass meadow and started up the road again. Meanwhile, Pilgrim
Sun nearly broke up with amusement, the Handsome Monkey King
almost collapsed with laughter. "This coolie!" he said. "Even those
wide open eyes couldn't recognize one of his own!"

Dear Great Sage! Shaking his body and changing again into a mole-
cricket, he attached himself firmly to Idiot's ear once more. After
walking four or five miles deep into the mountain, Idiot came upon in
a valley three square slabs of green rock, each about the size of a
table. Putting down his rake, Idiot bowed deeply to the rocks. Laughing silently to himself, Pilgrim said, "This Idiot! The rocks are no
humans; they know neither how to talk nor how to return his greet-

ing. Why bow to them? That's truly blind homage!" But Idiot, you see, pretended that the rocks were the T'ang monk, Sha Monk, and Pilgrim. Facing the three of them, Idiot was rehearsing what he would say. Said he, "This time when I go back to see Master, I'll say that there are monsters, should they ask me. And if they ask me what kind of mountain this is, I'll say that it's molded of clay, made of mud, wrought of tin, forged by copper, steamed with flour, plastered with paper, and painted with the brush. If they claim that I'm speaking idiotic words, I'm going to say some more. I'll say that this is a rocky mountain. If they ask me what sort of a cave there is, I'll say there is a rocky cave. If they ask me what kind of doors there are, I'll say there are sheet-iron doors studded with nails. If they ask me how deep is the cave inside, I'll say that there are some three sections in the dwelling. If they persist in trying to learn everything, such as how many nails there are on the door, I'll only say that old Hog is too pre-occupied to remember the exact number. Well, now that I have every-thing all made up, I'm going to go back to hoodwink that pi-ma-wên."

Having fabricated his story, Idiot dragged his rake along to retrace his steps. He did not know, however, that Pilgrim heard everything behind his ear. When Pilgrim saw him turning back, he stretched his wings and flew back first, changing back to his original form to see his master. "Wu-k'ung, so you have come back," said the master. "Why don't we see Wu-nêng also?" "He's just making up some lies," said Pilgrim, chuckling, "he'll be here soon." The elder said, "A person like him who has his eyes covered by his ears has to be a stupid fellow. What sort of lies can he make up? It's got to be some hum-buggery of yours again, trying to put the blame on him." "Master," said Pilgrim, "you are always covering up his faults. What I have to tell you, however, is based on evidence." He thereupon gave a com-plete account of how Idiot crawled into the clump of grass to sleep and was bitten by the woodpecker, and how he bowed to the rocks and made up the story on monster-spirits in the rocky mountain, in the rocky cave with the sheet-iron doors. After he finished, Idiot came walking back in a little while. As he was afraid that he might forget what he had made up, he was still rehearsing with head bowed when Pilgrim shouted at him: "Idiot, what are you reciting?" Sticking up his ears so that he could glance around, Pa-chieh said, "I'm back at the old homestead!" He went forward and knelt down, but the elder raised him up, saying, "Disciple, you must be tired!" "Yes," said Pa-chieh, "the person who walks or climbs mountains is the one most tired." "Are there any monsters?" said the elder. Pa-chieh said, "Yes, yes! There is a whole bunch of them!" "How did they treat you?" said the elder. Pa-chieh said, "They called me Ancestor Hog and Grandfather Hog; they also prepared some vegetarian food and soup noodles for me to eat, saying that they would put on a big parade to take us across this mountain." "Could this be your talking in your dreams, after you have fallen asleep in the grass?" said Pilgrim. When Idiot heard the question, he was so astounded that he almost lost two inches of his height, saying, "O Father! How could he know about my sleeping? . . ."

Pilgrim went forward and caught hold of him, saying, "You come over here! Let me ask you!" Idiot became even more alarmed; trembling all over, he said, "You can ask me anything. Why do you have to grab me like that?" "What kind of a mountain is there?" said Pilgrim. Pa-chieh said, "It's a rocky mountain." "What kind of a cave?" "It's a rocky cave," he said. "What kind of doors are there?" Pilgrim asked. "There are sheet-iron doors studded with nails," he said. "How deep is the cave inside?" "There are three sections inside," he said. "No need for you to say any more," said Pilgrim. "I can remember the last part quite clearly, but because I fear that Master still won't believe me, I'll say that for you." "You sneak!" said Pa-chieh. "You didn't even go with me! What do you know that you can say for me?" "How many nails are there on the doors?" said Pilgrim, laughing, "Just say that old Hog is too preoccupied to remember clearly. Isn't that about right?" Idiot was so frightened that he fell on his knees at once. Pilgrim said, "You bowed to the rocks and began speaking to them as if they were the three of us. Isn't that right? You also said, 'Let me make up this story so that I can go hoodwink that pi-ma-wên.' Isn't that right also?" "Elder Brother," said Idiot, kowtowing unceasingly, "could it be that you accompanied me when I went to patrol the mountain?" "You overstuffed coolie!" scolded Pilgrim. "This is an important area. We asked you to go patrol the mountain, and you went to sleep instead. If the woodpecker hadn't jabbed you up, you would still be sleeping there. After you were roused, you even made up such a big lie. You could completely ruin our important enterprise, couldn't you? Stick out your shanks at once, and you'll receive five strokes of the rod as a keepsake."

Horrified, Pa-chieh said, "That funeral rod is very heavy: a little touch and my skin will collapse, a little brush and my tendons will snap. Five strokes mean certain death for me." Pilgrim said, "If you are afraid of being beaten, why do you lie?" "Elder Brother," said Pa-chieh, "it's just this once. I'll never dare do that again." "All right," said Pilgrim, "I'll give you just three strokes this time." "O Father!" said Pa-chieh. "I can't even bear half a stroke!" Without any alternative, Idiot caught hold of the master and said, "You must speak for me." The elder said, "When Wu-k'ung told me that you were making up this lie, I would not believe him. Now that it is really so, you certainly deserve to be beaten. But we are trying to cross this mountain at the moment, and we need everyone whom we can use. So Wu-k'ung, you may as well spare him now. Let's cross the mountain first, and then you can beat him." Pilgrim said, "The ancients said, 'To obey the sentiments of one's parents is to perform a great filial act.' If Master tells me not to beat you, I'll spare you for the moment. You must go to patrol the mountain again. If you start lying and botch things up once more, I'll not spare you from even one stroke!"

Idiot had no choice but to scamper up and leave on the main road. Look at him! As he walked along this time, he was haunted by suspicion, supposing with every step of the way that the transformed Pilgrim was following him. As soon as he came upon an object or thing, he would immediately suspect that it was Pilgrim. After he had gone for about seven or eight miles, he saw a tiger running across the slope. Undaunted, he lifted up his muckrake and said, "Elder Brother, did you come again to listen to my fibs? I told you I wouldn't do that anymore." As he walked further, a violent mountain gust toppled a dead tree, which rolled up to him. Pounding his chest and stamping his feet, he cried, "Elder Brother! Why did you do this? I told you I would not try to deceive you anymore. Why did you have to change into a tree to strike at me?" He proceeded still further and saw in the air a white-necked old crow, which squawked several times overhead. He said again, "Elder Brother, aren't you ashamed of yourself? I told you I wouldn't lie anymore. Why did you still change into an old crow? Are you trying to eavesdrop on me again?" But this time Pilgrim, you see, did not follow him; he was simply ridden with suspicion and surmise, and we shall speak no more of him for the moment.

We now tell you about the mountain, which was named Level-Top Mountain, in which there was a cave called the Lotus-Flower Cave.

There were two fiends in the cave: one had the name of the Great King Golden Horn and the other, the Great King Silver Horn. As they sat in the cave that day, Golden Horn said to Silver Horn, "Brother, how long has it been since we patrolled the mountain?" Silver Horn said, "It's been half a month." "Brother," said Golden Horn, "go and patrol it today." Silver Horn said, "Why today?" "You don't know what I heard recently," said Golden Horn, "that the T'ang emperor in the Land of the East had sent his royal brother, the T'ang monk, to worship Buddha in the West. He has three other companions by the names of Pilgrim Sun, Chu Pa-chieh, and Sha Monk; including the horse, there are altogether five of them. Go see where they are and capture them for me." Silver Horn said, "If we want to eat people, we can catch a few anywhere. Where can these monks be? Let them pass." Golden Horn said, "You don't know about this. The year when I left the Heavenly Region, I heard people say that the T'ang monk is the incarnation of the Elder Gold Cicada, a man who has practiced religion for ten existences, and one who has not allowed any of his yang energy to be dissipated. If anyone can have a taste of his flesh, his age will be vastly lengthened." "If eating his flesh," said Silver Horn, "can lengthen our age and prolong our lives, what need we to practice sedentary[10] exercises, to cultivate the dragon and the tiger, or to achieve the union of the male and the female? We should just eat him. Let me go and catch him at once." Golden Horn said, "Brother, you are rather impulsive. Let's not hurry. If you walk out this door and grab any monk that comes along, you would be breaking the law unnecessarily if he were not the T'ang monk. I still recall how the real T'ang monk looks. Let's have portraits made of the master and his disciples which you can take along with you. When you see some monks, you can check whether they are the real ones." He thereupon had portraits drawn up, and the name of each person was written beside the picture. Taking the sketches with him, Silver Horn left the cave after calling up thirty little fiends to follow him to patrol the mountain.

We now tell you about Pa-chieh, on whom misfortune had fallen. As he walked along, he ran right into the various demons, who barred his way and asked, "Who is he that's approaching?" Raising his head and pushing his ears aside, Idiot saw that they were demons and he became quite frightened. He said to himself, "If I say that I'm a monk going to seek scriptures, they may want to seize me. I'd better say I'm only a traveler." The little fiends reported back to their master, saying, "Great King, it's a traveler." Among those thirty little fiends, there were some who did not recognize Pa-chieh. There were a few, however, who found his face somewhat familiar, and pointing at him, they said, "Great King, this monk looks like the portrait of Chu Pa-chieh." The old fiend told them at once to hang up the picture so that they could examine it more closely. When Pa-chieh saw it, he was greatly shaken, muttering to himself, "No wonder I feel somewhat dispirited of late! They have caught my spirit in this portrait!" As the little fiends held up the picture with their spears, Silver Horn pointed with his hand, saying, "This one riding the white horse is the T'ang monk, and this one with a hairy face is Pilgrim Sun." Hearing this, Pa-chieh said, "City Guardian, it's all right if I'm not included! I'll present you with three hog's heads, twenty-four portions of pure libation. . . ." Mumbling to himself repeatedly, he kept making all sorts of vows. The fiend, meanwhile, went on to say, "That long dark one is Sha Monk, and this one having a long snout and huge ears is Chu Pa-chieh." When Idiot heard what he said, he was so startled that he lowered his snout toward his chest and tried to conceal it. "Monk, stick out your mouth," cried the fiend. "It's a birth defect," said Pa-chieh. "I can't stick it out." The fiend told the imps to pull it out with hooks, and Pa-chieh became so alarmed that he stuck out his snout at once, saying, "It's no more than a homely feature! Here it is! If you want to look at it, just look. Why do you want to use hooks?"

Recognizing that it was Pa-chieh, the fiend took out his precious blade and hacked away. Idiot parried the blow with his rake, saying, "My child, don't be brazen! Watch my rake!" The fiend said with a chuckle, "This man became a monk in the middle of life." "Dear child!" said Pa-chieh. "You do have some intelligence! How do you know right away that your father became a monk in the middle of life?" "If you know how to use the rake," said the fiend, "you must have stolen it after hoeing the fields or gardens of some household." Pa-chieh said, "My child, you won't recognize the rake of your father, for it is not like any ordinary rake for hoeing the ground. We have here

Huge teeth made in the shape of dragon claws,
Adorned with gold and like a tiger formed.
When used in battle it draws down cold wind;
When brought to combat it emits bright flames.

It can for T'ang monk all barriers remove,
Catch all monsters on this road to the West.
When it's wielded, mists hide the sun and moon;
When it's held high, clouds make dim the pole stars.
It knocks down Mount T'ai and tigers panic;
It o'erturns oceans and dragons cower.
Though you, monster, may have many skills,
One rake will nine bloody holes produce!"

The fiend heard the words, but he was not ready to step aside. Wielding his sword of seven stars,[11] he charged Pa-chieh and they closed in again and again in the mountain. Even after some twenty rounds, neither appeared to be the stronger one. Growing more and more fierce, Pa-chieh began to fight as if he had no regard whatever for his life. When the fiend saw how his opponent flapped his huge ears and spat out saliva, whooping and yelling all the time, he became somewhat frightened. He therefore turned around to call up all his little fiends to do battle. Now, if it were a one-to-one combat, it would have been manageable for Pa-chieh. But when he saw all those little fiends approaching, he panicked and turned to flee. The road, however, was not very smooth and he immediately tripped over some vines and dried creepers along the way. As he was struggling to run, one of the little fiends made a flying tackle at his legs, and he hit the ground headfirst like a dog eating shit! The rest of the fiends swarmed all over him, pressing him on the ground, pulling at his mane and his ears, grabbing his legs, and tugging at his tail. Hauling him up bodily, they carried him back to the cave. Alas, thus it is that

Demons break out throughout the body, they are hard to destroy;
Ten thousand ills arise, they are tough to remove.

We do not know what happens to the life of Chu Pa-chieh, and you must listen to the explanation in the next chapter.

## Thirty-three

Heresy deludes the True Nature;
The Soul assists the Native Mind.

We were telling you about that fiend who hauled Pa-chieh into the cave, crying, "Elder Brother, we caught one!" Delighted, the old demon said, "Bring him here for a look." "Isn't this the one?" said the second demon. "Brother," said the old demon, "you caught the wrong one. This monk is useless." Pa-chieh at once jumped at this opportunity and said, "Great King, please release a useless monk and let him go. It's a crime!" "Elder Brother," said the second demon, "don't release him. Even if he's useless, he is part of the T'ang monk's company, and he's called Chu Pa-chieh. Let's soak him thoroughly in the pure water pool in the back; when the bristles are plucked and the hide peeled after the soaking, we can pickle him with salt and sun him dry. He'll be a good appetizer with wine on a cloudy day." When Pa-chieh heard these words, he said, "What rotten luck! I've met up with a monster who traffics in pickled food!" The little fiends hauled Pa-chieh inside and threw him into the water, and we shall speak of him no further.

We tell you now about Tripitaka sitting before the slope; his ears became flushed and his heart began to pound. Growing very restless, he called out, "Wu-k'ung, why is it that Wu-nêng has taken so long to patrol the mountain this time and hasn't returned?" Pilgrim said, "Master still doesn't know anything of how his mind works!" "How does it work?" said Tripitaka. "Master," said Pilgrim, "if this mountain truly has monsters, he will find it difficult to advance even half a step. Instead, he will run back to report to us with all sorts of exaggerations. I suppose, however, that there are no monsters, and he must have gone ahead directly when he found the road quiet and safe." "If he really has gone ahead," said Tripitaka, "where shall we meet him? This a wild, mountainous region, not like somewhere in a village or town." Pilgrim said, "Don't worry, Master, please mount up. That Idiot is rather lazy, and without doubt he moves very slowly. Urge your horse a little and we'll certainly catch up with him to proceed together again." The T'ang monk indeed climbed on his horse; as Sha Monk poled the luggage, Pilgrim led the way in front to ascend the mountain.

We tell you now instead about the old fiend, who said to the second demon, "Brother, if you have caught Pa-chieh, there must also be the T'ang monk somewhere. Go and patrol the mountain again, and make certain that you don't miss him." "At once! At once!" said the second demon, who immediately called up some fifty little fiends to go patrol the mountain with him. As they journeyed, they saw auspicious clouds and luminous ether circling. The second demon said, "Here comes the T'ang monk!" "Where is he?" asked the various little fiends. The second demon said, "Auspicious clouds will alight on the head of a virtuous man, whereas the black ether emitted from the head of a wicked man will rise up to the sky. That T'ang monk is actually the incarnation of the Elder Gold Cicada, a virtuous man who has practiced austerities for ten existences. That's why he is encircled by these auspicious clouds." Those little fiends, however, still could not perceive where the monk was. Pointing with his finger, the second demon said, "Isn't that he?" Immediately, Tripitaka on the horse shuddered violently; the demon pointed again, and Tripitaka shuddered once more. This went on for three times, and Tripitaka grew very anxious, saying, "Disciples, why am I shuddering like this?" "You must have an upset stomach," said Sha Monk, "and that's why you are feeling the chill." "Nonsense!" said Pilgrim. "Going through this tall mountain and rugged cliff must have made Master rather apprehensive, that's all. Don't be afraid! Don't be afraid! Let old Monkey put on a show for you with my rod to calm your fears somewhat." Dear Pilgrim! Whipping out his rod, he began to go through a sequence of maneuvers with the rod as he walked before the horse: up and down, left and right, the thrusts and parries were made in perfect accord with the manuals of martial arts. What the elder saw from the horse was a sight incomparable anywhere in the world!

As Pilgrim led the way toward the West, the monster, who was watching on top of the mountain, almost fell over with fear. Scared out of his wits, the monster blurted out: "I have heard about Pilgrim Sun for several years, but today I know that this is no false rumor." Drawing closer to him, the various fiends said, "Great King, why do you 'magnify the determination of others to diminish your own authority'? Of whom are you boasting?" "Pilgrim Sun," said the second demon, "truly possesses vast magical powers. We won't be able to eat the T'ang monk." "Great King," said the fiends, "if you don't have the abilities, let a few of us go and report to the Great, Great King. Ask him to call up all the fighters, young and old, of our cave, and we will all join to form a solid battle front. You fear that he'll be able to escape then?" "Can't you all see that iron rod of his?" said the second demon. "It's powerful enough to vanquish ten thousand foes. We have but four or five hundred soldiers in the cave, and they won't be able to take even a single stroke of his rod!" The fiends said, "If you put it that way, the T'ang monk certainly will not be our food. Doesn't that mean that we have also made a mistake in seizing Chu Pa-chieh? Let's return him to the monks." "We haven't quite made a mistake," said the second demon, "nor should we send him back so easily. In the end, we are determined to devour the T'ang monk, but we can't do it just yet." "If you put it that way," said the fiends, "should we wait for a few more years?" The second demon said, "No need for a few more years. I perceive now that that T'ang monk must be sought for with virtue and not be taken by violence. If we want to use force to catch him, we won't be able to get even a whiff of him. The only way we can move him is to feign virtue, so that his mind will be made to fuse with our minds, in the process of which we shall plot against him, exploiting the very virtue of his." The fiends said, "If the Great King wants to devise a plan to catch him, will you want to use us?" "Each of you may return to our camp," said the second demon, "but you are not permitted to report this to the Great King. If you disturb him and leak the news, my plan may be ruined. I have my own power of transformation, and I can catch him."

The various monsters dispersed; the demon by himself leaped down from the mountain. Shaking his body by the road, he changed into an aged Taoist. "How was he dressed?" you ask. You see

A shining star-patterned cap,
And tousled whitish hair;
A bird-feathered gown wrapped by sash of silk,
And Taoist shoes woven from yellow coir;
Refined features and bright eyes like a man divine;
A light, healthy frame as the Age Star's.
Why speak of the Taoist of the green buffalo?[1]

He's as strong as the master of the white tablet² —
A specious form disguised as the true form,
Falsehood feigning to be the honest truth!

By the side of the main road, he masqueraded himself as a Taoist with a bloody, broken leg, whimpering constantly and crying, "Save me! Save me!"

We were telling you about Tripitaka, who, relying on the strength of Great Sage Sun and Sha Monk, was proceeding happily when they heard repeatedly the cry, "Master, save me!" When this reached the ears of Tripitaka, he said, "My goodness! My goodness! There is all around not a single village in the wilderness of this mountain. Who could it be that's calling? It must be, I suppose, someone terrified by the tiger or the leopard." Reining in his fine horse, the elder called out, "Who is the person that's facing this ordeal? Please show yourself." The fiend crawled out of the bushes and at once banged his head on the ground without ceasing, facing the elder's horse. When Tripitaka saw that it was a Taoist, and an elderly one at that, he felt sorry for him. Dismounting at once, he tried to take hold of him with his hands, saying, "Please get up! Please get up!" The fiend said, "It hurts! It hurts!" When Tripitaka released his hold, he discovered that the man's leg was bleeding. "O Teacher," said the startled Tripitaka, "where did you come from? How is it that your leg is wounded?" With clever speech and specious tongue, the fiend answered falsely, saying, "Master, west of this mountain is a clean and secluded temple, of which I am a Taoist." Tripitaka said, "Why are you not tending the incense and fires or rehearsing the scriptures and the rituals in the temple? Why are you walking around here?" "A patron at the southern part of this mountain," said the demon, "invited the Taoists to pray to the stars and distribute the blessings day before yesterday. Last night my disciple and I were walking home when we ran into a ferocious striped tiger in a deep canyon. It seized my disciple and dragged him away in its mouth, while your terrified Taoist, madly attempting to flee, broke his leg when he fell on a pile of rocks. I couldn't even find my way back. But it must be a great Heavenly affinity that caused me to meet Master today, and I beseech you in your great compassion to save my life. When I get to our temple, I will repay your profound kindness even if it means selling myself into slavery!" When Tripitaka heard these words, he thought they were the truth and said to him, "O Teacher, we two belong to the same calling—I'm a monk and you're a Taoist. Though our attire may differ, the principles in cultivation, in the practice of austerities, are the same. If I don't save you, I shouldn't be ranked among those who have left the family. But though I intend to save you, I see that you can't walk." "I can't even stand up," said the fiend, "so how can I walk?" "All right, all right!" said Tripitaka. "I can still walk. I'll let you take my horse for this distance. When you get to your temple, you can return the horse to me." The fiend said, "Master, I'm grateful for your profound kindness, but my inner thigh is hurt. I can't ride." Tripitaka said, "I see," and he said to Sha Monk, "Put the luggage on my horse, and you carry him." "I'll carry him," said Sha Monk.

Stealing a quick glance at Sha Monk, the fiend said, "O Master, I was so terrified by that ferocious tiger. Now that I see this priest with such a gloomy complexion, I'm even more frightened. I dare not let him carry me." "Wu-k'ung," said Tripitaka, "you carry him then." Pilgrim immediately answered, "I'll carry him. I'll carry him." Having made certain that it was Pilgrim who would carry him, the monster became very amiable and did not speak anymore. "You cockeyed old Taoist!" said Sha Monk, laughing. "You don't think it's good for me to carry you, and you want him instead. When he is out of Master's sight, he'll smash even your tendons on a sharp, pointed rock!" Pilgrim, meanwhile, had agreed to put the monster on his back, but he said, chuckling, "You brazen demon, how dare you come to provoke me! You should have made some inquiry on how many years old Monkey has been around! Your fib can deceive the T'ang monk, but do you really think you could fool me? I can tell that you are a fiend of this mountain who wants to eat my master, I suppose. But is my master an ordinary person, someone for you to eat? And even if you want to devour him, you should at least have given a larger half to old Monkey!" When the demon heard Pilgrim muttering like this, he said, "Master, I am the descendant of a good family who has become a Taoist. It's my misfortune this day to have met this adversity of the tiger. I'm no monster." "If you fear the tiger and the wolf," said Pilgrim, "why don't you recite the Classic of the Northern Dipper?"[3] When Tripitaka heard these words just as he was mounting, he chided, "This wanton ape! 'Saving one life is better than erecting a seven-tiered pagoda.' Isn't it enough that you carry him? Why speak of the Classic of the Northern Dipper or the Classic of the Southern Dipper?" When Pilgrim heard him, he said, "Lucky for this fellow!

My master happens to be someone who is inclined toward compassion and virtue, but also someone who prefers external appearance more than inward excellence. If I don't carry you, he'll blame me, so I'll carry you, all right. But I have to make it clear to you: if you want to piss or shit, tell me first. For if you pour it down my back, I can't take the stink, and there is no one around to wash and starch my clothes when they are soiled." "Look at my age," said the fiend, "you think I don't understand what you said?" Only then did Pilgrim pull him up and put him on his back before setting out on the main road to the West with the elder and Sha Monk. When they reached a spot in the mountain where the road became bumpy, weaving up and down, Pilgrim took care to walk more slowly, allowing the T'ang monk to proceed first.

Before they had gone four or five miles, the master and Sha Monk descended into a fold of the mountain and became completely out of sight. More and more annoyed, Pilgrim thought to himself, "Master is such a fool even though he's a grown man! Traveling this great distance, one gets weary even if one were empty-handed—and he tells me instead to carry this monster! I wish I could throw him off! Let's not say he's a monster; even if he were a good man, he should die without regret for having lived so long. I might as well dash him to the ground and kill him. Why carry him any further?" As the Great Sage was about to do this, the monster knew instantly of his plan. Knowing how to summon mountains, he resorted to the magic of Moving Mountains and Pouring out Oceans. On Pilgrim's back he made the magic sign with his fingers and recited the spell, sending the Sumeru Mountain into midair and causing it to descend directly on Pilgrim's head. A little startled, the Great Sage bent his head to one side and the mountain landed on his left shoulder. Laughing, he said, "My child, what sort of press-body magic are you using to pin down old Monkey? This is all right, but a lopsided pole is rather difficult to carry." The demon said to himself, "One mountain can't hold him down." He recited a spell once more and summoned the O-mei Mountain[4] into the air. Pilgrim again turned his head and the mountain landed on his right shoulder. Look at him! Carrying two mountains, he began to give chase to his master with the speed of a meteor! The sight of him caused the old demon to perspire all over, muttering to himself, "He truly knows how to pole mountains!" Exerting his spirit even more, he recited another spell and sent up the

T'ai Mountain to press down on Pilgrim's head. With this magic of
the T'ai Mountain Pressing the Head, the Great Sage was over-
powered as his strength ebbed and his tendons turned numb; the
weight was so great that the spirits of the Three Worms[5] inside his
body exploded and blood spouted from his seven apertures.[6]

Dear monster! After he used his magic power to pin down Pilgrim,
he himself mounted quickly a gust of violent wind to catch up with
the T'ang monk. From the edge of the clouds, he stretched down his
hand to try to seize the rider of the horse. Sha Monk was so startled
that he threw away the luggage and whipped out his fiend-routing
staff to block the attempt. Wielding the sword of the seven stars, the
demon met him head on and it was some battle!

The sword of seven stars,
The fiend-routing staff,
All flashed golden beams as lightning bright.
This one, eyes glowering, seemed the black god of death;
That one, iron-faced, was the true Curtain-Raising Captain.
The fiend before the mountain showed his power,
Solely bent on catching Tripitaka T'ang.
This man, earnestly guarding the true monk,
Would not let go e'en at the threat of death.
The two belched fog and cloud to reach Heaven's Palace;
They sprayed dirt and dust to cover the stars.
They fought till the red sun grew dim and lost its light—
The great earth, the cosmos, turned dusky all.
Back and forth they scuffled for eight, nine rounds:
'Twas quick defeat for which Sha Monk was bound!

The demon was exceedingly ferocious; the thrusts and slashes of his
sword fell on his opponent like meteor showers. Growing weaker by
the moment, Sha Monk could no longer withstand him and turned to
flee, when the precious staff was forced aside and he was seized by a
huge hand. Wedging Sha Monk beneath his left arm, the demon
dragged Tripitaka off the horse with his right hand; with the tip of his
feet hooked on to the luggage and his mouth tugging at the mane of
the horse, he used the magic of removal and brought them all to the
Lotus-Flower Cave in a gust of wind. Shouting at the top of his voice,
he cried, "Elder Brother, all the monks are caught and brought here!"

When the old demon heard these words, he was very pleased, saying, "Bring them here for me to have a look." "Aren't these the ones?"

said the second demon. "Worthy brother," said the old demon, "you caught the wrong ones again." "But you told me to catch the T'ang monk," said the second demon. The old demon said, "It was the T'ang monk, all right, but you did not manage to catch the able Pilgrim Sun. We have to catch him first before we can enjoy eating the T'ang monk. If we haven't caught him, be sure not to touch any of his companions. That Monkey King, you see, has vast magic powers and knows many ways of transformation. If we devour his master, you think he'll accept that? He will certainly come to quarrel with us at our door and we will never be able to live in peace." "Elder Brother," said the second demon with a laugh, "you know only how to exalt others! According to your words, that monkey is unique on Earth, and rare even in Heaven. But as I see him, he's so-so only, with not many abilities." "You caught him then?" said the old demon. "He has already been pinned down by three large mountains that I summoned," said the second demon, "and he can't move even an inch. That's how I managed to transport the T'ang monk, Sha Monk, the white horse, and even the luggage back here." When the old demon heard these words, he was filled with delight, saying, "What luck! What luck! Only after we have caught this fellow can the T'ang monk be food in our mouths." He thereupon said to the little fiends, "Prepare some wine at once. Let's present to our Second Great King the goblet of merit." The second demon said, "Elder Brother, let's not drink wine yet. Let's order the little ones to scoop Chu Pa-chieh out of the water and hang him up." Pa-chieh was thus hung up in the east side of the cave, Sha Monk in the west side, and the T'ang monk in the middle. The white horse was placed in a stable while the luggage was brought inside the cave.

Smiling, the old demon said, "Worthy Brother, what marvelous ability! You went out twice and you caught three monks. Though Pilgrim Sun, however, has been pressed beneath the mountains, we must find a way to bring him here so that he can be steamed together with the others." The second demon said, "If Elder Brother wants to bring Pilgrim Sun here, there's no need for us to move. Please take a seat. We need only order two little monsters to put him in two treasures of ours and bring him here." "Which treasures should they take along with them?" asked the old demon. The second demon said, "Take my red gourd of purple gold and your pure mutton-jade vase." Bringing out the treasures, the old demon said, "Whom should we send?" The second demon said, "Let's send Sly Devil and Wily Worm, the two of them." He then gave the instructions to the two, saying, "Take these treasures and go to the tallest peak of the three mountains. Turn one of them upside down so that its mouth will face the ground and its bottom, the sky. Call out the name, 'Pilgrim Sun,' and if he answers, he will be sucked immediately inside. You will then seal the container with the tape bearing the words, 'May Lao Tzu Act Quickly According to This Command.'[7] In one and three-quarter hours, he will be reduced to pus." The two little fiends kowtowed before they left to fetch Pilgrim, and we shall speak no more of them for the moment.

We tell you now about the Great Sage, who was pressed beneath the mountains by the magic of the demon.

Suffering, he thought of Tripitaka;
In adversity, he recalled the holy monk.

He cried out with a loud voice, "O Master! I remember how you went to the Mountain of Two Frontiers to lift up the tape that had me pressed down, and it was then that old Monkey escaped his great ordeal to embrace the vow of complete poverty. Thanks to the Bodhisattva, I was given the dharma decree so that you and I could stay together and practice religion together, so that we would be brought under the same affinity and attain the same enlightenment and knowledge. How should I expect that we would run into such a demonic obstacle here, and that I would be pinned down again by his mountains. O pity it all! You may be fated to die, but pity Sha Monk, Pa-chieh, and the little dragon who took all that trouble of changing into a horse. Truly as the saying goes,

A tall tree beckons the wind, the wind will rock the tree;
A man lives for his name, his name will wreck the man."

When he finished this lamentation, tears fell down his cheeks like rain.

All that noise, however, immediately disturbed the mountain god, the local spirit, and the Guardians of Five Quarters, who came together with the Golden-Headed Guardian. The last one said, "Whose mountains are these?" "Ours," said the local spirit. "Do you know who it is that you have pinned down beneath the mountains?" "No, we don't," said the local spirit. "So, you don't know," said the Guardian, "but he happens to be the Great Sage, Equal to Heaven, the Pilgrim Sun Wu-k'ung who caused tremendous disturbance in Heaven five hundred years ago. Now he has embraced the right fruit to follow the

T'ang monk as his disciple. How could you permit the demon to borrow these mountains to pin him down? You are as good as dead! If he ever finds release and comes out, you think he'll spare you? Even if he lets you all go lightly, the local spirit will be demoted to an attendant in a post-house, the mountain god will be banished to military service, and even we will be placed under a terrible obligation." Only then did the mountain god and the local spirit become frightened; they said, "We really didn't know. All we heard was the spell for moving mountains recited by the demon and we transferred the mountains here. How could we know that it was the Great Sage Sun?" The Guardian said, "Don't be afraid now. The Law says, 'The ignorant will not be held culpable.' You and I can discuss the matter and see how we can release him without making him beat us." "This is becoming rather ridiculous," said the local spirit. "Will he beat us even after we have released him?" "You have no idea," said the Guardian, "that he possesses a compliant golden-hooped rod, a most powerful weapon indeed. One stroke of it means death; one touch, a bad wound! A small tap and the tendons snap, a tiny brush and the skin collapses!"

Growing more and more alarmed, the mountain god and the local spirit had a discussion with the Guardians of Five Quarters before walking up to the front of the three mountains and crying, "Great Sage, the mountain god, the local spirit, and the Guardians of Five Quarters have come to see you." Dear Pilgrim! Though he might be like a lean tiger at the moment, his courage remained. When he heard the announcement, he replied at once resolutely in a ringing voice, "Why do you want to see me?" The local spirit said, "Allow me to report this to the Great Sage. I ask your permission to move the mountains away so that the Great Sage might come out and pardon the crime of disrespect unknowingly committed by this humble deity." Pilgrim said, "Move the mountains away. I won't hit you." When he said this, it was as if an official pardon had been announced! The various gods began reciting their spells and the mountains were sent back to their original locations. Once released, Pilgrim leaped up; shaking off the dirt and tightening up his skirt, he whipped out his rod from behind his ear and said to the mountain god and the local spirit: "Stick out your shanks. Each of you will receive two strokes so that old Monkey may find some relief for his misery!" Terrified, the two gods said, "Just now the Great Sage promised to pardon us. How could you change

your word, now that you have come out, and want to hit us?" "Dear
local spirit! Dear mountain god!" said Pilgrim. "You are not afraid
of old Monkey, you are afraid of the monsters instead!" The local
spirit said, "Those demons have vast magical powers. With their incantations and spells, they would summon us into their cave and we
would have to take turns to be on duty."

When Pilgrim heard these two words "on duty," he, too, was quite
shaken. Lifting his head to face the sky, he cried in a loud voice, "O
Azure Heaven! Since the division of chaos and the creation of Heaven
and Earth, and since the Flower-Fruit Mountain gave birth to me, I
did search all around for the enlightened teacher to transmit to me
the secret formula for longevity. Think of it, I can change with the
wind, tame the tiger, and subdue the dragon; I even caused great
disturbance in the Celestial Palace and acquired the name, Great Sage.
But I never dared to be so insolent as to order a mountain god or a
local spirit around. These demons today are truly lawless! How could
they be so arrogant as to make the mountain god and the local spirit
their servants, forcing them to take turns to be on duty? O Heaven,
if you had given birth to old Monkey, why did you give birth to these
creatures also?"[8]

As the Great Sage was thus sighing, he saw in the distance beams
of light rising from a mountain valley. "Mountain god, local spirit,"
said Pilgrim, "since you have been on duty in the cave, you must
know what objects are those emitting the light." "They must be the
luminescent treasures of the demons," said the local spirit. "Some
monster spirits, I suppose, are coming with the treasures to subdue
you." Pilgrim said, "This is a lot more fun! Let me ask you quickly,
who would socialize with them in the cave?" The local spirit said,
"What they love are the firing of elixir and the refinement of herbs;
what they delight in are the Taoists of the Complete Truth Sect." "No
wonder he changed into an old Taoist to lure my master away," said
Pilgrim. "Since this is the case, your beating will be deferred for the
moment. You may leave, let old Monkey himself catch them." The
various deities rose into the air and left.

This Great Sage shook his body once and changed into an old adept.
"How was he dressed?" you ask.

His head had two buns of hair;
He wore a clerical robe;
He struck a bamboo fish;[9]

A Master Lü[10] sash circled his waist.
Reclining by the main road,
He waited for the little fiends.
In a while the fiends arrived;
The Ape King released his tricks.

In no time at all, the two little fiends came before him and Pilgrim stuck out his golden-hooped rod. Unprepared for this, one of the little fiends tripped on it and fell; only when he scrambled up did he see Pilgrim. "Villainy! Villainy!" he began to cry. "If our Great Kings didn't have a special fondness for your kind of people, I would scrap with you." "What's there to scrap about?" said Pilgrim, smiling amiably. "A Taoist meeting a Taoist, we are all in the same family!" "Why did you lie here," said the fiend, "and cause me to stumble?" Pilgrim said, "A Taoist youth like you, when you run into an aged Taoist like me, must take a fall—it's a sort of substitute for presenting an introductory gift." The fiend said, "Our Great Kings only demand a few ounces of silver as introductory gifts. Why do you insist on someone taking a fall? This must be the custom of another region, and you can't possibly be a Taoist from around here." "Indeed, I'm not," said Pilgrim, "for I came from P'êng-lai Mountain." The fiend said, "But P'êng-lai is an island in the territory of immortals." "If I'm not an immortal," said Pilgrim, "who's an immortal?" Turning all at once from anger to delight, the fiend approached him and said, "Old Immortal, Old Immortal! We are of fleshly eyes and mortal stock, and that's why we can't recognize you. Our words have offended you. Please pardon us." "I don't blame you," said Pilgrim, "for as the saying goes, 'The immortal frame does not tread on ground profane.' How could you know? The reason why I have landed on your mountain today is that I want to enlighten a good man to become an immortal, to understand the Tao. Which of you is willing to follow me?" Sly Devil said, "Master, I'll follow you," while Wily Worm also said, "Master, I'll follow you."

Though he knew the reason already, Pilgrim nonetheless asked, "Where did you two come from?" "From the Lotus-Flower Cave," said one of the fiends. "Where are you going?" "Our Great Kings have ordered us," said the fiend, "to go capture Pilgrim Sun." "To capture whom?" said Pilgrim. "To capture Pilgrim Sun," said the fiend again. Pilgrim said, "Could it be Pilgrim Sun, the one who's following the T'ang monk to seek scriptures?" "Exactly, exactly," said the fiend.

"You know him too?" "That monkey is rather rude," said Pilgrim. "I know him all right, and I am a little mad at him. I'll go with you to capture him; we'll consider this my assisting you in making merit." "Master," said the fiend, "no need for you to assist us in making merit. Our Second Great King has considerable magic powers: he summoned three huge mountains and had that monkey pinned down, unable to move even an inch. He then told us to come with treasures to store him up." "What kind of treasures?" said Pilgrim. Sly Devil said, "Mine is a red gourd, while his is a pure jade vase." "How do you plan to store him up?" said Pilgrim. The little fiend said, "Turn my treasure upside down so that its mouth will face the earth and its bottom the sky. I'll then call him once, and if he answers me, he will at once be sucked inside. I will then seal the treasure with a tape bearing the words, 'May Lao Tzu Act Quickly According to This Command.' In one and three-quarter hours, he will be reduced to pus."

When Pilgrim heard that, he said to himself in secret alarm, "Formidable! Formidable! Previously the Day Sentinel said that they had five treasures, and these must be two of them. I wonder what sort of things are the other three?" He smiled and said to the two of them, "Could you two permit me to have a look at the treasures?" Completely unsuspecting, the little fiends took out from their sleeves at once the two treasures and presented them to Pilgrim with two hands. When Pilgrim saw them, he was delighted, saying to himself, "Marvelous things! Marvelous things! I could wag my tail once and leap clear of this place, making off with the treasures as if they had been presented to me as gifts." He then thought to himself: "It's no good! I can rob them of these things, but old Monkey's reputation will be ruined. This is nothing but committing robbery in broad daylight." He therefore returned the treasures to the fiends, saying, "You haven't seen my treasure yet." One of the fiends said, "What kind of treasure does Master have? Would you permit us profane people to have a look, to ward off calamities perhaps?"

Dear Pilgrim! Stretching forth his hand, he pulled off a piece of hair from his tail and gave it a squeeze, crying "Change!" It changed at once into a huge red gourd of purple gold, about seventeen inches tall. He took it out from his waist, saying, "You want to see my gourd?" Having received it in his hands and examined it, Wily Worm said, "Master, your gourd is big, and it has nice form. It's good to look at all right, but I'm afraid that it's not good to use." "What do you mean by not good to use?" said Pilgrim. The fiend said, "Each one of our treasures can store up to a thousand people." "So," said Pilgrim, "yours can store up people. What's so rare about that? This gourd of mine can even store up Heaven!" "It can?" said the fiend. "Indeed," said Pilgrim. "I'm afraid you are lying," said the fiend. "Store it up for us to see and we'll believe you; otherwise, we'll never believe you." "If Heaven irritates me," said Pilgrim, "I usually store it up seven or eight times within a single month. If it doesn't bother me, I will not store it up for as long as half a year." "Elder Brother," said Wily Worm, "a treasure that can store up Heaven! Let's exchange ours with his." Sly Devil said, "How would he be willing to exchange his with ours, which can only store up people?" "If he's unwilling," said Wily Worm, "we'll make it good with our vase also." Secretly delighted, Pilgrim thought to himself:

A gourd repays a gourd,

We add a vase of jade.

Two things exchanged for one:

That's what I call fair trade!

He therefore went forward and caught hold of Wily Worm, saying, "If I store up Heaven, you will trade with me?" "If you do, yes," said the fiend. "If I don't, I'll be your son!" "All right! All right!" said Pilgrim. "I'll store it up for you to see."

Dear Great Sage! Bowing his head and making the magic sign, he recited a spell which brought him the God of Day Patrol, the God of Night Patrol, and the Guardians of Five Quarters, to whom he gave the following instruction: "Report for me at once to the Jade Emperor and say that old Monkey has embraced the right fruit to accompany the T'ang monk to acquire scriptures in the Western Heaven. Our path has been blocked at a tall mountain, where my master encounters grievous calamity. I would like to entice certain demons, who possess some treasures, into trading with me. I therefore beseech His Majesty with due reverence to let old Monkey borrow Heaven to be stored up for half an hour so that I may accomplish my task. If he but utters half a 'No,' I shall ascend to the Divine Mists Hall and start a war!"

The deities went past the South Heavenly Gate and stood below the Hall of Divine Mists to report to the Jade Emperor. "This impudent ape!" said the Jade Emperor. "He still speaks in such an unruly manner. Some time ago when Kuan-yin came to inform us that he had been released to accompany the T'ang monk, we even sent him the Guardians of the Five Quarters and the Four Sentinels to take turns to minister to him. Now he even wants to borrow Heaven to be stored up! How could Heaven be stored up?" Hardly had he finished speaking when the Third Prince Naṭa stepped forward from the ranks and memorialized, saying, "Your Majesty, Heaven, too, can be stored up." "How?" inquired the Jade Emperor. Naṭa said, "When Chaos first divided, that which was pure and light became Heaven, and that which was heavy and turbid became Earth. Heaven, then, is a round mass of clear ether which nonetheless supports the Jasper Palace and the Heavenly ramparts. In principle, therefore, Heaven cannot be stored up. However, the matter of Pilgrim Sun's accompaniment of the T'ang monk journeying westward to acquire scriptures is itself a source of blessings great as Mount T'ai and deep as the sea. Today we should help him to succeed." The Jade Emperor said, "How would our worthy minister help him?" "Let Your Majesty issue a decree," said Naṭa, "and ask Chên-wu, the Lord of the North at the North Heavenly Gate, to lend us his banner of black feathers, which should then be unfurled across the South Heavenly Gate. The sun, the moon, and the stars will be covered, and it will be so dark on Earth that people cannot see each other even if they are standing face to face. The fiends will be deceived into thinking that Heaven has been stored up, and that is how we may help Pilgrim to succeed." The Jade Emperor gave his consent to this suggestion, and the prince received the command to go to the North Heavenly Gate, where he gave the account to Chên-wu. The patriarch at once handed the banner to the prince.

Meanwhile, the Day Patrol God swiftly returned to the Great Sage and whispered in his ear, "Prince Naṭa has come to help you." Looking up, Pilgrim saw auspicious clouds looming up: indeed a deity was approaching. He turned to the little fiends, saying, "I'm going to store up Heaven." "Go ahead," said one of them. "Why keep dragging your feet?" "I was just exercising my spirit and reciting a spell," said Pilgrim. The two little fiends stood there wide-eyed and determined to find out how he was going to store up Heaven. Pilgrim gave the specious gourd a mighty heave and tossed it up into the air. Think of it: that gourd was changed from a piece of hair. How heavy could it be? Lifted up by the mountain wind, it drifted here and there for at least half an hour before dropping down. Meanwhile, Prince Naṭa at the South Heavenly Gate flung wide the black banner and in one instant covered the sun, the moon, and all the planets. Truly

The cosmos seemed dyed by ink,

The world was made indigo.

Astounded, the little fiends said, "It was just about noon when we were talking. How is it that it's dusk already?" "Heaven has been stored up," said Pilgrim. "You can't tell time! How can it not be dusk?" "Why is it so dark?" they cried. Pilgrim said, "The sun, the moon, and the stars are all contained inside. There's no light outside. How can it not be dark?" "Master," said one of the little fiends, "where are you speaking?" "Am I not in front of you?" said Pilgrim. The little fiend stretched out his hand to try to touch him, saying, "I can hear you, but I can't see your face. Master, where are we?" To deceive them further, Pilgrim said, "Don't move. This is the shore of the Gulf of Chihli. If you stumble and fall into the sea, you won't reach bottom even after seven or eight days." "Stop! Stop! Stop!" cried the horrified fiends. "Release Heaven, please! We know now how it is stored up. If we fool around anymore and drop into the sea, we'll not get home."

Dear Pilgrim! When he saw that they took the whole thing for the truth, he recited the spell again to alert the prince, who rolled up the banner and the sunlight of noon was seen once more. "Marvelous! Marvelous!" cried the little fiends, laughing. "Such fantastic treasure, if we don't exchange for it, we are certainly no better than bastards!" Sly Devil at once took out the gourd and Wily Worm the pure vase; both of them then handed the treasures to Pilgrim. In return, Pilgrim gave them the specious gourd. After the exchange, Pilgrim wanted to make certain that the bargain stuck. Pulling off a piece of hair from beneath his belly, he blew on it and it changed into a copper penny. "Young man," he said, "take this penny and buy us a piece of paper." "What for?" said the little fiend. "So that I can draw up a contract with you," said Pilgrim. "The two of you used your human-storing treasures to exchange with me a single piece of Heaven-storing treasure. I fear that you may not consider that quite fair and that after a few years you will come to regret our deal. That's why I want a contract for all of us." "We don't even have brush or ink around here," said one of the fiends. "Why bother about writing a document? Let's exchange vows instead." "What kind of vow?" said Pilgrim. The two little fiends said, "We gave two human-storing treasures to you in exchange for one Heaven-storing treasure. If we ever regret our decision, may we be stricken with plague in all four seasons." "I'll never regret mine," said Pilgrim with laughter. "If I do, may I also be stricken like you." After he made this vow, he leaped up and with one wag of his tail arrived before the South Heavenly Gate, where he thanked Prince Naṭa for unfurling the banner and lending him assistance. The prince then went back to the palace to report to the Jade Emperor and to return the flag to Chên-wu. Pilgrim, meanwhile, stood in the air and looked at those little fiends. We do not know what happens thereafter, and you must listen to the explanation in the next chapter.

## Thirty-four

The Demon King's crafty scheme entraps the Mind Monkey;
The Great Sage, ever versatile, wangles the treasures.

We were telling you about those two little fiends who took the specious gourd in their hands and, for some time, fought to examine it. Raising their heads, they suddenly discovered that Pilgrim had vanished. "Elder Brother," said Wily Worm, "even an immortal would lie. He said that after we had exchanged our treasures he would enlighten us to become immortals. Why did he leave without even telling us?" Sly Devil said, "When you tally up the score, we are the ones who have by far the greater gain. Why worry about his leaving? Give me the gourd. Let me store up Heaven, just for practice!" He indeed tossed the gourd up into the air, but it plopped down again immediately. "Why doesn't it work?" said a startled Wily Worm. "Could it be that Pilgrim Sun had changed into a false immortal and used a specious gourd to trade off our real one?" "Don't talk nonsense!" said Sly Devil. "Pilgrim Sun is pinned down by those three mountains. How could he come out? Give it to me again. Let me recite those few words of the spell he said and see if it will store up Heaven." Again the fiend tossed the gourd up into the air, crying, "If there is but half a 'No,' we shall ascend to the Divine Mists Hall and start a war." Before he had even finished saying that, the thing plopped down again. "It doesn't work! It doesn't work!" shrieked the little fiends. "It's got to be a fake!"

As they were clamoring like this, the Great Sage Sun saw and heard everything in midair. Fearing that they might learn the truth if they played with the thing too long, he shook his body and retrieved the piece of hair which had been changed into the gourd. The two fiends were left with four empty hands. "Brother," said Sly Devil, "give me the gourd." "You were holding it," said Wily Worm. "My God! How come it disappeared?" They searched madly on the ground and in the bushes; they stuck their hands into their sleeves and slapped their waists. But there was nothing to be found. Stupefied, the two fiends mumbled, "What shall we do? What shall we do? The Great King at the time gave us the treasures and told us to capture Pilgrim Sun. Not only have we not caught Pilgrim Sun, but we have even lost the treasures now. How dare we go back to give our report? We will simply be beaten to death. What shall we do? What shall we do?" After a while, Wily Worm said, "We'd better go." "Where?" said Sly Devil. "Never mind where," said Wily Worm. "If we go back and say that we have no treasures, we will lose our lives for sure." Sly Devil said, "Don't run away, let's go back instead. The Second Great King is ordinarily quite good to you; I'll put a little blame on you. If he is in the mood to be somewhat lenient, our lives may be spared; if not, we'll at least be beaten to death at home but we won't be left dangling here. Let's go. Let's go." After they had discussed the matter, the fiends began their walk back to their mountain.

When Pilgrim in midair saw them leaving, he shook his body again and changed into a fly to follow them. If he changed into a fly, you might ask, where did he put those treasures? If he left them by the road, or even if he hid them in the grass, people could pick them up if they saw them, and all his efforts would have been in vain. No, he had to take them with him, carrying the treasures on his body. But a fly is no bigger than the size of a pea. How could he carry them? The treasures, you see, were just like his golden-hooped rod; they were also called compliant Buddha-treasures. They would transform according to the size of the body: they could become large or small, and that was why even a tiny body like a fly could hold them. With a buzz, Pilgrim thus flew down and steadfastly followed the fiends till they reached the cave in no time.

The two head demons were sitting there and drinking wine when the little fiends faced them and knelt down. Pilgrim alighted on the door frame and listened. "Great Kings," said the little fiends. "Have you returned?" said the second demon, putting down his cup. "Yes," said the little fiends. "Have you caught Pilgrim Sun?" he asked again. The little fiends began to kowtow, not daring to make a sound. The old demon asked again, but they did not dare reply; all they did was to kowtow. Questioned again and again, they finally prostrated themselves on the ground and said, "Please pardon your little ones for the crime of ten thousand deaths! Please pardon your little ones for the crime of ten thousand deaths! When we took the treasures and reached the middle of the mountain, we ran into an immortal from

P'êng-lai Mountain. He inquired where we were going and we told him that we were going to catch Pilgrim Sun. When the immortal heard this, he said that he, too, was mad at Pilgrim Sun and wanted to give us assistance. We told him that there was no need for his assistance and explained how our treasures could store up humans. That immortal also had a gourd most capable of storing up Heaven. Moved by vain hopes and illicit desires, we thought we should exchange our treasures, which could only store up people, with his, which could store up Heaven. Originally, we wanted to exchange gourd for gourd, but Wily Worm decided to make good the deal by adding the pure vase. We had no idea that his immortal object could not be touched by the hands of the profane. Just as we were experimenting with it, it disappeared completely with the man also. We beseech you to pardon our mortal offense." When the old demon heard this, he was so aroused that he bellowed thunderously, "Undone! Undone! This has to be Pilgrim Sun who masqueraded himself as an immortal to dupe them. That ape has great magic powers and vast acquaintances. I don't know which clumsy deity has let him out, and he has wangled our treasures."

The second demon said, "Don't be so angry, Elder Brother. I didn't expect that ape head to be so insolent. If he has the ability, he can escape and that's all right. Why did he have to wangle our treasures? If I don't catch him, I'll never be a monster on this road to the West!" "How will you catch him?" said the old demon. The second demon said, "We have five treasures; two are gone but we still have three others. We must make certain that Pilgrim Sun will be caught by one of these." "Which three do we have now?" said the old demon. "I still have with me the sword of the seven stars and the palm-leaf fan," said the second demon, "but the yellow-gold rope is kept at the Crush-Dragon Cave of the Crush-Dragon Mountain, the place of our aged mother. We should now send two little fiends to invite mother to come to dine on the T'ang monk's flesh, and tell her at the same time to bring that yellow-gold rope to capture Pilgrim Sun." The old demon said, "Whom should we send?" "Not these useless creatures," said the second demon, and then he shouted to them, "Get up!" "Lucky! Lucky!" said the two of them. "We were neither beaten nor scolded. We are let go just like that!" The demon said, "Ask Hill-Pawing Tiger and Sea-Lolling Dragon who often accompany me to come here." The two little fiends arrived and knelt down. "You must be careful," instructed the second demon. "We shall be careful," they replied. "You two must be cautious." "Yes, we shall be cautious," they replied. "Do you know where the Old Madam's home is?" asked the second demon again. "Yes, we do," they replied. "If you do, get there quickly, and when you reach her house, inform her reverently that she is invited to come here to dine on the flesh of the T'ang monk. Tell her also to bring along the yellow-gold rope in order that we may catch Pilgrim Sun."

The two little fiends obeyed and raced out of the cave; they did not know that Pilgrim on one side had heard everything clearly. Stretching his wings, he flew out of the cave, caught up with Hill-Pawing Tiger, and landed on his body. After they had gone for two or three miles, he was about to slay them when he thought to himself, "To kill them is hardly difficult, but that Old Madam of theirs has the yellow-gold rope, and I don't know where she lives. Let me question them a bit first before I slaughter them." Dear Pilgrim! He darted away with a buzz and allowed the little fiends to walk ahead for about a hundred steps. Then with one shake of his body he also changed into a little monster wearing a fox-skin cap and a tiger-skin skirt hitched up to the waist. Running up to them, he said, "You on the road, wait for me." Turning around, Sea-Lolling Dragon said, "Where did you come from?" "Dear Brother," said Pilgrim, "you can't even recognize someone from the same clan?" "You are not in our clan," said the little fiend. "What do you mean?" said Pilgrim. "Take another look." "You don't look familiar at all," said the little fiend. "We haven't met before." "Indeed," said Pilgrim, "you have never seen me. I belong to the external division." The little fiend said, "I haven't met any officer from the external division at all. Where are you going?" Pilgrim said, "The Great King told you two to invite Old Madam to dine on the flesh of the T'ang monk as well as to bring along the yellow-gold rope to capture Pilgrim Sun. But he fears that the two of you would not walk fast enough, and your love of play would delay this important enterprise. That's why he sent me along also to tell you to hurry." When the little fiends saw that his words went straight to the bottom of the truth, they did not suspect anything, thinking instead that Pilgrim indeed was a member of the same clan. Hurriedly, they sprinted forward for eight or nine miles. "We have run too fast," said Pilgrim. "How far have we gone since we left home?" "About sixteen miles," said the little fiend. Pilgrim said, "How far more do we have to go?" Pointing with his finger, Sea-Lolling Dragon said, "Inside the dark forest up ahead—that's it." Pilgrim raised his head and saw a large dark forest not far away, and he figured that the old fiend had to be within that vicinity. He stood still, allowing the other two little fiends to proceed; then he caught up with them and gave them a swiping blow with the iron rod. Alas, they were no match for the rod at all and were reduced instantly to two meat patties! Pilgrim picked them up and hid them inside some bushes by the road. Pulling off a piece of hair, he blew on it a magic breath, crying "Change!" It changed at once into Hill-Pawing Tiger, while he himself changed into Sea-Lolling Dragon. The two specious monsters then proceeded directly to the Dragon-Crushing Cave to invite the old madam. This is what we call

Seventy-two ways of changing, what vast magic power!

Versatile with things—that's great ability!

With four, five leaps, he bounded right into the forest. As he was looking around, he saw two stone doors half-closed nearby. Not daring to enter abruptly, he had to call out: "Open the door, open the door." A female monster standing guard inside opened wide the door and asked: "Where did you come from?" Pilgrim said, "I came from the Lotus-Flower Cave of the Level-Top Mountain with an invitation for Old Madam." "Inside," said the female monster. When Pilgrim reached the second door, he stuck his head inside to take a look and found an old woman sitting squarely in the middle. "How did she look?" you ask. You see

Snow-white hair all tousled,

And starlike eyes all aglow.

Her face, though ruddy, has many wrinkles;

She's full of spirit though few teeth remain.

Charming—like the frosted chrysanthemum;

Rugged—like the old pine after the rain.

A scarf of fine-spun white silk wraps her head,

And bejeweled gold rings hang from her ears.

After he had seen her, the Great Sage Sun did not go inside at once. Instead, he remained crestfallen outside the second door and began to weep silently. "Why did he weep?" you ask. Could it be that he was afraid of her? Even if he were, he would hardly weep. Moreover, he was courageous enough to have bilked the monsters of their treasures and slain the little fiends. Why then did he weep? In times past, he could have entered a giant tripod of boiling oil, and even if he had been fried for seven or eight days, he would not have shed half a tear. It was, however, the thought of the misery inflicted on him on account of the T'ang monk's going to acquire scriptures that moved him to tears. He thought to himself, "If old Monkey had displayed his ability and changed into a little fiend to invite this aged monster, there would be absolutely no reason for him to speak standing up. I must kowtow when I see her! A hero all my life, I have only kowtowed to three persons: I bowed to Buddha of the Western Heaven, Kuan-yin of the South Sea, and four times to Master when he saved me at the Mountain of Two Frontiers. For him I have used up even my innards and my bowels! Ah, how much could a roll of scripture be worth? Yet, I'm forced to prostrate myself before this fiend today. If I don't, I'll be discovered for sure. O misery! In the last analysis, Master is in sad straits and that's why I have to bear such humiliation." When he came to that point in his thoughts, he had no choice but to race inside and kneel down, facing her. "Madam," he said, "please receive my kowtow."

The fiend said, "My child, stand up." "Fine! Fine! Fine!" said Pilgrim to himself. "That's an honest address!" "Where did you come from?" asked the old fiend. "From the Lotus-Flower Cave of the Level-Top Mountain," said Pilgrim. "I received the order of the two Great Kings to invite Madam to go and dine on the flesh of the T'ang monk. You have also been requested to bring along the yellow-gold rope to catch Pilgrim Sun." Exceedingly pleased, the old fiend said, "What filial sons!" She at once called for her sedan-chair. "O my child!" said Pilgrim to himself. "Even monsters ride in sedan-chairs!" From behind two female monsters carried out a sedan-chair made of fragrant rattan, on which they hung curtains of blue silk. The old fiend walked out of the cave and sat in the chair, followed by several little female monsters carrying toilet boxes, mounted mirrors, towels, and a perfume box. "Why did you all have to come out?" said the old fiend. "I'm going to my own home, and you think that there will be no one there to serve me? We don't need your big mouths there. Go back! Shut the doors and look after the house!" Those few little monsters indeed went back, and only two remained to pole the sedan-chair. "What are the names of those two who have been sent here?" asked the old fiend. "He's called Hill-Pawing Tiger," said Pilgrim quickly, "and my name is Sea-Lolling Dragon." The old fiend said, "Walk in front, the two of you. Shout and clear the way for me." "This had to be my misfortune!" thought Pilgrim. "We have not yet acquired the scriptures, but I have to be her slave at this moment!" He did not dare refuse; walking ahead, he shouted to clear the way.

After they had gone for five or six miles, he sat down on a slab of stone to wait for the two carrying the sedan-chair. When they arrived, Pilgrim said, "How about resting a while? Your shoulders must be getting sore." The little fiends did not suspect anything, of course, and they put down the sedan-chair. Walking behind it, Pilgrim pulled off a piece of hair from his chest and changed it into a huge biscuit, which he held and began to munch on. "Officer," said one of the chair carriers, "what are you eating?" "I'm embarrassed to tell you," said Pilgrim, "but we have walked all this distance to invite Old Madam, and she didn't give us any reward. I'm getting hungry, and that's why I'm eating some of our own dried goods before we move again." "Please give us some too," said the carriers. Pilgrim said, "Come on. We all belong to the same family. Why do you ask?" Not knowing any better, the little fiends both surrounded Pilgrim to divide the dried food. Whipping out his iron rod, Pilgrim gave their heads a terrific blow: the one hit directly was reduced at once to pulp, while the other who was swiped by the rod did not die immediately and was still moaning. When the old fiend heard someone moan and stuck her head out to look, Pilgrim leaped before the sedan-chair and slammed the rod down on her head. Brains burst out and blood spurted in every direction from the gaping hole. Pilgrim dragged her from the sedan-chair and discovered that she was a nine-tailed fox.[1] "Cursed beast!" said Pilgrim, laughing. "Who are you that you should be called Old Madam? If you are addressed as Old Madam, you should call old Monkey as your great, grand ancestor!" Dear Monkey King! He searched and found the yellow-gold rope, which he stuffed into his own sleeve, saying happily, "Those lawless demons may be powerful, but three treasures now belong to him whose name is Sun." He yanked off two pieces of hair which he changed into Hill-Pawing Tiger and Sea-Lolling Dragon, and two more which he changed into the fiends who carried the sedan-chair. He himself changed into the form of the old woman and sat in the sedan-chair. They then started out on the main road once more.

In a little while, they reached the entrance of the Lotus-Flower Cave. Those little fiends which were changed from the hairs cried out in front, "Open the door! Open the door!" The little fiends inside who

were guarding the door opened it and said, "Hill-Pawing Tiger and
Sea-Lolling Dragon, have you two returned?" "Yes," said the pieces
of hair. "Where is Old Madam whom you were to invite?" "Isn't she
there inside the sedan-chair," said the pieces of hair, pointing. "Stay
here," said one of the little fiends. "Let me go and report." When the
two head demons heard the announcement, "Great King, Old Madam
has arrived," they gave the order at once that an incense table be
prepared to receive her. When Pilgrim heard this, he was delighted,
saying to himself, "What luck! Now it's my turn to be somebody!
When I first changed into a little fiend to go invite that old monster, I
kowtowed to her once. But now that I have changed into the old
monster, who is supposed to be their mother, they must perform the
ceremony of four bows. It may not be much, but I'm reaping the
profit of two heads kowtowing to me!" Dear Great Sage! He descended
from the sedan-chair and, shaking off the dirt from his clothes,
retrieved the four pieces of hair onto his body. The little fiends who
stood guard at the door carried the empty sedan-chair inside, and he
followed them slowly from behind, mincing all the while to imitate
the gait of the old fiend. When they went inside, the entire flock of
monsters, old and young, all came to receive him, as drums and flutes
were played harmoniously and curls of fragrant smoke rose from the
Po-shan urn.[2] He arrived at the main hall and sat down, facing south;
the two head demons knelt before him and kowtowed, saying,
"Mother, your children are bowing." "My sons," said Pilgrim, "please
rise."

We tell you now about Chu Pa-chieh, who, hanging there on the
beam, suddenly let out a guffaw. "Second Brother," said Sha Monk,
"this is quite marvelous! They hang you till you laugh out loud!"
"Brother," said Pa-chieh, "I have a reason for laughing." Sha Monk
said, "What reason?" "We were afraid," said Pa-chieh, "that when
Madam arrived, we would be steamed and eaten. Now I see that it's
not Madam; it's the dear old thing." "What dear old thing?" said Sha
Monk. "Pi-ma-wên is here," said Pa-chieh, chuckling. Sha Monk said,
"How could you recognize him?" "When he bent his back to return
their greetings, saying, 'My sons, please rise,'" said Pa-chieh, "that
monkey tail of his flipped up from behind. I'm hung higher than you,
and that's why I can see more clearly." Sha Monk said, "Let's not
talk, let's hear what he has to say." "You are right, you are right,"
said Pa-chieh.

Sitting in the middle, the Great Sage Sun asked, "My sons, why did you invite me here?" "Dear Mother," said one of the demons, "for days your children have not had the opportunity to fulfill our filial responsibilities. This morning we managed to catch the T'ang monk from the Land of the East, but we dared not eat him all by ourselves. We therefore invited Mother to come so that he might be presented live to you, and then he will be steamed as your food to prolong your life." "My sons," said Pilgrim, "I'm not at all keen to dine on the T'ang monk's flesh, but I hear that the ears of one Chu Pa-chieh are quite marvelous. Why don't you cut them down and fix them up as appetizers for my wine?" Startled by what he heard, Pa-chieh said, "Plague on you! Did you come here to cut down my ears? If I announce aloud who you are, it won't sound very good!"

Alas! This one careless statement of Idiot at once unmasked the transformation of the Monkey King. Just then, a few little fiends who went to patrol the mountain and a few others who stood guard at the door all rushed in also, saying, "Great King, disaster! Pilgrim Sun has beaten to death Old Madam, and he disguised himself to come here." When the head demon heard these words, he did not wait for any further report; pulling out his sword of seven stars, he slashed at the face of Pilgrim. Dear Great Sage! He shook his body once, and brilliant red light filled the cave as he made his escape. Such abilities made the whole episode fun and games for him. For truly he had mastered this secret: coming together he took on form, but dispersing he became ether. So shaken were the inhabitants of the cave that the old demon's spirit left him, and the various monsters bit their fingers and shook their heads. "Brother," said the old demon, "take the T'ang monk, Sha Monk, Pa-chieh, the white horse, and the luggage—take them all and return them to Pilgrim Sun. Let's shut the door on conflict." "What are you saying, Elder Brother," said the second demon. "You have no idea how much effort I spent in devising this plan to bring back all those monks. And now intimidated by Pilgrim Sun's trickery you want to return them to him unconditionally. You have become, in fact, a person who fears the knife and shuns the sword. Is that manliness? You sit down and don't be afraid. I heard you say that Pilgrim Sun had vast magic powers; though I met him, I have yet to wage a contest with him. Bring me my armor. Let me fight three rounds with him: if he can't defeat me in those three rounds, the T'ang monk is still our food. If I cannot prevail against him in those three rounds, there is still time then for us to return the T'ang monk to him." The old demon said, "You are right, Worthy Brother." He immediately ordered the armor be brought out.

After the various fiends hauled out his armor, the second demon suited up himself properly and walked out the door, holding the treasure sword. "Pilgrim Sun," he cried, "where have you gone to?" At the time, you see, the Great Sage had already reached the edge of the clouds. When he heard his name called, he turned quickly and saw that it was the second demon. "How is he dressed?" you ask.

He wears a phoenix helmet whiter than snow
And an armor made of bright Persian steel.
The belt on his waist is dragon's tendon.
Plum-flower shaped gaiters top his goat-skin boots.
He seems the living Master of Kuan-k'ou;[3]
He looks no different from Mighty Spirit.[4]
He holds in his hands the sword of seven stars—
Stern and imposing in a towering rage.

"Pilgrim Sun," cried the second demon, "give us back quickly our mother and our treasures. I'll let you and the T'ang monk go to acquire scriptures." Unable to contain himself any longer, the Great Sage roared, "This impudent monster! You've made a mistake in thinking that your Grandpa Sun will let you go so easily! Return at once my master, my younger brothers, the white horse, and our luggage, and give us, moreover, some travel money for us to take on our road to the West. If half a 'No' leaks through your teeth, you might as well hang yourself with rope. That'll save your Grandpa from having to raise his hands." When the second demon heard these words, he leaped up to the clouds swiftly and stabbed with the sword. Pilgrim met him face to face with the uplifted iron rod, and it was some battle between the two of them in midair.

The chess master finding his match,
The general meeting a good warrior—
Finding his match the chess master can't suppress his joy;
Meeting a good warrior the general must apply himself.
When those two divine fighters come together,
They seem like tigers brawling on South Mountain
Or dragons striving in North Sea.
As dragons strive,
Their scales sparkle;
When tigers brawl,

Teeth and claws strike madly.
Teeth and claws strike madly like silver hooks,
And sparkling scales upturn like iron leaves.
This one all in all
Uses a thousand ways to attack;
That one back and forth
Does not let up for half a moment.
The golden-hooped rod
Is only three-tenths of an inch from the head.
The seven-stars sword,
Poised at the heart, needs only one thrust.
The imposing air of this one chills the Great Dipper;
The angry breaths of that one menace like thunder.

The two of them fought for thirty rounds but no decision was reached.

Secretly delighted, Pilgrim said to himself, "This lawless monster does manage to withstand the iron rod of old Monkey. But I have already acquired three of his treasures. If I continue to fight bitterly like this with him, won't it just delay what I want to do? Perhaps I should use the gourd or the pure vase to store him up." He then thought further: "No good! No good! The proverb says, 'Each thing has its master.' If I call him and he doesn't answer, it will just defeat my purpose. Let me use the yellow-gold rope to lasso his head." Dear Great Sage! He used one hand to wield his iron rod while his other hand whipped out the rope and lassoed the demon's head. The demon, however, knew a Tight-Rope Spell and a Loose-Rope Spell. If the rope had bound another person, he would recite the Tight-Rope Spell and that person would not be able to escape. But if the rope had been fastened on one of his own, he would recite the Loose-Rope Spell and no harm would come to the person. When he saw, then, that it was his own treasure, he recited at once the Loose-Rope Spell; the rope loosened itself and he came out of the noose. Taking the rope, he threw it at Pilgrim instead and it caught hold of the Great Sage instantly. The Great Sage was about to exercise his magic of thinning the body when the demon recited the Tight-Rope Spell and it had him firmly bound. It was impossible for him to escape, for when the rope was drawn down to his neck, one end of it changed into a gold ring tightly enclosing him. The fiend then gave the rope a tug and pulled Pilgrim down before he gave that bald head seven or eight blows with the sword. The skin on Pilgrim's head did not even redden at all.

"This monkey," said the demon, "has quite a hard head! I won't hack at you anymore. Let me take you back to the cave first before I hit you again. But you'd better return my other two treasures right now." "What treasures have I taken from you?" said Pilgrim, "that you should ask me for them?" The demon searched Pilgrim carefully and found both the gourd and the vase. Using the rope as a leash, he brought Pilgrim back to the cave, saying, "Elder Brother, I've caught him." The old demon said, "Whom did you catch?" "Pilgrim Sun!" said the second demon. "Come and look! Come and look!" The old demon took one look and recognized that it was indeed Pilgrim. He smiled happily and said, "It's he! It's he! Tie him up with a long rope to the pillar just for fun." They indeed had Pilgrim tied to a pillar, after which the two demons went to the hall in the back to drink.

As the Great Sage was crawling around beneath the pillar, he was seen by Pa-chieh. Hanging on the beam, Idiot laughed loudly, saying, "Elder Brother, you can't quite manage to eat my ears!" "Idiot," said Pilgrim, "are you comfortably hung up there? I'll get out right now, and you can be certain that I'll rescue all of you." "Aren't you ashamed of yourself?" said Pa-chieh. "You can't even escape yourself, and you want to rescue others. O, let it be, let it be! Master and disciples might as well die together so that we could ask for our way in the Region of Darkness." Pilgrim said, "Stop babbling nonsense! You watch me leave here." "I'll see how you leave here," said Pa-chieh. Though the Great Sage was talking to Pa-chieh, his eyes were fixed on those two demons. He saw that they were drinking inside, and there were a few little fiends running madly back and forth to bring in the dishes and to pour wine. When their guard lapsed momentarily and no one stood near the Great Sage, he at once exercised his divine powers. Slipping out his rod, he blew on it, saying, "Change!" and it changed instantly into a file of pure steel. Gripping the gold ring on his neck, he filed it through with four or five strokes and freed himself by pulling the ring apart. Yanking off a piece of hair, he commanded it to change into a specious form of himself tied to the pillar; his true self, however, changed with one shake of the body into a little monster and stood to one side. "Bad news! Bad news!" cried Pa-chieh once more on the beam. "The one tied up is a false product. The one hanging is genuine." Putting down his cup, the old demon asked, "What's that Chu Pa-chieh yelling about?" Pilgrim, who had changed into a little monster, went forward to say, "Chu Pa-chieh is trying to persuade Pilgrim Sun to escape by transformation, but Sun isn't willing. That's why Chu is hollering." "And we say that Chu Pa-chieh is without guile!" said the second demon. "Now I see what a sneak he is! He should have his mouth caned twenty times."

Pilgrim indeed went to get a cane for the beating. "You better hit me lightly," said Pa-chieh. "If the strokes are even slightly heavy, I'll yell again that I recognize you." Pilgrim said, "It's for the sake of all of you that old Monkey has undergone the transformation. Why did you have to let the truth leak out? All the monster-spirits of this cave can't recognize me. Why does it have to be you who can recognize me?" "Though you have changed your features," said Pa-chieh, "your ass hasn't been changed! Aren't those two patches of red still on your buttocks? That's why I can recognize you." Pilgrim slipped out to the kitchen and wiped some soot off the pots to blacken his buttocks before returning to the front. When Pa-chieh saw him, he said, chuckling, "This monkey must have gone somewhere to mess around so that he has now come back with a black ass!"

Pilgrim still remained standing there for he wanted to steal their treasures. Indeed a clever person, he walked up the hall and half-knelt to the fiend saying, "Great King, look how that Pilgrim Sun is crawling all over the pillar. The yellow-gold rope, I fear, may be ruined by all that rubbing and stretching. We should get something thicker to tie him up." "You are right," said the old demon, and he took off a belt with a lion buckle from his own waist to hand to Pilgrim. Taking the belt, Pilgrim fastened his false form to the pillar, but the rope he stuffed instantly into his own sleeve. Then he pulled off another piece of hair, which with one blow of his breath he changed into a fake yellow-gold rope, and which he presented with both hands to the fiend. Eager only for his wine, the fiend did not bother to examine it before putting it away. This is what we mean by

The Great Sage, ever versatile, displays his skills:
The hair is now exchanged for the golden rope.

As soon as he had acquired this treasure, he leaped out the door and changed back into his true form. "Monster!" he shouted. A little fiend guarding the door asked, "Who are you, that you dare shout here?" "Go in quickly," said Pilgrim, "and report to those lawless demons that a Grimpil Sun is here." The little fiend indeed made the report as he was told. Highly startled, the old demon said, "We have caught Pilgrim Sun already! How is it that there is a Grimpil Sun?" "Elder

Brother," said the second demon, "Why fear him? The treasures are all in our hands. Let me take the gourd out and have him stored up." "Brother," said the old demon, "do be careful." The second demon took out the gourd and walked out the door, where he encountered someone who seemed to be an exact image of Pilgrim Sun but only a little shorter. "Where did you come from?" he asked. Pilgrim said, "I'm the brother of Pilgrim Sun. When I heard that you caught my elder brother, I came to settle the score with you." "Yes, I caught him all right," said the second demon, "and he's locked up in the cave. Now that you have arrived, you want to fight with me, I suppose, but I won't cross swords with you. Let me call your name once. Do you dare answer me?" "Even if you call me a thousand times, I won't be afraid," said Pilgrim. "I'll answer you ten thousand times!" Leaping into the air with his treasure held upside down, the demon called out: "Grimpil Sun!" Pilgrim dared not reply, thinking to himself, "If I answer him, I'll be sucked inside." "Why don't you answer me?" said the demon. "My ears are a little stuffed up," said Pilgrim, "and I can't hear you. Call louder." The fiend indeed shouted, "Grimpil Sun!" Squeezing his fingers together to do some calculations down below, Pilgrim thought to himself, "My real name is Pilgrim Sun, but this Grimpil Sun is a fake name that I've made up. With the real name I can be sucked inside, but how could it work with a false name?" He could not refrain from answering, and instantly he was sucked into the gourd, which was then sealed by the tape. That treasure, you see, had no regard for whether the name called out was true or false: if one even breathed an answer, one would be sucked inside instantly.

When the Great Sage arrived inside the gourd, he found only total darkness. He tried to push up with his head but to no avail at all, for whatever was stopping the mouth of the gourd was exceedingly tight. Growing anxious, he thought to himself, "Those two little fiends I met on the mountain at the time told me that if a man was sucked into either the gourd or the vase, he would be reduced to pus in one and three-quarter hours. Could I be dissolved like that?" He thought further to himself: "It's nothing. I can't be dissolved! When old Monkey caused great disturbance in the Celestial Palace five hundred years ago and was refined for forty-nine days in the eight-trigram brazier of Lao Tzu, the process in fact gave me a heart strong as gold and viscera hardy as silver, a bronze head and an iron back, fiery eyes and diamond pupils. How could I be reduced to pus in one and three-quarter hours? Let me follow him inside and see what he does."

The second demon went inside with the gourd, saying, "Elder Brother, I've caught him." "Caught whom?" said the old demon. The second demon said, "Grimpil Sun has been stored up in the gourd by me." Delighted, the old demon said, "Worthy Brother, please take a seat. Don't move the gourd. We'll shake it after a while and we'll lift the seal only if it swashes." Hearing this, Pilgrim thought to himself: "If my body remains like this, how could it swash? I have to be reduced to liquid before the gourd can swash when shaken. Let me leave some urine here; when he shakes it and it swashes, he will certainly lift up the seal and I can then beat it!" But he thought again: "No good! No good! The urine can make the noise, but my shirt will be soiled. I'll wait until he shakes the gourd, and then I'll spit out a lot of saliva. All that drippy mess will deceive him into lifting the seal, and old Monkey can then escape." The Great Sage made this preparation, but the fiend was busy drinking and did not try to shake the gourd at all. Devising another plan to deceive them, the Great Sage suddenly cried out, "Heavens! My shanks have dissolved!" The demons did not shake the gourd, and the Great Sage cried out again, "O Mother! Even my pelvic bones are gone!" "When his waist is gone," said the old demon, "he's almost finished. Lift up the seal and take a look."

When the Great Sage heard this, he pulled off a piece of hair, crying "Change!" It changed into half a body stuck at the bottom of the gourd, while his true self was changed into a tiny insect attached to its mouth. As soon as the second demon lifted up the seal, the Great Sage flew out at once and with a roll changed instantly again into the form of Sea-Lolling Dragon, that little fiend who was sent formerly to fetch the Old Madam. He stood to one side, while the old demon took hold of the gourd and peered inside. Half a body was squirming down below, and he did not wait to determine whether it was genuine or not before he shouted, "Brother, cover it up, cover it up! He hasn't been completely dissolved yet." The second demon again taped on the seal, not realizing that the Great Sage on one side was snickering to himself, saying, "You don't know that old Monkey is right over here!"

Taking the wine pot, the old demon poured a full cup of wine and presented it with both hands to the second demon, saying, "Worthy

Brother, let me toast you with this cup." The second demon said, "Elder Brother, we have drunk wine for quite a while already. Why do you have to toast me with the cup now?" "It's no big thing, perhaps, that you caught the T'ang monk, Pa-chieh, and Sha Monk," said the old demon, "but you even managed to tie up Pilgrim Sun and store up Grimpil Sun. For making such great merit, you should be toasted with many cups more." When the second demon saw how his elder brother sought to honor him, he dared not refuse, but he dared not accept the cup with one hand either, for he was holding the gourd with the other. Quickly passing the gourd to Sea-Lolling Dragon, he then received the cup with both hands. Little did he realize, of course, that Sea-Lolling Dragon was in fact the transformed Pilgrim Sun. Look at him! He waited on the demons with great attentiveness. After the second demon took the wine and drank it, he wanted to return the toast. "No need to toast me," said the old demon. "Here, I'll drink a cup with you." The two of them kept exchanging niceties like that for some time, while Pilgrim holding the gourd fixed his eyes on them. When he saw them passing the wine cup back and forth without the slightest regard for what he was doing, he slipped the gourd into his sleeve and used another piece of hair to form a specious gourd exactly the same as the genuine one. The demon, after presenting wine for a while, took the gourd out of Pilgrim's hands without bothering to examine it. They sat down at their tables again and continued to drink as before. Having acquired the treasure again, the Great Sage turned and left, highly delighted and saying to himself,

Though this demon has his wizardry,

The gourd's still owned by the Sun family!

We do not know what he had to do thereafter to exterminate the fiends and rescue his master, and you must listen to the explanation in the next chapter.

## Thirty-five

Heresy uses power to oppress the righteous Nature;
The Mind Monkey, bagging treasures, conquers evil demons.

His nature's perfect, he himself knows the Way.
Turning round, he leaps clear of the net and snare.
To learn transformation's no easy thing,
Nor is it common to gain longevity.
He changes with fortune to things impure or pure;
He breaks up at will the kalpas set by fate.
For countless aeons he is wholly free—
A ray divine fixed forever on the void.

The meaning of this poem, you see, subtly corresponds to the wonders of the Tao attained by the Great Sage Sun. Since he had acquired the true treasure from that demon, he concealed it in his sleeve, saying happily to himself: "Though that lawless demon tries so hard to capture me, his efforts are no better than the attempt to fish the moon out of water. But when old Monkey wants to catch him, it's as simple as melting ice over fire!" Hiding the gourd, he slipped out the door and changed back into his original form. "Monster spirits," he shouted, "open the door!" A little fiend said, "Who are you that you dare make noises here?" Pilgrim answered, "Report at once to those old lawless demons that a Sun Pilgrim has arrived."

The little fiend dashed inside to make the report, saying, "Great King, there is a so-called Sun Pilgrim showing up outside our door." "Worthy Brother," said the old demon, deeply shaken, "that's bad! We have stirred up a whole nest of pestilence! Look! The yellow-gold rope has caught a Pilgrim Sun, while the gourd has stored up a Grimpil Sun. How can it be that there is another Sun Pilgrim? It must be that they have several brothers and they have all arrived." "Relax, Elder Brother," said the second demon. "This gourd of ours can hold up to a thousand people, and we have only one Grimpil Sun inside. Why worry about another Sun Pilgrim? Let me go out and take a look. I'll store him up also." "Do be careful, Brother," said the old demon.

Look at that second demon! Holding the specious gourd, he walked out the door as resolutely and confidently as before. "Who are you," he cried, "that you dare make noises around here?" Pilgrim said, "So, you don't recognize me!

I lived at Flower-Fruit Mount.
My home: the Water-Curtain Cave.
For disturbing Heaven's Palace
I ceased to strive a long time.
Lucky to be freed of my woes,
I left Tao and followed a monk
To reach Thunderclap with faith,
To seek scriptures and right knowledge.[1]
When I meet wild, lawless demons,
I work with my mighty magic.
Return my monk of Great T'ang
That we may go West to see Buddha,
Our conflict will then be ended,
And each one can enjoy his peace.
Don't stir up old Monkey's ire,
Or your stale life will expire!"

"You come over here for a moment" said the demon, "but I'm not going to fight with you. I'm about to call your name once. You dare answer me?" "If you call me," said Pilgrim, chuckling, "I'll answer you. But if I call you, will you answer me?" "I call you," said that fiend, "only because I have a treasure gourd which can store up people. What do you have that makes you want to call me?" Pilgrim said, "I, too, have a little gourd." "If you do," said the fiend, "take it out for me to have a look." Pilgrim took the gourd out of his sleeve, saying, "Lawless demon, you look!" He waved it once and stuffed it immediately back into his sleeve, for he was afraid that the demon might want to snatch it away.

When the demon caught sight of the gourd, he was greatly shaken, saying, "Where did that gourd of his come from? How is it that it is exactly like mine? Even if it grew from the same branch, there ought to be some difference in size or shape. How could they be exactly alike?" With complete seriousness, he said, "Sun Pilgrim, where did your gourd come from?" Pilgrim, of course, did not know the history of the gourd, but he turned the question around and asked instead, "Where did yours come from?" Not realizing that it was a trick, the demon thought that it was an honest query and he proceeded to give a complete account of its origin, saying, "This gourd of mine came into existence during the time when chaos divided and Heaven and Earth were created. There was then a Supreme Primordial Old Patriarch,[2] who through death changed himself into Nü Kua[3] and took on her name. She melted stones in order to repair the heavens and save the mundane world. When she reached a crack in the northwest region at the base of the K'un-lun Mountain, she discovered a strand of immortal creeper on which was formed this red gourd of purple gold. It is, therefore, something handed down by Lao Tzu until now." When the Great Sage heard this story, he at once used it as a model for his own account, saying, "My gourd also came from the same spot." "How so?" said the demon. "Since the division of the pure and the turbid," said the Great Sage, "Heaven was incomplete at the northwest corner, and Earth was incomplete in the southeast corner. The Supreme Primordial Taoist Patriarch through death changed himself into Nü Kua. After she had repaired the heavens, she journeyed to the base of the K'un-lun Mountain, where there was a strand of immortal creeper on which two gourds had formed. The one I have is a male, while yours is a female." The fiend said, "No need to distinguish the sexes; if it can store up people, it's a good treasure." "You are right," said the Great Sage, "I'll let you try first."

Highly pleased, the fiend leaped into the air, held up the gourd, and cried, "Sun Pilgrim!" When he heard the call, the Great Sage replied in one breath eight or nine times without stopping, but nothing happened to him at all. Dropping down from the air, the demon beat his breast and stamped his feet, crying, "Heavens! And we say that life has changed in the world! Even a treasure like this is afraid of her mate: when the female meets the male, it ceases to be effective!" "Why don't you put yours away," said Pilgrim, laughing, "for it's old Monkey's turn to call you." Swiftly somersaulting into the air, he turned the gourd upside down and took aim at the demon, crying, "Great King Silver Horn!" Not daring to close his mouth, the fiend made his reply, and instantly he was sucked into the gourd, which was then sealed by Pilgrim with the tape bearing the words, "May Lao Tzu Act Quickly According to This Command." Secretly pleased, Pilgrim said, "My child, you are going to try something new today!"

He descended from the cloud, holding the gourd, and headed straight for the Lotus-Flower Cave, every thought of his set on rescuing his master. The road on that mountain, you see, was pockmarked with holes, and he, moreover, was somewhat bowlegged. As he scurried along, the gourd was shaken repeatedly, and soon there came from within a loud swashing sound continuously. "How is it that it swashes already?" you ask. The Great Sage, you see, had a body which had been thoroughly refined and he could not be dissolved speedily. On the other hand, the fiend might know some such paltry magic as mounting the clouds and riding the fog, but he had not been completely delivered from his mortal constitution. The moment he was sucked into the treasure, he was dissolved. Pilgrim, however, did not quite believe that that had been the case. "O my child," he said, laughing, "I don't know whether you are pissing or gargling! But this sort of business is most familiar to old Monkey. Not until after seven or eight days, when you have become thin liquid, will I lift the cover to look. Why hurry? What's the rush? When I think of how easily I got out, I wouldn't spy on you for a thousand years!" As he held the gourd and talked to himself like that, he soon arrived at the entrance of the cave. He gave the gourd a shake and it was swashing even more loudly. "This sounds like the rattle of a fortune-telling tube," he said. "Old Monkey should make an inquiry to see when Master can come out of this door." Look at him! He shook the thing in his hand constantly while reciting, "The *I Ching* of King Wên, Great Sage Confucius, Master Chou of *Lady Peach-Blossom*,[4] Master Kuei-ku Tzŭ[5]. . . ."

When the little fiends in the cave saw that, they cried, "Great King, disaster! Sun Pilgrim has stored up our Second Great King in the gourd and he's using that for fortune-telling now." When the old fiend heard these words, he was so horrified that his spirit left him and his soul fled, his bones weakened and his tendons turned numb. He fell on the ground and began to wail, crying, "O Worthy Brother! When you and I left the Region Above in secret and found our lives in this mortal world, our hope was to enjoy together riches and glory as permanent lords of this mountain cave. How could I know that, because of this monk, your life would be taken away and our fraternal bond be broken!" The various fiends of the entire cave all began to wail aloud.

When Chu Pa-chieh, hanging there on the beam, heard the wailing of the whole family, he could not refrain from calling out: "Monster, don't cry! Let old Hog tell you something. The Pilgrim Sun who arrived first, the Grimpil Sun who came next, and finally the Sun

Pilgrim who came last—all three of them are in fact a single person, my elder brother. He is very versatile, knowing seventy-two ways of transformation. It was he who stole your treasure and had your brother stored up. Since your brother is now dead, there is no need for you to mourn like that. You should clean up your pots and pans quickly and fix up some dried mushrooms, fresh button mushrooms, bean sprouts, bamboo shoots, soybean cakes, wheat glutens, wood ears, and vegetables. Invite us master and disciples for a meal, and we will be pleased to recite for you once the *Receive Life Sūtra*." Infuriated by what he heard, the old demon said, "I thought Chu Pa-chieh was a guileless person, but he's actually most sassy. He dares to make fun of me at this moment! Little ones, stop mourning. Untie Chu Pa-chieh and steam him until he's soft and tender. Let me have a full stomach first, and then I'll go catch Pilgrim Sun to avenge my brother." Turning to Pa-chieh, Sha Monk chided him, saying, "Isn't that nice? I told you not to talk so much! Now your talking means that you'll be steamed and eaten." Idiot himself became somewhat alarmed, but a little fiend then spoke up, saying, "Great King, it's not good to steam Chu Pa-chieh." "Amitābha Buddha!" said Pa-chieh. "Which elder brother is trying to pile up secret merits? I'm indeed no good if I'm steamed." Another fiend said, "After he's skinned, he'll then be good to steam." Horrified, Pa-chieh said, "I'm all right! I'm all right! Though my bones and skins are coarse, I'll be tender the moment the water boils."

As they were speaking, another little fiend came from the front door to report: "Sun Pilgrim is reviling us at our door!" "This fellow," said a startled old demon, "abuses us because he thinks there is nobody here." He then gave the order: "Little ones, hang up Chu Pa-chieh as before, and find out how many treasures there are still in the house." A little fiend, who was the housekeeper, said, "There are three treasures yet in the cave." "Which three?" asked the old demon. "The sword of seven stars," said the housekeeper, "the palm-leaf fan, and the pure-jade vase." "That vase is useless!" said the old demon. "It was supposed to store up anyone who answered when his name was called, but the formula was somehow passed on to that Pilgrim Sun and now our own brother has been put away. I won't use the vase; leave it here at home. Bring me quickly the sword and the fan." The housekeeper handed over the two treasures to the old demon, who stuck the fan into his collar behind his neck and held the sword in his hand. He then called up about three hundred monsters, young and old, and told all of them to arm themselves with spears, clubs, ropes, and knives. The old demon himself also put on helmet and cuirass, covered with a flaming red silk cape. As the monsters rushed out the door, they lined up in battle formation intent on catching the Great Sage Sun. Knowing by now that the second demon had been dissolved in the gourd, the Great Sage fastened the gourd to the belt around his waist while his hands held high the golden-hooped rod to prepare for combat. As red banners unfurled, the old fiend leaped out the door. How was he dressed?

His helmet's tassle shimmered on his head,
And from his belt fresh, radiant colors rose.
He wore a cuirass knit like dragon scales,
Topped with a long red cape like crackling flames.
His round eyes opened wide and lightning flashed;
Wiry whiskers flared up like turbid fumes.
His hand held lightly the seven-star sword,
His shoulder half-hidden by the palm-leaf fan.
He moved like clouds rushing past the ocean's peaks;
Like thunder his voice shook mountains and streams.
An awesome Heaven-defying warrior,
Leading many monsters, he stormed out of the cave.

After ordering the little fiends to take their battle stations, the old demon shouted, "You ape! You are utterly wretched! You murdered my brother and broke up our fraternal bond. You are truly despicable!" "Monster, you are the one who's asking for death!" replied Pilgrim, "Do you mean to tell me that one life of a monster spirit is worth more than those of four creatures like my master, my younger brothers, and the white horse? You think that I can bear the thought of their being hung up in the cave at this moment? That I would agree to that? Bring them out at once and return them to me. You can add also some travel expenses and send off old Monkey amiably. Then I might spare this cur-like life of yours!" The fiend, of course, would not permit any further exchanges; lifting his treasure sword, he slashed at the head of the Great Sage, who met him with uplifted iron rod. This was quite a battle outside the entrance of the cave. Aha!

The seven-star sword and the golden-hooped rod
Clashed, and sparks flared up like lightning bright;
The spreading cold air brought oppressive chill

As vast dark clouds concealed the peaks and cliffs.
This one because of his fraternal bond
Would not let up a bit.
That one on account of the scripture monk
Would not slow down one whit.
Each one hated with the same kind of hate;
Both parties cherished such hostility.
They fought till Heaven and Earth darkened, scaring gods and
    ghosts;
The sun dimmed, the smoke thickened, as dragons and tigers
    quaked.
This one ground his teeth like filing down jade nails;
That one grew so mad that flames leaped out his eyes!
Back and forth they showed their heroic might,
And kept on brandishing both sword and rod.

The old demon fought with the Great Sage for twenty rounds, but neither could gain the upper hand. Pointing with his sword, the old demon shouted: "Little fiends, come up together!" Those three hundred monster-spirits rushed up together and completely surrounded Pilgrim. Dear Great Sage! Not in the least afraid, he wielded his rod and lunged left and right, attacking with it in front and protecting himself in the rear. Those little fiends, however, all had some abilities; the longer they fought, the more ferocious they became— like cotton floss sticking to one's body, they tackled Pilgrim at the waist and tugged at his legs, refusing to be beaten back. Alarmed, the Great Sage resorted to the magic of the Body beyond the Body. He plucked off a handful of hairs from under his left arm, chewed them to pieces, and spat them out, crying, "Change!" Every piece of the hair changed into a Pilgrim. Look at all of them! The tall ones wielded rods, the short ones boxed with their fists, and the tiniest ones grabbed the monsters' shanks and began to gnaw on them. They fought till all the fiends were scattered in every direction, crying, "Great King, we're finished! We can't fight anymore! The mountain is full of Pilgrim Suns!" The magic of the Body beyond the Body thus sent the flock of monsters into a hasty retreat: only an old demon was left in the middle, surrounded on all sides, sorely pressed but with no way to run at all.

Terribly frightened, the demon switched the treasure sword to his left hand; with his right, he reached behind his neck and pulled out the palm-leaf fan. Facing the direction of due south (which is the direction of fire), he made a sweeping motion with the fan from the left and fanned at the ground once. Flames leaped up instantly from the ground. The treasure, you see, could produce fire just like that. An unrelenting person, the fiend fanned at the ground for seven or eight more times, and a fierce fire raged everywhere. Marvelous fire!

The fire was neither the fire of Heaven
Nor the fire of a brazier;
Neither the wild fire on the meadows
Nor the fire inside an oven.
It was a spark of spiritual light taken naturally from the Five
    Phases.
The fan also was no common thing in the mortal world,
Nor was it made by any human skill.
It was a true treasure formed since the time chaos parted.
When the fan was used to start this fire,
Bright and brilliant,
It was like the red bolts of lightning;
Clear and ablaze,
It seemed mists iridescent.
There was not even a strand of blue smoke,
Only a mountain full of scarlet flames.
It burned till the summit pines became fire trees,
And cedars changed into lanterns before the cliff.
The beasts of the caves, eager to live,
Dashed to the east and the west;
The birds of the woods, zealous for their feathers,
Flew high and retreated wide.
This divine, air-filling holocaust
Burned till rocks broke, rivers dried up, and all the ground turned
    red!

When the Great Sage saw how ferocious the fire was, he, too, became quite shaken, crying, "It's bad! I can stand it myself, but my hairs are no good. Once they fall into the fire, they will be burned up." Shaking his body once, he retrieved all his hairs except one piece, which he used to change into a specious form of himself, pretending to flee the fire. His true body, making the fire-resisting sign with his fingers, somersaulted into the air and leaped clear of the blaze. He then headed straight for the Lotus-Flower Cave with the intent of rescuing his

master. As he sped up to the entrance of the cave and lowered the
direction of his cloud, he saw a hundred-odd little fiends outside the
door, every one of them with head wounds or broken legs, with lesions
and bruises. They were the ones injured by his magic of the Body
beyond the Body, all standing there whimpering and in pain. When
the Great Sage saw them, he could not suppress the savagery in his
nature; lifting up the iron rod, he fought all the way inside. How
pitiful it was that he should bring at once to nothing

The fruits of bitter exercise to acquire human forms!
They all became again old pieces of hair and hide!
After the Great Sage had finished off all the little fiends, he raced into
the cave with the intent of untying his master. Just then he saw again
a fiery glow inside, and he became terribly flustered, crying, "Undone!
Undone! If this fire is starting again even at the back door, old Monkey
will find it hard to save Master." As he was thus in alarm, he looked
again more carefully. Ah! It was not the glow of fire, but actually a
beam of golden light. Composing himself, he walked inside to have
another look and found that the source of the glow was the pure
mutton-jade vase. Filled with delight, he said to himself, "What a
lovely treasure! This vase was glowing also when the little fiends took
it up the mountain. Then old Monkey got it, only to have it taken
away again by the monster. It's hidden here and today it's still glowing." Look at him! He stole the vase at once and turned quickly to
walk out of the cave, not even bothering to try to rescue his master.
As soon as he came out the door, he ran into the demon returning
from the south, holding the treasure sword and the fan. The Great
Sage did not have time to hide himself, and the demon lifted his sword
instantly to slash at his head. Mounting his cloud-somersault, the
Great Sage leaped up and vanished immediately.

When the fiend arrived at his own door, he saw corpses lying
everywhere, all the monster-spirits under his command. He was so
stricken that he lifted his face toward Heaven and sighed loudly before
bursting into tears, crying "O misery! O what bitterness!" For him
we have a testimonial poem, and the poem says:

Hateful are the sly ape and the froward horse!
The seeds divine who came to the world of dust,
For one erring thought of leaving Heaven,
Fell on this mountain and destroyed themselves.
What bitter grief when flocks of birds break up!

How tears flow when monster troops are wiped out!
When will the scourge end, the chastisement cease,
That they may return to their primal forms?

Overborne by grief, the old demon wailed step by step into the cave;
he saw that the furniture and other belongings remained, but not
even a single person was in sight. In this total silence, he became
sadder than ever: as he sat all by himself in the cave, he placed his
head on a stone table, his sword he leaned against the table, and the
fan he stuck back into his collar. Soon, he fell into a deep sleep, just
as the proverb says:

Your spirit is full when you are happy;
Once dejected you tend to be sleepy!

We tell you now about the Great Sage Sun, who turned the direction
of his cloud-somersault around and stood before the mountain, thinking again of trying to rescue his master. Fastening the vase tightly to
his belt, he returned to the entrance of the cave to see what was
happening. The two doors he found wide open, but not a sound could
be heard. With light, stealthy steps he slipped inside and discovered
the demon sleeping soundly, leaning on the stone table. The palm-
leaf fan was sticking out of his collar, half covering the back of his
head, while the sword of seven stars was placed against the table. He
tiptoed near the demon, pulled out the fan, and turned at once to flee
outside. The fan, however, scraped against the hair of the fiend when
it was pulled out, rousing him from his sleep. When he lifted his head
to look and found that his fan had been stolen by Pilgrim Sun, he gave
chase at once with the sword. The Great Sage leaped out the door
and, having stuck the fan into his waist, met the fiend with both hands
wielding the iron rod. This was a marvelous battle!

The maddened demon king,
His cap raised by angry hair,
Wanted to swallow with one gulp his foe—
But e'en that was no relief!
He reviled the monkey thus:
"You mock me far too much!
You took our many lives.
You steal my treasure now.
This time I'll not spare you,
I'll see that you are dead!"

The Great Sage rapped the demon:

"You don't know what's good for you!
A student wants to fight old Monkey?
How could an egg smash up a rock?"
The treasure sword came,
The iron rod moved:
The two would no longer cherish kindness.
Again and again a contest they waged;
Over and over they used their martial skill.
Because of the scripture monk
Who sought at Spirit Mount a place,
Fire and Metal clashed in disaccord;
The Five Phases, confused, lost their harmony.
They showed their awe-inspiring, magic power;
They kicked up dust and stones to flaunt their might.
They fought till the sun was about to sink:
The demon grew weak and retreated first.

The demon fought with the Great Sage for more than thirty rounds; when the sky darkened, the demon fled in defeat and headed for the southwest in the direction of the Crush-Dragon Cave. We shall speak no more of him for the moment.

Lowering the direction of his cloud, the Great Sage dashed into the Lotus-Flower Cave and untied the T'ang monk, Pa-chieh, and Sha Monk. After they were freed, they thanked Pilgrim while asking, "Where did the demons go?" "The second demon has been stored up in the gourd," said Pilgrim, "and he must be completely dissolved by now. The old demon was defeated by me just now and he fled toward the Crush-Dragon Cave in the southwest. Over half of the little fiends of the cave have been killed by the body-division magic of old Monkey, and the rest who were defeated have also been wiped out by me. Only after that could I come in here to rescue and free all of you." Profoundly grateful, the T'ang monk said, "Disciple, you must have worked awfully hard!" "Indeed," said Pilgrim, laughing, "though all of you had to bear the pain of being hung up, old Monkey hasn't been able even to rest his legs! I had to be on the go even more frequently than the postal messenger: coming in and getting out, there was never a moment's pause. Only after having managed to steal his treasures could I defeat the demons." "Elder Brother," said Chu Pa-chieh, "take out the gourd and let us have a look inside. The second demon, I suppose, must have been dissolved by now." The Great Sage first untied the pure vase; he then took out the gold rope and the fan before he held the gourd in his hands. Then he said, "Don't look! Don't look! Just now he had old Monkey stored up, and only after I deceived him into opening the lid by feigning some gargling noise did I escape. We must not, therefore, lift up the lid, for he may still pull some tricks and escape." Thereafter master and disciples happily searched the cave and found some of the monsters' rice, noodles, and vegetables; after heating and washing some of the pots and pans, they prepared a vegetarian meal and ate their fill. They rested in the cave for the night and soon it was morning again.

We tell you now about that old demon, who went straight to the Crush-Dragon Mountain and gathered together all the female fiends, to whom he gave a thorough account of how his mother was beaten to death, how his brother was sucked into the gourd, how his monster soldiers were wiped out, and how his treasures had been stolen. The female fiends all burst into tears, wailing for a long time. Then the old demon said, "Stop crying, all of you. I still have with me the sword of seven stars, and I plan to go with all of you, female soldiers, to the back of this Crush-Dragon Mountain to borrow some more troops from my maternal relative. I'm determined to capture that Pilgrim Sun to exact vengeance." Before he had even finished speaking, a little fiend came from the door to report, saying, "Great King, your Venerable Maternal Uncle from behind the mountain has led his troops here." When the old demon heard this, he quickly changed into mourning garments of plain white silk and bowed to receive his visitor. The Venerable Maternal Uncle, you see, was the younger brother of his mother who went by the name, Great King Fox Number Seven. Because he had already received the report from some of his monster soldiers out on patrol that his elder sister was beaten to death by Pilgrim Sun, who then changed into the form of his sister to swindle treasures from his nephew, and that there had been fighting for several days on the Level-Top Mountain, he called up some two hundred soldiers from his own cave to offer his assistance. He stopped first at his sister's home to find out whether indeed she had died. The moment he walked in the door, however, he saw the old demon in mourning garments, and the two of them burst into loud wailing. After some time, the old demon knelt down to give a complete account of what had taken place. Growing very angry, Number Seven ordered the old demon to take off his mourning garments, to pick up his treasure sword, and to call up all the female monsters. Together they mounted the wind and the cloud, speeding toward the northeast.

The Great Sage just then was telling Sha Monk to prepare breakfast so that they could journey after the meal, when suddenly he heard the sound of the wind. Walking out the door, he found a horde of fiendish troops approaching from the southwest. Somewhat startled, Pilgrim dashed inside, calling to Pa-chieh, "Brother, the monster-spirit has brought fresh troops to help him." When Tripitaka heard these words, he paled with fright, saying, "Disciple, what shall we do?" "Relax, relax!" said Pilgrim, chuckling. "Give me all of his treasures." The Great Sage fastened the gourd and the vase to his waist, stuffed the gold rope into his sleeve, and stuck the palm-leaf fan into his collar. Wielding the iron rod with both hands, he told Sha Monk to stand and guard their master sitting in the cave, while he and Pa-chieh holding the muckrake went out to meet their adversaries.

The fiendish creatures ranged themselves in battle formation, and the one at the very forefront was the Great King Number Seven, who had a jadelike face, a long beard, wiry eyebrows, and knifelike ears. He wore a golden helmet on his head and a knitted cuirass on his body; his hands held a "square-sky" halberd.[6] In a loud voice he shouted: "You audacious, lawless ape! How dare you oppress people like that! You stole our treasures, slaughtered our relatives, killed our soldiers, and you even had the nerve to take over our cave dwelling. Stick out your neck quickly and accept death, so that I can avenge my sister's murder!" "You reckless hairy lump!" cried Pilgrim. "You don't know what your Grandpa Sun can do! Don't run away! Take a blow from my rod!" The fiend stepped aside to dodge the blow before turning again to meet him with the halberd. The two of them fought back and forth on the mountain for three or four rounds, and the fiend grew weak already. As he fled, Pilgrim gave chase and encountered the old demon, who also fought with him for three rounds. Then the Number Seven Fox turned around and attacked once more. When Pa-chieh on this side saw him, he quickly stopped him with the nine-pronged rake; so, each of the pilgrims took on a monster and they fought for a long time without reaching a decision. The old demon shouted for all the monster soldiers to join the battle also.

We tell you now about the T'ang monk, who was seated in the cave when he heard earth-shaking cries coming from outside. "Sha Monk," he said, "go and see how your brothers are doing in the battle." Lifting high his fiend-routing staff, Sha Monk gave a terrific cry as he raced outside, beating back at once many of the monsters. When Number Seven saw that the tide was turning against them, he spun around and ran, only to be caught up by Pa-chieh who brought down the rake hard on his back.

This one blow caused nine spots of bright red to spurt out;
Pity one spirit's true nature going to the world beyond.
When Pa-chieh dragged him aside and stripped off his clothes, he found that the Great King, too, was a fox spirit.

When the old demon saw that his maternal uncle was slain, he abandoned Pilgrim and attacked Pa-chieh with the sword. Pa-chieh blocked the blow with the muckrake; as they fought, Sha Monk charged near and struck with his staff. Unable to withstand the two of them, the demon mounted wind and cloud to flee toward the south with Pa-chieh and Sha Monk hard on his heels. When the Great Sage saw that, he swiftly leaped into the air, untied the vase, and took aim at the old demon, crying, "Great King Golden Horn!" The fiend thought that it was one of his defeated little demons calling him, and he turned to give his reply. Instantly he was sucked also into the vase, which was then sealed by Pilgrim with the tape bearing the words, "May Lao Tzu Act Quickly According to This Command." The sword of seven stars dropped to the ground below and it, too, became the property of Pilgrim. "Elder Brother," said Pa-chieh, coming up to meet Pilgrim, "you've got the sword. But where's the monster-spirit?" "Finished!" said Pilgrim, chuckling, "He's stored up in this vase of mine." When they heard this, Sha Monk and Pa-chieh were utterly delighted.

After they had completely wiped out the ogres and monsters, they went back to the cave to present the good news to Tripitaka, saying, "The mountain has been purged of all monsters. Let Master mount up so that we may journey again." Highly pleased, Tripitaka finished the morning meal with his disciples, whereupon they put in order the luggage and the horse and found their way to the West. As they walked, a blind man suddenly appeared from the side of the road and caught hold of Tripitaka's horse, saying, "Monk, where are you going? Give me back my treasures!" Horrified, Pa-chieh cried, "We are finished! Here's another old monster coming to ask for his treasures!" Pilgrim looked at the man carefully and saw that he was actually Lao

Tzu. Hurriedly he drew near and bowed, saying, "Venerable Sir, where are you going?" The old patriarch swiftly mounted his jade throne, which rose and stopped in midair. "Pilgrim Sun," he said, "return my treasures." The Great Sage also rose into the air saying, "What treasures?" "The gourd," said Lao Tzu, "is what I use to store elixir, while the pure vase is my water container. The treasure sword I use to subdue demons; the fan is for tending my fires; and the rope is actually a belt of my gown. Those two monsters happen to be two Taoist youths: one looks after my golden brazier, while the other my silver brazier. I was just searching for them, for they stole the treasures and left the Region Above. Now you have caught them, this will be your merit." The Great Sage said, "Venerable Sir, you are not very honorable! That you would permit your kin to become demons should make you guilty of oversight in the governance of your household." "It's really not my affair," said Lao Tzu, "so don't blame the wrong person. These youths were requested by the Bodhisattva from the sea three times; they were to be sent here, transformed into demons, to test all of you and see whether master and disciples are sincere in going to the West." When the Great Sage heard these words, he thought to himself, "What a rogue is this Bodhisattva! At the time when she delivered old Monkey and told me to accompany the T'ang monk to procure scriptures in the West, I said that the journey would be a difficult one. She even promised that she herself would come to rescue us when we encounter grave difficulties, but instead, she sent monster-spirits here to harass us. The way she double-talks, she deserves to be a spinster for the rest of her life!" He then said to Lao Tzu, "If Venerable Sir didn't show up personally, I would never have returned these things to you. But since you have made the appearance and told me the truth, you can take them away." After receiving the five treasures, Lao Tzu lifted the seals of the gourd and the vase and poured out two masses of divine ether. With one point of his finger he transformed the ether again into two youths, standing on his left and right. Ten thousand strands of propitious light appeared as

They all drifted toward the Tushita Palace;
Freely they went straight up to Heaven's canopy.

We do not know what happens thereafter, how the Great Sun accompanies the T'ang monk, or at what time they reach the Western Heaven, and you must listen to the explanation in the next chapter.

*Thirty-six*

When the Mind Monkey is rectified, the nidānas[1] cease;[2]

When the side door[3] is punctured, the bright moon is seen.

We were telling you about Pilgrim, who lowered the direction of his cloud and presented to his master a thorough account of how the Bodhisattva requested for the youths and how Lao Tzu took back his treasures. Tripitaka was deeply grateful; he redoubled his efforts and determination to go to the West at all costs. He mounted the horse once more, while Chu Pa-chieh poled the luggage, Sha Monk took hold of the bridle, and Pilgrim Sun took up his iron rod to lead the way down the tall mountain. As they proceeded, we cannot tell you in full how they rested by the waters and dined in the wind, how they were covered with frost and exposed to the dew. Master and disciples journeyed for a long time and again they found a mountain blocking their path. "Disciples," said Tripitaka loudly on the horse, "Look how tall and rugged is that mountain. We should be most careful, for I fear that there may be some demonic miasmas coming to attack us." Pilgrim said, "Stop thinking foolish thoughts, Master. Compose yourself and keep your mind from wandering; nothing will happen to you." "O Disciple," said Tripitaka, "why is it so difficult to reach the Western Heaven? I remember that since leaving the city Ch'ang-an, spring has come and gone on this road several times, autumn has arrived to be followed by winter—at least four or five years must have gone by. Why is it that we still haven't reached our destination?" "It's too early! It's too early!" said Pilgrim, roaring with laughter. "We haven't even left the main door yet!" "Stop fibbing, Elder Brother," said Pa-chieh. "There's no such big mansion in this world." "Brother," said Pilgrim, "we are just moving around in one of the halls inside." Laughing, Sha Monk said, "Elder Brother, stop talking so big to scare us. Where could you find such a huge house? Even if there were, you wouldn't be able to find cross beams that were long enough." "Brother," said Pilgrim, "from the point of view of old Monkey, this blue sky is our roof, the sun and moon are our windows, the five sacred mountains our pillars, and the whole Heaven and Earth is but one large chamber." When Pa-chieh heard this, he sighed: "We're finished! We're finished! All right, move around some more and we'll go back." "No need for this kind of silly chatter," said Pilgrim. "Just follow old Monkey and move."

Dear Great Sage! Placing the iron rod horizontally across his shoulders, he led the T'ang monk firmly up the mountain road and went straight ahead. As the master looked around on the horse, he saw some lovely mountain scenery. Truly

The rugged summits touch the dipper stars,
And treetops seem to join the sky and clouds.
Within piles of blue mist
The ape cries oft arise from the valley;
In the shades of riotous green
You hear the cranes calling beneath the pines.
Howling mountain ghosts stand up in the streams
To mock the woodsman;
Aged fox spirits sit beside the cliff
To frighten the hunter.
Marvelous mountain!
Look how steep it is on all sides,
How precipitous everywhere!
Strange knotty pines topped by green canopies;
Dried, aged trees dangling creepers and vines.
The stream surges,
Its piercing cold chills e'en the hairs of man;
The peak rears up,
Its eye-smarting clear wind makes one skittish.
Frequently you listen to big cats roar;
Now and then you hear mountain birds call.
Flocks of fallow deer cut through the brambles,
Leaping here and there;
Hordes of river deer seeking food of the wilds
Run back and forth.
Standing on the meadow,
One can't see any traveler;
Walk in the canyons
And there are wolves on all sides.
It's no place for Buddha to meditate,
Wholly the domain of darting birds and beasts.

With fear and trembling, the master entered deep into the mountain. Growing more melancholy, he stopped the horse and said, "O Wu-k'ung! Once

I was resolved⁴ to make that mountain trip,
The king did not wait to send me from the city.
I met on the way the three-cornered sedge;
I pushed hard my horse decked with bridle bells.
To find the scriptures I passed meadows and streams;
To yield to Buddha's spirit I scaled the peaks.
If myself I guard to complete my tour,
When may I go home to bow to the Court?"

When the Great Sage heard these words, he roared with laughter, saying, "Master, don't be so anxious and impatient. Relax and push forward. In due time, I assure you that 'success will come naturally when merit's achieved.'" As master and disciples enjoyed the mountain scenery while they walked along, the red orb soon sank toward the west. Truly

No traveler walked by the ten-mile arbor,
But stars appeared in the ninefold heavens.
Boats of eight rivers returned to their piers;
Seven thousand towns and counties shut their gates.
The lords of six chambers and five bureaus all retired;
From four seas and three rivers fish-lines withdrew.
Gongs and drums sounded on two tall towers;
One orb of bright moon filled the universe.

As he peered into the distance on the back of the horse, the master saw in the fold of the mountain several multistoreyed buildings. "Disciples," said Tripitaka, "it's getting late now and we are fortunate to find some buildings over there. I think it must be either a Taoist temple or a Buddhist monastery. Let's go there and ask for lodging for the night, and we can resume our journey in the morning." Pilgrim said, "Master, you are right. Let's not hurry, however; let me examine the place first." Leaping into the air, the Great Sage stared intently and found that it was indeed a Buddhist monastery. He saw

Eight-word brick wall⁵ painted muddy red;
Doors on two sides studded with nails of gold;
Rows of tiered-terrace sheltered by the peak;
Buildings, many storeyed, hidden in the mount.
The Wan-fo Tower⁶ faced the Tathāgata Hall;
The Morning-Sun Tower met the Great Hero⁷ Gate.

Clouds rested on a seven-tiered pagoda,
And glory shone from three honored Buddhas.[8]
Mañjuśri Platform faced the monastic house;
Maitreya Hall joined the Great Mercy Room.
Blue light danced outside the Mountain-Viewing Lodge;
Purple clouds bloomed above the Void-Treading Tower.
Pine retreats and bamboo courts—fresh, lovely green.
Abbot rooms and Zen commons—clean everywhere.
Gracefully, quietly the services were held.
Solemn but joyful, the priests walked the grounds.
Zen monks lectured in the Zen classrooms,
And instruments blared from music halls.
Udumbara petals dropped before the Wondrous-Height Terrace;
Pattra[9] leaves grew beneath the Law-Expounding Platform.
So it was that woods sheltered this land of the Three Jewels,
And mountains embraced this home of a Sanskrit King.
Half a wall of lamps with flickering lights and smoke;
A row of incense obscured by fragrant fog.

Descending from his cloud, the Great Sage Sun reported to Tripitaka, saying, "Master, it's indeed a Buddhist monastery. We can go there to ask for lodging."

The master urged his horse on and went straight up to the main gate. "Master," said Pilgrim, "what monastery is this?" "The hoofs of my horse have just come to a stop, and the tips of my feet have yet to leave the stirrups," said Tripitaka, "and you ask me what monastery this is? How thoughtless you are!" Pilgrim said, "You, your venerable self, have been a monk since your youth, and you must have studied the Confucian classics before you proceeded to lecture on the dharma sūtras. You must have mastered both literature and philosophy before you received such royal favors from the T'ang Emperor. There are big words on the door of this monastery. Why can't you recognize them?" "Impudent ape!" scolded the elder. "You mouth such senseless words! I was facing the west as I rode and my eyes were momentarily blinded by the glare of the sun. There might be words on the door, but they are covered by grime and dirt. That's why I can't make them out." When Pilgrim heard these words, he stretched his torso and at once grew to over twenty feet tall. Wiping away the dirt, he said, "Master, please take a look." There were seven words in large characters: "Precious Grove Monastery Built by

Imperial Command." After Pilgrim changed back into his normal size, he said, "Master, which one of us should go in to ask for lodging?" "I'll go inside," said Tripitaka, "for all of you are ugly in your appearance, uncouth in your speech, and arrogant in your manner. If you happen to offend the local monks, they may refuse our request, and that won't be good." "In that case," said Pilgrim, "let Master go in at once. No need for words anymore."

Abandoning his priestly staff and untying his cloak, the elder straightened out his clothes and walked inside the main gate with folded hands. There he found behind red lacquered railings a pair of Vajra-guardians,[10] whose molten images were fearsome indeed:

One has an iron face and steel whiskers as if alive;
One has bushy brows and round eyes that seem real.
On the left, the fist bones like raw iron jut out;
On the right, the palms are cragged like crude bronze.
Golden chain armor of splendid luster;
Bright helmets and wind-blown sashes of silk.
Offerings in the West to Buddha are bounteous:
In stone tripods the incense fires glow red.

When Tripitaka saw this, he nodded and gave a lengthy sigh, saying, "If in our Land of the East there are enough people who would mold such huge bodhisattvas with clay and worship them with fires and incense, this disciple would have no need to go to the Western Heaven." As he was saying this to himself, he reached the second gate, where he discovered inside the images of the Four Devarājas: Dhṛtarāṣṭra, Vaiśravaṇa, Virūḍhaka, and Virūpākṣa, each of them, stationed according to his position in the east, north, south, and west, was also symbolic of his powers to make the winds harmonious and the rains seasonal. After he entered the second gate, he saw four tall pines, each of which had a luxuriant top shaped like an umbrella. As he raised his head, he discovered that he had arrived before the Precious Hall of the Great Hero. Folding his hands with complete reverence, the elder prostrated himself and worshipped; afterwards, he arose and went past the Buddha platform to reach the rear gate. There he found the image of the reclining Kuan-yin who proffered deliverance to the creatures of South Sea. On the walls were carvings —all done by skillful artisans—of shrimps, fishes, crabs, and turtles; sticking out their heads and flapping their tails, they were frolicking in the billows and leaping over the waves. The elder again nodded his head four or five times, sighing loudly: "What a pity! Even scaly creatures would worship Buddha! Why is it that humans are unwilling to practice religion?"

As he was thus speaking to himself, a worker emerged from the third gate. When he saw the uncommon and handsome features of Tripitaka, he hurried forward and bowed, saying, "Where did the master come from?" "This disciple," said Tripitaka, "was sent by the Throne of the Great T'ang in the Land of the East to go to the Western Heaven and seek scriptures from Buddha. It was getting late when we arrived at your honored region, and I came to ask for lodging for one night." "Please do not be offended, Master," said the worker, "but I can't assume responsibility here. I'm just a manual laborer in charge of sweeping the grounds and tolling the bell. There's an old master inside who is the head of the household. Let me go in and report to him; if he wishes to ask you to stay, I'll come out to give you the invitation; if not, I dare not detain you." Tripitaka said, "Sorry for all that inconvenience."

The worker hurried to the abbot chamber and reported: "Venerable Father, there's someone outside." The monk-official arose immediately, changed his clothes, adjusted his Vairocana hat, and put on a cassock before he went to open the door to receive his visitor. "What man has arrived?" he asked the worker, who pointed with his finger and replied, "Isn't that a man there behind the main hall?" Bald-headed, wearing a Bodhidharma gown that was in shreds and a pair of sandals muddy and wet, Tripitaka was reclining by the door. When the monk-official saw him, he became enraged, saying, "Worker, you deserve to be flogged! Don't you know that a monk-official like me would come out and receive only the gentlemen from the cities who come here to offer incense? For this sort of a monk, why did you give me a phony report and ask me to receive him? Just look at his face! He can't be an honest man! He has to be some kind of mendicant who wants to sleep here now that it's getting late. You think I'm going to permit him to mess up our abbot chamber? Tell him to squat in the corridor. Why bother me?" He turned around and left immediately.

When the elder heard these words, tears filled his eyes and he said, "How pitiful! How pitiful! Truly 'a man away from home is cheap!' This disciple left home from his youth to become a monk. I did not

Do penance while eating meat with wicked glee,
Or read scriptures in wrath to soil the mind of Zen.
Nor did I
Cast tiles and stones to damage Buddha's hall,
Or rip down the gold from an arhat's face.
Alas, how pitiful! I don't know which incarnation it was that I had
offended Heaven and Earth, so that I have to meet unkind people so
frequently in this life. Monk, if you don't want to give us lodging, that's
all right. But why must you say such nasty things, telling us to go and
squat in the corridors? I'd better not repeat these words to Pilgrim,
for if I did, that monkey would come in and a few blows of his iron
rod would break all your shanks. All right! All right! The proverb
says, 'Man must put propriety and music first.' Let me go inside and
ask him once more and see what he really intends to do with us."

Following the tracks of the monk-official, the master went up to the
door of the abbot chamber, where he found the monk-official who,
having taken off his outer garments, was sitting inside, still panting
with rage. He was not reciting the sūtras, nor was he drawing up any
service for a family; all the T'ang monk could see was a pile of papers
on a table beside him. Not daring to walk inside abruptly but standing
instead in the courtyard, Tripitaka bowed and cried out: "Old Abbot,
this disciple salutes you." Somewhat annoyed by the fact that Tripitaka followed him inside, the monk only pretended to return the
greeting, saying, "Where did you come from?" "This disciple," replied
Tripitaka, "has been sent by the Throne of the Great T'ang in the
Land of the East to go to the Western Heaven and seek scriptures from
the Living Buddha. I passed through your honored region, it was
getting late, and I came to ask for lodging for one night. Tomorrow,
I'll leave before daybreak. I beseech the Old Abbot to grant me this
request." Only then did the monk-official get up from his seat and say,
"Are you that Tripitaka T'ang?" Tripitaka said, "Yes." "If you are
going to the Western Heaven to acquire scriptures," said the monk-
official, "how is it that you don't even know your way?" Tripitaka
said, "Your disciple has never passed through your honored region
and that's why he doesn't know the way here." "Due west of here,"
he said, "about four or five miles is a Thirty-Mile Inn, in which there
is also someone selling food. It will be convenient for you to stay there,
whereas it's not convenient here for me to entertain a monk like your-

self who has come from a great distance." "Abbot," said Tripitaka
with hands folded, "the ancients declared that 'A Taoist temple or a
Buddhist monastery all may be considered a lodge for a priest, who
has a claim for three percent of the food the moment he sees the
temple gate.' Why do you refuse me?" "You mendicant monk!"
shouted the monk-official angrily. "All you know is how to cajole and
wheedle!" Tripitaka said, "What do you mean by cajole and
wheedle?" The monk-official said, "Remember what the ancients
said?

A tiger comes to town;
Each house will shut the door.
Though no one is bitten,
Its name's already poor!"

"What do you mean by 'Its name's already poor'?" said Tripitaka. "A
few years ago," said the monk-official, "there was a group of mendi-
cants who arrived and sat in front of our monastery gate. I took pity
on their hardship when I saw how destitute they were, everyone of
them bald-headed and barefooted, shoeless and in rags. So I invited
them into the abbot chamber, gave them honored seats, and fed them
a vegetarian meal. Moreover, I even gave each of them an old suit of
clothes to wear and asked them to stay for a few days. How would I
know that they could become so greedy for easy food and clothing
that they would remain for seven or eight years, never giving a
thought to leaving again? I didn't mind even their staying, but they
indulged in all sorts of shabby activities." "What shabby activities?"
asked Tripitaka, and the monk-official said, "Just listen to my tale:

When idle they threw tiles along the pale;
When bored they pulled nails off the wall.
In winter they ripped window panes to feed the fires,
Unhinging doors in summer to leave on the road.
They tore flag-cloth to make foot-wraps;
They stole in hunger our green turnips.
Often from glass vases they poured our oil,
And made games of grabbing bowls and dishes!"

When Tripitaka heard these words, he said to himself: "How pitiful!
Is this disciple that kind of spineless monk?" He was about to cry, but
he was also afraid that the old monk in the monastery would laugh at
him. Swallowing his pride and his anger while wiping away his tears
secretly with his robe, he walked out quickly and met his three

disciples. When Pilgrim discovered how angry his master looked, he went forward to ask: "Master, did the monks in the monastery strike you?" "They didn't," said the T'ang monk. "They must have done so," said Pa-chieh, "for if they haven't, why is your voice cracking?" "Have they scolded you?" said Pilgrim. The T'ang monk said, "They haven't either." "If they haven't struck you," said Pilgrim, "or scolded you, why are you upset? You must be getting homesick." "Disciples," said the T'ang monk, "they say that it's not convenient here." "They must be Taoists here, then?" said Pilgrim, laughing. "Only a Taoist temple has Taoists," said the T'ang monk with rage. "There are only monks in a monastery." Pilgrim said, "You are useless! If they are monks, they are the same as we. The proverb says,

Gathered in Buddha's assembly
Are all men of affinity.

You sit here, and let me go inside to look around."

Dear Pilgrim! Giving the fillet on his head a squeeze and tightening the skirt around his waist, he went straight up to the Precious Hall of the Great Hero, holding his iron rod. There he pointed at the statues of the three Buddhas and said, "You are actually idols molded with clay and adorned with gold. You don't possess one whit of efficacy inside! Or do you? Old Monkey, who is accompanying the T'ang monk to go to the Western Heaven and seek the true scriptures from Buddha, has come here tonight specially to ask for lodging. You'd better hurry and announce my arrival. If you don't put us up, my rod will smash the golden bodies and reveal your original forms of mud!"

As the Great Sage was making his threats and intimidations, a worker in charge of vespers arrived with several sticks of lighted incense to be placed in the urn before the images of Buddha. One snarl of Pilgrim sent him tumbling; when he scrambled up and saw the face, he fell down again. Stumbling all over, he fled into the abbot chamber and made the report, saying, "Holy Father, there's a monk outside." "All of you workers deserve to be flogged!" said the monk-official. "I told you people before that they should be sent to squat in the corridors up front. Why make another announcement? One more word and I'll give you twenty lashes!" "Holy Father," said the worker, "this monk is not the same as the other one; he's mean and fierce looking." "How does he look?" said the monk-official. The worker said, "He's someone with round eyes, forked ears, a face full of hairs, and a beak like the thunder god's. He has a rod in his hands, furiously grinding his teeth to find someone to beat." "Let me go out and take a look," said the monk-official.

The moment he opened the door, he saw Pilgrim barging in. It was a hideous sight indeed! A bumpy, scabrous face, a pair of yellow eyeballs, a sunken forehead, and long, protruding fangs—he seemed virtually an overcooked crab with meat inside and cartilage outside! So panic-stricken was the old monk that he slammed shut the door of the abbot chamber at once. Pilgrim, however, rushed up to it and smashed it to pieces, crying, "Hurry up and clean out one thousand rooms! Old Monkey wants to take a nap!" As he attempted to hide in the room, the monk-official said to the worker, "No wonder he's so ugly! Talking big has caused him to end up with a face like that! Our place here, including abbot chambers, Buddha halls, bell-and-drum towers, and the two corridors, has barely three hundred rooms. He wants a thousand for him to take a nap. Where are we going to get these rooms?" "Master," said the worker, "I'm a man whose gall has been busted by fear. I'll let you answer him any way you please." Trembling all over, the monk-official said in a loud voice, "The elder who wants lodging, please hear me. It's truly inconvenient for this small, humble monastery of ours to entertain you. Please go somewhere to stay."

Pilgrim transformed his rod until it had the circumference of a basin's; then he stuck it straight up in the courtyard. "Monk," he said, "if it's inconvenient, you move out." The monk-official said, "We have lived here since our youth; our grand-masters passed the place on to our masters, and they in turn to us. We want to give it to our heirs. What sort of a person is he that he would so rashly ask us to move?" "Venerable Father," said the worker, "we can't muddle through like this. Why not move out? That pole of his is going to come smashing in!" "Stop babbling!" said the monk-official. "We have altogether five hundred monks here, old and young. Where are we going to move to? Even if we do move out, we have no other place to stay." Hearing this, Pilgrim said, "Monk, if you have no place to move, one of you must come out and be caned." The old monk said to the worker, "You go out and take the caning for me." Horrified, the worker said, "O Father! With that huge pole, and you ask me to take the caning!" The old monk said, "As the proverb says, 'It may take a thousand days to feed an army, but only one day to use it.' Why don't you go out?" "Don't speak of being caned by that huge pole," said the worker. "Even if it just falls on you, you'll be reduced to a meat patty." "Yes," said the old monk, "let's not speak of falling on someone. If it remains standing in the courtyard, one can crack his head bumping into it at night if one forgets it's there." "Master," said the worker, "if you know that's how heavy it is, why do you ask me to go out and take the caning for you?" whereupon the two of them began to quarrel between themselves.

Hearing all that noise, Pilgrim said to himself, "They really can't take it. If I kill each of them with one blow of my rod, Master will accuse me again of working violence. Let me find something to strike at and show them what I can do." He lifted his head and discovered a stone lion outside the door of the abbot chamber. Raising up the rod, he slammed it on the lion and reduced it to powder. The monk caught sight of the blow through a tiny hole in the window and, almost paralyzed with fear, began crawling under the bed while the worker tried desperately to creep into the opening of the kitchen range, yelling all the time: "Father! The rod's too heavy! The rod's too heavy! I can't take it! It's convenient! It's convenient!" Pilgrim said, "Monk, I won't hit you now. I'm asking you, how many monks are there in this monastery?" Shaking all over, the monk-official said, "There are two hundred and eighty-five chambers back and front, and we have altogether five hundred certified monks." "Go quickly and call up every one of those five hundred monks," said Pilgrim. "Tell them to put on their long robes and receive my master in here. Then I won't hit you." "Father," said the monk-official, "if you won't hit us, we'll be glad even to carry him inside." "Go now!" said Pilgrim. The monk-official said to the worker, "Don't tell me that your gall has been busted by fear. Even if your heart is busted, you still have to go and call up these people to welcome the Holy Father T'ang."

With no alternative at all, the worker had to risk his life. He dared not, however, walk out the door, but crawled out instead in the back through the dog hole from where he went to the main hall in front. He began striking the bell on the west and beating the drum on the east. The sounds of these two instruments soon aroused all the monks living in their quarters along the two corridors. They arrived at the main hall and asked, "It's still early. Why do you beat the drum and strike the bell?" "Change your clothes quickly," said the worker, "and line yourselves up to follow Old Master to go out of the gate in order to welcome a Holy Father from the T'ang court." The various monks indeed arranged themselves in order to go out the gate for the reception; some of them put on their cassocks, while others put on their togas. Those who had neither wore long, bell-shaped gowns, while the poorest ones folded up their skirts and draped them over both their shoulders. When Pilgrim saw them, he asked, "Monks, what kind of clothes do you have on?" When the monks saw how fierce and ugly he looked, they said, "Father, don't hit us. Let us tell you what we have on. The cloth was donated to us by the families in the city. As we don't have any tailor around here, we have to make our own clothes. The style is called A Wrap of Woe."

Smiling silently to himself when he heard these words, Pilgrim guarded the monks and saw to it that each one of them walked out the gate and kneeled down. After he kowtowed, the monk-official cried out: "Venerable Father T'ang, please go to the abbot chamber and take a seat." When Pa-chieh saw what was happening, he said, "Master is so incompetent! When you walked inside just now, you returned not only with tears, but you were pouting so much that you looked as if two flasks of oil had been hung on your lips. Now, what sort of cunning does Elder Brother have that makes them kowtow to receive us?" "You Idiot!" said Tripitaka. "You don't know what's going on! As the proverb says, 'Even ghosts are afraid of nasty people.'" When the T'ang monk saw them kowtowing, he was very embarrassed and he approached them, saying, "Please rise, all of you." The various monks continued to kowtow, saying, "If the Venerable Father could speak on our behalf to your disciple and ask him not to hit us with that pole, we would be willing to kneel here for a whole month." "Wu-k'ung," cried the T'ang monk, "don't hit them." "I haven't," said Pilgrim, "for if I did, they would have been exterminated." Only then did those monks get up; some went to lead the horse while others took up the pole of luggage. They lifted up the T'ang monk, carried Pa-chieh, and took hold of Sha Monk—all crowded inside the monastery gate and headed for the abbot chamber in the back.

After the pilgrims took their seats, the monks came again to do obeisance. "Abbot, please rise," said Tripitaka. "There's no need for you to go through such ceremony anymore, or your poor monk will find it much too burdensome. You and I, after all, are all disciples within the gate of Buddha." "The Venerable Father," said the monk-official, "is an imperial envoy of a noble nation, and this humble monk has not properly welcomed you when you reached our desolate mountain. Our vulgar eyes could not recognize your esteemed countenance, though it was our good fortune that we should meet. Permit me to ask the Venerable Father to tell me whether he was eating meat or vegetarian food on the way. We can then prepare your meal." "Vegetarian food," said Tripitaka. "Disciples," said the monk-official, "this Holy Father prefers vegetarian food." Pilgrim said, "We, too, have been eating vegatarian food. We have maintained such a diet, in fact, even before we were born." "O Father!" exclaimed that monk. "Such violent men would eat vegetarian food too?" Another monk, who was slightly more courageous, drew near and asked again: "If the Venerable Fathers prefer vegetarian food, how much rice should we cook?" "You cheapskates!" said Pa-chieh. "Why ask? For us family, cook a picul of rice." The monks all became frightened; they went at once to scrub and wash the pots and pans and to prepare the meal. Bright lamps were brought in as they set the table to entertain the T'ang monk.

After master and disciples had eaten the vegetarian dinner, the monks took away the dishes and the furniture. "Old Abbot," said Tripitaka, thanking him, "we are greatly indebted to you and your hospitality." "Not at all, not at all," said the monk-official, "we haven't done anything for you." Tripitaka said, "Where should we sleep?" "Don't be impatient, Venerable Father," said the monk-official. "This humble cleric has everything planned." He then asked: "Worker, do you have some people there who are free to work?" "Yes, Master," said the worker. The monk-official instructed them, saying, "Two of you should go and get some hay to feed the horse of Venerable Father T'ang. The rest can go to the front and clean up three of the Zen rooms; set up bedding and mosquito nets so that the Venerable Fathers can take their rest."

The workers obeyed and each of them finished the preparation before returning to invite the T'ang monk to go take his rest. Master and disciples led the horse and toted the luggage; they left the abbot chamber and went to the door of the Zen rooms, where they saw inside brightly lit lamps and four rattan beds with bedding all laid out. Pilgrim asked the worker who brought the hay to haul it inside the Zen rooms, where they tied up the white horse also. The workers were then told to leave. As Tripitaka sat down beneath the lamps, two rows of monks—all five hundred of them—stood on both sides and waited upon him, not daring to leave. Tripitaka got up and said, "Please go back, all of you. This humble cleric can then rest comfortably." The monks refused to retire, for the monk-official had given them the instruction that they were not to leave until every need of the Venerable Father T'ang was provided for. Only after Tripitaka said, "I'm all cared for, please go back," did they dare disperse and leave.

The T'ang monk stepped outside the door to relieve himself, and he saw a bright moon high in the sky. "Disciples," he called out, and Pilgrim, Pa-chieh, and Sha Monk all came out to wait on him. Moved by the bright, pure light of the moon—a round orb loftily hung to illumine the great Earth—and filled with longing for his homeland, Tripitaka composed orally a long poem in the ancient style. The poem said:

> The bright soul above hangs like a jeweled glass,
> Her radiance pervades the entire world:
> Jasper halls, jade towers filled with clear light;
> An ice tray or silver pan swathed in ether crisp.
> O'er ten thousand miles her pure rays extend;
> This night her beams are the year's most luminous.
> She seems a cake of frost leaving the dark blue sea,
> Or a wheel of ice nailed to the jade-green sky.
> By the wayside inn's cold transoms a lone guest mourns;
> In a mountain town's rural lodge an old man sleeps.
> She comes abruptly to the Han court to shock autumnal hair;
> She hastens evening makeup when she climbs the towers of Ch'in.[11]
> For her Yü Liang[12] has poems for the *History of Tsin*;
> For her Yüan Hung[13] stays up to sail his river boat.
> Floating on cup rims she's a cold, languid light;
> Shining cleanly on the garden, she's strong as a god.
> On each window pane one can sing of white snow;[14]
> In every household one can press the icy strings.[15]
> Tonight to a monastery her quiet pleasure comes.
> When will she join me to return to our home?

When Pilgrim heard these words, he approached him and said, "Master, all you know is that the moonlight fills you with longing for home, but you don't understand that the moon may symbolize the rules and regulations of nature's many modes and forms.[16] When the moon reaches the thirtieth day, the metal in its yang spirit is completely dissolved, whereas the water of its yin soul is filled to the brim of the orb. This is the reason for the designation of that day with the

term Obscure,[17] for the moon is completely dark and without light.
It is at this moment also that the moon copulates with the sun, and
during the time of the thirtieth day and the first day of the month, it
will become pregnant by the light of the sun. By the third day, one
[stroke][18] of the yang will appear, and two [strokes] of the yang will
be born by the eighth day. At this time, the moon will have half of
its yang spirit in the middle of its yin soul, and its lower half is flat like
a rope. That is the reason why the time of the month is callled the
Upper Bow. By the fifteenth day, all three [strokes] of the yang will be
ready, and perfect union will be achieved. That is why this time of the
month is called To Face.[19] On the sixteenth day, one [stroke] of the
yin will be born, and the second stroke will make its appearance on
the twenty-second day. At that time half of the yin soul will be in the
middle of the yang spirit, and its upper half is flat like a rope. That is
the reason why this time of the month is called the Lower Bow. By
the thirtieth day, all three [strokes] of the yin will be ready, and the
moon has then reached the state of obscurity once more. All this is
the symbol of the process of cultivation practiced by nature. If we can
nourish the Two Eights[20] until we reach the perfection of Nine Times
Nine,[21] then it will be simple for us at that moment to see Buddha,
and simple also for us to return to our home. The poem says:

After the First Quarter and before the Last Quarter:
The medicine's taste is blended, the condition's complete.
What you acquire from picking, refine in the stove—
The fruit of determination is the Western Heaven."[22]

When the elder heard what he said, he was immediately enlightened
and understood completely these words of realized immortality. Filled
with delight, he thanked Wu-k'ung repeatedly. On one side, Sha
Monk smiled and said, "Though Elder Brother spoke most appro-
priately concerning how the first quarter of the moon belonged to the
yang and the last quarter belonged to the yin, and how in the midst
of yin and in the middle of yang one could obtain the metal of water,
he did not mention

Water and fire blended, each is to the other drawn;
They depend on Earth Mother to make such a match.
Three members are thus fused without war or strife:
The water's in the Long River and the moon's in the sky."

When the elder heard that, his dull mind was again opened up. Thus
it was that

Truth, grasped by the heart's one channel, clears up a thousand
    channels.
Once you solve the riddle of no birth, you are a god.
Then Pa-chieh walked up to the elder and tugged at him, saying,
"Master, don't listen to all their babblings and delay your sleep. This
moon,
    After it wanes, will soon grow round again.
    Like me it was born none too perfectly!
    At meals I'm disliked for too large a maw;
    I drool too much, they say, on the bowls I hold.
    They have their blessings earned through cleverness;
    I have affinity stocked by foolishness.
    I tell you that
    By fetching scriptures you'll fulfill the three karmic paths,
    And, wagging your head and tail, go straight up to Heav'n!"
"All right, Disciples," said Tripitaka, "you must be tired from all this
journeying. You may go to sleep first, and let me meditate on this roll
of scripture." "Master, you must be mistaken," said Pilgrim. "You
left the family in your youth to become a monk. How could you not
be completely familiar with all the scriptures you studied when you
were young? Then you received the command from the T'ang emperor
to go to the Western Heaven and see Buddha for the True Canon of
Mahāyāna. But at this moment, your merit has not been perfected,
you have not seen the Buddha, and you have not yet acquired the
scriptures. Which roll of scripture do you want to meditate on?"
Tripitaka said, "Since I left Ch'ang-an, I have been traveling day
and night, and I fear that the scriptures I learned in my youth might
slip away from me. Tonight there's a little time, and I want to do some
reviewing." "In that case," said Pilgrim, "we'll go to sleep first." The
three disciples indeed lay down on three of the rattan beds. Closing
the door of the Zen hall and turning up the lamp, the elder opened his
roll of scripture and began to read and meditate in silence. Truly it
was that
    The first watch struck from a tower and human bustle ceased,
    When fishing-boat fires by the wild banks went out.
We don't know how that elder will depart from the monastery, and
you must listen to the explanation in the next chapter.

*Thirty-seven*

The Ghost King visits Tripitaka T'ang at night;

Wu-k'ung, through wondrous transformation, leads the child.

We were telling you about Tripitaka sitting in the Zen hall of the Precious Grove Monastery. He meditated for a while beneath the lamps on the *Water Litany of King Liang*,[1] and he read for a while the *True Sūtra of the Peacock*. Not until about the hour of the third watch did he wrap up the scriptures again in his bag. He was just about to get up and walk over to his bed when he heard the weird moan of a strong gust outside the door. Fearing that it might blow out the lamp, he tried hurriedly to shade it with the sleeve of his gown. When he saw the lamp flicker, he began to tremble, but at the same time, he was overcome by fatigue and soon dozed off with his head resting on the reading desk. Though his eyes were closed, he still seemed to be half conscious, able to hear all the time the continuous sighing of the dark wind outside his window. What a wind! Truly it

Whistled and whiffled—
It swayed and scattered—
It whistled and whiffled as fallen leaves flew;
It swayed and scattered the floating clouds.
Heaven's stars and planets were all darkened;
The whole Earth's dust and sand were strewn afar.
For a while it was fierce;
For a while it was mild.
When it was mild, bamboos and pines beat out their pure rhymes;
When it was fierce, waves of lakes and rivers heaved and churned.
It blew till mountain birds grew restless, their voices choked,
And sea fishes had no peace as they tossed and turned.
Windows and doors fell off in both east and west halls;
Gods and ghosts glowered in hallways front and back.
The Buddha Hall's flower vase was blown to the ground;
The oil chalice tumbled and wisdom-lamp grew faint;
The incense urn turned over and ashes spilled out;

The candlesticks were tilted as flames changed to smoke.

Banners, sacred canopies were all awry.

Bell-and-drum towers were shaken to the roots!

In his dream the elder seemed to hear, after the wind had passed, a faint voice outside the Zen hall crying, "Master!" He raised his head in his dream to look and discovered a man standing outside the door who was soaked from head to toe. As tears rolled down from his eyes, he kept calling: "Master!" Tripitaka rose up and said, "Could you be a goblin or a ghost, a fiend or a demon, coming to mock me at the depth of night? I am neither a rapacious nor a wrathful person, but rather an honest and upright priest. Having received the imperial decree from the Great T'ang in the Land of the East, I am on my way to the Western Heaven to seek scriptures from Buddha. I have three disciples under my command, all valiant men able to tame tigers and subdue dragons, heroic warriors capable of repelling demons and extirpating monsters. If they see you, you will be reduced to powder and dust. Take note, therefore, of my compassionate intent and my mind which knows how to use skillful means.[2] Leave this place, go somewhere far away while there's still time, and don't come up to the door of our Zen hall." Reclining firmly by the door of the hall, the man said, "Master, we are not a demon or monster, nor are we a goblin or bogie." "If you are not that kind of a creature," said Tripitaka, "why are you here so late in the night?" "Open wide your eyes, Master," said the man, "and look at us." The elder indeed fixed his gaze on his visitor. Ah!

His head had on it a rising-to-Heaven cap;

A green-jade belt he tied around his waist.

He wore on his body a reddish brown robe with dancing phoenixes
    and flying dragons;

His feet trod on a pair of carefree boots of embroidered cloud
    pattern;

His hands held a white jade-token adorned with planets and stars.

His face seemed the immortal King of T'ai Mountain;

His form was like the civilized King Wên-ch'ang.[3]

When Tripitaka saw this, he paled with fright and hurriedly bowed low before his visitor, crying with a loud voice, "Which dynasty do you belong to, Your Majesty? Please take a seat." He then tried to take hold of his visitor's hands, only to find that he succeeded in grasping nothing but thin air. Spinning around, he sat down and looked: there was the man again. The elder asked once more: "Your Majesty, in what region are you a king? Of what empire are you a ruler? Could it be that there is strife in your kindgom and you are so oppressed by treacherous ministers that you have to flee for your life and arrive here at night? What do you have to say? Please tell me." Only then did the man,

As tears rolled down his cheeks, describe events of old;

As sorrow constringed his brow, disclose the former cause.

"Master," he said, "our home is located due west of here, only about forty miles away, where there is a city, the place we founded our kingdom." "What is its name?" said Tripitaka. "To tell you the truth," said the man, "when we established our reign, we gave it the name Black Rooster Kingdom." "Why is it that Your Majesty seems so frightened," said Tripitaka, "and for what reason did you come to this place?" The man said, "O Master! Five years ago we had a drought here, so severe that no vegetation could grow and the people were all starving to death. It was dreadful."

When Tripitaka heard these words, he nodded and smiled, saying, "Your Majesty, the ancients said, 'When the kingdom is rectified, then even the Mind of Heaven is agreeable.' You must not have been treating your subjects with compassion. If there were drought and famine in the land, how could you forsake your domain? You should have opened up your warehouses in order to bring relief to the people; you should repent of all the sins you have committed and try to do good henceforth. When you have freed and pardoned those who were unjustly accused and condemned, then the Mind of Heaven will be pacified and the winds and the rains will become timely and auspicious once more." "The warehouses in my kingdom," said the man, "were all empty and both our revenue and food were exhausted. The salaries for our civil and military officials had to be stopped, and there was not meat in our royal diet. I attempted to imitate the way King Yü conquered the flood, by suffering with our people, by ritual cleansing, maintaining a vegetarian diet, and practicing abstinence. Night and day we offered prayers and incense to Heaven. This went on for three years, but all we had as a result were parched rivers and dried wells. As we reached our most desperate moment, there came to us suddenly from Chung-nan Mountain a Taoist of the Complete Truth sect,[4] who was able to summon the wind and call for rain, to transform rock into gold.[5] He first presented himself to the civil and

military officials, and then he met with us. We, of course, invited him
to ascend the liturgical platform and offer prayers, which were indeed
efficacious. As he struck aloud his ritual placard, torrential rain came
down in a moment. We thought that three feet of rain would be quite
sufficient, but he said that since the drought had been so severe for
such a long time, he would ask for an extra two inches. When we
saw how magnanimous he was, we went through the ceremony of
Eight Bows with him and became bond-brothers." "This," said Tripitaka, "is the greatest joy for Your Majesty." "What joy is there?" said
the man. Tripitaka said, "If the Taoist has that kind of abilities, you
can tell him to make rain when you want rain, and to make gold
when you want gold. What need is there for you to leave the city and
come here?" "We shared our food and rest with him for two years,"
said the man, "when it was the time of spring again. As flowers
bloomed seductively on the apricot and peach trees, every household
in the kingdom was going out to enjoy the lovely scenery. At that
time when our officials retired to their residences and our consorts to
their chambers, the Taoist and we walked hand-in-hand into the
imperial garden. When we came near our well with octagonal marble
walls, he threw something in it which emitted myriad shafts of golden
light and tricked us into approaching the side of the well to see what
sort of treasure was in it. Moved to treachery all at once, he pushed
us into the well which he then covered with a slab of stone. He sealed
off the entire well with mud and dirt, and he even transplanted a
plantain tree on it. Alas, pity us! We have been dead now for three
years,[6] a ghost who lost his life in the well and whose wrong has yet
to be avenged."

When the T'ang monk heard that the man was in fact a ghost, he
turned numb with fear as his hairs stood on end. He had, however,
no choice but to ask his visitor further, saying, "Your Majesty, there
is something unreasonable in what you have just said. If you have
been dead indeed for three years, how could those civil and military
officials, those consorts of three palaces, not miss you and seek you
when they had to attend court once every third morning?" The man
said, "Master, when one speaks of the Taoist's abilities, they are truly
rare in the world. Since he murdered us, he shook his body once in
the garden and transformed himself into an exact image of us. Then
and there he took over our empire and usurped our kingdom. Our
two divisions of civil and military officials—some four hundred court

ministers—and the consorts and ladies of three palaces and six chambers now all belong to him." "Your Majesty," said Tripitaka, "you are too timid." "Why timid?" said the man. Tripitaka said, "Your Majesty, that fiend indeed must have some magic powers in order to change into your form and usurp your kingdom. The civil and military officials might not recognize him, and the consorts might not realize what has happened. But you understand, even though you have died. Why didn't you file suit against him before King Yama in the Region of Darkness? You can at least give an account of the wrongs perpetrated." "His magic powers are great indeed, said the man, "and he's intimate with most of the divine officials. The city's tutelary guardian drinks with him frequently; the ocean's dragon kings are his relatives; Equal to Heaven of the T'ai Mountain[7] is his dear friend, and the Ten Kings of Hell happen to be his bond-brothers. That's why we have no place to go even to file suit."

Tripitaka said, "Your Majesty, if you cannot bring suit against him in the Region of Darkness, why do you come here to the World of Light?" "O Master," said the man, "you think that this wronged soul of yours would dare approach your gate? Before this monastery you have the various tutelary devas, the Six Gods of Darkness and the Six Gods of Light, the Guardians of Five Quarters, the Four Sentinels, and the Eighteen Guardians of the Faith, all of them closely watching over you and your horse. Just now it was the Night Patrol God who brought us in here with a gust of divine wind. He said that our water ordeal of three years is now fulfilled, and that we should come to seek an audience with you. He told us that you have under your command a senior disciple, the Great Sage, Equal to Heaven, who is able to slay fiends and subdue demons. We have come with all sincerity to plead with you. We beseech you to go to our kingdom and seize the demon, so that the true and the deviate can properly be distinguished. To repay the kindness of Master, we shall imitate those who express their gratitude by weaving grass ropes or holding bracelets in the mouth."[8] "Your Majesty," said Tripitaka, "so you came here to ask my disciple to get rid of those monsters for you?" "Exactly! Exactly!" said the man. Tripitaka said, "My disciple may not be good in doing something else, but if you ask him to subdue demons and catch fiends, the work will suit him to a tee. But Your Majesty, though you may order him to seize the monster, I fear that he may find it difficult to carry out." "Why should it be difficult?" said the man. Tripitaka said, "If that fiend indeed possesses such great magic powers that he has managed to transform himself into an exact image of you, then it will mean also that all the civil and military officials of the court and all your consorts have been nothing but friendly and amiable toward him. Though my disciple may be able, he would not engage in warfare recklessly. For if we were caught by the officials, who should accuse us of plotting against the kingdom and charge us with the crime of treason, we would be imprisoned in your city. Wouldn't our efforts then be like the vain attempt of drawing a tiger or carving a heron?"[9]

"I still have someone in the city," said the man. Tripitaka said, "That's good, that's good! He must be, I suppose, an hereditary prince of the first order, dispatched to a command post somewhere." "No," said the man, "I have in the palace a prince, an heir apparent of my own begetting." "Has the prince been banished by the demon?" asked Tripitaka. "Not yet," said the man, "but he has been asked to remain in the Hall of Golden Chimes, either to discuss the classic texts with one of the secretaries, or to sit on the throne with the Taoist. For these three years, the prince was forbidden to enter the palace and unable to see his mother." Tripitaka said, "For what reason?" The man said, "This was a plan of that fiend, for he feared that if mother and son had a chance to meet, their casual conversations might lead them to discover the truth." "Though your ordeal no doubt has been preordained of Heaven," said Tripitaka, "it is nonetheless similar to what I had to undergo. Long ago my father was killed by a pirate, who also took my mother by force. After three months, she gave birth to me, and I escaped with my life in the waters. It was my good fortune that a gracious master at the Gold Mountain Monastery reared me till I was grown. Come to think of it,

I had neither father nor mother when I was young,

And the prince at this place has lost his parents.

How pitiful indeed! But let me ask you, though you may have a prince still in court, how can I possibly get to meet him?" "Why not?" asked the man. Tripitaka said, "He's now guarded by the demon, and he cannot even see his own mother. I'm only a monk. For what reason would I be able to have an audience with him?" The man said, "But he is leaving the court tomorrow." "What for?" asked Tripitaka. The man said, "During the time of the early court tomorrow, the prince plans to lead three thousand men and horses, together with falcons and dogs, to go hunting outside the city. Master will certainly have a chance to meet him; when you do and if you are willing to tell him what I told you, he will believe you.'' "He's of fleshly eyes and mortal stock," said Tripitaka. "Having been deceived by the demon into remaining in the hall, was there a day when he did not address the spurious ruler as father king? How could he possibly believe my words?" "If you are afraid that he won't believe you," said the man, "we shall leave with you a sign to indicate that you are telling the truth." "What kind of sign?" said Tripitaka. The man put down the white jade-token inlaid with gold he had in his hands and said, "This thing can be a sign." "What's the significance of this thing?" said Tripitaka. The man said, "After the Taoist had changed into our form, all he lacked was this treasure. When he entered the palace, he claimed that the rain-making Taoist had robbed him of this jade-token, which for three years now he had not been able to recover. If our prince sees it, the sight of the thing will remind him of its true owner, and our wrongs will be avenged." "All right," said Tripitaka, "let me have it, and I'll ask my disciple to take care of you. Will you wait here?" "We dare not," said the man. "We plan to ask the Night Patrol God to use another gust of divine wind and send us into the inner palace, where we shall appear in a dream to our true queen of the central palace. We want to make certain that mother and son will be of one mind with all of you." Tripitaka nodded in agreement and said, "Please go."

The wronged soul bowed to take leave of Tripitaka, who was trying to walk outside to send him off. Somehow he tripped and fell, and when Tripitaka started up, it was all a dream. As he faced the dim, flickering lamp in fear, he cried repeatedly, "Disciples! Disciples!" "What's all this hollering for the local spirit?"[10] mumbled Pa-chieh, beginning to stir. "I used to be a man of might dedicated to passing my days by devouring humans, and I loved the taste of blood and meat. What enjoyment! You have to leave the family and ask us to protect you on a journey. I thought I was to be a monk, but in fact I'm a slave! During the day I have to pole the luggage and lead the horse, while at night, I have to carry the night pot and smell someone's stinky feet by sharing his bed. And even at this hour, you are not asleep! What are you calling disciples for?" "Disciples," said Tripitaka, "just now I fell asleep on the table and had a weird dream." Leaping up all at once, Pilgrim said, "Dreams arise from your thoughts. Before you ascended a mountain, you were afraid of monsters already. You worried over the distance to Thunderclap which you have yet to reach; you also thought of Ch'ang-an and wondered when you would be able to return. When your mind is restless, you have many dreams. But look at old Monkey! With true single-mindedness I seek to see Buddha in the West, and that's why I don't have even the tiniest dream!" Tripitaka said, "Disciple, this dream of mine is not a homesick dream. When I closed my eyes just now, a violent gust of wind brought into my view a king standing outside the door of our chamber. He said that he was the ruler of the Black Rooster Kingdom, but his whole body was dripping wet and he was weeping." He then proceeded to give a thorough account of their conversation in the dream to Pilgrim.

"No need to say anything more," said Pilgrim, chuckling. "If he appears in this dream of yours to you, he's plainly trying to take care of old Monkey by giving me some business. There must be a fiend there trying to usurp the throne and seize the kingdom. Let me distinguish the true from the false for those people. When my rod reaches that place, success is assured." "But disciple, said Tripitaka, "he said that the fiend has great magic power." "Don't be afraid of whatever greatness he has!" said Pilgrim. "Just remember that when old Monkey arrives, he'll have no place to run." Tripitaka said, "I also remember that he left us something as a sign." "Master, don't fool around," said Pa-chieh. "It's just a dream. Why keep up this chit-chat?" Sha Monk said, "As the saying goes,

You don't believe the honesty of the honest,
You guard against the unkindness of the kind.
Let us fetch some torches and open our door, then we can see what has happened."

Pilgrim indeed opened the door, and as they looked together, they saw in the light of the stars and moon there was truly a white jade-token inlaid with gold placed on the steps. Pa-chieh walked forward and picked it up, saying, "Elder Brother, what is this?" "This is a treasure usually held by a king," said Pilgrim, "and it's called a jade-token. Master, since we do have such a thing, the matter of your dream has to be true. You can depend entirely on old Monkey for catching the fiend tomorrow. But I want you to face three unlucky things." "Fine! Fine! Fine!" said Pa-chieh. "It's enough to have a dream. You have to tell him about it, too! Since when has this fellow

failed to play tricks on people? Now he wants you to face three unlucky things." As he walked back inside, Tripitaka said, "What three
things?" Pilgrim said, "Tomorrow I want you to take the blame, take
abuse, and catch the plague." "Just one of these is bad enough," said
Pa-chieh, laughing. "How could one bear all three of them?" The
T'ang monk, after all, was an intelligent elder. He therefore asked:
"Disciple, can you tell me more about what these three things
involve?" "No need to tell you," said Pilgrim, "but first let me give
you these two objects."

Dear Great Sage! Pulling off one of his hairs, he blew on it a mouthful of divine breath and cried, "Change!" It changed instantly into a
red lacquered box plated in gold. After he placed the white jade-token
inside the box, he said, "Master, in the morning, you should hold this
thing in your hands and put on your brocade cassock. Then go to sit
in the main hall and recite some sūtras. Let me go first to the city to
have a look; if there is indeed a fiend, I'll slay him so that we can
achieve some merit at this place. But if there is no fiend, we ought not
to incur calamity on ourselves." "Exactly! Exactly!" said Tripitaka.
Pilgrim said, "If the prince doesn't leave the city, then there may not
be much that I can do. But if he indeed comes out of the city in
accordance with your dream, I will certainly bring him here to see
you." "What shall I say to him when I see him?" said Tripitaka.
Pilgrim said, "When he arrives, let me first come in and announce
him. You can then pull open slightly the cover of the box, and I shall
change into a tiny monk about two inches tall so that I, too, can be
placed inside the box. You can hold the whole thing in your hands.
When the prince enters the monastery, he will most certainly want to
pay homage to Buddha. Let him bow all he wants, but don't you pay
him any attention. When he sees that you do not even rise before him,
he will surely order you seized. Let him do that—in fact, let him beat
you, tie you up, or execute you." "Hey!" said Tripitaka. "He's someone of high military command. If he truly wants to have me executed,
what shall I do?" "No fear, for I'm around," said Pilgrim. "When you
get to the crucial moment, I'll be there to protect you. If he asks who
you are, you can identify yourself as a monk sent by imperial decree
from the Land of the East to present treasures to Buddha and to
acquire scriptures from him in the Western Heaven. If he asks what
sort of treasure you have, you can tell him about the brocade cassock
of yours. Say to him, however, that that is only a third-class treasure,

and that you have in your possession good things which belong to the first and second classes. When he asks you some more, you can then tell him that there is a treasure in this box, which has knowledge of the past five hundred years, the present five hundred years, and the future five hundred years. All in all, this treasure has complete knowledge of the events of past and future for a period of one thousand five hundred years. Let old Monkey come out then, and I shall tell the prince what you heard in your dream. If he believes me, I'll go catch the demon, so that his father king may be avenged and our reputation may be established at this place. If he doesn't believe me, we can then show him the white jade-token. I fear that he might be a bit young even to recognize the token." When Tripitaka heard these words, he was very pleased, saying, "O Disciple, this is a most marvelous plan! But talk about these treasures, one will be called brocade cassock and the other white jade-token. What shall be the name of that treasure you will change into?" "Let's call him, King-Making Thing," said Pilgrim. Tripitaka agreed and kept these words in his heart. That whole night master and disciples did not, of course, have any sleep. Impatiently waiting for the dawn, they wish they could

By nodding their heads call forth the eastern sun,
And with one breath disperse all Heaven's stars.

In a little while, the eastern sky paled with light. Pilgrim thereupon gave the following instruction to Pa-chieh and Sha Monk: "Don't disturb the monks, so that they won't be milling about in the monastery. When I have accomplished what I must do, then we'll journey again." He took leave of them and somersaulted at once into the air. Opening wide his fiery eyes to look toward the West, he discovered that there was indeed a city. "How could he see it so readily?" you ask. The fact of the matter was that the city, as we told you before, was only forty miles away. So, the moment Pilgrim rose into the air, he saw it immediately.

As Pilgrim drew near the city and stared at it carefully, he saw that it was shrouded by unending layers of eerie mists and battered by constant gusts of demonic wind. Sighing to himself in the air, Pilgrim said,

If a true king ascends his precious throne,
Auspicious light and clouds will this place enfold.
Since a fiend has usurped the dragon seat,
Rising black mist seals up the doors of gold.

He was thus speaking to himself when he heard the loud booms of cannons. As the eastern gate swung open, a troop of men and horses appeared, indeed a hunting corps most fearsome in appearance. You see them:

Leaving the capital at dawn,
They go to hunt on the meadow.
Bright banners unfurl in the sun;
White stallions race against the wind.
The lizard-skin drums roll and roll
As tasseled lances strike in pairs.
The falconers are ferocious,
And whippers-in both mean and strong.
Fire cannons rattle the heavens
And birdlime poles glow in the sun.
Each one props up his arrows;
Every man holds up his carved bows.
They spread their nets beneath the slope
And pull taut the ropes in the paths.
At one crack like a thunderclap,
A thousand steeds charge the leopards and bears.
Tricky hares cannot save their lives;
Wily deer are at their wits' end;
Foxes are fated to expire;
Antelopes perish in the midst.
If pheasants can't fly to escape,
Could wild fowls find refuge from harm?
All of them ransack the mountain range to capture wild beasts,
And cut down the forest to shoot at flying things!

After those people had come out of the city, they spread out in the countryside toward the east, and in a little while they reached the rice fields on the highland some twenty miles away. In the midst of the troops there was a young warrior, who

Wore a helmet
And a cuirass;
A cummerbund, too,
Of eighteen layers.

His hands held a treasure sword of blue steel and he rode a brown war-horse. A fully strung bow also hung from his waist. Truly

He seemed faintly like a king,
A ruler with noble looks.

His features were not uncouth:

Like a true dragon he moved.

Secretly pleased in the air, Pilgrim said to himself, "That one has to be the crown prince. Let me tease him a little." Dear Great Sage! He lowered his cloud and darted straight into the army of the prince. Shaking his body once, he changed instantly into a little white rabbit, scampering about before the prince's horse. When the prince saw it, he could not have been more delighted. Pulling out an arrow, he stretched his bow to the full and shot the rabbit squarely with it.

The Great Sage, of course, had made it possible for the prince to hit him; being quick of hand and eye, he actually had caught the arrow. After dropping some of the arrow's feathers on the ground, he turned and sped away. When the prince saw the arrow had found its mark on the rabbit, he urged his horse on to give chase all by himself. He did not realize that he was being led away deliberately: when the horse galloped, Pilgrim ran like the wind, but when the horse slowed down, Pilgrim also took up a more leisurely pace just to stay slightly ahead of him. Mile after mile it went on like this, until the prince was lured right up to the gate of the Precious Grove Monastery. Changing back into his true form (the rabbit thus disappeared and only the arrow was stuck on the doorpost), Pilgrim raced inside yelling to the T'ang monk, "Master, he's here, he's here!" He changed again, this time into a tiny monk about two inches tall and crawled at once into the red box.

We now tell you about the prince, who chased his prey right up to the monastery gate; he could not find the white rabbit, but he saw an eagle-plumed arrow stuck on the doorpost. Greatly startled and turning pale, the prince said, "Strange! Strange! I clearly shot the white rabbit with my arrow. How could the rabbit disappear, and only the arrow be seen here? It must be that after years and months, the rabbit has turned into a spirit." He pulled out the arrow and raised his head to look: there on top of the gate of the monastery were written seven words in large characters, "Precious Grove Monastery Built by Imperial Command." "Now I know," said the prince. "Years ago my father king, I recall, did send some officials from the Hall of Golden Chimes to take some gold here so that the monks could redecorate the images and the halls. I didn't expect that I would be here today. Truly,

There, in a bamboo-shaded walk,

With a good monk I fell to talk.

So in this tedious mortal round
One afternoon of peace I found.[11]
Let me go inside for a walk.''

Leaping down from the horse, the prince was about to enter the monastery, when those three thousand men and horses who were accompanying him also arrived. As they crowded into the monastery, the resident monks hurriedly came kowtowing to receive them into the main hall so that they could pay homage to the images of Buddha. Afterwards, they raised their eyes to look about, intending to tour the corridors and enjoy the scenery, when they suddenly discovered that there was a monk sitting right in the middle of the hall. Becoming enraged at once, the prince said, "This monk is terribly rude! Half a throne of this dynasty has entered this monastery. Though I have issued no decree for this visit so that he has been spared from meeting us at a great distance, he should now at least get up when soldiers and horses are at the door. How dare he sit there unmoved? Seize him!" He said "Seize," and the guards on both sides immediately attempted to catch hold of the T'ang monk so that they could bind him with ropes. Sitting in the box, Pilgrim recited in silence a spell, saying, "You various Guardians of the Faith, the Six Gods of Darkness and the Six Gods of Light, I am drawing up a plan to subdue a fiend. This prince, ignorant of the matter, is about to have my master bound with ropes. All of you must protect him. If he's really bound, you all will be found guilty." When the Great Sage gave such an order in secret, who would dare disobey him! The deities indeed gave protection to Tripitaka in such a way that those people could not even touch his bald head. It was as if a brick wall had come between them, so that they could not approach him at all.

"Where did you come from, monk," said the prince, "that you dare use this magic of body concealment to mock me?" Tripitaka walked up to him instead and saluted him, saying, "This poor monk does not know any magic of body concealment. I am the T'ang monk from the Land of the East, a priest going to present treasures to Buddha and to acquire scriptures from him in the Western Heaven." The prince said, "Though your Land of the East is actually the central plains, it is incomparably poor. What kind of treasures do you have? You tell me!" "The cassock I have on my body," said Tripitaka, "is a treasure of the third class. But I have in addition those of the first and second classes as well, and they are even better things." "That garment of yours," said the prince, "covers only one side of your body, while your arm sticks out on the other side. How much could it be worth that you dare call it a treasure?" Tripitaka said, "Though this cassock does not completely cover the body, I have several lines of a poem which will reveal its excellence. The poem says:

The Buddha's gown's a half robe, there's no need to say.
It hides within the Real, free of worldly dust.
Countless threads and stitches perfect this right fruit;
Eight treasures and nine pearls fuse with the primal soul.
Maidens divine did make it reverently
To give to a monk to cleanse his sullied frame.
It's all right to see but not to greet the Throne.
But you, your father's wrong unrequited, have lived in vain!"

When the prince heard these words, he grew very angry, saying, "This brazen monk is talking rubbish! Your clever mouth and slippery tongue may boast all you will of that half a piece of garment. But since when have I not requited my father's wrong? You tell me." Taking a step forward, Tripitaka folded his hands and said, "Your Highness, how many favors does a man receive as he lives in this world?" "Four favors," said the prince. "Which four?" said Tripitaka. "The favor of shelter and support provided by Heaven and Earth," said the prince, "the favor of the luminous presence of the sun and the moon, the favor of provisions from the ruler and his land, and the favor of his parent's breeding and nurture." With a smile, Tripitaka said, "The words of Your Highness are not quite right. A man has only the shelter and support of Heaven and Earth, the luminous presence of the sun and the moon, and the provisions from the land of his king. Where does he get his parent's breeding and nurture?" "This monk," said the prince angrily, "is an idle and ungrateful man, who shaves his hair only to commit treason! If a man has no parental breeding and nurture, where does his body come from?" "Your Highness," said Tripitaka, "this humble monk does not know the answer, but inside this red box is a treasure, called the King-Making Thing. He has knowledge of events of the past five hundred years, the present five hundred years, and the future five hundred years. All in all, he knows completely the events of past and future for a period of one thousand five hundred years, and he knows that there is no such favor of parental breeding and nurture. It is he who has ordered your poor monk to wait here for you for a long time."

Hearing this, the prince gave the order: "Bring him here for me to see." Tripitaka pulled open the box's cover; Pilgrim leaped out and began to hobble all over the place. The prince said, "This little midget! What can he know?" When Pilgrim heard this remark about his size, he at once resorted to magic. Straightening up his torso, he grew about three and a half feet instantly. "If he can grow that rapidly," said the soldiers, highly startled, "it will only be a few days before he pierces the sky." When Pilgrim reached his normal height, however, he stopped growing. Then the prince asked him: "King-Making Thing, this old monk claims that you have the knowledge of past and future, of good and evil. Do you divine by the tortoise shell, by the stalks of plants, or do you use books to determine human fortunes?" "None of these," said Pilgrim, "for

I need my three-inch tongue solely,

When I know all things completely."

"This fellow, too, is babbling!" said the prince. "Since the time of antiquity, the book, *I Ching*, of Chou has proved to be supremely marvelous in determining throughout the world good and evil for man to seek or avoid. Therefore tortoise shells or plant stalks are used for divination. But if one relies solely on your words, what evidence is there? Your empty words on luck or misfortune can only vex the minds of people."

Pilgrim said, "Please do not be hasty, Your Highness. You are actually a prince begotten of the King of the Black Rooster Kingdom. Five years ago, you had a severe drought here and all the people were in such great suffering that your king and his subjects had to offer fervent prayers. Though not a drop of rain came, a Taoist arrived from the Chung-nan Mountain, who was an expert in summoning wind and rain and in transforming stone into gold. The king was so fond of him that he became his sworn brother. Is all this true?" "Yes, yes, yes!" said the prince. "Say some more." Pilgrim said, "After three years, the Taoist disappeared, and who is he now who uses the royal 'we'?" The prince said, "There was indeed a Taoist, with whom father king swore to be his brother. In fact, they ate together and rested together. Three years ago when they were enjoying the sights of the imperial garden, the Taoist used a gust of magic wind and transported back to Chung-nan Mountain the gold inlaid white jade-token that father king had in his hands. Even now, however, father king still misses him, and because of his absence, has closed down the garden for three years. But who is now ruling, if not my father king?"

When Pilgrim heard these words, he began to snicker. The prince asked him again, but instead of replying, he only continued to snicker some more. "Why don't you speak when you should?" said the prince angrily. "Why do you snicker like that?" "I still have plenty to say," said Pilgrim, "but there are so many people around and it's not convenient for me to speak up." When the prince saw that there might be some reason for such a statement, he waved his sleeve once to dismiss the soldiers. The captain of the guards immediately gave the order to have the three thousand men and horses stationed outside the monastery gate. The hall was thus nearly emptied of people, with only the prince sitting in the middle, the elder standing before him, and Pilgrim to his left. After even the resident monks retired, then Pilgrim went forward and said to him soberly, "Your Highness, the one who left with the wind is actually your true father, but the one who occupies the throne now is the Taoist who made rain." "Rubbish! Rubbish!" said the prince. "Since the departure of the Taoist, my father has governed so well that the wind and rain are seasonal, the country is prosperous, and the people are secure. But if what you say is true, then the present ruler is not my father king. It's a good thing that I am young and I can be somewhat tolerant. If my father king hears such treasonous words from you, he will have you seized and hewn to pieces." He dismissed Pilgrim with a snort. Turning to the T'ang monk, Pilgrim said, "You see? I said that he wouldn't believe me, and indeed he does not. Take the treasure now and present it to him. After certifying our rescript, we can proceed to the Western Heaven." Tripitaka handed the red box over to Pilgrim, who having received it, shook his body and the box disappeared. It was, you see, actually the transformation of his hair which was retrieved by him. With both hands, Pilgrim presented the white jade-token to the prince.

When he saw the object, the prince shouted, "What a monk! What a monk! You were the Taoist of five years ago who came to cheat our household of this treasure. Now you are disguised as a monk to present it back to us? Seize him!" When he shouted the order like that, the elder was so frightened that he pointed at Pilgrim and said, "You pi-ma-wên! You have a special knack for causing trouble and bringing calamity on me!" "Don't shout!" said Pilgrim, walking up to the prince to stop him. "Don't let this thing leak out. I'm not called

King-Making Thing, for I have a real name." "You come up here!" said the prince angrily. "Answer me with your real name so that I can send you to the bureau of justice to sentence you."

Pilgrim said, "I'm the senior disciple of this elder, and my name is Wu-k'ung Pilgrim Sun. Because my master and I were on our way to acquire scriptures in the Western Heaven, we arrived last night and found lodging here. My master was reading the sūtras in the night, and at about the hour of the third watch, he dreamed that your father appeared to him. Your father claimed that he was harmed by that Taoist, who pushed him into the octagonal well with the marble wall in the imperial garden. The Taoist changed into the form of your father, and this was not known to any of the court officials nor to you since you were so young. You were forbidden to enter the inner palace, and the garden was shut down so that the truth could not be discovered, I suppose. Your father king came specially in the night to ask me to subdue this demon. At first, I was afraid that the murderer was not a demon, but when I surveyed the city in midair, I could see that there was a monster-spirit all right. I was about to seize him when you came out of the city to hunt. The white rabbit which you shot with your arrow happened to be this old Monkey, who led you here to the monastery to see my master. Every word that we have said to you is the truth. If you could recognize this white jade-token, how could you possibly not think of your father's care and love and seek vengeance for him?" When the prince heard these words, he became grief stricken, thinking to himself sorrowfully, "Even if I don't believe him, his words seem to have at least thirty percent truth. But if I believe him, how could I face the father king now in the palace?" This is what we call

To advance or retreat is hard, so the mind asks the mouth;

To think thrice, to have patience—as the mouth asks the mind.

When Pilgrim saw how perplexed he was, he said again, "Your Highness, there's no need for perplexity. Let Your Highness return to your kingdom, and make inquiry of your queen mother. Ask her whether the feelings between her and her husband are the same as three years before. Just this one question will reveal the truth." Persuaded by this, the prince said, "Yes, let me go and inquire of my mother." Leaping up, he took hold of the white jade-token and wanted to leave. Pilgrim, however, tugged at him, saying, "If all these men and horses of yours return with you, someone is bound to leak out information, and it'll

be hard for me to succeed. You must, therefore, go back alone, and
don't make a show of yourself. Don't go through the Central Gate of
the Sun, but enter the palace through the Rear Gate of the Servants.
When you get to see your mother in the palace, you must remember
not to speak loftily or loudly; you must speak quietly and in a subdued
manner. For I fear that the fiend has great magic powers, and if he
ever gets wind of the news, it'll be difficult to preserve the lives of you
and your mother." The prince obeyed this instruction; walking out
the door, he gave this order to the officers; "Stay and camp here.
Don't move. I have something to attend to. When I return, we shall
go back to the city together." Look at him!

He gave the command for the troops to pitch camp,

While he sped to his city on a flying horse.

As he left, we do not know what they have to say when he sees his
mother, and you must listen to the explanation in the next chapter.

*Thirty-eight*

The child, questioning his mother, knows the perverse
   and the true;
Metal and Wood, reaching the deep, see the false
   and the real.

Meeting you I'll speak only of the cause of birth,
You'll then be a member of Ju-lai's[1] assembly.
One calm thought sees Buddha in this realm of dust;
The whole world watches the god who subdues.
If you would know today's true, enlightened lord,
You must ask your own mother of former years.
There's another world which you have never seen,
For each step in life may bring something new.
We were telling you about the prince of the Black Rooster Kingdom,
who, after he took leave of the Great Sage, soon returned to his city.
Indeed he did not approach the gate of the court, nor did he dare
announce his arrival. Going instead to the Rear Gate of the Servants,
he found that it was guarded by several eunuchs. When they saw the
prince approaching, however, they dared not stop him and let him
pass. Dear prince! Pressing his horse, he galloped inside and went
straight up to the Brocade Fragrance Pavilion, in which the queen
was seated, with scores of palace maidens waving their fans on both
sides. The queen, however, was reclining on the carved railings of the
pavilion and shedding tears. "Why was she shedding tears?" you ask.
For at the hour of the fourth watch, you see, she, too, had a dream,
but she could remember only half of it. She was trying very hard to
recall the other half when the prince dismounted and knelt beneath
the pavilion, saying, "Mother!" Forcing herself to appear delighted,
the queen cried out: "Son, what joy! What joy! For these two or three
years, you have been staying in the front palace to study with your
father king and I have not been able to see you. How I have thought
of you! How is it that you have the leisure today to come see me
instead? This is truly my greatest joy, my greatest joy! O son, why do
you sound so sad? Your father king, after all, is getting on in his
years. There will be a day when the dragon returns to the jade-green

sea and the phoenix will go back to the scarlet heavens. You will then inherit the throne. What could there possibly be to make you unhappy?" The prince kowtowed before he said, "Mother, permit me to ask you: who is he that is on the throne now? Who is the man who uses the royal 'we'?" When the queen heard this, she said, "This child is getting mad! The one who is ruling is your father king. Why do you ask such questions?" Again kowtowing, the prince said, "I beseech my mother to grant her son a pardon first. Only then would I dare present a further question. If you do not, I'll dare not ask." "Between mother and son," said the queen, "how could there be any criminal offense? Of course, I'll pardon you. Speak up, quickly!" The prince said, "Let me ask you this: are your relations with your husband just as warm and intimate as three years before?"

When the queen heard this question, her spirit left her and her soul fled. She dashed out of the pavilion and embraced the prince tightly as tears fell from her eyes. "My child," she said, "I haven't seen you for such a long time. Why do you come to the palace today and ask this question?" "Mother," said the prince, growing angry. "If you have something to say, say it. If you don't speak up, you might jeopardize a very important affair." Only then did the queen dismiss all her attendants and spoke, quietly weeping, "This matter, if you, son, did not ask me, would never have come to light even when I reached the Nine Springs[2] down below. Since you have asked me, listen to what I have to say:

Three years ago he was loving and warm;
For three years now he has been icy cold.
By the pillows I've pressed him long and hard;
He said, 'I'm weak, I'm feeble, I'm growing old!'"

When the prince heard these words, he at once struggled free and mounted his horse once more. Clutching at him desperately, the queen said, "Child, what are you doing? Why do you leave before we finish speaking?" Again the prince knelt on the ground and said, "Mother, I dare not speak, though I must! During the time of the early court this morning, I went out by imperial decree to hunt with falcons and dogs. By chance I met a sage monk sent by the Throne in the Land of the East to fetch scriptures. He has under him a senior disciple by the name of Pilgrim Sun, who is an expert in the subjugation of fiends. I was told that my real father king had been murdered in the imperial garden; he died, in fact, in the well with the octagonal marble walls. It was the Taoist, who falsely changed into the form of father king and usurped his dragon seat. Last night, father king appeared to the monk in a dream and asked him to send his disciple to the city to catch this fiend. Your child did not dare believe them completely and that was why I came specially to question you. Now that mother has spoken like this, I know that there must be a monster-spirit here." "O son," said the queen, "how could you take the words of some stranger outside as the truth?" The prince said, "I did not, but father king left them a sign." When the queen asked what sort of sign it was, the prince took out that white jade-token inlaid with gold and handed it to her. Recognizing at once it was a treasure which had belonged to the king, the queen could not hold back the torrents of tears. "My lord!" she cried. "How could you not come to see me first, if you had been dead for three years? How could you go to see the sage monk first, and then the prince afterwards?" "Mother," said the prince, "what are you saying?" The queen said, "My child, I also had a dream last night at about the hour of the fourth watch. I dreamed that your father king stood before me dripping wet, and he told me himself that he was dead. His spirit, he said, had gone to plead with the T'ang monk to subdue the specious king and to save his former body. I clearly recall these words, but there is another half of the dream which I just cannot remember. I was speculating just now by myself when you arrived with your questions and this treasure. Let me put away the jade-token for the moment. You should go and ask the sage monk to do what he must do quickly, so that the demonic miasma may be dispelled and the perverse and true can be distinguished. That's the way you can repay your father king's kindness in rearing you."

Swiftly mounting his horse, the prince went out of the Rear Gate of the Servants and slipped away from the city. Truly

Holding back his tears, he kowtowed to leave the queen;
In grief he went to bow again to the T'ang monk.

In a little while, he was out of the city gate and went straight to the gate of the Precious Grove Monastery, where he dismounted. As the soldiers came to receive him, the sun began to set. The prince gave the order for the soldiers to remain where they were stationed. Again by himself, he walked inside after straightening out his clothes to solicit Pilgrim's assistance. Just then the Monkey King swaggered out from the main hall, and the prince at once went to his knees, saying,

"Master, I've returned." Pilgrim went forward to raise him, saying, "Please rise. Did you ask anyone when you reached the city?" "I did," said the prince, and he gave a complete account of the conversation with his mother. Smiling gently, Pilgrim said, "If he is that cold, he must be the transformation of some kind of cold-blooded creature. Don't worry! Don't worry! Let old Monkey get rid of him for you. But it's getting late now, and I can't move. You go back first, and I'll arrive tomorrow morning." Kowtowing repeatedly, the prince said, "Master, I'll stay here to wait upon you until tomorrow, and then I can travel with you." "That's no good," said Pilgrim. "If we enter the city together, the fiend would become suspicious; instead of a chance meeting, he'll think that you have gone somewhere especially to fetch me. The whole arrangement will make him blame you, will it not?" "Even if I go back now," said the prince, "he will still blame me." "Why?" said Pilgrim. The prince said, "I was commanded during the early court to lead this number of men and horses, of falcons and dogs, to leave the city. But when I go back today, I have no game to present to the throne. If he accuses me of being incapable and has me jailed in Yu-li,³ whom would you rely on when you enter the city in the morning? There is no one, after all, in the ranks who knows about this." "That's nothing!" said Pilgrim. "You should have told me earlier about this, and I'd have found some game."

Dear Great Sage! Look at the way he shows off before the prince! With a bound he leaped straight up to the clouds, made the magic sign, and recited the spell, Let *Oṃ* and *Ram* purify the Dharma-realm,⁴ which summoned a mountain god and a local spirit, they arrived and bowed to him in midair, saying, "Great Sage, what is your wish when you command these humble deities to appear?" Pilgrim said, "Old Monkey arrives here in the company of the T'ang monk, and he now intends to catch a wicked demon. Unfortunately, the prince did not catch any game during the hunt and he dared not return to the court. I am, therefore, going to ask you for a small favor. Please find for us some fallow deer, antelopes, wild hares, and fowls—a few pieces of each kind—so that we can send him off." Not daring to disobey when they heard this instruction, the mountain god and the local spirit inquired as to how many heads of wild game were needed. "It doesn't matter," said the Great Sage, "just bring us some." The two deities, leading the demon soldiers under their command, called up a strong gust of dark wind to round up the wild animals. They caught some grouse and pheasants; horned deer and fat fallow deer; foxes, badgers, and hares; tigers, leopards, and wolves—all in all, several hundred of these which they brought before Pilgrim. Pilgrim said, "Old Monkey has no need of these. Pull out their leg tendons and place them on both sides of the forty-mile road leading back to the city. Those people will then be able to take them back without having to use falcons and dogs, and this will be counted as your merit." The deities obeyed; calming the dark wind, they placed the game beside the road.

Pilgrim dropped down from the clouds and said to the prince, "Your Highness, please go back. There is game on the road which you may collect." After having seen the kind of power Pilgrim displayed on top of the clouds, the prince had no doubts whatever. He kowtowed to take leave of Pilgrim before walking out of the monastery gate to order the soldiers to return to the city. As they journeyed, they found indeed a large number of wild game laid out on both sides of the road. Without releasing falcons and dogs, the soldiers caught them by merely lifting their hands. All of them, therefore, shouted bravos and congratulated the prince, saying that it was his great luck that brought them the game, but not knowing, of course, that it was the might of old Monkey. Listen to their songs of triumph as they proceeded back to the city!

Pilgrim, meanwhile, returned to protect Tripitaka. When those monks in the monastery saw how intimate the pilgrims had become with the prince, how could they dare not be reverent? They again prepared a vegetarian meal to serve to the T'ang monk, who then rested once more in the Zen hall. By about the hour of the first watch, Pilgrim, who had something on his mind, was unable to fall asleep. Rolling off his bed, he dashed up to the T'ang monk and cried, "Master." The elder at this time actually was not yet asleep, but knowing that Pilgrim could be rather restless and frenetic, he pretended that he was and did not respond. Pilgrim caught hold of his bald head and started to shake it violently, crying, "Master, how is it that you are already asleep?" "You rascal!" said the T'ang monk, growing angry. "You aren't going to sleep at this hour? What are you clamoring for?" "Master," said Pilgrim, "I have a little matter that I want to discuss with you." "What matter?" said the elder. Pilgrim said, "During the day I boasted to the prince that my abilities were higher than a mountain and greater than an ocean. To catch that monster-spirit, I said, was as easy as reaching for something in my pocket—all I had to do was to stretch forth my hand and take it. Now I can't sleep, and when I think about the matter, I find that there's some difficulty." "If you say that it's going to be difficult," said the T'ang monk, "then let's not try to catch him." "We still have to," said Pilgrim, "but we cannot justify our action." The T'ang monk said, "This ape is babbling again! The monster-spirit has usurped the throne of a ruler. What do you mean that we cannot justify our action?" Pilgrim said, "Your venerable self only knows how to recite sūtras and worship Buddha, how to sit and meditate. Since when have you ever seen the legal principles established by Hsiao Ho?[5] The proverb says, 'If you arrest a thief, you must seize him with the stolen goods.' That fiend has been a king for three years, but he has not permitted his secret to leak out in any way. He has slept with the ladies of the three palaces, and he has ruled amiably with his two rows of civil and military officials. Even if old Monkey has the ability to arrest him, it will not be easy to convict him of his crime." "Why not?" said the T'ang monk. Pilgrim said, "Even if he is a mouthless gourd, he will have a row with you for a while. Can't you hear him? 'I'm the king of the Black Rooster Kingdom. What offense against Heaven have I committed that you dare come to arrest me?' What evidence do I have with which I can argue with him?" "What do you plan to do, then?" said the T'ang monk.

With a chuckle, Pilgrim said, "The plan of old Monkey is already made, but one obstacle I have to face right now is that you, Dear Sir, have a tendency to dote on people." "What do you mean?" said the T'ang monk. Pilgrim said, "Pa-chieh is rather stupid, but you are somewhat partial to him." "How am I partial to him?" said the T'ang monk. "If you are not," said Pilgrim, "then you should try to be more courageous and stay here with Sha Monk. Let old Monkey and Pa-chieh take this opportunity now to go into the Black Rooster Kingdom first and find the imperial garden. We will break open the marble well and fish out the corpse of the true king which we will wrap in our bags. When we enter the city tomorrow, we won't bother with having our rescript certified; as soon as we see the fiend, I'll attack him with my rod. If he has anything to say, we'll show him the skeleton and tell him: 'You killed this man!' We can tell the prince to come out and mourn his father, the queen to give recognition to her husband, and the various officials to see their true lord. Old Monkey and the brothers, meanwhile, can lift our hands to fight. Now, that's what I

call a worthwhile litigation because there's something we can go on!"
Secretly pleased by what he heard, the T'ang monk said nevertheless,
"My only fear is that Pa-chieh is unwilling to go with you." "You
see!" said Pilgrim, laughing. "I told you that you doted on him! How
did you know that he would be unwilling to go? Perhaps you think
that he'll be like you when I called you just now, and after half an
hour, I would give up. But watch me! If you let me go near him, I'll
use only my healthy, three-inch tongue to persuade him. Never mind
that he is Chu Pa-chieh; even if he were Chu Chiu-chieh,[6] I would
have the ability to make him go with me." "All right," said the T'ang
monk, "you may go and rouse him."

Walking away from his master, Pilgrim went straight up to the side
of Pa-chieh's bed and shouted, "Pa-chieh! Pa-chieh!" Idiot, after all,
was a man overcome by travel fatigue: once he put his head down,
he snored so hard that nothing could wake him. Pilgrim finally
grabbed his ears and took hold of his bristles; giving a terrific pull, he
yanked Pa-chieh right up while shouting, "Pa-chieh!" Idiot was still
shuddering when Pilgrim hollered again. Idiot said, "Let's sleep!
Don't play around! We have to travel tomorrow." "I'm not playing,"
said Pilgrim. "There's some business that you and I have to attend
to." "What business?" said Pa-chieh. Pilgrim said, "Did you happen
to hear what the prince said?" "I haven't even seen him," said Pa-
chieh, "I haven't heard what he had to say." "The prince told me,"
said Pilgrim, "that that monster-spirit had in his possession a treasure
that could overwhelm ten thousand warriors. When we enter the city
tomorrow, we can't avoid doing battle with him; but if that fiend
brings out his treasure and defeats us, that won't be good. So, I
thought that if we couldn't vanquish him, we should do something
first. You and I, in fact, should go and steal his treasure. Isn't that
much better?" "Elder Brother," said Pa-chieh, "you are trying to persuade me to be a thief! Well, I know this sort of business, so I can be
your customer. But let me say this to you clearly first: when we have
stolen the treasure and subdued the monster-spirit, I won't put up
with this niggardly practice of dividing the loot. I'm going to keep the
treasure." "What for?" said Pilgrim. "I'm not eloquent like all of
you," said Pa-chieh, "and it's not easy for me to beg for food. This
body of old Hog is sluggish, and his words are dull. Moreover, I can't
even recite sūtras. When I get to those wild, uninhabited places, I
have hopes that I can exchange the treasure for food." Pilgrim said,
"Old Monkey is only concerned with acquiring a reputation, not a

treasure. Of course, I'll give it to you." When Idiot heard that it was to be given to him, he was delighted and scrambled up at once. Climbing into his clothes, he left with Pilgrim. Truly as the saying goes:

Even clear wine reddens a man's face,

And yellow gold moves the mind of Tao.

The two of them opened the door stealthily and slipped away from Tripitaka; mounting the auspicious luminosity, they headed straight for the city.

In a little while, they reached their destination; as they lowered their clouds, they heard the sound of the second watch struck from a tower. "Brother," said Pilgrim, "it's the second watch." "Just right!" said Pa-chieh. "Everybody is sleeping soundly inside." Instead of heading for the Central Gate of the Sun, the two of them went to the Rear Gate of the Servants, where they heard also the sound of the rattle struck by guards on patrol. "Brother," said Pilgrim, "the front and rear gates are all tightly guarded. How can we get in?" Pa-chieh said, "Have you ever seen a thief walking through a door? Let's just jump over the wall." Pilgrim agreed and leaped at once onto the palace wall, followed by Pa-chieh. Sneaking inside, the two of them searched for their way to the imperial garden.

As they walked along, they came upon a towered gate with triple eaves and flying white banners. Painted on top of the gate were three large words that were luminescent in the light of the stars and moon: "The Imperial Garden." When Pilgrim drew near and saw that the gate was locked and sealed with several layers of crossed strips of paper, he told Pa-chieh to go to work. Idiot lifted up his iron rake and brought it down on the gate as hard as he could: the gate was pulverized at once. Pilgrim led the way to enter the garden, but no sooner had he stepped inside when he began to jump up and down, whooping and shouting. Pa-chieh was so startled that he ran forward to tug at him, saying, "Elder Brother, you scare me to death! I have never seen a thief bellowing like that! If you wake up the people and they catch us and send us to court, even if we are not executed we would be banished to our native province for military service." "Brother," said Pilgrim, "you may wonder why I'm making such a fuss. Just look at those

Carved and painted railings in ruin;

Bejeweled sheds and towers crumbling;

Banks of sedges and smart-weeds all buried in dirt;

Peonia and *t'u-mi*[7] both wilted.
The scent of jasmines and roses is slight;
Tree-peonias and lilies bloom vainly.
Hibiscus, a few kinds, give way to bushes and shrubs;
Rare flowers and plants all perish.
Artificial rock mountains collapse;
Ponds dry up and fishes decline.
Green pines, purple bamboos—they're like dried firewood;
Wormwood and artemisia grow rank on the paths.
From cassia and peach trees branches break off;
The roots of pear and plum trees are upturned.
There is green moss on the bridge-head's winding path:
Such, the scene of this garden desolate!"

"Why waste your breath in this lamentation?" said Pa-chieh. "Let's go finish our business quickly." Though Pilgrim was saddened by what he saw, he also thought of the dream of the T'ang monk, when he was told that the well could be found only beneath a plantain tree. As they walked along, they saw indeed such a tree, whose luxuriant growth was quite different from the other plants. Truly she is

A fine, spiritual root of a kind,
Her empty self's[8] Heaven-endowed.
Every branch is thin like paper;
Every leaf can fold like a petal;
A thousand fine strands of green
Enclose one cinnabar heart within.
She grieves when saddened by night rain
And droops for fear of autumn's wind.
She grows in the primal strength of Heav'n;
Her nurture's the work of Creation.
A parchment forms her wondrous usage;
As a fan she makes rare merit.
How could phoenix plumes approximate her?
Could e'en phoenix tails resemble her?
Bathed in droplets of light dew,
Swathed in slender wisps of smoke,
Her green shade shrouds windows and doors;
Her green shadow mounts curtains and screens.
Wild geese aren't allowed to perch here,
Nor may horses be ticd to her.

A frigid sky will make her dejected,
A moonlit night her colors faint.
She can only dispel high heat
And protects from the scorching sun.
Bashful for lacking the peach and pear's charm,
She stands alone east of the white wall.

"Pa-chieh," said Pilgrim, "let's get started. The treasure's buried beneath the plantain tree." Idiot lifted his rake with both hands and toppled the plantain tree, after which he used his snout to burrow into the ground. After digging up some three or four feet of dirt, he discovered a slab of stone. Delighted, Idiot said, "Elder Brother, we're lucky! There's indeed a treasure here, covered by a slab of stone. I wonder if it's contained in a jar or a box." "Lift the stone up and take a look," said Pilgrim. Idiot indeed used his snout to give the slab of stone a shove; immediately, glimmering shafts of light shot up. Laughing, Pa-chieh said, "Lucky! Lucky! The treasure's glowing." He went forward to take another careful look and saw that it was actually the glow of the stars and moon reflected in the water of a well. "Elder Brother," said Pa-chieh, "when you want to do something, you ought to get to the bottom of it." "How so?" said Pilgrim. Pa-chieh said, "This is a well. If you had told me in the monastery that the treasure would be found in a well, I would have brought along those two ropes we use to tie our bags. Then we would have been able to find a way to lower old Hog down there. Now we're empty-handed. How could we go down there to fetch the thing up here?" "You want to go down there?" said Pilgrim. "Of course," said Pa-chieh, "but we have no ropes." "Take off your clothes," said Pilgrim, "and I'll give you the means." Pa-chieh said, "I don't have any good clothes! All I have to do is untie this shirt."

Dear Great Sage! He took out his golden-hooped rod and gave both its ends a pull, crying, "Grow!" It grew to about seventy or eighty feet long. "Pa-chieh," he said, "you grab hold of one end, and I'll let you down the well." "Elder Brother," said Pa-chieh, "you can do that, but when we reach the surface of the water, you stop." "I know," said Pilgrim. Idiot then wrapped himself around the rod at one end, and with no effort at all Pilgrim picked him up and lowered him into the well. In a little while, they reached the edge of the water and Pa-chieh said, "We're touching water." When Pilgrim heard that, he gave the rod a plunge downward and with a loud splash Idiot fell into the water headfirst. Abandoning the iron rod, he began at once to tread water, muttering to himself: "Damn him! I told him to stop when we reached water, but he gave me a plunge instead." Pilgrim retrieved his rod and said, laughing, "Brother, is there any treasure?" "What treasure?" said Pa-chieh, "only a well of water!" Pilgrim said, "The treasure has sunk deep into the water. Why don't you go below and feel around." Idiot indeed knew well the nature of water; he ducked his head under the surface and dove straight down. Ah, the well was extremely deep! He plunged hard a second time before opening his eyes to look around, and he saw all at once a towered edifice, on which were written the three words, "Water Crystal Palace." Highly shaken, Pa-chieh said, "Undone! Undone! I got on the wrong way. I must have fallen into the ocean, for only the ocean has a Water Crystal Palace. How could there be one in a well?" Pa-chieh, you see, did not know that this happened to be the palace of the Well Dragon King.

As Pa-chieh was speaking to himself, a yakṣa on patrol opened the gate of the palace. When he saw what he saw, he ran inside to report, saying, "Great King, disaster! From the well above fell a monk with a long snout and huge ears, stark naked and without a stitch of clothing. He isn't dead yet, and he is talking." When the Well Dragon King heard this, he was greatly startled. "This must be the Marshal of Heavenly Reeds. Last night the Night Patrol God came here by imperial decree from above to take the soul of the king of the Black Rooster Kingdom to see the T'ang monk. They were to ask the Great Sage, Equal to Heaven, to subdue a fiend. This has to be the Great Sage and the Marshal of Heavenly Reeds. We should not treat them rudely. Hurry, we must welcome them."

Straightening out his clothes, the dragon king led his water kinsmen out the door and cried in a loud voice: "Marshal of Heavenly Reeds, please take a seat inside." Pa-chieh became very pleased and said to himself, "So there's a friend here!" Without regard for etiquette or decency, Idiot walked right into the Water Crystal Palace and, still stark naked, took the honored seat above. "Marshal," said the dragon king, "I heard recently that your life was spared when you embraced the Buddhist faith to accompany the T'ang monk to acquire scriptures in the Western Heaven. For what reason have you come here?" "I was just about to tell you that," said Pa-chieh. "My elder brother, Sun

Wu-k'ung wanted to send you his most earnest greetings. He told me to come to ask you for a certain treasure." "That's pitiful!" said the dragon king. "Where do I have any treasure around here? I'm not like those other dragon kings of such big rivers as the Yang-tzu, the Yellow River, the Huai, and the Chi. When they can fly and soar through the air most of the time to transform, they will have treasures. I have been stuck here for a long time; I can't even get to see the sun and the moon regularly. Where would I get any treasures?" "Don't refuse me," said Pa-chieh. "If you have any, bring them out." "I do have just one treasure," said the dragon king, "but I can't bring it out. The Marshal himself will have to go and take a look. How about it?" "Wonderful! Wonderful! Wonderful!" said Pa-chieh. "I'll go and take a look."

The dragon king walked in front, while Idiot followed. They passed the Water Crystal Palace and came upon a long corridor, inside of which they found lying there a six-foot corpse. Pointing with his finger, the dragon king said, "Marshal, that's the treasure." Pa-chieh went forward to look at it. Ah, it was actually a dead king; still wearing a rising-to-Heaven cap, a reddish brown robe, a pair of carefree boots, and a jade belt, he lay there stiff as a board. "Hard! Hard! Hard!" said Pa-chieh, chuckling. "This can't be considered a treasure! When I recall the time when old Hog was a monster in the mountain, this thing was frequently used as food. Don't ask me how many such things I have seen—even as far as eating was concerned, I have consumed countless numbers. How could you call this a treasure?" "So you don't know, Marshal," said the dragon king, "that he is actually the corpse of the king of the Black Rooster Kingdom. Since he reached the well, I have embalmed him with a feature-preserving pearl so that he won't deteriorate. If you are willing to carry him out of here on your back to see the Great Sage, Equal to Heaven, who, by the way, may have the wish to revive him, don't speak of treasures—you can have anything you want." "In that case," said Pa-chieh, "I'll carry him out on my back for you. But how much cartage are you going to pay me?" The dragon king said, "I don't have any money." "You want to use people free!" said Pa-chieh. "If you really don't have any money, I won't carry him." "If you don't," said the dragon king, "please go." Pa-chieh left at once. The dragon king, however, ordered two powerful yakṣas to haul the corpse out of the Water Crystal Palace's gate. They threw him down, took off the water-repelling pearl, and water began to close in on all sides noisily.

Turning around quickly to look, Pa-chieh could no longer see the gate of the Water Crystal Palace. When he stretched out his hands, all he could lay hold of was the corpse of the king, the touch of which made his legs weaken and his tendons turn numb with fear. He darted up to the surface of the water; with his hands clinging to the wall of the well, he shouted, "Elder Brother, stick your rod down here to save me!" "Is there any treasure?" said Pilgrim. Pa-chieh said, "There isn't any! Beneath the water, however, there's a Well Dragon King, who told me to carry a dead man on my back. I wouldn't do it, and he sent me out the door; that was when his Water Crystal Palace disappeared also. When I felt that corpse, I was so scared that my hands grew weak and my tendons turned numb; I could hardly move. Elder Brother, for good or ill please save me." "That's precisely the treasure," said Pilgrim. "Why won't you carry him up here?" Pa-chieh said, "He must have been dead for quite a while. Why should I carry him on my back?" "If you won't," said Pilgrim, "I'll go back." "Where?" said Pa-chieh. "I'm going back to the monastery," said Pilgrim, "to get some sleep with Master." "You mean I can't go with you?" said Pa-chieh. Pilgrim said, "If you can climb up here, I'll take you back with me; if you can't, well that's it!" Pa-chieh was horrified, for how could he possibly climb up the well. "Take a look," he yelled. "Even the city wall was hard to scale already, whereas this well is large down below with a small mouth on top. All around the circular wall is straight up and down. Moreover, it has been such a long time since anyone has bailed water from this well that it's covered with moss everywhere. It's terribly slippery. How could I possibly climb it? Elder Brother, let's not upset our fraternal feelings, let me go and carry him up on my back." "Exactly," said Pilgrim. "Do it quickly, and I'll go back with you to sleep." Idiot put his head under water again and dove straight down; after he found the corpse, he pulled it onto his back and shot back up to the surface. Supporting himself on the wall of the well, he cried, "Elder Brother, I'm carrying him." Pilgrim stared into the well and saw that the body was indeed placed on Pa-chieh's back. Only then did he lower the golden-hooped rod into the well. A man who had been sorely tried, Idiot opened his mouth and held on to the tip of the iron rod with his teeth; he was then lifted up out of the well by Pilgrim with no effort at all.

Putting down the corpse, Pa-chieh grabbed his own clothes and put them on. When Pilgrim took a look, he found that the features of the dead king had not altered in the slightest—it was as if he were still alive. "Brother," said Pilgrim, "this man has been dead for three years. How could his features not deteriorate?" "You have no idea about this," said Pa-chieh. "This Well Dragon said to me that he had embalmed the corpse with a feature-preserving pearl, and that's why it has not deteriorated." "Lucky! Lucky!" said Pilgrim. "This has to mean that his wrong has yet to be requited, and that we are fated to succeed. Brother, put him on your back quickly again and we'll leave." "Where do you want me to carry him?" said Pa-chieh. "To see Master," said Pilgrim. Pa-chieh began to grumble, saying, "How am I going to live with this? I was sleeping nicely when this monkey fooled me with his clever talk into doing this so-called business with him. It turns out to be this sort of enterprise—carrying a dead man on my back! When I carry him, some putrid stinking fluid is bound to drip on me and soil my clothes, and there is no one ready to wash and starch them for me. The few patches on my garment may even turn damp again when the sky is grey. How can I wear them?" "Look, you just carry him," said Pilgrim, "and when we get to the monastery, I'll exchange clothes with you." "Aren't you ashamed of yourself?" said Pa-chieh. "You have hardly anything to wear, and you are going to exchange clothes with me?" Pilgrim said, "Oh, you are so smart mouthed! You aren't going to carry him?" "No!" said Pa-chieh. "Stick out your shanks then," said Pilgrim, "and I'll give you twenty strokes of my rod!" Horrified, Pa-chieh said, "Elder Brother, that's a heavy rod! If you give me twenty strokes, I'll be like this king!" "If you are afraid of being beaten," said Pilgrim, "then hurry up and put him on your back so that we can leave." Pa-chieh indeed was afraid of being beaten; rather listlessly, he yanked the corpse over and put it on his back before turning to walk out of the garden.

Dear Great Sage! Making the magic sign with his fingers, he recited a spell and sucked in a mouthful of air facing the ground in the southwest. When he blew it out, a violent gust immediately arose and lifted Pa-chieh out of the palace. They left the city instantly; as the wind subsided, the two of them dropped to the ground and proceeded slowly on foot. Nursing his rage in silence, Idiot planned to repay Pilgrim in kind, saying to himself, "This monkey has pulled a nice prank on me, but when I get to the monastery I'm going to pull one on him, too. I'm going to persuade Master to insist on restoring the king back to life. If that monkey can't do it, I'll make Master recite that

Tight-Fillet Spell until this monkey's brains burst. That will give me
some relief!" He walked along and thought further to himself: "No
good, no good! If you make him heal the man, all he has to do is to go
and ask King Yama for the soul, and the man will live again. I must
set the conditions so that he won't be permitted to go to the Region
of Darkness; the king has to be restored to life through some means
found in the World of Light. Only such a plan is good."

Hardly had he finished speaking to himself when they reached the
gate of the monastery. Pa-chieh walked right through it and went up
to the door of the Zen hall, where he threw down the corpse and cried,
"Master, get up and look at this." Unable to sleep, Tripitaka was just
chatting with Sha Monk on how Pilgrim had deceived Pa-chieh into
going with him, and how they did not return after such a long time.
When he heard the call, the T'ang monk quickly arose and said,
"Disciple, what do you want me to look at?" "The grandpa of Pilgrim,"
said Pa-chieh, "whom old Hog has brought back on his back." "You
pie-eyed Idiot!" said Pilgrim. "Where do I have a grandpa?" "Elder
Brother," said Pa-chieh, "if he isn't your grandpa, why did you ask old
Hog to bear him here? You don't know how much energy I've
wasted!"

The T'ang monk and Sha Monk opened the door to look, and they
discovered that the countenance of the king had not altered at all.
Turning sad all at once, the elder said, "Your Majesty, in which
previous existence did you incur an enemy who had to catch up with
you in this one and cause you to lose your life? Alas, you left your
wife and your child, unknown to all the civil and military officials!
Pity your wife who's still in the dark! Who will burn incense or pour
tea for you?" He was so broken up that he could not speak anymore
as tears rained down his cheeks. "Master," said Pa-chieh, laughing,
"what does his death have to do with you? He isn't one of your
ancestors. Why weep for him?" "O disciple!" said the T'ang monk,
"the fundamental principle of life for those who have left the family is
compassion. How could you be so hardhearted?" "I'm not hardhearted," said Pa-chieh, "for Elder Brother told me that he could
restore him to life. If he couldn't, I wouldn't have carried him back
here." This elder, after all, had a head full of water! Shaken by these
few words of Idiot, he said at once: "Wu-k'ung, if you indeed have the
ability to restore this king to life, you would have accomplished something greater than building a seven-storeyed stūpa. And even we

would have been benefited as if we had worshipped Buddha in the Spirit Mountain." Pilgrim said, "Master, how could you believe the nonsense of this Idiot! When a man dies, he can pass through the periods of three times seven or five times seven; at most, he may wait for seven hundred days, when after having suffered for all the sins committed in the World of Light, he will proceed then to the next incarnation. This man here died three years ago. How could I save him?" When Tripitaka heard these words, he said, "Oh, all right!" Still bitterly resentful, however, Pa-chieh said, "Master, don't believe him. He's a little sick in his brain! Just recite that little something of yours, and you are certain to get a living man." The T'ang monk indeed began to recite the Tight-Fillet Spell, and the monkey had such a headache that his eyes bulged. We do not know how he managed to heal the dead king, and you must listen to the explanation in the next chapter.

*Thirty-nine*

One pellet of cinnabar elixir found in Heaven;

A king, dead three years, lives again on Earth.

We were telling you about the Great Sage Sun, who could hardly bear his headache. "Master," he pleaded pitifully, "stop reciting! Stop reciting! Let me try to heal him." "How?" asked the elder. Pilgrim said, "All I need to do is to go to the Region of Darkness and find out in which of the Ten Kings' chambers his soul is residing. I'll fetch it and he'll be saved." "Master, don't believe him," said Pa-chieh. "He told me originally that he needn't go to the Region of Darkness, that his real ability could not be seen unless a cure was found in the World of Light." Believing in such perverse tattle, the elder began to recite the Tight-Fillet Spell once more. Pilgrim was so horrified that he had to say repeatedly, "I'll find some means in the World of Light! I'll find some means in the World of Light!" "Don't stop," said Pa-chieh, "just keep reciting!" "You idiotic cursed beast!" chided Pilgrim. "You are just trying to coax Master into putting that spell on me!" Laughing until he nearly collapsed, Pa-chieh said, "O Elder Brother! You only know how to pull tricks on me, but you don't realize that I can do the same on you." "Master, please stop," said Pilgrim, "and let old Monkey find a cure in the World of Light for the king." "Where would you find it in the World of Light?" said Tripitaka. "With a single cloud-somersault," said Pilgrim, "I shall penetrate the South Heavenly Gate, but I'll not go into the Big Dipper Palace nor into the Divine Mists Hall. Instead, I shall go straight up to the Thirty-third Heaven, to the Tushita Palace of the Griefless Heaven. When I see Lao Tzu there, I shall beg him for one pellet of his Soul-Restoring Elixir of Nine Turns, which will certainly make this man live again."

When Tripitaka heard these words, he was very pleased and said, "Go quickly and come back." "It's about the hour of the third watch at this moment," said Pilgrim, "but by the time I get back, it'll be dawn. The trouble with this man sleeping here like that is that the whole atmosphere seems so dull and heartless. Someone here should mourn him and that'll be more like it." "It goes without saying," said Pa-chieh, "that this monkey would like me to mourn the king." "Yes, but I'm afraid that you won't," said Pilgrim. "If you won't, I can't heal him either!" "Elder Brother," said Pa-chieh, "you may go. I'll mourn him." Pilgrim said, "There are several ways of mourning: when you merely open your mouth to make noises, that's called howling; when you squeeze out some tears, that's weeping. When you mourn with both tears and feelings, then we may call that wailing." "I'll give you an example of how I can wail!" said Pa-chieh, who pulled out a scrap of paper from somewhere and rolled it into a thin strip, which he stuck into his nostrils twice. Look at him! After sneezing a few times, tears and snivel all came out and he began to wail, mumbling and muttering protests all the time as if someone in his family had actually died. He bawled lustily, and when his passion rose to a terrific pitch, even the T'ang elder was moved to tears. "That's the sort of grief I want you to show," said Pilgrim with a laugh, "and you are not permitted to stop. For if you, Idiot, think that you can quit mourning after I leave, you are mistaken, for I can still hear you. You'll be all right if you keep this up, but the moment I discover that your voice has stopped, your shanks will be given twenty strokes." "You go!" said Pa-chieh, chuckling. "Once I start to mourn, it will take me a couple of days to finish." When Sha Monk heard how stern Pilgrim's reprimand of Pa-chieh was, he went and lit a few sticks of incense to bring to offer to the dead king. "Fine! Fine! Fine!" said Pilgrim, laughing. "When the whole family shows reverence like that, old Monkey can then exert his efforts."

Dear Great Sage! At this hour of midnight, he took leave of master and disciples, the three of them; mounting the cloud-somersault, he entered at once the South Heavenly Gate. Indeed, he did not go before the Treasure Hall of Divine Mists, nor did he ascend to the Big Dipper Palace. Treading on his cloudy luminosity, he went straight to the Griefless Heaven, the Tushita Palace of the Thirty-third Heaven. The moment he walked inside the door, he discovered Lao Tzu sitting in the elixir chamber: in the process of making elixir, he and a few divine youths were tending the fires with plantain fans. When he saw Pilgrim approaching, he immediately instructed the youths with these words: "Take care, each of you. The thief who once stole our elixir is here." Bowing to him, Pilgrim said with laughter, "Venerable Sir, don't be so silly! Why take such precaution against me? I don't do those things anymore!" "Monkey," said Lao Tzu, "when you caused great disruption in Heaven five hundred years ago, you stole and consumed countless efficacious elixirs of mine. And when we sent the Little Sage Erh-lang to arrest you and bring you to the Region Above, you were sent to be refined in my elixir brazier for forty-nine days and made me squander who knows how much charcoal. You were lucky to have regained your freedom when you embraced the Buddhist fruit and resolved to accompany the T'ang monk to the Western Heaven to acquire scriptures. But even then, you were still giving me a hard time when I asked you for my treasures after you had subdued the demons some time ago on the Level-Top Mountain. What are you doing here today?" "I didn't give you a hard time," said Pilgrim. "Old Monkey at the time gave you back your five treasures without delay. Why are you still so suspicious?" "Why aren't you on the road then?" said Lao Tzu. "Why did you sneak into my palace?"

Pilgrim said, "After we parted, we proceeded toward the West until we came to the Black Rooster Kingdom. The king there had been murdered by a monster-spirit masquerading as a Taoist able to summon wind and rain. The monster then changed himself into the form of the king, and now he sits in the Hall of Golden Chimes. When my master read the sūtras during the night before last in the Precious Grove Monastery, the king's spirit appeared to him and requested earnestly for old Monkey to subdue the fiend for him. When old Monkey considered the problem of evidence, he went to the imperial garden with Pa-chieh to look for the burial site. Within a well of octagonal marble walls, we fished out his corpse, which was perfectly preserved. When we brought him back to my master, he was moved by compassion and wanted me to revive him. The condition was set, however, that I could not go to the Region of Darkness to fetch his soul, and that I must find some means to revive him in the World of Light. I concluded that there was no other remedy available, and that was why I came especially to see you. I beseech the Patriarch of Tao to be merciful and lend me one thousand tablets of your Soul-Restoring Elixir of Nine Turns, so that old Monkey can save the king." "This ape is babbling!" said Lao Tzu. "What are you saying—one thousand tablets, two thousand tablets! You eat them like rice? You think they are kneaded with mud? That easy? No! Go quickly! I have none!" "All right," said Pilgrim chuckling, "how about a hundred tablets?" "I don't have any," said Lao Tzu. "Just ten tablets, then," said Pilgrim. "This wretched ape is an absolute pest!" said Lao Tzu angrily. "I don't have any. Get out! Get out!" "You really don't have any?" said Pilgrim, laughing. "I'll go somewhere to look for help then." "Go! Go! Go!" shouted Lao Tzu. Turning around, the Great Sage strode out at once.

Lao Tzu suddenly thought to himself: "This monkey is a rogue! When I told him to go, he left, but I fear that he might sneak back in and start stealing." He ordered a divine youth to call Pilgrim back at once, saying, "You ape, you have itchy hands and feet! I'll give you one tablet of my Soul-Restoring Elixir." "Venerable Sir," said Pilgrim, "if you know the talent of old Monkey, you will bring out your golden elixir at once and divide up what you have with me equitably. That'll be your good fortune! Otherwise, I'm going to swipe them clean for you." Taking out his gourd, the patriarch turned it upside down and poured out one pellet of golden elixir. He handed it over to Pilgrim, saying, "That's all I have. Take it, take it! I'm *giving* it to you, you know, and when that king is revived, it'll be counted as your merit." Pilgrim took it and said, "Let's not hurry! I'm going to have a taste of it first, for I'm not going to be duped by some bogus pill!" He popped it into his mouth at once. The old patriarch was so startled that he dashed forward and grabbed the skin on Pilgrim's head. Holding high his fist, he shouted, "You wretched ape! If you dare swallow it, I'll kill you!" "Shame on you!" said Pilgrim, laughing. "Don't be so petty! Who's going to eat your stuff! How much could it be worth, this flimsy stuff? Isn't it right here?" The monkey, you see, had a little pouch just beneath his jowl, and that was where he kept the golden elixir. After the patriarch had felt it with his fingers, he said, "Go away! Don't bother me here anymore!" Then the Great Sage thanked the old patriarch and left the Tushita Heavenly Palace. Look at him!

In countless hallowed beams he left the arches of jade;
On myriad auspicious clouds he went to the world of dust.

In a moment, he left the South Heavenly Gate behind and, as the sun came up, he dropped from the clouds and arrived at the gate of the Precious Grove Monastery. Pa-chieh's weeping could still be heard when he approached, crying, "Master." "Wu-k'ung has returned," said Tripitaka, delighted. "Do you have any elixir or medicine?" "I do," said Pilgrim. "He couldn't possibly not have it!" said Pa-chieh. "He would have brought back something even if he had to steal it!" "Brother," said Pilgrim, chuckling, "you can get out of the way, I

don't need you anymore. Wipe away your tears, or you can go somewhere to weep." Sha Monk, please fetch me some water." Sha Monk
hurried to the well in the rear where there was a buckct nearby. He
bailed out half an alms bowl of water and brought it to Pilgrim. After
he took it, Pilgrim spat out the elixir and placed it inside the lips of the
king. Then with both hands, he pulled the jaws of the king apart, and
using a mouthful of clean water, he flushed the golden elixir down to
the king's stomach. After about half an hour, loud gurgling noises
came from the belly of the king, although his body remained immobile. "Master," said Pilgrim, "even my golden elixir seems unable
to revive him! Could it be that old Monkey's going to be finished off by
blackmail?" Tripitaka said, "Nonsense! There's no reason for him not
to live. How could he swallow that water if he had been only a corpse
dead for a long time? It had to be the divine power of that golden
elixir, which entrance into his stomach now causes the intestines to
growl. When that happens, it means that circulation and pulse are in
harmonious motion once more. His breath, however, is still stopped
and cannot flow freely. But that's to be expected when a man has been
submerged in a well for three years; after all, even raw iron would be
completely rusted. That's why his primal breath is all used up, and
someone should give him mouth-to-mouth resuscitation." Pa-chieh
walked forward and was about to do this when he was stopped by
Tripitaka. "You can't do it," he said, "Wu-k'ung still should take
over." That elder indeed had presence of mind, for Chu Pa-chieh, you
see, had been a man-eater since his youth, and his breath was un-
clean. Pilgrim, on the other hand, had practiced self-cultivation since
his birth, the food which sustained him being various fruits and nuts,
and thus his breath was pure. The Great Sage, therefore, went forward
and clamped his thundergod beak to the lips of the king: a mighty
breath was blown through his throat to descend the tiered towers.[1]
Invading the bright hall, it reached the cinnabar field and the jetting-
spring points beyond before it reversed its direction and traveled to
the mud-pill chamber of the crown. With a loud swoosh, the king's
breath came together and his spirit returned; he turned over and at
once flexed his hands and feet, crying, "Master!" Going then to his
knees, he said, "I remember my soul as a ghost did see you last night,
but I did not expect this morning my spirit would return to the World
of Light." Tripitaka hurriedly tried to raise him, saying, "Your
Majesty, I didn't do anything. You should thank my disciple."

"Master, what are you saying?" said Pilgrim with laughter. "The proverb says, 'A household does not have two heads.' You should accept his bow."

Greatly embarrassed nonetheless, Tripitaka raised the king up with both hands and they went together into the Zen hall. The king insisted on greeting Pilgrim, Pa-chieh, and Sha Monk before he would take a seat. The resident monks of the monastery had just finished preparing the morning meal and they were about to present it when they discovered a king with soaking wet garments. Everyone became frightened; each of them began to speculate. Pilgrim Sun, however, leaped into their midst and said, "Monks, don't be so alarmed. This is in fact the king of the Black Rooster Kingdom, the true ruler of all of you. Three years ago he was murdered by a fiend, but old Monkey revived him last night. We plan to go with him to the city presently to distinguish the perverse from the true. If you have some vegetarian food prepared, bring it here, so that we can start our journey after we eat." The monks then presented hot water also so that the king could wash up and change his clothes. The royal reddish brown robe was discarded, and he put on instead two cloth shirts given to him by the monk-official. They took off the jade belt and tied him up with a yellow silk sash; after the carefree boots were removed, he was given a pair of old monk sandals. Then they had their vegetarian breakfast before going to saddle the horse.

"Pa-chieh," said Pilgrim, "how heavy is your luggage?" "I've been toting it everyday," said Pa-chieh, "and I really don't know how heavy it is." Pilgrim said, "Divide one and let the king take up the other one. We should get to the city early to do our work." Delighted, Pa-chieh said, "Lucky! Lucky! When I brought him here on my back, I used up a lot of my strength. I had no idea that he could be my substitute after he had been healed." Resorting at once to mischief, Idiot divided the luggage; he carried the lighter load with a flat pole which he acquired from the monastery, whereas the heavier load he gave to the king to pole. "Your Majesty," said Pilgrim with a chuckle, "I hope you don't mind our treatment, dressing you in that manner and asking you to pick up a pole to follow us?" Kneeling down immediately, the king said, "Master, you are like parents who have given me a new birth. Don't mention anything about poling some luggage. I'm even willing to pick up the whip and hold the stirrups to look after the Venerable Father and follow him all the way to the Western Heaven."

Pilgrim said, "There's no need for you to do that, but I have a reason for making you do this at the moment. You can help us carry the luggage for these forty miles until we have entered the city and caught the monster-spirit. Then you can become a king again, and we will go and fetch our scriptures." Hearing this, Pa-chieh said, "In that case, he is going to pole for only forty miles. After that, old Hog will remain as a long-term laborer!" "Brother, no more foolish talk!" said Pilgrim. "Get out there and lead the way."

Pa-chieh indeed walked with the king in front to lead the way, while Sha Monk helped his master to mount the horse and Pilgrim took up the rear. Arranged in an orderly formation, the five hundred monks of that monastery followed them all the way to the gate, playing and blowing their musical instruments. Smiling, Pilgrim said, "No need for you monks to accompany us any further. I fear that if any of this is leaked to the officials, our enterprise will be ruined. Go back quickly! Go back quickly! Only see to it that the king's clothing and belt are cleaned and prepared. Send them to the city either late tonight or early tomorrow morning. I'll ask for some reward for you." The monks obeyed and returned to their quarters, while Pilgrim in big strides caught up with his master to proceed with him. So it is that

The West has mystery, it's good to seek the truth.
Wood and Metal in concord, then spirit can be refined.
The elixir mother recalls in vain a foolish dream;
The child deplores deeply how powerless he is.
You must seek at a well's bottom the enlightened lord,
And then bow to Lao Tzu in the Hall of Heaven.
Back to your own nature once you see form's emptiness,[2]
You're thus truly a Buddha-led man of affinity.

It did not take master and disciples even half a day on the road when they saw a city approaching. "Wu-k'ung," said Tripitaka, "I suppose that must be the Black Rooster Kingdom ahead of us." "Exactly," said Pilgrim, "let's enter the city quickly so that we can do our business." After they entered the city, master and disciples found the population well-mannered and a great deal of bustling activities. As they walked along, they soon came upon the phoenix bowers and dragon towers, exceedingly grand and ornate edifices for which we have a testimonial poem. The poem says:

These outland buildings are like the sovereign state's;[3]
Like those of old T'ang, people sing and dance.

Flowers greet jeweled fans trailed by roseate clouds;
Fresh robes, sun-lit, glimmer in jade-green fog.
Peacock screens open and fragrant mist pours out;
Pearly shades unrolled, colored flags unfurl.
A picture of peace most worthy of praise:
Quiet rows of nobles but no memorials.

"Disciples," said Tripitaka as he dismounted, "we might as well go right into the court to have our rescript certified and not be bothered by some bureaucratic office." "That's reasonable," said Pilgrim. "We brothers will go in with you; it's easier to talk when you have more people on your side." The T'ang monk said, "If all of you are going inside, you must not be rowdy. Let's go through the proper ceremony of greeting a ruler before we do any talking." "If you want to go through that," said Pilgrim, "it means that you have to prostrate yourself." "Exactly," said the T'ang monk, "we have to undertake the grand ceremony of five bows and three kowtows." "Master, you are too insipid!" said Pilgrim with a chuckle. "It's so unwise of you to want to pay homage to that character! Let me go in first, for I know what I'm going to do. If he has anything to say to us, let me answer him. If I bow, you all can bow with me; if I crouch, you crouch also." Look at that mischievous Monkey King! He went straight up to the gate of the court and said to the guardian official, "We have been sent by the Throne of the Great T'ang in the Land of the East to go worship Buddha in the Western Heaven and to acquire scriptures from him. Having arrived in this region, we would like to have our rescript certified. May we trouble you to report this to the king so that the act of virtuous fruit will not be delayed." The Custodian of the Yellow Gate went at once to the gate of the main hall and knelt before the vermilion steps to memorialize, saying, "There are five monks outside the gate of the court, who claim that they have been sent by imperial decree from the T'ang nation in the Land of the East to go to see Buddha for scriptures in the Western Heaven. They would like to have their rescript certified, but they dare not enter the court, and they await your summons."

The demon king at once gave the order to summon them inside. The T'ang monk then proceeded to walk inside the court followed by the king who had been revived. As they walked, the king could not stop the tears from rolling down his cheeks, thinking to himself: "How pitiful indeed! My bronze-guarded empire, my iron-clad domain had been secretly taken over by him." "Your Majesty," said Pilgrim softly, "you must not show your sorrow at this moment, for we may reveal everything. The rod in my ear is getting rather restless. In a moment, it will achieve a great merit by beating a demon to death and banishing all perversity. Your empire will soon be returned to you." The king dared not disobey; pulling up his robe to wipe away the tears, he followed them resolutely up to the Hall of Golden Chimes.

The rows of civil and military officials, some four hundred of them, all stood there with great sobriety and noble looks. Pilgrim led the T'ang monk up to the white jade steps; he then stood still and remained erect. All those officials beneath the steps became terrified, saying, "This monk is most foolish and base! When he sees our king, why does he not prostrate himself, nor does he express his praise? He does not even give a bow! How audacious and rude!" Before they even finished speaking, the demon king asked: "Where did this monk come from?" Pilgrim replied boldly, "I am from the Great T'ang nation in the Land of the East, in the South Jambūdvīpa Continent, someone sent by imperial decree to go seek the living Buddha in the Great Thunderclap Monastery of India in the Western Territories for true scriptures. Having reached this region, I do not want to pass through it without having our travel rescript certified." When the demon king heard what he said, he became angry, saying, "So what if you are from the Land of the East! We are not paying tribute in your court, nor have we any intercourse with your nation. How dare you neglect your etiquette and not bow to us?" Laughing, Pilgrim said, "Our Heavenly court in the Land of the East was established in antiquity, and ours had been called the superior state for a long time. Yours is only a state of the hinterlands in an inferior region. Haven't you heard the ancient adage? 'The king of the superior state is father and ruler, whereas the king of the inferior state is son and subject.' You haven't even received me properly, and you dare chide me for not bowing to you?" Infuriated, the demon king shouted to the civil and military officials: "Seize this wild monk!" When he said, "Seize," all the officials surged forward. Pointing immediately with his finger, Pilgrim cried, "Cease!" That, you see, was the magic of immobilization, which made the various officials unable to move at all. Truly

The captains before the steps looked like idols of wood,
And marshals in the palace resembled men of clay.

When the demon king saw how Pilgrim had rendered immobile all the officials, he leaped up from the dragon couch and was about to seize Pilgrim himself. Secretly delighted, the Monkey King thought: "Good! Exactly what old Monkey wanted! The moment you come near, your head, even if it's made of raw iron, is going to have a gaping hole when my rod finds it." He was about to strike, when suddenly a saving star appeared from one side. "Who was it?" you ask. It was none other than the prince of the Black Rooster Kingdom. Dashing up to tug at the demon king's garment, the prince knelt before him and said, "Let the anger of father king subside." "What do you want to say, my child?" asked the monster-spirit. "Let me report this to father king," said the prince. "Three years ago I heard already that there was a sage monk sent by the Throne of the T'ang in the Land of the East to seek scriptures from Buddha in the Western Heaven, but I did not expect that he would arrive this day. The honored nature of father king is powerful and ferocious, I know. But if you seize this monk and have him executed, the great T'ang could be greatly angered if ever they should learn of this one day. Remember that Li Shih-min who, since he established his throne, did succeed in uniting his empire. Still not content, he went on various expeditions of conquest to foreign lands. If he discovers that our king has murdered the sage monk, his bond-brother, he will most certainly call up troops and horses to war with us. When we realize then how small is our army and how weak our generals are, it will be too late for regrets. Let the father king approve the memorial of his son, let him make a thorough investigation of the background of these four monks. We must first establish why they would not pay homage to the Throne before we convict them."

This whole speech, you see, was motivated by the prince's caution, who feared that the T'ang monk might be hurt and that was why he deliberately stopped the demon. The prince, of course, did not know that Pilgrim was about to strike. Consenting indeed to the words of the prince, the demon king stood before the dragon couch and loudly asked: "When did this monk leave the Land of the East? For what reason did the T'ang emperor ask you to seek scriptures?" Again Pilgrim replied boldly, "My master is the bond-brother of the T'ang emperor, and his honorific is Tripitaka. There is a prime minister before the T'ang throne whose name is Wei Chêng, and who has by the decree of Heaven beheaded an old dragon of the Ching River. Because of this, the Great T'ang emperor also had to tour the Region of Darkness in his dream, and after he was revived, he opened wide the plot of truth by giving a Grand Mass of Land and Water to redeem the wronged souls and damned spirits. As my master recited and performed the sūtras to magnify the power of compassion, the Bodhisattva Kuan-shih-yin of South Sea revealed to him suddenly that he should journey to the West. Making a grand promise, my master accepted the commission freely and gladly to serve his nation, and that was when the emperor bestowed on him the rescript. On the third day before the fifteenth, during the ninth month of the thirteenth year in the Chên-kuan period of the Great T'ang, he left the Land of the East. When he reached the Mountain of Two Frontiers, he accepted me as his disciple. My surname is Sun, and my name is Wu-k'ung Pilgrim. Next, we arrived at the Kao Family Village of the Tibet Kingdom, where my master made his second disciple; his surname is Chu, and his name is Wu-nêng Pa-chieh. At the Flowing Sand River, the third disciple joined the fold; his surname is Sha, and his name is Wu-ching Monk. The day before yesterday at the Precious Grove Monastery Built by Imperial Command, we newly acquired a mendicant Taoist who now helps us with poling the luggage."

After the demon king heard this speech, he found it difficult to turn up an excuse for examining further the T'ang monk, and it was even more difficult for him to try to overwhelm Pilgrim with deceptive interrogation. Glowering, he said, "You, monk! When you first left the Land of the East, you were all by yourself, but then you accepted all these four persons into your company. Those three monks may be all right, but this Taoist looks most suspicious. This mendicant must have been kidnapped from somewhere. What is his name? Does he have a certificate of ordination? Bring him up here and let him make a deposition." Trembling all over, the king said, "O Master! How shall I make this deposition?" Giving him a pinch, Pilgrim said, "Don't be afraid. Let me do it for you."

Dear Great Sage! He strode forward and said to the fiend in a loud voice, "Your Majesty, this old Taoist is not only dumb, but he is also somewhat deaf. We took him on because he knew the way to the Western Heaven, having gone there himself in his younger days. I know everything about him—his background, his origin, his rise and fall. I beg your Majesty's pardon, but let me make the deposition for him." "Do it quickly and truthfully," said the demon king, "lest he be convicted of a serious offense." Pilgrim said:

Of this deposition the mendicant's quite old;
Deaf, dumb, and dim-witted, he's also poor!
A man whose native home was in this place,
He met defeat and ruin five years ago.
With no rain from the sky,
Folks turned shriveled and dry.
King and subjects all abstained and fasted;
They bathed and burned incense to pray to Heav'n,
But no cloud was seen for ten thousand miles.
While people starved as though hung upside down,
There came from Chung-nan a Complete Truth fiend
Who called up wind and rain to show his power,
And then took in secret the king's own life.
The victim was pushed down a garden well;
The dragon seat was taken unknown to man.
Luckily I came.
My merit was great:
No snag it was to bring life back from death.
Willing to submit as a mendicant,
He would follow the monk to face the West.
That specious king is a Taoist in fact;
This Taoist is in truth the rightful king.

When that demon king on the Hall of Golden Chimes heard this
speech, he became so frightened that his heart pounded like the feet
of a young deer and his face was flushed with red clouds. He wanted
to run away at once, but he did not even have a weapon in his hands.
Turning around, he saw one of the captains of palace guards, who
had a scimitar buckled to his waist and who had been rendered a
dumb and stupid person standing there by Pilgrim's magic of immobilization. Dashing up to him, the demon king took this scimitar
and then immediately mounted the clouds to escape in the air. Sha
Monk and Chu Pa-chieh were so annoyed by this turn of events that
they screamed at Pilgrim: "You impatient ape! Why did you have to
say all those things at once? You could have tricked him into staying
if you had used a slower approach. Now that he has mounted the
clouds and escaped, where would you go to search for him?" "Don't
scream madly like that, brothers," said Pilgrim with laughter. "Let
me ask the prince to come out and bow to his father and the queen
to greet her husband first. Let me then recite another spell to release

those ministers from my magic so that they can learn the truth about what has happened and pay homage to the real king. Then I can go look for him." Dear Great Sage! After he had disposed of everything he said he would do, he told Pa-chieh and Sha Monk: "Take care to guard ruler and subjects, father and son, husband and wife, and our master. I'm off!" Hardly had he finished speaking before he was completely out of sight.

Rising straight up to the clouds of the ninefold Heaven, Pilgrim opened wide his eyes to stare all around: the demon king, having escaped with his life, was fleeing toward the northeast. Pilgrim caught up with him in no time, shouting, "Fiend, where are you going? Old Monkey's here." Swiftly turning around, the demon king brought out his scimitar and said with a loud voice, "Pilgrim Sun, what a rogue you are! I took the throne of another man, but that didn't concern you. Why did you have to be involved in someone's affairs and reveal my secret?" Roaring with laughter, Pilgrim said, "You audacious, lawless fiend! You think you ought to be permitted to be a king? If you recognized old Monkey, you should have fled at the earliest opportunity to the farthest place. How dare you try to give my master a hard time, asking for that so-called deposition? That deposition I gave you just now, was that accurate or not? Don't run away now! If you're a man, have a taste of old Monkey's rod!" The demon king stepped aside to dodge the blow before he wielded the scimitar to meet his opponent. The moment their weapons joined, it was a marvelous battle. Truly

The Monkey King is fierce,
The demon king is strong—
Rod and scimitar dare each other oppose.
This day the Three Regions are bedimmed by fog,
All for a king's restoration to his court.

After the two of them fought for a few rounds, the demon king could no longer withstand the Monkey King and fled instead back into the city on the way he came. Hurling himself into the two rows of civil and military officials before the white jade steps, the demon king gave his body a shake and changed into an exact image of Tripitaka T'ang, both of them standing hand-in-hand before the steps. The Great Sage arrived and was about to strike with the rod when the fiend said, "Disciple, don't hit me! It's I!" Pilgrim turned the rod toward the other T'ang monk who also said, "Disciple, don't hit me! It's I!"

There were two T'ang monks exactly alike and most difficult to distinguish. Thinking to himself, "If I kill the monster spirit with one blow of the rod, it would be my merit, all right; but what would I do if that blow happens to kill my true master?" Pilgrim had to stop and ask Pa-chieh and Sha Monk: "Which is the fiend and which is our master? Point him out to me so that I can strike at him." "You two were yelling and fighting in midair," said Pa-chieh, "and when I blinked my eyes, I saw two masters the next moment. I don't know who is real and who is false."

When Pilgrim heard these words, he made the magic sign with his fingers and recited a spell, which called together the various deva guardians, the Six Gods of Darkness and the Six Gods of Light, the Guardians of Five Quarters, the Four Sentinels, the Eighteen Guardians of the Faith, the local spirit, and the mountain god of that region. He said to them, "Old Monkey is trying to subdue a monster here, who has changed himself into the likeness of my master. Both their form and substance seem exactly the same and it's difficult to tell them apart. But you may be able to distinguish them in secret; if so, make my master walk up the steps into the main hall so that I can catch this demon." The fiend, you see, was accomplished in magic; when he heard these words of Pilgrim, he quickly bounded into the Hall of Golden Chimes. Pilgrim raised his rod and brought it down hard on the T'ang monk. Alas! If it had not been for desperate efforts of those several deities summoned to this place, the blow would have reduced even twenty T'ang monks to meat patties! Fortunately the various deities managed to block the blow, saying, "Great Sage, the fiend knows his magic. He has gone up to the hall first." Pilgrim gave chase at once, and the demon king ran outside the hall to catch hold of the T'ang monk once more in the crowd. After this confusion, they again could not be distinguished.

Pilgrim was highly displeased, and when he saw, moreover, that Pa-chieh was snickering on one side, he became enraged, saying, "What's the matter with you, stupid coolie? Now you have two masters whose calls you must answer and whom you must serve. Are you overjoyed?" Laughing, Pa-chieh said, "Elder Brother, you say I'm dumb; well, you're even dumber! If you can't recognize who is the real master, why waste all this energy? You try to endure a little pain on your head for a moment and ask Master to recite that little something of his. Sha Monk and I will each hold on to one of them and listen: that person who does not know how to recite the spell must be the monster. What's so difficult about that?" "Thank you, Brother," said Pilgrim. "You've got it. That little something indeed is known only to three persons: born of the very mind of our Buddha Tathāgata, it was transmitted to the Bodhisattva Kuan-shih-yin, who then imparted it to my master. There is no other person who has knowledge of it. All right, Master, start your recital." In truth the T'ang monk began to recite, but how could the demon king know what to do. All he could do was mumble something, and Pa-chieh said, "This one mumbling is the monster!" He let go and raised his muckrake to strike at the demon king, who leaped up and tried to flee treading the clouds.

Dear Pa-chieh! With a shout, he mounted the clouds also to give chase. Sha Monk hurriedly abandoned the T'ang monk and brought out his precious staff to do battle. Only then did the T'ang monk stop reciting his spell; the Great Sage Sun, enduring his headache, dragged his iron rod up to midair. Ah, look at this battle! Three fierce monks have surrounded a brazen demon!

The demon king, you see, was attacked left and right by Pa-chieh with his rake and Sha Monk with his staff. Chuckling to himself, Pilgrim said, "If I go attack him face to face, he will try to escape as he is already somewhat afraid of me. Let old Monkey get up higher and give me a garlic-pounding blow from the top down. That'll finish him off!"

Mounting the auspicious luminosity, the Great Sage rose to the ninefold Heaven and was about to show his decisive hand when a loud voice came from a petal of colored cloud in the northeast: "Sun Wu-k'ung, don't do it!" When Pilgrim turned to look, he discovered the Bodhisattva Mañjuśrī. Quickly putting away his rod, he drew near and bowed, saying, "Bodhisattva, where are you going?" "I came," said Mañjuśrī, "to put away this fiend for you." Pilgrim thanked him and said, "I'm greatly obliged." Taking out an imp-reflecting mirror from his sleeve, the Bodhisattva aimed it at the fiend and the image of its original form became visible at once. Pilgrim called Pa-chieh and Sha Monk to come to greet the Bodhisattva and to look into the mirror. Exceedingly ferocious in appearance, that demon king had

Eyes like large goblets of glass;
A head like a cooking vat;
A body of deep summer green;

And four paws like autumn's frost;
Two large ears that flipped downward;
A tail as long as a broom;
Green hair full of fighting ardor;
Red eyes emitting gold beams;
Rows of flat teeth like jade slabs;
Round whiskers rearing up like spears.
The true form seen in the mirror
Was Mañjuśrī's lion king.

"Bodhisattva," said Pilgrim, "so this is the green haired lion who serves as your beast of burden. How was it that he had been turned loose so that he could become a spirit here? Aren't you going to make him submit to you?" "Wu-k'ung," said the Bodhisattva, "he was not turned loose. He had been sent by the decree of Buddha to come here." Pilgrim said, "You mean that this beast's becoming a spirit to usurp the throne of a king was a decree of Buddha? If that's the case, old Monkey, who is accompanying the T'ang monk through all his trials, should have been given several imperial documents!"

The Bodhisattva said, "You don't know that this king of the Black Rooster Kingdom was dedicated to virtue and to the feeding of monks at first. The Buddha sent me to lead him to return to the West so that he could attain the golden body of an arhat. I could not, of course, reveal myself to him in my true form, and so I changed myself into an ordinary mortal monk to beg some food from him. During our conversation a few words of mine put him on the spot; not realizing that I was a good man after all, he tied me up with a rope and sent me into the imperial moat. I soaked in there for three days and nights before the Six Gods of Darkness rescued me back to the West. Tathāgata therefore sent this creature here to push him down the well and have him submerged for three years, in order to exact vengeance for my water adversity of three days. Thus 'not even a sup or a bite is not foreordained,' and we had to wait for all of you to arrive and achieve this merit."

"You might have repaid the private grievance of your so-called one sup or one bite," said Pilgrim, "but who knows how many human beings that fiendish creature has harmed." "He has not," said the Bodhisattva. "In fact, these three years after his arrival have seen nothing but winds and rains in season, prosperity for the kingdom and peace for the inhabitants. Since when has he harmed anyone?"

"Even so," said Pilgrim, "those ladies of the three palaces did sleep with him and rise with him. His body has defiled many and violated the great human relations countless times. And you say that he has not harmed anyone?" The Bodhisattva said, "He has not defiled anyone, for he's a gelded lion." When Pa-chieh heard this, he walked near and gave the creature a pat, saying with a chuckle, "This monster-spirit is truly a 'red nose who doesn't drink'! He bears his name in vain!" "All right," said Pilgrim, "take him away. If the Bodhisattva did not come here himself, I would never have spared his life." Reciting a spell, the Bodhisattva shouted, "Beast, how long are you going to wait before you submit to the Right?" The demon king at once changed back to his original form, after which the Bodhisattva released the lotus flower seat to be placed on the back of the lion. He then mounted the lion, who trod on the auspicious luminosity and left. Aha!

He went straight to the Wu-t'ai Mountain;[4]

To hear sūtras explained before the lotus seat.

We do not know finally how the T'ang monk and his disciples leave the city, and you must listen to the explanation in the next chapter.

## Forty

By the child's tricky transformations the Zen Mind's
   confused;
Ape, Horse, Spatula, and Wood Mother—all are lost.

We were telling you about the Great Sage Sun and his two brothers,
who lowered their clouds and returned to the court. They were met
by the king, the queen, and their subjects—all of them lined up in
rows to bow and to express their thanks. Pilgrim then gave a complete account of how the Bodhisattva came to subdue the monster,
and all the officials in court touched the top of their heads to the
ground in adoration. As they were thus rejoicing, the Custodian of
the Yellow Gate arrived to announce: "My lord, there are four more
monks who have arrived at the gate." A little apprehensive, Pa-chieh
said, "Elder Brother, could it be that the monster-spirit, having used
magic to disguise himself as the Bodhisattva Mañjuśri to deceive us,
has now changed again into some kind of monk to match wits with
us?" "How could that be?" said Pilgrim, who then asked that the
monks be summoned inside.

After the civil and military officials transmitted the order and the
visitors entered, Pilgrim saw that they were monks from the Precious
Grove Monastery, who came bearing the rising-to-Heaven cap, the
green-jade belt, the brownish yellow robe, and the carefree boots.
Highly pleased, Pilgrim said, "It's wonderful that you've come!" He
asked the Taoist to step forward: his head-wrap was taken off and the
rising-to-Heaven cap was placed on his head; the cloth garment was
stripped off and he put on the brownish yellow robe instead; after he
untied the silk sash and took off the monk sandals, he buckled on the
jade-green belt and climbed into the carefree boots. The prince was
then told to bring out the white jade-token so that the king might hold
it in his hands, and he was asked to ascend the main hall to be the
king once more. As the ancient proverb said, "The court should not
be one day without a ruler." But the king absolutely refused to sit on
the throne; weeping profusely, he knelt on the steps and said, "I've
been dead for three years, and I'm indebted to Master for making me

return to life. How could I dare assume such honor again? Let one of these masters be the ruler; I'll be perfectly content to go with my wife and child outside the city to live as a commoner." Tripitaka, of course, would have none of this, for he was intent on going to worship Buddha and to acquire the scriptures. The king then turned to Pilgrim, who said to him, smiling, "To tell you the truth, if old Monkey wanted to be a king, he would have been one throughout the myriad kingdoms in the world. But all of us are used to the leisurely and carefree existence of monks. If I become a king, I will have to let my hair grow again; I won't be able to retire when it's dark, nor will I be able to sleep beyond the hour of the fifth watch. I'll be anxious when reports from the borders arrive; I'll have endless worries when there are disasters or famines. How could I live with these things? So, you may as well be the king, and we shall continue to be monks to cultivate our merit." After pleading with them bitterly to no avail, the king had no choice but to ascend the treasure hall once more to face south and resume the use of the royal "we." After giving a general pardon throughout his empire, he also bestowed huge rewards on the monks of the Precious Grove Monastery before they left. Then he opened up the eastern palace to give a banquet to honor the T'ang monk; at the same time, painters were summoned into the palace to make portraits of the four pilgrims, so that these could be permanently revered in the Hall of Golden Chimes.

After they had securely established the kingdom, master and disciples, reluctant to stay too long, were about to take leave of the throne to face the West. The king, the queen, the prince, and all their subjects took out the crown treasures together with gold, silver, and silk to present to the master as tokens of gratitude, but Tripitaka refused to accept any of these. All he wanted was to have his travel rescript certified so that he could tell Wu-k'ung and his brothers to saddle the horse and leave. Feeling very keenly that he had not expressed his gratitude in an adequate manner, the king called for his imperial chariot and invited the T'ang monk to sit in it. The two rows of civil and military officials were told to lead the way in front, while he, the prince, and the ladies of the three palaces pushed the chariot themselves. Only after they had gone out of the city wall was the T'ang monk permitted to descend from the dragon chariot to take leave. "O Master," said the king, "when you have reached the Western Heaven and retrace your steps with your scriptures, you must pay our region a visit." "Your disciple obeys you," said Tripitaka, and the king went back to the city tearfully with his subjects. The T'ang monk and his three disciples again took up the labyrinthine path, their minds intent only on bowing at the Spirit Mountain. It was now the season of late autumn and early winter, and they saw

Frost blighting the maples to make each forest sparse,
And rain-ripened millet, plenty everywhere.
Warmed by the sun, summit plums spread their morning hues;
Rocked by the wind, mountain bamboos voice their chilly plaint.

After they left the Black Rooster Kingdom, master and disciples journeyed during the day and rested at night; they had been on the road for more than half a month when they came upon another tall mountain, truly Heaven-touching and sun-obstructing. Growing alarmed on the horse, Tripitaka quickly pulled in his reins to call Pilgrim. "What do you want to say, Master?" said Pilgrim. "Look at that huge mountain with those rugged cliffs before us," said Tripitaka. "You must take caution and be on your guard, for I fear that some deviate creature all of a sudden will come to attack me again." "Just get moving," said Pilgrim with a chuckle, "Don't be suspicious. Old Monkey has his defense." The elder had to banish his worries and urged his horse to enter the mountain, which was truly rugged. You see

Whether tall or not,[1]
Its top reaches the blue sky;
Whether deep or not,
A stream with depth like Hell down there.
Before the mountain often are seen endless rings of white clouds
    rising
And boiling waves of dark fog;
Red plums and jadelike bamboos;
Verdant cedars and green pines;
Behind the mountain are soul-rending cliffs ten thousand yards
    deep,
Behind which are strange, grotesque, demon-hiding caves,
Where water drips down from rocks drop by drop
And leads to a winding, twisting brooklet down below.
You see also fruit-bearing apes prancing and leaping,
And deer with horns forked and zigzagged;
Dull and dumbly staring antelopes;

Tigers which climb the hills to seek their dens at night;
Dragons that churn the waves to leave their lairs at dawn.
When steps at the cave's entrance snap and crackle,
The fowls dart up with wings loudly beating.
Look also at these beasts walking through the woods with paws
    noisily scratching.
When you see this bunch of birds and beasts,
You will be given a heart-pounding fear.
The Due-to-Fall Cave faces the Due-to-Fall Cave;
The cave facing the Due-to-Fall Cave faces a god.
Green rocks are dyed like a thousand pieces of jade;
Blue-green gauze enshrouds ten thousand piles of mist.

As master and disciples became more and more apprehensive, they saw a red cloud rising up from the fold of the mountain ahead of them; after it reached midair, it condensed and took on the appearance of a fireball. Greatly alarmed, Pilgrim ran forward to catch hold of one of the T'ang monk's legs and pulled him from the horse, crying, "Brothers, stop! A monster is approaching!" Pa-chieh and Sha Monk quickly took out their muckrake and precious staff and surrounded the T'ang monk.

Let us now tell you that there was indeed a monster-spirit inside the ball of red light. Several years ago he heard people saying that the T'ang monk sent from the Land of the East to acquire scriptures from the Western Heaven was the incarnation of the elder, Gold Cicada, a good man who had practiced austerities for ten existences. Any person who could taste a piece of his flesh, they said, would be able to prolong his life until it became the same as Heaven and Earth. Every morning, therefore, he waited in the mountain, and suddenly he found that the pilgrim had arrived. As he watched in midair, he saw that the T'ang monk beside the horse was surrounded by three disciples, all ready to fight. Marveling to himself, the spirit said, "Dear monk! This white-faced, chubby cleric riding a horse was just coming into my view, when all of a sudden these three ugly monks had him surrounded. Look at them! Everyone is rolling up his sleeves, stretching out his fists and wielding his weapon—as if he is about to fight with someone. Aha! One of them with some perception, I suppose, must have recognized me. Well, if it's going to be like this, it'll be difficult for anyone trying to get a taste of the T'ang monk's flesh." As he thought to himself, questioning his mind with mind like that, he said, "If I try to overpower them, I may not even get near them, but if I try to use the good to deceive them, I may succeed. As long as I am able to beguile their minds, I can trick them even with the good. Then I'll catch them for sure. Let me go down and tease them a little."

Dear monster! He made the red light disperse and lowered his cloud toward the fold of the mountain. Shaking his body, he changed immediately into a little mischievous boy, about seven years of age and completely naked, who was bound by a rope and suspended from the top of a pine tree. "Help! Help!" he cried without ceasing.

We were just telling you about the Great Sage Sun, who raised his head and found that the red cloud had completely dissipated and the flames all vanished. He therefore said, "Master, please mount up again for the journey." "You just told us that there was a fiend approaching," said the T'ang monk. "Do we dare proceed now?" "A little while ago," said Pilgrim, "I saw a red cloud rising up from the ground, and by the time it reached midair, it condensed into a flaming ball of fire. It had to be a monster-spirit. But now the red cloud has dissipated, and so it must be a monster who's a passerby and who does not dare harm people. Let's go." "Elder Brother is truly clever with words," said Pa-chieh, chuckling, "even monster-spirits can be passersby!" "How would you know?" said Pilgrim. "If some demon king of a certain cave in a certain mountain has sent out invitations to spirits of sundry mountains and caves to attend a festival, monster-spirits from all quarters—north, south, east, and west—would respond. Perhaps he's just interested in going to the festival and not in harming people. That's a monster-spirit who's a passerby."

When Tripitaka heard these words, he was only half-convinced, but he had little alternative other than to climb on his saddle to journey into the mountain. As they proceeded, they heard suddenly repeated cries of "Help!" Highly startled, the elder said, "O Disciples! Who's calling out in the midst of this mountain?" Pilgrim walked forward and said to him, "Master, keep moving. Don't harp on such things as human carriage,[2] donkey carriage, open carriage, or reclining carriage. Even if there were a carriage in a place like this, there wouldn't be anyone to carry you." "I'm not talking about carriages," said the T'ang monk, "I'm referring to someone calling us." "I know," said Pilgrim with laughter, "but mind your own business. Let's move on."

Tripitaka agreed and urged his horse forward once more. Before they had traveled a mile, they heard again the call, "Help!" "Disciple," said the elder, "the sound of this call can't be that of a demon or a goblin, for if it were, there would be no echo. Just listen to it: there was a call a moment ago, and now we have another one. It must have come from a man in dire difficulty. Let's go and help him." Pilgrim said, "Master, please put away your compassion just for today! When we have crossed this mountain, you can be compassionate then. If you know those stories about strange plants and possessed vegetations, you should know that every thing can become a spirit. In most cases, they may not be too dangerous, but if you should run into something like a python which has become an evil spirit after prolonged self-cultivation, you'd be in trouble. A spirit like that can even possess knowledge of a person's nickname. If he should call out, hiding in the bushes or in the fold of the mountain, a person may get by if he does not answer him, but if he does answer, the spirit can snatch away his primal soul, or he can follow that person and take his life that night. Let's get away! Let's get away! As the ancients said, 'If you escape, just thank the gods.' Please don't listen to this call."

The elder had little alternative but to agree and he whipped his horse to go forward. Pilgrim thought to himself, "I wonder where this brazen fiend is hollering. Let old Monkey give him a taste of 'Cancer in opposition to Capricornus' so that the two will never meet." Dear Great Sage! He said to Sha Monk, "Hold onto the horse and walk slowly. Old Monkey's going to take a leak." Look at him! He let the T'ang monk walk slightly ahead and then recited a spell to exercise the magic of shortening the ground and moving the mountain. He pointed his golden-hooped rod backward once, and master and disciples immediately went past the peak of the mountain, leaving behind the fiendish creature. In big strides, the Great Sage caught up with the T'ang monk and they proceeded. Just then Tripitaka heard again a call coming from the mountain behind him, crying "Help!" The elder said, "O Disciple! That person in adversity truly has no affinity, for he has not run into any of us. We must have passed him, for you can hear that he is crying out from the mountain behind us." "Or he may be still ahead of us," said Pa-chieh, "but perhaps the wind has changed." "Never mind whether the wind has changed or not," said Pilgrim, "just keep moving." As a result, everyone fell silent and concentrated on trying to pass the mountain, and we shall speak no more of them for the moment.

We tell you instead about that monster-spirit in the mountain valley: he cried out for three or four times but no one appeared. He thought to himself: "When I saw the T'ang monk just now, he couldn't have been more than three miles away. I've been waiting for him all this time. Why hasn't he arrived? Could it be that he had taken another road down the mountain?" Shaking his body, he loosened the rope at once and mounted the red light once more to rise into the air. Unwittingly the Great Sage Sun was looking back with head upturned, and when he saw the light, he knew that it was the fiendish creature. Once more he grabbed the legs of the T'ang monk and pushed him off the horse, crying, "Brothers, take care! Take care! That monster-spirit is approaching again!" Pa-chieh and Sha Monk were so alarmed that they wielded their rake and staff to surround the T'ang monk as before.

When that spirit saw what happened in midair, he could not stop marveling, saying to himself: "Dear monks! I just saw that white-faced priest riding on the horse. How is it that he is now surrounded again by the three of them? Now I realize, after what I've seen, that I must overthrow the one who has perception before I can seize the T'ang monk. If not,

My exertions are vain for I can't get my thing;
My efforts notwithstanding, all is nothing!"

He lowered his cloud and transforming himself as before, he hung himself high on top of a pine tree. This time, however, he positioned himself only about half a mile away.

We tell you now about the Great Sage Sun, who when he raised his head and found that the red cloud had dispersed, requested once more that his master mount up and proceed. "You just told us that the monster-spirit was approaching again," said Tripitaka. "Why do you ask me to move on?" Pilgrim said, "This monster-spirit is a passerby. He doesn't dare bother us." The elder grew angry and said, "You brazen ape! You're just playing with me! When there is a demon, you say it's nothing. But when we are in this peaceful region, you are out to frighten me, yelling all the time about a monster-spirit. There's more falsehood than truth in your words, and without regard for good or ill, you grab my legs and throw me off the horse. Now you come up with an explanation about this monster-spirit who's a so-called passerby! If I got hurt from the fall, would you be able to live with yourself? You, you . . ." "Please don't be offended, Master," said Pilgrim. "If your hands and feet got hurt from the fall, we could still take care of you, but if you were abducted by a monster-spirit, where would we go to look for you?" Enraged, Tripitaka would have recited the Tight-Fillet Spell had not Sha Monk desperately pleaded with him. Finally he mounted his horse and proceeded once more.

Before he could even sit properly on the saddle he heard another cry: "Master, please help me!" As he looked up, the elder found that it came from a little child, completely naked, who was suspended on top of a tree. He pulled in the reins and began to berate Pilgrim, saying, "You wretched ape! How villainous you are! You don't have the tiniest bit of kindness in you! Every thought of yours is bent on making mischief and working violence! I told you that it was a human voice calling for help, but you have to spend countless words to claim it was a monster. Look! Isn't that a person hanging on the tree?" Seeing how the master was putting the blame on him and also the form before his face, the Great Sage lowered his head and dared not reply, for there was nothing he could do at the moment and he was afraid that his master would recite the Tight-Fillet Spell. He had little choice, in fact, but to permit the T'ang monk to approach the tree. Pointing with his whip, the elder asked, "Which household do you belong to, child? Why are you hung here? Tell me, so that I can rescue you." Alas! Clearly this is a monster-spirit who has transformed himself in this manner, but that master is a man of fleshly eyes and mortal stock, completely unable to recognize what he saw.

When that demon heard the question, he became even more bold in his chicanery. With tears welling up in his eyes, he said, "O Master! West of this mountain there is a Withered Pine Brook, by the side of which there is a village where my family is located. My grandfather's name is Red, and because he has amassed a huge fortune, he was given the name Red Millions. He has, however, been dead for a long time after having lived to a ripe old age, and his estate was left to my father. Recent business reversals have gradually fribbled away our possessions, and my father for that reason has changed his name to Red Thousands. He has been, you see, befriending many men of valor, to whom he had lent gold and silver with the hope of reaping some profits. Little did he realize that these were all rootless men out to swindle him, and he lost both principal and interest. My father there-

fore vowed that he would never lend out another penny, but those
borrowers, after having squandered what they had, banded together
and plundered our house in broad daylight, holding lit torches and
staffs. Not only did they rob us of all our money and possessions, but
they killed my father also. And when they saw that my mother was
somewhat attractive, they decided to abduct her and take her with
them to be some kind of camp lady. Unwilling to abandon me, my
mother carried me along in her bosom and, weeping, followed the
thieves to this mountain, where they wanted to kill me also. Fortunately, my mother pleaded with them and I was spared the knife; I
was tied with ropes and hung here to die of hunger and exposure
instead. I don't know what sort of merit I've accumulated in another
existence that brings me the luck of meeting Master here. If you are
willing to be compassionate and save my life so that I can return
home, I shall try to repay your kindness even if I have to sell myself.
Even when the yellow sand covers my face, I will not forget your
kindness."

When Tripitaka heard these words, he thought they were the truth
and immediately asked Pa-chieh to loosen the ropes and rescue the
child. Not knowing any better either, Idiot was about to act when
Pilgrim on one side could not restrain himself any longer. "You
brazen thing!" he shouted. "There's someone here who recognizes
you! Don't think you can use your humbuggery to hoodwink people!
If your possessions were stolen, if your father was killed and your
mother taken by thieves, to whom would we entrust you once we
rescued you? With what would you thank us? Your fables don't add
up!" When the fiend heard these words, he became frightened,
realizing that the Great Sage was an able man to be reckoned with.
Trembling all over, the fiend spoke as tears flowed down his face:
"Master, though my parents are lost and gone, and though the wealth
of our family is reduced to nothing, I still have some land and
relatives." "What sort of relatives do you have?" said Pilgrim. The
fiend said, "The household of my maternal family lives south of this
mountain, while my aunties reside north of the peak. Li Four at the
head of the brook is the husband of my mother's sister, and Red Three
in the forest is a distant uncle. I have, moreover, several cousins living
here and there in the village. If Venerable Master is willing to save me
and take me to see these relatives at the village, I shall certainly give
them a thorough account of your kindness, and you will be handsomely rewarded when we sell some of our land."

When Pa-chieh heard what he said, he pushed Pilgrim aside, saying, "Elder Brother, this is only a child! Why keep on interrogating him? What he told us was that the thieves had robbed them of their liquid assets. They couldn't take their houses and land, could they? If he will speak to his relatives, we may have huge appetites, but we can't eat up the price of ten acres of land. Let's cut him down." Idiot, of course, thought only of food; he had no further regard for good or ill, and using the ritual razor, he ripped open the ropes to free the fiend. Facing the T'ang monk tearfully, the fiend knelt beneath the horse and kept on kowtowing. A compassionate man, the elder called out: "Child, get up on the horse. I'll take you there." "O Master," said the fiend, "my hands and feet are numb from the hanging, and my torso hurts. Moreover, I'm a rural person and not used to riding horses." The T'ang monk at once asked Pa-chieh to carry him, but the fiend, after glancing at Idiot, said, "Master, my skin is frostbitten, and I dare not let myself be carried by this master. He has such a long mouth and large ears, and the hard bristles behind his head can be frightfully prickly!" "Let Sha Monk carry you then," said the T'ang monk. After glancing at him also, the fiend said, "Master, when those robbers came to plunder our house, each one of them had his face painted; they wore false beards and they held knives and staffs. I was terribly frightened by them, and now when I see this master with such a gloomy complexion, I'm even more intimidated. I just don't dare to ask him to carry me." The T'ang monk therefore told Pilgrim Sun to put the fiend on his back. Laughing uproariously, Pilgrim said, "I'll carry him! I'll carry him!"

Secretly pleased, the fiendish creature gave himself willingly to Pilgrim to carry. When Pilgrim pulled him up from the side of the road to test his weight, he found that the fiend weighed no more than three catties and ten ounces. "You audacious fiend!" said Pilgrim, laughing. "You deserve to die today! How dare you pull tricks before old Monkey? I recognize you to be 'that something'." "I'm the offspring of a good family," said the fiend, "and it is my misfortune to face this great ordeal. What do you mean by 'that something'?" "If you are an offspring of a good family," said Pilgrim, "why are your bones so light?" "They are small," said the fiend. "How old are you now?" said Pilgrim, and the fiend said, "I'm seven years old." "Even if you put on only one catty of weight per year," said Pilgrim, "you should now weigh seven catties. How is it that you are not even a full four catties?" "I didn't get enough milk when I was a baby," said the fiend.

Pilgrim said, "All right, I'll carry you, but if you want to piss, you must tell me." Tripitaka then walked in front with Pa-chieh and Sha Monk, while Pilgrim followed behind with the child on his back. As they proceeded toward the West, we have a poem as a testimony, and the poem says:

> Though virtue's lofty, demonic blocks are high.
> Zen's cause is stillness, but stillness breeds fiends.
> The Lord of the Mind's upright, he takes the middle way;
> Wood Mother's[3] mischievous, he walks another path.
> The Horse of the Will's silent, holding want and greed;
> Yellow Hag's wordless, nursing his own unease.
> The Guest-Error succeeds but his joys are vain—
> At last they will, through the Right, all melt away.

As the Great Sage Sun carried the demon on his back, he began to brood over his resentment toward the T'ang monk, thinking to himself: "Master truly does not know how difficult it is to traverse this rugged mountain; it's hard enough to do so when you are empty-handed, but he has to ask old Monkey to carry someone else, not to mention a fellow who's a monster no less. Even if he were a good man, it would be worthless to carry him along, since he had already lost both parents. To whom would we carry him? I might as well smash him dead!" At once the fiendish creature became aware of what Pilgrim was thinking and he, therefore, resorted to magic: taking four deep breaths from the four quarters, he blew them on to the back of Pilgrim, and his bearer immediately felt as if a weight of a thousand pounds were on him. "My child," said Pilgrim, chuckling, "you are using the heavy-body magic to crush your venerable father?" When the fiend heard those words, he became afraid that the Great Sage might harm him. He liberated himself from his corpse and his primal soul rose into the air and stood there, while the weight on Pilgrim's back grew heavier. Growing angry, the Monkey King grabbed the body on his back and hurled it against some rocks at the side of the road; the body was reduced to a meat patty. Fearing that it would still be resistant, Pilgrim tore off the four limbs and smashed them to pieces also by the road.

When the fiend saw clearly what happened in midair, he could not restrain the fire leaping up in his heart, saying to himself, "This monkey monk! How villainous of him! Even if I am a demon plotting to harm your master, I have yet to raise my hand. How could you do such violence to me like that? It's a good thing that I have enough foresight to leave with my spirit; otherwise, I would have unwittingly lost my life. I might as well make use of this opportunity to seize the T'ang monk, for if I delay any further, he might get even smarter." Dear monster! He at once caused to rise in midair a truly fierce whirlwind, which threw up rocks and kicked up dirt. Marvelous wind!

Angrily it whipped up clouds and waters rank,
As rising black ether blotted out the sun.
All summit trees were pulled out by their roots;
Wild plums were wholly leveled with their branches.
Yellow sand dimmed the eyes, so men could not walk.
Strange rocks battered the road, how could it be smooth?
It churned and tossed to darken all the plains
While birds and beasts were howling throughout this mount.

The wind blew until Tripitaka could hardly stay on the horse, until Pa-chieh refused to look up and Sha Monk lowered his head and covered his face. Only the Great Sage Sun knew that it was a wind sent up by the fiend, but when he ran forward to try to catch up with the others, the fiend riding on the head of the wind had already caught hold of the T'ang monk and taken him away. Instantly they vanished without a trace, so that there was no way for the disciples to know even where to look for them.

In a little while, the wind began to subside and sunlight appeared once more. Pilgrim walked forward and saw that the white dragon horse was still trembling and neighing uncontrollably; the load of luggage was thrown by the road; Pa-chieh lay sprawled beneath a ledge moaning and Sha Monk was making noises while crouching on the slope. "Pa-chieh!" shouted Pilgrim. When Idiot heard the voice of Pilgrim and looked up, the violent wind had calmed. He scrambled up and tugged at Pilgrim, saying, "O Elder Brother, what a terrific wind!" Sha Monk also came up and said, "Elder Brother, this is a whirlwind." Then he asked: "Where's Master?" Pa-chieh said, "The wind was so strong that we all hid our heads and covered our eyes, each trying to find shelter. Master seemed to have put his head down also on the saddle." "But where is he now?" said Pilgrim. "He must have been made of straw," said Sha Monk, "and got blown away!"

Pilgrim said, "Brothers, it's time for us to disband." "Exactly," said Pa-chieh, "while there's still time. It's better for each of us to find our own way off. The journey to the Western Heaven is endless and limit-

less! When will we ever get there?" When Sha Monk heard these
words, he was so shocked that his whole body began to turn numb.
"Elder Brother," he said, "how could you say something like that?
Because we committed crimes in our previous lives, we were lucky to
be enlightened by the Bodhisattva Kuan-shih-yin, who touched our
heads, gave us the commandments, and changed our names so that
we could embrace the Buddhist fruit. We willingly accepted the commission to protect the T'ang monk and follow him to the Western
Heaven to worship Buddha and acquire scriptures, so that our merits
would cancel out our sins. Today we are here and everything seems
to come to an end abruptly when you can talk about each of us finding
our own way off, for then we would mar the good fruits of the
Bodhisattva and destroy our virtuous act. Moreover, we would provoke the scorn of others, saying that we know how to start but not
how to finish." "Brother," said Pilgrim, "what you say is right, of
course, but what are we to do with Master, who refuses to listen to
people. I, old Monkey, can with this pair of fiery eyes and diamond
pupils discern good and evil. Just now this wind was called up by that
child hanging on the tree, for I could tell that he was a monster-spirit.
But you didn't know, nor did Master; all of you thought that he was
an offspring of some good family and told me to carry him along
instead. Old Monkey was planning to take care of him when he tried
to crush me with the heavy-body magic. Then I smashed his body to
pieces, but he resorted to the magic of the liberation of the corpse and
kidnapped Master with the whirlwind. Because Master so frequently
refused to listen to my words, I became terribly discouraged and that
was why I said we should disband. Now that you, Worthy Brother,
have shown such faithfulness, old Monkey finds it difficult to make up
his mind. Well, Pa-chieh, what exactly do you want to do?" Pa-chieh
said, "I was stupid enough just now to mouth some foolish words, but
we truly should not disband. We have no choice really, Elder Brother,
but to listen to Younger Brother Sha and try to find the monster and
save Master." Brightening up all at once, Pilgrim said, "Brothers, we
shall unite our minds to do what we must; after we have picked up
the luggage and the horse, we shall ascend this mountain to find the
monster and save Master."

Pulling at creepers and vines, descending into ravines and crossing
streams, the three of them journeyed for some seventy miles without
turning up anything. That mountain did not have a single bird or

beast, though old cedars and pines were often sighted. Growing more and more anxious, the Great Sage Sun leaped up to the summit with a bound and shouted: "Change!" He changed into someone with three heads and six arms, just as he did when he caused great disturbance in Heaven. Waving the golden-hooped rod once, he changed it into three rods, which he wielded and began to strike out madly in both directions of east and west. When Pa-chieh saw him, he said, "Sha Monk, this is bad! Elder Brother is so mad because he can't find Master that he's having a fit."

After a while, the mock combat of Pilgrim brought out a band of indigent deities, all dressed in rags; their breeches had no seats and their trousers had no cuffs. Kneeling before the mountain, they cried, "Great Sage, the mountain gods and the local spirits are here to see you." Pilgrim said, "How is it that there are so many mountain gods and local spirits?" Kowtowing, the various deities said, "Let us report to the Great Sage, this mountain has the name of Roaring Mountain[4] of the Six-Hundred-Mile Awl-Head Peak. There are one mountain god and one local spirit for each ten-mile distance; altogether we have, therefore, thirty mountain gods and thirty local spirits. We heard yesterday already that the Great Sage had arrived, but since we could not assemble all at once, we were tardy in our reception and caused the Great Sage to be angry. Please pardon us." "I'll pardon you for the moment," said Pilgrim, "but let me ask how many monster-spirits there are in this mountain." "O Father!" said the deities, "there's only one monster-spirit, and he has just about worn our heads bald! He has been such a plague that we have little incense and no paper money, that we are completely without offerings. Every one of us has hardly enough clothes to wear and food for our mouths. How many more monster-spirits could we stand?" Pilgrim said, "Where is this monster-spirit living, before or behind the mountain?" "Neither place," said the deities, "for in this mountain is a stream, which has the name of Dried Pine Stream. By the stream is a cave, which has the name of Fiery Cloud Cave. In the cave there is a demon king of vast magic powers, who frequently abducts us local spirits and mountain gods there to do such menial tasks for him as tending fire, guarding the door, beating the rattle, and shouting passwords at night. The little fiends under him also ask us frequently for payola." "You are the immortals of the Region of Darkness," said Pilgrim. "Where would you have money?" "Exactly," said the deities, "we don't have any money to give them, and all we can do is to catch a few mountain antelopes or wild deer to pay off this gang of spirits now and then. If we don't have any presents for them, they will come to wreck our temples and strip our garments, giving us such harrassment that we can't possibly lead a peaceful existence. We beseech the Great Sage to stamp out this monster for us and rescue the various living creatures on this mountain." "If all of you are under his thumb so that you have to be in his cave frequently," said Pilgrim, "you must know the name of this monster-spirit and where he is from." "When we speak of him," said the deities, "perhaps even the Great Sage knows of his origin. He is the son of the Bull Demon King, reared by Rākṣasī. After he had practiced self-cultivation at the Blazing Flame Mountain for three hundred years, he perfected the true fire of Samādhi and his magic powers were great indeed. The Bull Demon King told him to come and guard this Roaring Mountain; his childhood name is Red Boy, but his fancy title is Great King Holy Child."

Highly pleased by what he heard, Pilgrim dismissed the local spirits and mountain gods and changed back into his original form. Leaping down from the summit, he said to Pa-chieh and Sha Monk, "Brothers, you may relax. No need to worry anymore. Master won't be harmed, for the monster-spirit is related to old Monkey." "Elder Brother," said Pa-chieh with a laugh, "don't lie! You grew up in the East Pūrvavideha Continent, but this place here belongs to the West Aparagodānīya Continent. The distance is great, separated by ten thousand waters and a thousand hills, and by at least two oceans. How could he be related to you?" Pilgrim said, "Just now this bunch of deities that appeared to me happens to be the local spirits and mountain gods of this region. When I questioned them on the origin of the monster, they told me that he was the son of the Bull Demon King reared by Rākṣasī. His name is Red Boy, and he also has the fancy title of Great King Holy Child. I remember that when old Monkey caused great disturbance in Heaven five hundred years ago, I made a grand tour at the time of the famous mountains in the world to search for the heroes of this great Earth. The Bull Demon King at one time joined old Monkey and others to form a fraternal alliance of seven; of the some five or six demon kings in this alliance, only old Monkey was quite small in size. That was the reason why we addressed the Bull Demon King as big brother. Since this monster-spirit is the son of the Bull Demon King, who is an acquaintance of mine, I should be regarded as his old uncle if we begin to talk about relations. How would he dare harm my master? Let's get to his place quickly." With laughter, Sha Monk said, "O Elder Brother! As the proverb says,

Three years not showing at the door,

A relative is one no more.

You were parted from him for five, perhaps six hundred years; you haven't even drunk a cup of wine with him, nor have you exchanged invitations or seasonal gifts. How could he possibly think of himself as your relative?" "How could you measure people this way?" said Pilgrim. "As the proverb says,

If one leaf of lotus can to the ocean flow,

Will men not meet everywhere as they come and go?

Even if he doesn't admit the fact that we are relatives, it will still be unlikely that he would harm my Master. If we don't expect him to give us a banquet, we most certainly may expect him to return to us the T'ang monk whole." So, the three brothers in all earnestness led the horse, which carried the luggage on its back, and found the main road to proceed.

Without stopping night or day, they came upon a pine forest after having traveled for over a hundred miles. Inside the forest was a winding brook in which clear green water swiftly flowed. At the head of the brook there was a stone-slab bridge, which led directly up to the entrance of a cave dwelling. "Brothers," said Pilgrim, "look at that craggy cliff over there with all those rocks. It must be the home of the monster-spirit. Let me discuss the matter with you: which of you is going to stand and guard the luggage and the horse, and which of you will follow me to subdue the fiend?" Pa-chieh said, "Elder Brother, old Hog can't sit still for too long. Let me go with you." "Fine! Fine!" said Pilgrim. "Sha Monk, hide the luggage and the horse deep in the forest, and guard them carefully. The two of us will go up there to search for Master." Sha Monk agreed; Pa-chieh then followed Pilgrim to move forward, each of them holding his weapon. Truly

The child's yet unrefined and demonic fire triumphs,

But Wood Mother and Mind Monkey support each other.

We don't know what will be the outcome when they walk up to the cave, and you must listen to the explanation in the next chapter.

*Forty-one*
Monkey of the Mind is defeated by fire;
Wood Mother is captured by demons.

Good and evil, the false thoughts of a moment;
Shame and honor, neither should concern you.
Failure, success, leisure, or work—let it come and go;
Live in accord with your needs and your lot.
Composed, you have peace deep and lasting;
Muddled, you'll be besieged by demons.
The Five Phases blocked will break the spell of meditation,
As certainly as chill comes when the wind rises.

We were telling you about the Great Sage Sun, who, along with Pa-chieh, took leave of Sha Monk. Leaping over the Dried Pine Stream, they went before a cliff full of strange rocks and discovered that there was indeed a cave dwelling. The scenery all around was most unusual. You see

A winding old path secluded and quiet;
E'en wind and moon listen to the black cranes' cries.
White clouds divide and the whole river's bright;
Water flows past a bridge to make the scene divine.
Apes and birds call amid rare flowers and plants
And rocks entwined by creepers and orchids fair.
The rustling green of canyons disperses mist and smoke;
Verdant pines and bamboos the phoenix beckon.
Distant summits rise like screens stuck up;
Facing stream and mountain's a true immortal cave,
Its source coming from the K'un-lun ranges,
To be enjoyed only by one preordained.

When they went up to the entrance of the cave, they found a slab of stone on which an inscription was written in large letters: "Fiery Cloud Cave, Dried Pine Stream, Roaring Mountain." Before the entrance was a mob of little imps prancing around with swords and spears. In a loud voice, the Great Sage Sun cried out: "Youngsters! Go quickly and report this to your cave master. Tell him to send out our T'ang monk at once, so that the lives of all these spirits in your cave may be spared. If you whisper but half a 'No,' I'll overturn your residence and level your cave!" When those little fiends heard these words, they turned and dashed inside the cave, slamming shut the two doors of stone. Then they ran to make this report: "Great King, disaster!"

We now tell you about that fiend, who captured Tripitaka and brought him back to the cave. The monk was stripped of his garments, hog-tied with all four limbs behind his back, and left in the rear yard. The little fiends were ordered to scrub him clean with water so that he might be steamed and eaten. When the announcement of disaster was suddenly heard, the demons stopped their activities and went to the front to ask: "What disaster is there?" "A monk with a hairy face and a thunder-god beak," said one of the little fiends, "leading another monk with large ears and long snout, is demanding the return of their master, someone by the name of the T'ang monk, in front of our cave. If we but whisper half a 'No,' they said, they would overturn our residence and level our cave." Smiling scornfully, the demon king said, "These two happen to be Pilgrim Sun and Chu Pa-chieh. They truly know where to look! From the spot halfway in the mountain where I caught their master to our place is a distance of some one hundred and fifty miles. How did they manage to find our door so quickly?" He then gave this order: "Little ones, those of you who look after the carts, push them out!" Several of the little fiends opened the door and pushed out five small carts. When he saw them, Pa-chieh said, "Elder Brother, these monster-spirits must be afraid of us. They have hauled out their carts to move to another place." "No," said Pilgrim, "look at the way they are placing the carts over there." The little fiends indeed placed the carts at five locations corresponding to the Five Phases of metal, wood, water, fire, and earth; five of the fiends stood guard beside the carts while five others went inside again to make their report. "Everything set?" asked the demon king. "All set," they replied. "Bring me my lance," he ordered. Those fiends who looked after weapons had two of them carry out an eighteen-foot fire-tipped lance to hand over to the monster king. With no other armor except a battle kilt of embroidered silk and with naked feet, the

monster king took up the lance and walked outside. When Pilgrim
and Pa-chieh raised their heads to look, they found a fiendish creature
who had

A face as if it had been powdered white,
And lips so ruddy, they seemed brushed with paint.
No dye could create such dark, lovely hair;
His eyebrows curved like new moons carved with knives.
Phoenix and dragon coiled on his battle kilt;
More husky than Naṭa's a frame he had.
With air imposing he lifted up his lance
And walked out the door, swathed in hallowed light.
He roared like thunder in the time of spring;
His striking eyes flashed like lightning bright.
If one would know his true identity,
Remember Red Boy, a name of lasting fame.

After that Red Boy monster had emerged from the door, he shouted:
"Who is here making all these noises?" Smiling as he drew near,
Pilgrim said, "My worthy nephew! Stop fooling around! This morning
when you were hung high on top of a pine tree by the mountain road,
you presented yourself as a thin, frightened boy with jaundice and
deceived my master. I carried you on my back with all good intention,
you know, but you used a little wind to abduct my master here. Even
though you appear before me now like this, you think I can't recognize you? You might as well send my master out quickly. Stop behav-
ing like a callow youth and take care not to upset the feelings of
kinship. For I fear that if your father gets wind of this, he might blame
old Monkey for oppressing youth with age, and that wouldn't be quite
right." Enraged by the words he heard, the fiend shouted back, "You
brazen ape! What feelings of kinship do I share with you? What sort
of balderdash are you mouthing around here? Who's your worthy
nephew?" "O brother!" said Pilgrim. "You wouldn't know, would
you? At the time when your father and I became bond-brothers, we
didn't even know where you were." "This ape is babbling more
nonsense!" said the fiend. "Where do you come from, and where do
I come from? Think about this! How could my father and you become
bond-brothers?"

"Of course, you wouldn't know about this," said Pilgrim. "I am
Sun Wu-k'ung, the Great Sage, Equal to Heaven, who greatly disturbed the Heavenly Palace five hundred years ago. But before I

caused such disturbance, I made extensive tours of all the Four Great Continents, and there was not a spot on Earth or in Heaven that I did not set foot on, for I was most eager to befriend all the valiant and heroic persons. Your father, the Bull Monster King, called himself the Great Sage, Parallel with Heaven. He and old Monkey formed a fraternal alliance of seven, and we all made him the big brother.[1] There were also a Dragon Monster King, who called himself the Great Sage, Covering the Ocean, and became the second brother; a Garuda Monster King, who called himself Great Sage, United with Heaven, and became the third brother; a Lion Monster King, who called himself the Great Sage, Mover of Mountains, and became the fourth brother; a Female Monkey King, who called herself the Fair Wind Great Sage and became the fifth member; and a Giant Ape Monster King, who called himself the God-Routing Great Sage and became the sixth brother. Old Monkey, the Great Sage, Equal to Heaven, was rather small in size, and so he was number seven. At the time when we old brothers were having fun, you weren't even born!"

Refusing to believe a word he heard, the fiend lifted up his fire-tipped lance to stab at Pilgrim. An expert, as they said, would not be exercised, and Pilgrim at once stepped aside to dodge the blow before striking out with his iron rod, yelling at the same time, "You little beast! You don't know what's good for you! Watch my rod!" The monster-spirit also parried the blow, yelling at the same time, "Brazen ape! You are so ignorant of the ways of the world! Watch my lance!" The two of them thus refused to give any consideration for kinship relation; changing colors all at once, they used their magic and leaped to the edge of the clouds. What a fight!

Pilgrim enjoyed great fame;
The demon king had vast powers.
One raised up the golden-hooped rod sideways;
One lunged forward with the fire-tipped lance.
Mist spread out to shroud the Three Regions;
Clouds spewed forth to hide the four quarters.
Violent air and savage noise did fill the sky;
The sun, the moon, the stars—all lost their light.
Not one kind word was spoken,
They felt such hatred and scorn.
That one's contempt made him lose all manners;
This one's wrath killed all regard for relations.

The rod struck with increasing might;
The lance came with growing fury.
One was the primordial, true Great Sage;
One was Child Sudhana[2] of the right fruit.
They drove themselves, each trying hard to win,
All for the T'ang monk, who would greet the dharma king.

The demon and the Great Sage Sun fought for more than twenty rounds without reaching a decision. Standing on one side, Chu Pa-chieh saw clearly what was going on: although the monster-spirit was not about to be defeated, he was only parrying the blows left and right, and did not attack his opponent at all; and, although Pilgrim did not seem able to prevail all at once, he was, after all, such an adroit and skillful warrior that the rod back and forth never seemed to leave the vicinity of the monster's head. Pa-chieh thought to himself, "That's good! Pilgrim is so tricky! He could fake something and deceive the demon into drawing closer. One blow of that iron rod then would wipe out my chance of making any merit!" Look at him! He roused his spirit, lifted up his nine-pronged rake, and brought it down hard on the monster-spirit's head. Terrified by what he saw, the fiend quickly turned around and fled, dragging his lance behind him. "Chase him! Chase him!" shouted Pilgrim to Pa-chieh.

The two of them gave chase up to the entrance of the cave, where they saw the monster-spirit standing in one of the five carts, the one set up in the middle. With one hand he held on to his fire-tipped lance; with the other fist, he gave his own nose a couple of punches. Laughing, Pa-chieh said, "Shame on him! This fellow's indulging in roguery! He wants to bust his own nose, make himself bleed a little, and smear his face red so that he may go somewhere and file suit against us." After that demon gave himself two punches, he recited a spell and immediately flames shot out from his mouth as thick smoke sprouted from his nose. In an instant, flames darted up from all five carts. The demon opened his mouth a few more times and a huge fire shot up to the sky, burning so fiercely that the entire Fiery Cloud Cave was hidden from sight by the flames and smoke. Horrified, Pa-chieh said, "Elder Brother, it's getting sticky! Once we are caught in that fire, we are finished. Old Hog will be roasted, and after some spices are added, they can just enjoy me! Quickly! Run!" He said he would run, and the next moment he had already crossed the stream without any regard for Pilgrim.

Pilgrim, however, had vast magic powers; making the fire-repellent sign with his fingers, he hurled himself into the fire to search for the fiend. When the fiend saw him approaching, he spat out a few more mouthfuls of flame and the fire grew even more intense. Marvelous fire!

Torrid and fierce, a blaze reaching the sky;
Hot and brilliant, it reddens the whole earth.
It's like a fiery wheel flying up and down,
Like charcoals aglow dancing east and west.
This fire is not from Sui-jên's[3] boring into wood,
Or from Lao Tzu's refining the elixir;
It's not fire from Heaven,
Nor is it a wild fire.
It's the realized samādhi fire[4] born of the demon's self-cultivation.
The five carts conform to the Five Phases,
Which grow and transform to beget the flame.
The liver's wood[5] can make the heart's fire strong;
The heart's fire can calm the earth of the spleen;
The spleen's earth begets metal, which changes into water;
Water can beget wood, thus the magic's complete.
Growth and transformation, all are caused by fire,
For all things flourish when fire fills the sky.[6]
The fiend, long enlightened, summons samādhi.
He rules the West forever as number one.

Because the fire and smoke were so intense, Pilgrim could not even see the way before the cave's entrance and therefore he could not search for the fiend. Turning quickly, he leaped clear of the blaze at once. Having seen clearly what took place before his own cave, the monster-spirit retrieved his fire equipment after Pilgrim left, and led the various fiends back inside. After the stone doors were shut, the little fiends were told to prepare for a victory celebration, and we shall speak no more of them for the moment.

We tell you instead about Pilgrim, who vaulted over the Dried Pine Stream. As he dropped from the clouds, he heard Pa-chieh and Sha Monk conversing loudly in the pine forest. "You idiot!" shouted Pilgrim as he approached Pa-chieh. "You haven't one whit of manliness! You could be so terrified by the demonic fire that you would abandon old Monkey to flee for your own life. It's a good thing that I can still take care of myself!" "Elder Brother," said Pa-chieh chuckling, "what that monster-spirit said of you was certainly correct, for you truly are ignorant of the ways of the world. The ancients said, 'He who knows the ways of the world shall be called a hero.' The monster-spirit did not want to talk kinship with you, but you insisted on presenting yourself as his kin. When he fought with you and let loose that kind of ruthless fire, you wouldn't run but still wanted to tangle with him." "How's the fiend's ability compared with mine?" asked Pilgrim. "Not as good," said Pa-chieh.

"How about his skill with the lance?"

"No good, either," said Pa-chieh. "When old Hog saw that he had a hard time withstanding you, I came to lend you a little assistance with my rake. Little did I expect that he was so puny that he would retreat in defeat at once and start the fire in such an unconscionable way." Pilgrim said, "Indeed you shouldn't have stepped forward. I was about to find a way to give him a blow with my rod after a few more rounds. Wouldn't that have been better?" The two of them gave themselves entirely to discussing the ability of the monster-spirit and the viciousness of his fire, but Sha Monk, leaning on the trunk of a pine tree, was laughing so hard that he could barely stand up. "Brother," said Pilgrim, after he noticed him, "why are you laughing? If you had the ability to capture that demon and destroy his fire defence, that would be a benefit to all of us. As the proverb says, a few feathers will make a ball. If you could seize the demon and rescue our master, it would be your great merit." "I don't have that kind of ability," said Sha Monk, "nor can I subdue the fiend. But I am laughing because both of you are so absentminded." "What do you mean?" said Pilgrim. Sha Monk said, "Neither the ability of that monster-spirit nor his skill with the lance can be a match for you, but the only reason why you two cannot prevail against him is because of his fire. If I have anything to say about this, I'll say that you should overcome him by mutual production and mutual conquest.[7] What's so difficult about that?" When Pilgrim heard these words, he roared with laughter and said, "Brother, you are right! Indeed, we are absentminded, and we have forgotten about the whole matter. If we consider the principles of mutual production and mutual conquest, then it is water which can overcome fire. We must find some water somewhere to put out this demonic fire. We would be able to rescue Master then, wouldn't we?" "Exactly," said Sha Monk. "No need for further delay." Pilgrim said, "Stay here, the two of you, but don't fight with him. Let old Monkey go to the Great Eastern Ocean and request some dragon soldiers to come with water. After we have put out the demonic fire, we will rescue Master." "Elder Brother," said Pa-chieh, "feel free to go. We can look after ourselves here."

Dear Great Sage! Mounting the clouds to leave that place, he arrived at the Eastern Ocean in a moment. He was too busy, however, to linger and enjoy the scenery; using the water-division magic, he opened up a pathway for himself through the waves. As he proceeded, he ran into a *yakṣa* on patrol. When the *yakṣa* saw that it was the Great Sage Sun, he went quickly back to the Water-Crystal Palace to report to the old Dragon King. Ao-kuang immediately led the dragon sons and grandsons together with shrimp soldiers and crab lieutenants to meet his visitor outside the gate. Pilgrim was invited to take a seat inside and also tea. "No need for tea," said Pilgrim, "but I do have a matter that will cause you some trouble. My master who's on his way to the Western Heaven to seek scriptures from Buddha happens to be passing through the Fiery Cloud Cave at the Dried Pine Stream of the Roaring Mountain. A Red Boy monster-spirit, with the fancy title of the Great King, Holy Child, has captured my master. When old Monkey made his search up to his door and fought with him, he let out some fire which we couldn't put out. Since we thought of the fact that water could prevail over fire, I came especially to ask you for some water. You can start a big rain storm for me to put out that fire so that the T'ang monk will be delivered from this ordeal." "You are mistaken, Great Sage," said the Dragon King, "for if you want rain water, you shouldn't have come to ask me." "You are the Dragon King of Four Oceans, the principal superintendent of rain and dew. If I don't ask you, whom should I ask?" The Dragon King said, "Though I'm in charge of rain, I can't dispense it as I will. We must have the decree of the Jade Emperor, specifying where and when, the number of feet and inches, and the hour when the rain is to begin. Moreover, three officials have to raise their brushes to draft the document which then must be dispatched by the North Star. Thereafter, we must also assemble the Thunder God, the Lightning Mother, the Wind Uncle, and the Cloud Boy, for as the proverb says, 'The dragon can't move without clouds.'" "I have no need for wind, cloud, thunder, or lightning," said Pilgrim, "only some rainwater to put out a fire." "In that case," said the Dragon King, "I still would not be able to help you all by myself. Let my brothers give you a hand to achieve this merit for you. How about that?" "Where are your brothers?" asked Pilgrim. The Dragon King said, "They are Ao-ch'in, Dragon King of the Southern Ocean, Ao-jun, Dragon King of the Northern Ocean, and Ao-shun, Dragon King of the Western Ocean." Laughing, Pilgrim said, "If I have to go and tour the three oceans, I might as well go to the Region Above to ask for the Jade Emperor's decree." The Dragon King said, "There's no need for the Great Sage to go there. All we have to do here is to beat our iron drum and sound the golden bell, and they will arrive momentarily." Hearing this, Pilgrim said, "Old Dragon King, please beat the drum and sound the bell."

In a moment, the three Dragon Kings rushed in and asked, "Big Brother, why did you summon us here?" Ao-kuang said, "The Great Sage Sun is here asking for our assistance; he needs rain to subdue a fiend." The three brothers were led to greet Pilgrim, who then gave an account of why he needed water. Each one of the deities was willing to oblige. They at once called up

The shark, so ferocious, to lead the troops,
And the big-mouthed shad to be the vanguard.
The carp marshal leaped through the tide and waves;
The bream viceroy spewed forth wind and fog;
The mackerel grand marshal screamed passwords in the east;
The culter-fish commander urged the troops in the west;
Red-eyed mermaids danced along in the south;
Black-armored generals rushed forward from the north;
The sturgeon sergeant took command at the center;
Soldiers of five quarters were all valiant.
Astute and clever, the sea-turtle lord chancellor;
Shrewd and subtle, the tortoise counselor;
Full of plots and wisdom, the iguana minister;
Agile and able, the sand-turtle commander.
Wielding long swords, crab warriors walked sideways;
Stretching heavy bows, shrimp amazons leaped straight up.
The sheat fish vice-director checked his books with care
To call up the dragon soldiers to leave the waves.
We have also a testimonial poem which says:
Dragon Kings of four seas are pleased to help
At the Great Sage, Equal to Heaven's request;
When Tripitaka meets an ordeal on the way,
Water is sought to put out the fiery red.

Leading those dragon troops, Pilgrim soon arrived at the Dried Pine Stream on the Roaring Mountain. "Worthy Ao Brothers," said Pilgrim, "I'm sorry for asking you to traverse such a distance. This is the habitat of the demon. Please remain for the moment in the air and do not reveal yourselves. Let old Monkey go fight with him; if I win, there's no need for you to catch him, and even if I lose, there's no need for all of you to help me. Only when he starts his fire will I call on you, and then you can send down your rain." The Dragon Kings all agreed to heed his command.

Pilgrim lowered his cloud and went straight into the pine forest, where he shouted "Brothers" to Pa-chieh and Sha Monk. "Elder Brother," said Pa-chieh, "you've returned very quickly. Have you been able to fetch the Dragon Kings?" "They are all here," said Pilgrim. "You two had better be careful not to let the luggage get wet by the torrential rain. Old Monkey will go fight with him." Sha Monk said, "Go right ahead, Elder Brother, we'll take care of everything here."

Leaping over the stream, Pilgrim dashed up to the entrance of the cave and shouted: "Open the door!" The little fiends went at once to report: "Great King, Pilgrim Sun is here again." Raising his head, Red Boy laughed aloud and said, "That monkey, I suppose, has not been burned by the fire and that's why he has returned. Well, I'll not spare him this time, for I won't stop until his skin is charred and his flesh is seared." As he leaped up to take hold of his lance, he gave the order: "Little ones, push out the carts!" After he rushed out the door, he said to Pilgrim, "Why are you here again?" "Return my master," said Pilgrim. "Monkey head," said the fiend, "you are indeed obtuse! If the T'ang monk can be your master, can't he also be our hors d'oeuvre for wine? Forget him! Forget him!" When Pilgrim heard these words, he was infuriated; pulling out his golden-hooped rod, he struck at the fiend's head. The monster-spirit quickly raised his fire-tipped lance to parry the blow, and their battle this time was not the same as theirs last time. Marvelous battle!

The wild demon, greatly angered;
The Monkey King, highly incensed.
This one wished only to save the scripture monk;
That one would eat Tripitaka T'ang.
Their minds had changed, they quelled all kinship feelings;
Feeling estranged, they granted no concession.

> This one wished he could be caught and skinned alive;
> That one wished he could be seized and dipped in sauce.
> Truly so ferocious!
> Indeed so headstrong and fierce!
> The rod blocked by the lance, thus the contest raged;
> The lance met by the rod, each strove to win.
> They raised their hands to fight for twenty rounds,
> Both men's abilities were just the same.

The demon king fought Pilgrim for some twenty rounds, and when he
saw that he could not prevail, he made a fake thrust with his lance
and turned quickly to give his own nose two punches with his fist.
Fire and smoke poured out at once from his eyes and mouth as a huge
blaze leaped up from the carts set before the cave's entrance. Turning
his head skyward, the Great Sage Sun shouted: "Dragon Kings,
where are you?" Leading their aquatic kin, the Dragon King brothers
sent a torrential downpour of rain toward the fire of the monster-
spirit. Marvelous rain! Truly

> Drizzling and sprinkling—
> Pouring and showering—
> Drizzling and sprinkling,
> It's like the meteors falling from the sky;
> Pouring and showering,
> It's like waves churning in a sea upturned.
> At first the rain drops seem the size of a fist;
> In a while they fall by the buckets and pans.
> The whole earth's o'erflowed with duck-head green,[8]
> And tall mountains are washed blue like Buddha's head.[9]
> Water flies down the canyon like sheets of jade;
> The stream swells in a thousand silver strands.
> Roads forked three ways are all filled up;
> So is a river which has nine bends.
> The T'ang monk facing an ordeal is helped by dragons divine
> Who o'erturn Heaven's river and pour it down.

The rain descended in torrents but it could not extinguish the fiend's
fire at all. The fact of the matter was that what the Dragon Kings let
loose happened to be unauthorized rain, capable of putting out worldly
fires. How could it extinguish the true fire of samādhi cultivated by
that monster-spirit? It was, in fact, like adding oil to the fire, making
the blaze all the more intense. "Let me make the magic sign," said the
Great Sage, "and penetrate the flames." Wielding the iron rod, he

searched for the fiend. When the fiend saw him approaching, he blew a mouthful of smoke right at his face. Pilgrim tried to turn away swiftly, but he was so dazed by the smoke that tears fell from his eyes like rain. This Great Sage, you see, could not be hurt by fire but he was afraid of smoke. For during that year when he greatly disturbed the Heavenly Palace, he was placed in the eight-trigram brazier of Lao Tzu, where he had been refined for a long time.[10] He managed to crawl into the space beneath the compartment which corresponded to the Sun trigram and was not burned. The smoke whipped up by the wind, however, gave him a pair of fiery eyes and diamond pupils, and that was the reason why even now he was afraid of smoke. Once more, the fiend spat out a mouthful of smoke and the Great Sage could no longer withstand it. Mounting the clouds, he fled hurriedly while the demon retrieved his fire equipment and returned to his cave.

His whole body covered by flame and smoke, the Great Sage found the intense heat unbearable and he dove straight into the mountain stream to try to put out the fire. Little did he anticipate that the shock of the cold water was so great that the heat caused by the fire was forced inward into his body and he fainted immediately. Alas!

His breath was caught in his chest, his tongue and throat grew cold;
His spirit fled, his soul left, and his life was gone!

Those Dragon Kings of the Four Oceans were so terrified that they put a stop to the rain and yelled loudly: "Marshal Heavenly Reeds and Curtain-Raising Captain! Stop hiding in the forest! Start looking for your elder brother!"

When Pa-chieh and Sha Monk heard that they were addressed by their holy titles, they quickly untied the horse and poled the luggage to dash out of the forest. With no regard for the mud and slush, they began searching along the banks of the stream when the bubbling currents swept down from above the body of a person. When Sha Monk saw it, he leaped into the water fully clothed and hauled the body back to shore. It was the body of the Great Sage Sun. Alas, look at him!

His four limbs were bent and they could not be stretched;
His whole body up and down was cold as ice.

"Elder Brother," said Sha Monk as tears filled his eyes, "what a pity you have to go like that! You were
Someone who never aged through countless years.
Now you have died young in the middle of the way."

With a chuckle, Pa-chieh said, "Brother, stop crying. This ape is pretending to be dead, just to scare us. Feel him a little and see if there's any warmth left in his breast?" "The whole body has turned cold," said Sha Monk. "Even if there were a little warmth left, how could you revive him?" Pa-chieh said, "If he is capable of seventy-two transformations, he has seventy-two lives. Listen, you stretch out his legs while I take care of him." Sha Monk indeed straightened Pilgrim's legs while Pa-chieh lifted his head and straightened his upper torso. They then pushed his legs up and folded them around the knees before raising him into a sitting position. Rubbing his hands together until .they were warm, Pa-chieh covered Pilgrim's seven apertures and began to massage him. The cold water, you see, had had such a traumatic effect on Pilgrim that his breath was caught in his cinnabar field[11] and he could not utter a sound. He was lucky, therefore, to have all that rubbing, squeezing, and kneading by Pa-chieh, for in a moment his breath went through the three regions,[12] invaded the bright hall,[13] and burst through his apertures. "O Master," he began to say. Sha Monk said, "Elder Brother, when you were alive, you lived for Master, and his name's on your lips even when you are dead! Wake up first. We are all here." Opening his eyes, Pilgrim said, "Are you here, Brothers? Old Monkey's a loser this time!" "You fainted," said Pa-chieh chuckling, "and if old Hog hadn't saved you, you would have been finished. Aren't you going to thank me?" Pilgrim got up slowly and raised his head, saying, "The Ao Brothers, where are you?" The Dragon Kings of Four Oceans replied in midair, "Your little dragons wait upon you here." "I am sorry to have caused you to travel all this distance," said Pilgrim, "but we have not accomplished our merit. Please go back first and I shall thank you again in another day." The Dragon Kings led their large group of followers to return to their residences, which need not concern us here.

Sha Monk then supported Pilgrim and led him back into the pine forest to sit down. In a little while, Pilgrim felt more collected and his breathing became more even, but he could not restrain the tears from rolling down his cheeks. Again he cried out, "O Master!

Think of your leaving the Great T'ang that year,
When you saved me from woe beneath that mount.
On waters and hills we face demonic foes;
Our bowels are torn by ten thousand pains.
We eat with an alms bowl, whether bare or filled;

In houses or woods we meditate at night.

Our hearts are set on achieving the right fruit.

How could I know I would be hurt this day?"

Sha Monk said, "Elder Brother, please do not worry. Let us devise a plan soon and see where we can go to ask for help to rescue Master." "Where shall we go to seek help?" said Pilgrim. Sha Monk said, "I remember when the Bodhisattva first gave us the instruction that we should accompany the T'ang monk, she also gave us the promise that when we called on Heaven, Heaven would respond, or when we called on Earth, Earth would reply. We just have to decide where we should go to seek help." "When I caused great disturbance in the Heavenly Palace," said Pilgrim, "all those divine soldiers were no match for old Monkey. This monster-spirit, however, has considerable magic powers, and so our helper must be someone stronger than even old Monkey. Neither the gods in Heaven nor those deities on Earth will be adequate. If we want to catch this demon, we must go to ask the Bodhisattva Kuan-yin. But unfortunately, my bones and muscles are sore and my torso is weak. I can't perform my cloud-somersault. How can I go?" "If you have any instruction," said Pa-chieh, "tell me. I'll go." Smiling, Pilgrim said, "All right! You can go, but when you appear before the Bodhisattva, don't stare at her face. You must lower your head and bow with reverence, and when she asks you, you may then tell her the names of this place and the fiend and beseech her to come to rescue Master. If she's willing, the fiendish creature will, of course, be taken." After Pa-chieh heard this, he mounted the clouds and mists at once and headed toward the south.

We now tell you about that demon king, who was celebrating in his cave. Merrily he said to his subjects, "Little ones, Pilgrim Sun truly has suffered loss this time. Though he may not die, he will be in a big coma! Holla! I fear that they might want to go find help somewhere. Open the doors quickly! Let me see where they are going." The fiends opened the doors and when the monster-spirit rose into the air to look all around, he discovered Pa-chieh heading toward the south. The south, the monster-spirit thought to himself, could mean only one thing: Pa-chieh was going to seek the help of the Bodhisattva Kuan-yin. Dropping quickly from the clouds, the fiend cried, "Little ones, find that leather bag of mine and take it out. It hasn't been used for quite some time and I fear that the rope around its mouth is not strong enough. Change the rope for me and place the bag beneath the second door. Let me go and capture Pa-chieh by deception; when he is brought back here, we'll store him in the bag. Then he'll be steamed until he's flaky so that all of you may enjoy him with wine." The monster-spirit, you see, had a compliant leather bag, which those little fiends took out and a new rope was fastened to its mouth. They placed it beneath the second door as they were told, and we shall speak no more of them.

We tell you instead about that demon king, who had lived in this place for a long time; the whole region, in fact, was familiar to him, and he knew which route to South Sea was the shorter one and which, the longer. Taking the shorter route, he mounted the clouds and at once went past Pa-chieh. He then lowered himself onto a tall ridge, sat down solemnly, and changed into a specious form of Kuan-shih-yin to wait for Pa-chieh.

Treading his clouds, Idiot was on his way when he saw suddenly the Bodhisattva. He could not, of course, distinguish the true from the false; like foolish men of the world, he regarded all images as real Buddhas! Stopping his cloud, Idiot bowed low and said, "Bodhisattva, your disciple, Chu Wu-nêng kowtows to you." The monster-spirit said, "Why aren't you protecting the T'ang monk on his way to fetch scriptures? Why have you come to see me?" "It was because your disciple and his master met on their way a Red Boy monster-spirit, who resided in the Fiery Cloud Cave by the Dried Pine Stream in the Roaring Mountain. He abducted our master, but your disciples found the way to his door and fought with him. He happened to be someone who knew how to start a fire; during our first battle, we could not prevail, and during our second one, we could not extinguish the fire even after we asked the Dragon Kings to assist us with rain. Since Elder Brother suffered burns so severe that he could not move, he asked me to come to plead with the Bodhisattva. We beg you to be merciful and save our master from his ordeal." "That master of the Fiery Cloud Cave," said the monster-spirit, "is not prone to take human lives. It must be that you have offended him." "Not I," said Pa-chieh, "but Elder Brother did offend him. The fiend changed himself at first into a small child hung on a tree to test Master. Our Master, of course, had a most kindly disposition; he told me to untie the child and Elder Brother to carry him for a distance. Elder Brother wanted to dash him to the ground, and that was when he abducted Master." The monster-spirit said, "Get up, and follow me into the cave to see the cave-master. I'll speak on your behalf, and you can salute him; the two of us will ask him then to release your master." "O Bodhisattva," said Pa-chieh. "If he's willing to return our master, I'll be glad to kowtow to him." "Follow me then," said the demon king.

Idiot, of course, did not know any better; instead of proceeding to the South Sea, he followed the fiend right back to the entrance of the Fiery Cloud Cave. When they reached the cave, the monster-spirit proceeded to walk inside, saying, "Don't be suspicious, for he's my acquaintance. You come in, too." Idiot had no choice but to stride inside also. With a terrific shout, the various fiends seized him all at once and stuffed him into the leather bag. After the rope around its mouth was pulled tight, the bag was drawn up high to a beam and hung there. Changing back into his true form, the monster-spirit took a seat in the middle and said, "Chu Pa-chieh, what sort of abilities do you have that you dare accompany the T'ang monk to acquire scriptures? That you dare go ask the Bodhisattva to subdue me? Open your pair of eyes, take a good look, and see if you recognize me, the Great King Holy Child! Now you are caught, you'll be hung for four or five days before you'll be steamed and served as hors d'oeuvre to my little fiends for their wine." When Pa-chieh heard these words, he began screaming inside the bag, saying, "You brazen fiend! Don't you dare be so insulting! So, you've plotted and planned to deceive me, but if you dare eat me, everyone of you will be stricken with the Heaven-sent plague of swollen head!" Idiot thus persisted in his expostulation for a long time, but we shall speak no more of him for the moment.

We tell you instead about the Great Sage Sun who sat in the forest with Sha Monk. A gust of putrid wind blew past and, sneezing immediately, he said, "Bad! Bad! This wind betokens misfortune more than good luck! Chu Pa-chieh, I think, must have taken the wrong way." "If he did," said Sha Monk, "couldn't he ask someone?" Pilgrim said, "He must have run into the monster-spirit." "If he ran into the monster-spirit," said Sha Monk, "couldn't he run back to us?" "It's not right," said Pilgrim. "You sit here and guard our belongings. Let me dash over the stream and find out what's going on over there." Sha Monk said, "Your body is still sore, Elder Brother, and I fear that you'll be hurt even more by him. Let me go." "You won't do," said Pilgrim, "let me go instead."

Dear Pilgrim! Gritting his teeth to endure the pain, he took up his iron rod and ran across the stream to reach the entrance to the Fiery Cloud Cave. "Brazen monster!" he cried, and those fiends guarding the door ran inside to report: "Pilgrim Sun is shouting again at the door!" The demon king gave the order for him to be seized, and all those little fiends, teeming with spears and swords, rushed out the door shouting, "Seize him! Seize him!" Pilgrim indeed was too weak to fight and he dared not oppose them. Diving to one side of the road, he recited a spell, crying, "Change!" He changed at once into a cloth wrapper adorned with gold. When the little fiends saw it, they took it inside and reported, "Great King, Pilgrim Sun is scared. When he heard the word 'seize,' he was so frightened that he dropped this wrapper and fled." Laughing, the demon king said, "That wrapper is not worth much! All it contains must be the torn shirts of those monks and their old hats. Bring it in and wash it clean; the piece of material can be used for mending or lining." One of the little fiends put the wrapper on his back to carry it inside, not knowing that it was the transformation of Pilgrim. Pilgrim said, "That's good! That's how you ought to carry this cloth wrapper adorned with gold!" Not thinking much about the thing, the monster-spirit left it inside the door.

Dear Pilgrim! Even in the midst of falsehood he knew greater falsehood, and each fakery of his produced more fakery! He pulled off one piece of his hair on which he blew a mouthful of divine breath: it changed at once into the wrapper, while his true body took on the form of a tiny fly which alighted on the door post. Then he heard Pa-chieh moaning and muttering somewhere in a muffled voice, somewhat like a hog stricken with plague! With a buzz, Pilgrim flew up to look around and saw at once that there was a leather bag hung high up on the beam. When he alighted on the bag, he heard Pa-chieh expostulating the demon in all sorts of vile language. "Wretched fiend," he said, "how dare you change yourself into a specious Bodhisattva Kuan-yin to trick me here? How dare you hang me up and want to eat me? One day, when my Elder Brother

Uses his boundless power, equal to Heav'n,
All monsters of this mountain will then be caught.
When I'm freed after this leather bag's untied,
I'll rake you a thousand times before I stop!"

When Pilgrim heard these words, he laughed silently, saying to himself, "Though the idiot must be suffocating in there, he hasn't dropped his banner or spear yet! Old Monkey must catch hold of this fiend! If I don't, I'll not be able to rid myself of my hostility!"

He was just trying to think of a plan to rescue Pa-chieh when he heard the call of the demon king: "Where are the six mighty commanders?" There were, you see, six little fiends who became special friends of his, and these spirits received the appointment of mighty commander. Their names were: Cloud-in-Fog, Fog-in-Cloud, Quick-as-Fire, Swift-as-Wind, Hurly-Burly, and Burly-Hurly. The six mighty commanders went forward and knelt down. The demon king said, "Do you all know the way to the house of the Venerable Great King?" "We do," they said. The demon king said, "Go at once, and journey in the night if you have to, to give this invitation to the Venerable Great King. Tell him that I have caught the T'ang monk, who will be steamed and served for him to eat so that his age may be lengthened a thousandfold." Obeying this order, the six fiends swarmed out of the door and left. With a buzz, Pilgrim flew away from the bag and followed those fiends to leave the cave. We do not know whom they want to invite to come here, and you must listen to the explanation in the next chapter.

## Forty-two

The Great Sage in diligence calls at South Sea;
Kuan-yin with compassion binds the Red Boy.

We were telling you about those six mighty commanders, who walked out of the cave entrance and followed the road directly toward the southwest. Pilgrim thought to himself: "They wanted to extend an invitation for the Venerable Old King to eat my master, and that Venerable Old King has to be the Bull Demon King. Since old Monkey met him that year, our friendship was a deep one, as ours were the most congenial spirits and sentiments. Now I have returned to the path of rectitude; though he's still a perverse demon, I can remember his looks despite our lengthy separation. Let old Monkey transform himself into the Bull Monster King and see if they could be deceived." Dear Pilgrim! He slipped away from those six little fiends; spreading his wings, he flew to a distance of some ten miles ahead. With one shake of his body he changed into the form of Bull Monster King and, pulling off several strands of hair, he cried, "Change!" They changed into several little fiends who were mounting falcons, leading hounds, and brandishing bows and arrows as if they were hunting in the fold of the mountain. There they waited for the six mighty commanders.

As that motley crew stumbled along, they suddenly saw the Bull Monster King seated before them. So startled were Burly-Hurly and Hurly-Burly that they fell to their knees at once, crying, "Venerable Great King is here!" Since Cloud-in-Fog, Fog-in-Cloud, Quick-as-Fire, and Swift-as-Wind were all of fleshly eyes and mortal stock, how could they possibly distinguish between the true and the false? They all knelt down also and kowtowed, saying, "Father, these little ones have been sent by the Great King Holy Child from the Fiery Cloud Cave. We are here to invite Father Venerable Great King to dine on the flesh of the T'ang monk, so that your age will be lengthened a thousandfold." "Children," rejoined Pilgrim, "get up. Follow me home; I'll go with you after I've changed my clothes." Kowtowing again, the little fiends said, "We beg our Father not to stand on ceremony. There's no need to return to your residence. The distance is great, and we fear that our Great King will chide us for our delay. We beseech you to begin your journey at once." Laughing, Pilgrim said, "What nice children you are! All right, all right! Clear the way and I'll go with you." The six fiends roused their spirits and shouted to clear the way, while the Great Sage followed them.

In no time at all they returned to their own place. Swift-as-Wind and Quick-as-Fire dashed into the cave, crying, "Great King, Father Venerable Great King has arrived." Delighted, the monster king said, "All of you are quite useful! You've returned so quickly!" He at once gave the order for all his captains to arrange their troops and to unfurl the flags and drums to receive the Venerable Great King. The fiends of the entire cave all obeyed this command and they formed an orderly formation all the way out to the entrance. Shaking his body once to retrieve his hairs who were leading dogs and falcons, Pilgrim with chest thrust forward walked loftily inside in big strides. After he took a seat in the middle facing south, Red Boy faced him and knelt down to kowtow to him. "Father King," he said, "your child gives you obeisance." Pilgrim said, "My child is exempted from such ceremonies." Only after he had prostrated himself four times did the monster king rise from the ground and stand below the seat of Pilgrim. "My child," said Pilgrim, "why did you ask me to come here?" Bowing again, the monster king said, "Though your child is not talented, he has managed to capture a certain person yesterday, a monk from the Great T'ang in the Land of the East. I have often heard people say that he is someone who has practiced self-cultivation for ten incarnations. If anyone eats a piece of his flesh, this person will enjoy the same age as an immortal from P'êng-lai or Ying-chou. Your foolish boy does not dare eat the T'ang monk by himself. That is why I have invited Father King especially to enjoy with me the flesh of the T'ang monk, so that your age may be lengthened a thousandfold." When Pilgrim heard these words, he shuddered and said, "My child, which T'ang monk is this?" "The one journeying to the Western Heaven to acquire scriptures," said the monster king." "My child," said Pilgrim, "is he the master of Pilgrim Sun?" 'Indeed," said the monster king. Waving his hand and shaking his head, Pilgrim said, "Don't provoke him! You can provoke others, but you don't know what sort of person that Pilgrim Sun happens to be! My worthy boy, you haven't met him, I suppose? That monkey has vast magic powers and knows many ways of transformation. Once when he caused great disturbance in the Heavenly Palace, the Great Jade Emperor sent against him one hundred thousand celestial soldiers, but they did not succeed in capturing him even after they had set up the cosmic nets. How dare you want to eat his master? Quickly, send him back to his disciple, and don't provoke that monkey. If he finds out that you have eaten his master, he need not come to fight with you; all he has to do is to use that golden-hooped rod of his to drill a hole halfway into the mountain and he will shovel it right out of its roots! My child, where will you find shelter then? Who will take care of me when I grow old?"

"Father King," said the monster king, "what are you saying? You are magnifying the powers of others to belittle the abilities of your son. Though that Pilgrim Sun and his two brothers—altogether three of them—attempted to lead the T'ang monk to cross our mountain, they permitted me to use a transformation to abduct their master back here. Afterwards, he and Chu Pa-chieh searched their way to our door, and he then made some such foolish claim that he was a kin of ours. I grew angry and fought with him, though the several rounds we went through did not indicate that he was such a hot shot! Chu Pa-chieh stepped in from the side to join the fray, and that was when your child spat out his true fire of samādhi and defeated them all at once. They were so frightened, in fact, that they went to ask the Dragon Kings of the Four Oceans to assist them with rain, but the rainwater, of course, could not extinguish my true fire of samādhi. Pilgrim Sun was so severely burned this time that he went into a little coma! Then he told Chu Pa-chieh to seek help from the Bodhisattva Kuan-yin of the South Sea. I changed into a specious Kuan-yin and tricked Pa-chieh back here; he's now hung in our compliant bag waiting to be steamed and fed to the little ones. This morning, that Pilgrim returned to our door to make noises once more; when I gave the order to seize him, he was so frightened that he even abandoned a wrap of his and fled. It was then that I decided to invite Father King to come here so that you can see him live before he is steamed for food. My hope is for your age to lengthen, so that you will enjoy long life without ever growing old."

Chuckling, Pilgrim said, "My worthy boy! You know only that you can overpower him with your true fire of samādhi. You don't know that he knows seventy-two ways of transformation." "He can change into whatever he wants to," said the monster king, "but I can still recognize him. I don't think he dares enter our door." "My child," said Pilgrim, "you may recognize him when he changes into something big, and that will be difficult indeed for him to get inside your door. But if he changes into something small, it will be difficult for you to recognize him." "Let him!" said the monster king. "Every door of mine here has four or five little fiends standing guard over it. How could he possibly enter?" Pilgrim said, "So you don't know about this! He is able to change into a fly, a mosquito, a flea, or a bee, a butterfly, a mole-cricket, or some such creature. He can even change into a form like me! How could you possibly recognize him?" "Don't worry!" said the monster king. "Even if he had a gall of iron and a heart of bronze, he wouldn't dare approach my door."

"According to what you have told me, my worthy boy," said Pilgrim, "you certainly are more than able to withstand him, and this explains why you are eager to invite me to come and dine on the T'ang monk's flesh. Unfortunately, however, I can't eat it today." "Why not?" asked the monster king. Pilgrim said, "I'm feeling my age these days, and your mother often tells me to do some good deeds. There's not much I can do, I thought, but I have decided to keep a vegetarian diet." The monster king said, "Is Father King keeping a permanent one or a monthly diet?" "Neither," said Pilgrim, "but mine is called a 'Thunder Vegetarian Diet,' and I keep it for only four days in a month." "Which four?" asked the monster king. Pilgrim said, "During those three days when the celestial stem *hsin* appears in the sexagesimal representations[1] and during the sixth day of the month. Today happens to be the day of *hsin-yu*: I should maintain a vegetarian diet in the first place, and in the second place, a *yu* day means that I myself should not meet any guests. Therefore, let's wait until tomorrow; I'll personally see to it that the T'ang monk is scrubbed clean to be steamed and enjoyed along with all of you."

When the monster king heard these words, he thought to himself: "My Father King has always fed on humans; that's been his livelihood, in fact, for over a thousand years. How is it that he has taken up a vegetarian diet now? He has, after all, committed many evil acts. How could three or four days of vegetarian diet atone for them? His words make no sense! Something's fishy!" He turned at once and walked out the second door, calling together the six mighty commanders to ask them: "Where did you find the Venerable Great King?" The little fiends said, "On our way." "I remarked that you all returned so quickly," said the monster king. "Didn't you reach his house?" "No," said the little fiends, "we did not." "That's bad!" said the monster king. "We have been deceived by him! This is no Venerable Great King." All those little fiends knelt down immediately, saying, "Great King, can't you even recognize your own father?" "The features and the gestures seem genuine," said the monster king, "but he doesn't talk like him. I fear that we may be deceived by him and become his victim. Take care, all of you: those who use swords unsheath your swords; those who use spears keep your spears sharp; those who use staffs and ropes have them ready. Let me question him some more and see how he talks. If indeed he is the Venerable Great King, we can wait even a month until he is pleased to eat the T'ang monk. But if his words are not right, I'll give a yell and all of you will attack together." The various demons obeyed.

This monster king went inside again and bowed once more to Pilgrim. "My child," said Pilgrim, "there's no need to stand on ceremony in the family. No need to bow to me. If you have something to say, say it." Prostrating himself on the ground, the monster king said, "Your foolish boy invited you to come here for two reasons: first, I wanted to present to you the flesh of the T'ang monk, and second, I have a small question to ask you. Some days ago, I was taking a leisure trip; as I mounted the auspicious luminosity to rise to the ninefold Heaven, I ran suddenly into Master Chang Tao-ling, the Taoist Patriarch."[2] "Is he the Heavenly Preceptor?" said Pilgrim. "Yes," said the monster king. Pilgrim said, "What did he have to say?" "When he saw how well formed my features were," said the monster king, "and how level were my shoulders, he inquired after the hour, date, month, and year of my birth. Your child, however, was too young to remember the exact time. An expert in astrological divination, the Master wanted to tell my fortune through calculations based on the five planets. That is the reason why I have asked Father King to come here. Please tell me the times of my birth, so that I can ask him to tell my fortune the next time I see him." When Pilgrim heard these words, he sat smiling to himself, thinking, "Dear monster! Since old Monkey has returned to the Buddhist fruit, I have caught, as a guardian of Master T'ang, several monster-spirits on our way, but none of them matches this one for jugglery! If he asks me about some trivial matters in the household, I can fabricate an answer with whatever comes into my mind. But now he wants to have the date, month, and year of his birth! How could I know?" Dear Monkey King! He was most resourceful indeed! Sitting augustly in the middle, he did not betray the slightest fear; instead, his face beaming with pleasure, he said smiling, "My worthy boy, please rise. Because of my age, I have been troubled by all sorts of things of late, and I have quite forgotten the exact time of your birth. Let me ask your mother when I return home tomorrow."

The monster king said to himself, "Father King has never stopped talking about the eight nativity characters³ of my birth, saying that I have an age as lengthy as Heaven's. How could he forget them today? Nonsense! He has to be false!" He gave a yell, and the various fiends rushed forward to hack at Pilgrim's head and face with their spears and swords. Using the golden-hooped rod to parry the blows, this Great Sage changed back into his original form and said to the monster-spirit, "My worthy child! How unreasonable you are! How could a son attack his own father?" Filled with embarrassment, the monster king did not even dare look at him, as Pilgrim transformed himself into a beam of golden light and left the cave dwelling. "Great King," said the little fiends, "Pilgrim Sun has escaped." The monster king said, "All right, all right! Let him go! I'll admit defeat this time! Let's shut the door and say nothing to him. We will wash and scrub the T'ang monk so that he can be steamed and eaten."

We now tell you about that Pilgrim who held on to his iron rod and walked toward the stream, roaring with laughter. When Sha Monk heard him, he quickly left the woods to meet him, saying, "Elder Brother, you have gone for nearly half a day, and you have returned laughing. Could it be that you have succeeded in rescuing Master?" "Brother," said Pilgrim, "though I have not rescued Master, I have won a round." "What do you mean?" said Sha Monk. Pilgrim said, "Chu Pa-chieh, you see, was tricked by that fiend, who changed himself into the form of Kuan-yin. He is caught and hung now in a leather bag. I was trying to devise a plan to rescue him when I heard that these so-called six mighty commanders were sent to invite a Venerable Great King to dine on Master's flesh. Old Monkey thought that that Great King had to be the Bull Monster King; so I changed into his form, bluffed my way in, and took the seat in the middle. The fiend called me Father King, and I answered him; he kowtowed to me, and I accepted it. It was a pleasure indeed! That was the round I won." "Elder Brother," said Sha Monk, "the way you are greedy of small advantages will make it difficult, I fear, for Master's life to be preserved." "Don't worry," said Pilgrim, "let me go and ask the Bodhisattva to come here." "But your torso is still sore," said Sha Monk. "Not anymore!" said Pilgrim. "The ancients said, 'A happy affair cheers one's spirit.' You look after the luggage and the horse; let me go." "You've given that monster a grudge against you," said Sha Monk, "and I fear that he might harm our master. Go and come back quickly." Pilgrim said, "I'll come back quickly all right! In the time of a meal, I'll be back."

Dear Great Sage! As he was speaking, he slipped away from Sha Monk; using his cloud-somersault, he headed straight for the South Sea. It took him much less than half an hour in the air when he saw the scenery of the Potalaka Mountain. In a moment, he lowered his cloud and dropped down on the mountain cliff, where he was met by a group of twenty-four devas who asked: "Where are you going, Great Sage?" After Pilgrim bowed to them, he said, "I want to see the Bodhisattva." "Wait a moment," said the devas, "and let us announce you." Then the deva Kuei-tzu-mu went before the Cave of Tidal Sound to announce: "Let the Bodhisattva know that Sun Wu-k'ung is here to have an audience with you." When the Bodhisattva heard the announcement, she ordered him to enter. Straightening out his attire, the Great Sage walked inside solemnly and prostrated himself before the Bodhisattva. "Wu-k'ung, why aren't you leading Master Gold Cicada to the West to seek scriptures?" said the Bodhisattva. "Why are you here?" Pilgrim said, "Permit me to make this known to the Bodhisattva. Your disciple was accompanying the T'ang monk on his journey, when we reached the Fiery Cloud Cave by the Dried Pine Stream at the Roaring Mountain. There is a monster-spirit called Red Boy, whose name is also the Great King Holy Child, and who has abducted my master. Your disciple and Chu Wu-nêng found our way to his door and fought with him. He let loose his samādhi fire and we could not prevail against him nor could we rescue Master. I went swiftly to the Great Eastern Ocean and managed to return with the Dragon Kings of the Four Oceans. They gave us rainwater, but we still could not win. In fact, your disciple was burned so badly that he almost lost his life." The Bodhisattva said, "If his is the samādhi fire and if he has such magic powers, why did you go seek the aid of the Dragon Kings? Why did you not come see me?" "I was about to come," said Pilgrim, "but your disciple was badly hurt by the smoke, unable to mount the clouds. I therefore told Chu Pa-chieh to come and seek the assistance of the Bodhisattva." "But Wu-nêng has never appeared," said the Bodhisattva. "Indeed he hasn't reached your treasure mountain," said Pilgrim, "for he was deceived by that monster-spirit, who changed into your image and has taken Wu-nêng into his cave. Right now, Wu-nêng is hanging in a leather bag, about to be steamed and eaten."

Hearing this, the Bodhisattva grew terribly angry, crying, "How dare that brazen fiend change into my image!" As she cried, she flung into the ocean the immaculate porcelain vase set with precious pearls which she held in her hand. Pilgrim was so startled that his hairs stood on end, and he stood up at once to stand in waiting down below, saying to himself, "This Bodhisattva still has quite a fiery temper! Well, old Monkey should have known better than to speak like that and provoke her into ruining her virtue by smashing the immaculate vase. What a pity! What a pity! If I had known it earlier I would have asked her to give it instead to old Monkey. That would be some gift, wouldn't it?"

Hardly had he finished speaking when the vase appeared again at the crest of some gigantic waves swelling up in the middle of the ocean. The vase, you see, was borne on the back of a strange creature, which Pilgrim stared at intently. How does this creature look?

The "Helper of Mud" is his primal name,
He adds luster to water to show his might.
Reclusive, he knows the laws of Heav'n and Earth;
Retired, he sees yet the mysteries of ghosts and gods.
Safely he hides once his head and tail withdraw,
But legs outstretched will make him fly and soar.
As King Wên drew trigrams and Tsêng Yüan divined,
He frequented, too, the courtyards of Fu Hsi.[4]
His nature displays a thousand charms
When he frolics and plays in the rising tide.
His armor's woven by strands of golden cord;
Spot by spot, that's how his shell has been adorned.
His robe shows Eight Trigrams and Nine Palaces,

And richly ornate is his gown of green.
Brave when he's living—so he's loved by Dragon Kings;
The Buddha's tablet he bears e'en after death.
If you want to know this strange creature's name,
He's the fierce black tortoise who makes winds and waves.

Carrying the vase on his back, the tortoise climbed ashore and nodded his head at the Bodhisattva twenty-four times to indicate that he had given her twenty-four bows.

When Pilgrim saw him, he smiled and thought to himself: "So the guardian of the vase is here. If the vase ever gets lost, I suppose we can ask him for it." The Bodhisattva said, "Wu-k'ung, what are you saying down there?" "Nothing," said Pilgrim. "Then bring the vase up here," commanded the Bodhisattva. Pilgrim went forward at once to pick up the vase. Alas! He could not do so at all! It was as if a dragonfly attempted to rock a stone pillar—how could he even budge it? Pilgrim approached the Bodhisattva and knelt down, saying, "Your disciple cannot pick it up." "Monkey head," said the Bodhisattva, "all you know is how to brag! If you can't even pick up a small vase, how can you subdue fiends and capture monsters?" "To tell you the truth, Bodhisattva," said Pilgrim, "I might be able to do it ordinarily, but today I just can't pick it up. I must have been hurt by the monster-spirit, and my strength has weakened." The Bodhisattva said, "Normally it's an empty vase, but once it has been thrown into the ocean, it has traveled through the three rivers, the five lakes, the eight seas, and the four big rivers. It has, in fact, gathered together from all the aquatic bodies in the world an oceanful of water which is now stored inside it. You may be strong, but you don't possess the strength of upholding the ocean. That's why you cannot pick up the vase." Pressing his hands together before him, Pilgrim said, "Yes, your disciple is ignorant of this."

Walking forward, the Bodhisattva used her right hand and picked up the immaculate vase with no effort at all and placed it on the middle of her left palm. The tortoise nodded his head again before he crawled back into the water. "So this is a coolie who serves the household and looks after the vase!" said Pilgrim. After the Bodhisattva took her seat again, she said, "Wu-k'ung, the sweet dew in my vase is not like that unauthorized rain of the Dragon Kings; it can extinguish the samādhi fire of the monster-spirit. I want you to take it with you, but you are unable to pick up the vase. I want the Dragon

Girl of Goodly Wealth to go with you, but I fear that you are not a person of kindly disposition. All you know is how to hoodwink people. When you see how beautiful my Dragon Girl is, and what a treasure is my immaculate vase, you will try to steal it. If you succeed, where would I find time to go look for you? You'd better leave something behind as a pledge." "How pitiful!" said Pilgrim. "Bodhisattva, you are so suspicious! Since your disciple embraced complete poverty, he has never indulged in such activities. You tell me to leave a pledge, what shall I use? This silk shirt on my body is a gift from you. And this tiger-skin skirt, how much can it be worth? The iron rod—well, I need it for protection night and day. Only this little fillet on my head is made of gold, but you used some tricks to make it grow on my head so that it could not be taken down. If you want a pledge, I'm willing now to give that to you as a pledge. You can recite a Loose-Fillet Spell and take it off from me. Otherwise, what shall I use as a pledge?" "You are rather smug, aren't you?" said the Bodhisattva. "I don't want your clothes, your iron rod, or your gold fillet. Pull off one strand of that life-saving hair behind your head and give it to me." Pilgrim said, "These hairs were also your gift; I fear that if I pull one off, they will be broken up in such a way that they will no longer be able to save my life." "You ape!" scolded the Bodhisattva. "You are so stingy that you won't even pull one hair! That makes it difficult for me to dispense my Goodly Wealth!" Laughing, Pilgrim said, "Bodhisattva, you are truly suspicious! But as the saying goes, 'If you don't have regard for the monk at least have regard for the Buddha.' I beg you to save my master from his ordeal." Then the Bodhisattva

Freely and gladly left the lotus seat

And walked up the rocky cliff with scented steps.

Since the holy monk was threatened with harm,

She would subdue the fiend and give him help.

Highly pleased, the Great Sage Sun followed Kuan-yin out of the Tidal Sound Cave, as the various devas stood attention on the Potalaka Peak. "Wu-k'ung," said the Bodhisattva, "let's cross the ocean." Pilgrim bowed and said, "Let the Bodhisattva go first." "You go first," said the Bodhisattva. Kowtowing, Pilgrim said, "Your disciple dares not display his power before the Bodhisattva. If I use the cloud-somersault, my clothes may flip up and reveal my body, and I fear that the Bodhisattva will take offense at my irreverence." When the Bodhisattva heard these words, she told the Dragon Girl of Goodly

Wealth to pick from the lotus pond one petal of lotus flower and drop it into the ocean below the mountain ridge. Then she said to Pilgrim, "Get up on that lotus flower petal and I'll send you across the ocean." When Pilgrim saw the flower, he said, "Bodhisattva, this petal of flower is so light and thin. How could it bear me up? I'll tumble into the water for sure, and won't my tiger-skin skirt be soaked? If it loses its tan, how can I wear it when the weather turns cold?" "Get up there and see what happens!" shouted the Bodhisattva. Not daring to disobey, Pilgrim risked his life and jumped onto the flower. At first, it did seem rather light and small, but when he alighted on it, he found that the flower was actually somewhat larger than a small boat. Delighted, Pilgrim said, "Bodhisattva, it should hold me." "In that case," said the Bodhisattva, "why can't you cross the ocean?" Pilgrim said, "There is neither pole nor oar, neither sail nor mast. How could I cross the ocean?" "No need for that," said the Bodhisattva, who blew a mouthful of air lightly onto the lotus flower and immediately it drifted away from the shore. Another breath of the Bodhisattva sent Pilgrim across the bitter sea of the Southern Ocean until he reached the other shore. When his feet touched solid ground again, Pilgrim laughed and said, "This Bodhisattva truly knows how to display her powers! She's able to summon old Monkey hither and thither with no effort at all!"

The Bodhisattva then gave instructions for all the devas each to stand guard in his station, and for the Dragon Girl of Goodly Wealth to shut the gate of the cave. Mounting the auspicious cloud, she departed from the Potalaka Peak. When she reached the backside of the mountain, she called out: "Hui-an, where are you?" Hui-an, you see, whose common name was Mokṣa, happened to be the second prince of the Pagoda Bearer Devarāja Li, and he, as the pupil taught personally by the Bodhisattva, never strayed from her side. His name was Disciple Hui-an, the Dharma Guardian. Pressing his hands together before him, Hui-an bowed to the Bodhisattva, who said to him, "Go quickly to the Region Above and borrow the Swords of Constellations from your Father King." "How many swords do you want, Teacher?" said Hui-an. "The entire set," said the Bodhisattva.

Obeying her command, Hui-an mounted the clouds and went through the South Heavenly Gate to reach the Palace of Cloudy Towers. He kowtowed to his Father King, who asked him: "Why has my son come here?" Mokṣa replied, "Sun Wu-k'ung came to ask my teacher to subdue a fiend; she in turn told your child to borrow the Swords of Constellations from Father King." The devarāja at once asked Naṭa to take out the swords, all thirty-six of them, to hand over to Mokṣa, who said to Naṭa, "Brother, please go and bow to mother. I have urgent business; when I return the swords, I shall kowtow to her then." They parted hurriedly; Mokṣa mounted the auspicious luminosity and returned to South Sea, where he presented the swords to the Bodhisattva.

After she received them, the Bodhisattva threw them into the air as she recited a spell: the swords were transformed into a thousand-leaf lotus platform. Leaping up, the Bodhisattva sat solemnly in the middle. On one side, Pilgrim snickered to himself: "This Bodhisattva is so prudent and penurious! In that pond of hers she has her own five-colored treasure lotus platform, but she can't bear to use it. She has to borrow someone's things!" "Wu-k'ung," said the Bodhisattva, "stop talking! Follow me!" They all mounted the clouds and left the ocean, the white cockatoo flying ahead while Great Sage Sun and Hui-an followed from behind.

In a moment, they reached the peak of a mountain. "This is the Roaring Mountain," said Pilgrim, "and from here to the door of the monster-spirit is a distance of approximately four hundred miles." When the Bodhisattva heard this, she lowered her auspicious cloud and recited a spell that began with the letter, Oṁ. At once various deities and demons appeared from the left and right of the mountain, all local spirits and mountain deities of the region. They came to kowtow before the Bodhisattva's treasure lotus seat. "Don't be alarmed, all of you," said the Bodhisattva. "I'm here to seize this demon king, but I want you all to sweep this area clean. Not a single living creature is to remain within three hundred miles around here. Take the small beasts in their lairs, the young creatures in their nests, and send them up to the peak so that their lives may be preserved." The various deities obeyed and left; they returned momentarily to report that their work was done. The Bodhisattva said, "If the region is cleared, all of you may return to your shrines." She turned her immaculate vase upside down and all at once a torrent of water thundered forth. Truly it

Surged over the summit,
And dashed over the stone walls.
Surging over the summit it seemed the swelling sea;

Dashing over stone walls it seemed the vast ocean.
Black mists arose, damping the entire sky;
Green waves reflecting the sun beamed chilly light.
The whole cliff gushed jadelike sprays;
The whole sea sprouted gold lotus.
The Bodhisattva let loose her awesome might,
Her sleeve revealed the Dharmakāya of Zen.[5]
This place was changed to Potalaka's scene,
Truly a perfect image of South Sea.
Young *t'an*[6] blossoms sprang from lovely rushes;
Fresh palmyra leaves spread from scented grass.
On purple bamboos the cockatoo paused;
Amid some green pines red partridges called.
Waves ten thousand fold and lotus all around,
Hear the wind roar, the water surging up to Heav'n.

When the Great Sage Sun saw this, he marveled to himself: "Truly
a Bodhisattva of great mercy and compassion! If old Monkey had this
kind of dharma power, he would simply pour the little vase on the
mountain. Who cares about fowls and beasts, crawling or winged
creatures!" "Wu-k'ung," cried the Bodhisattva, "stretch forth your
hand." Hurriedly rolling up his sleeve, Pilgrim stretched out his left
hand. The Bodhisattva pulled out a twig of her willow branch after
having dipped it in the sweet dew of her vase and wrote on his palm
the word "Delusion." She said to him, "Hold your fist and go quickly
to provoke battle with the monster-spirit. You are permitted not to
win but to lose; let him defeat you and chase you back here. I have
my power to subdue him."

Obeying the instruction, Pilgrim turned his cloudy luminosity and
headed straight for the entrance of the cave. Holding his left hand in
a fist and the iron rod with his right, he shouted, "Fiends, open the
door." Those little fiends again went inside to report: "Pilgrim Sun is
here again." "Shut the door tightly," said the monster king, "and
don't mind him." "Dear boy!" shouted Pilgrim. "You chased your
old man out the door, and you still wouldn't open up!" The little
fiends reported again: "Pilgrim Sun is using that little something to
insult you." All the monster said was, "Don't listen to him!" After
he had shouted for a couple of times and found the door still tightly
shut, Pilgrim became enraged. He lifted the iron rod and with one
blow punched a big hole in the door. The little fiends were so terrified

that they ran inside, crying, "Pilgrim Sun has smashed our door!"
When the monster king heard these reports and discovered that the
front door was smashed, he bounded out the door and, holding the
lance, yelled at Pilgrim: "You ape! You really don't know when to
stop! I let you take some advantage of me and you are still not
content. You dare come again to oppress me by smashing my door.
What sort of punishment should you receive?" "My child," said
Pilgrim, "you dare chase your old man out your door. What sort of
punishment should *you* receive?"

Embarrassed as well as angered, the monster king picked up his
lance and stabbed at Pilgrim's chest, who also lifted his iron rod to
parry and return the blow. They fought for four or five rounds when
Pilgrim, still making a fist, retreated with his rod trailing behind him.
The monster king stood still before the mountain and said, "I'm
going to wash and scrub the T'ang monk instead." "My dear boy,"
said Pilgrim, "Heaven is watching you! Won't you come?" When the
monster-spirit heard these words, he grew even more enraged. With
a yell, he dashed before Pilgrim and attempted to stab him with the
lance once more. Our Pilgrim wielded his iron rod and fought with
him for several rounds before retreating again. "Monkey," scolded
the monster king, "you were able to fight before for at least twenty or
thirty rounds. Why are you running away now when we are just
settling down to do battle? Why?" "Worthy child," said Pilgrim,
chuckling, "your old man is afraid that you will start a fire!" The
monster-spirit said, "I'm not going to start the fire. You come up
here." "If you are not," said Pilgrim, "step over here. A gallant fellow
should not beat up people in front of his own house." The monster-
spirit, of course, did not know that this was a trick; he lifted his lance
indeed and gave chase once more. Dragging his rod, Pilgrim opened
up his left fist and the monster king was completely deluded; all he
had in mind was to give chase to his adversary. The one running
ahead was like a falling meteor; the one chasing from behind was like
an arrow leaving the bow.

In less than a moment, they saw the Bodhisattva. Pilgrim said,
"Monster-spirit, I'm scared of you. Let me go. You have chased me to
the South Sea, the residence of the Bodhisattva Kuan-yin. Why
aren't you turning back?" The monster king refused to believe it;
gritting his teeth, he persisted in his chase. Pilgrim with one shake of
his body slipped into the divine luminosity that surrounded the body

of the Bodhisattva and disappeared. When the monster-spirit suddenly discovered that Pilgrim was gone, he walked up to the Bodhisattva with bulging eyes and said to her, "Are you the reinforcement Pilgrim Sun brought here?" The Bodhisattva did not reply. Rolling the lance in his hands, the monster king bellowed, "Hey! Are you the reinforcement Pilgrim Sun brought here?" Still the Bodhisattva did not reply. The monster-spirit lifted his lance and jabbed at the heart of the Bodhisattva, who at once changed herself into a beam of golden light and rose into the air. Pilgrim followed her on her way up and said to her, "Bodhisattva, you are trying to take advantage of me! The monster-spirit asked you several times. How could you pretend to be deaf and dumb and not make any noise at all? One blow of his lance, in fact, chased you away, and you have even left behind your lotus platform." "Don't talk," said the Bodhisattva, "let's see what he will do." At this time, Pilgrim and Mokṣa both stood in the air shoulder to shoulder and stared down; they found the monster-spirit laughing scornfully and saying to himself: "Brazen ape, you're mistaken about me! What sort of person do you think that I, Holy Child, happen to be? For several times you could not prevail against me, and then you had to go and fetch some namby-pamby Bodhisattva. One blow of my lance now has made her vanish completely. Moreover, she has even left the treasure lotus platform behind. Well, let me get up there and take a seat." Dear monster-spirit. He imitated the Bodhisattva by sitting in the middle of the platform with hands and legs folded. When he saw this, Pilgrim said, "Fine! Fine! Fine! This lotus platform has been given to some-one else!" "Wu-k'ung," said the Bodhisattva, "what are you saying again?" "Saying what? Saying what?" replied Pilgrim. "I'm saying that the lotus platform has been given to someone else. Look! It's underneath his thighs. You think he's going to return it to you?" "I *wanted* him to sit there," said the Bodhisattva. "Well, he's smaller than you," said Pilgrim, "and it seems that the seat fits him even better than it fits you." "Stop talking," said the Bodhisattva, "and watch the dharma power."

She pointed the willow twig downward and cried, "Withdraw!" All at once, flowers and leaves vanished from the lotus platform and the auspicious luminosity dispersed entirely. The monster king, you see, was sitting actually on the points of those swords. The Bodhisattva then gave this command to Moksa: "Use your demon-routing cudgel and strike back and forth at the sword handles." Dropping from the clouds, Mokṣa wielded his cudgel as if he were demolishing a wall: he struck at the handles hundreds of times. As for that monster-spirit,

Both his legs were pierced till the points stuck out;
Blood spouted in pools as flesh and skin were torn.

Marvelous monster! Look at him! Gritting his teeth to bear the pain, he abandoned the lance so that he could use both hands to try to pull the swords out from his body. "O Bodhisattva," said Pilgrim, "that fiendish creature is undaunted by the pain. He's still trying to pull out the swords." When the Bodhisattva saw this, she said to Mokṣa, "Don't harm his life." She then pointed downward again with her willow twig and recited a spell beginning with the letter, Oṁ. Those Swords of Constellations all changed into inverted hooks, sharp and curved like the teeth of wolves, which could not be pulled out at all. Only then was the monster-spirit overcome by fear. Holding onto the points of the swords, he pleaded in pain and pitifully: "Bodhisattva, your disciple has eyes but no pupils, and he could not perceive your vast dharma power. I beseech you to be merciful and spare my life. I'll never dare practice violence again. I'm willing to enter the gate of dharma to receive your commandments."

When the Bodhisattva heard these words, she lowered her golden beam and approached the monster-spirit with her two disciples and the white cockatoo. "Are you willing to receive my commandments?" she asked. Nodding his head as tears fell, the monster king said, "If you spare my life, I'm willing to receive the commandments." The Bodhisattva said, "You wish to enter my fold?" "If you spare my life," said the monster king, "I'm willing to enter the dharma gate." "In that case," said the Bodhisattva, "I'll touch your head and give you the commandments." She took out from her sleeve a golden razor and approached the fiend. With a few strokes, she shaved his hair off and turned it into the style of the T'ai Mountain Crowning the Head: the top was completely bald, but three tufts of hair were left around the edge so that they could be knotted together into three tiny braids. Grinning broadly on one side, Pilgrim said, "How unfortunate for this monster-spirit! He looks like neither boy nor girl! I don't know what he looks like!" "Since you have received my commandments," said the Bodhisattva, "I won't treat you lightly. I'll call you the Boy of Goodly Wealth. How's that?" The fiend nodded his head in agreement, for all he hoped for was that his life be spared. The Bodhisattva pointed with her finger and called out: "Withdraw!" The Swords of Constellations dropped to the ground, and the boy did not bear even a single scar on his body.

Then the Bodhisattva said, "Hui-an, you take the swords back to Heaven to return them to your Father King. You needn't return here to meet me, but go back to the Potalaka Peak to wait for me with the other devas." Mokṣa obeyed and sent the swords back to Heaven before returning to the South Sea, and we shall speak no more of him.

We tell you now that the wildness in that boy had not been wholly removed. When he saw that his pains were gone and that his thighs had healed and, moreover, that the hair on his head had been made into three tiny braids, he picked up the lance and said to the Bodhisattva, "You don't have any true dharma power to subdue me! It's a kind of chicanery, that's all! I won't take your commandments! Watch the lance!" He lunged at the face of the Bodhisattva, and Pilgrim was so mad that he wielded his iron rod and was about to strike. "Don't hit him," the Bodhisattva cried, "I have my punishment for him." She took out from her sleeve a golden fillet, saying, "This treasure used to belong to our Buddha, who gave it to me when he sent me to search for the scripture pilgrim in the Land of the East. There were three fillets altogether: the Golden, the Constrictive, and the Prohibitive. The Constrictive Fillet was given to you first to wear, while the Prohibitive Fillet was used to make the guardian of my mountain submit.[7] I have been unwilling to part with this Golden Fillet. Now that this fiend is so audacious, I'll give it to him." Dear Bodhisattva! She took the fillet and waved it at the wind once, crying, "Change!" It changed into five fillets, which she threw at the body of the boy, crying, "Hit!" One fillet enveloped the boy's head, while the rest caught his two hands and two feet. "Stand aside, Wu-k'ung," said the Bodhisattva, "and let me recite for a while the Golden-Fillet Spell." Horrified, Pilgrim said, "O Bodhisattva, I asked you to come here to subdue a fiend. Why do you want to cast that spell on me?" "This spell," said the Bodhisattva, "is not the Tight-Fillet Spell, which is the spell cast on you. It is the Golden-Fillet Spell, reserved especially for that boy." Greatly relieved, Pilgrim stood to one side of her to listen to the Bodhisattva's recital. Making the magic sign with her fingers, she went through her recitation several times, and the monster-spirit scratched his ears and clawed at his cheeks;

he curled himself into a ball and rolled all over the ground. Truly

    One word could reach the whole region of sand,

    This dharma power so vast, boundless, and deep.

We do not know how that boy manages to make his submission, and you must listen to the explanation in the next chapter.

## Forty-three

An evil demon at Black River captures the monk;
The Dragon Prince of the Western Ocean catches the iguana.

We were telling you about the Bodhisattva, who went through her recitation several times before she stopped. As the pain subsided, the monster-spirit collected himself and sat up to discover that there were golden fillets clasped tightly around his neck, his wrists, and his ankles. He wanted to take them off, but he could not even move them one whit. The treasure, you see, had taken root in the flesh, and the more he tried to loosen the fillets, the more painfully tight they felt. Laughing, Pilgrim said, "Darling boy! The Bodhisattva fears that you can't be reared. That's why she has made you wear a necklace and some bracelets!" Enraged by this remark, the youth picked up the lance once more and stabbed madly at Pilgrim. Dashing immediately behind the back of the Bodhisattva, Pilgrim cried: "Recite the spell! Recite the spell!"

The Bodhisattva dipped her willow twig in the sweet dew and sprinkled it at the youth, crying, "Close!" Look at him! He dropped the lance all at once, and his two hands were pressed together so tightly before his chest that he could not move them apart at all. This is thus the origin of the "Kuan-yin Twist," a posture assumed by the attendant of the Bodhisattva which you can see in portraits and paintings to this day. When the youth found that he could not use his hands nor could he pick up the lance, he realized at last how deep and mysterious the dharma power was. He had no alternative but to bow his head in submission. The Bodhisattva then recited some magic words as she tilted the immaculate vase to one side; the oceanful of water was retrieved entirely and not half a drop was left behind. She said to Pilgrim, "Wu-k'ung, this monster-spirit is vanquished, but his unruliness has not been completely eliminated. Let me make him take a bow with each step of the way—all the way back to the Potalaka Mountain—before I call off my power. Go quickly now into the cave to rescue your master." Turning to kowtow to her,

Pilgrim said, "I thank the Bodhisattva for taking the trouble of traveling for so great a distance. Your disciple should escort you for part of the journey." "No need for that," said the Bodhisattva, "for I don't want to jeopardize master's life." When Pilgrim heard these words, he was delighted and kowtowed again to take leave of the Bodhisattva. The monster-spirit thus returned to the right fruit; with fifty-three bows,[1] he made submission to Kuan-yin.

We tell you no more about the Bodhisattva's making a disciple of the youth. Instead, we speak of Sha Monk, who sat in the woods for a long time and waited in vain for Pilgrim to appear. At last, he put the luggage on the back of the horse, and with one hand holding the reins and the other the fiend-routing treasure staff, he left the pine forest to look toward the south. Momentarily, he found a happy Pilgrim approaching. Sha Monk went forward to meet him, saying, "Elder Brother, why did it take you until now to return from your trip to seek assistance from the Bodhisattva? I almost died from the anxious waiting!" "You are still dreaming!" said Pilgrim. "Old Monkey has not only brought the Bodhisattva here, but she has also subdued the fiend already." Then he gave a thorough account of the Bodhisattva's exercise of her dharma power, and Sha Monk was exceedingly pleased, saying, "Let's go then to rescue Master!"

The two of them leaped across the stream and dashed up to the cave entrance. After tying up the horse, they lifted their weapons together and broke into the cave to exterminate all the fiends. They then lowered the leather bag to free Pa-chieh. "Elder Brother," said Idiot after having thanked Pilgrim, "where is that monster-spirit? Let me rake him a few times, just to relieve my feelings!" Pilgrim said, "Let's find Master first." The three of them went to the rear and found their master bound in the courtyard, all naked and weeping. Sha Monk hurriedly untied the ropes and Pilgrim brought forth clothes for him to wear. The three of them then knelt down and said, "Master, you have suffered!" Tripitaka thanked them, saying, "Worthy disciples, you've worked hard! How did you manage to subdue the demon?" Pilgrim again gave a thorough account of how the Bodhisattva came to make submission of the youth, and when Tripitaka heard this, he quickly knelt down to bow towards the south. Pilgrim said, "No need to thank her, for we also have been instrumental in providing her with the blessing of making submission of a youth." This is thus the basis of the story which we hear even today, about the boy who gave fifty-three bows to Kuan-yin, and who was given the vision of Buddha after three bows.

Thereafter, Sha Monk was told to pick up all the treasures stored in the cave, while the rest of the disciples found some rice to prepare for their master. That elder

Retained his life, all because of the Great Sage Sun;

And acquired true scriptures, helped by the Handsome Monkey-
Spirit.

Master and disciples, after leaving the cave, found their way again and headed steadfastly toward the West.

They had traveled for more than a month when all at once the sound of flowing water filled their ears. "O disciples!" cried Tripitaka, highly startled, "where is this sound of water coming from?" "You old Master!" said Pilgrim, chuckling, "you are so full of worries! There are four of us altogether, but only you happen to hear some sort of water sound. You have quite forgotten again the *Heart Sūtra*." "The *Heart Sūtra*," said the T'ang monk, "was imparted to me orally by the Crow's Nest Zen Master of the Pagoda Mountain.[2] It has fifty-four sentences, all in all, two hundred and seventy characters. I memorized it at the time and up till now, I have recited it often. Which sentence do you think I have forgotten?" Pilgrim said, "Old Master, you have forgotten the one about 'no eye, ear, nose, tongue, body, or mind.' Those of us who have left the family should see no form with our eyes, should hear no sound with our ears, should smell no smell with our noses, should taste no taste with our tongues; our bodies should have no knowledge of heat or cold, and our minds should gather no vain thoughts. This is called the extermination of the Six Robbers.[3] But look at you now! Though you may be on your way to seek scriptures, your mind is full of vain thoughts: fearing the demons you are unwilling to risk your life; desiring vegetarian food you arouse your tongue; loving fragrance and sweetness you provoke your nose; listening to sounds you disturb your ears; looking at things and events you fix your eyes. You have, in sum, assembled all the Six Robbers together. How could you possibly get to the Western Heaven to see Buddha?" When Tripitaka heard these words, he fell into silent thought for a long time before he said, "O disciple!

Since I left our sage ruler that year,

I've moved most diligently night and day:

My sandals sweep open the mountain mists;

My coir hat bursts through the summit clouds.

At night the apes wail to make me sigh;
I can't bear to hear in moonlight the bird cries.
When will I complete the work of Double Three[4]
And acquire Tathāgata's wondrous scripts?"
When Pilgrim heard this, he could not refrain from clapping his hands
and roaring with laughter, saying, "So Master just can't get rid of his
homesickness! If you want to complete the work of Double Three,
there's no difficulty! The proverb says, 'Success will come when
meritorious service is done.'" "Elder Brother," said Pa-chieh, "if
we have to face all these evil barriers and wicked miasmas, we'll
never finish our meritorious service even after a thousand years!"
Sha Monk said, "Second Elder Brother, you and I are very much
alike, and we shouldn't rub Big Brother the wrong way with our
foolish tongues and stupid mouths. Just concentrate on carrying
the loads on our backs; there will be a day when the service is
completed."

As master and disciples conversed, they proceeded steadily when
they saw before them all at once a huge body of surging black water
blocking the path of the horse. Standing at the shore, the four of them
stared at the water carefully and they saw

Tiers of dense billows;
Layers of turbid waves;
Tiers of dense billows like dark sap spilling;
Layers of turbid waves like black oil rolling.
No reflection appears when you walk near;
No trees or woods you can see from afar.
Boiling, an earth full of ink!
Rippling, a thousand miles of ashes!
Like piles of charcoal water bubbles float;
Like o'erturned coals the breakers undulate.
Cattle and sheep will not drink here;
Crows and magpies cannot fly over.
Cattle and sheep won't drink, disdaining the black;
Crows and magpies can't fly, fearing the opaque.
Only the shore's reeds and rushes know the seasons,
And the bank's flowers and grass display their green.
There are lakes, streams, and rivers in all the world,
And many brooks and lagoons both great and small,
Which one in one's life may come upon.
But who has seen the Black River of the West?

As the T'ang monk dismounted, he said, "Disciples, why is the water so black?" Pa-chieh said, "Some families must have overturned their dye barrels!" "If not," said Sha Monk, "it has to be someone washing his brushes and ink-stones." Pilgrim said, "Stop speculating and babbling, both of you! We have to find a way to get Master across." "If old Hog wants to cross this river, said Pa-chieh, "it's not difficult: all I need to do is to mount the clouds or tread the waters, and I shall cross it in the time of a meal." "If you ask old Sand," said Sha Monk, "I, too, need only to mount the clouds or ride the waters, and I'll cross it in no time." Pilgrim said, "Of course, it's easy for us, but it'll be difficult for Master." "Disciples," said Tripitaka, "how wide is the river?" "Approximately ten miles," said Pa-chieh. Tripitaka said, "You three had better determine which of you will carry me across." Pilgrim said, "Pa-chieh can do it." "No, I can't," said Pa-chieh, "for if I carry him on my back and try to mount the clouds, I can't even rise three feet from the ground. As the proverb says, 'A mortal is heavier than a mountain!' If I carry him and tread water, he will push me down below with him."

While master and disciples were having this discussion by the river, they saw suddenly a man approaching from the upper reach of the river and rowing a small boat. Delighted, the T'ang monk said, "Disciples, we have a boat. Ask him to take us across." Shouting loudly, Sha Monk said, "Boatman, come and ferry us across this river." The man in the boat said, "I don't have a ferry boat. How could I take you across?" Sha Monk said, "In Heaven or on Earth, the most important thing is to perform deeds of kindness to others. Though yours may not be a ferry boat, we are not people who will often bother you. We are the sons of Buddha sent by imperial command in the land of the East to acquire scriptures. Please be kind to us and take us across the river. You will have our gratitude." When the man heard these words, he rowed the boat near the shore and, holding his oar, he said, "Master, my boat is small and there are many of you. How could I take you all across?" When Tripitaka walked closer and took a look, he saw that the boat was actually a canoe dug out of a log, and its hull could at most seat only two persons besides the boatman. "What shall we do?" said Tripitaka. "With this boat," said Sha Monk, "we will have to take two trips." Always sly and slothful, Pa-chieh immediately said, "Wu-ching, you and Big Brother can remain here to watch the luggage and the horse. Let me escort

Master and cross over first. Then the boat can return to take you and the horse. Big Brother can simply leap across." Nodding, Pilgrim said, "You are right."

After Idiot had helped the T'ang monk into the boat, the boatman punted the boat away from shore and began rowing it forward. As they approached the middle of the river, a violent gust of wind suddenly arose with a roar, whipping up the waves to darken the sky and the sun. Marvelous wind!

In midair a band of dark clouds rises up;
In midstream black waves surge a thousand tiers tall.
At both banks flying sand blots out the sun;
On all sides trees fall to this Heav'n-shaking howl.
Seas and rivers o'erturned, dragon gods take fright;
Mud and dirt flown up, plants and flowers fade.
The wind roars like thunder in times of spring,
And growls like a famished tiger on and on!
Crabs, turtles, shrimps, and fishes bow their heads;
Fowl and beast have all lost their nests and lairs.
The sailors of Five Lakes are victims all;
The households of Four Seas all fear for their lives.
If fishers in the stream can't lower their hooks;
How could the river's boatmen punt their poles?
With tiles and bricks upturned the houses fall;
With Heav'n and Earth shaken, the T'ai Mountain quakes.

This wind, you see, was called up by the man rowing the boat, who happened to be a fiendish creature in this Black River. The disciples saw with their own eyes that the T'ang monk and Chu Pa-chieh along with the boat were sinking into the water. In no time at all, they vanished without a trace.

Deeply dismayed on the shore, Sha Monk and Pilgrim cried, "What shall we do? The old master faces adversity every step of the way. He just escaped from one demonic ordeal and journeyed safely for a little while before he is in the clutches again of these black waters." Then Sha Monk said, "Could it be that the boat has capsized? Perhaps we should search for them downstream." "No," said Pilgrim, "it couldn't be, for if the boat had capsized, Pa-chieh with his aquatic skills could easily have picked up Master and trod water to carry him out. Just now I thought I saw something perverse about that boatman. I suppose that fellow must have called up the wind and dragged

Master beneath the water." When Sha Monk heard these words, he said, "Elder Brother, why didn't you speak up earlier? You watch the luggage and the horse. Let me go into the water to search for them." Pilgrim said, "The color of this water is hardly normal. I don't think you should go in there." "You think this water's more formidable than my Flowing-Sand River?" said Sha Monk. "I can go! I can go!"

Dear monk! Taking off his shirt and his socks, he lifted up his fiend-routing treasure staff and dove into the waves with a splash. Opening up the water before him, he went forward in big strides. Just as he was walking, he heard the sound of someone speaking. Sha Monk stepped to one side to sneak a glance around and he discovered ahead of him a pavilion; across its front door were written these large characters: "Hêng-yang Ravine, Residence of the Black River God." Then he heard the fiendish creature, sitting in the pavilion, say, "I have gone through some hard times and only now have I found something nice. This monk is a good man who has practiced self-cultivation for ten incarnations. If I manage to eat a piece of his flesh, I'll be a man of longevity who never grows old. I have waited for him long enough, and today I have realized my hopes. Little ones, bring out the iron cages quickly. Steam these two monks whole, while I prepare an invitation card to be sent to our second uncle. We want to celebrate his birthday for him." When Sha Monk heard these words, he could not restrain the fire leaping up in his heart. Lifting his treasure staff, he banged madly at the door, crying, "Brazen creature! Send out quickly my master, the T'ang monk, and my brother Pa-chieh." The little demons standing guard at the door were so frightened that they dashed inside to report: "Disaster!" "What sort of disaster?" said the old fiend. The little fiends said, "There's a monk with gloomy complexion outside. He's banging on our door and demanding the return of some monks."

When the fiend heard these words, he at once asked for his armor, which was brought out by the little fiends. After the old fiend suited himself up properly, he took up in his hands a steel riding crop with bamboolike joints.[5] As he walked out the door, he looked mean and vicious indeed! You see

A square face and round eyes flashing colors bright;
Curled lips and a mouth like a bloody bowl.
A few sparse whiskers wave like iron wires;
His temple's flanked by hair like cinnabar.

He has the form of Jupiter revealed
And the face of an angered thunder god.
He wears a suit of iron flower-adorned,
A gold helmet with jewels thickly set.
He holds the steel crop with bamboolike joints,
And violent wind churns as he walks along.
At birth he was a creature of the waves;
He shed his origin. What fearsome change!
You ask for this fiend's true identity:
Small iguana-dragon is his former name.

"Who is beating on my door?" bellowed the fiend. Sha Monk said, "You ignorant brazen fiend! How dare you use your paltry magic and change into a ferryman to abduct my master here with your boat? Return him at once, and I'll spare your life." The fiend roared with laughter and said, "This monk doesn't care about his life! Your master has been caught by me, all right, and now I'm about to have him steamed to be served to my invited guests. You come up here and match strength with me. If you can withstand me for three rounds, I will return your master. If you can't withstand me, I'll have you steamed and eaten also. Don't bother to dream about your going to the Western Heaven!" Maddened by what he heard, Sha Monk brought the treasure staff down on the fiend's head, but the latter raised his steel crop to parry the blow. The two of them thus began a fierce battle at the bottom of the river.

With fiend-routing staff and crop of bamboo joints
Two men, growing enraged, both strove to win.
One, a thousand-year-old fiend of the Black River;
One, a former immortal of Divine Mists Hall.
This one longed to devour Tripitaka's flesh;
That one sought to save the T'ang monk's piteous life;
At the river's bottom they met to fight,
Each craving success and nothing else.
They fought till pairs of shrimp and fish concealed themselves,
Till crabs and turtles in twos withdrew their heads.
Listen! The water-home's many fiends all beat their drums
And monsters shouted madly before their gate.
This dear, true Wu-ching of utter poverty
Did show all by himself his prowess and strength!
Waves tossed and churned and they fought to a draw

As the crop met and tangled with the staff.
Think of it! It was all for the monk of T'ang
Who would seek scriptures and bow in Buddha's Heav'n.

The two of them fought for some thirty rounds and neither proved to be the stronger. Sha Monk thought to himself: "This fiendish creature is indeed my match. Since I cannot prevail, I may as well entice him out of the waters so that my elder brother can beat him." Making one final feeble blow, Sha Monk turned quickly and ran with the staff trailing behind him. The monster-spirit, however, did not give chase and said instead, "You may go! I'm not going to fight with you any-more, for I have to prepare a card to invite a guest." Panting heavily, Sha Monk leaped out of the water and said to Pilgrim, "Elder Brother, this creature is unruly!" "Since you were down there for quite a while, did you find out what sort of monster he is?" asked Pilgrim. "Have you seen Master?"

"There's a pavilion down there," said Sha Monk, "and across the top of the gate outside are written these large characters: Hêng-yang Ravine, Residence of the Black River God. I sneaked up to it and heard him speaking inside, telling his little ones to wash and scrub some iron cages so that Master and Pa-chieh can be steamed alive. He also wanted to invite his uncle to come for a birthday celebration. I got mad and pounded at the door; that was when the fiendish creature came out with a steel crop with bamboolike joints. He fought with me for this half a day, about thirty rounds in all, and it was a draw. I faked defeat, thinking that I could lure him out here so that you could help me. But that fiendish creature was quite smart. He refused to chase me; all he wanted to do was to prepare his card to invite his guest. I came back up then." "What sort of a monster is he?" said Pilgrim. Sha Monk said, "He looks like a big turtle, or else he has to be an iguana." "I wonder," said Pilgrim, "who is his uncle?"

Hardly had he finished speaking when a man emerged from a bend downstream. Kneeling down at a distance, he cried: "Great Sage, the water god of the Black River kowtows to you." "Could you be that monster who rowed the boat," said Pilgrim, "returning to deceive me again?" The old man kowtowed and wept, saying, "Great Sage, I'm not a monster. I'm the true god of this river. It was the fifth month of last year during high tide that this monster-spirit arrived from the Western Ocean, and he immediately waged a battle against me. An old and feeble person like myself could not withstand him, of course, and he therefore took by force my official residence, the Hêng-yang Ravine. Since he had also taken the lives of many of my water kin, I had no choice but to file suit against him in the ocean. I didn't expect that the Dragon King of the Western Ocean was his maternal uncle, who threw out my plaint and told me instead that I should allow the monster to stay in my home. I wanted to go to Heaven to bring charges, but a humble deity and minor official like me would not get an audience with the Jade Emperor. When I heard that the Great Sage had arrived, I came especially to see you. I beg the Great Sage to exert his great power on my behalf and avenge my wrongs."

When Pilgrim heard these words, he said, "According to what you have said, the Dragon King of the Western Ocean is definitely guilty. Now this monster-spirit has abducted my master and my younger brother, boasting that he wants to have them steamed and served to his maternal uncle for his birthday. I was about to try to seize this fiend when luckily you came to inform me. All right, river god, you stay here and stand guard with Sha Monk. Let me go into the ocean to bring the Dragon King here so that he can capture the creature." "I'm deeply indebted to the Great Sage's kindness," said the river god.

Pilgrim at once mounted the clouds and went straight to the Western Ocean. He stopped his somersault and, making the water-repellent sign with his fingers, he divided the waves and walked right in. As he traveled, he ran into a black fish-spirit, holding a golden box and darting up like an arrow from the depths down below. Pilgrim whipped out his iron rod and gave his head a terrific blow: alas, the brains burst out and the jaw bones cracked open. With a swish, the corpse drifted up to the water surface. When Pilgrim opened the box, he saw an invitation card inside on which this message was written:

Your foolish nephew, Clean Iguana, touches his head to the ground a hundred times to inform you, Venerable Mr. Ao, my esteemed Second Uncle. Frequently I have enjoyed your goodly gifts, for which I am most grateful. I have recently acquired two creatures, who happen to be monks from the Land of the East. Since they are rare treasures in the world, your nephew dares not enjoy them by himself. As I recall that Uncle's sacred birthday is near, I have specially prepared a small banquet to wish you the addition of a thousand years. It is my earnest hope that you will honor us with your presence.

"This fellow," said Pilgrim chuckling to himself, "has presented the complaint first to old Monkey!" He put the card in his sleeve and proceeded. Soon a yakṣa on patrol saw him and darted quickly back to the Water-Crystal Palace to make the report: "Great King, Father Great Sage, Equal to Heaven, has arrived." The Dragon King Ao-shun at once led his water kinsmen out of the palace to receive his visitor. "Great Sage," he said, "please enter this small palace and take a seat, so that we may present you with tea." "I haven't yet drunk your tea," said Pilgrim, "but you have drunk my wine first." Smiling, the Dragon King said, "Since the Great Sage has made submission in the gate of Buddha, he no longer touches meat or wine. Since when have you invited me to drink?" "You haven't gone to drink wine," said Pilgrim, "but you have committed a crime of drinking nonetheless." Greatly startled, Ao-shun said, "What kind of crime has this small dragon committed?" Taking the card out of his sleeve, Pilgrim handed it over to the Dragon King.

When the Dragon King read it, his spirit left him and his soul fled. Hurriedly going to his knees, he kowtowed and said, "Great Sage, please pardon me! That fellow is the ninth child of my sister. Because my brother-in-law had made an error in administering wind and rain by not releasing the prescribed amount, the Heavenly Judge issued a decree and he was beheaded by the human judge, Wei Chêng, during a dream.[6] My sister had no place to go and it was your little dragon who brought her here and had her cared for. Year before last she died of illness, but since her son did not have a home. I told him to stay at the Black River where he could nourish his nature and practice the arts of the realized immortal. I did not expect him to commit such wicked crimes. This little dragon will send someone immediately to arrest him." "How many sons did your sister have?" said Pilgrim. "Are they all monsters somewhere?" The Dragon King said, "My sister has altogether nine sons, but eight of them are good ones. The first, Little Yellow Dragon, lives in the Huai River; the second, Little Black Dragon, lives in the Chi River; the third, Blue-Backed Dragon, lives in the Yangtze River; the fourth, Red-Whiskered Dragon, lives in the Yellow River; the fifth, Futile Dragon, strikes the bell for the Buddhist Patriarch; the sixth, Reclining-Beast Dragon, guards the roof beam in the palace of the Taoist Patriarch; the seventh, Reverent Dragon, guards the imperial commemorative arches for the Jade Emperor; and the eighth, Sea-Serpent Dragon, remains at the place of my elder brother and guards the T'ai-yüeh Mountain of Shanhsi Province. The ninth son is the Iguana Dragon; because of his youth and lack of official appointment, he was told last year to live in the Black River to nourish his nature. When he acquired a name, I would have transferred him to another post. I didn't anticipate that he would disobey my decree and offend the Great Sage."

When Pilgrim heard these words, he smiled and said, "How many husbands did your sister have?" "Only one," said Ao-shun, "and he was the Dragon King of the Ching River who was beheaded. My sister lived here as a widow and died year before last." "One husband and one wife," said Pilgrim, "how could they manage to produce so many different kinds of offspring?" Ao-shun said, "This is what the proverb means when it says that 'A dragon will produce nine species, and each species is different from the others.'"

Pilgrim said, "Just now I was so vexed that I was about to use the invitation card as evidence and file suit against you at the Heavenly court, charging you with conspiracy with a fiend and kidnapping. But according to what you have told me, it's really the fault of that fellow who disobeys your instructions. I'll pardon you this time—for the sake of my relationship with you and your brothers, and on account of the fact that that dragon is young and ignorant after all. And also, you have no knowledge of that matter. Quickly dispatch someone to arrest him and rescue my master. We'll then decide what to do next."

Ao-shun at once gave this command to the prince, Mo-ang: "Call up immediately five hundred young soldiers of shrimps and fishes; arrest that iguana and bring him back here for indictment. Meanwhile, let us prepare some wine and a banquet as our apology to the Great Sage." "Dragon King," said Pilgrim, "you needn't be so edgy. I told you just now that I would pardon you. Why bother to prepare wine and food? I must go now with your son, for I fear that Master may be harmed and my brother is waiting for me."

Unable to detain his guest with even desperate pleadings, the old dragon asked one of his daughters to present tea. Pilgrim drank one cup of the fragrant tea while standing up and then took leave of the old dragon. He and Mo-ang led the troops from the Western Ocean and soon arrived in the Black River. "Worthy Prince," said Pilgrim, "take care to catch the fiend. I'm going ashore." "Have no worry,

Great Sage," said Mo-ang, "this little dragon will arrest him and take him up here for the Great Sage to convict him of his crime. Only after your master has been sent up also will I dare take him back to the ocean to see my father." Very pleased, Pilgrim left him and made the water-repellent sign with his fingers to leap out of the waves. As he reached the eastern shore, Sha Monk who led the river god to meet him said, "Elder Brother, you left by the air but why did you return from the river?" Pilgrim gave a thorough account of how he slew the fish-spirit, acquired the invitation card, confronted the Dragon King, and led troops back here with the dragon prince. Sha Monk was exceedingly pleased; all of them then stood on the bank to wait to receive their master, and we shall speak no more of them for the moment.

We tell you now about Prince Mo-ang, who sent a soldier of his to go before the water residence and make this announcement to the fiend: "Prince Mo-ang has been sent here by the Venerable Dragon King of the Western Ocean." The fiend was sitting inside when he heard this report and thought to himself: "I sent the black fish-spirit to present an invitation card to my second maternal uncle, and I haven't received any answer since. Why is it that my uncle has not come? Why has he sent my elder cousin instead?" As he was thus deliberating with himself, a little fiend sent out to patrol the river also returned to make this report: "Great King, there is a regiment of soldiers stationed to the west of our water residence, and one of the banners has these words clearly written: Young Marshal Mo-ang, Crown Prince of the Western Ocean." "This elder cousin is indeed arrogant," said the fiend. "I suppose my uncle cannot come, and that's why he has been sent in his place to attend our banquet. But if he's coming for a banquet, why bring along soldiers and warriors? Aha! I fear that there's another reason behind this. Little ones, bring out my armor and have my steel crop ready, for I fear that he may turn violent suddenly. Let me go out to receive him and see what's happening." Having received this instruction, all the little fiends rubbed their fists to prepare themselves.

When the iguana-dragon walked out of the door, he saw that there was in truth a regiment of marine soldiers encamped on the right. He saw

Banners with sashes aflutter;
Halberds arranged in bright mists;

Treasure swords amassing luster;
Long lances twirling flower tassels;
Curved bows like many new moons;
Arrows as wolves' teeth stuck up;
Scimitars big and gleaming;
Short cudgels both rough and hard.
Sea serpents, oysters, and whales,
Crabs, turtles, fishes, and shrimps—
Big and small they stood in order,
Their weapons dense and thick like hemp.
If the gen'ral did not command it,
Who'd dare step out of line one bit?

The iguana fiend went before the gate of the camp and cried out in a loud voice: "Big Cousin, your younger brother awaits you respectfully. Please come out." A snail on patrol in the camp went hurriedly to the middle tent to report: "Your Highness, the iguana-dragon is outside calling for you." Pressing down the golden helmet on his head and tightening the treasure belt around his waist, the prince picked up a three-cornered club[7] and ran out of the camp in great strides. "Why did you ask me to come out?" he asked. Bowing, the iguana-dragon said, "Your younger brother sent an invitation card to Uncle this morning. But I suppose he has declined my invitation and sent you instead. If my Big Cousin is here for the banquet, why have you called up the troops? You did not enter the water residence but you pitched camp here instead. And you even put on armor and held a weapon. Why?" "Why did you invite your uncle to come?" said the prince. "It was his kindness which bestowed this place on me as a residence, but I have not seen him for a long time nor have I had an opportunity to express my filial love for him. Yesterday I happened to have caught a monk from the Land of the East who, so I have heard, possesses an original body which has practiced self-cultivation for ten incarnations. If a person eats him, his age will be lengthened. I was hoping to ask Venerable Uncle to look this monk over before I put him in an iron cage and have him steamed for Venerable Uncle to celebrate his birthday."

"You are so dim-witted!" shouted the prince. "Who do you think this monk is?" "He is a monk from the T'ang court," said the fiend, "a priest on his way to the Western Heaven to acquire scriptures." The prince said, "You know only that he is the T'ang monk, but you don't know how formidable his disciples are." The fiend said, "He has under him a monk with a long snout, whose name is Chu Pa-chieh. I have caught him also and am about to have him steamed and eaten together with the T'ang monk. There is another disciple of his by the name of Sha Monk, a fellow rather dark in color and gloomy in complexion who uses a treasure staff. Yesterday this monk made a demand in front of my door for the return of his master, but I called out the river troops to face him. Several blows from my steel crop made him flee for his life. I don't see how he could be called formidable!"

"You are ignorant!" said the prince. "The T'ang monk still has another disciple, his eldest, who happens to be the Great Sage, Equal to Heaven, a golden immortal of the Great Monad who did cause great disturbance in the Celestial Palace five hundred years ago. Now he is the guardian of the T'ang monk on his way to acquire scriptures in the Western Heaven, and his name has been changed to Pilgrim Sun Wu-k'ung at the time of his conversion by the great and merciful Bodhisattva Kuan-yin of the Potalaka Peak. Don't you have any other thing to do but to cause such a great disaster as this? It was that Pilgrim Sun who ran into your messenger in our ocean; he took your invitation card and went straight into the Water-Crystal Palace, charging us father and son with the crimes of 'conspiracy and kid-napping.' You'd better send the T'ang monk and Pa-chieh back to the shore of the river immediately and return them to the Great Sage Sun. You can then rely on my apologies to him to preserve your life. But if you utter only half a 'No,' you might as well forget about your life or any further opportunity to live in this place!"

When the fiend heard this statement, he grew terribly angry, saying, "I'm an intimate first cousin of yours. How could you side with someone else? If I listen to you, I'll have to send out the T'ang monk—just like that! You think there's such an easy thing in this whole wide world? You may be afraid of that Sun Wu-k'ung, but you think I'm afraid of him, too? If he has any ability, let him come to the front of my water residence and fight with me for three rounds. I'll return his master then, but if he can't withstand me, I'll capture him also and have him steamed together with his master. I won't recognize any relative, nor will I invite any more guests! I'll shut my door and ask my little ones to sing and dance. I'll take the honored seat above to enjoy myself. You bet I'll eat his mother's!"

When the prince heard this, he opened his mouth wide and expostulated: "You brazen demon! You are truly audacious! Let's not ask the Great Sage Sun to face you. Do you dare hold a contest with me?" "If I want to be a hero," said the fiend, "you think I'll be afraid of any contest?" He shouted to his little fiends: "Bring me my armor!" His cry immediately made those little fiends on his left and right bring up his armor and the steel crop. Changing their colors all at once, the two of them unleashed their strength and gave the order for the drums to sound on both sides. This battle was quite different from the previous one in which Sha Monk took part. You saw

Flags and banners luminous;
Spears and halberds ablaze.
On that side the camps were quickly broken;
On this side the doors were widely open.
Prince Mo-ang held high his golden club,
Met by fiend iguana wielding his crop.
The cannon's one boom made river soldiers fierce;
Three strokes of the gong aroused marine troops.
Shrimps fought with shrimps;
Crabs strove with crabs;
The whale swallowed the red carp;
The bream downed the yellow *chang*;[8]
The shark devoured the mullet and the mackerel fled;
The rock oyster caught the clam and the mussel panicked.
Hard like an iron rod was the stingray's whip;
Sharp like a razor was the swordfish's jaw.
The sturgeon chased the white eel;
The whitebait seized the black pomfret.
A riverful of water fiends took up the fight;
Dragon troops on both sides did join the fray
And brawled for a long time as billows churned.
Mighty as Indra was the prince Mo-ang,
Who with a cry brought down his golden club
And caught the king of mischief, the iguana fiend.

Holding his three-cornered club, the prince feigned an opening and the monster-spirit, not realizing that it was faked, lunged forward to attack. Sidestepping quickly from his opponent's charge, the prince brought the club down hard on the monster-spirit's right arm and knocked him to the ground. The prince rushed up to him and gave him another kick that sent him sprawling. The marine soldiers all surged forward to pin the monster-spirit to the ground; his arms were hog-tied behind his back and his chest bone was pierced and bound with an iron chain. He was taken up to the shore to appear before Pilgrim Sun, as the prince said, "Great Sage, your little dragon has caught the monster iguana. Let the Great Sage decide what shall be done with him."

When Pilgrim saw this, he said to the monster-spirit, "You have been disobedient to what you were told. When your Venerable Uncle gave you permission to live here, he intended for you to nourish your nature to preserve your body. At the time when you acquired a name, he would have transferred you to another post. How dare you use force to occupy the residence of the water god and abuse the kindness of your elders? How dare you exercise your paltry magic to deceive my master and my younger brother? I would like to give you a stroke of my rod, but this rod of old Monkey is quite heavy. One slight touch and your life will be finished. Let me ask you instead, where have you placed my master?" Kowtowing without ceasing, the fiend said, "Great Sage, this little iguana has no knowledge of the Great Sage's reputation. Just now, I violated reason and morality to resist my elder cousin, who had me arrested. Now that I have seen you, I am eternally grateful to the Great Sage for sparing my life. Your master is still tied up in the water residence. I beg the Great Sage to loosen my iron chain and untie my hands. Let me go into the river and escort him out here." On one side Mo-ang said, "Great Sage, this is a rebellious fiend and most devious. If you turn him loose, I fear that he may plot something wicked." "I know his residence," said Sha Monk, "let me go and find Master."

He and the river god at once leaped into the waves and went to the water residence down below, where they found the doors wide open but not a single little fiend. When they walked inside to reach the pavilion, they found the T'ang monk and Pa-chieh still bound there and completely naked. Sha Monk hurriedly untied his master as the river god loosened the ropes on Pa-chieh, after which they placed the freed prisoners on their backs and darted back to the surface of the water. When Pa-chieh discovered the monster-spirit on the shore all tied up with ropes and chains, he lifted his rake and wanted to strike him, crying, "You perverse beast! You still want to eat me?" Pilgrim tugged at him, saying, "Brother, let's spare him, Have regard for the feelings of Ao-shun and his son." Bowing, Mo-ang said, "Great Sage, your little dragon dares not linger any longer. Since we have succeeded in rescuing your master, I must bring this fellow back to see my father. Though the Great Sage has spared his life, my father will most certainly not permit him to go unpunished. He will dispose of him in some way, I'm sure, and then we shall report to the Great Sage along with our apologies once more."

"In that case," said Pilgrim, "you may take him and leave. Please bow to your Honored Father for me and I shall thank him in person another time." The prince at once led the marine soldiers and the monster-spirit into the water, where they found their way directly back to the Great Western Ocean and we shall speak no more of them.

We tell you now about the river god of the Black River, who gave thanks to Pilgrim, saying, "I am deeply indebted to the Great Sage for the recovery of my water residence." The T'ang monk said, "Disciples, we are still stranded on the eastern shore. How shall we cross this river?" The river god said, "Venerable Father, please do not worry and mount your horse. This humble deity will open up a path for Venerable Father to cross the river." The master indeed climbed onto the white horse, while Pa-chieh held the reins, Sha Monk poled the luggage, and Pilgrim took up the rear. The river god then exercised his magic of blocking the water; as the upper reaches of the river were dammed up, the lower part of the river soon turned dry, and a wide road was thus created. Master and disciples walked safely to the western shore and, after thanking the river god, they proceeded to high ground to set out again on their way. So it was that

With assistance the Zen monk could face the West;
With the earth waterless, they could cross Black River.
We do not know how finally they manage to see Buddha and acquire scriptures, and you must listen to the explanation in the next chapter.

*Forty-four*

The dharma-body in primary motion meets the strength
    of the cart;
When the mind conquers demons and imps, they cross the
    spine-ridge pass.

The poem says:
    To seek scriptures and freedom they go to the West,
    An endless toil through countless mounts of fame.
    The days fly by like darting hares and crows;
    As petals fall and birds sing the seasons go.
    A little dust—the eye reveals three thousand worlds;
    The priestly staff—its head has seen four hundred isles.
    They feed on wind and rest on dew to seek their goal,[1]
    Not knowing which day they may all return.
We were telling you about Tripitaka T'ang, who was fortunate
enough to have the dragon prince subdue the fiend and the god of
Black River open a path for him. After they crossed the Black River,
master and disciples found the main road to the West. Truly they had
to face the wind and brave the snow, to be capped by the moon and
cloaked by the stars. They journeyed for a long time and soon it was
the time of early spring. You see
    The return of triple *yang*;[2]
    The radiance of all things.
    The return of triple *yang*
    Makes all heavens beguiling like a painted scroll;
    The radiance of all things
    Means flowers spread brocade through all the earth.
    The plums fade to few specks of snow;
    The grains swell with the valley clouds.
    Ice breaks gradually and mountain streams flow;
    Seedlings sprout completely and unparched.
    Truly it is that
    The God of the Year rides forth;
    The God of the Woods takes a drive.
    Warm breezes waft floral fragrance;

Light clouds renew the light of the sun.
Willows by the wayside spread their curvate green;
The rains give life; all things bear the looks of spring.

As master and disciples traveled slowly along the road, enjoying the scenery as they proceeded, they suddenly heard a loud cry that seemed the roar of ten thousand voices. Tripitaka T'ang was so startled that he immediately pulled in his reins and refused to go forward. Turning back, he said, "Wu-k'ung, where did that terrible din come from?" "Yes, it sounded as if the earth were splitting apart and the mountains were toppling," said Pa-chieh. "More like the crack of thunder I would say," said Sha Monk. Tripitaka said, "I still think it's men shouting or horses neighing." With a chuckle, Pilgrim Sun said, "None of you has guessed correctly. Stop here and let old Monkey go take a look."

Dear Pilgrim! He leaped up at once and rose into midair, treading on the cloudy luminosity. He peered into the distance and discovered a moated city; when he looked more carefully, he saw that it was veiled by auspicious luminosity after all and not by any baleful vapor. This is a nice place, Pilgrim thought to himself. Why should there be such an ear-splitting roar? There are no banners or spears in sight in the city, and what we heard couldn't possibly be the roar of cannons. Why is it then that we hear this hubbub of men and horses? As he was thus thinking to himself, a large group of monks came into his sight: on a sandy beach outside the city gate they were trying to pull a cart up a steep ridge. As they strained and tugged, they cried out in unison to call on the name of the Bodhisattva King Powerful for help, and this was the noise that startled the T'ang monk.

Pilgrim lowered his cloud gradually to take a closer look. Aha! The cart was loaded with bricks, tiles, timber, earth clods, and the like. The ridge was exceedingly tall, and leading up to it was a small narrow path flanked by two perpendicular passes, with walls like two giant cliffs. How could the cart possibly be dragged up there? Though it was such a fine warm day that one would expect people to dress lightly, what the monks had on were virtually rags. They looked destitute indeed! Pilgrim thought to himself: "I suppose they must be trying to build or repair a monastery, and since a region like this undoubtedly yields a bountiful harvest, it must be difficult for them to find part-time laborers. That's why these monks themselves have to work so hard." As he was thus speculating, he saw two young

Taoists swagger out of the city gate. "How were they dressed?" you ask.

Star caps crowned their heads;
Brocades draped their bodies;
Luminous star caps crowned their heads;
Colorful brocades draped their bodies.
Cloud-headed boots³ held up their feet;
Fine silk sashes tied up their waists.
Like full moons their faces were handsome and bright;
They had the fair forms of jade-Heaven gods.

When the monks saw the two Taoists, they were terrified; every one of them redoubled his effort to pull desperately at the cart. "So, that's it!" said Pilgrim, comprehending the situation all at once. "These monks must be awfully afraid of the Taoists, for if not, why should they be tugging so hard at the carts? I have heard someone say that there is a place on the road to the West where Taoism is revered and Buddhism is destroyed. This has to be the place. I would like to go back and report this to Master, but I still don't know the whole truth and he might blame me for bringing him surmises, saying that even a smart person like me can't be counted on for a reliable report. Let me go down there and question them thoroughly before I give Master an answer."

"Whom would he question?" you ask. Dear Great Sage! He lowered his cloud and with a shake of his torso, he changed at the foot of the city into a wandering Taoist of the Complete Truth sect, with an exorcist hamper hung on his left arm. Striking a hollow wooden fish with his hands and mumbling some Taoist chants, he walked up to the two Taoists near the city gate. "Masters," he said, bowing, "this humble Taoist raises his hand." Returning his salute, one of the Taoists said, "Sir, where did you come from?" "This disciple," said Pilgrim, "has wandered to the corners of the sea and to the edges of Heaven. I arrived here this morning with the sole purpose of collecting subscriptions for good works. May I ask the two masters which street in this city is favorable towards the Tao, and which alley is inclined towards piety? This humble Taoist would like to go there and beg for some vegetarian food." Smiling, the Taoist said, "O Sir! Why do you speak in such a disgraceful manner?" "What do you mean by disgraceful?" said Pilgrim. "If you want to *beg* for vegetarian food," said the Taoist, "isn't that disgraceful?" Pilgrim said, "Those who have left the family live by begging. If I didn't beg, where would I have money to buy food?" Chuckling, the Taoist said, "You've come from afar, and you don't know anything about our city. In this city of ours, not only the civil and military officials are fond of the Tao, the rich merchants and men of prominence devoted to piety, but even the ordinary citizens, young and old, will bow to present us food once they see us. It is, in fact, a trivial matter, hardly worth mentioning. What's most important about our city is that His Majesty, the king, is also fond of the Tao and devoted to piety." "This humble cleric is first of all quite young," said Pilgrim, "and secondly, he is indeed from afar. In truth I'm ignorant of the situation here. May I trouble the two masters to tell me the name of this place and give me a thorough account of how the king has come to be so devoted to the cause of Tao—for the sake of fraternal feelings among us Taoists?" The Taoist said, "This city has the name of the Cart Slow Kingdom, and the ruler on the precious throne is a relative of ours."

When Pilgrim heard these words, he broke into loud guffaws, saying, "I suppose that a Taoist has become king." "No," said the Taoist. "What happened was that twenty years ago, this region had a drought, so severe that not a single drop of rain fell from the sky and all grains and plants perished. The king and his subjects, the rich as well as the poor—every person was burning incense and praying to Heaven for relief. Just when it seemed that nothing else could preserve their lives, three immortals suddenly descended from the sky and saved us all." "Who were these immortals?" asked Pilgrim. "Our masters," said the Taoist. "What are their names?" said Pilgrim. The Taoist replied, "The eldest master is called the Tiger-Strength Great Immortal; the second master, the Deer-Strength Great Immortal; and the third master, Goat-Strength Immortal." "What kinds of magic power do your esteemed teachers possess?" asked Pilgrim. The Taoist said, "Summoning the wind and the rain for my masters would be as easy as flipping over one's palms; they point at water and it will change into oil; they touch stones and change them into gold, as quickly as one turns over in bed. With this kind of magic power, they are thus able to rob the creative genius of Heaven and Earth, to alter the mysteries of the stars and constellations. The king and his subjects have such profound respect for them that all of us Taoists are claimed as royal kin." Pilgrim said, "This ruler is lucky, all right. After all, the proverb says, 'Magic moves ministers!' He certainly can't lose to claim kinship with your old masters, if they possess such powers. Alas! I wonder if I had even that tiniest spark of affinity, such that I could have an audience with the old masters?" Chuckling, the Taoist replied, "If you want to see our masters, it's not difficult at all. The two of us are their bosom disciples. Moreover, our masters are so devoted to the Way and so deferential to the pious that the mere mention of the word, Tao, would bring them out of the door, full of welcome. If we two were to introduce you, we would need to exert ourselves no more vigorously than to blow away some ashes."

Bowing deeply, Pilgrim said, "I am indebted to you for your introduction. Let us go into the city then." "Let's wait a moment," said one of the Taoists. "You sit here while we two finish our official business first. Then we'll go with you." Pilgrim said, "Those of us who have left the family are without cares or ties; we are completely free. What do you mean by official business?" The Taoist pointed with his finger at the monks on the beach and said, "Their work happens to be the means of livelihood for us. Lest they become indolent, we have come to check them off the roll before we go with you." Smiling, Pilgrim said, "You must be mistaken, Masters. Buddhists and Taoists are all people who have left the family. For what reason are they working for our support? Why are they willing to submit to our roll call?"

The Taoist said, "You have no idea that in the year when we were all praying for rain, the monks bowed to Buddha on one side while the Taoists petitioned the Pole Star on the other, all for the sake of finding some food for the country. The monks, however, were useless, their empty chants of sūtras wholly without efficacy. As soon as our masters arrived on the scene, they summoned the wind and the rain and the bitter affliction was removed from the multitudes. It was then that the Court became terribly vexed at the monks, saying that they were completely ineffective and that they deserved to have their monasteries wrecked and their Buddha images destroyed. Their travel rescripts were revoked and they were not permitted to return to their native regions. His Majesty gave them to us instead and they were to serve as bondsmen: they are the ones who tend the fires in our temple, who sweep the grounds, and who guard the gates. Since we have some buildings in the rear which are not completely finished, we have ordered these monks here to haul bricks, tiles, and timber for the construction. But for fear of their mischief, indolence, and unwillingness to pull the cart, we have come to investigate and make the roll call."

When Pilgrim heard that, he tugged at the Taoist as tears rolled
from his eyes. "I said that I might not have the good affinity to see
your old masters," he said, "and true enough I don't." "Why not?"
asked the Taoist. "This humble Taoist is making a wide tour of the
world," said Pilgrim, "both for the sake of eking out a living and for
finding a relative." "What sort of relative do you have?" said the
Taoist. Pilgrim said, "I have an uncle, who since his youth had left
the family and shorn his hair to become a monk. Because of famine
some years ago he had to go abroad to beg for alms and hadn't
returned since. As I remembered our ancestral benevolence, I decided
that I would make a special effort to find him along the way. It's very
likely, I suppose, that he is detained here and cannot go home. I must
find him somehow and get to see him before I can go inside the city
with you." "That's easy," said the Taoist. "The two of us can sit here
while you go down to the beach to make the roll call for us. There
should be five hundred of them on the roll. Take a look and see if your
uncle is among them. If he is, we'll let him go for the sake of the fact
that you, too, are a fellow Taoist. Then we'll go inside the city with
you. How about that?"

Pilgrim thanked them profusely, and with a deep bow he took
leave of the Taoists. Striking up his wooden fish, he headed down to
the beach, passing the double passes as he walked down the narrow
path from the steep ridge. All those monks knelt down at once and
kowtowed, saying in unison, "Father, we have not been indolent. Not
even half a person from the five hundred is missing—we are all here
pulling the cart." Snickering to himself, Pilgrim thought: "These
monks must have been awfully abused by the Taoist. They are
terrified even when they see a fake Taoist like me. If a real Taoist goes
near them, they will probably die of fear." Waving his hand, Pilgrim
said, "Get up, and don't be afraid! I'm not here to inspect your work,
I'm here to find a relative." When those monks heard that he was
looking for a relative, they surrounded him on all sides, everyone of
them sticking out his head and coughing, hoping that he would be
claimed as kin. "Which of us is his relative?" they said. After he had
looked at them for a while, Pilgrim burst into laughter. "Father," said
the monks, "you don't seem to have found your relative. Why are you
laughing instead?" Pilgrim said, "You want to know why I'm
laughing? I'm laughing at how immature you monks are! It was
because of your having been born under an unlucky star that your
parents, for fear of your bringing misfortune upon them or for not

bringing with you additional brothers and sisters, turned you out of the family and made you priests. How could you then not follow the Three Jewels and not revere the law of Buddha? Why aren't you reading the sūtras and chanting the litanies? Why do you serve the Taoists and allow them to exploit you as bondsmen and slaves?" "Venerable Father," said the monks, "are you here to ridicule us? You must have come from abroad, and you have no idea of our plight." "Indeed I'm from abroad," said Pilgrim, "and I truly have no idea of what sort of plight you have."

As they began to weep, the monks said, "The ruler of our country is wicked and partial. All he cares for are those persons like you, Venerable Father, and those whom he hates are us Buddhists." "Why is that?" asked Pilgrim. "Because the need for wind and rain," said one of the monks, "caused three immortal elders to come here. They deceived our ruler and persuaded him to tear down our monasteries and revoke our travel rescripts, forbidding us to return to our native regions. He would not, moreover, permit us to serve even in any secular capacity except as slaves in the household of those immortal elders. Our agony is unbearable! If any Taoist mendicant shows up in this region, they would immediately request the king to grant him an audience and a handsome reward; but if a monk appears, regardless of whether he is from nearby or afar, he will be seized and sent to be a servant in the house of the immortals." Pilgrim said, "Could it be that those Taoists are truly in possession of some mighty magic, potent enough to seduce the king? If it's only a matter of summoning the wind and the rain, then it is merely a trivial trick of heterodoxy. How could it sway a ruler's heart?" The monks said, "They know how to manipulate cinnabar and refine lead, to sit in meditation in order to nourish their spirits. They point to water and it changes into oil; they touch stones and transform them into pieces of gold. Now they are in the process of building a huge temple for the Three Pure Ones, in which they can perform rites to Heaven and Earth and read scriptures night and day, to the end that the king will remain youthful for ten thousand years. Such enterprise undoubtedly pleases the king."

"So that's how it is!" said Pilgrim. "Why don't you all run away and be done with it?" "Father, we can't!" said the monks. "Those immortal elders have obtained permission from the king to have our portraits painted and hung up in all four quarters of the kingdom. Although the territory of this Cart Slow Kingdom is quite large, there is a picture of monks displayed in the marketplace of every village, town, county, and province. It bears on top the royal inscription that any official who catches a monk will be elevated three grades, and any private citizen who does so will receive a reward of fifty taels of white silver. That's why we can never escape. Let's not say monks—but even those who have cut their hair short or are getting bald will find it difficult to get past the officials. They are everywhere, the detectives and the runners! No matter what you do, you simply can't flee. We have no alternative but to remain here and suffer."

"In that case," said Pilgrim, "you might as well give up and die." "Venerable Father," said the monks, "many of us *have* died. There were altogether some two thousand monks caught and brought here: some six or seven hundred of them have perished because they could not bear the suffering and the persecution, or because they could not endure the cold or adjust to the climate. Another seven or eight hundred committed suicide. Only we five hundred failed to die." "What do you mean by that?" said Pilgrim. The monks said, "When we tried to hang ourselves, the ropes snapped; when we tried to cut ourselves, the blades were blunt; when we hurled ourselves into the river, we floated back up instead; and when we took poison, nothing happened to us." Pilgrim said, "You are very lucky! Heaven must be desirous of prolonging your lives!" "The last word is not quite right, Venerable Father," said the monks, "for surely you mean prolonging our torments! Our daily meals are thin gruel made of the coarsest grains, and at night, we have nowhere to rest but this exposed piece of sandy beach. When we close our eyes, however, there will be deities here to protect us." "You mean the hard work during the day," said Pilgrim, "causes you to see ghosts at night." "Not ghosts," said the monks, "but the Six Gods of Darkness and Six Gods of Light, together with the Guardians of Monasteries. When night falls, they will appear to protect us and, in fact, prevent those who want to die from dying." Pilgrim said, "These gods are rather unreasonable. They should rather let you die early so that you could reach Heaven at once. Why are they guarding you like that?" The monks said, "They try to comfort us in our dreams, telling us not to seek death but to endure our suffering for a while until the arrival of the holy monk from the Great T'ang in the Land of the East, the arhat who is journeying to the Western Heaven to acquire scriptures. Under him, we are told, there is a disciple who is the Great Sage, Equal to Heaven, and who has vast magic powers. He is, moreover, a person of rectitude and kindness, one who will avenge the injustices of the world, assist those who are needy and oppressed, and comfort the orphans and the widows. We are told to wait for his arrival, for he will reveal his power and destroy the Taoists, so that the teaching of Zen and complete poverty will be honored once more." When Pilgrim heard these words, he said silently to himself, smiling,

> Don't say old Monkey has no abilities,
> For gods proclaim in advance his fame.

Turning quickly and striking up again the wooden fish, he left the monks to return to the city gate to meet the Taoists. "Sir," said the Taoists as they greeted him, "which of them is your relative?" "All five hundred of them are relatives of mine," said Pilgrim. Laughing, the two Taoists said, "How could you have that many relatives?" "One hundred are neighbors to my left," said Pilgrim, "and one hundred are neighbours to my right; one hundred belong to my father's side, and one hundred belong to my mother's side. Finally, one hundred happen to be my bond-brothers. If you are willing to let these five hundred persons go, I'll be willing to enter the city with you. If you are not, I won't go with you." The Taoists said, "You must be a little crazy, for all at once you are babbling! These monks happen to be gifts from the king. If we want to release even one or two of them, we will have to go first before our masters to report that they are ill. Then, we have to submit a death certificate before we can consider the matter closed. How could you ask us to release them all? Nonsense! Nonsense! Why, not to speak of the fact that we would be left without servants in our household, but even the court might be offended. The king might send some officials to look into the work here or he himself might come to investigate. How could we dare let them go?" "You won't release them?" said Pilgrim. "No, we won't!" said the Taoists. Pilgrim asked them three times and his anger flared up. Whipping out his iron rod from his ear, he squeezed it once in the wind and it had the thickness of a rice bowl. He tested it with his hand before slamming it down on the Taoists' heads. How pitiful! This one blow made

> Their heads crack, their blood flow, their bodies fall;
> Their skin split, their necks snap, their brains flow out!

Those monks on the beach, when they saw in the distance that he had slain the Taoists, all abandoned the cart and ran towards him, crying, "It's disastrous! You've just killed royal kin." "What royal kin?" said Pilgrim. The monks had him completely surrounded, crying, "Their masters would not bow when they walk into court, and when they walk out, they would not take leave of the king. His Majesty addresses them constantly as Royal Preceptors, Elder Brothers, and Masters. How could you cause such a terrible disaster? Their disciples came out here to supervise our work and they did not offend you. How could you beat them to death? If those immortal elders claimed that you were here only to supervise our labor and that we were the ones who took their lives, what would happen to us? We must go into the city with you and have you confess your guilt first." "Stop hollering, all of you," said Pilgrim, laughing. "I am no mendicant Taoist of the Complete Truth sect. I'm here to save you." "You have murdered two men," said the monks, "and we are likely to be blamed for it. Look what you have added to our burdens! How could you be our savior?"

Pilgrim said, "I am Pilgrim Sun Wu-k'ung, the disciple of the holy monk of the Great T'ang. I have come especially to save your lives." "No! No!" cried the monks. "You can't be, for we can recognize that Venerable Father." "You haven't even met him," said Pilgrim, "so how could you recognize him?" The monks said, "We have met in our dreams an old man who identified himself as the Gold Star Venus. He told us over and over again how Pilgrim Sun was supposed to look so that we wouldn't make a mistake in identifying him." "What did he tell you?" said Pilgrim. The monks said, "He said that the Great Sage has

A bumpy brow, and golden eyes flashing;
A round head and a hairy face jowl-less;
Gaping teeth, pointed mouth, a character most sly;
He looks more weird than a thunder god.
An expert with a golden-hooped iron rod,
He once broke open Heaven's gates.
He now follows Truth and protects a monk,
Ever a savior from mankind's distress."

When Pilgrim heard these words, he was both pleased and annoyed; pleased, because the gods had spread wide his fame, but also annoyed, because those old rogues, he thought, had revealed to mortals his primal form. He blurted out all at once: "Indeed all of you can see that I am not Pilgrim Sun, but I am a disciple of his, just learning how to cause some trouble for fun! Look over there! Isn't that Pilgrim Sun who is approaching?" He pointed to the East with his finger and tricked the monks into turning their heads. As they did so, he revealed his true form, which the monks recognized immediately. Every one of them went to his knees, saying, "Father, we are of fleshly eyes and mortal stock, and we failed to know that you appeared to us in transformation. We beg Father to avenge our wrongs and dispel our woes by entering the city quickly and exterminating the demonic ones." "Follow me," said Pilgrim, and the monks all followed him closely.

The Great Sage walked to the beach and exerted his power: he picked up the cart and sent it hurtling through the two passes and up the steep ridge before crashing into pieces. He then tossed all those bricks, tiles, and timber down a ravine. "Go away!" he bellowed to the monks. "Don't crowd around me. Let me see the king tomorrow and destroy those Taoists." "O Father!" said those monks. "We dare not go very far away, for we fear that we might be caught by the officials. Then we would be brought back for beatings and for ransom, and there would be no end to our woes." "In that case," said Pilgrim, "let me give you some means of protection."

Dear Great Sage! He plucked a handful of hairs which he chewed into small pieces. To each of the monks he gave a piece with the instruction: "Stick it into the nail of your fourth finger and then make a fist. You can walk as far as you want. Don't do anything if no one comes to seize you, but if there should be someone trying to arrest you, hold your fist up tightly and cry, 'Great Sage, Equal to Heaven.' I will come at once to protect you." "Father," said the monks, "if we walk too far away and you can't see or hear us, what good will it do?" "Relax," said Pilgrim, "for even if you are ten thousand miles away, I guarantee you that nothing will happen to you."

One of the monks who was somewhat courageous indeed held up his fist and whispered: "Great Sage, Equal to Heaven." At once a thunder spirit stood in front of him, holding an iron rod. He looked so formidable that not even a thousand cavalry would dare charge near him. Several scores of the monks made the call also, and several scores of Great Sages at once appeared. The monks kowtowed, crying, "Father, truly an efficacious manifestation!" "When you want it to disappear," said Pilgrim, "all you have to say is the word, 'Cease.'" They cried, "Cease!" and the hairs appeared again in their nails. The monks were overjoyed and began to disperse. "Don't go too far away," said Pilgrim, "but listen for news of me in the city. If a proclamation requesting for monks to return to the city is published, you may then enter the city and give me back my hairs." Those five hundred monks then scattered in all directions, and we shall speak no more of them for the moment.

We tell you now instead about the T'ang monk by the wayside. When he waited in vain for Pilgrim to come back with a report, he told Chu Pa-chieh to lead the horse forward toward the West. As they proceeded, they met some monks hurrying by, and when they drew near the city, they saw Pilgrim standing there with a dozen or so monks who had not dispersed. Reining in his horse, Tripitaka said, "Wu-k'ung, you were sent here to find out about the strange noise. Why did it take you so long and still you didn't return?" Leading those monks to bow before the T'ang monk's horse, Pilgrim gave a thorough account of what had happened. Horrified, Tripitaka said, "If this is the situation, what shall we do?" "Please have no fear, Venerable Father," said those monks. "Father Great Sage Sun is an incarnation of a heavenly god, and his vast magic powers will no doubt prevent you from coming to any harm. We are priests of the Wisdom Depth Monastery of this city, an edifice built by imperial command of the late king, the father of the present ruler. Since the image of the late king is still inside the monastery, it has not been torn down along with all the other monasteries, big and small, of the city. Let us invite the Venerable Father to go into the city and rest in our humble dwelling. We are certain that the Great Sage Sun will know what to do by the time of the morning court tomorrow." "What you say is quite right," said Pilgrim. "All right! We might as well enter the city first."

The elder dismounted and went up to the city gate. The sun was setting as they walked across the drawbridge and inside the triple gates. When people on the streets saw that priests from the Wisdom Depth Monastery were toting luggage and leading a horse, they all drew back and avoided them. Before long they reached the entrance of the monastery, where they saw hanging high above the gate a huge plaque on which was written in gold letters: "The Wisdom Depth Monastery, Built by Imperial Command." Pushing open the gates, the monks led them through the Vairocana Hall. They then opened the door to the main hall; the T'ang monk draped the cassock over his body and prostrated himself before the golden image. Only after he had paid homage to Buddha in this manner did he walk inside the main hall. "Hey you who are looking after the house!" cried the monks, and an old priest emerged. When he saw Pilgrim, he fell on his knees at once and cried, "Father, have you arrived?" "Who am I?" said Pilgrim. "Why should you address me and honor me in this manner?" "I recognize you to be the Great Sage, Equal to Heaven, the Father Sun," said the priest. "Every night we dream of you, for the Gold Star Venus frequently appears to us in our dreams, telling us that we can preserve our lives only when you come to us. Today, I can tell immediately that you are the one whom we saw in our dreams. O Father, I'm so glad that you have arrived in time. After one or two more days, we may all become ghosts!" "Please rise! Please rise!" said Pilgrim with laughter. "Tomorrow you will see some results!" The monks all went to prepare for them a vegetarian meal, after which they swept clean the abbot's residence for the pilgrims to rest.

Pilgrim, however, was so preoccupied that he could not sleep even by the time of the second watch. From somewhere nearby also came the sound of pipes and gongs, and he became so aroused that he rose quietly and slipped on his clothes. He leaped into midair to have a better look and at once discovered that there was the bright glare of lamps and torches due south of him. Lowering his cloud, he peered intently and found that the Taoists of the Three Pure Ones Temple were making supplications to the stars. He saw

The spiritual realm of a tall chamber;
The blessed place of a magic hall.
The spiritual realm of a tall chamber,
August like the features of Mount P'êng-lai;
The blessed place of a magic hall,
Immaculate like the Palace of Transformed Joy.
Taoists on both sides played their strings and pipes;
Masters at the center held up their tablets of jade.
They expounded the *Woe-Dispelling Litany*;
They lectured on the *Tao Tê Ching*.
To raise dust[4] a few times they wrote out their charms;
To make the supplication they prostrated themselves.
With spell and water they sent a dispatch
As flames of torches shot up to the Region Above.

They sought and questioned the stars
As fragrant incense rose through the azure sky.
Before the stands were fresh offerings;
On top of tables were victuals sumptuous.

On both sides of the hall's entrance was hung a pair of yellow silk scrolls on which the following parallel couplet in large letters was embroidered:

For wind and rain in due season,
We invoke the Honorable Divines' boundless power.
As the empire's peaceful and prosperous,
May our lord's reign exceed ten thousand years.

There were three old Taoists resplendent in their ritual robes, and Pilgrim thought they had to be the Tiger-Strength, Deer-Strength, and Goat-Strength Immortals. Below them there was a motley crew of some seven or eight hundred Taoists; lined up on opposite sides, they were beating drums and gongs, offering incense, and saying prayers. Secretly pleased, Pilgrim said to himself, "I would like to go down there and fool with them a bit, but as the proverb says,

A silk fiber is no thread;
A single hand cannot clap.

Let me go back and alert Pa-chieh and Sha Monk. Then we can return and have some fun."

He dropped down from the auspicious cloud and went straight back to the abbot's hall, where he found Pa-chieh and Sha Monk asleep head to foot in one bed. Pilgrim tried to wake Wu-ching first, and as he stirred, Sha Monk said, "Elder Brother, you aren't asleep yet?" "Get up now," said Pilgrim, "for you and I are going to enjoy ourselves." "In the dead of night," said Sha Monk, "how could we enjoy ourselves when our mouths are dried and our eyes won't stay open?" Pilgrim said, "There is indeed in this city a Temple of the Three Pure Ones. Right now the Taoists in the temple are conducting a mass, and their main hall is filled with all kinds of offerings. The buns are big as barrels, and their cakes must weigh fifty or sixty pounds each. There are also countless rice condiments and fresh fruits. Come with me and we'll go enjoy ourselves!" When Chu Pa-chieh heard in his sleep that there were good things to eat, he immediately woke up, saying, "Elder Brother, aren't you going to take care of me too?" "Brother," said Pilgrim, "if you want to eat, don't make all these noises and wake up Master. Just follow me."

The two of them slipped on their clothes and walked quietly out the door. They trod on the cloud with Pilgrim and rose into the air. When Idiot saw the flare of lights, he wanted immediately to go down there had not Pilgrim pulled him back. "Don't be so impatient," said Pilgrim, "wait till they disperse. Then we can go down there." Pa-chieh said, "But obviously they are having such a good time praying. Why would they want to disperse?" "Let me use a little magic," said Pilgrim, "and they will."

Dear Great Sage! He made the magic sign with his fingers and recited a spell before he drew in his breath facing the ground toward the southwest. Then he blew it out and at once a violent whirlwind assailed the Three Pure Ones Hall, smashing flower vases and candle stands and tearing up all the ex-votos hanging on the four walls. As lights and torches were all blown out, the Taoists became terrified. Tiger-Strength Immortal said, "Disciples, let's disperse. Since this divine wind has extinguished all our lamps, torches, and incense, each of us should retire. We can rise earlier tomorrow morning to recite a few more scrolls of scriptures and make up for what we miss tonight." The various Taoists indeed retreated.

Our Pilgrim leading Pa-chieh and Sha Monk lowered the clouds and dashed up to the Three Pure Ones Hall. Without bothering to find out whether it was raw or cooked, Idiot grabbed one of the cakes and gave it a fierce bite. Pilgrim whipped out the iron rod and tried to give his hand a whack. Hastily withdrawing his hand to dodge the blow, Pa-chieh said, "I haven't even found out the taste yet, and you're trying to hit me already?" "Don't be so rude," said Pilgrim. "Let's sit down with proper manners and then we may treat ourselves." "Aren't you embarrassed?" said Pa-chieh. "You are stealing food, you know, and you still want proper manners! If you were invited here, what would you do then?" Pilgrim said, "Who are these bodhisattvas sitting up there?" "What do you mean by who are these bodhisattvas?" chuckled Pa-chieh. "Can't you recognize the Three Pure Ones?" "Which Three Pure Ones?" said Pilgrim. "The one in the middle," said Pa-chieh, "is the Honorable Divine of the Origin; the one on the left is the Enlightened Lord of Spiritual Treasures; and the one on the right is Lao Tzu." Pilgrim said, "We have to take on their appearances. Only then can we eat safely and comfortably." When he caught hold of the delicious fragrance coming from the offerings, Idiot could wait no longer. Climbing up onto the

tall platform, he gave the figure of Lao Tzu a shove with his snout and
pushed it to the floor, saying, "Old fellow, you have sat here long
enough! Now let old Hog take your place for a while!" So Pa-chieh
changed himself into Lao Tzu, while Pilgrim took on the appearance
of the Honorable Divine of the Origin and Sha Monk became the
Enlightened Lord of Spiritual Treasures. All the original images were
pushed down to the floor. The moment they sat down, Pa-chieh began
to gorge himself with the huge buns. "Could you wait one moment?"
said Pilgrim. "Elder Brother," said Pa-chieh, "we have changed into
their forms. Why wait any longer?"

"Brother," said Pilgrim, "it's a small thing to eat, but giving ourselves away is no small matter! These holy images we pushed on the
floor could be found by those Taoists who had to rise early to strike
the bell or sweep the grounds. If they stumbled over them, wouldn't
our secret be revealed? Why don't you see if you can hide them
somewhere?" Pa-chieh said, "This is an unfamiliar place, and I don't
even know where to begin to look for a hiding spot." "Just now when
we entered the hall," Pilgrim said, "I chanced to notice a little door
on our right. Judging from the foul stench coming through it, I think
it must be a Bureau of Five-Grain Transmigration. Send them in
there."

Idiot, in truth, was rather good at crude labor! He leaped down,
threw the three images over his shoulder, and carried them out of the
hall. When he kicked open the door, he found a huge privy inside.
Chuckling to himself he said, "This pi-ma-wên truly has a way with
words! He even bestows on a privy a sacred title! The Bureau of Five-
Grain Transmigration, what a name!" Still hauling the images on his
shoulders, Idiot began to mumble this prayer to them:

O Pure Ones Three,
I'll confide in thee:
From afar we came,
Staunch foes of bogies.
We'd like a treat,
But nowhere's cozy.
We borrow your seats
For a while only.
You've sat too long,
Now go to the privy.
In times past you've enjoyed countless good things

By being pure and clean Taoists.
Today you can't avoid facing something dirty
When you become Honorable Divines Most Smelly!

After he had made his supplication, he threw them inside with a splash and half of his robe was soiled by the muck. As he walked back into the hall, Pilgrim said, "Did you hide them well?" "Well enough," said Pa-chieh, "but some of the filth stained my robe. It still stinks. I hope it won't make you retch." "Never mind," said Pilgrim, laughing, "you just come and enjoy yourself. I wonder if we could all make a clean getaway!" Idiot changed back into the form of Lao Tzu; the three of them took their seats and abandoned themselves to enjoyment. They ate the huge buns first; then they gobbled down the side dishes, the rice condiments, the dumplings, the baked goods, the cakes, the deep-fried dishes, and the steamed pastries—regardless of whether these were hot or cold. Pilgrim Sun, however, was not too fond of anything cooked; all he had were a few pieces of fruit, just to keep the other two company. Meanwhile Pa-chieh and Sha Monk went after the offerings like comets chasing the moon, like wind mopping up the clouds! In no time at all, they were completely devoured. When there was nothing left for them to eat, they, instead of leaving, remained seated there to chat and wait for the food to digest.

Alas! This was what had to happen! There was, you see, in the east corridor a young Taoist, who, just when he had lain down, scrambled up again all at once when he thought to himself: "I left my handbell in the hall. If I lost it, the masters would rebuke me tomorrow." He said to his companion, "You sleep first. I've got to go find something." Without even putting on his under garments, he threw a shirt on himself and went to the main hall to search for his bell. Groping this way and that in the darkness, he finally found it. As he was turning to leave, he suddenly heard sounds of breathing. Terribly frightened, the Taoist began to rush out of the hall, and as he did so, he stepped on a lychee seed, which sent him crashing to the floor and the bell was smashed to pieces. Unable to restrain himself, Chu Pa-chieh burst into roars of laughter, frightening the little Taoist out of his wits. He scrambled up only to fall down once more; stumbling all over, he managed to reach the master residence. "Grand-Masters," he screamed as he pounded on the door, "It's terrible! Disaster!" The three old Taoists had not yet fallen asleep.

They opened the door to ask: "What disaster?" Trembling all over, the young Taoist said, "Your disciple left behind his handbell, and he went to the main hall to search for it. I heard someone roaring with laughter, and it almost frightened me to death." When the old Taoists heard these words, they cried, "Bring some light. Let's see what kind of perverse creature is around." The Taoists sleeping along the two corridors, old and young, were all aroused, and they at once scrambled up to the main hall with lamps and torches. We do not know what was the result, and you must listen to the explanation in the next chapter.

*Forty-five*

At the Three Pure Ones Temple the Great Sage leaves his
   name;
At the Cart Slow Kingdom the Monkey King reveals
   his power.


We now tell you about the Great Sage Sun, who used his left hand to
give Sha Monk a pinch, and his right to give Chu Pa-chieh a pinch.
Immediately understanding what he meant, the two of them fell
silent and sat with lowered faces on their high seats. They allowed
those Taoists to examine them back and front with uplifted lamps and
torches, but the three of them seemed no more than idols made of
clay and adorned with gold. "There are no thieves around," said the
Tiger-Strength Immortal, "but then, why are all the offerings eaten?"
"It definitely looks as if humans have eaten them," said the Deer-
Strength Immortal. "Look how the fruits are skinned and their stones
spat out. Why is it that we don't see any human form?" "Don't be
too suspicious, Elder Brothers," said the Goat-Strength Immortal. "I
think that our piety and sincerity and the fact that we are reciting
scriptures and saying prayers here night and day, all in the name of
the Court, must have aroused the Honorable Divines. The Venerable
Fathers of the Three Pure Ones, I suppose, must have descended to
earth and consumed these offerings. Why don't we take advantage of
the fact that their holy train and crane carriages are still here and
make supplication to the Honorable Divines. We should beg for some
golden elixir and holy water with which we may present His Majesty.
Wouldn't his long life and perpetual youth be in fact our merit?" "You
are right," said the Tiger-Strength Immortal. "Disciples, start the
music and recite the scriptures. Bring us our ritual robes. Let me tread
the stars to make our supplication." Those little Taoists all obeyed and
lined themselves up on both sides. At the sound of the gong, they all
recited in unison the scroll of *True Scriptures of the Yellow Court*. After
having put on his ritual robe, the Tiger-Strength Immortal held high
his jade tablet and began to dance. Intermittently he would fall to the
ground and prostrate himself. Then he intoned this petition:

318

In fear and dread,
We bow most humbly.
To stir up our faith
We seek Purity.
Vile priests we quell
To honor the Way.
This hall we build
The king to obey.
Dragon flags we raise,
And off'rings display;
Torches by night,
Incense by day.
One thought sincere
Doth Heaven sway.
Chariots divine
Now come to stay.
Grant unto us some elixir and holy water,
Which we may give to His Majesty
That he may gain longevity.

When Pa-chieh heard these words, he was filled with apprehension.
"This is our fault! We've eaten the goods and should be on our way.
Now, how shall we answer such supplication?" Pilgrim gave him
another pinch before suddenly opening his mouth and speaking out
loud: "You immortals of a younger generation, please stop your
recitation. We have just returned from the Festival of Immortal
Peaches, and we have not brought along any golden elixir or holy
water. In another day we shall come to bestow them on you." When
those Taoists, old and young, heard that the image had actually
spoken, everyone of them trembled violently. "O Fathers!" they cried,
"the living Honorable Divines have descended to earth. We must not
let them go. We must insist on their giving us some sort of magic
formula for eternal youth." Then the Deer-Strength Immortal went
forward also to prostrate himself and intone this supplication:

Our heads to the dust,
We pray earnestly.
Your subjects submit
To the Pure Ones Three.
Since we came here,

The Way was set free.
The king is pleased
To seek longevity.
This Heavenly Mass
Chants scriptures nightly.
We thank the Honorable Divines
For revealing their presence holy.
O hear our prayers!
We seek your glory!
Do leave some holy water behind,
That your disciples long life may find!

Sha Monk gave Pilgrim a pinch and whispered fiercely, "Elder Brother! They are at it again! Just listen to the prayer!" "All right," said Pilgrim, "let's give them something." "Where could we find it?" muttered Pa-chieh. "Just watch me," said Pilgrim, "and when you see that I have it, you'll have it too!" After those Taoists had finished their music and their prayers, Pilgrim again spoke out loud: "You immortals of a younger generation, there's no need for your bowing and praying any longer. I am rather reluctant to leave you some holy water, but I fear then that our posterity will die out. If I gave you some, however, it would seem to be too easy a boon." When those Taoists heard these words, they all prostrated themselves and kowtowed. "We beseech the Honorable Divines to have regard for the reverence of your disciples," they cried, "and we beg you to leave us some. We shall proclaim far and near the Way and the Power. We shall memorialize to the king to give added honors to the Gate of Mystery." "In that case," said Pilgrim, "bring us some vessels." The Taoists all touched their heads to the ground to give thanks. Being the greediest, the Tiger-Strength Immortal hauled in a huge cistern and placed it in the hall. The Deer-Strength Immortal fetched an earthenware garden vase and put it on top of the offering table. The Goat-Strength Immortal pulled the flowers from a flowerpot and placed it in the middle of the other two vessels. Then Pilgrim said to them, "Now leave the hall and close the shutters so that the Heavenly mysteries will not be seen by profane eyes. We shall leave you some holy water." The Taoists retreated from the hall and closed the doors, after which they all prostrated themselves before the vermilion steps.

Pilgrim stood up at once and, lifting up his tiger-skin skirt, filled the flowerpot with his stinking urine. Delighted by what he saw, Chu Pa-chieh said, "Elder Brother, you and I have been brothers these few years but we have never had fun like this before. Since I gorged myself just now, I have been feeling the urge to do this." Lifting up his clothes, our Idiot let loose such a torrent that it sounded as if the Lü-liang Cascade[1] had crashed onto some wooden boards! He pissed till he filled the whole garden vase. Sha Monk, too, left behind half a cistern. They then straightened their clothes and resumed their seats solemnly before they called out: "Little ones, receive your holy water."

Pushing open the shutters, those Taoists kowtowed repeatedly to give thanks. They carried the cistern out first, and then they poured the contents of the vase and the pot into the bigger vessel, mixing the liquids together. "Disciples," said the Tiger-Strength Immortal, "bring me a cup so that I can have a taste." A young Taoist immediately fetched a tea cup and handed it to the old Taoist. After bailing out a cup of it and gulping down a huge mouthful, the old Taoist kept wiping his mouth and puckering his lips. "Elder Brother," said the Deer-Strength Immortal, "is it good?" "Not very good," said the old Taoist, his lips still pouted, "the flavor is quite potent!" "Let me try it also," said the Goat-Strength Immortal, and he, too, downed a mouthful. Immediately he said, "It smells somewhat like hog urine!" Sitting high above them and hearing this remark, Pilgrim knew that he could no longer fool them. He thought to himself: "I might as well display my abilities and leave them our names too." He cried out in a loud voice:

O Taoists, Taoists,
You are so silly!
Which Three Pure Ones
Would be so worldly?
Let our true names
Be told most clearly.
Monks of the Great T'ang
Go West by decree.
We came to your place
This fine night carefree.
Your offerings eaten,
We sat and played.
Your bows and greetings
How could we repay?

That was no holy water you drank.

'Twas only the urine we pissed that stank!

The moment the Taoists heard this, they barred the door; picking up pitchforks, rakes, brooms, tiles, rocks, and whatever else they could put their hands on, they sent these hurtling inside the main hall to attack the imposters. Dear Pilgrim! Using his left hand to catch hold of Sha Monk and his right to take hold of Pa-chieh, he crashed out of the door and mounted the cloudy luminosity to go straight back to the Wisdom Depth Monastery. When they arrived at the abbot's residence, they dared not disturb their master; each went to bed quietly and slept until the third quarter of the fifth watch. At that time, of course, the king began to hold his morning court, where two rows of civil and military officials—some four hundred of them—stood in attention. You see

Bright lamps and torches midst purple gauze;

Fragrant clouds rising from treasure tripods.

As soon as Tripitaka T'ang woke up, he said, "Disciples, help me to go and have our travel rescript certified." Rising quickly, Pilgrim, Sha Monk and Pa-chieh slipped on their clothes and stood to one side to wait on their master. They said, "Let it be known to our master that this king truly believes only the Taoists and is eager to exalt the Way and to exterminate the Buddhists. We fear that any ill-spoken word may cause him to refuse to certify our rescript. Let us therefore accompany Master to enter the court."

Highly pleased, the T'ang monk draped the brocaded cassock on himself while Pilgrim took out the travel rescript; Wu-ching was told to hold the alms bowl and Wu-nêng to take up the priestly staff. The luggage and the horse were placed in the care of the monks of the Wisdom Depth Monastery. They went before the Five-Phoenix Tower and saluted the Custodian of the Yellow Gate. Having identified themselves, they declared that they were scripture pilgrims from the Great T'ang in the Land of the East, who wished to have their travel rescript certified and would therefore like the custodian to announce their arrival. The official of the gate went at once into court and prostrated himself before the golden steps to memorialize to the king, saying, "There are four Buddhist monks outside who claim that they are scripture pilgrims from the Great T'ang in the Land of the East. They wish to have their travel rescript certified, and they now await Your Majesty's decree before the Five-Phoenix Tower." When the king heard this, he said, "These monks have nowhere to court death and, of all places, they have to do it here! Why didn't our constables arrest them at once and bring them here?" A Grand Preceptor before the throne stepped forward and said, "The Great T'ang in the Land of the East is located in the South Jambūdvīpa Continent; it's the great nation of China, some ten thousand miles from here. As the way is infested with monsters and fiends, these monks must have considerable magic powers or they would not dare undertake this westward journey. I implore Your Majesty to invite them in and certify their rescript so that they may proceed, for the sake of the fact that they are the distant monks from China and for the sake of not destroying any goodly affinity."

The king gave his consent and summoned the T'ang monk and his followers before the Hall of Golden Chimes. After master and disciples arrived before the steps, they presented the rescript to the king. The king opened the document and was about to read it, when the Custodian of the Yellow Gate appeared to announce: "The three National Preceptors have arrived." The king was so flustered that he put away the rescript hurriedly and left the dragon seat. After having ordered his attendants to set out some embroidered cushions, he bent his body to receive his visitors. When Tripitaka and his followers turned around to look, they saw those three great immortals swagger in, followed by a young acolyte with two tousled pigtails. Not daring even to lift their eyes, the two rows of officials all bowed deeply as they walked by. After they ascended the Hall of Golden Chimes, they did not even bother to salute the king. "National Preceptors," said the king, "we have not invited you. How is it that you are pleased to visit us today?" "We have something to tell you," said one of the old Taoists, "and that's why we're here. Those four monks down there, where do they come from?" The king said, "They were sent by the Great T'ang in the Land of the East to fetch scriptures, and they presented themselves here to have their travel rescript certified."

Clapping their hands together, the three Taoists burst out laughing and said, "We thought they had fled. So they are still here!" Somewhat startled, the king said, "What do you mean, Preceptors? When we first heard of their arrival, we wanted to arrest them and send them to serve you, had not our Grand Preceptor on duty intervened and presented a most reasonable memorial. Since we had regard for the fact that they had traveled a great distance, and since we did not wish to destroy our goodly affinity with China, we summoned them in here to verify their rescript. We did not expect you to raise any question about them. Could it be that they have offended you in some way?"

"Your Majesty wouldn't know about this," said one of the Taoists, chuckling. "Hardly had they arrived yesterday when they slew two of our disciples outside the eastern gate. The five hundred Buddhist prisoners were all released and the cart was smashed to pieces. As if that weren't enough, they sneaked into our temple last night, vandalized the holy images of the Three Pure Ones, and devoured all the imperial offerings. We were fooled by them at first, thinking that the Honorable Divines had descended to Earth. We therefore even asked them to give us some golden elixir and holy water with which we might present Your Majesty, so that you would be blessed with eternal youth. We hardly expected that they would trick us by leaving us their urine. We found out all right, after each of us had tasted a mouthful! Just when we were about to seize them, they managed to escape. We didn't think that they would dare remain here today. As the proverb says, 'The road for fated enemies is narrow indeed!'"

When the king heard this, he became so irate that he would have had the four priests executed at once. Pressing his palms together, the Great Sage Sun cried out in a loud voice, saying, "Your Majesty, let your thunderlike wrath subside for the moment and permit this monk to present his memorial." "You offended the National Preceptors!" said the king. "Do you dare imply that their words might be erroneous?"

Pilgrim said, "He claimed that we slaughtered yesterday two of his disciples outside the city. But who could be a witness? Even if we were to confess to this crime, and that would be a gross injustice, only two of us need be asked to pay with our lives, and two of us should be released so that we might proceed to acquire the scriptures. He claimed further that we wrecked their cart and released their Buddhist prisoners. Again, there is no witness, and moreover, this is hardly a mortal offense and only one of us should be punished for this if it were true. Finally, he charged us with vandalizing the images of the Three Pure Ones and caused disturbance in their temple. This is clearly a trap they set for us." "How could you say that it's a trap?" said the king.

"We monks are from the Land of the East," said Pilgrim, "and we've just arrived in this region. We can't even tell one street from

another. How could we know about the affairs of their temple, and at
night no less? If we could leave them our urine, they should have been
able to arrest us right then and there. Why did they wait until this
morning to accuse us? In this whole wide world, there are countless
people who use false identities. How could they know for certain that
we are guilty? I beg Your Majesty to withhold your anger and make
a thorough investigation." The king, after all, had always been rather
muddle-headed. When he heard this lengthy speech by Pilgrim, he
became more confused than ever.

Just then, the Custodian of the Yellow Gate again came to make
this announcement: "Your Majesty, there are outside the gate many
village elders who await your summons." "For what reason?" asked
the king. He ordered them brought in, and thirty or forty village elders
came before the hall. "Your Majesty," they said as they kowtowed,
"there has been no rain this year for the entire spring, and we fear that
there will be a famine if it remains dry like this through the summer.
We have come especially to request that one of the Holy Fathers, the
National Preceptors, to pray for sweet rain that will succor the entire
population." The king said, "Let the village elders withdraw. Rain will
be forthcoming." The village elders gave thanks and left.

Then the king said, "You, priests of the T'ang court, why do you
think that we honor the Tao and seek to destroy Buddhism? It was
because in years past, the monks of this dynasty attempted to pray for
rain, and they could not produce even a single drop. It was our good
fortune that these National Preceptors descended from Heaven and
saved us from our bitter affliction. Now all of you have offended the
National Preceptors no sooner than you arrived from a great distance,
and you should be condemned. We shall pardon you for the moment,
however, and ask whether you dare to have a rainmaking competition
with our Preceptors. If your prayers could bring us the rain to assuage
the needs of the people, we would pardon you, certify your rescript,
and permit you to journey to the West. If you fail in your competition
and no rain comes, all of you will be taken to the block and beheaded
publicly." With a laugh, Pilgrim said, "This little priest has some
knowledge of prayers, too!"

When the king heard this, he at once asked for an altar to be built.
Meanwhile, he also gave the command that his carriage be brought
out. "We want personally to ascend the Five-Phoenix Tower to
watch," he said. Many officials followed the carriage up the tower and
the king took his seat. Tripitaka T'ang, followed by Pilgrim, Sha

Monk, and Pa-chieh, stood at attention down below, while the three
Taoists also accompanied the king and took their seats on the tower.
In a little while, an official came riding with the report: "The altar is
ready. Let one of the Father National Preceptors ascend it."

Bowing with his hands folded before him, the Tiger-Strength Immortal took leave of the king and walked down the tower. "Sir," said
Pilgrim, barring his way, "where are you going?" "To ascend the
altar and pray for rain," said the Great Immortal. "You do have a
sense of self-importance," said Pilgrim, "absolutely unwilling to defer
to us monks who have come from a great distance. All right! As the
proverb says, 'Even a strong dragon is no match for a local worm!'
But if the master insists on proceeding first, then he must make a
statement first before the king." "What statement?" said the Great
Immortal. Pilgrim said, "Both you and I are supposed to ascend the
altar to pray for rain. When it comes, how could anyone tell whether
it's your rain or mine? Who could tell whose merit it is?" When the
king above them heard this, he was secretly pleased and said, "The
words of this little priest are quite gutsy!" When Sha Monk heard this,
he said to himself, smiling, "You don't know that his stomach's full of
gutsiness! He hasn't shown much of it yet!"

The Great Immortal said, "There's no need for me to make any
statement. His Majesty is quite familiar with what I am about to do."
"He may know it," said Pilgrim, "but I am a monk who came from a
distant region. I have never met you and I'm not familiar with what
you are about to do. I don't want us to end up accusing each other
later, for that wouldn't be good business. We must settle this first
before we act." "All right," said the Great Immortal, "when I ascend
the altar, I shall use my ritual tablet as a sign. When I bang it loudly
on the table once, wind will come; the second time, clouds will gather;
the third time, there will be lightning and thunder; the fourth time,
rain will come; and finally the fifth time, rain will stop and clouds will
disperse." "Marvelous!" said Pilgrim, laughing. "I have never seen
this before! Please go! Please go!"

With great strides, the Great Immortal walked forward, followed by
Tripitaka and the rest. As they approached the altar, they saw that it
was a platform about thirty feet tall. On all sides were flown banners
with the names of the Twenty-Eight Constellations[2] written on them.
There was a table on top of the altar, and on the table was set an urn
filled with burning incense. On both sides of the urn were two candle

stands with huge, brightly lit candles. Leaning against the urn was a
tablet made of gold, carved with the names of the thunder deities.
Beneath the table were five huge cisterns full of clear water and afloat
with willow branches. To the branches was attached a thin sheet of
iron inscribed with the charms used to summon the agents of the
Thunder Bureau. Five huge pillars were also set up around the table,
and written on these pillars were the names of the barbarian thunder
lords of Five Quarters. There were two Taoists standing on both sides
of each pillar; each of the Taoists held an iron bludgeon used for
pounding on the pillar. There were also many Taoists drawing up
documents behind the altar. Before them there were set up a brazier
for burning papers and several statues, all representing the mes-
sengers of charms, the local spirits, and patron deities.

The Great Immortal, without affecting the slightest degree of
modesty, walked straight up to the altar and stood still. A young
Taoist presented him with several charms written on yellow papers
and a treasure sword. Holding the sword, the Great Immortal recited
a spell and then burnt a charm on the flame of a candle. Down below
several Taoists picked up a document and a statue holding a charm
and had these burned also. With a bang the old Taoist high above
brought down his ritual tablet on the table and at once a breeze could
be felt in the air. "O dear! O dear!" muttered Pa-chieh. "This Taoist
is certainly quite capable! He bangs his tablet once and indeed the
wind's rising." "Be quiet, Brother," said Pilgrim. "Don't speak to me
anymore. Just stand guard over Master here and let me do my
business."

Dear Great Sage! He pulled off a piece of hair and blew on it his
immortal breath, crying, "Change!" It changed at once into a spurious
Pilgrim, standing next to the T'ang monk. His true body rose with his
primal spirit into midair, where he shouted, "Who is in charge of the
wind here?" He so startled the Old Woman of the Wind that she
hugged her bag while the Second Boy of the Wind pulled tight the rope
at the mouth of the bag. They stepped forward to salute Pilgrim, who
said, "I am accompanying the holy monk of the T'ang Court to go to
acquire scriptures in the Western Heaven. We happen to pass through
the Cart Slow Kingdom and are now waging a rainmaking contest
with that deviant Taoist. How could you not help old Monkey and
assist that Taoist instead? I'll pardon you this time, but you'd better
call in the wind. If there's just the tiniest breeze to make the whiskers of

the Taoist flutter, each of you will receive twenty strokes of the iron rod!" "We dare not! We dare not!" said the Old Woman of the Wind, and so, there was no sign of any wind. Unable to contain himself, Pa-chieh began to holler: "You Sir, please step down! You've banged aloud the tablet. How is it that there's no wind? You come down, and let us go up there."

Holding high his tablet, the Taoist burned another charm before bringing down his tablet once more. Immediately, clouds and fog began to form in midair, but the Great Sage Sun shouted again, "Who is spreading the clouds?" He so startled the Cloud-Pushing Boy and the Fog-Spreading Lad that they hurriedly came forward to salute him. After Pilgrim had given his explanation as before, the Cloud Boy and the Mist Lad removed the clouds, so that

The sun came out and shone most brilliantly;
The sky was cloudless for ten thousand miles.

With laughter, Pa-chieh said, "This master may deceive the king and befool his subjects. But he hasn't any real abilities! Why, the tablet has sounded twice! Why is it that we don't see any clouds forming?"

Becoming rather agitated, the Taoist loosened his hair, picked up his sword, and recited another spell as he burned a charm. Once more he brought down his tablet with a bang, and immediately the Heavenly Lord Têng arrived from the South Heavenly Gate, trailed by the Squire of Thunder and the Mother of Lightning. When they saw Pilgrim in midair, they saluted him, and he gave his explanation as before. "What powerful summons," he said "brought you all here so quickly?" The Heavenly Lord said, "The magic of five thunder exercised by that Taoist was not faked. He issued the summons and burned the document, which alerted the Jade Emperor. The Jade Emperor sent his decree to the residence of the Primordial Honorable Divine of All-Pervading Thunderclap in the Ninefold Heaven. We in turn received his command to come here and assist with the rainmaking by providing thunder and lightning." "In that case," said Pilgrim, "just wait a moment. You can help old Monkey instead." There was, therefore, neither the sound of thunder nor the flash of lightning.

In sheer desperation, that Taoist added more incense, burned his charms, recited more spells, and struck his tablet more loudly than ever. In midair, the Dragon Kings of Four Oceans arrived all together, only to be met by Pilgrim, who shouted, "Ao-kuang, where do you think you're going?" Ao-kuang, Ao-shun, Ao-ch'in, and Ao-jun all went forward to salute him, and Pilgrim gave his explanation as before. He thanked the Dragon Kings moreover, saying, "I needed your help in times past, but we have not yet reached our goal. Today, I must rely on your assistance once more." "We all obey you," said the Dragon Kings. Turning to Ao-shun, Pilgrim said, "I must also thank you for sending your son to seize that fiend and rescue my master." "That fellow, by the way, is still chained in the ocean," said the Dragon King, "and I dare not decide what to do with him. I was, in fact, about to ask the Great Sage and see how you would like to dispose of him." "You may do whatever you wish," said Pilgrim, "but it's far more important that you should help me achieve this merit right now. That Taoist has struck his tablet four times, and it's now old Monkey's turn to do business. But I don't know how to burn charms, issue summons, or strike any tablet. So all of you must play along with me."

The Heavenly Lord Têng said, "If the Great Sage gives us the order, who would dare disobey? You must, however, give us a sign, so that we may follow your instructions in an orderly manner. Otherwise, thunder and rain may be all mixed up, and that will not be to the credit of the Great Sage." Pilgrim said, "I'll use my rod as the sign." "O Dear Father!" cried the Squire of Thunder, horrified. "How could we take the rod?" "I'm not going to strike you," said Pilgrim, "all I want from you is to watch the rod. If I point it upwards once, you'll make the wind blow." "We'll make the wind blow!" snapped the Old Woman of the Wind and the Second Boy of the Wind in unison.

"When the rod points upward a second time, you'll spread the clouds." "We'll spread the clouds! We'll spread the clouds!" cried the Cloud-Pushing Boy and the Mist-Spreading Lad.

"When I point the rod upwards for the third time, I want thunder and lightning." "We'll provide the service! We'll provide the service!" said the Squire of Thunder and the Mother of Lightning.

"When I point the rod upwards the fourth time, I want rain." "We obey! We obey!" said the Dragon Kings.

"And when I point the rod upwards the fifth time, I want sunshine and fair weather. Don't make any mistake!"

After he had given all these instructions, Pilgrim dropped down from the clouds and retrieved his hair back to his body. Being of fleshly eyes and mortal stock, how could those people know the difference? Pilgrim then cried out with a loud voice, "Sir, please stop! You have struck aloud the tablet four times, but there's not the slightest sign of wind, cloud, thunder, or rain. You should let me take over." The Taoist had no choice but to leave his place and come down the altar for Pilgrim to take his turn. Pouting, he went back to the tower to see the throne. "Let me follow him," said Pilgrim, "and see what he has to say." He arrived and heard the king asking the Taoist, "We have been listening here most eagerly for the sounds of your tablet. Four times it struck and there was neither wind nor rain. Why is that?" The Taoist said, "Today the dragon deities are not home." Pilgrim shouted with a loud voice, "Your Majesty, the dragon deities are home all right, but the magic of your National Preceptor is not efficacious enough to bring them here. Allow us priests to summon them here for you to see." "Ascend the altar at once," said the king, "and we shall wait for the rain here."

Having received this decree, Pilgrim dashed back to the altar and tugged at the T'ang monk, saying, "Master, please go up to the altar." "Disciple," said the T'ang monk, "I don't know how to pray for rain." "He's trying to set you up," said Pa-chieh, laughing. "If there's no rain, they'll put you on the pyre and finish you off with a fire." Pilgrim said, "Though you may not know how to pray for rain, you know how to recite scriptures. Let me help you." The elder indeed ascended the altar and solemnly took a seat on top. With complete concentration, he recited silently the *Heart Sūtra*. Suddenly an official came galloping on a horse with the question, "Why are you monks not striking the tablet and burning charms?" Pilgrim answered in a loud voice, "No need for that! Ours is the quiet work of fervent prayers." The official left to give this reply to the king, and we shall mention him no further.

When Pilgrim heard that his old master had finished reciting the sūtra, he took out his rod from his ear and one wave of it in the wind gave it a length of twelve feet and the thickness of a rice bowl. He pointed it upwards in the air; when the Old Woman of the Wind saw it, she immediately shook loose her bag as the Second Boy of the Wind untied the rope around its mouth. The roar of the wind could be heard instantly, as tiles and bricks flew up all over the city and stones and dust hurtled through the air. Just look at it! It was truly marvelous wind, not at all similar to any ordinary breeze. You saw

Snapped willows and cracked flowers;
Fallen trees and toppled woods;

Nine-layered halls with chipped and broken walls;
A Five-Phoenix Tower of shaken pillars and beams;
The red sun losing its brightness in Heav'n;
The yellow sand taking wings on Earth;
Alarmed warriors before the martial hall;
Frightened ministers in the letters bower;
Girls of three palaces with frowzy locks;
Beauties of six chambers with tousled hair.
Tassels dropped from gold caps of marquis and earls;
The prime minister's black gauze did spread its wings.
Attendants had words but they dared not speak;
The Yellow Gate held papers which could not be sent.
Gold fishes and jade belts stood not in rows;
Ivory tablets and silk gowns had broken ranks.
Colored rooms and turquoise screens were all damaged;
Green windows and scarlet doors were all destroyed.
Tiles of Golden Chimes Hall flew off with bricks;
Carved doors of Brocade-Cloud Hall all fell apart.
This violent wind was violent indeed!
It blew till king and subjects, fathers and sons, could not meet,
Till all streets and markets were emptied of men,
And doors of ten thousand homes were tightly shut.
As this violent gust of wind arose, Pilgrim Sun further revealed his
magic power. Giving his golden-hooped rod a twirl, he pointed it
upwards a second time. You saw
The Cloud-Pushing Boy,
The Fog-Spreading Lad—
The Cloud-Pushing Boy showed his godly power
And a murky mass dropped down from Heav'n;
The Fog-Spreading Lad displayed his magic might
And dense, soaring mists covered the Earth.
The three markets all grew dim;
The six avenues all turned dark.
With wind clouds left the seas
And K'un-lun, trailing the rain.
Soon they filled Heav'n and Earth
And blackened this world of dust.
'Twas opaque like chaos of yore;
None could see Phoenix Tower's door.

As thick fog and dense clouds rolled in, Pilgrim Sun gave his golden-
hooped rod another twirl and pointed it upwards a third time. You
saw

The Squire of Thunder raging,
The Mother of Lightning irate—
The Squire of Thunder, raging,
Rode a fiery beast backward as he came from Heaven's pass;
The Mother of Lightning, irate,
Wielded gold snakes madly as she left the Dipper Hall.
Hu-la-la cracked the thunder,
Shattering the Iron Fork Mountain;
Hsi-li-li flashed the scarlet sheets,
Flying out of the Eastern Ocean.
Loud rumbles of chariots came on and off;
Like fires and flames the grains and rice shot up.
Myriad things sprouted, their spirits revived.
Countless insects were from dormancy aroused.[3]
King and subjects both were terrified;
Traders and merchants were awed by the sound.

P'ing-p'ing, P'ang-p'ang, the thunder roared so ferociously that it
seemed as if mountains were toppling and the earth was splitting
apart. So terrified were the city's inhabitants that every house lighted
incense, that every home burned paper money. "Old Têng," shouted
Pilgrim. "Take care to look out for those greedy and corrupt officials,
those churlish and disobedient sons. Strike down many of them for
me to warn the public!" The peal of thunder grew louder than ever.
Finally, Pilgrim pointed the iron rod once more and you saw

The dragons gave order,
And rain filled the world,
Strong as Heaven's river spilling o'er the dikes,
Quick as the clouds rushing through a channel.
It pattered on top of towers;
It plashed outside the windows.
The Silver Stream ran down from Heav'n,
And whitecaps surged through the streets.
It spurted like vases upturned;
It gushed forth like basins poured out.
With houses almost drowned in hamlets,
The water rose to rural bridges' height.

> Truly mulberry fields became vast oceans,
> And billows all too soon raced through the land.
> Dragon gods came to lend a helping hand
> By lifting up the Yangtze and throwing it down!

The torrential rain began in the morning and did not stop even after the noon hour. So great was the downpour that all the streets and gulleys of the Cart Slow Kingdom were completely flooded. The king therefore issued this decree: "The rain's enough! If we had any more, it might damage the crops and that would have made things worse." An official messenger below the Five-Phoenix Tower at once galloped through the rain to make this announcement: "Holy monk, we have enough rain." When Pilgrim heard this, he pointed the golden-hooped rod upwards once more and, instantly, the thunder stopped and the wind subsided, the rain ended and the clouds dispersed. The king was filled with delight, and not one of the various civil and military officials could refrain from marveling, saying, "Marvelous priest! This is truly that 'for the strong, there's someone stronger still!' Even when our National Preceptors were capable of making the rain, a fine drizzle would go on for virtually half a day before it stopped completely. How is it that the weather can turn fair the moment the priest wants it to be fair? Look, the sun comes out instantly and there is not a speck of cloud anywhere!"

The king gave the command for the carriage to be returned to the palace, for he wanted to certify the travel rescript and permit the T'ang monk to pass through. Just as he was about to use his treasure seal, the three Taoists all went forward and stopped him, saying, "Your Majesty, this downpour of rain cannot be regarded as the monk's merit, for it still owes its origin to the strength of Taoism." The king said, "You just claimed that the Dragon Kings were not home and that was why it didn't rain. He walked up there, exercised his quiet work of fervent prayers, and rain came down at once. How could you strive with him for credit?"

The Tiger-Strength Immortal said, "I issued my summons, burned my charms, and struck my tablets several times after I ascended the altar. Which Dragon King would have the courage to absent himself? It had to be that someone else somewhere was also requesting their service, and that was the reason that the Dragon Kings along with the officers of the other four bureaus—of wind, cloud, thunder, and lightning—did not show up at first. Once they heard my summons, however, they were in a hurry to get here, and by that time it happened that I was leaving the altar already. The priest, of course, made use of the opportunity and it rained. But if you thought about the matter from the beginning, the dragons were those which I summoned here and the rain was that which we called for. How could you regard this, therefore, as their meritorious fruit?" When that dimwitted king heard these words, he became again all confused.

Pilgrim walked one step forward, and pressing his palms together, he said, "Your Majesty, this trivial magic of heterodoxy is hardly to be considered anything of consequence. Let's not worry about whether it's his merit or ours. Let me tell you instead that there are in midair right now the Dragon Kings of the Four Oceans; because I have not dismissed them, they dare not withdraw. If that National Preceptor could order the Dragon Kings to reveal themselves, I would concede that this was his merit." Very pleased, the king said, "We have been on the throne for twenty-three years, but we have never laid eyes on a living dragon. Both of you can exercise your magic power, regardless whether you are a monk or a Taoist. If you could ask them to reveal themselves, it would be your merit; if you couldn't, it would be your fault."

Those Taoists, of course, had no such power or authority. Even if they were to give the order, the Dragon Kings would never dare show themselves on account of the presence of the Great Sage. So, the Taoists said, "We can't do this. Why don't you try?"

Lifting his face toward the air, the Great Sage cried out in a loud voice: "Ao-kuang, where are you? All of you brothers, show your true selves!" When those Dragon Kings heard this call, they at once revealed their original forms—four dragons dancing through clouds and mists toward the Hall of Golden Chimes. You see them

Soaring and transforming,
Encircling clouds and mists.
Like white hooks the jade claws hang;
Like bright mirrors the silver scales shine.
Whiskers float like white silk, each strand's distinct;
Horns rise ruggedly, each prong is clear.
Those craggy foreheads;
Those brilliant round eyes.
They, hidden or seen, can't be fathomed;
They, flying or soaring, can't be described.

Pray for rain, and rain comes instantly;
Ask for fair sky, and it's here at once.
Only these are the true dragon forms, most potent and holy,
Their good aura surrounds the court profusely.

The king lighted incense in the hall, and the various officials bowed down before the steps. "It was most kind of you to show us your precious forms," said the king. "Please go back, and we shall say a special mass another day to thank you." "All of you deities may now retire," said Pilgrim, "for the king has promised to thank you with a special mass on another day." The Dragon Kings returned to the oceans, while the other deities all went back to Heaven. Thus this is

The true magic power, so boundless and vast;
The side door's[4] cut down by nature most enlightened.

We don't know how the deviant is finally exorcised, and you must listen to the explanation in the next chapter.

## Forty-six

Heresy, exercising its strength, makes mockery of orthodoxy;
Mind Monkey, displaying his saintliness, destroys the deviates.

We were telling you that when the king saw Pilgrim Sun's ability to
summon dragons and command sages, he immediately applied his
treasure seal to the travel rescript. He was about to hand it back to the
T'ang monk and permit him to take up the journey once more, when
the three Taoists went forward and prostrated themselves before the
steps of the Hall of Golden Chimes. The king left his dragon throne
hurriedly and tried to raise them with his hands. "National Preceptors," he said, "why do you three go through such a great ceremony
with us today?" "Your Majesty," said the Taoists, "we have been
upholding your reign and providing security for your people here for
these twenty years. Today this priest has made use of some paltry
tricks of magic and robbed us of all our credit and ruined our reputation. Just because of one rainstorm, Your Majesty has pardoned even
their crime of murder. Are we not being treated lightly? Let Your
Majesty withhold their rescript for the moment and allow us brothers
to wage another contest with them. We shall see what happens then."

That king was in truth a confused man: he would side with the east
when they mentioned east, and with the west when they mentioned
west. Indeed, putting away the travel rescript, he said, "National
Preceptors, what sort of contest do you wish to wage with them?" "A
contest of meditation," said the Tiger-Strength Great Immortal.
"That's no good," said the king, "for the monk is reared in the religion
of meditation. He must be well trained in such mysteries before he
dares receive the decree to acquire scriptures. Why do you want to
wage such a contest with him?" "This contest," said the Great Immortal, "is not an ordinary one, for it has the name of The Manifestation of Saintliness by the Cloud Pillar." "What do you mean by that?"
said the king. The Great Immortal said, "We need one hundred tables,
fifty of which will be made, by piling one on top of the other, into an
altar of meditation. Each contestant must ascend to the top without

using his hands or a ladder, but only with the help of a cloud. We shall also agree on how many hours we shall remain immobile while sitting on the top of the altar."

When he learned that it was to be such a difficult contest, the king put the question to the pilgrims, saying, "Hey, monks! Our National Preceptor would like to wage with you a contest of meditation, called The Manifestation of Saintliness by the Cloud Pillar. Can anyone of you do it?" When Pilgrim heard this, he fell silent and gave no reply. "Elder Brother," said Pa-chieh, "why aren't you saying anything?" "Brother, to tell you the truth," said Pilgrim, "I'm quite capable of performing such difficult feats as kicking down Heaven or overturning wells, stirring up oceans or upending rivers, carrying mountains or chasing the moon, and altering the course of stars and planets. I'm not afraid, in fact, of even having my head split open or cut off, of having my stomach ripped open and my heart gouged out, or of any such strange manipulations. But if you ask me to sit and meditate, I'll lose the contest even before I begin! Where could I, tell me, acquire the nature to sit still? Even if you were to chain me to an iron pillar, I would still try to climb up and down. I can never manage to sit quietly and unmoved." "But I know how to sit and meditate," the T'ang monk blurted out suddenly. "Marvelous! Just marvelous!" said Pilgrim, highly pleased. "How long can you do this?" "I met some lofty Zen masters when I was young," said Tripitaka, "who expounded to me the absolutely crucial foundation of quiescence and concentration in order to preserve my spirit. Shut up alone in the so-called Life-and-Death Meditative Confinement, I had managed to sit still for two or three years at least." "If you do that, Master," said Pilgrim, "we won't need to go acquire scriptures! At most, I don't think it will be necessary for you to sit for more than three hours here before you will be able to come down." "But Disciple," said Tripitaka, "I can't get up there." "You step forward and accept the challenge," said Pilgrim. "I'll send you up there." Indeed the elder pressed his palms together before his chest and said, "This humble priest knows how to sit in meditation." The king at once gave the order for the altars to be built. Truly, a nation has the strength to topple mountains! In less than half an hour, two altars were built on the left and right of the Hall of Golden Chimes.

Coming down from the hall, the Tiger-Strength Great Immortal went to the middle of the courtyard. He leaped into the air and at once a mat of clouds formed under his feet and took him up to the altar to

the west, where he sat down. Pilgrim meanwhile pulled off one strand
of his hair and caused it to change into a spurious form of himself,
standing down below to accompany Pa-chieh and Sha Monk. He
himself changed into an auspicious cloud of five colors to carry the
T'ang monk into the air and lift him to sit on the altar to the east. He
then changed himself into a tiny mole-cricket and flew to alight on
Pa-chieh's ear to whisper to him, "Brother, look up and watch Master
with care. Don't speak to the substitute of old Monkey!" Laughing,
Idiot said, "I know! I know!"

We tell you now about the Deer-Strength Great Immortal sitting on
the embroidered cushion in the hall, where he watched the two con-
testants for a long time and found them quite equally matched. This
Taoist decided to give his elder brother some help: pulling a stubby
piece of hair from the back of his head, he rolled it with his fingers into a
tiny ball and filliped it on to the head of the T'ang monk. The piece of
hair changed into a huge bedbug and began to bite the elder. At first,
the elder felt an itch, after which it changed to pain. Now, one of the
rules in meditation is that one cannot move one's hands; when one
does, it is an immediate admission of defeat. As the elder found the
itch and pain to be quite unbearable, he sought to find relief by
wriggling his head against the collar of his robe. "O dear!" said Pa-
chieh. "Master is going to have a fit!" "No," said Sha Monk, "he might
be having a headache." Hearing this, Pilgrim said, "My master is an
honest gentleman. If he said he knew how to practice meditation, he
would be able to do it. A gentleman does not lie! Stop speculating, the
two of you, and let me go up to take a look."

Dear Pilgrim! He buzzed up there and alighted on the head of the
T'ang monk, where he discovered a bedbug about the size of a bean
biting the elder. Hurriedly, he removed it with his hand, and then he
gave his master a few gentle scratches. His itch and pain relieved, the
elder once more sat motionless on the altar. "The bald head of a
priest," thought Pilgrim to himself, "can't even hold a louse! How
could a bedbug get into it? It must be, I suppose, a stunt of that Taoist,
trying to harm my master. Ha! Ha! Since they haven't quite reached
a decision yet in this contest, let old Monkey give him a taste of his
own tricks!" Flying up into the air until he reached a height beyond
the roof of the palace, he shook his body and changed at once into a
centipede at least seven inches in length. It dropped down from the
sky and landed on the Taoist's upper lip before his nostrils, where it

gave him a terrific bite. Unable to sit still any longer, the Taoist fell
backwards from the altar head over heels and almost lost his life. He
was fortunate enough to have all the officials rush forward to pull him
up. The horrified king at once asked the Grand Preceptor before the
Throne to help him go to the Wên-hua Pavilion to be washed and
combed. Pilgrim, meanwhile, changed himself again into the
auspicious cloud to carry his master down to the courtyard before the
steps, where he was declared the winner.

The king wanted to let them go, but the Deer-Strength Great
Immortal again said to him, "Your Majesty, my elder brother has been
suffering from a suppressed chill; when he goes up to a high place, the
cold wind he's exposed to will bring on his old sickness. That was why
the monk was able to gain the upper hand. Let me now wage with
them a contest of guessing what's behind the boards." "What do you
mean by that?" asked the king. Deer-Strength said, "This humble
Taoist has the ability to gain knowledge of things even if they were
placed behind boards. Let's see if those monks are able to do the same.
If they could outguess me, let them go; but if not, then let them be
punished according to Your Majesty's wishes so that our fraternal
distress may be avenged and that our services to the kingdom for these
twenty years may remain untainted."

Truly that king is exceedingly confused! Swayed by such fraudulent
words, he at once gave the order for a red lacquered chest to be
brought to the inner palace. The queen was asked to place a treasure
in the chest before it was carried out again and set before the white-
jade steps. The king said to the monks and the Taoists, "Let both sides
wage your contest now and see who can guess the treasure inside the
chest." "Disciple," said Tripitaka, "how could we know what's in the
chest?" Pilgrim changed again into a mole-cricket and flew up to the
head of the T'ang monk. "Relax, Master," he said, "let me go take
a look." Dear Great Sage! Unnoticed by anyone, he flew up to the
chest and found a crack at the base, through which he crept inside.
On a red lacquered tray he found a set of palace robes: they were the
empire blouse and cosmic skirt. Quickly he picked them up and shook
them loose; then he bit open the tip of his tongue and spat a mouthful
of blood onto the garments, crying, "Change!" They changed
instantly into a torn and worn-out cassock; before he left, however,
he soaked it with his bubbly and stinking urine. After crawling out
again through the crack, he flew back to alight on the T'ang monk's

ear and said, "Master, you may guess that it is a torn and worn-out cassock." "He said that it was some kind of treasure," said Tripitaka. "How could such a thing be a treasure?" "Never mind," said Pilgrim, "for what's important is that you guess correctly."

As the T'ang monk took a step forward to announce what he guessed was in the chest, the Deer-Strength Great Immortal said, "I'll guess first. The chest contains an empire blouse and a cosmic skirt." "No! No!" cried the T'ang monk. "There's only a torn and worn-out cassock in the chest." "How dare he?" said the king. "This priest thinks that there is no treasure in our kingdom. What's this worn-out cassock that he speaks of? Seize him!" The two rows of palace guards immediately wanted to raise their hands, and the T'ang monk became so terrified that he pressed his palms together and shouted, "Your Majesty, please pardon this humble priest for the moment. Open the chest; if it were indeed a treasure, this humble priest would accept his punishment. But if it were not, wouldn't you have wrongly accused me?" The king had the chest opened, and when the attendant to the throne lifted out the lacquered tray, sitting on it was indeed one torn and worn-out cassock! "Who put this thing here?" cried the king, highly incensed, and from behind the dragon seat the queen of the three palaces came forward. "My lord," she said, "it was I who personally placed the empire blouse and the cosmic skirt inside the chest. How could they change into something like this?" "Let my royal wife retire," said the king, "for we are well aware of the fact that all the things used in the palace are made of the finest silk and embroidered materials. How could there be such an object?" He then said to his attendants: "Bring us the chest. We ourselves will hide something in it and try again."

The king went to his imperial garden in the rear and picked from his orchard a huge peach, about the size of a rice bowl, which he placed in the chest. The chest was brought out and the two parties were told to guess once more. "Disciples," said the T'ang monk, "he wants us to guess again." "Relax," said Pilgrim, "let me go and take another look." With a buzz, he flew away and crawled inside the chest as before. Nothing could have been more agreeable to him than what he found: a peach. Changing back into his original form, he sat in the chest and ate the fruit so heartily that every morsel on both sides of the groove was picked clean. Leaving the stone behind, he changed back into the mole-cricket and flew back onto the T'ang monk's ear, saying, "Master, say that it's a peach's pit." "Disciple," said the elder, "don't make a fool of me! If I weren't so quick with my mouth just now, I would have been seized and punished. This time we must say it's some kind of treasure. How could a peach's pit be a treasure?" "Have no fear," said Pilgrim. "You'll win, and that's all that matters!"

Tripitaka was just about to speak when the Goat-Strength Great Immortal said, "This humble Taoist will guess first: it is a peach." "Not a peach," said Tripitaka, "but a fleshless peach's pit." "It's a peach we put in ourselves," bellowed the king. "How could it be a pit? Our third National Preceptor has guessed correctly." "Your Majesty," said Tripitaka, "please open the chest and see for yourself." The attendant before the throne went to open the chest and lifted up the tray: it was in truth a pit, entirely without any peel or flesh. When the king saw this, he became quite frightened and said "O National Preceptors, don't wage any more contests with them. Let them go! The peach was picked by our own hands, and now it turns out to be a pit. Who could have eaten it? The spirits and gods must be giving them secret assistance." When Pa-chieh heard the words, he smiled sardonically to Sha Monk, saying, "Little does he realize how many years of peach eating are behind this!"

Just then, the Tiger-Strength Great Immortal walked out from the Wên-hua Pavilion after he had been washed and combed. "Your Majesty," he said as he walked up the hall, "this monk knows the magic of object removal. Give me the chest, and I'll destroy his magic. Then we can have another contest with him." "What do you want to do?" said the king. Tiger-Strength said, "His magic can remove only lifeless objects but not a human body. Put this Taoist youth in the chest, and he'll never be able to remove him." The youth indeed was hidden in the chest, which was then brought down again from the hall to be placed before the steps. "You, monk," said the king, "guess again what sort of treasure we have inside." Tripitaka said, "Here it comes again!" "Let me go and have another look," said Pilgrim. With a buzz, he flew off and crawled inside, where he found a Taoist lad. Marvelous Great Sage! What readiness of mind! Truly

Such agility is rare in the world!
Such cleverness is uncommon indeed!

Shaking his body once, he changed himself into the form of one of those old Taoists, whispering as he entered the chest, "Disciple." "Master," said the lad, "how did you come in here?" "With the magic of invisibility," said Pilgrim. The lad said, "Do you have some instructions for me?" "The priest saw you enter the chest," said Pilgrim, "and if he made his guess a Taoist lad, wouldn't we lose to him again? That's why I came here to discuss the matter with you. Let's shave your head, and we'll then make the guess that you are a monk." The Taoist lad said, "Do whatever you want, Master, just so that we win. For if we lose to them again, not only our reputation will be ruined, but the court also may no longer revere us." "Exactly," said Pilgrim. "Come over here, my child. When we defeat them, I'll reward you handsomely." He changed his golden-hooped rod into a sharp razor, and hugging the lad, he said, "Darling, try to endure the pain for a moment, Don't make any noise! I'll shave your head." In a little while, the lad's hair was completely shorn, rolled into a ball, and stuffed into one of the corners of the chest. He put away the razor, and rubbing the lad's bald head, he said, "My child, your head looks like a monk's all right, but your clothes don't fit. Take them off and let me change them for you." What the Taoist lad had on was a crane's-down robe of spring-onion white silk, embroidered with the cloud pattern and trimmed with brocade. When he took it off, Pilgrim blew on it his immortal breath, crying, "Change!" It changed instantly into a monk shirt of brown color, which Pilgrim helped him put on. He then pulled off two pieces of hair which he changed into a wooden fish and a tap. "Disciple," said Pilgrim, as he handed over the fish and the tap to the lad, "you must listen carefully. If you hear someone call for the Taoist youth, don't ever leave this chest. If someone calls 'Monk,' then you may push open the chest door, strike up the wooden fish, and walk out chanting a Buddhist sūtra. Then it'll be complete success for us." "I only know," said the lad, "how to recite the *Three Officials Book*, the *Northern Dipper Book*, or the *Woe-Dispelling Book*. I don't know how to recite any Buddhist sūtra." Pilgrim said, "Can you chant the name of Buddha?" "You mean Amitābha," said the lad. "Who doesn't know that?" "Good enough! Good enough!" said Pilgrim. "You may chant the name of Buddha. It'll spare me from having to teach you anything new. Remember what I've told you. I'm leaving." He changed back into a mole-cricket and crawled out, after which, he flew back to the ear of the T'ang monk and said, "Master, just guess it's a monk." Tripitaka said, "This time I know I'll win." "How could you be so sure?" said Pilgrim, and Tripitaka replied, "The sūtras said, 'The

Buddha, the Dharma, and the Sangha are the Three Jewels.' A monk therefore is a treasure."

As they were thus talking among themselves, the Tiger-Strength Great Immortal said, "Your Majesty, this third time it is a Taoist youth." He made the declaration several times, but nothing happened nor did anyone make an appearance. Pressing his palms together, Tripitaka said, "It's a monk." With all his might, Pa-chieh screamed: "It's a monk in the chest!" All at once the youth kicked open the chest and walked out, striking the wooden fish and chanting the name of Buddha. So delighted were the two rows of civil and military officials that they shouted bravos repeatedly; so astonished were the three Taoists that they could not utter a sound. "These priests must have the assistance from spirits and gods," said the king. "How could a Taoist enter the chest and come out a monk? Even if he had an attendant with him, he might have been able to have his head shaved. How could he know how to take up the chanting of Buddha's name? O Preceptors! Please let them go!"

"Your Majesty," said the Tiger-Strength Great Immortal, "as the proverb says, 'The warrior has found his equal, the chess player his match.' We might as well make use of what we learned in our youth at Chung-nan Mountain and challenge them to a greater competition." "What did you learn?" said the king. Tiger-Strength said, "We three brothers all have acquired some magic abilities: cut off our heads, and we can put them back on our necks; open our chests and gouge out our hearts, and they will grow back again; inside a cauldron of boiling oil, we can take baths." Highly startled, the king said, "These three things are all roads leading to certain death!" "Only because we have such magic power," said Tiger-Strength, "do we dare make so bold a claim. We won't quit until we have waged this contest with them." The king said in a loud voice, "You priests from the Land of the East, our National Preceptors are unwilling to let you go. They wish to wage one more contest with you in head cutting, stomach ripping, and going into a cauldron of boiling oil to take a bath."

Pilgrim was still assuming the form of the mole-cricket, flying back and forth to make his secret report. When he heard this, he retrieved his hair which had been changed into his substitute, and he himself changed at once back into his true form. "Lucky! Lucky!" he cried with loud guffaws. "Business has come to my door!" "These three things," said Pa-chieh, "will certainly make you lose your life. How could you say that business has come to your door?" "You still have no idea of my abilities!" said Pilgrim. "Elder Brother," said Pa-chieh, "you are quite clever, quite capable in those transformations. Aren't those skills something already? What more abilities do you have?" Pilgrim said,

Cut off my head and I still can speak.
Sever my arms, I still can beat you up!
My legs amputated, I still can walk.
My belly, ripped open, will heal again,
Smooth and snug as a won-ton people make:
A tiny pinch and it's completely formed.
To bathe in boiling oil is easier still;
It's like warm liquid cleansing me of dirt.

When Pa-chieh and Sha Monk heard these words, they roared with laughter. Pilgrim went forward and said, "Your Majesty, this young priest knows how to have his head cut off." "How did you acquire such an ability?" said the king. "When I was practicing austerities in a monastery some years ago," said Pilgrim, "I met a mendicant Zen master, who taught me the magic of head cutting. I don't know whether it works or not, and that's why I want to try it out right now." "This priest is so young and ignorant!" said the king, chuckling. "Is head cutting something to try out? The head is, after all, the very fountain of the six kinds of yang energies in one's body. If you cut it off, you'll die." "That's what we want," said Tiger-Strength. "Only then can our feelings be relieved!" Besotted by the Taoist's words, the foolish ruler immediately gave the decree for an execution site to be prepared.

Once the command was given, three thousand imperial guards took up their positions outside the gate of the court. The king said, "Monk, go and cut off your head first." "I'll go first! I'll go first!" said Pilgrim merrily. He folded his hands before his chest and shouted, "National Preceptors, pardon my presumption for taking my turn first!" He turned swiftly and was about to dash out. The T'ang monk grabbed him, saying, "O Disciple! Be careful! Where you are going isn't a playground!" "No fear!" said Pilgrim. "Take off your hands! Let me go!"

The Great Sage went straight to the execution site, where he was caught hold of by the executioner and bound with ropes. He was then led to a tall mound and pinned down on top of it. At the cry "Kill," his head came off with a swishing sound. Then the executioner gave the head a kick, and it rolled off like a watermelon to a distance of some forty paces away. No blood, however, spurted from the neck of Pilgrim. Instead, a voice came from inside his stomach, crying, "Return, head!" So alarmed was the Deer-Strength Great Immortal by the sight of such ability that he at once recited a spell and gave this charge to the local spirit and patron deity: "Hold down that head. When I have defeated the monk, I'll persuade the king to turn your little shrines into huge temples, your idols of clay into true bodies of gold." The local spirit and the god, you see, had to serve him since he knew the magic of the five thunders. Secretly, they indeed held Pilgrim's head down. Once more Pilgrim cried, "Return, head!" But the head stayed on the ground as if it had taken root; it would not move at all. Somewhat perturbed, Pilgrim rolled his hands into fists and wrenched his body violently. The ropes all snapped and fell off; at the cry "Grow," a head sprang up instantly from his neck. Every one of the executioners and every member of the imperial guards became terrified, while the officer in charge of the execution dashed inside the court to make this report: "Your Majesty, that young priest had his head cut off, but another head has grown up." "Sha Monk," said Pa-chieh, giggling, "we truly had no idea that Elder Brother has this kind of talent!" "If he knows seventy-two ways of transformation," said Sha Monk, "he may have altogether seventy-two heads!"

Hardly had he finished speaking when Pilgrim came walking back, saying, "Master." Exceedingly pleased, Tripitaka said, "Disciple, did it hurt?" "Hardly," said Pilgrim, "it's sort of fun!" "Elder Brother," said Pa-chieh, "do you need ointment for the scar?" "Touch me," said Pilgrim, "and see if there's any scar." Idiot touched him and he was dumbfounded. "Marvelous! Marvelous!" he giggled. "It healed perfectly. You can't feel even the slightest scar!"

As the brothers were chatting happily among themselves, they heard the king say, "Receive your rescript. We give you a complete pardon. Go away!" Pilgrim said, "We'll take the rescript all right, but we want the National Preceptor to go there and cut his head off too! He should try something new!" "Great National Preceptor," said the king, "the priest is not willing to pass you up. If you want to compete with him, please try not to frighten us." Tiger-Strength had no choice but to go up to the site, where he was bound and pinned to the ground by several executioners. One of them lifted the sword and cut off his head, which was then kicked some thirty paces away. Blood did not spurt from his trunk either, and he, too, gave a cry, "Return, head!" Hurriedly pulling off a piece of hair, Pilgrim blew on it his immortal breath, crying, "Change!" It changed into a yellow hound, which dashed into the execution site, picked up the Taoist's head with its mouth, and ran to drop it into the imperial moat. The Taoist, meanwhile, called for his head three times without success. He did not, you see, have the ability of Pilgrim, and there was no possibility that he could produce another head. All at once, bright redness sprouted from his trunk. Alas!

Though he could send for wind and call for rain,
A realized immortal how could he match?

In a moment, he fell to the dust, and those gathered about him discovered that he was actually a headless tiger with yellow fur.

The officer in charge of the execution went again to memorialize. "Your Majesty," he said, "the Great National Preceptor's head was cut off, but it could not grow back again. He perished in the dust and then he became a headless tiger with yellow fur." On hearing this, the king paled with fright and stared at the remaining two Taoists with unblinking eyes. Rising from his cushion, Deer-Strength said, "My Elder Brother must have been fated to die at this particular moment. But how could he be a yellow tiger? This has to be that monk's roguery. He is using some kind of deceptive magic to change my elder brother into a beast. I won't spare him now. I insist on having a competition of stomach ripping and heart gouging."

When the king heard this, he calmed down and said, "Little priest, our Second National Preceptor wants to wage another contest with you." "This little priest," said Pilgrim, "has not eaten much prepared food for a long time. The other day when we were journeying westward, a kind patron kept asking us to eat and I stuffed myself with more pieces of steamed bread than I should have taken. I have been having a stomachache since, and I fear that I may have worms. This contest, therefore, can't be more timely, since I want very much to borrow Your Majesty's knife to rip open my stomach, so that I may take out my viscera and clean out my stomach and spleen before I dare proceed to see Buddha in the Western Heaven." When the king heard this, he gave the order: "Take him to the execution site." A throng of captains and guards came forward to pull and tug at Pilgrim, who pushed them back, saying, "I don't need people to hold me.

I'm going to walk there myself. There's one thing, however. I don't want my hands tied, for I want to wash and clean out my viscera." The king at once gave the order: "Don't tie his hands."

With a swagger, Pilgrim walked down to the execution site. Leaning himself on a huge pillar, he untied his robe and revealed his stomach. The executioner used a rope and tied his neck to the pillar; down below, another rope strapped his two legs also to the pillar. Then he wielded a sharp dagger and ripped Pilgrim's chest downward, all the way to his lower abdomen. Pilgrim used both his hands to push open his belly, and then he took out his intestines which he examined one by one. After a long pause, he put them back inside, coil for coil exactly as before. Grasping the skins of his belly and bringing them together with his hands, he blew his magic breath on his abdomen, crying, "Grow!" At once his belly closed up completely. So astonished was the king that he presented with both his hands the rescript to Pilgrim, saying, "Holy monk, please do not delay your westward journey any further. Take your rescript and leave." "The rescript is a small matter," said Pilgrim, chuckling. "How about asking Second National Preceptor to go through with the cutting and ripping?" "Don't put the blame on us," said the king to Deer-Strength. "It's you who wanted to be his opponent. Please go! Please go!" "Relax!" said Deer-Strength. "I don't think I'll ever lose to him!"

Look at him! He even imitated the swagger of Pilgrim Sun as he headed for the execution site. There he was bound with ropes, and then his stomach was also ripped open by the dagger of the executioner. He, too, took out his guts and manipulated them with his hands. Pilgrim at once pulled off a piece of his hair, on which he blew a mouthful of his divine breath, crying, "Change." It changed into a hungry hawk; spreading its wings and claws, it flew up to the Taoist and snatched him clean of his guts. Then it flew off to somewhere to enjoy its catch leisurely, while the Taoist was reduced to

A drippy ghost of torn belly and empty trunk,

An aimless soul with less innards and no guts!

Kicking down the pillar, the executioner dragged the corpse over to have a closer look. Ah! It was actually a white-coated deer with horns.

The officer in charge of the execution again ran hurriedly to make the report: "Second National Preceptor is most unlucky! After his stomach was ripped open, his viscera were snatched away by a hungry hawk. After he perished, his corpse changed into a white-coated deer with horns." More and more alarmed, the king said, "How could he turn into a deer with horns?" The Goat-Strength Great Immortal said, "Yes, how could my elder brother die and turn into the form of a beast? It has to be the magic of that monk, used by him to plot against us. Let me avenge the deaths of my elder brothers." "With what magic can you triumph over him?" said the king, and Goat-Strength replied, "I'm going to wage with him the contest of bathing in a cauldron of hot oil." The king indeed sent for a huge cauldron filled with fragrant oil and told them to begin the contest. "I thank you for your kindness," said Pilgrim, "for this young priest has not had a bath for a long time. My skin, in fact, has been rather dried and itchy these past two days, and I must have it scalded to take away the irritation."

The attendant before the throne indeed lighted a great fire on a huge pile of wood, and the oil in the cauldron was heated to boiling. When he was asked to step into it, Pilgrim pressed his palms together in front of him and asked: "Will it be a civil or a military bath?" "What's the difference?" asked the king. Pilgrim said, "A civil bath means that I shall not remove my clothing. With my hands on my hips, I'll jump in and jump out again after one little roll, so swiftly in fact that the clothes are not permitted to be soiled. If there's the tiniest speck of oil on the garments, I lose. A military bath, however, will require a clothes rack and a towel. I'll undress before I dive in, and I shall be permitted to play in there as I wish, including doing somersaults and cartwheels." The king said to Goat-Strength, "How do you want to compete with him? A civil or a military bath?" "If we take the civil bath," said Goat-Strength, "I fear that his robes may have been treated so that oil will slide off him. Let's have the military bath." Stepping forward instantly, Pilgrim said, "Pardon me again for the presumption of taking my turn first." Look at him! He took off his shirt and untied his tiger-skin skirt. With a bound, he leaped straight into the cauldron, splashing and frolicking in the boiling oil as if he were swimming in it.

When Pa-chieh saw this, he bit his finger and said to Sha Monk, "We truly have misjudged this ape! During those sarcastic exchanges and the banter between us all this time, I thought he was simply joking! Little did I realize that he really had such ability!" They could hardly refrain from their marveling, but when Pilgrim saw them whispering back and forth to each other, he became highly suspicious and thought to himself: "That Idiot must be laughing at me! This is what the proverb means: 'Intelligence has its work and incompetence its leisure.' Old Monkey has to go through all this, and he's quite comfortable over there! Let me put some ropes on him and see whether he'll be more cautious!" As he bathed himself, he suddenly dove towards the bottom of the cauldron with a splash. There he changed himself into a small tack and all but disappeared.

The officer in charge of the proceedings went forward again to make the report: "Your Majesty, the young priest has been fried to death by the boiling oil." Delighted, the king gave the order for the bones to be fished out for him to see, and the executioner went forward to rake the oil with an iron strainer. The holes in the strainer, however, were quite large, whereas the tack into which Pilgrim had changed himself was very tiny, and repeatedly, it fell through the holes after it had been scooped up. The officer had no choice but to come back with this word: "The priest's body is tender and his bones are frail. He seems to have melted completely!"

The king at once shouted: "Seize those three monks!" Seeing how savage were the looks of Pa-chieh, the palace guards rushed at him first and threw him to the ground, tying both of his hands behind his back. Tripitaka was so terrified that he cried out in a loud voice: "Your Majesty, please pardon this humble cleric for the moment. Since that disciple of mine embraced our faith, he has made merit again and again. Today his affront to the National Preceptor has led to his death in a cauldron of oil, and this humble cleric certainly has no desire to cling to my own life. Moreover, just as the officials are ruling over the people, so are you the ruler above all, and if you as king ask me, your subject, to die, how could I dare not die? But the one who died first has already become a spirit, and this is the reason I beg you for a moment's grace. Grant me half a cup of cold water or a bowl of thin gruel; give me also three paper horses and permit me to go before the cauldron to present these offerings and to express my regard for him as a disciple. Then I will accept whatever punishment you have for me." On hearing this, the king said, "All right! The Chinese are a very loyal people indeed!" He asked that the T'ang monk be given the rice gruel and paper money.

The T'ang monk requested that Sha Monk go with him below the steps, while a few of the guards dragged Pa-chieh by the ears up to the cauldron. Facing it, the T'ang monk offered the following invocation:

My dear disciple, Sun Wu-k'ung!
Since taking your precepts at the grove of Zen,
What deep love you showed me on our westward way.
We hoped to reach together the Great Tao.
How could I know you would perish this day.
You lived for finding scriptures when alive;
In death you must on Buddha fix your mind.
Though far away your gallant soul should wait:
Your ghost from darkness will go to Thunderclap.

On hearing this prayer, Pa-chieh said, "Master, that's not the proper invocation. Sha Monk, hold up the rice offering for me. Let me pray!" Bound and pinned to the ground, Idiot panted out the words:

You brazen, disaster-courting ape!
You ignorant pi-ma-wên.
You brazen, death-deserving ape!
You deep-fried pi-ma-wên!
The monkey's finished!
The ma-wên's undone!

Pilgrim Sun was, of course, still in the bottom of the cauldron. When he heard these castigations from Idiot, he could no longer restrain himself and at once changed back into his original form. Standing up stark naked in the cauldron, he shouted, "You overstuffed coolie! Whom are you castigating?" "Disciple," said the T'ang monk when he saw Pilgrim, "you almost frighten me to death!" Sha Monk said, "Elder Brother simply loves to play dead!" The civil and military officials all rushed up the steps to report: "Your Majesty, that priest did not die. He has emerged again from the cauldron." Fearing that he might be found guilty of making a false report to the throne, the officer in charge of execution said, "He is dead all right. But today happens to be a rather inauspicious day and the ghost of that young priest is now making an appearance."

Maddened by what he heard, Pilgrim leaped out of the cauldron, dried himself from the oil, and threw on his clothes. Dragging that officer over, he whipped out his iron rod and one blow on the head reduced him to a meat patty. "What ghost is this who's making the appearance?" he huffed. Those officials were so terrified that they freed Pa-chieh at once and knelt on the ground, pleading, "Pardon us! Pardon us!" The king, too, wanted to leave his dragon throne, but he was caught by Pilgrim, who said, "Your Majesty, don't walk away. Tell your third National Preceptor to go into the cauldron also." Trembling all over, the king said, "Third National Preceptor, save our life. Go into the cauldron quickly so that the monk won't hit us."

Goat-Strength went down the steps from the hall and took off his clothes like Pilgrim. Leaping into the cauldron of boiling oil, he began to cavort and bathe himself.

Letting go of the king, Pilgrim approached the cauldron and told the fire tenders to add more wood while he put his hand into the oil. Aha! That boiling oil felt ice cold. He thought to himself: "It was very hot when I took the bath, but feel how cold it is now that he's washing in there. I know. It has to be some dragon king who is giving him protection here." Leaping into the air, he recited a spell which began with the letter *Oṁ* and instantly summoned the Dragon King of the Northern Ocean to his side. "You horn-growing earthworm!" said Pilgrim to him. "You scaly lizard! How dare you assist that Taoist by coiling a cold dragon around the bottom of the cauldron? You want him to display his power and gain the upper hand on me?" Terribly intimidated, the Dragon King stammered out his answer: "Ao-shun dares not do that! Perhaps the Great Sage has no knowledge of this: this cursed beast did go through quite an austere process of self-cultivation, to the point where he was able to cast off his original shell. He has acquired the true magic of the five thunders, while the rest of the magic powers he has are all those developed by heterodoxy, none fit to lead him to the true way of the immortals. The powers of both his associates have already been destroyed by the Great Sage and they had to reveal their original forms. The performance of this one right now is also part of the Great Illusion which he has learned in the Little Mao Mountain,[1] a cold dragon which he has managed to cultivate by himself. This can deceive the worldly folks, but it can never deceive the Great Sage. I shall arrest that cold dragon at once, and you can be certain that he will be deep-fried—bones, skins, and all!" "Take him away," said Pilgrim, "and you'll be spared a whipping!" Changing into a violent gust of wind, the Dragon King swooped down to the cauldron and dragged the cold dragon back to the ocean.

Pilgrim dropped down from the air and stood again before the steps with Tripitaka, Pa-chieh, and Sha Monk. They saw that the Taoist was bobbing up and down in the oil, but his desperate efforts to get out were all to no avail. Every time he climbed up the wall of the cauldron, he would slip back down; in no time at all, his flesh dissolved, his skin was charred, and his bones left his body.

"Your Majesty," another officer in charge of execution went forward to report, "the Third National Preceptor has passed away!" As tears streamed from his eyes, the king clutched at the imperial table before him and sobbed uncontrollably, crying:

The human form is hard, hard indeed, to get!
Make no elixir when there's no true guide.
You have the charms and water to send for gods,
But not the pill to lengthen, protect your life.
If perfection's undone,
Could Nirvāṇa be won?
Your life's precarious, your efforts are vain.
If you knew before such hardships you'd meet,
Why not abstain, stay safely in the mount?
Truly
To touch gold, to refine lead—of what use are they?
To summon wind, to call for rain—still all is vain!

We do not know what will happen to master and disciples, and you must listen to the explanation in the next chapter.

## Forty-seven

The sage monk at night is blocked at the Heaven-Reaching
  River;
Metal and Wood, in compassion, rescue little children.

We were telling you that the king, who was leaning on his dragon
table, wept without ceasing until night fell, his tears gushing forth
like a stream. Finally Pilgrim went up to him and shouted: "How could
you be so dim-witted? Look at the corpses of those Taoists: one happens to be that of a tiger and the other, a deer. Goat-Strength was, in
fact, an antelope. If you don't believe me, ask them to fish out his bones
for you to see. How could humans have skeletons like that? They
were all mountain beasts which had become spirits, united in their
efforts to come here and plot against you. When they saw that your
ascendancy was still strong, they dared not harm you as yet; but after
two or more years when your ascendancy would be in decline, they
would have taken your life and your entire kingdom would have been
theirs. It was fortunate that we came in time to exterminate these
deviates and save your life. And you are still weeping? What for?
Bring us our rescript at once and send us on our way." Only when he
had heard this from Pilgrim did the king return to his senses. The civil
and military officials also went forward to speak to him, saying, "The
dead indeed turn out to be a white deer and a yellow tiger, while bones
in the cauldron do belong to an antelope. It is unwise not to listen to
the words of the sage monk." "In that case," said the king, "we are
grateful to the sage monk. It's late already. Let the Grand Preceptor
escort the sage monks back to Wisdom Depth Monastery to rest.
During early court tomorrow, we shall open up the Eastern Pavilion
and command the Court of Imperial Entertainments to prepare a huge
vegetarian banquet to thank them." The priests were escorted back
to the monastery.

At the time of the fifth watch the following morning, the king held
court for many officials. He at once issued a decree to summon the
Buddhist monks to return to the city, and this decree was to be posted
on every road and on all four gates. After giving the order also for the

preparation of a huge banquet, he sent his imperial chariot to the Wisdom Depth Monastery to invite Tripitaka and followers back to the Eastern Pavilion for the feast, and we shall speak no more of that.

We tell you now instead about those monks who succeeded in escaping with their lives. When they heard of the decree that was promulgated, every one of them was delighted and began to return to the city to search for the Great Sage Sun, to thank him, and to return his hairs. Meanwhile, the elder, after the banquet was over, obtained the rescript from the king, who led the queen, the concubines, and two rows of civil and military officials out the gate of the court to see the priests off. As they came out, they found many monks kneeling on both sides of the road, saying, "Father Great Sage, Equal to Heaven, we are the monks who escaped with our lives on the beach. When we heard that Father had wiped out the demons and rescued us, and when we further heard that our king had issued a decree commanding our return, we came here to present to you the hairs and to thank you for your Heavenly grace." "How many of you came back?" asked Pilgrim, chuckling, and they replied, "All five hundred. None's missing." Pilgrim shook his body once and immediately retrieved his hairs. Then he said to the king and the lay people, "These monks indeed were released by old Monkey. The cart was smashed after old Monkey tossed it through the double passes and up the steep ridge, and it was Monkey also who beat to death those two perverse Taoists. After such pestilence has been exterminated this day, you should realize that the true way is the gate of Zen. Hereafter you should never believe in false doctrines. I hope that you will honor the unity of the Three Religions: revere the monks, revere also the Taoists, and take care to nurture the talented. Your kingdom, I assure you, will be secure forever." The king gave his assent and his thanks repeatedly before he escorted the T'ang monk out of the city.

And so, this was the purpose of their journey:

A diligent search for the three canons;

A strenuous quest for the primal light.

As they proceeded, they walked by day and rested by night; they drank when they were thirsty and ate when they were hungry. Spring ended, summer waned, and soon it was again the time of autumn. One day towards evening, the T'ang monk reined in his horse and said, "Disciples, where shall we find shelter for the night?" "Master," said Pilgrim, "a man who has left the family should not speak as one who remains in the family." Tripitaka said, "How would a man in the family speak? And how would a man who has left the family speak?" "In this time of the year," said Pilgrim, "a man who remains in the family will enjoy the benefits of a warm bed and snug blankets; he has his children in his bosom and his wife next to his legs. That's how comfortably he will sleep! Now, how could we who have left the family expect to enjoy such things? We must be cloaked by the stars and wrapped by the moon; we must dine on the winds and rest by the waters. We move on if there's a road, and we stop only when we come to its end." "Elder Brother," said Pa-chieh, "you know only one thing, but you can't see its implications. Look how treacherous is this road we're walking on! I have such a heavy load on me that I find it difficult even to walk. Please find some place where I can have a good night's rest and regain my strength. By morning, I can face the load once more. Otherwise, I'll die of fatigue!" "Let's move on a little further then in this moonlight," said Pilgrim, "and we can stop when we reach some place where there are houses." Master and disciples had no choice but to follow Pilgrim forward.

They did not journey long before they heard the sound of rushing water. "Undone!" said Pa-chieh. "We've come to the end of the road!" "We are blocked by a torrent of water," said Sha Monk. The T'ang monk said, "How could we get across?" "Let me test it to discover how deep it is first," said Pa-chieh. Tripitaka said, "Wu-nêng, don't speak such nonsense! How could you test the depth or shallowness of water?" "I'll find an egg-shaped pebble," said Pa-chieh, "and throw it in: if it splashes and foam comes up, it's shallow; if it sinks down with a gurgling sound, then it's deep." "Go and test it," said Pilgrim. Our Idiot groped on the ground and found a stone, which he threw into the water; all they heard was a gurgling sound as if fishes were releasing bubbles as the stone sank down to the bottom. "Deep! Deep! Deep!" he said. "We can't cross it!" "Though you may have discovered its depth," said the T'ang monk, "you may not know how wide it is." "Indeed not! Indeed not!" said Pa-chieh. Pilgrim said, "Let me have a look." Dear Great Sage! He somersaulted at once into the air and fixed his gaze on the water. He saw

The moon soaked in sheens of light;
The sky drenched in vasty deep;
A supernal branch able to down mountains;
A long river feeding a hundred streams;

A thousand layers of churning foams;
Ten thousand folds of mountainous waves;
No fisher-fires lit up the banks
But egrets rested by the beach.
An oceanlike vast expanse,
With no boundaries in sight.

He dropped down quickly from the clouds to the bank of the river,
saying, "Master, it's very wide! Very wide! We can't get across! These
fiery eyes and diamond pupils of old Monkey can discern good and evil
up to a thousand miles during the day, and even at night, they can
cover a distance of four or five hundred miles. Just now I couldn't even
see the other shore. How could I tell the width of the river?"

Horrified, Tripitaka could not say a word for a long time. Then he
sobbed out, "O Disciple! What shall we do?" "Master, please don't
cry," said Sha Monk. "Look over there! Isn't that a man standing by
the water?" Pilgrim said, "He could be a fisherman lowering his nets,
I suppose. Let me go and ask him." Holding his iron rod, he sprinted
forward to have a closer look. Ah! It was not a man, but only a stone
monument, on which were written three large words in seal script
and two rows of smaller words down below. The three large words
were: Heaven-Reaching River. The two rows of smaller words read:

A width of eight hundred miles
Which few, from days of old, have crossed.

"Master," Pilgrim called out, "come and look." When Tripitaka saw
the monument, tears rolled down his cheeks, saying, "O Disciple!
When I left Ch'ang-an that year, I thought that the way to the
Western Heaven was quite easy. How could I know of the obstacles of
demons and monsters, the long distance over mountains and waters!"

"Master," said Pa-chieh, "listen for a moment. Isn't that the sound
of drums and cymbals coming from somewhere? It must be that some
family is feasting the monks. Let's go over there and beg for some
vegetarian food and make inquiry concerning the possibility of finding
a boat to take us across tomorrow." Cocking his ears as he rode, Tripitaka indeed heard the sound of drums and cymbals. "These are not
the musical instruments of Taoists," he said. "It has to be some
religious service conducted by us Buddhists. Let us go over there."
Pilgrim led the horse in front and all of them proceeded toward where
the music was coming from. There was actually no road for them to
walk on, only a rolling sandy beach. Presently, they saw a group of

well-built houses, about four or five hundred of them altogether. They
saw that these houses were

    Close by the hill and the roads,
    Next to the shores and the stream.
    Everywhere the wooden fences wcrc shut;
    The bamboo yard of each house was closed.
    Egrets resting on sand dunes had peaceful dreams;
    Birds nesting on willows voiced their chilly tunes.
    The short flutes were silent;
    The washing flails had no rhythm.
    Prince's feathers quaked in the moonlight;
    Yellow rushes battled the wind.
    A village dog barked through sparse fences by the fields;
    An old fisher slept on his boat at the ford,
    Where lights were low,
    And human bustles, quiet.
    The bright moon seemed a mirror hung in the air,
    The scent of duckweed blossoms all at once
    Came from the far shore with the west wind.

As Tripitaka dismounted, he saw a house at the head of a path; before
the house was erected a pole with a banner flying, while the inside
was ablaze with lamps and candles and filled with fragrant incense.
"Wu-k'ung," said Tripitaka, "what we have here is certainly better
than either the fold of the mountain or the edge of the river. At least
the eaves of the roof can provide some shelter from the night mists,
and we can rest without fears. You, however, should stay behind first,
and let me go up to that patron's door to make known our request. If
he is willing to let us stay, I'll call for you; but if he's unwilling, all
of you are not to let loose any mischief. You are, after all, quite ugly
in your appearances, and I fear that you may frighten them. Offending
these people may mean that we shall have nowhere at all to stay."
"What you say is quite right," said Pilgrim. "Please go first, Master,
and we'll wait for you here."

    Taking off his broad-brimmed bamboo hat, the elder shook the dirt
from his clerical robe and went up to the door of the house, holding
the priestly staff in his hands. He found the door half-closed; not
daring to enter without permission, the elder stood still and waited for
a brief moment, when an old man, with some beads hanging around
his neck, emerged from the house, chanting the name of Buddha as he

walked. Seeing that the old man was about to shut the door, however, the elder hurriedly pressed his palms together and cried out: "Old Benefactor, this humble priest salutes you." Returning his greeting, the old man said, "You are too late, monk." "What do you mean?" said Tripitaka. "I mean that you won't get anything because you are late," said the old man. "If you had come earlier, you would have found that we were feasting the monks. After you have eaten your fill, you would then be given an additional three ounces of cooked rice, a bale of white cloth, and ten strings of copper pennies. Why do you come at this hour?" "Old Benefactor," said Tripitaka, bowing, "this humble priest is not here to be feasted." "If you are not," said the old man, "then why have you come here?" Tripitaka said, "I am some-one sent by imperial decree of the Great T'ang in the Land of the East to acquire scriptures in the Western Heaven. It was late when we arrived at your region. When we heard the sound of drums and cymbals from your house, we came to ask you for one night's lodging. We'll leave by morning." "Monk," said the old man, waving his hand gently, "a man who has left the family should not lie. The distance between our place here and your Great T'ang in the Land of the East happens to be fifty-four thousand miles. A single person like you, how could you come here all by yourself?" "That's an exceptionally accurate observation, Old Benefactor," said Tripitaka, "but I am not alone. I have three disciples, who have opened up a path through the mountains and built bridges when we came upon the waters. It was because of their being my escorts that I could arrive here today." "If you have disciples," said the old man, "why haven't they come with you? Please invite them forth at once! My house has enough room for all of you." Turning around, Tripitaka said, "Disciples, come here."

Now, Pilgrim was by nature rather impulsive; Pa-chieh was born without manners and Sha Monk, too, happened to be very impetuous. The moment the three of them heard their master beckoning, they rushed like a cyclone toward the house, dragging the horse and the luggage along. When the old man caught sight of them, he was so terrified that he fell on the ground, crying repeatedly, "Monsters are here! Monsters are here!" Raising him with his hands, Tripitaka said, "Don't be afraid, Benefactor. They are not monsters. They are my disciples." Trembling all over, the old man said, "Such a handsome master! Why did you take such ugly disciples?" "Though they are not good to look at," said Tripitaka, "they are quite knowledgeable in

taming tigers and subduing dragons, in seizing monsters and capturing fiends." Not fully believing what he heard, the old man supported
himself on the T'ang monk and walked slowly with him inside.

We tell you now about those three rogues, who dashed into the
hall, where they dropped their luggage and tied up the horse. There
were at that time several priests in the hall reciting sūtras. Sticking out
his long snout, Pa-chieh shouted at them, "Hey monks! Which sūtra
are you reciting?" On hearing this, those monks raised their heads
and all at once

They saw a visitor,
With long snout and huge ears,
A thick frame and wide shoulders,
A voice that boomed like thunder.
But Pilgrim and Sha Monk
Were in looks e'en uglier.
Of those priests in the hall
None was not in terror.
They tried to keep reciting
But were stopped by their leader.
They left their stones and bells
And forsook the graven Buddhas.
The lamps were all blown out,
And torches all smothered.
They scrambled and they stumbled,
The doorsills falling over.
Like gourds when props were down,
Their heads bumped one another.
A serene plot of Truth
Became a cause of great laughter!

When the three brothers saw how those priests stumbled and fell all
over, they clapped their hands and roared with laughter. More terrified
than ever, those priests banged into one another as they fled for their
lives and deserted the place. Tripitaka led the old man up the hall, but
the lights and lamps were completely out, while the three of them were
still in guffaws. "You brazen creatures!" scolded the T'ang monk.
"You are so wicked! Haven't I taught you every day, admonished you
every morning? The ancients said,

To be virtuous without instruction,
Is this not sagacity?

To be virtuous after instruction,
Is this not nobility?
To be virtueless even after instruction,
Is this not stupidity?

The way you have perpetrated mischief has just shown you to be people of the greatest baseness and stupidity! You barged into someone's door without any manners! You have frightened the old Benefactor and scattered the priests reciting the sūtras, completely spoiling the good works of others. Wouldn't I be blamed for all this?" He spoke with such vehemence that they dared not utter a word in reply, and only then did the old man become convinced that they were his disciples. He turned quickly to bow to Tripitaka, saying, "Venerable Father, it doesn't matter! It doesn't matter! They were putting out the lights just now because the ceremony was about done anyway." "If it's over," said Pa-chieh, "bring out the end-of-service feast so that we can enjoy it and sleep." "Bring out the lights! Bring out the lights!" cried the old man. Some of the members of his household, when they heard him, began to complain to themselves: "There are enough candles already in the hall for the religious service. Why is he calling for lights?" A few houseboys came out to see for themselves and they found the hall in complete darkness. Returning hurriedly with torches and lanterns, they suddenly saw the forms of Pa-chieh and Sha Monk. So terrified by the sight they were that they dropped their torches and dashed inside, slamming shut the mid-level door and shouting all the time, "There are monsters here! There are monsters here!"

Picking up one of the torches, Pilgrim re-lit the lamps and the candles before he pulled a chair to the middle of the hall for the T'ang monk to sit on. Then he and his brothers sat down on both sides and the old man took a seat in front of all of them. As they settled into their seats, they heard the inner door open and another old man walked out, supporting himself on a staff. "What kind of perverse demons are you," he said, "that you dare enter the door of a virtuous family in the dark of night?" The old man, who was seated, quickly arose and met him behind the screens, saying, "No need to clamor, Elder Brother. They are no perverse demons, but arhats sent to acquire scriptures by the Great T'ang in the Land of the East. Though they look vicious, they are actually quite gentle." Only then did the other old man put down his staff and bow to greet all four of the visitors, after which, he, too, took a seat in the front of the hall. "Bring out the

tea," he cried, "and prepare us some vegetarian food." He had to call
several times before several houseboys, still trembling, emerged,
though they still did not dare walk near the visitors.

Unable to contain himself, Pa-chieh said, "Old man, why are your
servants milling about on both sides?" "I told them to bring out some
vegetarian food to serve to the Venerable Fathers," said the old man.
Pa-chieh said, "How many are there to serve us?" "Eight of them,"
said the old man. "Which of us are they going to serve?" said Pa-
chieh. "Why, all four of you!" said the old man, and Pa-chieh said,
"That pale-faced master requires only one person to serve him; the
one with the hairy face and thunder-god beak needs only two. But
the one with the gloomy complexion will have to have eight persons,
and, as for me, nothing less than twenty attendants will do." "If I
understand you correctly," said the old man, "you are trying to tell
me that you have a large appetite." "It's passable, passable," said Pa-
chieh. "Well," said the old man, "there are plenty of people here."
Young and old, he managed to summon thirty some servants to come
out.

As the two old men spoke amiably with the monks, the rest of the
household felt more at ease. A table was set up in the middle of the
hall and the T'ang monk was asked to take the honored seat. Three
other tables were set up on both sides for the disciples, while the two
old men were seated at another table facing all of them. Fruits and
vegetables were presented first, after which they brought out
glutenous rice, rice, side dishes, and soup with vermicelli. After the
food was laid out properly, the elder T'ang lifted his chopsticks and
recited the *Fast-Breaking Sūtra*. Our Idiot, however, was an impulsive
eater for one thing, and he was hungry for another. Without waiting
for the T'ang monk to finish his recitation, he grabbed one of the red
lacquered wooden bowls and hurled a whole bowl full of rice into his
mouth. Every grain of it immediately vanished! One of the young
attendants on the side said, "This Venerable Father is not very smart!
If you want to snatch something and hide it in your sleeve, why don't
you take some steamed buns? Why do you snatch a bowl of rice
instead? Won't it soil your clothing?" "I didn't put it in my sleeve,"
said Pa-chieh, chuckling, "I ate it!" "You have hardly moved your
mouth," said the young man, "how could you have eaten it?" "Only
your son would lie!" said Pa-chieh. "Of course, I ate it! If you don't
believe me, I'll eat some more for you to see!" The young man indeed

picked up the bowl, filled it with rice once more, and handed the bowl
to Pa-chieh. Idiot took it, and instantly he gulped it all down with a
flick of his hand. When the houseboys saw this, they cried, "O Father!
You must have a throat lined with polished bricks! It's so level and
smooth!" Before the T'ang monk had finished reciting one sūtra,
Idiot had downed five or six bowls of rice. After that, they raised their
chopsticks to enjoy the other kinds of food. Without regard for
whether they were fruits, rice, glutenous rice, or side dishes, Idiot
simply scooped them all up with his hands and stuffed them into his
mouth, calling all the time, "More rice! More rice! Where are you all
disappearing to?" "Worthy Brother," said Pilgrim, "please don't eat
so much! We are already much better off than trying to endure hunger
in the fold of the mountain. It's good enough if you are half-filled."
"Never mind," said Pa-chieh. "As the proverb says,

   The priest half-fed
   Is worse than dead!"

"Take away the stuff," said Pilgrim. "Don't mind him!" Bowing, the
two old men said, "To tell you the truth, there is no problem whatever
if it is during the day, for we can easily feed over a hundred priests like
our big-bellied elder here. But it's late now. We have put away the
leftovers, and we have managed to steam only one stone of glutenous
rice and five barrels of plain rice together with a few tablefuls of
vegetarian food. We were about to invite a few neighbors to disperse
the blessings with the priests. When all of you arrived, the priests
became frightened and left, and we dared not even ask our neighbors
or kin to come here. Everything that had been prepared was already
presented to you. But if you are not yet filled, we can steam some
more." "Steam some more! Steam some more!" said Pa-chieh.

   After they finished eating, the tables and dishes were put aside.
Tripitaka stood up and bowed to the two old men to thank them for
the feast. Then he asked: "Old Benefactors, what is your honored
name?" One of them said, "Our surname is Ch'ên." Pressing his palms
together, Tripitaka said, "We share the same illustrious ancestors."
"So the Venerable Father also has the surname of Ch'ên?" said one
of the old men. "Yes," said Tripitaka, "that is the name of my secular
home. May I ask what kind of religious service was held just now?"
"Why do you ask, Master?" said Pa-chieh, laughing. "Can't you
guess? It has to be a service for harvest, or for peace, or for the com-

pletion of a building. Nothing more!" "No, no," said the old man. "Truly what was it for then?" asked Tripitaka again, and the old man said, "It's a preparatory mass for the dead." Laughing so hard that he could hardly remain seated, Pa-chieh said, "Grandpa, you aren't very perceptive! We are experts in half-truths, masters of humbug! How could you hope to deceive me with that fraudulent title? You think that monks are ignorant of masses and religious services? You may hold a preparatory mass for the transference of merit, or for the presentation of a votive offering. Since when was there ever a preparatory mass for the dead? There is no one in your house who has died. How could you have a mass for the dead?"

When Pilgrim heard these words, he was secretly pleased and thought to himself: "This Idiot is getting smarter!" Then he said, "Old Grandpa, you must have been mistaken. What is this preparatory mass for the dead?" Instead of replying at once, the two old men bowed and said, "How did all of you turn from the main road to acquire scriptures and arrive at our place?" Pilgrim said, "We were walking along the main road, but it was barred by a torrent of water and we could not cross it. Then we heard the sound of cymbals and drums, and that led us here to ask you for a night's lodging." "When you reached the edge of the water," said the old man, "did you see anything?" "Only a stone monument," said Pilgrim, "with the three-word inscription, Heaven-Reaching River. Below it, there were the words:

A width of eight hundred miles
Which few, from days of old, have crossed.
There was no other thing." "If you had gone about a mile inland from the monument," said one of the old men, "you would have come upon a temple of the Great King of Miraculous Power. But you didn't see it?" "We did not," said Pilgrim. "Tell us, old Grandpa, what is this Miraculous Power?"

At once the two old men began to shed tears as they said, "O Venerable Father! That Great King was
Powerful to move a region to build his shrine;
Miraculous to bless people far and near.
He sends us sweet rains from month to month,
And auspicious clouds from year to year."
Pilgrim said, "Sweet rains and auspicious clouds are good things, but

you are so sad and dejected when you speak of them. Why?" Beating
their chests and stamping their feet, the old men sighed deeply and
said, "O Venerable Father!

Though favors abound, there's also spite.
He will take lives even when he is kind.
He loves to eat the virgin boys and girls,
This god has no enlightened, upright mind!"

"So he likes to devour virgin boys and girls?" said Pilgrim. "Yes," said
the old men. Pilgrim said, "I suppose it's your family's turn now?"
"Indeed it is," said one of the old men. "Our village here consists of
over one hundred families, and it belongs to the Yüan-hui County of
the Cart Slow Kingdom. The name of this village of ours is the Ch'ên
Village. Every year this Great King requires the sacrifice of a virgin
boy and a virgin girl in addition to the offering of various kinds of livestock like hogs and sheep. When he has devoured all of these to his
satisfaction, he would bless us with wind and rain in due season. If
there is no such sacrifice for him, he will inflict upon us all kinds of
calamity." "How many esteemed sons do you have in your family?"
said Pilgrim. "Alas! Alas!" said the older of the two men, beating his
breast. "Why mention 'esteemed sons'? The term would only em-
barrass us to death! This is my brother, Ch'ên Ch'ing, and I am called
Ch'ên Ch'êng. He is fifty-eight and I am sixty-three, both badly off for
children. Since I had no children even when I was fifty, friends and
relatives urged me to take a concubine. I had no choice but to do so
and a girl was born later. Her name is One Load of Gold, and she is
barely eight this year." "What an expensive name!" said Pa-chieh.
"Why was she given it?" The old man said, "Since I was childless for
so many years, I persisted in repairing bridges and roads, in erecting
temples and stūpas, and in the feasting of monks. I kept a record of all
I spent—a few ounces here and a few ounces there—and by the time
my daughter was born, I had spent exactly thirty pounds of gold.
Thirty pounds make one load, and that was how she got her name."

"And does he have a son?" said Pilgrim. The old man said, "He has,
indeed, a son born also of a concubine. He is only seven years old, and
his name is Ch'ên Kuan-pao."[1] "Why such a name?" said Pilgrim,
and the old man said, "Because our family worships the Holy Father
Kuan, and the child was conceived after prayers were offered to the
Holy Father. That's why he has such a name. The joint age of my
brother and me is over one hundred and twenty, but we have only

these two children to perpetuate our families. How could we ever anticipate that the turn to provide the victims would fall on us! We dare not, of course, refuse, but it is difficult to give up our precious children. It was for the welfare of their souls that we established this plot of Truth in advance, and that was the reason I named it the preparatory mass for the dead."

When Tripitaka heard these words, he could not restrain the tears from rolling down his cheeks and he said, "Truly it's like what the proverb says:

Instead of yellow plums only green plums drop.

Old Heaven's doubly harsh to a childless man!"

Pilgrim, however, smiled and said, "Let me question him a bit more. Old Grandpa, how much property do you have?" The two old men said together, "Quite a bit. We have at least some seven hundred and fifty acres of paddy fields and over a thousand acres of dry fields. There must be some ninety pasture fields, three hundred water buffalos, some thirty horses and mules, and countless numbers of hogs, sheep, chickens, and geese. There is more grain in our warehouses than we can consume and more clothing in our houses than we can wear. Our property and our wealth, as you can see, are quite sizable." "If you own so much," said Pilgrim, "it's pathetic that you are so stingy!" "How did you come to that conclusion?" said one of the old men. Pilgrim said, "If you are so well-off, how could you permit your own children to be sacrificed? Throw away fifty ounces of silver and you can buy a virgin boy; throw away another hundred ounces and you can buy a virgin girl. You need spend no more than two hundred ounces of silver for all expenses and you will preserve posterity for you and your family. Isn't that much better?" Shedding copious tears, the two old men said, "Venerable Father! You aren't aware of the fact that the Great King is truly so powerful that he knows everything. Why, he even comes frequently to the families here." Pilgrim said, "When he came through, did you ever discover how he looked or how tall he was?" "We have never seen his form," said the two old men. "But whenever we felt a fragrant breeze, it was a sign that the Father Great King had arrived. Then we had to burn hurriedly lots of incense and all of us, young and old, had to bow toward the wind. He knows everything there is to know of our families here; he can remember even the birth dates and hours of young and old. He will not consider it a treat unless he can devour children who are truly ours. Don't speak of two or three hundred ounces of silver; even if we were to spend several thousand ounces, we had nowhere to purchase a boy or a girl of exactly the same appearance and age."

"So, that's how it is!" said Pilgrim. "All right, all right! Bring out your son and let me take a look at him." Ch'ên Ch'ing went inside at once and carried his son Kuan-pao out to the front hall, placing him before the lamps. The child, of course, was wholly unaware of the disaster that was about to descend on him. With two sleeves stuffed with preserved fruits and candies, he danced about as he munched on the goodies. On seeing him, Pilgrim recited a spell silently and shook his body: at once he changed into a boy with the exact appearance of that child Kuan-pao. Now there were two boys holding hands and dancing before the lamps! The old man was so startled that he fell on his knees, causing the T'ang monk to cry out: "Venerable Father, this is blasphemy! Blasphemy!" The old man said, "But this Venerable Father was just speaking to us. How did he manage to take on the appearance of my child all at once? Look, you give them a call, and both of them answer together! We are the ones who are not worthy! Please show your true form! Please show your true form!" With a wipe of his own face Pilgrim changed back into his true form. Remaining on his knees, the old man said, "So the Venerable Father has this kind of ability!" "Did I look like your son?" said Pilgrim, laughing. "Very much! Very much!" said the old man. "You had exactly the same features, the same voice, the same clothes, and the same height!" "You haven't even examined me closely," said Pilgrim. "Bring out the scale and see if I'm of the same weight as his." "Yes! Yes! Yes!" said the old man. "I could tell that you were exactly of the same weight." "You think I could serve as the sacrifice?" said Pilgrim. "It's marvelous! Just marvelous!" said the old man. "Of course, you could serve as the sacrifice."

Pilgrim said, "I'll exchange my life for your boy's so that your family's posterity will be preserved. I'll present myself as a sacrifice to that Great King." Kowtowing as he knelt on the ground, Ch'ên Ch'ing said, "If in your compassion you are willing to present yourself as a substitute, I shall present Father T'ang with a thousand ounces of white silver as his travel expenses to the Western Heaven." "And you are not going to thank old Monkey?" said Pilgrim. "If you are a sacrificial substitute," said the old man, "you will be finished." "What do you mean finished?" said Pilgrim. "The Great King will devour you," said the old man, and Pilgrim said, "Does he dare?" "If he doesn't eat you," said the old man, "it will only be because you are too smelly for his taste." "May Heaven's will be done!" said Pilgrim, chuckling. "If he eats me, it'll mean that I am to die young; if he does not, it's my luck. Anyway, I shall be your sacrificial substitute."

Ch'ên Ch'ing not only kowtowed to thank him, but also promised to give the monks an additional five hundred ounces of silver. Ch'ên Ch'êng, however, neither kowtowed nor gave thanks; leaning on one of the screens, he wept profusely. Understanding his plight, Pilgrim went up to tug at him and said, "Number One, you are not promising me anything nor are you thanking me. I suppose you must feel terrible about parting with your daughter?" Going to his knees at once, Ch'ên Ch'êng said, "Yes, I can't part with her. I am indebted to you, Venerable Father, for your kindness, and it should be enough that you have saved our nephew. But this old moron has no other children except his daughter. If I should die, she would weep bitterly, too! How could I ever part with her?" "Then go quickly and steam five more barrels of rice," said Pilgrim. "Prepare some fine vegetarian dishes also and let that long-snout master of ours enjoy himself. Then we can ask him to change into the form of your daughter, and we two brothers will be your sacrificial substitutes. By saving the lives of your daughter and son, we shall accrue to ourselves secret merit. How about that?" Horrified by what he heard, Pa-chieh said, "Elder Brother, you can show off your energy as you please! But don't drag me into this venture without any regard for my life!" "Worthy Brother," said Pilgrim, "the proverb says, 'Even chickens can eat only food they work for!' The moment we entered their house, they feted us with a huge banquet, while you were complaining that you were only half-filled! How could you be unwilling to assist them in their difficulties?" "O Elder Brother," said Pa-chieh, "I don't know anything about transformation." "What do you mean?" said Pilgrim. "You know thirty-six modes of transformation." "Wu-nêng," cried Tripitaka, "what your elder brother has just said is certainly right, and what he has proposed is most appropriate. The proverb says, 'The saving of one life is better than the construction of a seven-tiered pagoda.' In the first place, we should repay their great kindness to us; in the second, we should make merit whenever possible by the performance of good works. Since there is no other thing you must attend to in this cool night, you and your brother can go and have some fun." "Look at the way Master talks!" said Pa-chieh. "I may know how to change into a mountain, a tree, a rock, a scabby elephant, a water buffalo, or a stout fellow. But it'll be rather difficult for me to change into a small young girl!" "Don't believe him, Number One," said Pilgrim. "Bring out your precious daughter." Ch'ên Ch'êng dashed inside and brought out his child, One Load of Gold. At the same time, his whole family, including his wife and his concubine, young and old, all came out to the front hall to kneel before the monks and kowtow, begging them to save the girl's life.

The girl was wearing on her head a patterned emerald fillet with dangling pearl and precious stone pendants; she had on a coat of red silk shot with yellow, covered by a cape of mandarin green satin with chess-board patterned collar. Around her waist was tied a silk skirt with bright red flowers. She also had on a pair of gold-kneed trousers and a pair of light pink toad's-head patterned shoes made of hemp thread. And she, too, was munching on some fruits. "Pa-chieh," said Pilgrim, "that's the girl. Change into her form quickly, so that we can be sacrificed." "O Brother!" said Pa-chieh. "She's so delicate and lovely! How could I do it?" "Quick!" said Pilgrim. "Don't ask for a beating!" Alarmed, Pa-chieh said, "Elder Brother, don't beat me! Let me try and see what happens!"

This Idiot recited a spell and shook his head several times, crying, "Change!" Indeed, his head took on the features of the little girl, but his belly remained as big as ever so that his hulking frame bore hardly any resemblance to the girl's. "Change some more!" cried Pilgrim, laughing. "You can beat me all you want," said Pa-chieh, "but I can't change anymore. What am I to do?" "You can't take on the head of a girl," said Pilgrim, "and the body of a priest! You would be neither boy nor girl, and that wouldn't be good, would it? Why don't you assume the star posture and see what I can do for you." He blew a mouthful of magic breath on to Pa-chieh, whose body at once took on the form of the little girl. Then Pilgrim said to the two old men, "Please take your relatives, your son, and your daughter inside so that we will not be confused with them. I fear that after a while, my brother may become slothful and sneak inside, and it will be difficult for you to tell them apart. Give your children plenty of nice fruits and candies and make certain that they don't cry. I don't want that Great King to get wind of our plans. We two will have some fun and be off."

Dear Great Sage! He gave instructions for Sha Monk to stand guard over the T'ang monk, while he and Pa-chieh assumed the exact forms of Ch'ên Kuan-pao and One Load of Gold. After the two of them made all the preparations, Pilgrim asked, "How are we to be presented, trussed up or just bound? Steamed or chopped to pieces?" "Elder Brother," said Pa-chieh, "don't pull any more tricks on me! I don't have that kind of ability!" "No, No!" said one of the old men. "All we need are two red lacquered trays, on which we will ask both of you to sit. The trays will be placed on top of two tables, which will then be carried to the temple by some of our houseboys." "Fine! Fine!" said Pilgrim. "Bring out the trays and let us try them." The old man took out the lacquered trays; Pilgrim and Pa-chieh sat in them, after which four houseboys lifted up two tables and walked into the courtyard. Delighted, Pilgrim said, "Pa-chieh, a couple of turns like this and we shall be priests who have ascended the tray-platform!" "If they carry us inside," said Pa-chieh, "and carry us out again, I won't be afraid even if they go back and forth until tomorrow morning. But once they take us into the temple, we'll be devoured, and that's no game!" "Just watch me," said Pilgrim. "When he seizes me and tries to eat me, you can flee." "But how would I know whom he will eat first?" said Pa-chieh. "If he eats the virgin boy first, I can flee, of course. But if he wants to eat the virgin girl first, what am I to do?" "During one of the sacrifices some years ago," said the old man, "a few people courageous enough hid themselves behind the temple or beneath the offering tables. They saw that he ate the boy first before he devoured the girl." Pa-chieh said, "That's my luck! That's my luck!" As the brothers were talking, a loud din of gongs and drums could be heard outside the house, now lit up also by the light of many torches and lamps. The people of the same village came to pound at the front gate, crying, "Bring out the virgin boy and the virgin girl!" As the old men wept and wailed, the four houseboys lifted the tables and carried the two of them away. We truly do not know what happened to their lives, and you must listen to the explanation in the next chapter.

*Forty-eight*

The demon, raising a cold wind, sends a great snow fall;
The monk, intent on seeing Buddha, walks on layered ice.

We tell you now about those worshipers from the Ch'ên Village, who carried Pilgrim and Pa-chieh along with various offerings of livestock straight to the Temple of Miraculous Power. The virgin boy and girl were placed on top of the offerings. Pilgrim turned his head and saw that there were incense, flowers, and candles on the offering tables, in the middle of which there was also a tablet inscribed in gold letters with the title: "The God and Great King of Miraculous Power." There was no other image of any deity. After the worshipers had set out everything properly, they knelt down and kowtowed toward the tablet, saying in unison, "Great King Father, in this year, this month, this day, and this hour, Ch'ên Ch'êng, the one in charge of the sacrifice and the leader of all the faithfuls of the Ch'ên Village, young and old, does follow our annual custom and offer to you a virgin boy by the name of Ch'ên Kuan-pao and a virgin girl by the name of One Load of Gold. Hogs and sheep in the same number are presented to you also for your enjoyment. We pray that you will grant us rain and wind in due season and a rich harvest of the five grains." After they made this invocation, they burned paper money and horses before returning to their houses.

When Pa-chieh saw that the people had dispersed, he said to Pilgrim, "Let's go home, too." "Where's your home?" said Pilgrim. Pa-chieh said, "I want to go back to old Ch'ên's house to sleep." "Idiot," said Pilgrim, "you are babbling again! If you have agreed to do this for him, you have got to finish the job." "You call me an idiot," said Pa-chieh. "Aren't you the real idiot? We were supposed to have some fun with the Ch'êns and fool with them a bit. You can't be serious that you want us sacrificed?" "If we help someone," said Pilgrim, "we must help him to the end. We must wait until that Great King arrives and devours us, or it will not be a perfect finish! If he has no sacrifice, he will send calamities to the village, and that will not be right."

As he spoke, they heard the sound of a fierce wind outside. "O dear!" said Pa-chieh. "When the wind blows like that, it must mean that the thing is here!" "Shut up!" cried Pilgrim. "Let me do the talking!" In a moment, a fiend arrived at the door of the temple. Look at the way he appears:

Gold helmet and cuirass both bright and new;
A treasure sash like red clouds wrapped his waist.
His eyes seemed big stars blazing in the night;
His teeth resembled those of a heavy saw.
Mists in waves did encircle both his legs,
And steamy fog surrounded all his frame.
He walked and a cold wind stirred repeatedly;
He stood and baleful aura rose in tiers.
He looked like the Curtain-Raising Captain
Or the great god of a monastery's gate.

Standing right at the doorway, the fiend asked: "Which family this year is providing the sacrifice?" Smiling broadly, Pilgrim said, "Thank you for asking! Those in charge are Ch'ên Ch'êng and Ch'ên Ch'ing." Puzzled by this answer, the fiend thought to himself: "This virgin boy is not only bold, but also articulate. Usually the victims in the past could not even reply to the first asking, and they would be frightened out of their wits at the second asking. By the time I seized them with my hands, they were already as good as dead. How is it that this virgin boy today can still give such intelligent replies?" Not bold enough to seize his prey immediately, the fiend asked once more: "What are the names of the boy and the girl?" With a laugh, Pilgrim said, "The virgin boy is called Ch'ên Kuan-pao, and the virgin girl is called One Load of Gold." "This sacrifice," said the fiend, "happens to be an annual custom. Now that you have been offered to me, I'm going to eat you." "I dare not resist you," said Pilgrim. "Please feel free to enjoy yourself." When the fiendish creature heard this, he was even more reluctant to raise his hands. Standing there in the doorway, he shouted, "Don't you dare be impudent! In years past I would eat the virgin boy first. But this year, I'm going to eat the virgin girl first." "O Great King," said Pa-chieh, horrified, "please do it the usual way! Don't break an old custom!"

Without permitting for further discussion, the fiend stretched out his hands to seize Pa-chieh. With a bound Idiot leaped down from the offering table and changed back into his true form. Whipping out his rake, he brought it down hard on the hands of the fiend. The fiend retreated hurriedly and tried to flee, but not before the blow of Pa-chieh sent something to the ground with a clang. "I've punctured his armor!" shouted Pa-chieh. As he changed back into his true form also, Pilgrim stepped forward to have a look and found that there were two fish scales about the size of ice dishes. "Chase him!" he yelled, and the two of them leaped into the air. Since that creature thought he was coming to a feast, he brought no weapon along. With bare hands he stood on the edge of the clouds and asked, "Monks, where did you come from? How dare you come to oppress me here, rob me of my offerings, and ruin my name?" "So, you're an ignorant, brazen creature!" said Pilgrim. "We are disciples of the sage monk Tripitaka from the Great T'ang in the Land of the East, who was sent by royal decree to go to the Western Heaven for scriptures. When we stayed with the Ch'ên family last night, we heard that there was a perverse demon who falsely assumed the title of Miraculous Power. Every year he demands a virgin boy and a virgin girl as sacrifice. In compassion we wanted to save lives and arrest you, you lawless creature. Confess at once. How many years have you called yourself Great King of this place, and how many boys and girls have you devoured? Give us a detailed account, and we may spare your life." When that fiend heard these words, he turned and fled immediately. Pa-chieh tried to strike at him again with the muckrake but did not succeed, for the fiend changed into a violent gust of wind which faded into the Heaven-Reaching River.

"No need to chase him anymore," said Pilgrim. "This fiend has to be a creature of the river. Let's wait till tomorrow before we try to catch him and ask him to take Master across the river." Pa-chieh agreed and both of them returned to the temple and hauled all the offerings and livestock, including the tables on which they were laden, back to the Ch'ên house. At that time, the elder, Sha Monk, and the Ch'ên brothers were all waiting for some news of them, when suddenly, they saw the two disciples dumping the sacrificial animals and offerings in the courtyard. "Wu-k'ung," said Tripitaka, going forward to meet them, "how did the sacrifice go?" Pilgrim gave a thorough account of how they revealed their names and how the fiend disappeared into the river. The two old men were most pleased, and they at once gave the order for rooms to be made ready and bedding laid out for master and disciples to rest. There we shall leave them for the moment.

We tell you instead about that fiend, who escaped with his life and went back to his water palace. After he sat down, he fell completely silent for such a long time that his watery kinsfolk, young and old, all gathered about him to ask: "Great King, you are usually quite happy when you come home after the sacrifice. Why is it that you seem so annoyed this year?" "After I've satisfied myself in past years," said the fiend, "I usually managed to bring some leftovers for you to enjoy. Today, however, not even I myself got anything to eat. I was so unlucky that I ran into an adversary and almost lost my life." "Which adversary was that, Great King?" they asked. The fiend said, "A disciple of a holy monk of the Great T'ang in the Land of the East, who was on his way to seek scriptures from Buddha in the Western Heaven. He took on the form of a virgin girl, while another disciple became the boy, both sitting in the temple. When they changed back into their original forms, I was nearly killed by the two of them. I have long heard that Tripitaka T'ang happened to be a good man who had been practicing self-cultivation for ten incarnations. To eat even one piece of his flesh would prolong one's life indefinitely, but I didn't realize that he had such disciples under him. Not only has my reputation been ruined by them, but also the offerings due me were taken away. I would like very much to catch hold of that T'ang monk, but I fear that I may not be able to."

From among the watery kinsfolk stepped a stripe-coated perch-mother who wriggled and bowed toward the fiend, saying, "Great King, if you want to catch the T'ang monk, it isn't difficult at all. But I wonder if you would be willing to reward me with some wine and meat once you catch hold of him." "If you could devise a plan and succeed in capturing the T'ang monk," said the fiend, "I would become your bond-brother. We two shall share the same table to feast on him." After thanking him, the perch-mother said, "I've known for a long time that the Great King possesses the magic to summon winds and rains and to stir up seas and rivers. May I ask whether you are able to cause snow to descend?" "Of course," said the fiend, and she asked again: "How about making ice and causing things to freeze over?" The fiend said, "Certainly." "In that case," said the perch-mother, clapping her hands and laughing, "it's most easy! It's most easy!" "Tell me what it is that's most easy," said the fiend.

The perch-mother said, "When it is about the hour of the third watch this night, the Great King should exercise his power without

any further delay. Call up a cold wind and send down a great snow
fall so that the entire Heaven-Reaching River will be solidly frozen.
Those of us capable of transformation will assume human forms:
carrying luggage, holding umbrellas, and pushing carts, we will
follow the direction of the main road to the West and walk continuously on the ice on top of the river. That T'ang monk must be rather
impatient to get to the scriptures, and when he sees people walking
about like that, he, too, will want to cross the river by walking on the
ice. The Great King can sit quietly at the heart of the river; as soon as
you hear the sound of their footsteps, crack open the ice so that he
and his disciples will fall into the water. All of them will be captured
then." When that fiend heard these words, he was exceedingly
pleased. "Marvelous! Marvelous!" he cried, and he left his water
residence at once to rise into the air. There he began to raise up a cold
wind to bring snow and to cause everything to freeze up, but we shall
mention him no further.

We tell you now instead about the T'ang elder and his disciples, the
four of them, sleeping in the Ch'ên household. Just before dawn, all
of them began to feel the chill even inside their blankets and their
pillows turning cold. Sneezing and shivering, Pa-chieh could no longer
sleep, and he called out, "Elder Brother, it's very cold!" "Idiot, why
don't you grow up!" said Pilgrim. "Those who have left the family
cannot be touched by heat or cold. How could you be afraid of the
cold?" Tripitaka said, "Disciple, it is indeed cold. Look! Even the

Heavy quilts provide no warmth,
And hands in sleeves feel like ice.
Presently frost buds dangle from withered leaves,
And icy bells form on the hoary pines.
The ground cracks for the severe cold;
The pond's level as the water's frozen.
No old fisher is seen on any boat,
Nor a monk at the mountain temple.
Wood is scarce and the woodman's sad;
Charcoals added, and the noble's glad.
The soldier's beard is like iron;
The poet's brush is all hardened.
A leather coat still seems too thin;
A fur robe feels even too light.
On straw mats old priests turn stiff;

By paper screens no traveler can sleep.
Though brocade covers are heavy,
Your whole body shivers and shakes!"

Neither master nor disciples could sleep any longer; they scrambled up, and after putting on their clothes they opened the door to look outside. Ah! It was completely white, for it was snowing. "No wonder you were complaining of the cold," said Pilgrim. "It's snowing heavily!" The four of them stared at it. Marvelous snow! You see

Dark clouds densely formed—
Gray fog thickly gathered—
Dark clouds densely formed,
As a frigid wind howls throughout the sky;
Gray fog densely gathered,
As a great snow fall covers the earth.
Truly it is like
A flower that blooms six times,
Each petal a precious jasper;
Or a thousand-tree forest,
Each plant bedecked with jade.
In a moment: piles of flour!
In an instant: heaps of salt!
The white parrot has lost its essence;
The frosty crane can't boast of its cost.
You have suddenly the waters of Wu and Ch'u
Or something surpassing plum blossoms of the southeast.
Now it resembles defeated jade dragons, some three million
    strong—
Indeed like their torn scales and ripped armor flying through the
    air.
How could there be the shoes of Tung-kuo,[1]
The resting place of Yüan An,[2]
Or the reflected light by which Sun K'ang[3] studies?
Nor could one see Tzǔ-yu's boat,[4]
Wang Kung's robe,[5]
Or the blanket which feeds Su Wu.[6]
All you have are some village huts built with silver bricks,
And the countryside seems kneaded out of jade.
Marvelous snow!
Like willow fleeces they clog up the bridge;

Like pear blossoms they cover the houses.
Willow fleeces clog up the bridge
As a fisher hangs up his coir-coat by the bridge;
Pear blossoms cover the houses
As wild codgers burn tree roots in the houses.
The guest cannot buy wine;
The old servant can't find the plums.
Flitting and fluttering like butterfly wings;
Drifting and soaring like goose down;
Churning and rolling it follows the wind;
In heaps and mounds it hides the roads.
In waves the chilly might pierces the screens;
Soughing the cold air the curtains penetrates.
Auspicious omens of a good year descend from the sky,
Worthy to wish humans in their affairs success.

That snow came down fluttering, like flying silken threads and clipped off pieces of jade. After master and disciples gazed at it for a while, admiring its beauty, they saw the elder Ch'ên approaching as two houseboys swept open a path. Two more brought along hot water for them to wash their faces, after which, others presented hot tea and milk cakes. Then they carried charcoal fires into the parlor and invited master and disciples to sit inside. "Old Benefactor," asked the elder, "may I inquire whether the seasons of your region are divided into spring, summer, autumn, and winter?" With a smile, the elder Ch'ên said, "Though ours is a rather out-of-the-way region, only our people and our customs are different from those of a noble nation. But all the grains and livestock share the benefits of the same Heaven and the same sun. How could the four seasons be lacking?" "If so," said Tripitaka, "how is it that we have such a great snow fall at this time of the year and such a terrible cold?" The elder Ch'ên said, "Though this is only the seventh month, we just passed White Dew[7] yesterday, and that means that we are approaching the eighth month. In this place of ours, we have frost and snow during the eighth month." "That's quite different from our Land of the East," said Tripitaka, "for we never have snow back there until winter actually arrives."

As they conversed, the servants came forward once more to set the tables for them to dine on rice gruel. After the meal, the snow fell even more heavily, and soon it was two feet deep on the ground. Growing more and more anxious, Tripitaka began to weep. "Venerable Father, please do not worry," said the elder Ch'ên. "Please don't let the deep snow bother you. We have stored up in our house a considerable amount of food, and, I dare say, sufficient to feed all of you for quite a long time." Tripitaka said, "You don't understand my sorrow, Old Benefactor. In that past year when I was entrusted with the decree to acquire scriptures, His Majesty personally escorted me outside the capital. With his own hand holding the goblet to toast me, the T'ang emperor asked me: 'When can you return?' Not having any idea of the dangers of mountains and waters, this humble priest replied rather casually, 'After three years, I shall be able to return to our nation with the scriptures.' Since we parted, it has been seven or eight years, and I have yet to see the face of Buddha. I have great fear that I might have exceeded the imperial limit, and I also am troubled by the viciousness of demons and monsters. Today it is my good fortune to live in your great mansion. After the small service rendered you by my foolish disciples last night, I had hopes that I could ask you for a boat to cross the river. Little did I expect that Heaven would send down this great snow fall to block and cover all the roads. Now I wonder when I would attain my goal and be able to return home." "Relax, Venerable Father," said the elder Ch'ên, "for after all, many days of your journey have passed already. It does not matter if you spend a few more days here. When the weather clears and the ice melts, this old moron will see to it that you cross the river, even if I have to exhaust my wealth to do it."

Just then, a houseboy came to invite them to breakfast. After they finished that in the front hall, they hardly had time to converse when lunch was served also. Troubled by the sight of the elaborately prepared meal, Tripitaka said in great earnestness, "If you are kind enough to take us in, you must treat us as ordinary members of the family." "Venerable Father," said elder Ch'ên, "we are deeply indebted to you for saving our children's lives. Even if we were to feast you every day, we could never repay you sufficiently."

Thereafter the snow stopped, and people soon began to come and go once more. When the elder Ch'ên saw how unhappy Tripitaka appeared to be, he asked that the garden be swept out. After a huge brazier with fire was sent for, he invited the whole party to spend some time in a snow cave. "This old fellow doesn't quite use his head!" said Pa-chieh, laughing. "One can admire the garden in the second or the third month during the time of spring. But after such a big snow fall,

and it's so cold now, what's there for us to admire?" Pilgrim said,
"Idiot, you *are* ignorant! The scenery of snow quite naturally has a
mysterious calm, something which not only we can enjoy but which
also can console our master." "Exactly! Exactly!" said the elder
Ch'ên. Following his beckoning, they went to the garden and they saw

A scenery of late autumn,
When prospects of *La*[8] appeared.
Jadelike buds formed on hoary pines;
Silver blooms hung on lifeless willows.
Jade-moss beneath the steps heaped up powder;
Bamboos before the window sprouted jasper roots.
On artificial mountains—
In domestic fish ponds—
On artificial mountains
Pointed peaks were ranged like shoots of jade;
In domestic fish ponds
The clear, running water became ice trays.
By the banks the color of hibiscus faded;
Tender twigs of the *chin*[9] drooped near the ridge.
Begonia plants
Were completely crushed;
Winter-plum trees
Brought forth new branches.
The peony arbor,
The pomegranate arbor,
And the cassia arbor—
Every arbor was piled high with goose down;
The place of enjoyment,
The place of entertainment,
The place of amusement—
Each place was covered with butterfly wings.
Chrysanthemum by two fences: white jade framed in gold;
A few maple trees: lovely red lined with white.
Since countless courtyards were too cold to reach,
You might admire the snow cave chilly as ice.
In there was a brazier of elephant legs and adorned with faces of
    beasts,
In which a red-hot charcoal fire had just been started.

All around were some lacquered armchairs draped with tiger skins
So warm and soft set by the paper windows.
Inside the cave, there were hung on walls several old paintings by
famous hands, the themes of which all had to do with
The seven worthies going through the pass,[10]
The solitary fisher on a cold river,
And the snow-bound scenes of tiered mountain ranges;
Su Wu feeding on his blanket,
Breaking the plum to meet the messenger,
And the frigid art wrought by trees and plants of jade.
You can't begin to describe
The house by the waters where fishes are easily bought,
Or how scarce is wine when snow buries the roads.
Truly this is a place most worthy to linger in.
Think of it, and you needn't visit P'êng-hu.[11]

After they had admired the scenery for a long while, they sat down in the snow cave and chatted with some of the aged neighbors on the matter of acquiring scriptures. When they finished drinking some fragrant tea, the elder Ch'ên asked again: "Would the several Venerable Fathers take some wine?" "This humble cleric does not drink," said Tripitaka, "but my disciples may drink a few cups of vegetarian wine." Delighted, the elder Ch'ên at once gave the order: "Bring fruits and vegetables, and warm the wine. We would like to help our guests ward off the chill." The houseboys and servants brought forth tables and small braziers for heating the wine. The pilgrims and the neighbors each drank a few cups before the utensils were taken away.

Soon it was dusk, and they were taken back to the front hall again for dinner. Just then, someone walking on the street was heard saying, "What chilly weather! Even the Heaven-Reaching River is frozen!" On hearing this, Tripitaka said, "Wu-k'ung, if the river is frozen, what shall we do?" "This sudden cold," said the elder Ch'ên, "must have frozen only the shallow parts of the river near the bank." But the man walking on the street was saying, "All eight hundred miles across the river are so solidly frozen that its surface is smooth like a mirror. Even people are walking on it." When Tripitaka heard that there were people walking on the river, he immediately wanted to go and look. "Please be patient, Venerable Father," said the elder Ch'ên, "for it's getting late now. We shall go tomorrow." They took leave of the

neighbors, and after dinner, they rested in the parlors as they had the
night before.

   When they arose the next morning, Pa-chieh said, "Elder Brother,
last night was even colder. The river, I suppose, must be solidly
frozen." Facing the door, Tripitaka knelt down and bowed toward
Heaven, saying, "All you great Guardians of the Faith, your disciple
has with complete sincerity resolved to journey to the West to see
Buddha. Throughout the bitter experience of traversing mountains
and streams, I have never once complained. Having reached this
place, I thank Heaven for providing assistance by freezing the river.
Your disciples therefore wish to offer you our thanksgiving first. After
we have acquired the scriptures, we shall inform the T'ang emperor
so that he may repay this favor of yours with all due reverence."
After he finished praying, he ordered Wu-ching immediately to saddle
the horse so that they could walk on the ice to cross the river. "Please
be patient," said the elder Ch'ên again. "Wait for a few days until the
snow and ice melt away. This old moron will prepare a boat to take
you across." "I don't think we should settle on staying or leaving,"
said Sha Monk, "for what we hear is not as reliable as what we see.
Let me saddle the horse, but Master should go personally to the river
to have a look." "You are right," said the elder Ch'ên. "Little ones, go
and saddle six horses at once. But don't saddle Father T'ang's horse
yet."

   With six houseboys following, all of them went to the bank of the
river to look. Truly there were
   Snow piles rising up like hills,
   As sunlight broke up the clouds of dawn.
   The southern border froze and all the peaks were barren.
   Ice formed in lakes and rivers to make them flat and smooth.
   The wind was cold and biting;
   The ground was hard and slippery.
   Pond fishes cuddled the dense weeds;
   Wild birds hugged the dead branches.
   Travelers abroad all lost their fingers;
   The riverboatman's teeth madly chattered.
   Snake bellies split;
   Bird feet snapped.
   Truly the icebergs rose a thousand feet tall.
   Cold silver floated in countless ravines;

The whole river seemed one cold piece of jade.
The East might think that they produced silkworms,
But the North in truth had their caves of rats.
A place where Wang Hsiang[12] might have lain down;
A place where Kuang-wu[13] might have crossed over.
In one night e'en the river bottom solidified!
The winding stream became jagged layers;
The deep river turned frozen blocks.
Without a ripple throughout the water's width,
It seemed a road on land, only bright, clean, and smooth.

When Tripitaka and the others came up to the river's edge, they stopped the horses to look, and true enough, there were people walking on to the ice from the main road. "Benefactor," said Tripitaka, "where are those people going on the ice?" The elder Ch'ên said, "On the far side of the river is the Western Kingdom of Women, and these people must be traders. Things worth a hundred pennies on our side can fetch a hundred times more over there, and their things worth a hundred pennies can similarly fetch a handsome price over here. In view of such heavy profits, it is understandable that people want to make this journey without regard for life or death. Usually, five or seven people, and the number may even swell to more than ten, will crowd into a boat to cross the river. When they see that the river is frozen now, they are risking everything to try to cross it on foot." "Profit and fame," said Tripitaka, "are regarded as most important in the affairs of the world; for profit, men would give up their own lives. But the fact that this disciple strives so hard to fulfill the imperial decree may also be taken as his quest for fame. Am I so different really from those people?" He turned around and said, "Wu-k'ung, go quickly back to our Benefactor's home and pack. Saddle up the horse, too. Let's make use of the ice and leave for the West at once." Smiling broadly, Pilgrim obeyed.

"O Master," said Sha Monk, "the proverb says, 'In a thousand days, you only eat a thousand pecks of rice.' You are already indebted to the hospitality of Mr. Ch'ên. Why not stay a few more days and wait until the weather turns warmer, when we can cross with a boat? Otherwise, I fear that all this hurry may cause us to make mistakes." "Wu-ching," said Tripitaka, "how could you be so unthinking? If this were during the second month of the year, one might well expect the weather to warm up day by day and the snow to melt eventually.

But this is after all the eighth month, and it will grow colder and colder from now on. How could you expect the ice to break so readily? If we were to wait, wouldn't our trip be delayed, perhaps even up to half a year?"

Leaping down from the horse, Pa-chieh said, "Stop arguing, all of you, and let old Hog test it to see what's the thickness of the ice." "Idiot," said Pilgrim, "you threw a stone the other night and succeeded in testing the depth of the water. But the ice now is solid and heavy. How could you test it?" "Elder Brother," said Pa-chieh, "you don't realize that I can give the ice a blow with my rake. If it breaks open, it will be too thin for us to walk on, but if it does not, it will be thick enough. There's no reason for us not to want to walk on it." "Yes," said Tripitaka, "what you said is quite reasonable." Hitching up his robe and walking forward in great strides, Idiot went to the edge of the river. He raised the muckrake high with both hands and brought it down with all his might. A loud thud could be heard and nine white marks were left on the ice, while Idiot's hands were momentarily numbed by the impact. "You can walk on it! You can walk on it!" said he, laughing. "Even the bottom is solid!"

When Tripitaka heard this, he was very pleased. He went back hurriedly to the Ch'ên household and all he could say was that they had to leave at once. When those two old men found that all their earnest pleas for him to remain fell only on deaf ears, they had no alternative but to prepare some such dried food as baked biscuits and breads to give to the pilgrims. As the whole family came out to kowtow to them, the old men brought out also a tray of gold and silver. Going to their knees also, they said, "We thank you again, Venerable Fathers, for saving our children. Please take this, just for a meal on your way." Shaking his head and waving his hand, Tripitaka refused to accept it, saying, "This humble monk is a person who has left the family. I have no need of money. Even if I were to keep it, I wouldn't dare use it on our way, for begging is our proper means of livelihood. It is more than enough for us to take the dried goods." The two old men pleaded with him again and again; so Pilgrim stuck his finger into the tray and lifted up a tiny piece, approximately as heavy as four or five drams, which he handed over to the T'ang monk, saying, "Master, keep it as their offering so that these two will not be too disappointed."

They went to the river, but when the horse stepped on to the ice, it began to slip and slide and Tripitaka was almost thrown off its back. "Master, shouted Sha Monk, "we can't go!" "Stop for a moment," said Pa-chieh, "and let's ask Mr. Ch'ên for some straw." "What for?" said Pilgrim. Pa-chieh said, "You wouldn't have any idea about this! The straw will be used to wrap up the hoofs of the horse, so that Master won't fall down." When the elder Ch'ên heard on the shore what Pa-chieh said, he told someone to fetch the straw at once. After the T'ang monk returned to the bank and dismounted, Pa-chieh wrapped all four hoofs of the horse with straw and that enabled it to step on the ice without slipping.

Having taken leave of the Ch'ên clan at the edge of the river, they proceeded for no more than three or four miles when Pa-chieh handed the nine-ringed priestly staff to the T'ang monk, saying, "Master, put this across your saddle." "Idiot," said Pilgrim, "don't be so sly! You're supposed to carry this priestly staff. Why are you asking Master to do it?" "Since you have no experience in walking on ice," said Pa-chieh, "you will not think of this. Even the thickest of ice has holes; step on one of them and you will plunge into the water. Without something like this held crosswise, you will sink rapidly while the ice above closes in like a huge wok cover. You can never crawl out again unless you have something like this to stop your fall." Snickering, Pilgrim said to himself: "This Idiot must have walked on ice for years!" So, all of them followed what Pa-chieh told them to do: the elder held the staff crosswise across his saddle; Pilgrim and Sha Monk each carried his iron rod and his fiend-routing treasure staff across his shoulders. Pa-chieh, who was poling the luggage, tied the rake sideways at his waist. Master and disciples then felt perfectly safe to proceed.

They journeyed until evening; after eating some dried goods, they dared not stop at all. As the stars and the moon lighted up the ice, turning it into brilliant patches of white, they pressed forward. Indeed, the horse never stopped trotting for the entire night; master and disciples never once closed their eyes. By morning, they ate some more of their provisions and again set out toward the West. As they journeyed, a rending sound came from the bottom of the ice, so frightening the white horse that it almost fell. Greatly astonished, Tripitaka said "O Disciples, why was there such a sound?" "This river is so solidly frozen," said Pa-chieh, "that the ice formed from top to bottom must be grating the river bed. That may be the sound we heard." Astonished but pleased by what he was told, Tripitaka urged his horse on and they started out once more.

We now tell you about that fiend, who led various spirits from the water residence and sat waiting for a long time beneath the ice. Finally, when the sound of the horse's hoofs became audible, he at once exercised his magic power and caused the ice to break open. The Great Sage Sun managed to leap at once into the air, but his three companions and the white horse all plunged into the water.

After catching hold of Tripitaka, the fiend led the spirits back to the water residence, where he shouted aloud: "Where are you, perch-sister?" The old perch-mother met him at the door, bowing, and said, "Great King, I'm not worthy of it!" "Worthy Sister, why do you say that?" said the fiend. "For 'Even a team of horses cannot overtake the word that has left my mouth!' I promised you that if your plan could enable me to catch the T'ang monk, I would become your bond-brother. Today your marvelous plan did materialize, and the T'ang monk had been caught. You think I would retract my promise?" He then gave the order: "Little ones, bring out the tables and the sharp knives. Cut up this monk: take out his heart, skin him, and debone him. Meanwhile, start the music. I'm going to share him with my worthy Sister, so that both of us will gain longevity." "Great King," said the perch-mother, "let's not eat him yet, for I fear that his disciples may spoil our party should they come here to search for him. Wait a couple of days, and if no one appears, we can then cut him up. Great King can take your honored seat, while the watery kinsfolk can surround you with singing and dancing. His flesh will be presented to you, and you can take your time to enjoy your feast. Isn't that much better?" The fiend agreed; the T'ang monk was placed in a lidded stone box about six feet long which was then hidden in the rear of the palace, and we shall speak no more of him for the moment.

We tell you now about Pa-chieh and Sha Monk, who managed to recover the luggage in the water. After they had placed it on the white horse, they opened up a path in the water and trod on the waves to rise to the surface. Pilgrim saw them from midair and asked at once: "Where is Master?" "He changed his family name to Sink,"[14] said Pa-chieh, "and his given name is To-the-Bottom. We don't know where to look for him. Let's get to shore before we decide what to do." Pa-chieh, you see, happened to be the incarnation of the Marshal of Heavenly Reeds, who in past years was a commander of eighty thousand marines stationed in the Heavenly River. Sha Monk came from the Flowing-Sand River, and the white horse, too, was the descendant of Dragon King of the Western Ocean. That was why all of them felt so comfortable in the water. Led by the Great Sage in the air, they soon returned to the eastern shore, where they brushed down the horse and stripped themselves of their wet garments. After the Great Sage dropped down from the clouds, they went together to the Ch'ên Village. At once someone went to make this report to the two old men: "Four Fathers went to seek the scriptures, but only three have come back." The two brothers went quickly out the door to receive them, and they found the clothing of the pilgrims still dripping wet. "Venerable Fathers," they said, "we pleaded with you to stay and you refused. You would stop only when you came to this! Now, where is Father Tripitaka?" Pa-chieh said, "He's no longer named Tripitaka, for he has changed it to Sink To-the-Bottom." As tears fell, the two old men said, "How pitiful! How pitiful! We said we would prepare a boat for him to cross the river, but he absolutely refused and that cost him his life." "Old fellow," said Pilgrim, "it's no use worrying for the dead. But I have a hunch that Master is going to live for a long time yet. Old Monkey knows! It has to be that Great King of Miraculous Power, who has planned all this and abducted him. Don't worry now. Wash our clothes for us and dry our rescript. Make sure our white horse is fed, and let us brothers go and find that fellow. We will not only rescue our master, but we will root out also this evil for your entire village, so that you will be able to live peacefully forever." When the two brothers heard these words, they were delighted and asked for food for the pilgrims at once.

After the three brothers had a big meal, they gave the horse and the luggage to the Ch'ên family to look after. Each wielding his own weapon, they went straight to the river to search for their master and seize the fiend. Truly

They erred in stepping on thick ice, and nature was hurt.

Could there be perfection when the great elixir leaked?

We do not know in what way they succeeded in rescuing the T'ang monk, and you must listen to the explanation in the next chapter.

*Forty-nine*

Calamity-stricken, Tripitaka's sunk to a water house;
To bring salvation, Kuan-yin displays a fish basket.

We were telling you about the Great Sage Sun, Pa-chieh, and Sha Monk, who took leave of the elder Ch'ên and went to the edge of the river. "Brothers," said Pilgrim, "the two of you must decide which one will go first into the water." Pa-chieh said, "Elder Brother, neither of us is particularly capable. You are the one who should enter the water first." "To tell you the truth, Worthy Brother," said Pilgrim, "if this were a monster-spirit in a mountain, there would be no need for both of you to exert yourselves. But I can't quite handle doing business in water. If I were to go into the ocean or walk in a river, I would have to make the water-repelling sign with my fingers, or else I would have to change into a fish or a crab before I could go in. Since I had to make the sign, I would not be able to use my iron rod properly to attack the fiend. But both of you are used to water, and that's why I am asking you to go." "Elder Brother," said Sha Monk, "we can go in all right, but we don't know what to expect once we reach the river bottom. I think we should all go in; you can change into some kind of creature, and I can carry you along as I open up a path in the water. Once we find the lair of the fiend, you can then go inside and scout the place. If Master is still there unharmed, we can begin our assault at once with all our might. But if it were not this fiend who used the magic, or if Master had been drowned or eaten already by him, then there would be no need for us to engage in this bitter quest. We might as well go off in another direction as quickly as possible. How about that?" "What you said, Worthy Brother," said Pilgrim, "is most reasonable. Which one of you will carry me?" Secretly pleased, Pa-chieh thought to himself: "I don't know how many times this ape has made a fool of me! So he doesn't know how to handle himself in water. Let old Hog carry him and give him a taste of his tricks!" Laughing amiably, Idiot said, "Elder Brother, I'll carry you." At once perceiving his intentions, Pilgrim nonetheless played along with him, saying, "All right, that's fine. Your arms might be even a bit stronger than Wu-ching's." Thus Pa-chieh carried Pilgrim on his back.

As Sha Monk divided the water to make a path, the three brothers all plunged into the Heaven-Reaching River. After journeying for over a hundred miles towards the bottom, that Idiot was about to play a trick on Pilgrim, who at once pulled off a piece of hair which he changed into a spurious form of himself clinging to the back of Pachieh. His true self was changed into a hog louse securely lodged in one of Pa-chieh's ears. As Pa-chieh walked along, he suddenly and deliberately stumbled so that Pilgrim was sent flying over his head. The spurious form, however, was only a transformed piece of hair; once it left the back of Pa-chieh, it drifted away with the current and soon vanished. "Second Elder Brother," said Sha Monk, "how would you explain this? Why didn't you walk more carefully? It would have been all right if you had fallen in the mud. Now the jolt has sent Big Brother off to who knows where!" Pa-chieh said, "That monkey can't even stand a fall: just once and he's melted already. Brother, don't worry whether he's dead or alive. You and I can go search for Master." "It's no good," said Sha Monk, "for we must have him. Though he may not feel at home in water, he is far more agile than we. If he's not around, I shall not go with you." Unable to contain himself any longer, Pilgrim inside Pa-chieh's ear shouted with a loud voice: "Wu-ching, old Monkey's right here!" On hearing this, Sha Monk laughed and said, "O dear! This Idiot is as good as dead! How dared you try to play a trick on him? Now you can hear him but you can't see him. What are you going to do?" Pa-chieh became so frightened that he went to his knees in the mud and kowtowed, saying, "Elder Brother, it's my fault! Wait till we rescue Master, and I shall apologize to you once more on the shore. Where are you making all this noise from? I'm scared to death! Please reveal your original form. I'll carry you, and I'll never dare offend you again." Pilgrim said, "You are still carrying me, all right! I won't trick you. Let's get going quickly!" Still muttering his apologies, Idiot scrambled up and proceeded with Sha Monk.

They journeyed for another hundred miles or so when they came upon a towered building all at once, on which there was, in large letters, the inscription: "Sea-Turtle House." "This must be the residence of the monster-spirit," said Sha Monk, "but we don't know that for sure. How could we go up to the door to provoke battle?" "Wu-ching," said Pilgrim, "is there any water around the gate?" Sha Monk said, "No." "In that case," said Pilgrim, "the two of you go and hide on both sides of the door. Let Old Monkey go and scout around."

Dear Great Sage! Crawling free of Pa-chieh's ear, he shook his body once and changed again into a shrimp-mother with long legs. With two or three leaps, he bounded right inside the gate. As he looked around, he saw the fiend sitting up there while his watery kinsfolk stood in two rows beneath him. There was also a striped-coated perch-mother sitting by his side. They were all having a discussion on how to eat the T'ang monk. Pilgrim looked left and right with great care, but he could not find his master at all. Just then he saw a large-bellied shrimp-mother come out and stand still in the western corridor. Pilgrim leaped up to her and greeted her, saying, "Mama, the Great King is discussing with the others how to eat the T'ang monk. But where *is* the T'ang monk?" "He was captured yesterday," said the shrimp-mother, "after the Great King brought down the snow and created the ice. He is now imprisoned in a stone box at the rear of the palace. If by tomorrow his disciples do not show up to cause any trouble, we will make music and feast on him."

After he heard this, Pilgrim chatted further with her for a while before moving towards the rear of the palace. He looked, and sure enough there was a stone box, somewhat like a pigsty that people use in a pigpen or a stone coffin. Measuring it, he found it to be approximately six feet in length. He crawled on top of it and soon heard the pitiful sound of Tripitaka's weeping coming from inside. Not uttering a word, Pilgrim cocked his ear to listen. Grinding his teeth in sheer frustration, the master said:

I loathe River Float, a life plagued by woes!
How many water perils bound me at birth!
I left my mother's womb to be tossed by waves;
I plumbed the deep, seeking Buddha in the West.
I met disaster at Black River before;
Now in this ice-break, my life will expire.
I know not if my pupils can come here,
Or if with true scriptures I can go home.

Pilgrim could not refrain from calling out, "Master, don't be annoyed. The *Water-Calamity Book* says, 'Whereas earth is the mother of the Five Phases, water is their very fountain: there is no birth without earth, and no growth without water.' Old Monkey has arrived!" On hearing this, Tripitaka said, "O Disciple! Please save me!" "Try to relax," said Pilgrim. "Wait till we seize the monster-spirit and you will be freed from your ordeal." "Get moving quickly!" said Tripitaka. "One more day and I'll suffocate!" "That won't happen! That won't happen!" said Pilgrim. "I'm off!" Turning around, he leaped right out of the gate and changed back into his original form. "Pa-chieh!" he shouted. Idiot and Sha Monk drew near, saying, "Elder Brother, what did you find out?" "It was this fiend all right," said Pilgrim, "who captured Master. He is not yet hurt, but he is imprisoned in a stone box. The two of you should provoke battle at once after old Monkey has gone back up to the surface of the water. If you two can capture him, do so; but if you can't, feign defeat and entice him out to the surface. I'll attack him then." "Have no worry, Elder Brother," said Sha Monk. "You leave first and let us size up the situation." Making the water-repelling sign with his fingers, Pilgrim darted out of the river and stood on the bank of the river to wait for them.

Look how violent that Pa-chieh could become! Dashing up to the gate, he shouted in a severe voice: "Brazen fiend! Send my master out!" The little monsters inside the gate were so alarmed that they went hurriedly to report: "Great King, someone at the gate is demanding his master." "That must be one of those brazen monks," said the monster. "Bring out my armor!" The little fiends took it out quickly. After he was properly suited up, the monster picked up his weapon and walked out the gate. Facing him on the left and on the right were Pa-chieh and Sha Monk, who stared intently at him. Dear monster! Look at him!

His head wore a gleaming helmet of gold.
A gold cuirass he had that flashed red light.
Pearl- and jade-studded, a belt wrapped his waist.
His feet were shod in strange boots, tobacco brown.
The bridge of his nose rose high like a ridge.
His forehead was, like a dragon's, broad and wide.
His blazing eyes were both round and fierce.
His teeth, like steel swords, were even and sharp.
His tousled short hair did shoot up like flames.
His long beard was groomed like a golden awl.
His mouth held a pond weed, tender and green.
His hands gripped a nine-grooved mallet of red bronze.
As the gates swung wide open with a creak,

He bellowed like the thunder of triple spring.
Features like his are rare in the human world.
Hence he's called Great King of Miraculous Power.

After the fiend walked out of the gates, about a hundred little imps, all wielding lances and swords, followed him out and stood in two columns behind him. "From which monastery have you come," he asked Pa-chieh, "and why are you causing a disturbance here?" "You brazen creature!" shouted Pa-chieh. "You were almost beaten to death! You argued with me the other night, and yet you dare play ignorant and ask me again today? I am a disciple of a holy monk from the Great T'ang in the Land of the East, and a pilgrim journeying to see Buddha in the Western Heaven for scriptures. Befooling the people with your empty magic, you are even audacious enough to call yourself Great King of Miraculous Power and indulge in devouring virgin boys and girls from the Ch'ên village. I am One Load of Gold from the family of Ch'ên Ch'ing. Can't you recognize me?" "Monk," said the monster, "you are quite unreasonable! For taking on the form of One Load of Gold, you should be charged with the crime of false identity. Not only did I not eat you, but the back of my hand was also wounded by you. I have yielded to you already. How dare you come seeking trouble right up to my door?" "If you had yielded," said Pa-chieh, "then why did you raise up the cold wind and send down the great snow fall? Why did you make the ice to trap my master? Send him out quickly and all will be well. If but half a 'No' escapes from your teeth, I'll never spare you! Just look at this rake in my hands!" On hearing this, the fiend smiled sarcastically and said, "Monk, you are wagging your tongue and bragging! It was I, indeed, who brought the snow and froze the river to abduct your master. Now you are clamoring at my door and demanding his return, but this time, I fear, is not quite the same as the time before. Previously, I brought no weapon with me as I thought I was attending a feast, and you took advantage of me. Don't run away now, because I'm going to fight with you for three rounds. If you can withstand me, I will return your master; if you cannot, I'll eat you also."

"My darling child!" said Pa-chieh. "That's the way to talk! Take care, watch my rake!" "So you became a monk midway in your life," said the fiend. Pa-chieh said, "My dear boy, you do have a little miraculous power! How did you know that I became a monk midway in my life?" "Since you are using a rake," said the fiend, "you must have been hired as a gardener somewhere, and now you have stolen even your master's rake!" "Son," said Pa-chieh, "this rake of mine is no garden tool. Look!

> The huge teeth are forged like dragon claws;
> Its handle, white-gold wrapped, is serpent shaped.
> When it's used in battle, cold wind swoops down;
> When it's put to combat, bright flames spring up.
> Able to smite fiends for the holy monk,
> It catches monsters on the westward way.
> When I move it, mist hides the sun and moon.
> When I use it, bright, colored lights will shine.
> Mount T'ai's brought down, and a thousand tigers cringe.
> The sea's upturned, ten thousand dragons fear.
> Though you may have miraculous power,
> One blow will give you nine big, gaping holes!"

That fiend, of course, would not take such words seriously! He raised his bronze mallet and brought it down on Pa-chieh's head. Using his muckrake to parry the blow, Pa-chieh said, "You brazen creature! So, you too, became a spirit midway in your life!" "How could you tell that I became a spirit midway in my life?" said the fiend. "If you know how to use a bronze mallet," said Pa-chieh, "you must have been a laborer hired by some silversmith to tend the fires. You took advantage of him and stole his mallet!" The fiend said, "This is no mallet for forging silver. Look!

> Nine segments formed like the petals of a flower;
> A stem, though hollow, is made of evergreen.
> It's not anything of this mortal world,
> It has its birth and name in the house of gods.
> Green seeds and cases aged in the jasper pool;
> Pure scent and nature born of a jade-green pond.
> Since I toiled to temper and refine it,
> It's charged with magic and it's hard as steel.
> Swords, halberds, and spears—all can't rival it.
> Axes and lances—none can withstand it.
> Though your rake may be like a sharp-edged sword,
> My mallet will break it as it breaks a nail!"

When Sha Monk saw how the two of them engaged in such exchanges, he could no longer restrain himself from approaching them and shouting, "Fiend! Stop this boasting! The ancients said, 'What's spoken

proves nothing; only deeds are visible!' Don't run away. Have a taste
of my staff!" Using the mallet to parry the blow, the fiend said, "So,
you also are someone who became a monk midway in your life!"
"How did you know?" said Sha Monk. "The way you look," said the
fiend, "you resemble someone who used to work in a pastry shop."
Sha Monk said, "How could you tell that I used to work in a pastry
shop?" "If you didn't work there," said the fiend, "how could you
learn to use a rolling pin, like the one they made noodles with?" "You
cursed thing!" scolded Sha Monk. "Of course, you haven't seen anything like this before!

This kind of weapon is rare in the world;
That's why you don't know the treasure staff's name.
It came from the moon—the shadowless spot—
Carved from a piece of divine *śāla* wood.
Outside it's decked with jewels luminous;
Within a hub of gold's most glorious.
In bygone days it attended royal feasts;
Now it follows Right and guards the T'ang monk.
Few may know it on the way to the West;
Great fame it has in the Region Above.
It's called the fiend-routing treasure staff:
One blow and it will surely crack your skull!"

In no mood to talk further, the fiend charged him; the three of them
turned ferocious all at once and began a fierce battle at the bottom of
the river.

Bronze mallet, treasure staff, and muckrake:
Wu-nêng and Wu-ching both engaged the fiend.
One was the Heavenly Reeds descending to earth;
One was a divine warrior coming from the sky.
Both attacked the water fiend, displaying their power.
This one withstood alone the god-monks—a laudable show!
Proper affinity can perfect the great Tao:
Mutual growth or conquest holds Ganges' sand.
Earth conquers water,
And the bottom's seen when water dries up;
Water begets wood
Which, in ascendancy, will bloom.
Zen and Tao, cultivated, lead to the same essence;
Elixir, refined and forged, does tame the three faiths.

Earth is the mother
Causing golden shoots to sprout;
When gold grows in divine water the baby's born.
Water's the source
To moisten wood,
And wood, flourishing, brings forth strong, bright fire.
The Five Phases, crowded, will all differ:
That's why they strive, each changing his colors.
Look! Each section of that bronze mallet was fine and bright;
The treasure staff seemed hung with a thousand strands of silk.
The rake, made according to yin-yang and the stars,[1]
Dealt sundry blows without style or number.
They risked their lives for the monk's ordeal;
They courted death because of Śākyamuni.
The bronze mallet was kept busy all the time,
Blocking the staff on the left and the rake on the right.

The three of them fought for some two hours underneath the water and no decision could be reached. Supposing that they could not prevail against him, Pa-chieh winked at Sha Monk, and the two of them at once feigned defeat. They turned and fled, their weapons trailing behind them. "Little ones," ordered the fiend, "stay here. Let me catch up with these fellows and bring them back for you to eat." Look at him! Like the wind blowing dead leaves and the rain beating down the withered flowers, he pursued them right up to the surface of the water.

On the eastern shore, the Great Sage Sun was staring at the water with unblinking eyes. Suddenly huge waves arose in the river and there were shouts and roars. Pa-chieh was the first to leap ashore, crying "He's coming! He's coming!" Sha Monk, too, rushed up to the bank, crying, "He's coming! He's coming!" He was pursued by the fiend, who yelled: "Where are you running to?" No sooner did he clear the water, however, than he was met by Pilgrim, shouting, "Watch the rod!" Quickly swerving to dodge the blow, the fiend met him with up raised mallet. One of them churned up the waves near the edge of the river, while the other showed forth his power on the bank. Before they reached even three rounds after they closed in, the fiend had already weakened. With a splash he plunged back into the river and disappeared; the wind and the waves thus subsided.

Pilgrim went back to high ground and said, "Brothers, you've worked very hard!" "Elder Brother," said Sha Monk, "this monster-spirit might not do so well on land, but he was quite formidable beneath the water. Second Elder Brother and I attacked him left and right and both of us could only manage to fight him to a draw. What shall we do to rescue Master?" "Let's not dillydally," said Pilgrim, "for I fear that he may harm Master." "Elder Brother," said Pa-chieh, "we'll go and try to entice him to come out again. You be quiet and wait for him in midair. Once his head emerges, you give him one of those garlic-pounding blows squarely on the top of his skull. Even if you don't kill him, you'll knock him dazed. Old Hog can then finish him off with one blow of the rake." "Exactly! Exactly!" said Pilgrim. "That's what we call mutual cooperation. Only that can accomplish anything." The two of them dove into the water again, and we shall leave them for the moment.

We tell you now about that fiend, who fled in defeat and returned to his residence. As the various fiends met him, the perch-mother went up to him and said, "Great King, where did you chase those two monks to?" The fiend said, "I didn't realize that those monks have another helper, who, when they leaped ashore, tried to hit me with an iron rod. I dodged the blow and fought with him. God knows how heavy that rod of his is! My bronze mallet could not stand up to it at all. Before we finished three rounds, I had to flee in defeat." "Great King," said the perch-mother, "can you remember how that helper looked?" "He has a hairy face and a thunder-god beak," said the fiend, "forked ears and broken nose. A monk with fiery eyes and diamond pupils." When the perch-mother heard this, she shuddered and said, "O Great King! It was smart of you to flee, and you escaped with your life! Three more rounds and you won't live at all! I know who that monk is." "Who is he? said the fiend." "Some years back I was living in the Great Eastern Ocean," said the perch-mother, "and I heard the old Dragon King talking about him and his reputation. This monk is the Great Sage, Equal to Heaven, the Handsome Monkey King who is a golden immortal of the great monad and of the primal chaos in the Region Above. Five hundred years ago, he caused great havoc in the Celestial Palace, but now he has embraced Buddhism to accompany the T'ang monk to go to the Western Heaven for scriptures. He has changed his name to Pilgrim Sun Wu-k'ung. He has tremendous magic powers and knows many ways of transformation.

Great King, how could you tangle with him! From now on, you must not fight with him at all."

Hardly had she finished speaking when one of the little imps dashed in to report: "Great King, those two monks are here again to provoke battle." The monster-spirit said, "My worthy sister's opinion is very sound! I'm not going to face them again. See what they can do!" He gave hurriedly this order: "Little ones, shut the gates. As the proverb says,

You may call outside the door;
Your cries I'll wholly ignore!

They may even stay here for a couple of days, but when they get tired of it, they'll leave. Then we can freely and leisurely enjoy the T'ang monk." All those little fiends started to haul rocks and mud to seal up the entrance to the residence. When Pa-chieh and Sha Monk shouted repeatedly without receiving any reply, Idiot in perturbation began to batter the gates with his rake. The gates, of course, were tightly shut, but a few blows of the rake broke them down. Inside the gates, however, was a solid wall of mud and rocks piled sky-high. When Sha Monk saw it, he said, "Second Elder Brother, this fiend is terribly afraid, and that's why he shuts himself up and refuses to come out. You and I should go back up to shore and discuss the matter with Big Brother." Pa-chieh agreed and they returned to the eastern shore.

Halfway between cloud and fog, Pilgrim stood waiting and holding his iron rod. When he saw the two of them emerge without the fiend, he lowered his cloud and met them on the bank. "Brothers," he asked, "how is it that that thing has not come up?" Sha Monk said, "The fiend has shut his doors tightly and refused to come out to meet us. When Second Elder Brother broke the doors, we ran into a solid wall of mud and rocks inside. That's why we could not even do battle with him. We decided to return to talk to you and see how we could make plans to rescue Master." "If that's how he behaves," said Pilgrim, "it's quite hard to think of anything to overcome him. You two had better patrol the banks to make certain that he doesn't escape to another place. Let me make a trip." "Elder Brother," said Pa-chieh, "where are you going?" Pilgrim said, "I'm going to the Potalaka Mountain to make inquiry of the Bodhisattva. I want to find out the origin of this monster, his name, and how I may search out his ancestral home. After I have seized his kinsfolk and all his relations, I can return here to rescue Master." With a laugh, Pa-chieh said, "Elder Brother, the way you do things will waste a lot of time and energy!" "I won't waste any time or energy!" said Pilgrim. "I go, and I'll be back at once!"

Dear Great Sage! Mounting the auspicious luminosity quickly, he left the river and headed straight for the South Sea. In less than half an hour, the Potalaka Mountain came into sight as he lowered his cloud and went up to the summit. The Twenty-four devas, the Great Mountain-Guardian, the disciple Mokṣa, Child Sudhana, and the Pearl-Bearing Dragon Girl all came forward to greet him. "Why did the Great Sage come here?" they asked, and Pilgrim said, "I must see the Bodhisattva." "The Bodhisattva left the cave this morning," said the deities, "and forbade anyone to follow her. She went by herself into the bamboo grove, though she left word that you would arrive today and that we should be here to receive you. She said she would not be able to see you immediately and she asked you to be seated before the cliff for a while and wait for her to come out."

Pilgrim obeyed and before he had even taken a seat, the Child Sudhana approached him bowing and said, "Great Sage Sun, I must thank you for your past kindness. The Bodhisattva was gracious enough to take me in and I have been her constant companion, waiting upon her beneath her lotus platform. She has, in fact, shown me great favors." Recognizing that he was formerly the Red Boy, Pilgrim said with a laugh, "In the past you were gripped by demonic delusions. Now that you have attained the right fruit, you must realize that old Monkey is a good person!"

After having waited for a long time, Pilgrim grew very anxious, and he said, "Please make the announcement for me, all of you. If there's further delay, I do fear for my master's life." "We dare not," said the deities, "for the Bodhisattva gave specific instruction that you should wait for her to come out." As he had always been impulsive, Pilgrim, of course, could stand it no longer and dashed all at once into the bamboo grove. Aha!

This Handsome Monkey King
Was by nature most impulsive.
The devas could not detain him
When he wished to go inside.
Deep into the grove he strode,
His round eyes glanced furtively.
There the salvific Honored-One

Sat, cross-legged, on bamboo leaves.
Carefree and without makeup
She looked so gentle and mild.
Her tresses, undone, flowed down;
She had no headgear with fringes.
Her blue robe she did not wear,
But only a small waistcoat.
A silk skirt wrapped round her waist.
Her two feet were both naked.
Her cloak's silk sash was not tied;
Her two arms were wholly bare.
Her jadelike hand held a knife
With which she pared the bamboos.

When Pilgrim saw her, he could not refrain from calling aloud: "Bodhisattva, your disciple, Sun Wu-k'ung, pays you sincere homage." "Wait outside," commanded the Bodhisattva. Pilgrim went to his knees to kowtow, saying, "Bodhisattva, my master is facing a terrible ordeal. I came especially to ask you concerning the origin of the fiend at Heaven-Reaching River." "Go out of the grove," said the Bodhisattva, "and wait till I come out."

Not daring to force her, Pilgrim had no choice but to walk out of the bamboo grove and said to the various devas, "The Bodhisattva seems to be all wrapped up today in her domestic affairs. Why is she not sitting at her lotus platform? Why is she not made up? Why does she look so gloomy, making bamboo slips in the grove?" "We don't know," said the deities. "When she left the cave this morning, she went at once into the grove before she was even properly dressed. She told us also to wait for the Great Sage, and she must be doing something for your affairs." Pilgrim could do nothing but wait.

After a while, the Bodhisattva emerged from the grove, her hand holding a purple-bamboo basket. "Wu-k'ung," she said, "I'll go with you to rescue the T'ang monk." Kneeling down hurriedly, Pilgrim said, "Your disciple dares not press you. Let the Bodhisattva dress and ascend her seat first." "No need to dress," said the Bodhisattva, "I can go with you just like this." Abandoning the devas, the Bodhisattva mounted the auspicious clouds immediately and rose into the air. Great Sage Sun had to follow her!

In a moment, they arrived at the Heaven-Reaching River. On seeing them, Pa-chieh said to Sha Monk, "Elder Brother is so impulsive!

I wonder what sort of wild clamor he made at South Sea that forced an undressed and unadorned Bodhisattva to come here!" Hardly had he finished speaking when the Bodhisattva landed on the bank. Bowing, the two disciples said, "Bodhisattva, we have intruded upon you. Please forgive us!" Untying her sash from her vest, the Bodhisattva fastened it to the basket and rose halfway into the air on the clouds. She held the sash and lowered the basket into the river, pulling it towards the upper reach. Then she recited a spell, saying, "The dead depart; the living remain! The dead depart, the living remain!" She repeated this seven times and then lifted up the basket. Inside was a shiny goldfish, still blinking its eyes and twisting. "Wu-k'ung," cried the Bodhisattva, "go into the water quickly and rescue your master." "But we have not yet captured the fiend," said Pilgrim. "How could we rescue Master?" "Isn't the fiend in the basket?" said the Bodhisattva. Bowing, Pa-chieh and Sha Monk said, "How could the little fish get to be so powerful?" "He is a goldfish reared in my lotus pond," said the Bodhisattva. "Every day, he would float with the current to the surface to listen to my lectures, and his powers were acquired from his self-cultivation. That nine-sectioned bronze mallet is a stalk supporting an unopened lotus bud, which the process of his magic cultivation has made into a weapon. I don't know which day it was when high tide carried him to this place. When I watched my flowers leaning on the railing this morning, this fellow did not come out to greet me. I made calculations then by consulting the grooves on my fingers and learned that he had become a spirit here, seeking to harm your master. That was why I did not even bother to put on my clothes or jewels, for I was exercising my divine powers to fashion this basket to catch him."

"Bodhisattva," said Pilgrim, "please remain here for a moment. Let me go and call together the believers in the Ch'ên village so that they may gaze upon your golden visage. This will be your great favor towards them, and, moreover, the account of how you have captured the fiend will help these mortal humans to become your devout worshippers." "All right," said the Bodhisattva. "Go and call them together quickly." Pa-chieh and Sha Monk sprinted back to the village, screaming, "Come, all of you, to see the living Bodhisattva Kuan-yin!" The inhabitants of the entire village, young and old, all rushed to the edge of the river. Without regard for the mud and water, they all knelt down and kowtowed. Someone skilled in painting among them at once made a portrait of the goddess, and that was how the picture of the Kuan-yin with a fish basket came about. Thereafter, the Bodhisattva returned to South Sea.

Opening a path in the water, Pa-chieh and Sha Monk went straight to the Sea-Turtle House to search for their master. The watery fiends and fish spirits inside were all dead. They went to the rear of the palace and opened the stone box. Then they carried the T'ang monk to leave the waves and to be reunited with the others on the shore. Ch'ên Ch'ing and his brother in gratitude kowtowed to them, saying, "Venerable Father, you should have listened to our pleadings and you would not have had to undergo such suffering." "No need to say that anymore," said Pilgrim. "You people here will have no need to make any more sacrifices next year, for the Great King has been done away with. He will take no more lives. Mr. Ch'ên, now we must count on you to find a boat to take us across the river." "We have one! We have one!" said Ch'ên Ch'ing. He at once gave the order to build a boat; when the villagers heard this, everyone responded with enthusiasm. One of them said that he would purchase the mast and another volunteered to get the oars. Some of them wanted to bring the ropes, while still others promised to hire the sailors.

As they were making such clamor by the bank of the river, they suddenly heard this cry coming from the middle of the water: "Great Sage Sun, there is no need for a boat which will only be a waste of money and materials. I'll take you four across the river." When the people heard this, they were so frightened that the timid ones fled back to the village, while the more courageous among them, trembling all over, stole glances at where the voice was coming from. Instantly, out crawled a strange creature from the depths. "How did he look?" you ask. He is

A square-headed divine not of this world;
His name: a water god most subtle and shrewd.
His tail can life prolong a thousand years;
He hides himself in a hundred rivers deep.
Vaulting on waves and currents he comes to shore;
Facing the sun and wind he lies on the beach.
Truly enlightened he nourishes his breath,
An old turtle, scabby headed and white shelled.

"Great Sage," cried the old sea-turtle again, "don't build the boat. I'll take all of you, master and disciples, across the river." Raising high his iron rod, Pilgrim said, "Cursed creature! If you dare approach me, I'll kill you with one blow of my rod!" "I am grateful to the kindness of the Great Sage," said the old turtle, "and that's why I want to help all of you with the best intention. Why do you want to hit me instead?" "What kindness have I shown you?" said Pilgrim. The old turtle said, "Great Sage, you don't realize that the Sea-Turtle House down below happens to be my residence, a place my ancestors handed down to me from generation to generation. Since I had awakened to my source and origin, I succeeded in nourishing my spiritual breath and I have been practicing self-cultivation in this place. The house was rebuilt by me and named the Sea-Turtle House. Nine years ago, that fiend arrived during a huge tidal wave, and at once he let loose his violence and fought with me. He slew many of my children and robbed me of many of my kinsfolk. I was no match for him, and my house was taken away from me by force. Now I am truly indebted to the Great Sage, who in his attempt to rescue his master, has succeeded in bringing the Bodhisattva Kuan-yin here to disperse all the fiendish miasma. With the monster seized, the house belongs to me once again. Now I can be reunited with my kin, young and old; I can occupy my old home again without having to rest on earth or recline on mud. This favor of yours is indeed great as a mountain and deep as the sea. But it is not just I myself who am indebted to you. The entire village here has been exempted from ever having to make the annual sacrifice, and countless children's lives are spared. This is indeed a case of the double gain with a single move. Dare I not show my gratitude and try to repay you?"

Secretly pleased by what he heard, Pilgrim put away his iron rod and said, "Are you really sincere about this?" The old turtle said, "I'm a recipient of the Great Sage's profound kindness. How dare I play false?" "Swear to Heaven that you are telling the truth," said Pilgrim. Opening wide his huge red mouth towards the sky, the old turtle said, "If I do not truly intend to send the T'ang monk across the Heaven-Reaching River, may my body turn into blood!" "You come here then," said Pilgrim, chuckling. Swimming to the edge of the river, the old turtle then crawled up the bank. When the people gathered about him to take a look, they found a huge white globe of a shell, about forty feet in its circumference. "Master," said Pilgrim, "we can get on him and cross over." Tripitaka said, "Disciple, even that thick ice before gave us difficulty. I wonder if this turtle's carapace is safe at all." "Please do not worry, Master," said the old turtle, "I'm much safer than that thick ice! If I make even one slip, I'll not achieve my merit." "O Master!" said Pilgrim. "It is not likely for a creature who has acquired human speech to lie. Brothers, bring us the horse! Quick!"

As they went to the edge of the river, the whole Ch'ên village, young and old, all came to bow to them. After Pilgrim led the horse up on to the back of the old turtle, he asked the T'ang monk to stand to the left of the horse's neck, Sha Monk to the right, and Pa-chieh at the back. Pilgrim himself stood in front of the horse. Fearing that the turtle might cause trouble nevertheless, he untied the sash of his tiger-skin skirt and fastened it to the nose of the turtle, pulling it up like a rein. He placed one foot on the turtle's back and the other foot on its head; one hand held the iron rod and while the other held the rein. "Old Turtle," said he, "go slowly. One wrong move and I'll give your head a blow!" "I dare not! I dare not!" said the old turtle. Stretching forth his four legs, the turtle trod on the surface of the water as smoothly as if he were walking on level ground. The people on shore all burned incense and kowtowed, everyone chanting, "Namo Amitābha!" It was truly as if real arhats were descending to earth and living Bodhisattvas revealing themselves. The people worshipped until they could no longer see the pilgrims before they dispersed, and we shall speak no more of them.

We tell you instead about the master riding on the white turtle; in less than a day, they crossed the Heaven-Reaching River of eight hundred miles. With dry hands and feet, they went ashore, As Tripitaka landed, he pressed his palms together to give thanks, saying, "I have troubled you, old Turtle, but there is nothing I can give you. Let me acquire the scriptures first, and when I come back, I'll thank you then with a gift." The old turtle said, "There's no need for any gift from you, old Master. But I have heard that the Buddhist Patriarch in the Western Heaven has not only transcended the process of birth and death, but he has also the knowledge of past and future. I have practiced self-cultivation here for a full thirteen hundred years. Though I have lengthened my age and lightened my body, and I have also acquired the knowledge of human speech, I find it difficult to shed my original shell. When you get to the Western Heaven, I beg the old Master to inquire of the Buddhist Patriarch and see when I may cast off my original shell to acquire a human body." Tripitaka said, "I promise to ask. I promise to ask." Then the old turtle turned around and plunged back into the water. Pilgrim helped T'ang monk to mount the horse, Pa-chieh poled the luggage, and Sha Monk took up the rear. Master and disciples found the main road and started out again toward the West. Thus it was that

The holy monk sought Buddha by decree

Through a vast distance and many ordeals.

His mind was steadfast, undaunted by death;

He crossed Heaven River on a turtle's back.

We don't know exactly how far they still have to go, or whether good or evil befalls them, and you must listen to the explanation in the next chapter.

*Fifty*

Feelings grow chaotic and nature falls prey to desires;
Spirit's confused and the affected mind meets demons.

The poem says:
    Sweep frequently the grounds of the mind;
    Wipe out the dust of affections.
    Don't let the pit ensnare the Buddha-body true.
    When the essential self is pure,
    You may speak of the primal source.
    Nature's candle you must trim
    And breathe freely at Ts'ao-ch'i.[1]
    Keep the horse and the ape from sounding harsh.
    Work ceaselessly night and day,
    Then your technique's revealed.
The tune of this tz'ŭ poem is called the *Nan-k'o-tzŭ*, and it is meant to
describe the T'ang monk and how he escaped from his ordeal of ice in
the Heaven-Reaching River and how he ascended the other shore by
standing on the white turtle. Master and the disciples, the four of them,
followed the main road and set out again toward the West. It was the
time of midwinter and they saw
    The faint outlines of woodlands in the mists,
    The clear image of bare mountains in the stream.
As master and disciples walked along, they again came upon a huge
mountain blocking their way. The road turned exceedingly narrow
and the cliffs were tall; moreover, there were many rocks and the
ridges were so steep that it would be difficult for humans or horses to
proceed. Reining in his horse, Tripitaka called out: "Disciples."
Pilgrim led Chu Pa-chieh and Sha Monk forward, saying, "Master,
what do you have to say?" "Look how tall the mountain is ahead of
us," said Tripitaka. "I fear that tigers and wolves might run rampant
up there, or strange beasts might come out to attack us. Be careful!"
"Please do not worry, Master," said Pilgrim. "We three brothers are
united in a single effort to seek the Right and the Real. We will exer-

cise our power to disperse monsters and subdue fiends. You needn't be afraid of any tigers or wolves!" On hearing his words, Tripitaka felt more assured and urged his horse forward to ascend the cliff. As they did so, they glanced around and saw that it was quite a mountain indeed.

Rugged and soaring—
Pointed and towering—
Rugged and soaring it rises to the sky;
Pointed and towering it blocks the blue heavens.
Strange rocks piled high like tigers sitting;
Hoary pines aslant like dragons flying.
Atop the peak a bird sings a pretty song;
Before the cliff the plums waft a strong, sweet scent.
The brook swells and surges, its water cold;
The clouds assail the summit, dense and dark.
You also feel the drifting snow,
The biting wind,
And the roar of the hungry mountain tiger.
Jackdaws pick through the trees but they find no nest;
Wild deer search in vain for a place to rest.
Pity the travelers, they can hardly walk.
Crestfallen and downcast, they cover their heads!

Master and disciples, the four of them, braved the snow and cold to scale, shivering, the rugged peak. After they passed it, they saw in the distance a towered building in the fold of the mountain and some quaint houses nearby. Delighted, the T'ang monk said on his horse, "O Disciples, I feel so cold and hungry today! It's a good thing that there are in the fold of the mountain that building and the houses. It has to be either a village, a temple, or a monastery. Let's go and beg for some food. We can move on after we have a meal." When Pilgrim heard this, he opened wide his eyes to look and saw that the place was shrouded with baleful clouds and diabolical air. "Master," he turned to speak to the T'ang monk, "that's not a good place." "There are buildings and houses," said Tripitaka. "Why isn't it a good place?" "O Master," said Pilgrim, smiling, "how could you know? There are plenty of monsters and demons on the way to the West, and they are most capable of devising some form of houses or dwellings. It doesn't matter whether it is a towered building or a pavilion, or some such edifice; any one of these can be merely a transformation to deceive people. You have heard of the saying that 'a dragon can beget nine kinds of offspring.' One of them is the giant clam;[2] the breath this creature emits is luminous and takes on the appearance of buildings and houses. When a big river is caught in inclement weather, that's when the giant clam produces such a mirage. If some birds or crows happen to fly by and decide to rest their wings on these specious buildings, the clam will swallow them with one gulp. It's a vicious trap. When I see how baleful the aura is over there, I must tell you not to approach it."

"So, we can't go over there," said Tripitaka, "but I'm really hungry!" "If you are, Master, please dismount," said Pilgrim. "Sit here on level ground and let me go somewhere to beg some vegetarian food for you to eat." Tripitaka consented and dismounted. After Pa-chieh took hold of the reins, Sha Monk put down the luggage and untied the wrap to take out the alms bowl to hand over to Pilgrim. Taking it in his hand, Pilgrim gave this instruction to Sha Monk: "Worthy Brother, don't go forward. Just stand guard over Master sitting here. Wait until I come back with the food and we can then set out again to the West." Sha Monk obeyed, and Pilgrim said once more to Tripitaka, "Master, that place in front of us betokens more evil than good. Don't ever leave here and go elsewhere. Old Monkey is off to beg for food." "Don't talk anymore," said the T'ang monk. "Just go quickly and come back. I'll wait for you here." Pilgrim turned and was about to leave, but he walked back again to say, "Master, I realize you can't sit still for very long. Let me provide you with some means of safety." He took out his golden-hooped rod and drew on the level ground a large circle. The T'ang monk was asked to sit in its middle, while Pa-chieh and Sha Monk stood by either side of him. The horse and the luggage, too, were placed near them. Then Pilgrim pressed his palms together to bow to the T'ang monk, saying, "The circle drawn by old Monkey here is as strong as an iron wall. No matter what they are—tigers, wolves, ogres, or demons—they will not dare come near you. But you must not step out of the circle. Remain seated inside and no harm will come to you. But if you leave the circle, you will in all likelihood meet with danger. Please take heed of my words! Please take heed of my words!" Tripitaka agreed and all three of them sat down solemnly in the circle.

Mounting the clouds, Pilgrim went south to search for a place to beg for food. Suddenly he saw some tall, aged trees, near which was a village. He lowered his cloud and took a careful look. He saw

Snow abusing weak willows

And ice frozen in the square pond;

Sparse bamboos waving their blue;

Dense pine trees holding their green;

A few thatched huts half decked with silver;

A small, slanted bridge powder-dusted;

Half-bloomed narcissus by the fence;

Long icicles dangling beneath the eaves.

The piercing cold wind wafted a rare scent,

But snow hid the place where plum flowers bloomed.

As Pilgrim admired the scenery of the village, he heard one of the wooden gates open with a creak and out walked an old man, who wore a lamb's-wool hat, a long robe full of holes, and a pair of grass sandals. Supporting himself with a staff, he looked up to the sky and said, "Ah, the northwest wind is rising. It'll be fair tomorrow." Hardly had he finished speaking when a Pekingese ran out from behind him and barked furiously at Pilgrim. Only then did the old man turn around; Pilgrim stood before him holding the alms bowl and bowed, saying, "Old Benefactor, this priest happens to be someone sent by imperial decree of the Great T'ang in the Land of the East to the Western Heaven to seek scriptures from Buddha. We are passing through your region and my master is hungry. I have come to your honorable residence to beg you for some vegetarian food." When the old man heard this, he shook his head and struck the ground several times with his staff, saying, "Elder, you shouldn't beg for food just yet, for you have taken the wrong road." "I have not," said Pilgrim. The old man said, "The main road to the Western Heaven is due north of here, over a thousand miles away. You should go and find that road at once." Pilgrim laughed and said, "Yes, it *is* due north of here, and my master right now is sitting beside that road and waiting for me to beg for food." "This monk is babbling!" said the old man. "If your master is indeed waiting at the main road for you to beg for food, a distance of a thousand miles will require six or seven days of traveling one way, even if you happen to be an exceptionally adroit traveler. When you go back to him, it will take another week or so. By then, he would be long starved to death, wouldn't he?"

Pilgrim laughed again and said, "To tell you the truth, Old Benefactor, I left my master not long ago, and it took me no more than the time of drinking a cup of tea to get to this place. Once I succeed in begging some food, I shall rush back to serve it to him for lunch." On hearing this, the old man became terribly frightened, thinking to himself: "This priest is a ghost! A ghost!" He turned around and began to dash inside. Pilgrim made a grab at him and said, "Benefactor, where are you going? If you have some food, donate it to us." "It's not convenient! It's not convenient!" said the old man. "Go to some other family." "Benefactor," said Pilgrim, "you aren't very considerate! As you said, this place is over a thousand miles away from the main road. If I go to another family, it may take another thousand miles. Wouldn't my master be really starved to death then?"

"To tell you the truth," said the old man, "there are altogether six or seven people in my family, and we have just washed and placed three pints of rice in the cauldron. It's not even fully cooked yet. Please go somewhere else to look for your food." Pilgrim said, "As the ancients said, 'Walking to three other houses is not like sitting in one.' This humble priest will sit here and wait." When the old man saw how persistent Pilgrim was, he became angry; lifting his staff, he struck out at Pilgrim. Not the least intimidated, Pilgrim allowed the old man to hit his bald head seven or eight times without a flinch—it was as if someone were scratching an itch for him! "This is a priest with a collision-proof head!" said the old man. "Venerable Sir," said Pilgrim, chuckling, "you can hit me all you want. But you'd better remember the number of blows you give me: one blow will cost you one pint of rice! You can take your time and measure it!" On hearing this, the old man quickly dropped his staff and ran inside. He slammed the door shut, yelling, "A ghost! A ghost!" The entire household was so terrified that both the front and the back doors were at once tightly bolted. When Pilgrim saw that the doors were shut, he thought to himself, "This old rogue said that they had just washed the rice and placed it in the cauldron. I wonder if he was telling the truth. As the proverb says, 'The Taoists beg from the worthies but the Buddhists from the fools.' Let old Monkey go in and take a look." Dear Great Sage! He made the magic sign with his fingers and used the magic of invisibility to walk straight into the kitchen: steam was indeed rising from the cauldron, for there was inside it half a cauldron of dried rice. He stuffed the alms bowl into the cauldron and gave it a strong scoop to fill the alms bowl with rice. He then mounted the clouds to go back to his master, and we shall not speak of him for the moment.

We tell you now instead about the T'ang monk sitting in the circle. He waited for a long time without seeing Pilgrim returning. Half rising, he said dejectedly, "Where did that ape go to beg for food?" "Who knows!" said Pa-chieh on one side, snickering. "He must have gone somewhere to play around! You think he's going to beg for food! He just wants us imprisoned here!" "What do you mean by imprisoned?" said Tripitaka. "Don't you know, Master?" said Pa-chieh. "The ancients drew on the ground to establish a jail. That's what he did! He drew a circle with his rod, and he claimed that it was stronger than a wall of iron. But if some tigers or ferocious beasts really showed up, how could this circle protect us? We might as well give ourselves to them for food!" "Wu-nêng," said Tripitaka, "what would you want to do?" Pa-chieh said, "This place can't shelter us from the wind or the cold. If you agree with old Hog, we should follow this road and start out towards the West once more. If Elder Brother manages to get some food, he will no doubt return quickly, riding on his cloud. He should have no difficulty catching up with us, and when there is food, we can stop and eat first before we move on. Sitting here all this time will only make our feet grow cold!"

It was the evil fortune of Tripitaka to have heard these words! He agreed with Idiot and all of them walked out of the circle. Pa-chieh led the horse while Sha Monk poled the luggage; the elder did not even climb on the horse. Following the road, he walked right up to the towered building and found that it was an edifice facing south. Outside the door was a painted eight-word brick wall,[3] which connected with a small towered-gate decorated with carvings of lovebirds hung upside down and painted with five colors. The door of the building was half closed. Pa-chieh tied the horse to one of the stoneware door wedges, and Sha Monk put down his pole. As he was sensitive to the cold wind, Tripitaka sat on the threshold. "Master," said Pa-chieh, "this must be the residence of a nobleman or an official. If we can't see anyone near the front door, all the inhabitants must be inside warming themselves by the fire. You two sit here, and let me go inside to take a look." "Take care!" said the T'ang monk. "Don't offend people!" Idiot said, "I know! Since I was converted and entered the gate of Zen, I have acquired some manners! I'm not like one of those village fools!"

Tying the muckrake to his waist, Idiot straightened out his blue silk shirt and walked inside in a civil manner. He saw three large front halls with all the curtains drawn up; the whole place was quiet and without a trace of any human inhabitant. There were neither furniture nor utensils. Passing the screens, he walked further inside and came upon a long corridor, behind which was a tall, two storied building. The windows on top were half opened, and one could see parts of a set of yellow silk curtains in the room. "The people must be afraid of the cold," said Idiot to himself. "They are still sleeping!" With no regard for manners, Idiot strode right up to the second story of the building. When he drew the curtains apart to take a look, he was so startled that he stumbled and fell. Inside the curtains, you see, and lying on top of an ivory bed was a skeleton of sickly white. The skull was big as a jar and the leg bones, straight as poles, were about four feet long. After he had calmed down, Idiot could not restrain the tears rolling down his cheeks. Shaking his head and sighing, he said to the skeleton: "I wonder if you are

The form of a marshal of what nation,
Or a great general of which country or state.
Once you were a hero striving to win;
Today how piteously you show your bones.
Your children and wife aren't here to serve you;
No soldiers burn incense to honor you.
You are truly most lamentable a sight:
You, who used to seek rule by might or right!"

As Pa-chieh thus lamented, he suddenly saw a flare of light behind the curtains. "Someone must be here after all to offer incense to him," said Idiot. He went behind the curtains hurriedly to look and found that rays of light were coming through some screens set up in a side room. Behind the screens was a lacquered table, on which there were several garments made of embroidered silk brocade. When Idiot picked them up, he saw that they were three silk vests.

Without regard for good or ill, he took the vests and came down the building. He went back through the front halls to walk out the door. "Master," he said, "there's no trace of anyone living inside. It's in fact a residence of the deceased. Old Hog went inside and walked upstairs to the tall tower, where there was a skeleton inside some yellow silk curtains. In a side room there were three silk vests, which I've brought with me. This has to be our luck, at least a little of it! Since it's turning cold now, we can make good use of them. Master, take off your outer garment and put on one of those vests. Enjoy, so you won't feel the cold so much." "No! No!" said Tripitaka. "For the *Book of Law* says, 'To take things, whether in open or in secret, is thievery.' If someone found out and caught up with us, the officials would undoubtedly charge us with the crime of theft. Take them back and put them at the place you found them. We can sit here for a while to escape from the wind, and when Wu-k'ung arrives, we'll move on. Those of us who have left the family should not be so covetous of little things!" Pa-chieh said, "There's not a single person around, even dogs or chickens are unaware of our presence. Only we know what we have done. Who will file charges against me? Who will be a witness? It was as if we had picked up these vests from the road. What do you mean by taking in open or in secret?" "You act foolishly!" said Tripitaka. "Though man may not know it, will Heaven be ignorant of it? Yüan-ti left this instruction: 'One may act against conscience in a secret place, but the eyes of the god are like lightning.' Return them quickly! Don't be greedy for things which do not belong to you."

Idiot, of course, refused to listen. Laughing, he said to the T'ang monk, "O Master! Since I became a human, I have worn several vests, but none made with such lovely brocade. If you won't want to put it on, let old Hog put it on. I'm going to try something new, and I want to warm my back a bit. When Elder Brother arrives, I'll take it off and we'll move on." "If that's the way you put it," said Sha Monk, "I'll try one, too!" The two of them took off their shirts and put on the vests. They were just trying to tighten the straps when all of sudden they could no longer stand up and tumbled to the ground. The vests, you see, somehow turned out to be like two straitjackets; in an instant, the two of them had their arms twisted backwards and firmly bound behind their backs. Tripitaka was so taken aback that he stamped his feet and chided them; he then went forward to try to untie them, but it was all to no avail. As the three of them made continuous clamor over there, a demon was soon alerted.

That towered building, you see, had indeed been devised by a monster-spirit, who had spent the days ensnaring people at the place. As he sat in his own cave, he suddenly heard noises of complaint and expostulation. When he hurried out to have a look, he found two victims all tied up. The demon called up his little imps quickly and did away with the buildings and towers. The T'ang monk was seized along with the white horse and the luggage. Then they herded all of them, including Pa-chieh and Sha Monk, into the cave. After the old demon took his seat high in the middle, the little fiends pushed the T'ang monk forward and forced him to kneel down. "Where did you come from, monk?" asked the old demon. "How dared you be so bold as to steal my garments?" As tears rolled down, the T'ang monk said, "This poor monk is someone sent by the Great T'ang in the Land of the East to acquire scriptures in the Western Heaven. Stricken with hunger just now, I told my senior disciple to go to beg for food and he hasn't returned. He told us to remain seated in the mountain, and if we had listened to him, we would not have trespassed your immortal court to find shelter from the cold wind. It was here that these two young disciples of mine grew covetous of small things after they found your clothes. Your poor monk certainly had no evil intentions, and they were told to return the vests to where they were found. Refusing to listen to me, they wanted to wear them just to warm their backs, and that was how they fell into the traps set by the Great King. Since you have caught me, I beg you to be merciful and spare my life so that I may proceed to acquire the true scriptures. I shall always be grateful for your grace and kindness, which I shall forever proclaim when I return to the Land of the East."

"I have often heard," said the demon, chuckling, "that if anyone eats a piece of the T'ang monk's flesh, his white hair will turn black, and his fallen teeth will grow back once more. Today it is my good fortune that you have arrived without my beckoning. And you still expect me to spare you? What is the name of your big disciple? Where did he go to beg for food?" On hearing the question, Pa-chieh said loudly and boastfully, "My Elder Brother is Sun Wu-k'ung, the Great Sage, Equal to Heaven, who caused great havoc in Heaven five hundred years ago."

When the demon heard that declaration, he became rather apprehensive. Though he did not utter a word, he thought to himself: "I have heard for a long time that that fellow has vast magic powers. I didn't expect that I would meet him by chance like this." Then he gave the order: "Little ones, tie them up also with two new ropes. Put them all in the rear. Wait until I have caught their big disciple. Then we can steam them all together to eat them." The little fiends obeyed with a shout and tied up all three of them before they were carried to the rear. The white horse was chained in the stable and the luggage was left in the house. Then the various monster-spirits began sharpening their weapons to prepare to catch Pilgrim, and we shall leave them for the moment.

We tell you now about Pilgrim Sun, who after he had stolen an alms bowlful of rice from the village in the south, mounted his cloud to return to where he began. By the time he reached the slope of the mountain and lowered his cloud, he saw that the T'ang monk was gone. The circle he drew with his rod could be seen on the ground, but neither the people nor the horse were anywhere in sight. He quickly turned his head to look toward the towered buildings and found that these, too, had disappeared. All he saw were strange rocks and mountain ridges. Aghast, Pilgrim said, "That's it! They must have fallen into danger!" Following the tracks of the horse he hurried along the road toward the West.

He journeyed for about five or six miles, and as he became more and more dejected, he heard all at once someone speaking on the northern slope. When he looked, he saw that it was an old man, who had on a thick woolen robe, and his head was covered by a warm hat. On his feet he had on a pair of half-new leather boots which had been nicely waxed. He supported himself with a staff which had a dragon head, and he was followed by a young houseboy. The old man also carried a twig of winter-plum blossoms in his hand, and as he walked down the slope, he was humming some kind of song. Putting down his alms bowl, Pilgrim faced him and bowed, saying, "Old Grandpa, this humble priest salutes you." Returning his bow, the old man said, "Where did you come from, elder?" Pilgrim said, "We came from the Land of the East, on our way to seek scriptures from Buddha in the Western Heaven. Master and disciples, there were altogether four of us. Because my master was hungry, I was sent to beg for some vegetarian food. I told the three of them to sit on a level spot by the mountain slope back there to wait for me. By the time I came back, however, they had disappeared. I don't know which road they took. May I ask, Old Grandpa, whether you have seen them?" When the old man heard this, he snickered and said, "Was there someone with a long snout and huge ears among those three?" "Yes! Yes! Yes!" said Pilgrim.

"Was there also someone with a gloomy complexion tugging a white horse and leading a pale-faced stoutish monk?"

"Yes! Yes! Yes!" said Pilgrim. The old man said, "You have taken the wrong road, all of you! Don't bother to look for them. Each of you should flee for your life!" Pilgrim said, "The pale-faced one is my master, and those strange-looking priests are my younger brothers. They and I were united in our determination to go to the Western Heaven for scriptures. How could I not go to search for them?" "I passed through this region sometime ago," said the old man, "and I saw them taking the wrong road which had to lead them straight into the mouth of demons." "Old Grandpa," said Pilgrim, "please tell me what kind of a demon there is and where does he live, so that I may demand their return at his door." The old man said, "This mountain is named the Golden Helmet Mountain, and in it there is a Golden Helmet Cave. The master of the cave is the Great King One-Horn Buffalo, who has vast magic powers and who is most capable in the martial arts. Your three companions this time must have lost their lives, and if you go there to search for them, I fear that you, too, may get yourself killed. Perhaps it's better for you not to go. I don't want to keep you from going, but I certainly am not going to encourage you either. It's your decision."

Bowing again and again to thank him, Pilgrim said, "I am grateful to the Old Grandpa for his instructions. But I cannot possibly give up my search!" He was about to pour out the rice which he took from the village in the south to give to the old man so that he could put away the empty bowl when the old man lay down his staff and took away the alms bowl. All at once the houseboy and the old man both revealed their true forms and went to their knees to kowtow. "Great Sage," they cried in unison, "these humble deities dare not hide anything from you. We are the mountain god and the local spirit of this region, and we have come to receive you here. Let us keep the bowl and the rice for the moment, so that the Great Sage can exercise his power. When the T'ang monk is rescued, the rice will then be presented to him and he will appreciate what reverence and devotion the Great Sage has shown him."

"You are asking to be beaten, clumsy ghosts!" bellowed Pilgrim. "If you knew that I had arrived, why didn't you show up earlier to meet me? Why must you come in shabby disguises?" "The Great Sage is rather impetuous," said the local spirit, "and this humble deity dares not confront you directly. That's why we camouflage ourselves to report to you." Calming down more and more, Pilgrim said, "I'll only make a note of your beating this time! Take care of that alms bowl for me, and let me go and catch that monster-spirit." The local spirit and the mountain god obeyed.

Tightening his sash on his tiger-skin skirt which he hitched up, our Great Sage dashed into the mountain to look for the fiend's cave, holding high his golden-hooped rod. He passed one of the cliffs and saw more strange boulders and two stone doors just beneath a green ledge. In front of the doors were many little imps, wielding lances and waving swords. Truly there were

Mists in auspicious folds;
Moss in bluish clumps;
Strange rugged rocks stood in array;
Rough winding paths coiled round and round.
Apes cried and birds sang in this lovely scene;
Phoenixes, male and female, danced as in P'êng-Ying.[4]
A few plums, facing the east, began to bloom;
Warmed by the sun, the bamboos displayed their green.
Beneath the steep ridge—
Within the deep brook—
Beneath the steep ridge snow piled high like powder;
Within the deep brook water froze as ice.
Two groves of pines and cedars fresh for a thousand years;
Many bunches of mountain tea all glowing red.

As he did not go there merely to admire the scenery, our Great Sage strode up to the doors and cried out in a severe voice: "Little imps! Go inside quickly and tell your cave master that I am Sun Wu-k'ung, the Great Sage, Equal to Heaven, and the disciple of the holy monk from the T'ang court. Tell him to send out my master quickly so that all of your lives may be spared."

That group of fiends dashed inside to report: "Great King, there is a hairy-faced priest with a curved beak outside. He calls himself Sun Wu-k'ung, the Great Sage, Equal to Heaven, and he has come to demand the return of his master." When he heard this announcement, the demon king was delighted. "I wanted him to come!" he said. "Since I left my former palace and descended to earth, I have never had a chance to practice martial art. Today he is here and he will be a worthy opponent." He gave the order at once for his weapon to be brought out, and every one of those fiends, young and old, in the cave aroused himself. They hurriedly hauled out a twelve-feet-long spotted-

steel lance to present to the old fiend. Then the old fiend gave this
order: "Little ones, all of you must follow orders. Those who advance
will be rewarded; those who retreat will be executed." The fiends all
obeyed and followed the old demon, who, when he walked out of the
cave, asked aloud: "Who is Sun Wu-k'ung?" On one side Pilgrim took
a look at that demon king and saw that he was ugly and ferocious
indeed:

A jagged, single horn;
A pair of gleaming eyes;
Coarse skin swelling up from his head;
Dark flesh glowing beneath his ears.
A long tongue oft' licking his nose;
A wide mouth full of yellow teeth.
His hide is like indigo blue;
His tendons are tough as steel.
Rhino-like, though he can't light up the stream;[5]
Steer-like, though he can't plow the fields.
He has no use at all for tilling the soil,
Though he has the strength to shake Heav'n and Earth.
His two dyed-blue hands with tendons brown
Grasp firmly the long, straight, spotted-steel lance.
You'll see why, if you stare at his fierce form,
He's called the Great King One-Horned Buffalo.

Pilgrim Sun walked up to him and said, "Your Grandpa Sun is here!
Give me back my master quickly, and you will suffer no harm. Utter
but half a 'No,' and I'll see to it that you die faster than you can select
your burial ground!" "You audacious, brazen monkey-spirit!"
shouted the demon. "What abilities do you have that you dare indulge
in such tall talk?" "You brazen fiend," said Pilgrim, "it's only you who
has never seen the abilities of old Monkey!" The demon said, "Your
master stole some garments of mine and I caught him all right.
And now I am just about to have him steamed and eaten. What kind
of a warrior are you that you dare demand his return at my door?"
"My master is an honest and upright priest," said Pilgrim. "It's impossible that he should want to steal things from a fiend like you!"
The demon replied: "I created an immortal village beside the mountain, and your master sneaked into one of the buildings. What he saw
he coveted, and he took three of my vests of silk brocade and put them
on. I had proof derived from both the stolen goods and witnesses, and

that was why I seized him. If you indeed are able, you should try your hand with me. If you can withstand me for three rounds, I will spare your master's life. If you can't, I'll send you to the Region of Darkness!"

With a laugh, Pilgrim said, "Brazen creature! No need for this bravado! If you speak of trying my hand, you are after old Monkey's own heart. Come up here and have a taste of my rod!" The fiendish creature, of course, was in no wise afraid of any combat. Raising his lance, he stabbed at Pilgrim's face. This was quite a marvelous battle! Look at

The golden-hooped rod upraised—
The long-shafted lance going out—
The golden-hooped rod upraised
Is brilliant as the golden snakes of lightning.
The long-shafted lance going out
Is radiant like a dragon leaving the ink-dark sea.
The little imps beat the drums before the door
As they spread in formation to help the fight.
Over here our Great Sage uses his might
To reveal, back and forth, his abilities.
On that side there is a lance,
Alert and spirited;
On our side there is a rod—
Such lofty art of combat!
Truly a hero has met a hero true;
A foe has found another worthy foe.
That demon king belches purple breath like lightning coils;
This Great Sage's eyes flash forth rays like brocade clouds.
Because a Great T'ang monk faces an ordeal,
They, without forbearance, strive bitterly.

Closing again and again for more than thirty times, they could not reach a decision. When that demon king saw how perfect Wu-k'ung's style was in using his rod, how there was not even the slightest false move, he was so pleased that he shouted bravos repeatedly, saying, "Marvelous ape! Marvelous ape! Truly abilities like these are worthy to cause havoc in Heaven!" That Great Sage, too, was also pleased by the methodical way in which the demon king wielded his lance: as he parried left and right, every blow and every thrust were in perfect form. "Marvelous spirit! Marvelous spirit!" cried the Great Sage also. "Truly a demon capable of stealing elixir!" The two of them therefore fought for twenty more rounds.

Using the tip of his lance to point at the ground, the demon king shouted for the little imps to attack together. All those brazen fiends, wielding swords, scimitars, staffs, and spears, rushed forward at once and surrounded the Great Sage Sun completely. Entirely undaunted, Pilgrim only cried: "Welcome! Welcome! That's exactly what I want!" He used his golden-hooped rod to cover his front and back, to parry blows east and west, but that gang of fiends refused to be beaten back. Growing more agitated, Pilgrim tossed his rod up into the air, shouting, "Change!" It changed immediately into iron rods by the hundreds and thousands; like flying snakes and soaring serpents, they descended on to the fiends from the air. When those monster-spirits saw this, everyone was frightened out of his wits. Covering their heads and necks, they fled toward their cave for their lives. The old demon king, however, stood still and, laughing with scorn, said, "Monkey, don't be impertinent! Watch my trick!" He at once took out from his sleeve a white, shiny fillet and tossed it up in the air, crying, "Hit!" With a swish, all the iron rods changed back into a single rod, which was then sucked up by the fillet. The Great Sage Sun, completely empty-handed, had to use his somersault desperately in order to escape with his life. Thus

The demon, in victory, returned to his cave,

But Pilgrim, in a daze, knew not what to do.

Truly it is that

The Tao is one foot but demons are ten feet tall.

Nature lost, feelings confused, you seek the wrong home.

Pity the dharma-body who has no proper seat:

He made the wrong decision for his act that time!

We do not know what is the end of all this, and you must listen to the explanation in the next chapter.

# Abbreviations

Chou      Chou Wei 周緯, *Chung-kuo ping-ch'i-shih kao* 中國兵器史稿 (Peking, 1957).

*CTS*      *Ch'üan T'ang Shih* 全唐詩, 12 vols. (Ts'ui-wên t'ang 粹文堂 edition; repr. Tainan, Taiwan, 1974).

Dudbridge      Glen Dudbridge, *The Hsi-yu Chi: A Study of Antecedents to the Sixteenth-Century Chinese Novel* (Cambridge, Eng., 1970).

*HJAS*      *Harvard Journal of Asiatic Studies.*

*HYC*      *Hsi-yu chi* 西游記 (Peking, 1954). Abbreviation refers only to this edition.

*JW*      *The Journey to the West.*

Needham      Joseph Needham, *Science and Civilisation in China*, vol. 1–5/3 (Cambridge, England, 1954–76).

Porkert      Manfred Porkert, *The Theoretical Foundations of Chinese Medicine: Systems of Correspondence*, M.I.T. East Asian Science Series, Nathan Sivin, general editor (Cambridge, Mass., and London, 1974).

*SPPY*      *Szu-pu pei-yao* 四部備要.

*SPTK*      *Szu-pu ts'ung-k'an* 四部叢刊.

*STT*      *Hsin-k'ê ch'u-hsiang kuan-pan ta-tzŭ Hsi-yu chi* 新刻出像官板大字西游記 (Shih-tê t'ang 世德堂 edition, 1592).

*T.*      Taishō Tripiṭaka.

*TPKC*      *T'ai-p'ing kuang-chi* 太平廣記, 10 vols. (Peking, 1961).

*TT*      *Tao Tsang.*

References to all Standard Histories, unless otherwise indicated, are to the *SPTK Po-na* 百衲 edition.

# Notes

## CHAPTER TWENTY-SIX

1. The "sword" above the "heart": the first two lines of this poem are built on ideographic elements of the two Chinese characters, *jên* 忍 and *nai* 耐, which mean patience. The character *jên* is made of two words: *jên* 刃, which means a knife or sword, and *hsin* 心, which means the heart or mind. The second character, *nai*, is made also of two words: *êrh* 而, which means and or nevertheless, and *ts'un* 寸, which means an inch. The second line of the poem thus reads literally: in your conduct remember the "nevertheless" beside the "inch." Since this is meaningless in English, I have translated the line analogously.

2. "The noblest": literally the "highest type of men" (*shang-shih* 上 士), an allusion to the *Tao-tê Ching*, 41.

3. "The sage loves virtue": an allusion to *Analects*, 4, 11. The line in the Confucian classic actually reads: the princely man loves or thinks of virtue 君子懷德.

4. "The Joyful Festivities of Four Seasons": Pa-chieh is punning here on the word *ch'ing* 磬, which means sonorous stone, and the word *ch'ing* 慶, which means festivity or celebration.

5. Jade juice: according to the *Shan-hai ching* 山海經, the jade juice of certain mountains will transform a man into an immortal once he drinks a drop of it.

6. To tread the Dipper: a part of Taoist ritual in which the practitioner's prescribed movement imitates the shape of the seven stars in the Ursa Major.

7. Tung-fang Shuo: the famous thief of an old legend in which he stole divine peaches from the garden of the Queen of the West. His exploits in medieval China became the subject of a series of stage works. For his story, see the *Shih Chi* 史記, *chüan* 126; *Han Shu* 漢書, *chüan* 65; TPKC, *chüan* 6; Dudbridge, *Antecedents*, pp. 36–38; Burton Watson, *Courtiers and Commoners in Ancient China* (New York, 1974), pp. 79–106.

8. Pearl tree: a mythical tree found in fairyland; the wood resembles cedar but the leaves are pearls.

9. Red steel: *kun-wu* 錕鋙, a kind of red steel whose name is derived from *kun-wu* 昆吾, a legendary mountain in Western China where the ore is found. A sword made of this steel can "slice through jade as if it were mud." See the *Lieh Tzu* 列子, 5.

10. Part of a book: literally *i-p'in* 一品, the highest class or grade. But *p'in* also can refer to *varga*, a chapter of a sūtra. This latter meaning seems more appropriate in the present context.

11. Four Noble Truths: literally, in Chinese, *ssŭ-shêng* 四聖, the four sages or the four kinds of holy men: śravakas, pratyeka-buddhas, bodhisattvas, and buddhas. If this is the reference here, the line of the verse would read something like: "When the four sages are taught [*shou* 授], they will hear right fruit." But *ssŭ-shêng* can also refer to *ssŭ-shêng-ti* 四聖諦, *catvāri ārya-satyāni*, the four cardinal dogmas of Buddhism on suffering, its causes, its end, and its deliverance. I have chosen the second meaning for the translation here.

12. Six Stages: the six stages of rebirth for ordinary mortals.

13. Young grove: in Chinese, *shao-lin* 少林, which is commonly known as the name of a famous Buddhist monastery in Honan province. In the present context, however, the literal meaning (young forest or grove) seems more appropriate.

CHAPTER TWENTY-SEVEN

1. *Hai-t'ang*: *Malus balliana*.

2. *Analects*, 4, 19.

3. Liberation through the Corpse: *shih-chieh* 尸解, or the deliverance from the corpse. According to Needham 2: 141, "representations of the *hsien*, often in the form of feathered men, are not uncommon in Han art. One's body might appear to be left behind in the coffin, but it would be only a simulacrum feigned by an object such as a sword or a piece of bamboo, which had previously been prepared with special rites. This was called the 'deliverance of the corpse' (*shih chieh*), or the 'transmutation of the *hun*-soul' (*lien hun*). The process was thought of as similar to insect metamorphosis." He further notes in vol. 5, pt. 2, 106 that the distinction between *t'ien-hsien* (celestial immortals) and *ti-hsien* (earthly immortals) arose quite early. "Already in +20 Huan Than named five categories of spiritual beings. The mid +3rd-century *Thai Shang Ling-Pao Wu Fu Ching* lays great emphasis on *thien hsien* (empyreal immortals) as if to affirm their superiority. Ko Hung wrote in the *Pao Phu Tzu* book:

> The manuals of the immortals say that masters of the highest category (*shang shih*) are able to raise themselves high up into the aery void (*chü hsing shêng hsü*); these are called 'celestial immortals (*thien hsien*).' Those of the second category (*chung shih*) resort to the famous

mountains (and forests) and are called 'terrestrial immortals (*ti hsien*).' As for those of the third category (*hsia shih*) they simply slough off the body after death, and they are called 'corpse-free immortals (*shih chieh hsien*).'"

For stories of person who had attained immortality by departing in their spirits and leaving behind their bodies, see the *Yu-yang tsa-tsu* 酉陽雜俎, *chüan* 2; *TPKC, chüan* 58, 360.

4. P'êng Tsu: the Methuselah of China, he was an official in the reign of the legendary King Yao (ca. 2357–2255 B.C.), and he was supposed to have lived for over 800 years.

5. Jade stone: the *ch'ing* or sonorous stone.

6. "When the birds vanish . . .": a slightly abbreviated form of a famous statement attributed to Fan Li 范蠡, who used it to warn his friend, Chung 種, about the character of King Kou-chien 勾踐 of the State of Yüeh 越 in the Warring States Period (468–221 B.C.). After Kou-chien defeated his rival, King Fu-ch'a 夫差 of the State of Wu, he demanded the suicide of a minister like Chung who served him faithfully and helped him come to power. Hence the statement is often used to describe ingratitude. See the *Shih Chi* 史記, *chüan* 21.

7. Avīci Hell: the deepest layer of Buddhist Hell.

CHAPTER TWENTY-EIGHT

1. Dragon-drivers: i.e., immortals or gods.

2. Six kinds of trees are listed in this line. They are: the *ch'un* (*Cedrela odorata*), the *shan* (the common pine, *Cryptomeria japonica*), the *huai* (*Sophora japonica*), the *kuei* (Chinese juniper, *Juniperus chinensis*), the *li* (the chestnut tree, *Castanea vulgaris*), and the *t'an* (sandalwood, *Santalum album*).

3. Wolf-teeth arrows: a kind of arrow with a sharp head shaped like the fang of wolves, first introduced in the reign of Shen-tsung (1067–85) of the Sung dynasty. See the *Sung shih* 宋史, *ping-chih* 兵志, *chüan* 156, 6b.

4. Fire cannons: some kind of firearm using gunpowder was already in use, on both land and sea during the Sung dynasty. See the *Sung shih, ping chih, chüan* 150, 15b–16a. Cf. also Needham, IV/3, 476; L. Carrington Goodrich and Feng Chia-sheng, "The Early Development of Firearms in China," *Isis* 36 (1945–46): 114–23, 250–51; Wang Ling, "On the Invention and Use of Gunpowder and Firearms in China," *Isis* 37 (1947): 160–78; Herbert Franke, "Siege and Defense of Towns in Medieval China," in *Chinese Ways in Warfare*, ed. Frank A. Kierman and John K. Fairbank (Cambridge, 1974), pp. 171–73. For firearms in the Ming period, see the discussion and illustrations in Chou, pp. 270–71, and plate 83.

5. This *tz'ŭ* poem written to the tune of *Hsi-chiang yüeh* 西江月 (The West River's Moon) with an extra syllable tagged on in the last line, is con-

structed by means of puns on the names of various kinds of herbs. The names would be used for either their literal meanings or the borrowed meanings from their homophones. Thus: Line 1, dark heads: *wu-t'ou* 烏頭; literally, black head, it is also *Aconitum carmichaeli*, Chinese aconite tuber collected in the spring. Line 2, the winged horses: *hai-ma* 海馬; literally, sea horse, it is also *Hippocampus* used in Chinese medicine and a legendary horse with wings. Line 3, lords and nobles: *jên-shên* 人參 and *kuan-kuei* 官桂, they are *Panax ginseng* and *Cinnmomum cassia*, respectively. In the translation, *jên-shên* is read as 人紳, gentry, and *kuan-kuei* as 官貴, noble official. Line 4, cinnabar: *chu-sha* 硃砂, HgS. Line 5, fathers and sons: *fu-tzŭ* 附子, also *Aconitum carmichaeli*, Chinese aconite tuber collected in the autumn. In the translation, it is read as *fu-tzŭ* 父子, father and son. Line 6, fine men: *pin-lang* 檳榔, *areca catechu*. In the translation, it is read as *pin-lang* 斌郎, refined, elegant young man. Line 7, fell to the dust: *ch'ing-fên* 輕粉, HgCl, calomel. In the translation, it is read for *ch'ing-fên* 傾扮, fall [to the] dust. Line 8, rouged ladies: *hung-niang-tzŭ* 紅娘子; literally, red lady, it is also the *Huechys*, an insect belonging to the cicada family and used for medicinal purpose. For poems of a similar nature in another work of Chinese fiction of this period, see the *Chin P'ing Mei*, chaps. 33 and 61. I owe these references to Professor David Roy.

6. Drill ice for fire: in other words, "I'll do what's impossible to find food."

7. The moon had no base: i.e., it is only a reflection.

8. Nonetheless: literally, the words are *fên ming* 分明, quite clearly. But there is hardly anything in the poem which indicates that this is "an evil place." Hence this minor emendation.

9. The moon his third friend: an allusion to a famous poem by the T'ang poet, Li Po (701–62). In "Drinking Alone beneath the Moon," Li wrote:

A pot of wine among the flowers:
I drink alone, no kith or kin near.
I raise my cup to invite the moon to join me;
It and my shadow make a party of three.

See *Sunflower Splendor: Three Thousand Years of Chinese Poetry*, co-edited by Wu-chi Liu and Irving Lo (Bloomington, Ind., 1975), p. 109.

10. Spirit-Soothing Pillar: a euphemistic name of the stick used to tie someone about to be executed.

CHAPTER TWENTY-NINE

1. Precious Image: *Pao-hsiang* 寶象 can mean, literally, precious elephant. But the word *hsiang* is used frequently as *hsiang* 相, meaning image or likeness, in which case the phrase *pao-hsiang* may refer to the precious image of Buddha.

2. No less prosperous: i.e., than the T'ang nation.

3. Metal and liquid: an allusion to the phrase *chin-ch'êng t'ang-ch'ih* 金城湯池 , metal walls and moats of scalding liquid; i.e., a fortified city.

4. Great Ultimate Hall, etc.: the names of these halls and palaces are taken from actual buildings constructed in various periods of Chinese history. See G. Combaz, "Les temples impériaux de la Chine," *Annales de la Société Royale d'Archéologie* (Brussels) 21 (1907): 381 ff.; and Oswald Sirén, *The Imperial Palaces of Peking*, 3 vols. (Paris and Brussels, 1927).

5. A pair of hawks: possibly an allusion to two lines of poetry by the T'ang poet, Tu Fu (712–70), who wrote in "A Song of Weeping by the River 哀江頭,"
And an archer, breast skyward, shooting through the clouds
And felling with one dart a pair of flying birds.
(Translation by Witter Bynner.)

6. Necessary-to-be-sent document: a conventional phrase used frequently at the end of an official communication.

7. Hanlin Academy: the *Han-lin Yüan* 翰林院 was the College of Literature in the capital. In the Ming dynasty, it was headed by a Chancellor (*hsüeh-shih* 學士), a rank much lower than the Grand Secretary (*ta hsüeh-shih*), and the reference here in the narrative might have been carelessness on the part of the *JW* author. According to Charles O. Hucker, "Governmental Organization of the Ming Dynasty," *HJAS* 21 (1958): 37, the Academy "provided literary and scholarly assistance of all kinds to the Emperor and the court. Its personnel drafted and polished proclamations and other state documents, compiled imperially sponsored histories and other works, read and explained the classics and histories to the Emperor, and participated in state ceremonies and to some extent in governmental deliberations."

8. Fragrant wind: usually, demon kings are not associated with fragrant wind or auspicious luminosity (*hsiang-fêng* 香風 and *hsiang-kuang* 祥光), but this particular one is no ordinary monster. See chap. 31 below for his celestial origin.

9. Rattle: *pang* 梆, a piece of slightly convex wood, with a slit at the top and hollowed out; it is struck by the watchman or by the bugler either as an alarm signal or as a signal that the battle is over.

CHAPTER THIRTY

1. Second disciple: in the narrative, Sha Wu-ching is, of course, the third disciple of Tripitaka, but since the monster has no knowledge of Sun Wu-k'ung up to this point, it is only natural that Sha Monk is so identified. Ōta Tatsuo and Torii Hisayasu's emendation in their edition of the *Saiyuki*, Chūgoku koten bungaku taikei, vols. 31–32 (Tokyo, 1971), 1, 256, and

n. 1 on 264, is completely unwarranted, since they fail to take into account this simple authorial use of point of view.

2. Old Sand: Sha, in Chinese, means sand. See *JW*, 1, chap. 8, for the naming of this disciple.

3. Tzŭ-chien: Ts'ao Chih (192–232), the third son of the warlord Ts'ao Ts'ao (155–220), was an accomplished writer and poet. Legend has it that he could finish composing a poem after taking seven steps.

4. P'an An: P'an Yüeh, style An-jen, of the Tsin period. He was reputedly so handsome that women would line the streets and throw fruits at him when he went out. See the *Tsin Shu* 晉書, *chüan* 55.

5. Red threads: the Old Man in the Moon, the marriage broker par excellence in Chinese mythology, is supposed to tie the feet of fated lovers with scarlet threads.

6. *P'i-p'a*: a lutelike musical instrument with four strings.

7. Metal Squire: for the significance of this name and that of Wood Mother and Yellow Hag, see Introduction to *JW*, 1: 50–51.

CHAPTER THIRTY-ONE

1. Gate of undivided truth: the gate is the *dharma–paryāya*, the teachings of Buddha regarded as the gateway to enlightenment. Undivided truth refers to *advaya*, the one and undivided unity of all things, non-duality.

2. Sixfold Path: the six ways of reincarnation. See *JW*, 1, chap. 8, n. 7.

3. An unfilial act: a quotation from chap. 11 of the *Classic on Filial Piety* (*Hsiao Ching* 孝經), traditionally attributed to Tsêng Shên, a disciple of Confucius. The Five Punishments, according to ancient reckoning (e.g., *Shu Ching* 書經, *chüan* 6), refer to tattooing the face, cutting off the nose, cutting off the feet, castration, and death. Since about the sixth century A.D., however, the phrase means caning, whipping, penal servitude, exile, and death. Still more recently, it has meant monetary fines, hard labor of a set period, penal servitude of a set period, life imprisonment, and death.

4. "O my father": these four lines are quotations from a poem titled *Liao-o* 蓼莪, in the *Hsiao-ya* 小雅 section of the *Book of Odes*.

5. Śarīra: the relic or ashes of a Buddha or a saint after the person is cremated.

6. Nine Luminaries: for these and other gods following, see *JW*, 1, chap. 5.

7. Wood-Wolf Star: in the Chinese stellar divisions, constellation number 15, *k'uei* 奎 (Revatī), has the corresponding element of wood and the corresponding animal of wolf. Hence its name. The constellation is composed of the asterism *bēta* (Mirach), *délta, epsīlon, zēta, ēta, mū, nū, pē* Andromeda, *sīgma* (2), *tau, nū, phī, chī, psī* Pisces at longitude 17°48′12″.

CHAPTER THIRTY-TWO

1. *Hai-t'ang*: *Malus balliana*.

2. Purple Path: roads in the imperial city are frequently referred to as "purple paths" in classical Chinese verse. The series of images here is often used in poetry celebrating the enjoyment of flowers in the time of spring. See, for example, Liu Yü-hsi 劉禹錫 (772–841), "元和十一年自朗州召至京戲贈看花諸君子" 紫陌紅塵拂面來，無人不道看花回, … , … in *CTS*, *chüan* 365: 4114.

3. *Heart Sūtra*: see *JW*, 1, chap. 19.

4. Jade-white brows: Buddha's eyebrows (*ūrnā*) are supposedly of this color.

5. Nidānas: the twelve conditions of causation, according to Mahāyāna Buddhism, which give rise to all things, all phenomena.

6. Three Stars: i.e., the Stars of Longevity, Blessing, and Wealth. See chap. 26.

7. Chên-wu: the Lord of the North, a Taoist god whose original name was Hsüan-wu 玄武, but changed to Chên-wu during the Sung period. He had under his command the two famous generals of the turtle and the snake.

8. Mars: revered in China as the God of Fire.

9. "Clever talk and a pretentious appearance are seldom found in the good" (Waley's translation) is a quotation of *Analects*, 1, 3.

10. Sedentary exercises: this and the other phrases refer to the processes of alchemical self-cultivation.

11. Sword of seven stars: one of the five treasures possessed by the two monsters. See chap. 34 below.

CHAPTER THIRTY-THREE

1. Green buffalo: according to the *Shên-hsien Chuan* 神仙傳 (Lives of the Holy Immortals), one Fêng Chün-ta 封君達 practiced the taking of mercury, with the result that he had the appearance of a thirty-year-old person at the age of a hundred. He rode a green cow or bull, hence the name. See also the *Han Wu (Ti) Nei Chuan* 漢武帝內傳 in *TT*, 289. The text of the *HYC* is erroneous here: 清 (clear) should read 青 (green or blue).

2. Master of the white tablet: in the Chinese text of the *HYC*, the line has 素券先生, but the word *chüan* 券 = 劵 may be an error since it is an archaic form of 倦, meaning tired, weary, and fatigued. I have emended the word to *ch'üan* 券, which means a bond, a contract, or a deed written (in ancient times) on a tablet of wood or bamboo, with each party involved in the business transaction holding half of the document. The white deed or tablet (*su-ch'üan*) may refer to the charms or judgments written in divination and fortune-telling.

3. Classic of the Northern Dipper: the full name of this Taoist text is 北斗進命經 (Classic of the Northern Dipper for the Advancement of Life).

4. O-mei Mountain: a famous sacred mountain in Szechuan Province.

5. Three Worms: see *JW*, 1, chap. 15, n. 1.

6. Seven apertures: the eyes, the ears, the nostrils, and the mouth.

7. These words are frequently used in Taoist rituals of exorcism and healing; they are also written in charms and various incantations.

8. This last rhetorical question addressed to Heaven is a parody of the dying words of the strategist-general, Chou Yü 周瑜, who served the state of Wu in the novel, *San-kuo chih yen-i* (Romance of the Three Kingdoms). Though he and Chu-ko Liang, the master strategist serving Liu Pei, were temporary allies in their famous Red Cliff campaign against Ts'ao Ts'ao, Chou was completely outwitted by Chu-ko. When Chou died as a result of arrow wounds and the frustration of not being able to outmaneuver Chu-ko Liang, he asked, "If [you, Heaven] gave birth to Yü, why did you also give birth to Liang?" See chap. 57 of the novel.

9. Bamboo fish: a gong made of bamboo and shaped like a fish, to be struck in accompaniment to the recitation of scriptures.

10. Master Lü: Lü Tung-pin, one of the famous Eight Immortals, and revered as one of the supreme patriarchs of folk Taoism.

CHAPTER THIRTY-FOUR

1. Nine-tailed fox: a mythical animal which frequently takes on the form of a beautiful woman to seduce people in legends and fictions. See Kuo P'u 郭璞, *Shan-hai ching* 山海經,海外東經圖讚, 27a (*SPPY* edition).

2. Po-shan urn: an incense urn shaped like a mountainous island on top, with a dish at the bottom which is filled with hot water when the incense is burned. The steam will thus mingle with the rising incense fragrance. For a sketch of the urn, see the *Chung-wên ta tz'ŭ-tien*, 2808. 12.

3. Master of Kuan-k'ou: i.e., the god Erh-lang.

4. Mighty Spirit: for this god, see *JW*, 1, chap. 4.

CHAPTER THIRTY-FIVE

1. Right knowledge: literally, seeking scriptures by returning to the proper [source] of enlightenment (*chüeh-chêng* 覺正).

2. "Supreme . . . Patriarch": i.e., Lao Tzu.

3. Nü Kua: the sister and successor of the legendary King Fu Hsi, she was said to have a human head and a serpent body, to have made five-colored stones to repair the heavens, to have cut off a huge turtle's legs to establish the four quarters, and to have piled up reed ashes to stop the flood. See Ssŭ-ma Chên 司馬貞, *Pu Shih Chi* 補史記,三皇本紀.

4. Master Chou of the *Lady Peach-Blossom*: *Lady Peach-Blossom* (*T'ao-hua Nü* 桃花女) is the name of a Yüan drama, which tells the story of a woman exorcist by the same name and how she outwits the tricks of a devious fortune-teller, Master Chou.

5. Kuei-ku Tzŭ: see *JW*, 1, chap. 10, n. 23.

6. "Square-sky" halberd: the weapon has such a name probably because part of its head resembles the Chinese character, *t'ien* 天, meaning sky. See Chou Wei, plate 83, 14.

CHAPTER THIRTY-SIX

1. Nidānas: in Buddhist doctrine, the cycle of twelve causes or links in the chain of existence (*shih-êrh yin-yüan* 十二因緣), from which it is the aim of Buddhism to set men free. The cycle consists of ignorance (*avidyā*, *wu-ming* 無明), which causes the phenomenon of the aggregates (*saṁskāra*, *hsing* 行), which causes the phenomenon of consciousness (*vijñāna*, *shih* 識), which causes the phenomenon of name and form (*nāmarūpa*, *ming sê* 名色), which causes the phenomenon of the six senses (*ṣaḍāyatana*, *liu-ju* 六入), which causes the phenomenon of contact (*sparśa*, *ch'u* 觸), which causes the phenomenon of sensations (*vedanā*, *shou* 受), which causes the phenomenon of desire (*tṛṣnā*, *ai* 愛), which causes the phe-nomenon of grasping (*upādāna*, *ch'ü* 取), which causes the phenomenon of coming into existence (*bhava*, *yu* 有), which causes the phenomenon of birth (*jāti*, *shêng* 生), which causes the phenomenon of old age and death (*jarāmaraṇa*, *lao ssŭ* 老死), which causes again ignorance.

2. Cease: literally, *fu* 伏, to fall prostrate, to yield, to submit, and to be subdued.

3. Side door: *p'ang-mên* 傍門, metaphor for heterodoxy.

4. Like the poem in chap. 28 (see p. 38 and also n. 5), this *lü-shih* (regulated verse) poem is also written by means of puns on various names of herbs. The names would either be used for their literal meanings or their borrowed meanings from homophones. Thus- Line 1, resolved, *i-chih* (益智 , *alpinia sp.*) is intended for *i-chih* 一志, determined, single-mindedness. Line 2, the king did not wait, literally, the king did not ask me to remain, *wang-pu-liu-hsing* 王不留行, *vaccaria pyramidata*. Line 3, three-cornered sedge: *san-lêng-tzu* 三稜子, *scirpus yagara*. Line 4, bridle bells: *ma-tou ling* 馬兜鈴, also *aristolochia debilis*. Line 5, scriptures: *ching-chieh* 荆芥 , *nepeta japonica*, is read for *ching-chieh* 經戒, sūtras and command-ments. Line 6, Buddha's spirit: *fu-ling* 茯苓, *poria cocos*, is read for *fu* (*fo*)*-ling* 佛靈. Line 7, myself I guard: *fang-chi* 防己, *stephania tetrandra*. Complete my tour: *tsu-li*: 竹瀝, bamboo oil, is read for *tsu-li* 足歷, to finish a journey or complete a preordained experience. I thank Professor Chow Tse-tsung for suggesting the interpretation of this particular line.

Line 8, go home: *hui-hsiang* 茴香, *foeniculum vulgare*, is read for *hui-hsiang* 回鄉. For the names of the Chinese herbs, I have consulted the *Chung-yao chih* 中藥誌·, prepared by the *Chung-kuo i-hsüeh k'o-hsüeh yüan yao-wu yen-chiu so* 中國醫學科學院藥物研究所 (4 vols., Peking, 1959–61).

5. Eight-word brick wall: this could be a reference to the construction of a kind of wall with cut-away corners so that it resembles the Chinese word for eight, *pa* 八. On the other hand, it may also refer to eight words taken from the chapter on "Holy Conduct" (*shêng-hsing* 聖行) in the *Nirvāṇa sūtra*. The eight words declare that the doctrine of the sūtra is death, or nirvāṇa as entrance into joy 生滅滅已寂滅為樂.

6. Wan-fo Tower: i.e., the Tower of Ten Thousand Buddhas.

7. Great Hero: a title of Buddha, which signifies his great power and wisdom to overcome all demonic barriers.

8. Three honored Buddhas: i.e., Śākyamuni and the two most beloved disciples.

9. Pattra leaves: from the *Borassus flabelliformis* palm leaves used for writing.

10. Vajra-guardians: Karl L. Reichelt in *Truth and Tradition in Chinese Buddhism* (Shanghai, 1927), p. 195, calls these guardian deities "cherubs," but their appearances hardly resemble those of their Western counterparts.

11. Towers of Ch'in: commonly a name for brothels.

12. Yü Liang: 庾亮 (289–340), an official of the Tsin period and a passionate poet. See *Tsin shu* 晉書, *chüan* 73.

13. Yüan Hung: 袁宏 (328–76), another official and poet of the Tsin period. See *Tsin shu, chüan* 92.

14. White snow: the reference here is to the whiteness of the moonlight and to a song or tune by such a name. The complete title is *Yang-ch'un pai-hsüeh* 陽春白雪, a tune so lofty and noble that it is known only to a few persons. See the *Wên-hsüan* 文選,宋玉對楚王問.

15. Icy strings: *ping-hsien* 冰絃, refers to a lute (*p'i-p'a*) brought back from the region of Shu (Szechuan) by one Pai Hsiu-chên 白秀貞 and presented to the T'ang emperor, Hsüan-tsung, in the K'ai-yüan period (713–42). The instrument originated as an article of tribute from the territory of Sinkiang, the strings of which were said to be made from the silk of ice silkworms.

16. For some of the philosophical and religious ideas underlying Wu-k'ung's discourse here, see the *Ts'an T'ung Ch'i* 參同契, chaps. 10 and 41; Needham, 2: 329–35; Introduction, *JW*, 1: 48–49.

17. Obscure: i.e., *hui* 晦.

18. Stroke: in the writings of Ching Fang 京房 (77–37 B.C.) and Yü Fan 虞翻 (164–233), two early alchemical theorists, the stages of the lunar movement are correlated with the eight trigrams (*kua*). In traditional

interpretation, the broken lines of the trigrams belong to the yin, whereas the unbroken lines belong to the yang. Thus the *chên* trigram, associated with the third day of the month and the first quarter of the moon, is depicted by this symbol ☳, which has one unbroken or yang stroke. The *tui* trigram, associated with the eighth day, has this symbol ☱. For a chart of the complete correlation, see Liu Ts'un-yan, "Taoist Self-Cultivation in Ming Thought," in *Self and Society in Ming Thought*, ed. Wm. Theodore de Bary and the Conference on Ming Thought (New York and London, 1970), pp. 302–3.

19. To Face: i.e., *wang* 望. The full moon on the fifteenth day of the month is thought to be facing the sun perfectly.

20. Two Eights: *êrh pa* 二八. In the *Ts'an T'ung Ch'i* 參同契, there is the poem:

When the essences of Two Quarters are fused,

兩弦合其精

The cosmic substance is thus formed.

乾坤體乃成

Two Eights will make up one catty;

二八應一斤

The Way of Change is true and lasting.

易道正不傾

Though the commentary by Chu Hsi in the *Chou-I Ts'an T'ung Ch'i K'ao-i* 周易參同契考異, 11a (*SPPY* edition) interprets the numbers as the two periods of eight days during the first and the last quarter of the month, many works of the alchemists tend to follow what seems to be the literal meaning of line 3 and read *êrh-pa* as referring to two eight-ounce units of medicine or chemicals, which add up to one catty or Chinese "pound" of materials in alchemy. Thus two lines of a seven-syllabic *lü-shih* poem in the *Wu-chên p'ien* 悟眞篇 (in *TT.* 51:126, *chüan* 27, 24a, poem 32) by the Sung Taoist, Chang Po-tuan 張伯端, declare that

Medicine, weighing one catty, requires Two Eights;

藥重一斤須二八

To regulate the "fire times" one must depend on yin-yang.

調停火候托陰陽

"Fire times," according to Needham, 2: 330, may refer to either "the right moments for carrying out the chemical operations" or "the strength of the heating" in alchemical processes. For a different interpretation of *êrh-pa*, see Tai Yüan-ch'ang 戴源長, *Hsien-hsüeh tz'u-tien* 仙學辭典 (Taipei, 1962), pp. 14–15.

21. Nine Times Nine: the product is eighty-one, which in this narrative represents the number of perfection. See chap. 99 of *HYC* (p. 1116), where the Bodhisattva Kuan-yin explicitly declares that "in the gate of Buddha,

Nine Times Nine will lead one to return to the real" (*kuei-chên* 歸真).
Eighty-one as a number may refer to the eighty-one species of illusion or
misleading thoughts arising from pride, folly, wrath, and desire. There are
nine grades of such illusion, according to Buddhist teachings, in each of the
nine realms of desire.

22. This poem, with the exception of the last line, may be found in the
seven-syllabic *chüeh-chü* section of the *Wu-chên p'ien*. Other segments of the
*Tao Tsang* which contain this poem have been noted in the Introduction, *JW*, 1: 49, and n. 95. The last line of the original poem reads:
煉成溫養自烹煎 (After forging the warm nourishment, you your-
self can cook and fry). For the possible meaning of this poem, I refer the
reader to a commentary by one Tung Tê-ning 董德寧, in his *Wu-chên
p'ien chêng-i* 悟真篇正義, *chüan* 2, 12b–13a, collected in the *Tao Tsang
ching-hua-lu pai-chung* 道藏精華錄百種. The commentary reads: "The
line, After the First Quarter and before the Last Quarter, refers to the two
Quarters of the moon before and after the two eights in the month. This is
to symbolize the two *ch'is* of yin and yang within our bodies. The line, The
medicine's taste is blended, the condition's complete, points to the fact that
since we are able to acquire half of the metal and the water in each of the
quarters, the *ch'i* of all the medicinal materials are therefore mixed and
blended. Thus the condition of yin-yang is perfect and complete. Now those
who engage in the process of making elixir are those who pick the two
*ch'is* of metal and water and return them for refinement in the stoves and
reaction-vessels. The process goes on night and day, and there should be no
slackening morning or evening."

前弦之後後弦前者,謂月之二八前後兩弦,此喻吾身之陰
陽二氣也藥味平平氣象全者以兩弦之金水各得其半,為
藥物之氣均平,是陰陽之象完全也今修丹者,乃採取此金
水二氣,歸於鼎爐之中煆煉而晨昏無懈晝夜如斯.


## CHAPTER THIRTY-SEVEN

1. Water Litany: a vicious and envious woman when she was alive, the
wife of the ruler, Liang Wu-ti (502–49), appeared to him in his dreams as
a great serpent or dragon after she died. For her, the emperor had ten scrolls
of litany performed, after which his wife became a devī, thanked him, and
ascended to Heaven. See the *Nan Shih* 南史,梁武德郗皇后傳 and the
釋氏稽古史略.

2. "Mind . . . means": *fang-pien chih hsin* 方便之心, the mind or intelligence which uses skillful means to save others.

3. King Wên-ch'ang: the full name is *Wên ch'ang ti-chün* 文昌帝君,
who is also named *Tzu-t'ung ti-chün* 梓童帝君. He is worshiped as the

God who presides over the Bureau of Letters (wên-ch'ang fu 文昌府) and lives in the Great Bear. See the Kai-yü ts'ung-k'ao 陔餘叢考.文昌神.

4. Complete Truth sect: the ch'üan-chên 全真 sect is generally regarded as the Northern Division ( 北宗 ) of religious Taoism. Founded by Wang Chê 王喆 (1112–70), styled Chih-ming 知明, and hao Ch'ung-yang 重陽, of the early Chin 金 period, the sect's teachings promulgated the equality of the Three Religions, giving special emphasis to the teachings of loyalty and filial piety in Confucianism, the prohibitory commandments in Buddhism, and the spagyrical arts in Taoism. This is the reason for its name, Complete Truth. For its history and background, see T'ao Tsung-i 陶宗儀, Cho-kêng Lu 輟耕録全真教; Wan-yen Shou 完顏璹, Chung-nan Shan shên-hsien Ch'ung-yang chung-jen Ch'üan-chên Chiao chiao-tsu pei 終南山神仙重陽重人全真教教祖碑; Liu Tsu-ch'ien 劉祖謙, Chung-nan Shan Ch'ung-yang tsu-shih hsien-chi chi 終南山重陽祖師仙跡記; Ch'ên Yüan 陳垣, Nan-Sung ch'u Ho-pei hsin tao-chiao k'ao 南宗初河北新道教考 (Peking, 1958); Sun K'ê-k'uan 孫克寬, Sung Yüan Tao-chiao chih fa-chan 宋元道教之發展 (2 vols., Taichung, 1968), 2: 241–42; Kubo Noritada 窪德宗, Chūgoku no shūkyō kaikaku 中國の宗教改革 (Kyoto, 1967), pp. 71–141.

5. On aurification in China, see Needham, 5/2, 2–14, 62–71, 188–223.

6. Three years: the time scheme of the author at this point is not the most consistent. As the narrative has it, it should have been eight years ago when the drought began. The drought lasted for three years; then came the Taoist, who then murdered the king after two years. Three more years elapsed before the dead king appeared to Tripitaka. I have not, however, tried to emend the text.

7. Equal to Heaven: it was in the T'ang period that the worship of the T'ai Mountain gained momentum. The title of King Equal to Heaven 天齊王 was conferred in the thirteenth year of the K'ai-yüan reign period (726) to the mountain deity.

8. "Weaving grass ropes . . . mouth": a reference to two classic stories on how to repay the kindness of others. In the first story, a certain Wei K'o 魏顆 in the Spring and Autumn period had been told by his father that his favorite concubine should be allowed to remarry to someone should he die. Later, when the father became seriously ill, he reversed his decision and wanted the concubine buried alive with him. Reasoning, however, that he should obey his father's sane command given when he was well rather than the wish made in his delirium ( 疾病則亂吾從其治也 ), Wei K'o prevented the burial and married off the concubine. Hard pushed in battle afterwards, Wei was assisted by an old man, who entangled his foe's cavalry with ropes woven of grass. In his dream that night, he was told that the old man was the concubine's father. See the Tso Chuan 左傳.宣公.十五年.

In the second story, one Yang Pao 楊寶 was only nine years old when he rescued a yellow bird in the mountain from attack by kites and hawks. After staying with Yang for over three months and having fully recovered, the bird flew away. That night, a yellow-robed youth appeared to Yang, bowing repeatedly and saying, "I'm the messenger of the Lady Queen Mother of the West. In gratitude for your kindness and assistance, please accept these four white jade bracelets, which should preserve your descendants from vice and bring them prosperity and success." See the *Hsü Ch'i-hsieh chi* 續齊諧記.

9. "Drawing . . . heron": references to two common sayings, originating from the *Hou Han Shu* 後漢書, "Ma Yüan Chuan 馬援傳," on efforts exerted in vain. The sayings go: when one fails in the drawing of a tiger, it will look like a dog; and, when one fails in the carving of a heron, it will look like a duck.

10. Local spirit: a pun on the phrase *t'u-ti* 徒弟 (disciple), which is homophonous to local spirit, *t'u-ti* 土地.

11. A quotation of the last two lines of a *chüeh-chü* 絕句 poem by the T'ang poet, Li Shê 李涉. There is a small mistake in the *HYC* text, for the Tao-yüan 道院 (Taoist courtyard) of the first line should be *Chu-yüan* 竹院 (bamboo courtyard); our translation follows the original. See the *CTS, chüan* 477, 7: 5429, "題鶴林寺僧舍." The English translation is that by John A. Turner, S.J., in his *A Golden Treasury of Chinese Poetry*, comp. and ed. John J. Deeney (Hong Kong, 1976), p. 191.

CHAPTER THIRTY-EIGHT

1. Ju-lai: Buddha as Tathāgata, or he who comes as do all the other buddhas.

2. Nine Springs: a synonym for Hades or death.

3. Yu-li: 羑里, the name of a place where King Wên of Chou was imprisoned for private misgivings over the tyrannical policies of the last king of the Yin dynasty as well as for his reputed virtue. See *Shih chi* 史記, *chüan* 3 and 4. Yu-li is about nine miles north of what is now T'ang-yin hsien 湯陰縣 in Honan Province.

4. "Let . . . realm": a literal translation of the text, but I have not been able to locate the source or identity of this spell in Buddhist literature.

5. Hsiao Ho: 蕭何 (?–193 B.C.), who helped the first emperor of the Han to unify the nation as his prime minister, was the author of many laws. See the *Han Shu* 漢書, *chüan* 39.

6. Chiu-chieh: i.e., Nine Prohibitions. Pilgrim is making fun of the name Pa-chieh, which means Eight Prohibitions.

7. *T'u-mi*: 荼蘪 or 酴釄, the *Rubus commersonii*.

8. Empty self: the stalk of the plant is hollow, and thus its very nature may be made a symbol of emptiness or vacuity.

CHAPTER THIRTY-NINE

1. Tiered towers: for the meaning of this term and those that follow in the text, see *JW*, 1, chap. 22, n. 5, and chap. 19, nn. 6–9

2. Form's emptiness: "form is emptiness and emptiness is form" are the famous opening words of the *Heart Sūtra*. See *JW*, 1: 393–94.

3. Sovereign state: *shang-kuo* 上國 or *shang-pang* 上邦 sovereign or superior state has been used traditionally as a euphemistic term for China, particularly in relation to the surrounding nations beyond the borders.

4. Wu-t'ai Mountain: 五臺山. The mountain near the northeastern border of Shansi Province, its patron saint is Mañjuśrī.

CHAPTER FORTY

1. With only minor changes, this poem is a repetition of one found in chap. 20. See *JW*, 1: 403–4.

2. Human carriage: a pun on the homophonous words, to call and carriage, both of which are pronounced *chiao*.

3. Wood Mother: the text of the *HYC* here has the phrase, *pên-mu* 本母, meaning original Mother, which makes little sense. I follow the texts of the *Hsi-yu chên-ch'üan*, *Hsi-yu yüan-chih*, and the *Hsin-shuo Hsi-yu chi* and read *mu-mu* 木母 instead.

4. Roaring Mountain: a Hao Shan 號山 can be found in the *Shan-hai Ching* 山海經 *chüan* 2, 25a, but whether this is the source of the name of the mountain in the narrative is not apparent from its description in the classical text. I am indebted to Professor David Roy for this reference.

CHAPTER FORTY-ONE

1. See *JW*, 1: 109, 130.

2. Child Sudhana: shan-ts'ai t'ung-tzŭ 善財童子, the Boy of Goodly Wealth, so named because all kinds of rare jewels and treasures appeared with him at the time of his birth, according to the account in the *Avataṁsaka sūtra*. In Buddhist iconography, he and the Girl of Goodly Wealth (shan-ts'ai t'ung-nü) are often seen as the attendants of the Bodhisattva Kuan-yin (cf. chap. 42 below). In this inventive episode, the *JW* author is saying that the Child Sudhana prior to his submission to Buddhism was the demon, Red Boy.

3. Sui-jên: the legendary Prometheus of China, who invented fire.

4. Samādhi fire: see n. 3, chap. 7, in *JW*, 1: 511.

5. Liver's wood: in the literature of internal, or physiological, alchemy and in medical lore, the five viscera (heart, liver, spleen, lung, and kidney) are often correlated with the Five Phases, in the sense that the energy of fire is thought to be lodged in the liver, the energy of earth is lodged in the spleen, and so on. What the poem seems to express in these lines here is the "productive sequence" of the Five Phases, in which every Evolutive Phase,

in the words of Porkert, p. 51, is "conceived as the product or 'child' (*tzŭ* 子 ) of the precedent E.P., which in turn is considered its 'mother' (*mu* 母 )."

6.  Fire fills the sky: i.e., the sun.

7.  Mutual production and mutual conquest: (*hsiang-shêng hsiang-k'o* 相生相尅) these are two of several traditional views of how the Five Phases operate, either one phase acting as a parent of another (mutual production), or as that which overcomes or conquers another phase (mutual conquest). See Needham, 2: 255–61; Porkert, pp. 51–54.

8.  Duck-head green: the bright green feathers often seen around a certain part of a duck's neck, used to describe the color of water.

9.  Buddha's head: Buddha's hair is said to have the color of ultramarine. This line of poem is also an adaptation of another line by the Sung poet, Lin Pu 林逋 (967–1028). See his poem on the "West Lake 西湖": 春水淨於僧眼碧晚山濃似佛頭青 , in *Lin Ho-ching shih-chi* 林和靖詩集 (Shanghai, 1938), p. 21.

10.  See *JW*, 1: 167.

11.  Cinnabar field: i.e., the lower abdomen.

12.  Three regions: *San-kuan* 三關, traditionally understood as the upper, middle, and lower parts of the body. See *Huang Ti Nei Ching Su Wên, or The Yellow Emperor's Classic of Internal Medicine*, trans. and ed. Ilza Veith (Berkeley, 1972), pp. 186–93, for a description of the division and sub-divisions of these regions.

13.  Bright hall: the space, one inch inside the skull, between the eyebrows.

CHAPTER FORTY-TWO

1.  In the day-count of traditional Chinese culture, a cyclic system of sixty days is established by various alternate combinations made up of the series of ten celestial stems (*t'ien-kan* 天干) and twelve earthly branches (*ti-chih* 地支). The cycle begins anew after sixty combinations are reached. In any thirty-day period, therefore, it is likely that the stem *hsin* 辛, which is the eighth of the ten celestial stems, will appear three times in various combinations with the branches.

2.  Chang Tao-ling: master alchemist and Taoist theocrat of the second century (fl. A.D. 156), he had acquired so many followers that he was able to establish a semiautonomous government at the borders of Szechuan and Shensi provinces. See Needham, 2: 155–56; 5/3: 43–47.

3.  Eight nativity characters: eight words, made up of the various combinations of the stems and branches, which designate the hour, date, month, and year of a person's birth.

4. Fu Hsi: A legendary monarch of the Five Rulers Period (*Wu-ti chi*) who was said to have discovered the eight trigrams (*pa kua*) on the back of a tortoise. King Wên of the preceding line was also associated with the development of the use of the trigrams for fate-calculation and for plastromancy in legends. The Tsêng Yüan of the preceding line may not be the son of the famous Confucian Tsêng Shên, but a Sung official (full name, Tsêng Yüan-chung 曾元中 or 元忠) and a reputed expert on the calendar and the *I Ching*. For a discussion of the origin of plastromancy in China, see Shih Chang-ju 石璋如 , "Ku-pu yü kuei-pu t'an-yüan 骨卜與龜卜探源," *Ta-lu tsa-chih* 8 (May 1954): 9–13.

5. Dharmakāya of Zen: or the Dharmakāya of meditation, one of the five attributes of the "spiritual body" (*pañca-dharmakāya*) of Tathāgata, the Buddha. The dharmakāya of meditation indicates his quiescent or tranquil nature and his transcendence of all false ideas.

6. *T'an* blossoms: the flowers of the udumbara.

7. See *JW*, chap. 17.

CHAPTER FORTY-THREE

1. Fifty-three bows: an allusion to the story of how Child Sudhana, after having heard the discourse of Mañjuśrī, follows his instruction to gain enlightenment by visiting fifty-three wise ones. See the last chapter of the *Avataṁsaka sūtra*, *chüan* 46–60 in *T.* 9/689–788; *chüan* 62–80, in *T.* 10/333–444.

2. *Heart Sūtra*: see *JW*, 1: 392–94.

3. Six Robbers: see *JW*, 1: 306–14.

4. The work of Double Three: see n. 15 of chap. 1 in *JW*, 1: 505–6.

5. For a sketch of this weapon, see Chou, plate 63.

6. See *JW*, 1: 220–32.

7. Three-cornered club: it is actually called the *chien* 鐧, classified by Chou, plate 63, also as a whip or a crop. Since a whip implies usually something pliant, and this weapon is clearly something hard and firm, I have translated it as a club (actually, a swordlike cudgel with a handle). The illustration in the *STT* edition confirms the accuracy of Chou's sketch. See *STT*, *chüan* 9, 38b–39a.

8. *Chang* 鱨: a large, yellow fish described as having horns and able to fly.

CHAPTER FORTY-FOUR

1. Their goal: literally, purple path.

2. Triple *yang*: a metaphor for the first month of the lunar calendar, it is so named because it is correlated with the *ch'ien* 乾 trigram of the *I Ching*.

The symbol for this *kua* consists of three unbroken lines ☰ ; as every un-broken line is representative of the *yang*, the symbol is thus called *san-yang* 三陽 or triple *yang*.

3. Cloud-headed boots: a reference to the patterned embroidery on their boots, the tops of which are made of silk.

4. To raise dust: *yang-ch'ên* 揚塵, literally, to kick up dust. The phrase refers to a story in the *Shên-hsien chuan*, when the goddess Ma-ku 麻姑 told another immortal, Wang Fang-p'ing 王方平, that she had witnessed the Eastern Ocean 東海 transformed into land three times. "When I was journeying to P'êng-lai recently," she said, "I noticed that the water had receded by more than half. Could it be that the ocean is turning into land once more?" With laughter, Wang Fang-p'ing replied, "After all the Sages had declared that dust would fly again (*yang-ch'ên*) in the ocean." See the *Shên-hsien chuan* 神仙傳, *chüan* 7, 4a (Han-wei ts'ung-shu 漢魏叢書 edition); cf. also Wang Shih-chên 王世貞, *Lieh-hsien Ch'üan-chuan* 列仙全傳, *chüan* 3, 25b (facsimile edition; Taipei, 1974). As it is used in the poem here, the phrase refers thus to the Taoists' magic powers of trans-formation.

CHAPTER FORTY-FIVE

1. Lü-liang Cascade: 呂梁洪, a famous double waterfall located in Kiangsu Province, southeast of the county (*hsien*) T'ung-shan 銅山.

2. Twenty-Eight Constellations: see *JW*, 1: 145 for their names.

3. In the last four lines of the poem, the author is alluding to the phe-nomenon of spring storm; hence thunder is associated with *ching-chê* 驚蟄 (arouse the torpid), the third of the twenty-four solar terms (approx. March 5–20), when insects come out of their dormancy or winter quarters as the spring equinox approaches.

4. Side door: a metaphor for heterodoxy. See the titular couplet of chap. 36.

CHAPTER-FORTY-SIX

1. Little Mao Mountain: one of three mountains, also bearing the name Chü-ch'ü 句曲, in Kiangsu Province. Legend has it that one Mao Ying 茅盈 of the Han period came to the mountain and became an immortal, and he was followed by two brothers who also practiced austerities in the region. The mountain is therefore called the Three Mao Mountain: Big, Middle, and Little. See Liao Yung-hsien 廖用賢, *Shang-yu lu* 尚友錄, *chüan* 6.

CHAPTER FORTY-SEVEN

1. Kuan-pao: 關保 or literally, blessed of Kuan. The name refers to Kuan Yün-ch'ang 關雲長, the renowned fighter and bond-brother of Liu

Pei in the *Romance of the Three Kingdoms*. Kuan has been deified as a popular god and is worshiped for his rectitude and gallantry.

Chapter Forty-eight

1. The shoes of Tung-kuo: a reference to the story of Mr. Tung-kuo 東郭先生 in the *Shih Chi*. Before he was made an official, he was so poor that he dressed in rags and wore shoes that had only the tops but no bottoms when he walked through the snow. See the *Shih Chi* 史記, *chüan* 126.

2. Yüan An: 袁安, a man of the Eastern Han period. Prior to the time of his becoming an official he was already known for his uprightness. When a great snow fall in Lo-yang drove many of its inhabitants out to the streets to beg for food, Yuan refused to demean himself in such a manner and remained at home in bed instead. The magistrate of Lo-yang later found him nearly starved to death and, marveling at his virtue, awarded him the degree of *hsiao-lien* 孝廉. See the *Hou Han Shu* 後漢書, *chüan* 75.

3. Sun K'ang: 孫康, a scholar in the T'sin period, who was so poor that when he studied at night, he had to read by the reflected light of the snow.

4. Tzŭ-yu's boat: an allusion to Wang Tzŭ-yu 王子猷, son of the famous calligrapher, Wang Hsi-chih (4th century). Tzŭ-yu was such an unpredictable person that he once took a boat in a snowy night to see a friend. As he reached the door of his friend's house, however, he turned back at once. When asked why, Tzŭ-yu replied: "I felt like coming to see him when I started, but as I arrived, I no longer had the feeling. There's no reason therefore for me to see him!" See the *Tsin Shu* 晉書, *chüan* 80.

5. Wang Kung's robe: an allusion to the story of 王恭, an official of the Tsin period, reputedly so handsome that when he walked through the snow in a crane-feathered gown, a friend exclaimed: "Truly an immortal!" See the *Tsin Shu*, *chüan* 84.

6. Su Wu: 蘇武 (2d century B.C.), an emissary who spent nineteen years in captivity among the Huns. Banished by their leader to be a shepherd, Su had to drink melted snow and eat his blanket to keep from starvation. See the *Han Shu* 漢書, *chüan* 54.

7. White Dew: One of the twenty-four solar terms. See *JW*, 1: 505, n. 6, for a complete list.

8. *La*: the so-called People's New Year, which occurs on the third *hsü* day after winter Solstice (January 16–27). For a discussion of this annual beginning and its rituals, see Derk Bodde, *Festivals in Classical China* (Princeton and Hong Kong, 1975), pp. 49–138.

9. *Chin*: 槿 or *Hibiscus syriacus*.

10. Seven worthies going through the pass: 七賢過關, a common theme for paintings of snow scenes. The identity of the seven worthies is, however, controversial, though they are usually thought of as the Seven

Worthies of the Bamboo Grove 竹林七賢. See the *Tsin Shu, chüan* 49; *Shih-shuo hsin-yü* 世說新語, 28a (*SPPY* edition).

11. P'êng-hu: a variant name for P'êng-lai.

12. Wang Hsiang: 王祥, one of the twenty-four persons in Chinese culture famous for their exemplary acts of filial piety. Because his mother was fond of eating fresh carps, Wang went out to a frozen pond and lay there until two carps leaped out. See the *Tsin Shu, chüan* 33.

13. Kuang-wu: the first ruler (25–58) of the Later Han period. This is an allusion to the episode when Kuang-wu came upon a river during one of his expeditions. No boats were available, but the ice in the river drifted together and that was how he and his followers went across. See the *Hou-Han Shu, chüan* 1.

14. Sink To-the-Bottom: a pun on the homophones Ch'ên 陳, the surname of Hsüan-tsang, and *Ch'ên* 沉, meaning to sink.

CHAPTER FORTY-NINE

1. "According to Yin-yang . . .": i.e., according to the numerological symbolism of Yin-yang and of the stars.

CHAPTER FIFTY

1. Ts'ao-ch'i: see *JW*, 1: 513, n. 8.

2. Giant clam: this is the legendary *shên* 蜃, whose breath may present a watery mirage of buildings in the ocean. See the *Han shu* 漢書, *chüan* 26.

3. Eight-word brick wall: see chap. 36, n. 5.

4. P'êng-Ying: i.e., P'êng-lai and Ying-chou, two of the three famous island-abodes of immortals.

5. "Rhino-like . . . stream": an allusion to the story of Wên Chiao 溫嶠 of the Tsin period, who in one of his military campaigns came to a river, the depth of which was too deep to be measured. He was told, moreover, that there was an abundance of weird creatures in it. Whereupon Wên Chiao burned some rhinoceros horns to illumine the water and, soon after, he did catch sight of many strange watery creatures attempting to put out the fire. See the *Tsin Shu* 晉書, *chüan* 67.